SECRET AGENT "X"

THE COMPLETE SERIES

VOLUME 1

CONTAINING THE FIRST FOUR STORIES:

THE TORTURE TRUST
THE SPECTRAL STRANGLER
THE DEATH-TORCH TERROR
AMBASSADOR OF DOOM

WRITTEN BY
PAUL CHADWICK

BOSTON

ALTUS PRESS

2008

The Torture Trust originally appeared in
SECRET AGENT "X" (February 1934)

The Spectral Strangler originally appeared in
SECRET AGENT "X" (March 1934)

The Death-Torch Terror originally
appeared in SECRET AGENT "X" (April 1934)

Ambassador of Doom originally appeared in
SECRET AGENT "X" (May 1934)

Printed in the United States of America

First Edition — 2008

Visit AltusPress.com for more books like this.

THANKS TO
*Brian Earl Brown, Matthew Higgins, Tom Johnson,
Chris Kalb, Will Murray, Rick Ollerman,
Don O'Malley & Bill Thom.*

TABLE OF

CONTENTS

TOM JOHNSON

SECRET AGENT "X" was the ultimate spy! No one knew his name or face, and he only had one contact in government, a mysterious individual known as K-9. Only one woman was ever really close to him, Betty Dale, and she had seen his face just once. But she loved him, and often assisted him in dangerous investigations. "X" was the unknown factor, and criminals beware!

I first found Secret Agent "X" when my father was in the Dallas VA Hospital awaiting his death. I was stationed in California in 1972, and drove into Dallas to visit my father for the last time. I had been collecting *Doc Savage* and *The Shadow* for several years, and even picked up a number of pulps out in Los Angeles earlier. Leaving the hospital for a while, I visited an older used bookstore in downtown Dallas, and was surprised to see thousands of science fiction pulps stacked on the floor throughout the building. I mentioned to the owner that I was really looking for the hero stuff, like *Doc* and *The Shadow*. He said, "Oh, those are upstairs, but nothing under two dollars. And first issues are four bucks! But I don't have any *Shadows* or *Doc Savages*."

He took me upstairs, and left me alone in a single room the size of the whole downstairs, filled with pulps and comic books from the 1930s and '40s. I swear, I thought I had died and gone to pulp heaven! Being in the military at the time, I didn't have a lot of money, so I had to be careful how much I spent that day. The owner was wrong, though. I did find one *Shadow*. If I had had more time, I might have found more, maybe even a *Doc* or two. But time and money were both short.

I want you to use your imagination for a minute. Just think about going through stack after stack of pulp magazines, and finding so many beautiful gems that your heart skips a beat every few seconds. You find *Operator #5, The Black Hood, G-8, Masked Detective,*

Black Book Detective (with the Black Bat), *Captain Future, G-Men* (with Dan Fowler), *Public Enemy,* and *The Lone Eagle*. And comic books that I hadn't seen since the 1940s! Glorious covers, exciting titles, and I had to leave them all there!

I selected about fifty *Phantom Detectives,* all from the 1930s, many issues of *The Ghost/Green Ghost* (including a first issue), that one *Shadow* issue ("Isle of Death"), and a dozen *Secret Agent "X"* issues! This was my first real pulp collection. And it took me some time to read all those wonderful old stories, but I finally got through them. And I was fascinated with the character of Secret Agent "X"!

I had to return to California before my father died, but I returned to Dallas later and went back to that old store with money in my pocket. Unfortunately, this time the upstairs had been pretty well picked over. The comics and most of the pulps were gone. I picked up a few issues of *G-Men Detective,* and some other stuff, but was disappointed that I had missed the opportunity to go through those pulps one more time. The store later closed. I suspect the old gentleman had passed on. I can imagine some descendant tossing the books in a dumpster in the alley afterwards.

I began reading the "X" series and taking notes. Back then, there was very little known about any of the pulp heroes, except for Doc Savage and The Shadow. I also started looking through ads for missing issues for my collection. I paid four dollars for the second issue, coverless, from a book dealer somewhere. I was closing in on my set by the 1975 PulpCon, and I had asked Jack Irwin (I believe) to bring any "X" issues he had for sale, and let me look at them. He did, and I completed my set at that convention. However, those last few issues cost me something like $60.00 each! The prices had risen since interest for the lesser-known pulps were becoming greater.

It was prior to the convention that Will Murray contacted me. He had heard that I was researching the "X" series, and wanted to share data. I began sending him synopses of the stories, and my notes, and thoughts, and Will started adding two and two together, coming up with little known facts and data from his sources. After the convention, we put the history of the series together and sent it to Robert Weinberg for his Pulp Classics series. It remained in Robert's hands until 1980, when it was finally published—missing a number of pages. An updated version was finally published by Altus Press in 2007, *The Secret Agent "X" Companion,* complete with the previously-missing pages, and more professional binding.

Today, everyone is familiar with the character, and there's not much that isn't known about the series. But everything being said seems to stem from the research that Will and I did in the book so many years ago. And because of that early research, new writers are churning out new stories about the character that may not have ever read one of the original novels. Will originally identified the rewritten Captain Hazzard novel as one of the "X" stories as far back as the early 1970s, but lately I've seen mention of someone else identifying the novel. Sorry folks, credit belongs to Will Murray.

Secret Agent "X," an enigma to the underworld, his face a mystery, ready to lay his life down for his country. This was the character I first encountered back in 1972. I have heard that this was one of the early influences of Ian Fleming when he created James Bond! Notorious gangster Al Capone loved the pulp crime fighters like Secret Agent "X" and Dan Fowler.

The stories that you will find in this first volume are the ones that set the pace for the rest of the series. Although the authors will change from time to time, the editorial control will keep the stories on a fairly even path, just alternating the theme from time to time. There is a possibility that Paul Chadwick, the originator of the series, may have brought in a few ghosts in the early stages, but if so, he certainly went over their work and gave the final stories his own touch. It is only later that the publisher begins to bring in their writers to supplement Chadwick's stories, eventually replacing him completely. I think you will find the series as fascinating as I did back in 1972.

Happy reading!

Tom Johnson
Seymour, Texas
August 8, 2007

BOOK I

THE TORTURE TRUST

Men with skulls for faces—these were the victims of that terrible trio who met in a hidden room. And Secret Agent "X" went against them, daring the bottled torment of their deaf-mute slaves. In a desperate battle of wits at the gateway of destruction.

CHAPTER I

NIGHT GET-AWAY

THE PRISON GUARD'S feet made ghostly echoes along the dimly-lighted corridor of the State Penitentiary. The sound whispered weirdly through the barred chambers, dying away in the steel rafters overhead. The guard's electric torch probed the cells as he passed, playing over the forms of the sleeping men.

It was after midnight. All seemed quiet within the great, gloomy building that was one of society's bulwarks against a rising tide of crime.

The guard's figure passed through a door at the end of a corridor, and the echoes at last ceased their eerie whisperings.

Seconds of silence passed. Then a new sound came. It issued from cell No. 17—the sound of furtive movement.

The man who had been lying as still as death when the guard passed threw his blankets aside. His hard, shrewd eyes gleamed eagerly. His narrow-boned face took on the alertness of a prowling weasel.

Jason Hertz, down on the prison books as convict No. 1088, had not been asleep at all.

His thin, clawlike hands, which had dabbled in every sort of crime from blackmail to murder, became suddenly active. He drew the blankets apart, wadded one into the shape of a sleeping man, and stuffed it under the other. Then he reached beneath his bunk and drew out a roundish object the size of a melon.

It was a ball made from stale bread mixed with water and kneaded together. The bread he had saved for the last three days. He set it on the end of the bunk nearest the door, covering the top of it with scraps of loose hair collected from the floor of the prison barber shop. It looked like the touseled head of a sleeping man and would serve to mislead the guard when he made his next tour of inspection.

Hertz pulled other articles from beneath his bunk—articles which had been smuggled to him under mysterious circumstances. And, as he looked at them, an uneasy expression crossed his face. He recalled the visitor who had come to him the day before and on other days during the past several weeks—the tall, gray-haired man whose card bore the name "Crawford Gibbons, Attorney-at-Law."

He recalled the strangely compellent look in the lawyer's eyes, the forcefulness of his manner, the abrupt persuasiveness of his voice.

Who was Crawford Gibbons, and who was employing him? Why was he aiding Hertz to escape?

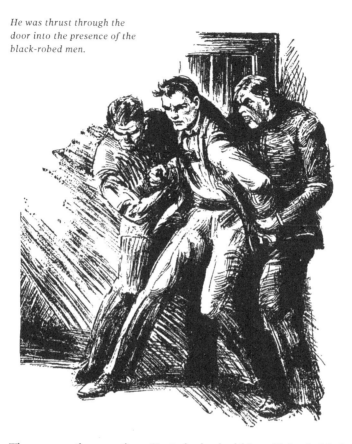

He was thrust through the door into the presence of the black-robed men.

These were the questions Hertz had asked himself, for, behind the guard's back, Gibbons had quietly slipped him a chamois-skin bundle. In it were tools and instructions making his get-away possible.

The prison authorities regarded Hertz as a desperate criminal. Among his vicious associates in crime, he was rated as being hard-boiled and as dangerous as a snake. But the lawyer, Gibbons, had put fear into Jason Hertz's heart. Gibbons had refused to answer questions, refused to reveal his motives. Yet, under the mysterious dominance of the man's personality, Hertz had felt his own will crumbling. It was as though Gibbons had cast a spell over him.

Conflicting impulses stirred in Hertz's mind; one, the desire to escape and go back to his underworld haunts; the other, the fear that he might be entering some sort of trap. He paused a moment fighting within himself. But it was useless. Something stronger than reason cried out that he must follow the lawyer's instructions.

With a cleverly shaped skeleton key that Gibbons had given him, he opened the door and stepped into the corridor, every nerve alert. He listened, but no sound came except the snores of sleeping men.

Shoes off, as silent as a fox, he walked away from the cell, turning into a branch corridor. He climbed a flight of steel stairs and reached the empty cell block above used for overflow prisoners. It was as deserted as a tomb. Hertz entered one of the empty cells, grasped the bars, and climbed up toward the metal ceiling with the agility of an ape. There was a galvanized iron roof above him. For a moment he struck a match, feet braced on a crossbar below.

The tiny flickering flame showed that the metal, seemingly intact, had been cut through with a fine hack saw—his own handiwork of the night before.

He lifted his hand, pressed against the galvanized iron, and a circular piece of metal moved upward. A dark opening appeared, large enough for a man to crawl through.

Hertz thrust his fingers up, caught the strong edge of the thick metal, and lifted himself. He braced his elbows, rested a moment, then strained again. In a second he was in the narrow "attic" of the prison, between the ceiling and the roof.

A faint gleam of light made by the night sky showed ahead. Hertz crept toward it, across the top of the metal ceiling, careful to step on the steel rafters to which the sheet iron was fastened. He came to the light—the square opening of a barred window—and used his hands again.

Drawing a hack saw set in a metal frame from his blouse, he attacked the bars before him with the skill of a man accustomed to the use of tools. The hardened chromium bit through the bars one by one and Hertz wrenched them loose.

He fastened a loop of strong line, which he also took from his blouse, to the stub of one bar, threw the end out the window, and crawled through feet first. Hand over hand, he lowered himself to the ground below.

Clouds obscured the stars. Hertz moved forward in utter darkness, his bare feet soundless on the earth.

HE stopped a moment to get his bearings, then walked on toward the southwest wall of the prison. Trembling violently, his fingers groping, he felt along the stone surface till his hand encountered a rope. He had been expecting it, but fear made him recoil for an instant as though the rope had been the dangling body of a snake. Then he approached it gingerly again. The mysterious lawyer, Crawford Gibbons, had kept his word.

Hertz seized the rope and began the ascent of the wall. It was an easy matter for him to draw himself up its side. With a skill born of experience, he avoided the two strands of electrically charged wire at its top. He balanced himself, stepped over them, and went down the rope on the other side.

His escape was an accomplished fact now. He was free, once again a potential menace turned loose upon an unsuspecting society. But fear still made his heart beat madly.

He had moved only a few yards ahead when he halted as abruptly as though a chain had been stretched across his path.

Somewhere close by in the darkness a whistle had sounded. It was a strange whistle, melodious yet unearthly, seeming to fill the whole air with a ventriloquistic note. It aroused in Hertz a stark, unreasoning terror.

His beady eyes sought to pierce the darkness. He almost cried out. Someone was standing directly ahead of him. He had caught sight of a vague silhouette.

"Follow me," said a low voice.

The words came out of the black vault of the night like an inexorable command from Fate itself. They had in them that compellent quality that paralyzed Hertz's will.

The clouds thinned a little, letting a ray of wan starlight through. He saw the quiet face and the silvery hair of the lawyer. He sensed again the unswerving fixity of the man's eyes upon him. Then, like a sleepwalker, he followed as the other turned and led the way.

Where was he going? He did not know. What strange purpose did the lawyer have? It was veiled in black mystery.

Hertz stumbled on through the darkness for what seemed a quarter of a mile. He knew he must be somewhere close to the road leading to the prison. Then he heard the faint sound of an automobile engine idling. The man ahead clicked on a flashlight no larger than a pencil. Its thin beam disclosed for an instant the lines of a low, powerful roadster parked by the highway.

Crawford Gibbons motioned for him to get in.

Hertz rebelled. Fear of the strange man had been growing in him. He set his jaw and blurted a question.

"What's the idea? Where you gonna take me?"

There was arrogance in his tone now. He was out of the prison. He might make a break for it and escape into the darkness, run away from this fear-inspiring man.

"Get in," said Gibbons harshly.

"What if I won't?" blustered Hertz.

The answer came so suddenly that he gasped. Powerful fingers clutched his arm. He was lifted off his feet, thrust into the car. Then the gray-haired man got in beside him, and the car moved ahead.

Fury and fear welled up in Jason Hertz's mind. His lips opened and he gave a loud, involuntary cry.

"Fool!" hissed the man beside him.

Hertz shrank back in his seat, afraid of what he had done. For his cry had echoed startlingly through the night. A light flashed somewhere on the wall of the prison—another and another. A siren rose like the voice of some monster, beginning with a throaty gurgle and lifting into a furious, spine-chilling wail. The purple shaft of a searchlight on one of the prison towers winked on. Its shimmering beam moved, swung downward, centering on the car. An instant later Hertz cried out again in a frenzy of fear.

For a flickering pinpoint of light leaped out on the wall of the prison. There was a staccato rattle like the drum taps of doom. And, in the air around the speeding car, there came the deathly whine of steel-jacketed bullets.

CHAPTER II

FORCED TESTIMONY

UNDER THE LAWYER'S hands, the roadster leaped ahead in the darkness like a live thing. A machine-gun bullet struck against the metal back of the car. Another passed screamingly between the two men's heads, slapped against the shatterproof windshield, and sent spider-web lines radiating in all directions.

Hertz, his face white and ghastly, crouched whimpering in his seat. He stole a sidewise glance at the lawyer's features, saw the hawk-like nose, the jutting chin, and deep-set eyes. The man was driving calmly, as though death were not riding the wind behind him.

They passed at last beyond the searchlight's range, and the bullets ceased to come. There would be pursuit; but it seemed nothing outside of a bullet could catch that speeding car. Under its long, low hood the smoothly running motor rose into a mighty paean of power. The speedometer needle swung to sixty, seventy, eighty as the car leaped ahead along the dark road. Hertz spoke again.

"You gotta tell me where I'm going. I won't stand for this."

"No?" The single word was ironic, mocking.

"Where you taking me—that's what I wanta know."

It seemed that a grim smile spread over the lawyer's face. He was silent, and leaden fear gnawed at Hertz's heart again. He only knew that they were leaving the city behind; that they had reached a country road. Then the car swung sidewise, turning off the smooth macadam. It passed along a dirt lane between rows of pines that moaned and whispered in the night wind. They came to a jarring stop.

"Get out!" said Gibbons.

The mystery of the night seemed to deepen. Hertz's nerves were almost at the breaking point. He crouched back, showing his teeth, his hands hooked like talons.

"I won't!" he shrieked. "I'll—I'll—"

Under the instrument-board light he found himself looking into the sinister muzzle of an automatic. His craven spirit weakened.

"All right I'll go. Take that gat away. Don't shoot!"

But the gun was not withdrawn. Hertz walked ahead, trembling, with the gun in his back, and the outlines of a house suddenly rose out of the blackness before him. It looked like a farmhouse, low and ramshackle.

A key grated in the lock. He was pushed inside and the door closed after him. There was the stuffy smell of deserted rooms and musty carpets. Gibbons appeared to know what he was about. He pushed Hertz into a rear chamber, struck a match and lighted an oil lamp. The windows of the room were tightly boarded up. Gibbons thrust a chair forward and motioned Hertz to sit down.

Alone with the mysterious lawyer, Hertz had a deeper sense of dread. The compelling eyes of Gibbons were upon him again. He sensed mystery behind them, and power. It was as though they were boring into his very soul. The voice of the lawyer sounded harshly.

"You are free of prison, Jason Hertz. In return you are going to give me information!"

So, that was it! A snarl rose on Hertz's lips. His eyes gleamed wickedly.

"I won't tell you nothing. I don't know nothing!"

The gray-haired man before him smiled again and drew a clipping from his pocket. He held it in front of Hertz's face. It had been cut from a newspaper—CATRELLA KILLED AT SCENE OF TORTURE MURDER.

"He was one of your pals, Hertz. You've seen the papers in prison. You know that murders are being committed—men tortured to death. Joe Catrella was in on it in some way. Give me the names of his friends."

The question came relentlessly; but Jason Hertz shook his head.

"I don't know nothing—I won't talk," he cried.

He'd heard rumors of the series of hideous killings that were baffling the police. Prominent people found dead—tortured. "The Torture Trust," the papers called it. Fear sealed his lips. He knew little; but he dared not tell even that. Death was the penalty meted out to a squealer in the underworld, and there was mystery and horror behind this murder wave that eclipsed anything he had ever heard of before. There was an uncanniness to it that made his spine crawl. He wished he had stayed in jail.

"I don't know nothing," he repeated wildly.

HIS voice died in a gasp. He found himself looking into the eyes of the lawyer, found himself unable to turn away. Like a bird staring at a snake, he was held fascinated.

The lawyer's face was coming closer to his—closer, closer. The lawyer's eyes were pools of blazing light.

Hertz cowered in his seat, pressing till the rungs of the chair cut into his back. Terror of the man before him rose in his throat and seemed to choke him. He sensed again that he was in the presence of a person who had powers beyond his knowledge—vast depths of strength and magnetism. It seemed that his own brain was being battered into submission.

"Think back, Jason Hertz. It is March, 1933. You have not been caught by the police as yet. You are not in jail. You are with Joe Catrella, plotting evil. What is your understanding with him? Who are his friends?"

The eyes of the lawyer were relentless. His voice went on droningly. Jason Hertz felt himself slipping—slipping into the mysterious depths of hypnosis.

From drowsiness, Hertz went into laxity of posture, slumping in his chair, staring with glassy eyes into the face of the man who called himself Crawford Gibbons. Then slowly his body became rigid; his fingers tightened around the arms of the chair; his legs pressed stiffly against the floor. He was in the third stage of the hypnotic state, the stage known as catalepsy; his will completely under the dominance of the strange man before him.

"You will speak, Jason Hertz. You will answer my questions."

Sweat broke out on the forehead of the escaped convict. Fear still fought for control of his subconscious mind. But the man in front of him substituted another fear, deeper, more imminent.

Gibbons reached around the side of Hertz, his forefinger extended. He pressed the tip of it against Hertz's spine.

"There's a machine gun at your back, ready to blow you to pieces, Hertz! You can feel it there, pressing, pressing. You must speak. Who were Catrella's friends? Who gave you your orders when you were with him?"

A gurgle came from Hertz's lips. They moved slowly. The cords in his neck stood out.

"I—don't—know!" he gasped. "The Bellaire Club. We hung around there. Panagakos, the manager, may have been—I got notes in the blue vase—telling me what to do—the vase on the dance floor. So did Catrella. We never knew—who the big shot was—the guy we was working for. We sent notes to him the same way. Don't kill me—for God's sake! That's all I know; I swear it. They got me—in that spaghetti-joint holdup—when I tried to make a little dough for myself on the side. I had a moll and she—"

Betty Dale

His voice trailed off. For the lawyer, Gibbons, had stopped listening and had taken his eyes away. A man in the hypnotic state tells the truth because he must. Jason Hertz had told all of interest that he knew!

Gibbons moved back and Hertz sat staring straight ahead of him. His labored breathing told that he was in the hypnotic trance. He might stay thus for hours.

Gibbons drew a pencil and notebook from his pocket. He placed the pencil in Hertz's fingers, put the notebook under his hand.

"Write, Jason Hertz! Write one of those notes to your boss—telling him you are out of prison, ready to serve him again."

The fingers of Jason Hertz moved mechanically. The pencil whispered across the paper like the pencil of a spiritualistic medium doing automatic writing. When the note was finished. Gibbons tore the page loose, folded it, and put it in his pocket.

Then he began a series of quick, mysterious movements.

HE brought the light nearer Hertz, studied his face, and, after a few seconds, walked to a cabinet standing against the wall. He opened the front and drew from it a collection of odd-shaped apparatus.

There was a magnesium flare set in the center of a silvered, parabolic reflector. There was a small movie camera, a dictaphonic machine driven by a spring motor, and a set of elaborate measuring instruments based on the formulae of the Bertillon System. He placed them in front of Jason Hertz.

Lighting the flare, he focused it on Hertz's face and body.

"Get up!" he ordered. "Walk around, Hertz."

The escaped convict obeyed, rising from his seat and moving about the room in the manner of a sleepwalker. But his muscles made characteristic movements that the lens of the movie camera in Gibbons' hands began to record.

"Sit down," said Gibbons after a time.

Again Hertz obeyed, and Gibbons brought the camera closer.

"Smile," he commanded, and Hertz did so. Then in quick succession Gibbons ordered the felon to scowl, laugh, register fear, surprise, and arrogance.

He set the camera down with a snap, turned off the magnesium light, and started the motor of the dictaphone machine.

"Now, Hertz—follow me. Repeat first the vowel sounds—aaa—ah—oh—ooo—ee! Now the consonants. Ker—ter—bur—mer—"

The needle of the dictaphone recorded the vibrations of Hertz's voice on the hard-rubber cylinder. Gibbons was using the science of phonetics, setting down every inflection of the convict's lips, throat, and tongue for future use. When he was satisfied that he had missed nothing, he closed the dictaphone and set to work with his measuring instruments, going over the planes of Hertz's face. He jotted down the widths of Hertz's eyes, mouth, and nostrils, the angle of his jaw, the slope of his forehead, the height of his cheek bones.

Satisfied at last, he put his apparatus away, keeping only the movie film, the cylinder from the dictaphone, and the figures he had set down.

He took up the notebook and pencil and began scribbling a brief note.

"You have betrayed your friends, Hertz," he wrote. "You know the penalty of betrayal in the underworld. There is murder abroad, torture, horror. Your only chance to live is to escape from the country. I am giving you that chance. To catch a wolf I am freeing a rat. In the enclosed envelope you will find a passport already filled out and a boat ticket to South America. Take them, go, and never come back."

The lawyer took a hundred-dollar bill from his pocket, put it in the note he had written, placed it in the envelope with the ticket and passport and pinned it to the front of Hertz's coat. Then he paused a moment, holding the pencil in his hand.

With a strange, grim smile on his face, he reached forward and made a mark on the envelope—a mysterious "X" that seemed to have no purpose or meaning.

But if Jason Hertz could have seen it, he would have understood more about the strange adventure he had been through. For the man whose symbol and trade-mark that "X" was had built up a reputation which had reached even behind prison walls. It was a reputation for swift movement, startling courage, masterly disguises that no man could penetrate—and mysterious motives that no man could fathom.

It was a reputation that baffled the police as well as the underworld. For the man who hid behind "X," symbol of the unknown quantity, seemed to be working against crime, even while classed as a criminal.

Gibbons turned then and strode through the door into the night, and behind him floated an eerie yet melodious whistle that had in it an unearthly quality like a voice from some other world.

THE AGENT'S HIDE-OUT

IT WAS AN hour later that Gibbons, the lawyer, parked his roadster and walked along a quiet street at the outskirts of the city. His movements were quick, eager. There was a strange, restless brightness in his eyes.

The silence of the night was punctured by the shrill cry of a newsboy, peddling an early morning edition. Gibbons bought a paper and the restlessness in his eyes deepened as he stared at the front page. Black headlines were spread across it. They told of another mysterious torture murder—a millionaire's son found dead in his penthouse apartment, his face eaten away by acid.

Somewhere down the block a police siren sounded and a green roadster whirled by. Gibbons, watching from the shadows, recognized the man in it—a detective from the homicide squad. Murder seemed to whisper through the darkness of the night. Menace lay like a pall over the city.

The lawyer's pace increased. Once he paused in his swift stride to press a hand to the left side of his chest. An old wound, received on a battlefield in the World War, had given him a momentary twinge of pain.

A harsh laugh fell from his lips. Years ago doctors had predicted that he had only a few months to live; but he had gone on living, defying death. Perhaps it was this closeness to death that made him so restless—or perhaps it was something else.

He reached a wealthy residential section at length. The river flowed beside him, millionaires' homes and expensive apartment buildings rose at his right. At the corner of the block he stopped. A high wall followed the line of the side street. A huge pile of masonry, bleak and austere, towered above the sidewalk, the windows of it boarded up. It was the old Montgomery mansion, facing the river, the house that the litigation of heirs, quarreling about the estate, had kept empty for years. Its luxurious rooms were gathering dust now. Mice moved unmolested across its polished floors. Moths were nibbling at the expensive rugs.

The man who called himself Gibbons turned and walked down the side street. There was no one in sight. He followed the wall as silently as a shadow. A few gaunt shrubs that had not been properly tended for years made a sparse fringe along the wall.

Suddenly the man stopped. He parted two shrubs and stepped behind them. His hands moved in the darkness for an instant. An old door leading into the ancient garden swung open. The door closed softly behind him.

He was in a place of ruin, decay, and desolation with the teeming life of the city shut away. Under the glow of the sky overhead, he picked his way through the garden, passed statues fallen from their pedestals, passed a tumble-down summerhouse, passed a fountain that had long since ceased to spray moisture.

He appeared to be at home, appeared to know where he was going, appeared to belong there. He came to the rear of the house, lifted the cover of the cellar door, and descended a flight of stone steps.

A key grated in the lock. In a moment he was inside. Then he paused by another door in a rear room of the old cellar. Flashing a tiny, electric light, he pried loose a piece of paneling and stared intently at a hidden dial.

A clocklike mechanism behind the dial moved a cylinder of paper slowly like the drum of a seismograph. There was a stylus poised over the paper. It recorded blows and footfalls. The paper drum was blank, showing that for the last twenty-four hours no one had passed through the hidden passageway behind the door that led down to the black waters of the river. The man nodded in satisfaction.

He moved up into the house, to a room that was hidden beneath the huge front staircase. It was in reality the false back of the old butler's pantry. The partition had been expertly moved forward and a door into the secret chamber was concealed by shelves that swung outward.

Here the man who had made the house his home could be as much shut away from the world as though he were in the black depths of a vault.

There were strange things in that secret room: a small chemical and photographic laboratory, jars, bottles, and mysterious boxes; a miniature arsenal, containing humane but efficient weapons; gas pistols that could knock a man unconscious within a radius of twenty feet; tiny, stupefying darts concealed in cigarette lighters; a concentrated tear bomb in the stem of a watch that would momentarily blind a man when he stooped to look at the time. There was also a mirror at the side of the wall under strong lights. It had three movable sides that would show every angle of a man's face, head, and body.

GIBBONS walked up to it and stood regarding himself. Then he moved away and seated himself at a shelf before another mirror. His long, restless fingers began to stray across his face. Beneath their tips a mysterious transformation took place. He plucked tiny plates of tissue-thin metal from his nostrils—plates that had made his nose hawk-like; peeled a transparent covering of fibrous, fleshlike material from his chin and cheeks; lifted the clever, mesh-thin toupee of gray hair from his head. His whole appearance had changed.

The mirror reflected him as he really was—as he was never seen by any living soul—as he never appeared except in the silence and secrecy of this one room. The face that stared back at him from the mirror was even-featured and boyish-looking. Gray eyes that held a hint of humor in them. Brown hair and a smooth-shaven skin.

It was only when he turned his head and the light fell on his face in a certain way that new lines were brought out—lines that made him look suddenly older, mature, poised—with the record of countless experiences written in them, and indications of restless energy and driving will power that would not let him be quiet.

A grim smile came as he looked at himself. Secret Agent "X." The man of a thousand faces—a thousand disguises—a thousand surprises! The man of whom it was whispered that he had the unofficial sanction of a great government in his fight on the criminal hordes preying upon society. The man said to be officially dead in the records of the Department of Justice—his supposed death arranged that he might disappear and fight crime in a new and startling way.

His real name and background were mysteries known, if at all, only to a chosen few. Who was Secret Agent "X"?[1]

Suddenly a frown crossed his face. He glanced at the telegram that lay open on a table in the strange room.

It was in code and it had been sent from Washington, D.C., to a certain Elisha Pond, care of the First National Bank. Its seemingly meaningless words were burned into his mind like a brand.

"Six victims claimed in Torture Trust," the code words of the telegram stated. "Why aren't you on the job?"

He picked the yellow sheet up and walked toward a metal strongbox that rested on a shelf. For a moment he hesitated.

Holding the telegram in his left hand, he ran the fingers of his right delicately along the lid of the strongbox till he reached a certain raised rivet head. He pressed this, and there was heard a faintly audible "click."

The rivet head corresponded to the safety catch on an automatic. But the forces that it held in leash were a thousand times more destructive. There were two pounds of trinitrotoluene concealed in a false bottom of the box which, unless the safety catch was pressed, would explode when the lid was raised. The terrible explosive guarded Agent "X's" secrets from any one who might penetrate his hide-out during his absence.

He laid the telegram for safe keeping on top of a special document that the box contained.

The document bore a governmental coat of arms. It was couched in brief and simple terms, but its words carried a strange portent.

> In recognition of brilliant work performed and faithful service rendered, we confer upon you the title of Secret Agent "X." Your way will be a lonely one. You will combat crime, fight ceaselessly against those who seek to destroy law, order, and the decencies of civilization. You will stand ready to risk your life in the cause of humanity as you did while serving your country in the Intelligence Division during the

---

1 AUTHOR'S NOTE: As intimation has come to me from reliable sources that Secret Agent "X" was, at the beginning of his career, seen entering the White House at the time when the "Crime Commission" was in session. It is my personal belief that he has the full though unacknowledged sanction of that body, backed by a very high government official, in his startling campaign against organized crime. More than that I am not in a position to state at the present time.

I have had many close contacts with the Secret Agent, many conversations even, but he has never chosen to reveal his past history to me by word of mouth. What I have learned I have learned by careful observation and by a process of gathering together small scraps of information and drawing deductions from them.

World War. For reasons, which you will comprehend, there can be no official acknowledgment of your work or sanction of your methods. Your funds, however, will be unlimited. Ten public-spirited men of great wealth, unknown to you and unacquainted with your name, have subscribed a fund for your use. A fraction of this fund is on deposit in the First National Bank. It can be drawn by you under the cognomen of Elisha Pond. This account will be replenished whenever it becomes low. Utilize it as you see fit.

With a quick movement, the Secret Agent closed the box and released the safety catch again. There were those who knew of his existence and had absolute faith in his methods. He would endeavor to live up to that faith.

He began going over his face again with quick, deft fingers. The boyish lines disappeared under the magic touch of his hands. Gray hairs appeared at the temples. The flabby contours and dignity of middle age came into being. He leaned forward and stared intently at his own reflection. The man of a thousand faces had again achieved a master disguise.

Jeffrey Carter, clubman and gentleman of leisure!

That was his role for the rest of the evening. It was after one o'clock, but he had no intention of going to bed. Sleep was a thing he seldom indulged in. Restless, dynamic forces seemed always driving him on. And tonight there was work to be done—a series of hideous murders to investigate.

He had taken the photographs, the sound record, and the measurements of Jason Hertz for a purpose. No pains were too great, no efforts too laborious in creating a new disguise. When the time came to impersonate Hertz, he would do it with the skill of an artist and a scientist. But the time for the impersonation had not come.

He rose, removed the clothes he had been wearing, and, from a closet containing a vast wardrobe, selected a trim tuxedo. It fitted perfectly his lithe, muscular figure; but, as he slipped into the coat, he winced again at the twinge of pain near his heart.

That and the scar on his chest, drawn into the lines of a crude X where a piece of shrapnel had ploughed, might sometime give him away. It was a risk he was prepared to take.

THE Secret Agent, alias Jeffrey Carter, took a taxi down town. He told the driver to swing left at Twenty-third Street, and he gave a number in a block of medium-priced apartment houses. Through the agent's mind a series of sentences were moving, repeating

With the instinctive response which had more than once saved his life, the Secret Agent twisted his body sidewise.

themselves again and, again. Bellaire Club! Panagakos! A blue vase on the dance floor!

He paid the driver, dismissed the cab, and walked forward. This was not a night-club section, but Agent "X" had special business. Halfway down the long, silent block he stepped back into an angle formed by the intersection of two walls. Here the deep shadows lay as black as ink.

For a moment the Agent's eyes narrowed. He was staring upward alone the brick facing of an apartment building opposite. There was a light showing behind the drawn shade in a window on the sixth floor.

The Agent fingered the black bat-wing tie above his immaculate shirt front, gave his silk muffler a deft twitch, then moved briskly out of the shadows and crossed the street.

He entered the building, passed through a small foyer where a switchboard operator was sitting, and ascended by an elevator. Walking left along a corridor, he pressed the button of apartment No. 6B.

There came a sound of high heels clicking over the parquet flooring inside. A moment later the door opened and a girl with blonde hair and a *petite* figure stood on the threshold.

She raised an uneasy hand, patted her gleaming *coiffure* nervously, and stared closely at Agent "X," her blue eyes narrowing in worried speculation.

"Miss Betty Dale, I believe," the Agent said. "May I come in?"

His voice now was cultured, softly modulated. The masterly disguise he had affected tonight hid his real identity. He was playing a part for a purpose.

"My name is Jeffrey Carter," he continued. "I'd like to talk to you a few moments if you can spare the time."

As he spoke, he watched the girl's face narrowly. It expressed uneasiness, doubt, perplexity. Obviously she did not know who he was. Obviously to her he was a perfect stranger and a suspicious one at that.

"Come in," she said at last, a note of reluctance in her tone.

She turned, her small pretty face screwed up in worry, and led the way into the sitting room.

The long, powerful hands of Jeffrey Carter moved then. One of them flickered out, the fingers holding something that was like a thin stick of pomade.

He made a quick movement close to the wall as he passed by, then slipped the mysterious stick back into his pocket. There was a faint smile on his face. His disguise had proven adequate under the gaze of a girl whose intelligence and cleverness he rated as high as her beauty.

He reached out and snapped off the electric light switch, plunging the room into darkness.

The girl gave a little gasp of surprise and fear; but the stranger's voice reassured her.

"A beacon shines for all good mariners," he said.

She turned. On the wall at her back was a glowing X, shimmering there with a strange eerie light. It was the mark of the Secret Agent—written in the purest radium paint—paint made by a secret formula and containing thousands of dollars' worth of the world's most expensive metal.[2]

"It is you then?" she said, relief in her voice.

The Secret Agent had given her many moments of worry in his desire to use her as a test. He had come to her in dozens of different disguises. She never felt sure of her ground until he gave her some characteristic, identifying sign.

His manner changed now. He was no longer the suave clubman. There was a tenseness in his attitude that the girl sensed. When they were seated in the next room, Jeffrey Carter talked quickly moving his long-fingered hands, restlessly.

"Blue vases are the devil's choice," he said suddenly.

The words were incomprehensible to the girl; but she relaxed in her chair, all uneasiness gone. The Agent generally spoke in metaphors and parables, the significance of which she learned in due time. Almost everything he said had some double meaning.

Respect and intense loyalty mingled in her blue eyes as she regarded the man who tonight called himself Jeffrey Carter. Whoever the Secret Agent really was, she knew that he had been a friend of her dead father's—the father who had been a police captain, slain by underworld bullets.

She had been brought up to feel an intense hatred of criminals. The death of her father had crystallized this feeling.

This man, her father's friend, was working against the underworld. She trusted him, relied upon him, knew that he was kindly and brave. There had been times when he had placed sums of money collected from criminals in her hands—to give to charity, to help the poor and those who had been victimized by underworld plots.

She knew that he kept nothing for himself, asked nothing but to live dangerously, recklessly, gambling with Fate. There were moments when wonder filled her as to what sort of face lay behind those brilliant disguises. Would she ever know? Or would death claim him before she had penetrated the secrets of his life?

---

2 AUTHOR'S NOTE: This paint of the Agent's is unmistakable. It is ten times brighter than the radium paint used on the faces of clocks and watches which contains only the minutest fraction of the priceless element. It is more luminous than any paint I have ever seen, and it is obvious that the expense and trouble entailed in its manufacture are sanctioned by the Agent as an insurance against imitation. He cannot afford to take chances.

The Agent spoke mysteriously again, his eyes gleaming with some hidden emotion.

"You are an accomplished dancer, Miss Dale, and to dance beautifully is an art. Tonight I ask you to dance with me."

She gave a start of surprise and flushed slightly. "What do you mean?"

"The Bellaire Club is calling us, Betty. There is music to be danced to and a blue vase to be looked at. Put on your best frock."

SHE shrugged, nodded, and flashed him a smile. Something deeper than caprice and a love of dancing, she knew, lay behind his words. And when, at the end of ten minutes, she emerged from her boudoir, she was a vision of loveliness.

Betty Dale was a girl who knew how to wear clothes. Poise and refinement were instinctive with her and that good taste which is something inborn and can never be taught. Because of these things, she had gotten ahead in the world. She had won a career for herself as a star reporter on the *Herald*. When she was covering society stuff, she could meet and hobnob with fashionable people on their own plane. This made her invaluable both to the paper and the Agent.

More than once she had helped him by going places with him when he needed a feminine companion, by carrying out his orders, and by getting information that he required.

Tonight she was clad in a white evening dress with a fur wrap draped over her shoulders. Together they went to the street and signaled a taxi.

They were whirled through the brightly-lighted thoroughfares of the great city to the doors of the Bellaire Club, which, for all its gaudy ostentation, was a place of ill repute, a place where sinister things had happened.

It was frequented by the fast, wealthy set, and by gangsters and gamblers who had made big money. There were gambling tables in the rear, a dance floor and a large orchestra in front, with tables for couples to sit at and drink.

The Secret Agent had asked Betty Dale to accompany him tonight because a lone man or woman coming to the Bellaire Club was at once an object of curiosity to Mike Panagakos, the flabby-jowled, sloe-eyed manager. The Agent did not want that.

He whirled Betty Dale around the room once, and his eyes

gleamed as he saw a blue vase on a low settee by one wall. It was a fine piece of Turkish pottery that somehow fitted in with the gaudy, exotic atmosphere of the club. It seemed to have been placed there as a receptacle for flowers, but it was empty now.

As they whirled past it, the Secret Agent's hand flicked out. The note he had made Jason Hertz write fell into the vase.

By that act he believed he was opening a trail that might lead him into the shadow of hideous murder and mysterious death.

When the dance had ended, they seated themselves at a table to watch the moving crowds about them; the sinuous, over-painted women, and the immaculately dressed men.

Then Betty Dale suddenly caught her breath, and the Secret Agent's head turned quickly.

Across the room a group of people had scattered. A woman gave a hoarse cry of fear.

From the center of the group, a man ran forward into the circular spot cast by an overhead light. He was holding his hands to his face, staggering drunkenly—and, as Agent "X" watched, he let forth a scream of agony that shivered through the air with the keenness of a knife thrust. Then he collapsed and lay writhing on the polished floor.

CHAPTER IV

POLICE NET

GASPS OF HORROR went up from those in the room. The orchestra, playing a languorous concert number, came to a discordant stop. Men and women crowded forward, craning their necks.

Agent "X" arose. There was a steely brightness in his eyes, tenseness in the low whisper of his voice.

"Satan has struck," he said.

Leaving the girl at the table, he moved across the floor to mingle with the crowd around the fallen man. Silently, swiftly, he pushed his way close. Looking over the shoulder of an elaborately dressed woman, he got a glimpse of the man on the floor.

The man's hands were still covering his face. Between the quivering fingers Agent "X" saw inflamed, mottled flesh, pockmarked and drawn together. Faint fumes curled up. The man's skin had been hideously burned. Someone had thrown acid at him

Agent "X" turned. He ran to the nearest table, grabbed a bottle of olive oil and shouldered his way back, kneeling by the fallen man. With quick, deft fingers, he poured the sweet oil over the man's tortured face.

It was a simple remedy, but, quickly applied, it might save the man from death or life disfigurement. The man moaned and twitched. One side of his coat fell away. The edge of a gleaming badge showed. He was a headquarters detective. He writhed again, pawing at his injured face, then went limp. Merciful unconsciousness had come.

The Secret Agent got up quickly. Mike Panagakos, the fat, sleek-haired manager, was pushing his way forward.

"Call an ambulance," said Agent "X" harshly. But another voice cut in on him.

"It's already been done. Everybody keep quiet. Don't try to leave the room. There are men stationed at the doors with orders to shoot."

The man who had spoken was heavy-set, stern-eyed. He looked out of character in the tuxedo that wrinkled baggily around his lumpy body. He was Detective-Sergeant Mathers of the Homicide Squad.

"It's a raid!" cried a woman, the quavers of hysteria in her voice.

"Raid is right! There's been a murder attempted. There's a killer in this room. Every man and woman of you is gonna get searched."

In Sergeant Mathers' words was a savage note. He glared at the people around him with a ferocity that was backed by bafflement and fear.

"The Torture Trust!" whispered somebody hoarsely. And a sudden silence descended on the room, broken only by the tense breathing of fear-stricken people. Horror seemed to creep out of the corners. The fat face of Mike Panagakos turned a sickly dough color. The whites of his eyes showed.

Agent "X's" quick brain grappled with the situation. Detectives, he realized, must have been posted in the room all evening. The police, too, must know that Joe Catrella had hung out at the Bellaire Club. They were leaving no stone unturned in their efforts to solve the hideous torture murders. And the "Torture Trust" in its campaign of terror had turned brutally on the police force itself.

Agent "X" looked around the big room. At the main entrance, a man with a police automatic in his hand was standing alertly. There was another close to the door of Panagakos' private office in the rear. A third guarded the window by the fire escape. Sergeant Mathers had worked quickly, efficiently.

"Squad cars are on the way," he barked. "There'll be policewomen to search the ladies. Inspector Burks himself is coming."

The imperious clanging of an ambulance bell sounded in the street outside. It stopped at the door of the Bellaire Club. A moment later, the detective at the main entrance stepped back as two white-coated internes entered, a stretcher in the hands of one.

Sergeant Mathers spoke again, pointing to the figure on the floor.

"Get that man to the hospital as fast as you can."

Secret Agent "X" developed the art of disguise into an exact science. Before his triple mirror in the secret sanctum of his room, miraculous transformations took place.

The internes moved like automata. Opening the collapsible stretcher, they lifted the unconscious detective, placed him on it, and carried him out of the room. The gong of the ambulance sounded again, growing fainter as it wound its way through traffic that had stopped as if frozen. The bell seemed to leave behind it a black pall of mystery and terror.

In staccato sentences, harsh as the crack of a whip, Sergeant Mathers began questioning Panagakos.

"Donelly was a good man. He's the third who's had stuff thrown in his face. The first one cashed in. Where was Donelly when he got his?"

Panagakos shook his head. He drew the back of his hand across lips that were moist and quivering.

"I—I didn't see nothing," he said. "I was in my office. When I heard the racket I came out."

A foreign-looking waiter in a short-tailed jacket came close to Sergeant Mathers. He made movements in the air with his hands.

"It was from the kitchen that he came, *señor*. It was there that I first saw him—the policeman. But I saw no one else."

Mathers pressed forward, the crowd following, led on by morbid curiosity, and Agent "X" followed, too.

HE saw Mathers round up and question the kitchen staff. Saw them shake their heads. They had seen no one. A hallway led to a big pantry and storeroom beside the kitchen. Agent "X" knew the angles of the building. He made it a business to learn such things. There was likely to be an air shaft in the storeroom. Why didn't Mathers search there? But he couldn't suggest it. It would attract attention to himself. The detectives would have to work their way. He would work his. But there was worry in his eyes.

Any moment cars filled with policemen and policewomen might arrive at the Bellaire Club. Every person in the room would be searched. It was something that Agent "X" did not care to risk. There were strange articles concealed in his clothing—articles that it would be embarrassing to have the police find. Sometimes quick changes of disguise were necessary. Painstaking care had gone into the creation of featherweight, portable make-up. Odd kinds of material were cleverly concealed in the linings of his coat and vest.[3]

To make matters worse, Inspector Burks of the Homicide Squad was a bitter enemy of the Agent's. Discrediting rumors that "X" was working against the underworld, the formal, routine-loving police inspector regarded the Agent as a particularly vicious criminal.

More than once their ways had crossed. More than once Agent "X" had led the inspector along the right path to apprehend some evil-doer. But he had done it so subtly, so deviously, that Burks never realized he had been aided. He had only redoubled his efforts to trap the man whose trademark was a gleaming "X." His suspicions would be aroused if he found hidden disguises on the man who tonight called himself Jeffrey Carter.

With a grim smile on his face, Agent "X" made his way back toward the table where he had left Betty Dale. He must get away and take the girl with him before Inspector Burks arrived. With armed

---

3 AUTHOR'S NOTE: Agent "X's" ability to make quick changes of disguises falls little short of genius. By means of nostril and mouth plates he is able to sculpture his features into new faces, and, using volatile plastic material laid over flesh-tint pigments, he has developed external make-up into an exact science.
It is my belief that in his strange and varied career he was at one time associated with some great character actor. He has never said so; but he has all the tricks of the stage at his command. In the art of impersonation he has even outrivaled Vidocs, the famous French detective who became the first "Chef de Police de Surete," in Paris.

men at every door and window, this seemed impossible. Only brilliant strategy could accomplish it.

There were fear shadows in Betty Dale's eyes as he approached her. One slim hand was pressed against her breast.

"We're trapped," she said. "They'll search you! What will you do?"

"Sometimes a leopard can change his spots," he said enigmatically.

Her eyes grew wide with wonder as she stared at him. Sergeant Mathers had said that no one was to be allowed to leave the room. No matter what disguise he wore, it would be the same, she thought. Even the Agent couldn't accomplish the impossible.

Close to their table was a heavy drapery across the front of the private booth for diners who wanted to be alone. The booth was empty tonight. The drapery was partially drawn back.

With the light of purpose in his eyes, the Agent stepped quietly into the booth. Inch by inch he edged the drapery across till the booth was covered—till he was out of sight.

The girl looked quickly about The men and women in the room were staring at Sergeant Mathers, following his every word and gesture as he cross-examined Mike Panagakos and the kitchen staff. No one had seen the Agent go behind the drapery. She looked toward the booth for an instant.

A faint light showed under the drapery's edge. The Agent was mysteriously at work. But fear and perplexity still mingled in her expression. Her ears were strained to catch the wailing of police sirens outside announcing the arrival of the headquarters' cars.

Then she gave a sudden gasp. The drapery in the front of the booth moved. A man stepped out—but not Jeffrey Carter, the clubman who had brought her to the Bellaire Club.

The man who emerged had a hard, pale face. His mouth was a thin line. There was a frown between his eyes. His eyebrows, in contrast to his white hair, jutted blackly. He carried himself with erect, military bearing. She had seen that man before. He was Inspector Burks of the Homicide Squad.

Betty Dale drew in her breath.

She could not be mistaken. One man had gone into the booth; another had stepped out—but she knew they were one and the same man—Secret Agent "X." She knew that his uncanny mastery of disguise had accomplished the impossible.

He didn't try to test his make-up this time. He looked at her, smiled an instant, and nodded. Then his face set again into grim lines. He gestured toward the front entrance and handed her her wrap. She understood.

With wildly beating heart, but covering her agitation, she walked toward the door.

The burly detective guarding it barred her way. "You heard the sergeant's orders, lady—nobody goes out!"

Then the detective gave a visible start. His eyes widened. He drew himself up respectfully and lowered the gun.

"It's all right," said a cold voice. "I'll show her to the street. See that nobody else leaves."

"Certainly, Inspector!"

The detective's puzzled frown indicated that he couldn't quite piece things together. He could only go by what he saw. Inspector Burks was at the girl's elbow. The Homicide Squad head must, it seemed, have come in the back way. He must have a good reason for making an exception in the girl's favor. The detective stood back, and Betty Dale and the Secret Agent moved unmolested down the carpeted stairs.

They did not hurry. The man at Betty Dale's side maintained his stiffly erect bearing.

But, at the downstairs entrance, his grip on her arm tightened. He gave a swift look right and left and suddenly drew her across the street. Up the block, headlights flared piercingly; a swift car shot around the corner; squealing rubber; and a siren rose into a screaming, pulsating wail.

"The police!" gasped Betty Dale, the words like a sob of fear in her throat.

CHAPTER V

THE ACID THROWER

THERE WASN'T TIME to do more than draw the girl into a dark areaway beside a stoop. Agent "X" did so, crouching beside her. To be seen now disguised as Inspector Burks would put an end to his plans.

He waited tensely as the car with the screaming siren came to a halt opposite. The real inspector was the first to get out, his erect, military bearing and pale face making him easy to identify. After him tumbled three plain-clothes men and two grim-faced police-women. They crossed the sidewalk and disappeared in the entranceway of the Bellaire Club.

A second squad car rounded the corner and came roaring down the block, sliding to a screeching halt behind the first. All the detectives in the city seemed to be concentrating on this one point. The sirens had attracted attention. Heads were peering out windows. A small crowd was collecting. Any moment sharp eyes might spy out Agent "X" and the girl beside him. But she was safe now. He motioned toward the street and she understood.

"You?" she said. "What will you do?"

"The spots of the leopard will change again," he replied.

Her face was pale and uneasy as she left him and mingled with the crowd on the street. A moment later she signaled a taxi, stepped into it and was whisked away.

The Agent turned his back. Head down amongst the shadows of the areaway, his long fingers began to move. They were working in the darkness now, working by instinct and the uncanny skill that past experience had developed.

He left the white hair on, but drew the jutting black eyebrows off and peeled away the plastic material from his face. He slipped rubber cheek plates against his gums to broaden his features, smoothed the frown of Inspector Burks from his forehead, then turned.

As he sauntered out into the light of the street, no one would have known him for either of the two men he had impersonated earlier in the evening. He looked older now, fatter—and the glittering nose glasses with a black cord attached that he slipped on heightened the effect of dignity and age.

The voices in the crowd around him were tense, electrified with fear. Rumors were running like wildfire. The "Torture Trust" had claimed another victim. A newspaper man with a flash-light camera was taking pictures of the front of the Bellaire Club. Soon the presses of the tabloids would be grinding out another story of mystery and horror for a thrill-loving public to devour at their leisure.

But the game that "X" was playing was a game of life and death.

He slipped through the crowd, moving along the side of the building to the mouth of an alley that tradesmen used. He stared down it, glanced back along the street, then plunged out of sight.

The dignity of his movements fell from him suddenly. He snapped the eyeglasses off, placed them in his pocket. His eyes were bright and piercing as bits of polished steel.

Above him were the lighted windows of the Bellaire Club. He followed the alley on up to the corner of the building. Ahead was a courtyard filled with boxes and barrels. A fire escape snaked up the side of the club, passing the windows of the kitchen, going on up to the roof.

"X" stood a moment, trying to locate the position of the air shaft he had figured was there. It was either by that or the fire escape that the acid thrower had entered and gone.

Then he drew in his breath. Far above him, silhouetted a moment against the starlit sky he saw faint movement. It might have been a man's head or hand. He couldn't be certain which; but he crouched back in the black shadows of the courtyard.

Then, swiftly as a cat, he crossed the flagstones and leaped up. His fingers caught the end of the weighted fire escape ladder. The ladder came down slowly, its rusty hinges squeaking.

Agent "X" paused and listened. No sound came from the darkness above. He mounted the ladder swiftly, up past the kitchen windows, reaching the darkness beyond just as one opened. Inspector Burks was on the job now and would be more thorough than Sergeant Mathers had been.

"X" took the iron steps two at a time. Speedily, silently, he reached the roof, while behind him a cop stepped out on the second-floor landing. The police, too, were going to search the roof. The Agent had escaped from one difficult situation only to be involved in another. His blood raced madly. Once again he was pitting his wits and courage against the forces of Fate. What if there was no other way down from the roof? What if the police trapped him?

But he didn't dwell on the dangers of the situation.

Lightly as a cat, he leaped to the coping of the roof and balanced there on the balls of his feet.

The top of the Bellaire Club stretched before him. Beyond was another building, higher still—a sheer cliff of offices closed for the day. But against its brick walls he saw vague movement again. A giant spider seemed to be creeping up its bare side.

The Agent's eyes had been trained to work in semi-darkness—to see things that other men missed. There was an iron ladder up the side of the building beyond. Someone was climbing it swiftly—a figure which, even at that distance, had something macabre and sinister about it.

Agent "X" started in pursuit. He was ahead of the police, one jump in advance on the trail of a would-be murderer. As he reached the higher building, he looked behind him across the roof of the Bellaire Club and saw the head and shoulders of the cop. Then his hands were on the ladder and his feet had found the rungs.

It ran straight up, a sheer hundred feet, to the roof above. It passed by unlighted windows, and, as he mounted, it was as though he were hanging in space.

THEN, far behind him, he heard a cry. A pinpoint of flame blossomed in the darkness. There was a sharp, whiplike report. Something struck the bricks beside him and screamed away into the night like a frightened banshee.

The Secret Agent smiled. It wasn't the first time he had been under fire. The cop on the roof below had glimpsed him just as he had glimpsed the man ahead. But there could be no accurate shooting. The policeman's second bullet went wider of its mark than the first. The cop was being blinded by the flash of his own gun.

Agent "X" continued to climb. The cop below turned on a flashlight, but its beam wouldn't reach. Agent "X" was too high up. A moment later, however, the iron ladder gave out faint vibrations, warning the Agent that the man below had reached it and was mounting, too.

"X" traversed the last rungs at dangerous speed. He vaulted over the edge of the roof and stood there like a man on top of the world. The twinkling lights of the city lay below him, peaceful as though murder were not stalking through the night

He turned and looked along the roof. All seemed quiet. He could see no movement now; but with quick, silent strides, he skirted the edge of the roof, then leaped forward.

At a point opposite where he had come up, another ladder went down. It had become a mad game of hide-and-seek on the rooftops of the city. There was no place up here for a man to hide. "X" tried the one skylight window and found that it was locked on the inside. The man ahead, whoever he might be, was showing that he knew his ground. His fiendish act tonight had been as deliberate as it was diabolical, planned with the cunning that characterized every movement of the "Torture Trust."

Agent "X" grasped the top of the second ladder and began the descent as quickly as he had climbed. Six stories below, his feet touched another, lower roof. He crossed it, reached the fire escape that mounted on the next building. He was moving along the block on the rooftops. He looked back again, and, far above, outlined against the high office building, he saw movement. The cop was close on his trail.

A sense of menace seemed to descend on him out of the night. He could outwit the police, but he was pitting himself against criminals as fiendish as they were cunning. He reached under his coat, drew out a pistol. It was one of the weapons he sometimes used in moments of emergency—not an ordinary gun. The Agent did not kill. To slaughter a man was a crude way of dealing with a situation. The Agent operated with finesse, ingenuity, and impetuous daring. The chambers of this gun contained concentrated anesthetizing gas of a high specific gravity. Even in the open, fired into a man's face, it could cause unconsciousness.

He gripped the pistol, climbed still faster. He was on the last flight of the fire escape now, with the roof of the third building ahead. He stared up twelve feet. And, as he did so, a black shape suddenly blotted, out the stars. So quickly that the Agent didn't have time to raise his gun, a man's arm flashed out.

With that instinctive response which had more than once saved his life, the Secret Agent twisted his body sidewise. He hung by one hand and foot, swaying perilously away from the iron ladder, out over dizzy space.

Something hissed by in the air close to his face. The stench and reek of chemicals made his nostrils quiver. Burning, acrid fumes made his eyes blink and smart. Then the flesh of his left wrist felt as if a red-hot brand had suddenly been pressed upon it. The pain was so excruciating that his muscles contracted and he almost let go his hold. The silhouette above disappeared.

Biting his lips with pain, the Secret Agent continued to climb. By a few inches only he had missed the liquid torture from the roof above. A few drops of the acid thrower's torment had struck his wrist, showing what terrible thing he had escaped.

His eyes glowing like points of steel, he went on up, peering cautiously over the roof, the gas gun in his fingers. But the roof was deserted now.

The Agent saw why. With a bound he crossed the tarred space to a heavy trapdoor cover. He tugged at it with tense fingers, but it was bolted inside. Then, stooping down, he placed his ear against the sheet metal. From below came the faint stir of descending footsteps. The acid thrower had made good his escape.

Philosophical always in defeat, biding his time, the Secret Agent stood up. He couldn't go back the way he had come. He walked across the building to the fire escape at the rear, and quickly began the descent.

This one seemed to end in a vacant courtyard below. He paused a moment listening. All was quiet.

He reached the bottom, dropped to the flagstones and started toward a fence in the rear, then suddenly crouched back. A bright beam pierced the darkness close ahead. The ray of a flashlight made his eyelids narrow.

"Stand still, guy," a harsh voice said.

Against the glow of a street light beyond the court Agent "X" got a sudden glimpse of the visored cap of a city cop.

CHAPTER VI

SINISTER SUMMONS

IT WAS A situation that he hadn't anticipated—a dangerous turn of events. The cop's voice held deadly purpose. The Agent knew that a gun was trained on him. He knew also that the police were nervous, fearful, and ready to shoot at the drop of a hat. Calmness would be necessary and brilliant strategy.

A slow smile spread over the Agent's face. He made his voice drawling.

"Don't be hasty, old man. Nothing to get excited about, you know."

With aggravating deliberation, he dusted his palms together, wiped a speck of dust from the front of his tuxedo and reached toward his vest pocket.

"Keep yer hands in sight," snarled the cop. "Go for a gat and I'll drill yer."

"Really!" said the Agent, poised and unruffled. "I don't think you fully grasp the situation."

With the tips of his fingers, he delicately drew his eyeglasses from his vest. He breathed upon them, wiped the gleaming lenses on his sleeve, and placed them carefully on his nose. Then he raised his head. Looking straight at the cop he spoke arrogantly.

"Now, my good man, I'd appreciate it if you'd take that light of yours out of my eyes. It's quite annoying."

The cop came closer, still tautly alert.

"What were yer doing on that roof? Who the hell are yer?"

"Names Claude Fellingsfort," said the Agent. "Thought I saw a fellow running around up top. Went up for a bit of a look. Heard that the police were having a man hunt. Thought I'd aid them."

"Yeah?"

"Quite—and now, if you'll just step aside, I'll be on my way."

"You'll be on your way right enough. You're gonna have a talk with the inspector. He's up the block. I've got my orders and I'm gonna follow 'em."

"The devil you say! You'd better give me your number. I intend to register a complaint about this."

The cop's gun thrust against his aide. "Move along where I tell yer! Keep your hands away from your pockets."

"You'll hear from me, my good man."

The Agent's voice was outraged now. His pose was that of the injured man-about-town; a citizen furious at the ingratitude of blundering officials. But he moved in the direction the cop indicated. He might learn something from a chat with the inspector.

The crowd in front of the Bellaire Club made way for the cop and his prisoner. They climbed the carpeted stairs to where Inspector Burks was standing just inside the door of the main room. The search of the fifty or more guests of the club was still in progress. The cop spoke harshly.

"I found this guy stepping off a fire escape down the block, chief. He handed me a line. I thought maybe you'd want to talk to him."

Inspector Burks focused the full glare of his black eyes on Agent "X." They were face to face—the official head of the world's greatest homicide squad and the man who worked outside the law for the cause of law and order. But the Agent was protected by his masterly disguise.

The inspector's pale, aquiline face registered no recognition. He was in a dangerous mood, though, ready to grasp at any straw that came his way. The press was clamoring that the "Torture Trust" be smashed. The police were being criticized.

"Who the devil are you?" he snapped.

The Secret Agent adjusted his glasses again, stroking the black cord.

"I told this fellow here," he drawled, gesturing toward the cop. "My name's Fellingsfort, in case you want to know."

"What do you do for a living?"

"A bit of financial work. Bond selling and that sort of thing."

"What have you got to prove it?"

The Agent reached into his coat pocket, drew out a wallet and opened it. He carried a dozen or more cards with him always, different names upon them. His disguises went more than skin deep. He avoided trouble by checkmating it in advance.

From a deep inner pocket in the wallet, he drew a card bearing the name Claude Fellingsfort, with the legend "High Grade Bonds" directly after it. With an elaborate flourish he presented it to the inspector. Burks glared at it suspiciously.

"What were you doing climbing down off the fire escape, Fellingsfort?"

"One couldn't stay on it forever," said Agent "X" suavely. "Since I went up, I had to come down."

"Why did you go up in the first place?"

"I thought I saw a fellow sneaking around up there as it were. It turned out I was right"

The inspector's eyes narrowed into aggressive pinpoints of light.

"What the hell do you mean?"

Deftly the Secret Agent stretched out his arm, pulled up his coat, and drew back his cuff. An inflamed spot showed on his wrist where the skin had been burned.

"The bally idiot threw acid down on me, you know. Sort of an unfriendly devil. I didn't linger to pursue our acquaintance."

"Acid!" Burks's voice had the sharpness of a whiplash.

"Quite. There's the spot—burned rather painfully if I do say so."

"Where did the man who threw it go?"

"Down the block—fifth house from the end. It might pay you, inspector, to send a couple of men to search the place."

For an instant the tone of the man who called himself Claude Fellingsfort changed. Then he resumed his irritating drawl.

"And now, if you've no objections, I'll be on my way."

Burks reply was icy.

"You'll go down to the station house, Fellingsfort. I'm going to hold you for investigation—check up on your credentials."

He gestured toward two husky cops.

"Take this man down to the station—keep him there till I come."

"I say!" protested Fellingsfort. "That's what I call gratitude! I'm late for an appointment now. I really can't sanction this!"

He drew a gold watch from his pocket and looked at it with a frown.

"Take him away, boys," was the inspector's answer.

The two cops stepped forward, one on each side of the Secret Agent. The watch was still in the Agent's hand, and suddenly a strange thing happened. His thumb moved delicately. There was a faint click inside the timepiece. Then the Agent's arm described a quick arc in the air before the two cops' faces and a thin jet of vapor spurted from the watch's stem.

With gasps the two policemen fell back, wiping their eyes, momentarily blinded by harmless tear gas. And, quick as a fleeing wraith, the Agent leaped to the door and ran down the stairs.

Inspector Burks cried out harshly and another cop at the entrance attempted to stop "X," but a second jet of gas sent the patrolman back. An instant later and the Secret Agent, alias Claude Fellingsfort, had run into the street and disappeared, lost in the crowd.

Inspector Burks stared again at the card Fellingsfort had given him, then gave a sudden gasp of amazement.

The card had turned black in his hands, the name disappearing. In the center of the card a glaring white figure stood out. It was a mysterious letter "X," come there as though by magic.[4]

IT wasn't until twenty-four hours later that Agent "X" returned to the Bellaire Club—and this time he went alone. In the meantime he had followed reports in the papers, questioned numerous people, and done all he could to trace down the hidden members of the "Torture Trust." But in each instance he had drawn a blank.

There was one lead still open, however—the most significant of all, the one upon which Agent "X" depended for success—or death.

As a news item, the escape of Jason Hertz from the State penitentiary had not been important. The story had been tucked away on the second and third pages of the metropolitan papers. The police hadn't linked up his break for liberty with the sinister activities of the "Torture Trust." But Agent "X" knew that somewhere in the city knowing eyes had read of Hertz's escape.

He returned therefore to the Bellaire Club disguised as a young

---

4 AUTHOR'S NOTE: The trick of "X's" is a simple one. He keeps certain cards in a special light-proof compartment of his wallet. These cards have a silver nitrate coating like photographic paper. But a small "X" is placed over the card before the silver wash is put on. Then the "X" is taken away and the card dried. Given five minutes of exposure to light and every part of the card except the uncoated "X" turns black.

man-about-town. But into his disguise he injected a sleekness of appearance, a sharp, hungry look, that any one acute enough would sense. He had the appearance of a man possessed with the gambling fever.

And only after he had lost two hundred dollars at cards, allaying the suspicions of Mike Panagakos and the detectives stationed around the room, did he seat himself at a table by the dance floor. He ordered a drink and sat hunched over it, smoking a cigarette morosely, like a man despondent at the loss he has suffered.

The table wasn't ten feet from the blue vase on its polished settee.

Minutes passed, and the Agent's hand moved to the cord of the table-light running below the cloth. No one noticed, but in his fingers was a pair of singularly shaped pliers. They bit down on the cord and did not sever it; but a needle point thrust itself through the outer silk covering into the two copper cables inside.

There was a small spark, a hiss, the odor of burned insulation, and every light in the room went out as the main fuses blew. "X" had deliberately caused a short circuit.

In the hubbub that followed he moved quickly. He crossed in the darkness to the blue vase, slipped his hand inside and withdrew it. In his fingers was a piece of paper.

He pulled the pliers from the light cord, stopping the short circuit. When the blown fuses had been replaced by someone in the kitchen, Agent "X" was again sitting quietly at his table. A half hour later, attracting little attention, he gathered up his coat and left.

It wasn't till he reached a secluded avenue that he opened the note in the hollow of his hand. Then his heart leaped with excitement.

"Come to Forty-four MacDonough Street, J. H., and ring the bell seven times," the note said. And Agent "X" knew that in those brief words lay the seeds of success—or hideous death—depending on his own wits and the cards that Fate dealt him.

CHAPTER VII

MASTERS OF DEATH

FOR HOURS THAT night, the Agent worked in his secret room in the old Montgomery mansion. Rats scuttled across the deserted floors. Mice squeaked in the walls of the ancient house. From outside came the occasional noises of the city. The rumble of a heavy truck. The faint blare of a taxi horn. But the Agent's chamber was like a little world in itself shut away from the lives of ordinary men.

He had been extraordinarily careful tonight. He had studied closely the faithful recording apparatus in the cellar, making sure that no one had disturbed the privacy of the house. He had taken special pains to throw any possible shadower off the track.

Now, feeling secure, he set to work methodically to achieve the most masterly disguise of his career. On its perfection his very life depended, and perhaps the lives of others, innocent victims of the "Torture Trust."

He took out the movie films, the sound record, and the measurements made during his interview with Jason Hertz. The film he had already developed in his small photographic laboratory.

He set a projector on a tripod, focused it on a silver screen, and switched off the lights in the room. Then he snapped on the bulb behind the projector and started the machine in motion.

Hertz's image appeared on the screen. Agent "X" studied it again and again, noting each movement and facial expression. He had made a series of still enlargements from the movie film, and these he studied also.

He placed the hard-rubber record on a phonographic machine and listened to Hertz's voice.

For twenty minutes he practised the vowel and consonant sounds, perfecting tongue and lip movements, until he had mastered the timbre and pitch—until it seemed that Hertz himself was speaking in the small room. Then he seated himself before his triple mirror, and, with the measurement chart at his side, began the elaborate make-up.

He used his finest pigments, built up his plastic material, working in thin layers with constant reference to the notes he had made. He reconstructed each plane and line of the ex-convict's features; then practised characteristic expressions. He laughed, frowned, registered fear, surprise, and arrogance as he had seen Jason Hertz do.

Even then he wasn't satisfied—not until he had risen and moved about the room, imitating Hertz's walk and arm movements. When at last he put his equipment away, Hertz's own mother wouldn't have known that the man in the room was not her son.

"X" dressed himself as a criminal and gunman: a cheap, flashy suit, a striped silk shirt, a tie that shouted to the world.

But, in the linings of the suit, he hid other articles. There was no telling what desperate emergencies might arise. He took one keen took at the little chamber before leaving. It might, for all he knew, be the last he would ever get.

A taxi sped him to within a few blocks of MacDonough Street. He got out and paid the driver, doubting that the cabman would recognize him as Hertz. The police heads would know him. The detective force would be tipped off. He must avoid representatives of the law. But he didn't fear citizens or ordinary cops except in the region that Jason Hertz had frequented.

MacDonough Street was in a dark, cluttered section near the river front. Number forty-four was in a block of ancient, unpainted houses that seemed like a stagnant backwater left by the city's swift progress northward.

The Secret Agent's heart beat faster as he climbed the stoop and pressed the bell of number forty-four seven times.

It was at least two minutes before the door opened. Then a slatternly old woman stood before him. Her beady, ratlike eyes were set in a face as evil as a witch's. She licked thin, toothless gums and stared at him out of the black pit of the hall. Then she jerked her head.

"Come in," she said harshly.

She hadn't asked him his name. He knew she had recognized him as Jason Hertz. He followed her along a dusty smelling corridor into a rear room. Here she switched the light on, closed the door after her, and left him alone.

But he had the uncanny sense that eyes somewhere were studying him. He waited breathlessly, and seconds later a closet door opened and a man stepped out.

The man was small, dressed in gray, and his face had the dead, listless color of putty. His eyes, too, were listless, reptile-like; but they focused on "X's" with cold, calculating intelligence.

For seconds the man studied "X" at close range, then took a pad from his pocket and the stub of a pencil. He scribbled a sentence on the pad and handed it to the Agent.

"Come with me," the sentence read.

And "X" realized with a start that the gray-clad man before him was a deaf-mute. Looking closer, he saw that the mask-like face of the man seemed to conceal some horrible inner maladjustment. Was he insane, or a drug addict? There was something chillingly sinister about him, as though he were the very emissary of death.

HE led the Agent out a rear door of the house, through a back yard into another street as evil looking as the one in front. A car was waiting at the curb. It was a dark-colored, closed vehicle, and at the wheel of it was another man of the same type as "X's" guide. His features were not the same; but there was a weird similarity of coloring and manner that puzzled the Agent.

He got into the car at a gesture from the guide. The auto moved away. It glided through deserted streets, passed narrow, one-way alleys, then, in a particularly black spot, the gray-clad man at "X's" side leaned forward. In his hand was a strip of dark cloth. He raised it, slid it across "X's" face and blindfolded him.

The act made the Secret Agent's nerves tingle with excitement. There was no fear in his heart—except the fear of possible failure. The precautions taken by the deaf-mute warned the Agent that he was coming in contact with some supercriminal who left nothing undone.

The car stopped at last. Agent "X," blindfolded, unable to see a step he took, was nevertheless making precise inner records. His uncanny memory was at work, his supersensitive faculties registering impressions.

He was drawn out of the car, guided by one of the evil gray men. He heard a door open, and marked in his mind the position of it. He was led along a passageway, and he kept track of each individual step. He turned to the right, went down a flight of stairs, up another, walked straight ahead through a second corridor.

His ears even registered the acoustic properties of the hall. Another flight of stairs and his guide stopped him. The Agent's eyes behind the cloth were bright. Brief as the time had been, he felt certain he could retrace his steps. The blindfold had failed of its purpose.

Then Agent "X" had a sense of chill, a sense of quiet, a sense that he was in some old, dark building where gloomy shadows lay. Slowly he was pushed to the center of a room. The blindfold was taken from his face; footsteps withdrew; he was left in absolute darkness.

For seconds that seemed endless, he stood there, wondering what was to come next. There was no movement in the room, no sound. Then suddenly a light flashed on. It was a bulb set in a reflector, a small searchlight, and it was focused directly on his face.

He waited, staring toward the light, certain that other eyes behind it were upon him, certain that he was being observed, analyzed, picked to pieces. Would his disguise stand the test?

Gradually his gaze adjusted itself to the brightness of the light. He could see the faint illumination it shed in other parts of the room. He could see the walls, the furniture. Then he gave an inner start. Perfectly coordinated nerves held it in abeyance. But he let his face muscles sag as Jason Hertz would have done. He registered an uneasiness he didn't feel.

For there were three black figures in the room. They sat on chairs like three ravens of death facing him. There were black hoods over their heads, trailing black cloth over their bodies. Through holes in the hoods he saw the evil glitter of eyes.

There was not one criminal, then, but three behind the murders that had taken place. He was in the presence of the "Torture Trust," the men whose inhuman brains had plotted hideous villainy.

A voice came out of the gloom, cold and precise and dangerous as the buzz of a rattler's tail.

"What have you got to say for yourself, Jason Hertz?"

The Agent gulped, stirred, and imitated Hertz's tone as he had learned it from the phonographic record.

"I—I lammed out of stir. I figured maybe you'd have something fer me to do. That's how come I dropped the note. A guy's gotta eat."

"We know you got out of the penitentiary. We have eyes. We read the papers. But we know your limitations, Hertz. It seems remarkable that you could have escaped without outside help. Will you please tell us exactly how you did it?"

The Agent knew at that moment how perilous was the ground upon which he stood. There were brains of diabolical cunning behind those sinister black hoods. His life hung upon the answer he made.

CHAPTER VIII

TERRIBLE SECONDS

S **LOWLY HE DREW** his lips into a smile. He straightened his body, threw out his chest, facing the spectral trio with the arrogance of a criminal proud of his handiwork.

He was a student of human psychology, and he acted now as he believed Jason Hertz would do in his shoes.

"You gotta hand it to me," he said. "You're king-pins an' you're smarter than me. But I pulled a fast one when I slipped outta the big house. There ain't many guys could 'a done it."

"You haven't answered our question, Hertz!" There was a relentless note in that cultured, measured voice.

These men, "X" sensed, were not ordinary criminals. They bore no relation to the underworld of thugs, gunmen, racketeers, and gamblers—except that they lived by death and the fear of it that their deeds inspired.

He smiled again. "You wanta hear about it right from the start?"

"That's what we want."

"Well, I bought a hack saw from a snowbird named Cooper. His brudder smuggled it to him, see? An' he was too shaky to use it. I give him money to buy coke instead. I snitched a key from a guard when he had his back turned talkin' to another guy. The key was on a chain. I stuck a piece of soap on it, see, and made a nifty pattern."

Agent "X," alias the convict, Hertz, chuckled again as though at his own cleverness.

"There was tools in the machine shop," he continued. "I was a good guy. They made me a trusty. I made me a key from the pattern in the piece of soap. When I got the chance I slipped out and went to the empty cell block up top. I cut a hole through the ceiling and got amongst the rafters. That's the way a guy they told about in the papers did it."

"Then," came a voice in the gloom, "you cut the bars of an end window—and climbed down to the yard. We read all that, Hertz. But how about the wall?"

"X" laughed again.

"You must 'a seen about the rope, too," he said. "I left it there. They's lots of things a trusty can do. I snitched that rope in the cellar, the one they used to haul ash cans out on a pulley. I tied a bolt to it an' slung it over the wall. There was a loop on it. I caught the loop on a brace that the wires on top of the wall was fastened to. I did a pretty slick job."

There was silence as he finished his tale. He knew that evil brains were debating, weighing the story he had told. He believed it rang true. Hertz had been a trusty. Convicts in the past had used exactly the methods he had described to escape.

But there was a slow constriction around his heart and he could feel his pulses pounding. What if he had aroused their suspicions?

Then another of the black-hooded trio spoke. His voice was lower, hoarser, but it, too, had a cultured note.

"You've done well, Jason Hertz. You are cleverer than we thought. We may be able to use you again. But for a time you will have to lie low. We will call you when we need you."

There was finality in the voice. The Agent's heart sank. He must find out something definite. He couldn't wait around for weeks while the hideous murders went on.

His disguise had worked. He was not suspected, but he had learned little. Who were these men? What faces lay behind those black hoods? Where did they live?

He stared again beyond the range of the searchlight, looked at the black-hooded figures with quick penetration. His eyes came to a focus on one.

The right foot of the middle man was thrust slightly forward. The toe of a shoe projected from under the black robe that dropped to the floor. On that shoe the sharp eyes of the Agent detected streaks of mud—mud that had caked recently, mud that formed an irregular pattern. And, in that brief glimpse, his astute brain registered an impression that was photographic.

The hooded men, so far as he could see, made no signal; but one of the mask-faced deaf-mutes returned. The Agent was familiar with the regular deaf-and-dumb language, but he could not follow the strange finger conversation that ensued between the trio and the mute. It must, he concluded, be in code.

The blindfold was slipped over his eyes again; the light in the room went out. He was led through darkness. The sinister trio obviously believed him to be Jason Hertz. But they were taking no chances. Besides themselves only the deaf-mutes were allowed to know the secrets of this hidden place.

Agent "X" was storing impressions again. He was being led out by a different route. The stairs were different, so were the corridors. The acoustic properties of the latter, responding to his footfalls, gave out different echoes.

WHEN they reached the street, he was pushed into a car and the blindfold wasn't removed until they had driven many blocks. But the Agent had been marking the intersections in his mind by the different sounds that the street openings made. They had passed four. The rumbling note of the wheels changed each time. They rounded a corner, went two more blocks, then another corner. The blindfold was taken off. The car slid into MacDonough Street.

He was motioned up the steps of No. 44 again, and a deaf-mute rang the bell, two longs and a short. Then the mute wrote on his pad: "Stay here," and thrust it under "X's" nose.

The witchlike landlady led "X" to a second-floor room. She lighted a gas jet and left him alone. He heard the deaf-mute descend the stoop and the car drive away.

He crossed the room quickly, thrusting his head out the door. He could hear the faint, shuffling steps of the landlady somewhere below. Taking off his shoes, he tiptoed out, walked down the hall and reached the front door. He made no sound. He kept close to the walls. In a moment he had opened the door and slipped out.

Thinking he was Jason Hertz, escaped convict, they would expect him to stay in the house, glad of a refuge. But the real Jason Hertz was far away, and the man impersonating him had a perilous task to perform.

He moved along the block like a wraith, ducked into a deserted alley, listened a moment, then set to work.

Under the quick movements of his skilled fingers, the brilliant disguise came away. It would take long minutes of patient labor to build it up again; but only a few seconds were required to remove it. And in his coat lining, he had another quick disguise ready.

When he emerged from the alley, he appeared as a young, red-headed street loafer. The silk shirt was gone. The sweater he had worn under it, surreptitiously, was in evidence, drawn up around his neck. His coat and trousers, specially tailored to be turned in-side out, had completed the change. He no longer remotely resem-bled Jason Hertz.

Keeping close to the shadows, he walked back along the way he had come. He thought out each step, turned the right corners as he came to them, pausing at last by a huge empty warehouse.

His pulses were tingling now. It was into this building that the deaf-mute had led him. It was out of it that the sinister trio must come.

Carefully, casually, he skirted the big warehouse. It occupied nearly the whole of a small block. Three sides of it were on streets. But there was a clutter of empty houses in the rear. Agent "X" moved by these. Then his heart beat faster.

In the street outside he saw the glint of moisture. A puddle, barely dried, reflected the light from a distant street lamp. The mud around the puddle was a light yellow. Dried, it would prob-ably appear white. It formed a precious clew.

He took up his position in the shadows across the street. There was no telling how many secret entrances the chamber in the ware-house had. The most subtle precautions had been taken to guard them. Yet the Agent felt certain that at least one of the trio had passed in through these old buildings in the rear. Might he not be expected to come out the same way?

Night wind moaned along the street. The stars glittered coldly. Somewhere far up on the warehouse a piece of loose tin flapped and groaned like a wounded vampire. The street was cold, bleak, and deserted. But the Secret Agent waited.

It was nearly an hour later that he crouched back in his hiding place. A door in one of the deserted buildings had at last opened. A man in a long ulster stepped quietly out, closing the door after him. His movements were not furtive. They were calm, assured. The man's face was even-featured and calm, too, and he was well dressed.

But the Agent leaned forward tensely. On the man's shoes were pale streaks of mud. He picked his way past the puddle as though a recent unpleasant experience had taught him to be careful.

Shadowing was one of "X's" specialties. He had done much of it in his life. He knew all the tricks. Yet it took every resource at his command to keep sight of the man in the gray ulster.

The man walked four blocks up the street at a rapid pace. He turned left, walked four blocks more to a main thoroughfare and waited for a taxi.

At a fast clip, hands in pockets, head bent low, the Agent walked on by him. His heart was beating rapidly with the excitement of the chase. What if another taxi did not come? What if he lost sight of the man in a traffic jam? These were risks a shadower must always take.

Then he saw a cab approaching from the other direction. He stepped into the street, signaled it. The driver seemed loath to stop because of "X's" unpresentable appearance. But "X" waved a bill in his face.

"Make a U turn," he said. "Then drive ahead slowly."

The driver did so and the Agent looked back. He saw another cab glide in to the curb and pick up the man behind. It came on up the street and passed.

"Follow that car," said the Agent.

THE driver of the cab obeyed. But the man ahead, as though it were part of a customary routine, changed cabs three times, walked many extra blocks, and used other tricks to throw off possible pursuit.

The trail led at last to a house in the suburbs—a house on a quiet, respectable street. There were no lights in it when the man in the gray ulster entered. But they flashed on soon after. He was evidently staying alone.

The Agent waited outside till long after midnight, till the lights finally went out for good. Then he slipped a handkerchief over his face crossed the street, and moved to the rear of the house. If he should be caught, he wanted to be thought a common burglar.

He took from his pocket a kit of tiny, chromium steel tools. There was a glass cutter with a full diamond point among them. He selected the windows of the library, placed a rubber suction disc against a pane, cut the glass noiselessly, and, holding the disc, drew the glass toward him with a faint snap.

In a moment he was in the library, playing the beam of a tiny flashlight over the walls and furniture. There were books, many of them, and a desk with papers on it.

From these he learned the name of the man who lived in the house. Professor Ronald Morvay, psychologist.

That was something. The Agent stored it in his memory. He rotated the beam of his flash, then stopped. It was focused on the wall, on the circular front of a small sunken safe.

The Agent walked to it quickly. House- and safe-breaking were included in his activities—when it was the house of a murderer he broke into and the safe of a murderer he opened.

But there were no clews as yet that would help unravel the plot behind the mysterious "Torture Trust." He knew it was an extortion racket. The police knew that, too. But what diabolical minds were back of it, and how could they be caught?

He knelt before the safe, touched the dial with his long fingers, put his ear to the metal. In the pursuit of criminals he had studied their methods, and he was familiar with the mechanics of safe-breaking. There were few that he could not open by listening to the faint movement of the lock tumblers.[5]

At the end of a minute he had the door of the wall safe in Professor Morvay's library swinging outward on its hinges. Then his hand reached inside.

A common burglar would have been disappointed, but the Agent felt rewarded. There were in the safe several small books, their pages filled with fine, close script. And as the Agent turned the beam of his flash on them and studied them, his eyes gleamed eagerly. He began to read—and read on, devouring the lines, page after page.

He was held in the grip of such appalling horror that his skin felt cold. Here was a record of human ingenuity and fiendishness beyond anything he had ever run into. No wonder the books had been placed in the safe!

They told of a series of experiments by a scientist—a psychologist—who used his knowledge for criminal purposes. They told of the experiments of Professor Morvay on that part of the human brain which harbors the sadistic tendencies—the lust to torture and kill. They told how men with a trace of sadism in their make-up could be trained into inhuman monsters. And Agent "X," grim-faced, thought of the gray-clad deaf-mutes with their sinister features. These were Professor Morvay's subjects, the men he had experimented on. These were the sadistic fiends who were only too glad to carry out the orders of their masters. These were the acid throwers!

---

5 AUTHOR'S NOTE: Because of his unlimited resources, the Secret Agent has access to information beyond the range of the average criminal. I have seen him, for instance, studying the charts and diagrams of the leading vault and safe makers, familiarizing himself with the various types of lock mechanisms. It is my belief that if the necessity arose, he could even open the most complicated bank vaults.

But the other two members of the murder trio were unknown to him. And there would have to be proof beyond this to convince any jury that the respectable Professor Morvay was a hideous criminal.

"X" began searching through the second book. Then he stopped. A faint noise had come. He put the books back in the safe, closed the door swiftly and started to turn toward the window. But instead, he held himself as though every muscle were frozen.

For the lights in the room suddenly flashed on, and standing in the door which he had silently opened stood Professor Morvay. There was an automatic in his hand, and its black, deadly muzzle was pointing straight at the Secret Agent's heart.

CHAPTER IX

THE MURDERERS STRIKE

IN THE SPACE of a second, the Agent knew what he faced. The menace of death hung heavy in the room. There was death in Professor Morvay's green-gray eyes and in the thin, cruel line of his lips. Legally he could find justification for shooting the Agent who appeared now as a common thief. Morvay would say to the police that he had shot in self-defense. Any instant the Agent expected to feel the impact of a bullet above his heart.

But the fear that gripped him was not for himself. It was for the success of his plans. Death would bring an end to them all.

But Morvay did not shoot. Instead, he came forward slowly, the gun held in fingers that were as tense as a bird's talons. His eyes were fixed upon the Agent, boring in, trying to penetrate behind the handkerchief.

"X" understood. Morvay was taking no chances. Curiosity was restraining the quick pressure of his trigger finger. The Agent appeared as a common burglar. But there was a chance that he might be someone else—a detective, for instance.

This doubt was the slender thread upon which the Agent's life hung. He would live until Morvay's curiosity was satisfied.

In those brief moments while the psychologist approached, "X" studied him. He saw the high, peaked forehead, the aquiline nose, the ruthless intelligence of the eyes. Morvay, he suspected, was an intellectual giant who had gone wrong, a man with erudition and a vast store of knowledge at his command. If the other members of the "Torture Trust" were like him, no wonder the police had been baffled. The professor and his colleagues were masters of death, cunning, pitiless, diabolical, laying the threads of their extortion racket like a sinister tarantula's web.

Morvay spoke then, and "X's" keenly attuned ears recognized

his voice as one of those he had heard in that mystery room where the deaf-mute had taken him.

"Stand still—lift your hands—or you die!"

Slowly the Secret Agent raised his arms. The acceleration of his pulses had stopped. They were normal now. An icy calm possessed him. His brain was working with the silent, faultless precision of some finely adjusted mechanism. He was matching his wits against death.

Holding the automatic in his right hand, standing only three feet from the Agent, Morvay reached out with his left. He drew the handkerchief down over the Agent's face. Whom he expected to see, "X" did not know. The Agent's disguise was that of a common thug—a street loafer lured into the byways of crime.

And, as Morvay studied him, the Agent saw curiosity give way to another emotion. A sinister message was flashing from the professor's eyes. The pupils had contracted. The whites glinted evilly. He had the look of a crouched jungle beast ready to spring. Morvay was planning to kill, planning it deliberately, ruthlessly, satisfied now that his nocturnal visitor had nothing to do with the police.

In "X's" right shoe was a weapon he might have used—a tiny air gun in the front of the sole, firing a stupefying dart, and discharged by pressing back in a certain way on his heel. It was one of many masterly defensive weapons he had devised. But he dismissed the idea of employing it now.

There was a greater issue than his own life at stake. There was the work to which he had dedicated that life. To use the dart now would give away to Professor Morvay that he wasn't what he appeared—a common burglar. Morvay, when he recovered from the dart's stupefying effect would be suspicious, on his guard ever after—and he would warn the other members of the "Torture Trust." They might disappear and carry on their fearful operations in some other community. "X" must stick to the role he had elected for himself.

With the quickness of a striking snake, he lashed outward and upward with his foot. He bent his body back, threw his whole weight forward, and the toe of his shoe struck Horvay's gun arm.

The gun exploded with a deafening report as Morvay's tense fingers jerked the trigger. The bullet went over the Agent's head, so close that he felt it nick the cloth of the cap he wore. His toe broke Morvay's hold on the weapon. It spun in the air, clattered to the floor, and Morvay staggered back with a cry of pain.

The man came toward her. On his face was a terrible smile—a smile of fiendish pleasure.

In an instant Agent "X" had swept up the gun and had reversed the direction of its muzzle. He snarled in his throat like a vicious thug.

"Stick 'em up, guy. Make any play and I'll burn yer guts. Thought yer was smart, didn't yer?"

His eyes glittering like those of a snake, the professor obeyed. Those eyes were upon "X" now, watching, calculating. And "X" knew that Morvay's suspicions were not entirely quieted. The Agent spoke again.

"Open that safe."

To emphasize his words, he thrust the gun closer, skinning his lips back from his teeth, making his face hideous.

"Open it, or I'll drill yer."

With a shrug Morvay turned. He knelt before the safe. His long fingers turned the dial. The safe's door swung outward.

"Stand back!"

With his gun, Agent "X" motioned Morvay against the wall. Then, his face greedy, he stepped forward and thrust his left hand into the safe. He withdrew it, fingers clutching the books. He thumbed them, stared at them closely, then flung them to the floor with a harsh curse.

"Where's the dough? What are yer tryin' to hand me?"

The professor was silent, and "X" pressed the gun savagely against his body.

"I'll give yer two minutes to come across."

Morvay nodded toward the desk. "You'll find money in there. The bottom left drawer."

Agent "X" backed away, crouched, fingers curled over the butt of the gun—the picture of a cash-crazed crook.

He jerked open the drawer of the desk with his left hand, pulled out an envelope. His fingers ripped it open, drew forth a sheaf of bills. There were many in there—tens, twenties, several hundred in cash, he estimated. Growling exultantly, he wadded the bills up, stuffed them in his pocket. There was a telephone on the desk. He yanked the cord loose, breaking it away from the box on the wall.

Then slowly, still holding the gun trained on Morvay, he backed toward the window. He thrust his feet out, eased his body backward, and in a moment the darkness had swallowed him.

HE was certain now that his acting had convinced Professor Morvay—certain that Morvay believed him to be a mere thief.

He crossed through several back yards, gliding between night-darkened houses. In the glow of a street lamp, he examined the roll of bills he had taken. There were more than he had thought—nearly four hundred dollars. It was money that he would turn over immediately to Betty Dale.

That was his practice when he took cash from criminals. There were worthy people upon whom the shadow of crime had fallen heavily. There was, for instance, the mother of a lad he knew, a boy who had foolishly taken part in a crap game that the police had raided. He had been sent to the workhouse for six months. The mother was destitute. This cash, taken from the murderer Morvay, would give her food and a roof over her head while her son was in jail. Betty Dale would see to that.

The Agent placed the sweater under his silk shirt again, making himself more presentable. He took a taxi to the block Betty lived on.

Walking along the block, he puckered up his lips and his strange, melodious whistle filled the air. It awoke echoes along the quiet street, piped eerily among the rooftops and whispered to silence in the dark areaways.[6]

He came to a stop opposite her apartment building, then stepped back into the shadows formed by an angle where two walls met. Looking upward, he saw that her windows were dark. Betty Dale was out or had gone to bed. He stood for a moment irresolutely.

Then something on the ground caught his eye. A whitish spot lay at his feet. He stooped down.

Close to one toe of his shoe was a cigarette stub. A little farther away was another. He had trained himself to observe small things, to miss nothing. What were these cigarette stubs doing here? Here in the spot where he always stood watching Betty's windows after whistling for her? He stared more closely.

There was a third stub just behind him. They told a story to the Agent. Someone else had stood here, waiting, watching—long enough to finish three cigarettes.

He struck a match and stooped down. Then he drew in his breath with a hiss. His fingers, suddenly tense, reached down and picked one of the stubs up. His eyes narrowed to steel-like pinpoints as he examined it.

On the cigarette butt were yellowish, uneven stains—the marks of the fingers that had grasped it. And the Agent's spine began to crawl with horror, with a slow, deepening dread.

His mind leaped back to those other hands he had seen—the hands of the gray-faced deaf-mutes—the acid throwers. Their fingers, he remembered, had been stained with the fumes of the liquid horror they carried. One of them must have been standing out here, watching Betty Dale's window.

He crossed the street at a run, entered the building. The night switchboard operator was lolling before his plugs, half asleep. The

---

6   AUTHOR'S NOTE: *The Agent's whistle is a sound which makes an unforgettable impression. I have heard it many times and am always startled. How he does it, I am not quite certain. It may be the peculiar formation of his lips which gives it its characteristic note. Or it may be the way he directs the column of air. In any event, he can vary its timbre and pitch as a great violinist varies the tone of his instrument while still retaining its essential quality. His whistle is always melodious, birdlike—but sometimes weird, sometimes menacing, sometimes questioning.*

Agent asked a question in a tone that brought the man up with a jerk.

"Miss Dale," "X" said. "Is she in?"

The switchboard operator shook his head.

"She got a call from her paper a half hour ago."

Dread deepened in the Agent's heart. The *Herald* seldom called Betty Dale at night.

"Get the paper at once," he said. "Let me speak to the night editor."

He went to the booth in the apartment's lobby, picked up the instrument. The operator at the switchboard plugged in a number. The crackling voice of the *Herald's* night editor came to the Agent's ears.

"Hello. Who is it?"

"Let me speak to Miss Betty Dale, please."

"Miss Dale? She's not here."

"Didn't you call her a half hour ago?"

"No—she works here in the day."

"You don't know where she is then?"

"Home, I guess—why? Who's calling?"

The Agent didn't answer. His hands trembled for a moment as he hung up. Fear possessed him—an icy fear that crept along his spine like the touch of some loathsome reptile—not fear for himself but for small, courageous Betty Dale, who had aided him so often.

Someone other than the *Herald's* editor had called her from the outside, lured her away. Someone had spied upon her movements, left cigarette butts with acid stains upon them—the badge of a hideous profession. Betty Dale had fallen under the black and awful shadow of the "Torture Trust"!

CHAPTER X

TORTURE!

WITH NO INKLING of the menace creeping upon her, Betty Dale had settled herself for a quiet evening at home. She had slipped into a comfortable and becoming pair of lounging pajamas, propped pillows on a sofa, and drawn the bookmark from an interesting new novel.

The reading light sprayed radiance on her gleaming blonde hair, touched her long lashes, caressed the soft contours of her face and figure. She lay back relaxing after a hard day at the office.

When at midnight the call from the *Herald* office came, it surprised her. She was seldom called at night.

"The editor wants you," said a voice. "A big story's broke. He thinks you can help—an' wants you to come right down."

With a sigh and a philosophical shrug, Betty Dale rose and dressed. Her career had been won by a lot of hard work and self-discipline. When the paper wanted her, she made it a point to be ready.

She powdered her face, gave her hat a smart tilt, dabbed lipstick on, and descended to the street. A proportion of her success had been gained by always appearing chic and alert.

She took a cab at the corner and told the driver to make it snappy. The paper had called. The presses were waiting. There was no time to lose.

The cab rolled swiftly through the deserted streets down to the block where the *Herald* building rose with the lights in its many windows gleaming cheerfully. Men in the linotype and composing rooms were hard at work.

She paid the driver and stepped smartly toward the building's entrance.

Then someone moved from the shadows beside the door. He held up his hand, signaled to her. He was a small man dressed in gray. She could not see his features, for he had a cap pulled down. They appeared to be strangely gray, masklike. She had never to her knowledge seen him before. Nevertheless she stopped.

And, in that instant, the man glided up to her. His movements were so quick, so purposeful, that she thought he was going to hand her something—thought that he must be an employee of the paper.

Instead, his fingers reached out, clutching her arm. With a quick movement that unbalanced her, he drew her back into the shadows. She started to scream, but he clapped a hand over her mouth. She tried to break away and something jabbed into her arm.

It was a sharp, keen pain like the prick of a needle. It was followed by a cool sensation in the surrounding flesh.

Betty Dale gasped and struggled and a wave of icy terror filled her. She felt a sudden roaring in her head, felt her knees giving way under her, felt as though the night were pressing in upon her from all sides. The lighted windows of the *Herald* building seemed to move in all directions. They seemed to explode, gyrate, whirl round and round like a galaxy of comets sweeping across an infinite sky. Then the roaring ceased. The comets grew dim. Betty Dale slipped into unconsciousness.

WHEN she awoke, feeling faint and dizzy, she sensed a jouncing motion. She tried to see, but something was over her eyes. She tried to speak and felt something else constricting her lips. She knew then that she was on the seat of a car, and she leaned back fighting the icy terror that possessed her. Her body still felt numb, paralyzed beyond the point of movement.

She realized that the sharp pain in her arm had been a hypodermic needle, an injection of some sort of drug. But who had pressed it in? Who was the strange, gray-faced man she had seen, and where was she being taken?

Fear rose in her mind. She had heard of unspeakable things, of the white slave traffic, of dark, slimy alleys of vice. Fear lay over her mind like a leaden pall.

She lost track of time. It might have been hours and it might have been minutes later that the car stopped. Then a door opened. She was propelled forward over a seemingly endless space, through an infinite duration of time. She was in some building, somewhere, but she couldn't see or cry out.

She was pushed into a chair. The covering was taken from her eyes, and a gag was removed from her mouth. But she was in utter darkness and could still see nothing. She drew in great gasps of air, but she did not cry out. She wasn't the sort of girl who screams or faints easily. She waited and listened in a frozen attitude of dread.

Then a light flashed on directly in her eyes. For minutes she could see nothing and no one spoke. More seconds passed and the light was suddenly dimmed. She could see around it now, behind it, and she caught her breath fearfully.

Two black-robed figures were sitting, regarding her. She saw the glitter of their eyes through slits in the black hoods that covered their faces. Somehow she sensed that she was in the presence of beings so evil that no human appeal would register. She did not speak. She waited to see what was to come.

A voice came out of the semi-gloom, out from behind a black hood. It was measured, impersonal. The tones were cultured.

"Miss Betty Dale! You are here to answer certain questions. A few nights ago you were seen at the Bellaire Club with a man who called himself Jeffrey Carter. There was a police raid. You left the club with a man who looked like Inspector Burks of the homicide squad. You were seen crossing the street with him into the shadows of a building. Shortly afterwards the real Inspector Burks arrived from headquarters. Who was the man who led you out? Who was Jeffrey Carter?"

Betty Dale sat still, her keen brain grappling with the situation. Were these men detectives? Was this a new kind of third degree?

"I don't know," she said at last. "I don't know who Jeffrey Carter really is."

The voice spoke again.

"Are he and the man who calls himself Secret Agent 'X' one and the same?"

Betty Dale gasped. Whoever these men were they seemed close to the truth. The facts dawned on her. Horror crept through her veins like a flow of icy water. These men were the heads of the hideous "Torture Trust." They had learned, or guessed, that the Agent was after them. But what could she tell them even if she cared to speak? She knew little about the Agent, and that little was a sedulously guarded secret. Courage and stubbornness overshadowed fear.

"I will tell you nothing," she said.

One of the hooded figures spoke again, his tone as dry and sinister as the scrape of a serpent's scales across stone.

"Others have said that. But there are things that will make any man or woman talk. There are things so terrible that human flesh crawls in the face of them. Things that make the human will crumble. Do you think that you, a mere girl, can endure such things?"

Betty Dale kept silent. She sat in her chair still frozen. They might wring the truth out of her, make her admit that Jeffrey Carter was the Secret Agent. She was not a superwoman. She might babble that if they forced her. But she knew it wouldn't satisfy them. They would want more, and she couldn't tell more. It was better to say nothing and let them think she knew all. It was better to stall for time.

She did not see either of the hooded men signal, but suddenly two men slipped into the room—two men dressed in gray, with faces as gray as their clothes. They were men with masklike expressions and reptilian cruelty in their lusterless eyes.

ONE of the hooded figures lifted his hands, making a series of motions in the air with his fingers—motions that the gray-faced men seemed to understand.

They drew Betty Dale from her seat and led her out of the room. The blindfold was slipped on again. She was led along corridors, down stairs, her numbed feet moving as though in a dream. She felt the damp coldness of a basement at last. She felt stone under her feet. Then she saw a light around the edges of the blindfold.

Suddenly she was tipped backwards, forced into what appeared to be a big chair. A scream of terror, her first, came from her lips as she felt cold bands of steel snapped over her wrists and ankles. The blindfold was removed and, glassy eyed, she stared about her.

The room she was in had a stone floor like a laboratory. The white shelves along the walls were loaded with bottles and tubes which heightened the effect. But the chair into which she had been thrust had no place in a laboratory. It was massive, heavy, made of steel and brass like a chair in a barber shop. The metal that encircled her arms and ankles was bolted to the sides of the chair. She was held as tightly as a prisoner in chains.

And a second look revealed that the room was not a laboratory. A laboratory would be devoted to science, research, human enlightenment. This room was dedicated to the opposite—to agony, fear, unspeakable horror. The room was a torture chamber.

One of the deaf-mutes was working at a shelf now. He had taken the stopper from a tall flask. He poured the contents into another flask, adding a few drops from still another.

Betty saw greenish, slow-moving fumes curling up like steam from a hideous witches' cauldron. They rose around the deaf-mute's face, but he didn't seem to mind. It was as though close proximity to evil had made him immune to the terrible things in which he dealt.

Betty screamed again, straining at the metal cuffs. But it was useless, hopeless, and the two men in the room could not even hear her cries. Their faces were impassive, devilish.

The man with the flask turned and came toward her. He held the flask in one hand and in the other was a stick with a swab on the end of it. He dipped the swab into the flask, brought it out, and she saw that it was wet with a green, sinister liquid.

Slow fumes wreathed up, curling lazily into the air, hideous and terrible as the quiet uncoiling of a serpent. The man moved the swab toward the fresh beauty of her face, toward her skin that was as smooth as the velvety petal of a rose. On his face for the first time was a definite expression. It was a terrible smile—a smile that seemed to take some of the lackluster from his eyes. It was a smile of fiendish pleasure, as though the thing he was about to do would give him exquisite delight.

Betty Dale screamed again. She screamed because she could not help it, because her eyes were fixed upon those lazy, terrible fumes, because terror seemed to writhe through her body like a living thing.

Then the wave of terror deepened. It engulfed her in a black flood that pressed against her heart. With a piercing, agonized scream on her lips, she fainted.

CHAPTER XI

A CRY IN THE DARK

THE SECRET AGENT, sensing the awful significance of Betty Dale's disappearance, sprang into action. There were times when he could be patient, times when he could wait, catlike, hour after hour to achieve some end. This was not one of them.

He felt responsible for the fate that had overtaken Betty Dale. If she had not aided him, been seen with him, this would not have happened.

He left the apartment building in long, quick strides. At the corner taxi stand where all-night cabs were available, he spoke to the drivers.

One was the cabman who had taken Betty Dale to the *Herald* building. He was taciturn at first under the Agent's sharp questioning, but a dollar bill loosened his tongue.

"Did Miss Dale go to the *Herald* office?" The Agent asked.

The cabman could not remember. He had gone on after collecting his fare, he said.

"Was there any one around—any other car near by?"

The taxi driver stroked his chin. Yes, he remembered now. There was a closed car parked down the block. It had made little impression on him. There were always cars around the *Herald* office.

The Agent nodded. There was the harsh glint of steel in his eyes. He jerked open the door of the cab, got in, and gave the driver a number.

Agent "X," unknown to any one but himself, had invested some of the funds intrusted to him in several cars. In his perilous work he needed one always handy. Each car was registered under a different name. He kept one, a sleek, fast roadster, in a mid-town garage.

The number he had given the driver was two blocks away from

the garage. When the cab stopped, he got out, paid the driver and disappeared into a shadowy areaway beside the street. There he affected another disguise. He was H. J. Martin now, the man in whose name the mid-town car was registered.

He strode quickly to the garage, and the night attendant got the car out for him. A minute more and he was speeding toward the West Side river front—toward the dark alleys and sinister dives around MacDonough Street.

The traffic lights had been turned off for the night. The streets were almost deserted. He drove with reckless abandon seemingly, but really with such skill as few men could duplicate. His face grim, his hands tense on the wheel, he rocketed around corners, plunged through side streets, raced against time. He passed through Mac-Donough Street and onward, a half dozen blocks to the vicinity of the warehouse.

There he slowed the car's speed, creeping forward, lights out, the engine barely turning over, till the big car was close to the vast bulk of the warehouse that rose silent and sinister into the night.

He parked the car in the blackest spot he could find near the row of dilapidated buildings in the warehouse's rear. Then, wraithlike, he slipped from it.

DEATH seemed to lurk in every hidden corner of the street. Death sounded in the soughing of the night wind, in the far-off whisper of the city. He was in a street of death and evil.

Once again, he took the kit of steel tools from his pocket. There were delicate skeleton keys hung on a metal ring. There were instruments that could open any door. These, combined with the Agent's uncanny skill, made every lock pregnable.

Moving close to the wall, he approached the door out of which he had seen Professor Morvay come. He kept so near to the building that the dim arc light at the street's corner did not even cast a shadow. He was no more than a darker blotch in the darkness of the night.

One of the small, gleaming tools was in his hand. His touch on the lock was as delicate as the touch of some skilled musician playing a beloved instrument. He moved the steel tool softly, turned it, probed. The knob of the door twisted in his hand. The door opened.

A moment more and he was inside the building. And the instant he entered it, he knew that it constituted a section of one of the routes along which he had been led. The faint acoustics of the walls were familiar.

But the darkness was like a black, evil pall, and at the end of the first corridor was another door. It, too, was locked, and the Agent paused to open it. He passed through it as easily as some disembodied spirit.

He stood listening, heard nothing, and winked on the beam of his pencil-thin flashlight. By twisting the end he could cut down its light as water is cut at the end of a garden hose by turning the nozzle. It cast a spot of radiance no bigger than a dime. He probed with it along the walls.

But he had to admit that he was at a loss. Where was Betty Dale? There was a chance, a terrible possibility, that she had not been brought here at all. There was another chance that she was being interviewed by one or more of the mysterious heads of the "Torture Trust."

He knew he could find again that chamber where he had first heard the voice of Professor Morvay. His mind had stored away directions for reaching it. To go there now seemed his only course.

In the darkness, picturing himself as still blindfolded, he began retracing his steps, going back along the way the deaf-mutes had led him. Up a flight of stairs, along another corridor, still on. He was in the warehouse proper now.

There was a feeling of solidity around him. A penetrating dampness in the air as of great, chill spaces. He was getting close to the secret council room, and every nerve in his body was taut.

Then he paused. It seemed to him that he heard a faint sound somewhere in the building. It was like an irrepressible whisper, coming through many thicknesses of walls.

He moved back quickly, half the length of the corridor. Then he listened again.

The sound came once more, and the hair on the Agent's head seemed to rise. The sound he had heard was a girl's scream of terror, faint, muffled, seemingly subterranean, but with such a note of agony in it that it was like a stifling, icy substance constricting his heart.

HE gave up any idea of going to the council chamber now. Betty was not there. Somewhere down in the dark sub-cellars of the warehouse she had been taken. He dared not think what they were doing to her, what had inspired that awful scream.

His ears were straining, his brain trying to locate the exact direction of the sound. He was desperately afraid that he might go the wrong way.

He reached a door along the corridor, opened it, turned on his flash, and saw that it led up. He ran on till he came to another. Dampness beat against his face as he swung the door back. There were stairs leading down.

He descended and found himself in a place that was like a series of catacombs. Each second seemed like a lost hour. He moved forward frantically, searching, groping, icy fear for the girl driving him on.

Ahead, nearer this time, the scream sounded again. There seemed to be only a few thicknesses of walls between it and himself. His ears had caught its exact location. He moved on with greater speed.

There was another door before him. He opened it with one of his master keys, melted through it, found himself in a dank corridor beyond. Running swiftly, he reached the corridor's end and stopped short. Directly ahead was a faint crack of light, the light below the edge of a door.

Silently as a shadow, he crept up to it. A third frenzied scream came from behind it, so close that it was like a knife stab.

The Agent had to steady his hand as he tried the knob. It, too, was fastened. He had never moved so quickly in his life as he did thrusting the key into the lock aperture. His hand grew steady again. In this crisis, nerves and muscles were cooperating. The crack of the door widened.

Swift as a streak of light, the Secret Agent was in the room. Then horror widened his eyes.

Betty Dale sat in a metal chair that was somehow reminiscent of a prison death house. He saw the metal bands that held her in, saw her face, white as parchment, her eyes stark with terror. He saw the gray-faced deaf-mute who bent over her, the swab of acid-soaked cotton in his hand.

And in that instant the Agent leaped across the floor. There was no time for subtle action. A drop of the greenish, horrible fluid had already fallen off the swab. It had fallen on Betty's dress close to her white neck. Fumes of it were curling up. Fumes from the swab itself were close to her nostrils, close to the satiny softness of her face, as the torturer brought it nearer.

Betty had come out of her faint only to find her tormenters waiting, ready to go ahead with their terrible deed. The Agent did not know this. He only knew that, mercifully, he had been in time.

So quickly that the mute in front of Betty did not see him until it was too late, he leaped forward. His hand struck the swab from the torturer's fingers. His other hand, balled into a hard fist, struck the gray-clad man in the side of the head, sending him reeling away.

The other mute whirled and came toward Agent "X" with a tube of acid in his hand. He flung it. Reeking fumes filled the air. But the Agent sidestepped and rushed in.

He swung again and sent the man crashing back against a shelf filled with bottles. The bottles leaped and fell with a clatter of breaking glass. More fumes filled the room.

From the corner of his eye, Agent "X" saw the first man he had struck rise and scuttle from the chamber like a streaking gray rat.

BUT there was no time to follow. The air was suffocating, deadly. He turned to Betty Dale. She was sitting in the chair, her face almost corpselike with the fear that had filled her. She could barely speak.

She watched him dumbly as he stared at the cuffs that held her. Seconds were precious. Where had the deaf-mute gone? To warn his masters? To get reinforcements?

"X's" hands were trembling—unusual for him. The steel bracelets presented difficulties. The keyholes in them were too small for any of his master keys.

Then he turned and leaped to the man who lay on the floor. The mute was breathing stertorously. He was unconscious. "X" fumbled in the man's pockets, exclaiming with relief when he found a ring of keys. Two of them were small, fragile.

He thrust one into the locks of the cuffs on Betty's wrists and ankles, and the cuffs snapped open. But it had taken time, and time was a precious thing.

He lifted her out of the chair, stood her on her feet, but she could not walk. Fear and the cramped position she had been in had stiffened her muscles.

He picked her up bodily; turned toward the door of the chamber. Somewhere in the vast building overhead, there was a faint noise. It was like a signal bell. Down a long corridor he saw a dim flicker of light. He didn't like it. Deaf-mutes could not hear, but they could see. What if there were others? There was no way of knowing how many of his terrible subjects Professor Morvay had trained.

Running as swiftly as he could, he carried Betty back the way he had come. But he found that one door had snapped shut again. He had to put her down and work with his master key. That took time.

At the level of the ground floor, at a junction of corridors he paused. There was a whisper of sound behind—the sound of running feet. Pursuers were coming out of the darkness. He and Betty would shortly be overwhelmed. The girl must be gotten away at all costs. If she were injured, burned with acid, it would haunt him to the end of his days.

He stooped and whispered to her.

"Rats are coming out of the night. A terrier may have to hold them in check. Do as the terrier says."

He carried Betty along a passage into the rear group of buildings. He set her down and found she could walk now. Then he spoke again, calmly, as though death were not close at their heels in the darkness behind.

"Go straight ahead and out the door. A car waits across the street. Drive away—as fast as you can. Go to the Hotel Graymont. Wait for the terrier there!"

He heard her breath come quickly, felt her fingers clutch him. She did not want to obey—did not want to desert him. But a steely touch of his hand on her arm gave accent to his order. He pushed her forward, heard her footsteps receding.

He was glad he had done it. The sounds in the corridor behind were close now. Betty Dale could not walk rapidly. Carrying her, he would have been overtaken surely. Her only chance of escape was for him to make himself a dyke against the human flood of evil and horror that was surging in upon him.

He waited tensely till the sounds of the running feet were close. Then he whipped out his gas pistol and fired. There were only six gas-filled shells in the gun. He discharged them all, laying a momentary barrage in the corridor.

There was the noise of a stumbling, falling body. Gasps of fear came out of the darkness and the footsteps receded. Then the gas cloud cleared and the fierce wave advanced again. The blackness vomited leaping, flying figures. There were a half-dozen of the gray-clad men.

Struggling fiercely, fighting against the human torrent that engulfed him, the Secret Agent went down in a flying welter of arms and legs and lashing fists.

CHAPTER XII

TRAPPED!

HE FOUGHT ON blindly in the darkness, expecting momentarily to have scalding drops of acid dashed into his face, to feel his eyeballs, nostrils, and lips being seared into shapeless lumps of quivering, pain-prodded flesh. But none came.

The gray-clad men seemed for the moment to have discarded the liquid horror that they dealt in. They wanted evidently to take him alive, uninjured.

He crashed a balled fist into a man's writhing face. He felt teeth snap, felt the skin of his knuckles rip. But the next instant two men were on his back and snake-like fingers were encircling his throat. He reached up, tried to break their hold, and someone butted him in the stomach, doubling him up in breathless agony. Then it seemed that a dozen vises had been clamped upon him. Hands pinioned him from all sides. The pressure on his throat increased till his breath was shut off, till he lay gasping.

With unconsciousness close at hand, he relaxed. The fingers on his throat were loosened slightly. He could breathe again feebly. A light was turned on and he saw a forest of legs around him.

The faces looking down at him were impassive, hideous as death masks in their reptilian immobility. One of the men lay moaning, nursing his bleeding gums, but there were five others.

They yanked the Secret Agent to his feet. A gun was pressed against his back so forcefully that it bruised the flesh. He was pushed along the corridor, back the way he had come.

He wondered dully why they didn't shoot, why they didn't kill him now, or throw acid in his face. Then he realized that these men were slaves, being disciplined in evil and committed to do the will of their masters. They were taking him upstairs again, to the council chambers.

Four of them held him outside the door while the fifth slipped inside. "X" had no doubt the man was telling in finger language to the hooded masters of death, the story of Betty Dale's escape and his own entry.

The fifth mute came back, his face still impassive, and Agent "X" was thrust through the door into the presence of the black-robed men. But there were only two now. The third had not returned. That one, the Agent guessed, was Morvay.

The spotlight was turned on his face again. He trusted to his disguise, but wondered what their reaction to it would be. He was posing as H. J. Martin now, a sandy-haired, plump-faced businessman.

The two men behind the black hoods stared at him, their eyes glittering through the slits. At a gesture from one of them, the deafmutes withdrew to the side of the room. "X" stood alone like a prisoner before the bar.

The voice of one of the hooded men came slowly, tauntingly.

"So—a young Sir Galahad who has rescued a fair lady in distress!"

The other one, his voice gruffer, asked a question.

"Who are you?"

The Agent answered bluntly, quickly, playing his part as always.

"My name's Martin. You devils can't get away with what you tried to do to Miss Dale. I came just in time."

A low, evil laugh sounded from behind the hood.

"She escaped—but nothing can save her now. She was only being frightened to make her talk. But she will be found now—wherever she is—and the beauty of her face will become a thing that men will turn their eyes from in loathing."

The Secret Agent clenched his fist. His voice was tense, high-pitched, as he continued his pose.

"Whoever you are, you can't get away with it, I say. You'll all go to jail, or the electric chair. You're devils, murderers."

They ignored his passionate speech.

"Tell us one thing—Mr. Martin. How did you find your way here? How did you get in?" There was a sneer in the voice—a taunting note.

The Agent sensed what it meant; but he kept up his bluff.

"You're not as clever as you think. Betty's a girl friend of mine.

I learned she'd gotten a phony call. I found she'd disappeared and I followed her."

"Yes?"

"Yes."

One of the hooded figures leaned forward. His hands were gripping the sides of his chair. His eyes were glittering points of light behind the eyeholes of his hood, and his voice was low, harsh and deadly.

"Don't think you can fool us—Martin. We know who you are. We know there is only one man who could have found his way to this place and come through the locked doors. We know there is only one man who could have saved Betty Dale!"

THE room was still as death for an instant. Then a low, dry chuckle sounded.

"We compliment you—Secret Agent 'X'! You have proved your cleverness. Your disguise is beyond reproach. So it was when you played the part of Jeffrey Carter—and when you impersonated Inspector Burks of the homicide squad. So, too, it was when you made us believe you were Jason Hertz. That was your master stroke, 'X.' But we had Hertz watched. When he so mysteriously disappeared from the refuge we had given him, we began to suspect we had been tricked."

Agent "X's" heart stood still. The voice of the hooded man droned on.

"What you did with Hertz we do not know. That is neither here nor there. We know that you helped him out of prison, impersonated him—so cleverly that you fooled us for a time. But you cannot go on fooling us as you can the police. Your methods are dashing, sensational, dramatic. You have annoyed us and will continue to do so if you are not curbed. But we have agents of our own. You have been watched, spied upon from the night you went to the Bellaire Club. Your impersonation of Inspector Burks was seen by the man you chased over the roof."

The chuckle came again.

"I am being frank with you, because I expect you to be frank with us. Your history is intriguing. Just who is employing you? For what particular cause are you working?"

The voice had become almost matter-of-fact now. It was as though "X's" answers were foregone conclusions. But he was silent. The voice behind the hood changed again. It had a steely, imperious note in it.

"You will give us all this information, Agent 'X.' It is necessary for us to know. There may be an effort made to replace you when—" The voice trailed off with sinister implication.

"Yes, death for you is inevitable. You are aware of that yourself. You are aware that you cannot leave this place alive. But we can give you a choice of two deaths—one quick, painless; the other so lingering, so horrible, so pregnant with agony that you will cease to be a man and will become a blind, babbling creature, a death so unthinkable that you would choose to die a thousand ordinary deaths."

Still the Agent was silent, standing stiffly erect, staring straight before him. Momentarily his will seemed suspended. Momentarily he could only wait and listen. The voice droned on.

"You have seen the faces of men who have been dead many days. Your face will be like that while you are still alive; the flesh eaten away, the eye sockets empty, the teeth skull-like."

Sweat broke out on the Secret Agent's forehead. It was not so much fear as fury against these men—a fury so terrible that it left him white and shaking. Then he grew calm again.

"What would you ask me to do?" he said.

"A small thing. We will provide you with pen and paper and a place to write. You will give us a report of all your activities. You will name your hide-outs, your methods, tell us exactly who you are and who is behind you. We know you work alone. We know that no one shares your secrets; but you are supplied with money. That is evident. There have been whispers that the government is backing you."

"Ask the police," said the Agent coldly.

"The police hunt you, too. They regard you as an enemy, a criminal—that is part of your game. But you will tell us—everything."

There was silence again, and the Agent could feel the eyes of the ravenlike pair before him boring into his own.

"What's your answer?" came a voice at last.

The Agent held himself more erect. His lips remained closed. He stared calmly, silently at his questioners.

"You will not speak! We are not surprised. You are clever in your disguises. You are confident of your ability. But there are things which will penetrate and destroy any disguise. There are acids hungry for the flesh of men. We will give you a small taste of what hell is like—then we will leave you poised on the brink of hell, and—who knows—you may be willing to talk—to avoid the last terrible plunge!"

CHAPTER XIII

THE PLUNGE

THE HOODED MAN'S hands moved in the air before him. His fingers made quick motions, delivering imperious orders. Four of the gray-clad mutes stepped forward and grasped the Agent's arms. The fifth man held the gun at his back. He was marched out of the room.

He had no plan of action. He saw at the moment no way of escape. He waited for that small, brief opportunity which might checkmate the awful fate ahead of him. He couldn't do what had been asked of him—betray the secrets that he guarded so jealously. Yet to keep them guarded he would have to submit to more than human flesh could endure. Would it be better, he wondered, to make a break now and invite a bullet in his back?

But he pictured himself lying wounded, helpless, with flesh-eating acid being poured into his face. There was nothing that these men would stop at.

He walked quietly downstairs and through the corridors. They had not blindfolded him—a tribute to his cleverness, to the knowledge that no blindfolds could keep him from knowing where he was. And it was evidence of the certainty that he was to die.

They came at last to the door of the torture chamber. The four men holding him redoubled the force of their grip on his arms. The man with the gun stepped forward, unlocking the door. He pressed a switch and light came from inside.

For the moment this fifth man with the gun was dead ahead, silhouetted against the light behind him. There would never be another opportunity. Within the next minute Agent "X" would be in the chair with the steel cuffs snapped over his legs and ankles—cuffs that no human strength or will could break. It was now or never.

His four captors didn't notice the motion of his foot, or if they did they mistook it for a shrinking back in fear. He lifted his toe, swayed his body sideways, bringing his full weight down on the right heel, pressing the rubber and flattening it so that the metal stud inside that was the trigger of the tiny air gun was pushed home.

They did not hear the faint hiss that came from the end of the minute tube concealed in the thick sole of his shoe.[7]

The man in the door of the torture chamber, the man with the gun, gave a throaty, inarticulate cry. His face registered intense surprise. He turned, slowly, stood swaying on his feet, and, just as slowly, his face changed. The masklike look came again. The face muscles sagged, knotted, and sagged again. The man's gun fell from his inert fingers and clattered to the stone floor. The man's knees buckled under him and he collapsed.

The four mutes holding Agent "X" stiffened with amazement. Their lusterless eyes showed utter incomprehension. Their grip on his arms relaxed for the fraction of a second. And, in that fraction of time, he put all the strength of his muscles into one mighty heave. He wrenched himself loose and leaped backwards.

He heard the pounding of feet behind him, saw lights flash again as a secret signal system was put into operation. The gray-clad men were swift runners, too. They sensed now that the collapse of the man with the gun had been a trick of the Agent's. Their fury was animal-like. He could hear their babbling, incoherent cries—the cries of mutes trying to give expression to inhuman rage.

He passed an open passageway and saw two more figures running toward him. He flashed past; but something streaked out, burning his leg so that for a moment the pain almost paralyzed him and forced him to slow down. A splash of acid hurled by one of the men in the corridor had struck his ankle. He ran on, his face contorted.

He had the feeling now that flitting gray shapes were everywhere, that another spray of acid might come out of any dark corner. But he could not see his way. He turned on the pencil-thin

---

7 *AUTHOR'S NOTE: It was my privilege once to examine this air gun of the Agent's. He did not explain its mechanism, but the general details of it were simple enough. The tube or barrel of the gun was made of flexible steel that straightened when his foot was lifted. The dart was no longer than a phonograph needle and had a tiny hollow at its end. In this hollow was a drop of the distilled essence of some drug like morphine. Its effect on the nervous system was, I gathered, almost instantaneous.*

beam of his flash for an instant. Directly ahead was the corridor leading through the jumble of buildings in the warehouse's rear. Beyond it was the street.

He reached the street with flying figures close behind him. He burst out the door into the cold night air. But Betty had taken his car as he had told her to. Death was close at his heels.

WINCING with pain, limping, he plunged along the street. Looking back he saw gray shapes moving behind him like wolves in the night. The "Torture Trust's" horrible horde was close behind. The street seemed to harbor death.

He put on a burst of speed that pumped blood into the burned spot on his ankle, increasing the pain until it was as though a hot rivet had been driven into his flesh.

He turned a corner, ran on with the pursuers gaining. It was late, the streets were deserted. Even if there were a cop in sight he would be of no aid. He would only meet a hideous death, too.

Two more blocks and the Agent saw something that made him increase his efforts. There was an all-night lunch room at the next corner. A taxi stood before it, its engine idling to keep warm. The driver was inside.

Even as he leaped into the cab's front seat, he heard the sound of another auto starting up behind, backing out of a garage. He remembered the car that had taken Betty Dale away from the *Herald* office, the car in which he had ridden to MacDonough Street.

He raced the taxi's engine, drew the shift lever back, released the clutch, and plunged forward. He heard the hoarse shout of a man behind him—the taxi driver running from the lunch room. But he had to take the cab. If anything happened to it, he'd see that the taxi company was reimbursed.

The taxi was an old one. Its valves needed grinding. The motor had poor pickup. The car was already shooting down the street, gaining. He shifted frantically, and pressed the accelerator down till the engine coughed. The taxi began to gain speed. It rumbled and jounced over the rough pavement. He spun the wheel, made a skidding turn around a corner, and roared on.

At the end of the block he heard the pursuing car duplicate his maneuver. The sound of the taxi's engine was rising in pitch now. The big cab was rolling ahead at ever mounting speed. The needle on the speedometer showed forty, fifty, fifty-five. He took another corner, heading toward the river to get out of the rough cross-town streets. Then he found himself on a long, wide avenue running parallel with the water. It too, was deserted, until a cop's whistle blew frantically. But the taxi lurched and roared past.

Agent "X" glanced over his shoulder through the rear window. The goggling lights of the car behind were increasing steadily in size. He pressed the accelerator down as far as it would go—and got up to fifty-five again. But the needle of the speedometer hung there, sliding forward a degree when the street slanted down, going back when there was a slight incline. The pursuing car was only a half block behind.

Then the warehouses and pier sheds to right and left echoed to the sudden staccato clatter of a sub-machine gun. Something whined by in the night. An explosive tinkle of breaking glass came from the rear window. He looked back and saw that it had disappeared. It was an old model car. Even the windshield was not shatterproof. The glass partition between the driver's seat and the passenger's compartment was the next to go. Then the windshield flew into crystal slivers before his face. Pieces of it whizzed by his head, pricked his skin.

The night wind beat against his eyes with a force that made them blink and burn. The cab was being torn to pieces, raked by bullets as the devilish chatter of the machine gun continued with a measured, precise regularity that had the finality of doom. In a matter of seconds only the law of averages would take effect, a steel-jacketed bullet would pierce him, and he would slump forward in his seat. The speeding cab would crash into a building, be demolished, burst into flame. The car behind had demonstrated its supremacy in speed.

He shot a glance to the left toward the river, his eyes bright as hot coals. Death by bullets was quick, painless. The old wound in his side had brought him near death often. He was on familiar terms with the Grim Reaper. But there was the cause for which he worked. There was the "Torture Trust" to be smashed, and there was Betty Dale! Unless he fought for her, saved her, she would be tracked down and hideously mutilated, perhaps killed.

He spun the wheel of the plunging cab viciously. It rocked to the left across the broad street. For an instant the raking stream of bullets left it. Then they found it again. The car behind had swerved, too. But Agent "X" pulled the wheel still farther. The fat tires squealed in protest. The cab groaned in every bolt. It skidded dangerously, then roared ahead. The yawning entrance to an open dock was directly before it; farther still the oily, chill waters of the river moved sluggishly. The cab lunged out across the clattering boards of the dock.

The machine gun ceased its chattering, but the car behind still followed. The Agent did not decrease his speed. He sat hunched low over the wheel, staring ahead through the shattered windshield.

A low protecting bulkhead rose at the end of the dock. There were capstans spaced at intervals for tugs and excursion boats to tie to. He aimed the blunt nose of the cab between them and put on a last burst of speed, holding the wheel steady.

The front tires of the cab struck the bulkhead and leaped up. The cab plunged on like a madly bucking horse, rearing its yellow shape over the end of the dock. An instant it seemed to hang in the air, then it plunged to the black river below and struck with a terrific splash. Steam hissed from the hot pipes of the engine. Yellow foam seethed and slithered sidewise. A second passed—two—and the cab filled and sank from sight.

CHAPTER XIV

THE MARK OF THE AGENT

THE HEADS OF the "Torture Trust" were assembled again in their secret council chamber. All were there, including the sinister Professor Morvay. There was tonight a question of singular importance to be discussed. First, however, one of the gray-clad deaf-mutes entered, stood before the black-robed trio, and began making motions in the air—the motions of his strange finger language.

He told for the benefit of Professor Morvay, who had not been present the night before, just what had taken place. He told of the escape of Betty Dale, of how they had pursued the Secret Agent, riddled his car with bullets, and seen him plunge to his death in the black waters of the river.

The fast-moving hand and fingers of the deaf-mute gave a graphic account of that wild chase through the night-darkened streets.

Morvay leaned forward, his eyes glowing behind the black hood. His long fingers answered in the same language, then asked a question.

"Are you certain he is dead? Did you wait to see whether he rose to the surface?"

"Yes," came the answer. "We waited, watched—there was no chance of his survival."

Morvay registered grim satisfaction. The deaf-mute was dismissed. One of the hooded trio spoke.

"You have heard what our slave reports. Secret Agent 'X' is dead. The girl escaped, but she knows nothing. The agent has no close confidante."

Morvay nodded.

"But to make sure," he said, "you are having the girl trailed? You will have her punished as soon as she is found."

The man he had questioned nodded.

"The *Herald* office and her apartment are being shadowed," he said. "She will turn up at one place or the other. We will make an example of her."

Again Morvay nodded. He hadn't seen Betty Dale, but he had been told that she was beautiful, piquant. She had chosen to interfere with the activities of the "Torture Trust." She was an ally of the Secret Agent. Because of that her beauty would be hideously destroyed. She would spend the remainder of her life looking forward to death. The secret strain of sadism that made Morvay the vicious criminal he was took delight in this prospect. He ran his tongue over thin, cruel lips.

"Let us forget the girl and the Agent now," he said. "One is dead—the other will shortly be disposed of. What of the business in hand?"

The other two men leaned forward. There was the glitter in their eyes of men whose greed for money and power amounts to fanaticism. Money—power! For these they had slaughtered, maimed, and spread terror. They had extorted thousands from fear-crazed millionaires. They began to picture themselves as czars of crime, masters of death, invincible rulers of the underworld. And, scorning the citizens of the underworld, they planned to organize its riffraff into a vast disciplined legion. That would come later, however, when they had more power. Tonight there was something concrete to go over— details of the most daring crime they had ever conceived.

"Fear of our organization is spreading," said the man on Morvay's right. "We are becoming famous. They call us the "'Torture Trust.'" A low laugh followed. "It will make our next move easier. We are known across the water."

THEY then began to discuss the plot they had in mind. It was stupendously daring, yet absurdly simple; but they never acted without long preliminary arguments, weighing each move with cold logic. They had the training, the discipline, of men in high positions. Each could have made a decent living in the world of honest men. But there was in each a hidden strain of criminality coupled with a ruthless thirst for power.

The plan under discussion tonight dealt with Sir Anthony Dunsmark, British financier; one of the heads of the great Bank of England; a man of international repute; a man whose opinions were taken as gospel truth and whose statements had to be issued guardedly because they had power to influence stock quotations in many countries. Dunsmark had shouldered his share of the financial burdens of the World War. He was on his way to America now to take part in a meeting of bankers, to do his bit toward helping along world recovery. Traveling on the liner *Victoria,* accompanied by one secretary, he would arrive in three days.

The hooded trio were like buzzards before a feast preparing for his arrival. So far their extortion racket had fallen on rich men in the city only. But here was an opportunity to extend operations.

What if Anthony Dunsmark disappeared upon arrival in America? What if his government should receive a letter demanding a vast sum which, if not paid over, would bring about the death of Dunsmark by the lingering horrors of acid?

No government would permit such a thing to happen to one of its best-known citizens. The sum asked would be paid, no matter how great it might be. To have Sir Anthony Dunsmark meet his death at the hands of American criminals would be a blot on the United States. America would contribute to his ransom if necessary. Thus the black-robed trio reasoned. But there were still details to be worked out. Dunsmark would be met at the dock by a police escort. There would be secret service operatives mingling in the crowd. To steal him away in spite of this was a big order. But the trio had confidence in their ability.

"There are many methods," said the man on Morvay's right. "Dunsmark will be lionized for days after his arrival. He will be invited everywhere. We will watch him ceaselessly and wait for an opportunity."

Morvay laughed softly.

"One of us," he said, "might even invite him to our own home. We are not without social position ourselves."

The man on his left growled an objection.

"There must be no hint of suspicion directed at us."

"We will meet again tomorrow night," Morvay answered. "I have feelers out. I will know then the names of some of the people who plan to have Dunsmark as a guest."

The others nodded assent. Discussion ceased. One by one they arose and left the council chamber, each leaving by a different route, Morvay passed through the buildings in the rear of the warehouse. He breathed easier now that the Secret Agent was gone. "X" was the only man so far who had given them any worry. The police were still wandering in confused circles and floundering in a bog of doubt.

It was raining as Morvay stepped into the dark street. He rolled his collar up and strode quickly along, his ulster flapping about his heels. He turned at the corner, heading toward the avenue four blocks away where it was his custom to pick up a taxi.

Then, shortly before he reached it he was pleased to see a cruising cab coming his way. The rain had increased. This was a bit of luck, he thought.

He held up a finger, signaled the cab, and climbed in. He gave the name of a hotel, one of the points where he sometimes changed taxis, in the routine that all of them followed to throw shadowers off the trail. He lit a cigarette and leaned back against the seat, going over in his mind the details of the daring crime planned.

The driver, sitting slumped behind the wheel, drove the cab on through the chill winter rain. Drops of moisture splattered against the glass in the door. Morvay was glad the windows were closed. He did not see the hands of the driver creep down to a small hidden lever beside his seat. He could not, for there was a front partition cutting off his view.

But he began to feel a slow dizziness creeping over him. The air in the cab seemed to be getting stale as though the exhaust had sprung a leak and carbon monoxide were seeping into the car's interior.

Morvay leaned forward, reaching toward a window. But the dizziness increased to such an extent that he swayed in his seat.

He tried to raise his hand and it seemed to weigh many pounds. His cigarette dropped from shaking fingers. He tried to cry out to the driver, but his voice sounded faint and far away.

He slumped sidewise in the seat, struggling frantically to preserve his faculties. For a moment his face turned toward the ceiling of the cab, and a sudden shudder of amazement passed through his body. He made a desperate effort to rise, but succeeded only in flopping to the floor where he lay, still staring toward the roof with glassy, horrified eyes.

Over his head, in the center of the fabric covering the taxi's roof, something glowed with an eerie, wavering light. It was a letter, an "X," written in some kind of radiant paint. And, as Professor Morvay slipped into unconsciousness, it seemed to hover before his gaze like an accusing, all-seeing eye.

CHAPTER XV

THE INSPECTOR ARRIVES

THE TAXI ROLLED on through the dreary, rain-swept night. In the rear compartment the inert body of Professor Morvay lurched grotesquely with every jounce the car gave. His still face and glassy eyes were like those of a corpse. But he was not dead.

The driver of the cab pressed the small lever beside his seat a second time, cutting off the flow of odorless anesthetizing gas that had swept Morvay into the dreamless depths of unconsciousness. The driver's face was expressionless, but under his visored cap his eyes glowed with piercing brightness.

Several times fares stepped to the curb, signaling him to stop, supposing the cab empty. But the cabman drove by them briskly. He avoided the lighted streets, turned west, and whirled into a long avenue that led uptown. He bore steadily ahead through the rain with the purposefulness of a man who has a definite objective.

Wheeling into the broad drive that skirted the river, he passed millionaires' homes and block upon block of expensive apartment houses, magnificent with their liveried doormen and glittering foyers.

Once he turned his head and glanced sidewise at a gloomy old house that rose on a corner. Its windows were boarded up. There was an air of decay and desolation about the place. It was the old Montgomery mansion which the litigation of heirs had kept empty for years.

A faint, grim smile twisted the mouth of the cabman, alias Secret Agent "X." In a chamber of that house he had achieved his present disguise. The past twenty-four hours had been exciting ones. A man rated as dead had come to life. The members of the hideous "Torture Trust" believed he had gone down with the speeding taxi that had plunged off the dock. Their sadistic slaves had watched for him to rise to the surface, and he had not risen. The crash of the cab had been something he had planned deliberately.

They did not know that he could hold his breath a full two minutes under water and swim with the swift, powerful strokes of a diving otter. They hadn't seen him when he reached the surface under the inky shadows of the dock. And they didn't know that he had communicated with Betty Dale, told her to keep under cover in her room at the Hotel Graymont.

There was tonight a glint of ironic amusement in the Agent's eyes. This was the second taxi he had driven within a space of twenty-four hours. The first he had stolen and destroyed. This one he had bought. But he preferred to consider the first a loan, for money from the account of Elisha Pond would pay for them both eventually. He wasn't a criminal, and when he found it necessary to destroy property he took pains to reimburse the owners. The present cab had been purchased for the purpose of installing the hidden tank of compressed gas, the lever control, and the outlet tube in the passenger's compartment. To aid in capturing a man like Morvay, to break the hideous "Torture Trust," the investment seemed legitimate.

But he was not taking Morvay to jail.

The cab passed on up the drive, turned east, then north, and continued through the heart of the city. Agent "X" drove with the ease of a man to whom all types of cars are familiar.

He came to the suburbs at last, but still forged on through the rain-swept night. Miles beyond the city limits, he turned off on a little dirt road. The cab jounced and pitched like a ship on a stormy sea. The body of Professor Morvay rolled with it, his glassy eyes still directed toward the ceiling and the "X" that glowed there. But the eyes were unseeing now.

Agent "X" stopped the cab. He opened the door and lifted Morvay out as though he had been a sack of meal. He carried him, arms and legs dangling, through the pelting rain, to the dim outlines of a house. It was an old, ramshackle farmhouse—the same to which he had taken Jason Hertz on the night Hertz escaped from prison.

He held Morvay over his shoulder with one hand for a moment. A key grated in the lock, the door opened, and Agent "X" and his prisoner were inside.

The rain drummed steadily on the worn shingles of the roof. There was the musty, stifling smell of old carpets and moldy walls. The Agent took Morvay to a back room and struck a light.

There he set to work quickly, eagerly, for he had much to do. He deposited Morvay in a chair, backed the chair to an upright supporting the big beams in the center of the room and, after drawing Morvay's inert arms about the upright, snapped handcuffs over his wrists. Morvay was now a prisoner, held erect in the chair by the metal cuffs.

Agent "X" went to a shelf and drew out a bottle and a piece of cotton. He dipped the cotton into the bottle and held it close to Morvay's nose. The pungent smell of carbonate of ammonia filled the room.

SLOWLY Morvay stirred and began to breathe more deeply as the powerful stimulant overcame the effects of the gas. In three minutes he lifted his head. His eyes opened, closed, and opened again. They were no longer glassy, but were alive, intelligent. Morvay had returned to consciousness.

But fear and horror overspread his features. He tugged at his manacled hands, strained till the cords stood out in his neck, then began cursing harshly. There was the look of an evil, predatory beast on his features.

The Agent's face was bleak, unyielding. His eyes under his visored cap glowed like coals of fire.

"Agent 'X'! You are still alive then?" said Morvay. "They did not kill you—the fools, the fools!" There was bitterness in his voice and fury that bordered on the insane. The blundering deaf-mutes were to be pitied if he ever got free.

Agent "X" came closer. He hadn't spoken, but his eyes were boring into those of the professor's. His voice was low, persuasive.

"You are a murderer, Professor Morvay—one of a trio of murderers. The electric chair awaits you. But there is one road of escape. It is a road which no man of decency or principle would think of following. But you have proved that you are neither. Therefore, I am offering you this road. Turn States' evidence, tell me the names of your two friends, your fellow criminals and murderers, and you will escape the death penalty."

Agent "X" knew it would be futile to employ the method he had used so effectively with Jason Hertz—the method of hypnosis. A man of Morvay's type, a psychologist and hard-headed intellectual, could never be hypnotized.

Morvay blinked at the Agent for a moment, as though weighing the proposition. Then his lips curled back in an ugly sneer and a mocking laugh came from them.

"Fool! Fool! I will tell you nothing! You have no evidence against me! No proof! You will never find out who my colleagues are, nor learn our secrets!"

His harsh laugh sounded again, and seconds passed as their eyes clashed. "X" might have resorted to torture to make Morvay talk. But that was not his way. He knew that men are not always truthful under torture—and the truth was what he wanted.

He stood frowning, irresolute, with Morvay's harsh laughter ringing in his ears. He might turn Morvay over to the police, but the evidence against him was still too weak. There were missing links in the chain; and it wasn't the Agent's concern to have individuals arrested. He wanted to smash the whole hideous pattern of the "Torture Trust."

He turned then, brought his movie camera out, and focused the calcium flare on Morvay's evil face. The professor cursed and struggled in his chair as the camera clicked. Before he realized what was being done, "X" had started the dictaphone machine also, making a record of his voice. Morvay grew wise suddenly, and ceased speaking. There was a light of fury in his eyes, and he followed every movement the Agent made like a tiger hoping for a chance to spring.

Agent "X," silent and intent, filled a hypo needle from a small vial in a rack. There were other vials beside it, marked with different hour numbers.[8] He selected one, the label of which read, "Thirty-six."

Morvay began cursing again as Agent "X" approached him with the hypo needle. He bared his teeth like a cornered animal and the light in his eyes was satanic. But calmly, deftly, the Agent thrust the point of the needle into his arm and pressed the plunger home.

Morvay's curses became incoherent, babbling. His lips quivered, his eyes closed again. In a few moments his head fell forward. For thirty-six hours he would be dead to the world.

Agent "X" unsnapped the handcuffs from about the upright and carried the professor to the attic. There he deposited him on a pile of straw and carefully went through his pockets, taking Morvay's keys, watch, and private papers. He descended to the first

---

8 *AUTHOR'S NOTE: Agent "X," I am convinced, has made a profound study of anesthesia and anesthetic compounds. He has often made use of them in his dangerous and daring work and can figure with remarkable exactitude how long a certain dose of a particular drug will hold a man under its influence.*

floor room, removed the record from the dictaphone machine, the film from the movie camera, and left the farmhouse, driving back through the rain to the city. His interview with Morvay had not been satisfactory. He had failed to learn the identities of the other members of the "Torture Trust." He was still working in a black pall of mystery.

For hours that night he labored in his hidden room in the old Montgomery mansion. Sleep seemed unnecessary to the Agent. Vital, nervous forces drove him on. He developed the movie film, wound it on a drying reel, put the dictaphone record under a phonograph needle, and listened to Morvay's voice.

Once he thrust a hand into his pocket and brought out a box of varicolored, transparent capsules. They were about an inch long, filled with various essences and strange looking substances. The Agent selected several and swallowed them.[9]

He continued his work until the slow, gray fingers of dawn crept across the street outside and made steely glints on the surface of the river.

BY the next evening Agent "X" had a disguise of Professor Morvay as perfect as the one he had done of Jason Hertz. He left the Montgomery mansion as twilight descended, and took a taxi to Morvay's house in that respectable street in the suburbs. There he once again opened the safe, and began a more comprehensive inspection of the books it contained. He found something he had not had time to investigate before—a lengthy paper written in code. It appeared meaningless, unintelligible. Groups of five letters were spaced at intervals across the page. Where did Morvay keep the code book which would make the paper understandable? He searched the room for a half hour without results.

Then, philosophically, with a box of cigarettes, a pencil and sheets of paper handy, he settled himself in a big chair under the light. Patience and perhaps hours of work lay ahead of him, but he

---

9   *AUTHOR'S NOTE: I was surprised and somewhat shocked when I first learned that Agent "X" lives almost entirely on synthetic concentrated foods. But he accidentally dropped some of his life-sustaining capsules during an interview I had with him. I took the liberty of having them analyzed by a skilled chemist and dietitian. They contained proteins, carbohydrates and vitamins concentrated into remarkable calorie-producing substances. I understood then that Agent "X" was not starving himself, and, I realized that at times in his strange work it must be a great advantage to have his meals always with him.*

knew how to go about the task in hand.[10]

In forty-five minutes, by use of word frequency tables, he had mastered the code of Morvay's paper. His eyes gleamed with excitement. Besides giving methods of work, countersigns, times of meeting, and types of acids used by the "Torture Trust," there were two names listed. The names were Albert Bartholdy and Eric Van Houten, M.D. Names which had a ring to them—names which seemed to carry dignity and prestige.

The Agent's face hardened. Crime in its most hideous form sometimes blossomed in high places just as the deadliest fungi grew in the richest soil. It was not always the spawn of the poor, the downtrodden, and suffering who turned to the byways of evil. Nature worked strange contrasts.

He put the paper away in his pocket and reached for the telephone book, then paused. There had come a sudden strident ringing of the front door bell. Supposing it were Van Houten or Bartholdy come to pay a social visit to their colleague in crime? His disguise would fool them, but could he play his part, knowing nothing of their relations with Morvay? With wildly beating heart he strode to the door, opened it, then stepped back, for once finding it difficult to maintain his composure. For the man who stood before him was Inspector John Burks of the city Homicide Squad.

10   AUTHOR'S NOTE: As a cryptographer and cryptoanalyst it is my belief that Secret Agent "X" has few equals in the world. I am sure that he was at one time associated with the famous Yardley of the American Secret Service. Certainly he has had much experience with codes, ciphers, and crypto-grams during his work in the Intelligence Service. I have seen him solve multiple-alphabetic-substitution ciphers, biliteral-monoalphabetic-substitution ciphers, ciphers written by means of the Vigniere table, combined substitution-transposition ciphers, the Playfair cipher with its diagraphic substitution, and all manner of one- and two-part codes.

CHAPTER XVI

THE TERRIBLE TRIO

TENSE AND ALERT, Agent "X" stared at the man before him. Then he noticed the expression on Burks's face. That expression was grave, thoughtful—not the look of a man who has come to make an arrest or cross-question a suspect. He waited for the inspector to speak first.

"You don't know me," the detective chief said. "I'm Inspector Burks. They told me about you at City College. They said you might be a good man to talk to."

Again the Agent found it difficult not to show amazement. A man of a thousand faces should expect to create strange situations. But this one was unbelievably fantastic.

"Come in, inspector," he said, making an effort to keep his voice casual.

The inspector entered stolidly, his pale, gaunt face composed.

"It's about these torture murders, Morvay," he said when they were seated. "I've got a theory I want to talk over with an expert—someone like you. These killings strike me as being the work of an abnormal man."

"A sadist," said the Agent quietly.

Burks leaned forward in excitement.

"That's the word. But would a man like that—a sadist who likes to hurt people, have enough brains to execute such a series of crimes? Wouldn't he be deficient mentally?"

The Agent leaned back in his chair, a cigarette in his long fingers, smoke curling lazily from his nostrils. He was enjoying the situation now. What would Burks do if he knew his real identity? It was grotesque, ironic, that the two men pursuing the same group of criminals should meet under such circumstances.

"Have you ever thought," he said, "that these acid throwers may be only the tools of some greater criminal, or criminals? The money extorted by the 'Torture Trust' has been gotten with the greatest cleverness. There are cunning brains behind this."

The inspector leaned forward, his eyes snapping.

"By God, I know it! And if there's a master criminal back of this racket, I know who it is!"

"You do?"

"Yes, a man who calls himself Secret Agent 'X.' A man who's as cunning as a fox."

For a moment there was silence so complete that the clock on the mantel seemed to give out sledge-hammer blows. Then the Agent spoke.

"Why not go after him?"

The inspector swore bitterly.

"I had him the other night. A cop caught him sneaking down a fire escape after an acid throwing. But he got away—I won't say how. There are twenty headquarters men out looking for him now."

"Tell them to keep at it," was the Agent's calm rejoinder.

Burks didn't catch the faintly mocking note, and if he had he wouldn't have understood. He asked another question relating to sadism. And Agent "X," posing as the psychologist Morvay, began a learned discussion of the subject.[11]

When Inspector Burks left, he was impressed with the fact that Morvay was a well-informed man.

THE instant the door had closed, Agent "X" sprang out of his chair and set to work again on Morvay's desk. All his casualness of manner had left him. A fierce inward fire seemed to be driving him on. He hadn't forgotten those terrible moments in the subterranean corridors of the black-robed trio's hide-out. He hadn't forgotten the haggard, terror-stricken look on Betty Dale's face when he had come in time to save her from awful mutilation. And at any moment the "Torture Trust" might strike again. The threat of it was a black, ever present menace. The inspector's words had brought home to him the utter bafflement of the police.

11 AUTHOR'S NOTE: I am certain that Agent "X" has a vast fund of information on the theory of criminal behavior as well as his practical knowledge concerning criminals themselves. From scrapes of conversation, I gather that he is familiar with the works of Steckle, Freud, Adler, Jung, as well as all of the better known criminologists from Lombrose to Robert Anderson.

He finished with the desk and took out Morvay's wallet. It contained sixty dollars in bills, membership cards to several exclusive clubs, a driver's license. Then, in an inside pocket, he found a crumpled newspaper clipping.

It was marked by pencil and announced the sailing to America on board the steamship *Victoria* of Sir Anthony Dunsmark, distinguished official of the Bank of England.

For long seconds the Agent stared at the clipping, his eyes glowing strangely.

He reached again for the telephone book. Albert Bartholdy and Doctor Eric Van Houten were both listed, their addresses given. The Agent paused in doubt. He was faced with one of the biggest problems of his life.

If Bartholdy and Van Houten were the other members of the trio, he would have to proceed with the greatest caution. A false step now would put them on their guard. Yet he would have to act quickly, before the disappearance of Morvay was suspected. That tiny clipping mentioning the coming of Dunsmark might be the key to the situation. Why was Morvay interested in Dunsmark?

The Agent left Morvay's house and went first to the address of Albert Bartholdy. He changed his disguise, on the way to H.J. Martin.

Bartholdy lived in a fashionable apartment building. Posing as a credit investigator, Agent "X" learned from the apartment manager that Bartholdy was a lawyer employed as an assistant in the district attorney's office. That explained the trio's uncanny knowledge of police movements.

He got his car out of the mid-town garage, drove to Doctor Van Houten's address, and his eyes brightened. It was a private home.

He parked his car far up the block, then, under cover of the darkness he slipped through a servant's alley, crossed a back yard and circled the house till he located the windows of what appeared to be an office.

Using fingers and toe holds and risking a fall, he climbed stealthily up the side of the building till he got a view into the window under the narrow space below the shade.

A thin, gray-haired man inside was sitting at a desk interviewing a lady. "X" could not hear what was being said, but the thin man's manner was studied, professional. He drew a prescription pad from a drawer of the desk, wrote something on it, and handed it to the lady, as "X" watched. The man was unquestionably Doctor Van Houten.

The Agent studied him carefully. Van Houten, too, had a face of intelligence; but the nostrils were thin, the mouth small, and the eyes narrow and close-set. High, flat cheek bones and a cleft chin gave the features a look of power—but it was a face that might harbor brutality and greed—the face of a possible criminal.

The Agent slid noiselessly to the ground and began a patient vigil in the shadows across the street. If an immediate crime were being plotted, the trio would surely meet again.

IT was close to ten-thirty when he saw the figure of Doctor Van Houten emerge. Many patients had gone in and come out. The doctor's office hours were over.

With the skfll of long experience, the Agent shadowed his man. His heart beat faster. Doctor Van Houten was getting into a cab.

At a safe distance the Agent followed. Where was Van Houten bound? The doctor's next move convinced him. For Van Houten got out, dismissed the cab and walked several blocks. Then, after a glance around him, signaled another taxi.

The Agent overtook the cab, passed it, and went on out of sight. He pressed the gas button down and drove his roadster like a demon. He glanced at the clock on the instrument board. It was twenty minutes to eleven. Could it be that a meeting was scheduled to take place in the mysterious council chamber at that hour? Van Houten's furtive movements seemed an affirmative answer.

He raced ahead of the doctor, reaching the deserted warehouse at ten minutes of eleven. Somewhere inside the sinister deaf-mutes might be lurking, but there was one route through which the Agent felt he could go unmolested. Morvay always entered by the rear buildings, and Morvay would not be present tonight.

Using his master keys, he let himself in through the now familiar door. The place seemed silent and deserted. But "X" sensed the presence of death and horror. He stopped a moment, his reasoning faculties working.

The trio always wore black hoods and robes. Was it to hide their identities from their victims? Or did they want to remain unknown to their slaves, the deaf-mutes, as well. Morvay had not had the weird garments with him when he had emerged. They must be stored close at hand, for, if they were to protect Morvay from the gaze of the deaf-mutes, he would not want to traverse the corridors without them.

Risking detection, Agent "X" probed carefully with the beam

of his flash. Then he stepped forward. Reason had led him aright. There was a locked closet close to the first door. He groped, opened it, and drew forth the hood and robe—symbols of darkness and death.

Standing in the blackness of the corridor, he adjusted them over his body and walked forward. Twice he turned on the flash light, fearless now of being discovered by the mutes.

He was the first to reach the council chamber and he had a strange sense of eeriness as he settled himself into the middle chair. He was taking a terrible chance tonight, going into the very jaws of death. A slip might betray him—some overt act that he couldn't anticipate.

A tiny bulb flashed on, throwing dim shadows around the room. He stared at the floor, saw a slight bulge in the carpet close by his foot and understood then how secret signals had been flashed to the mutes.

The seconds seemed to pass with crawling slowness. He heard no sound in the room or in the vastness of the building outside. Had he been right about Van Houten? Was the man coming here tonight?

Slow footfalls approached. They sounded first as a ghostly whisper, measured, precise. They made his scalp crawl.

Waiting tensely in the dimly lit room, he did not know what the next few minutes would bring.

A faint noise came from the door. It opened slowly and another hooded figure came in. Without sign or word of greeting, the figure moved across the room to a chair at "X's" right and sat down. Eyes met the Agent's from behind the black hood. Was this Van Houten or Albert Bartholdy, he wondered?

The man did not move or speak, and when minutes had passed, a third figure entered. It was only then that the first man opened his lips.

"What news?" he said in a low, harsh voice. "Are there any new plans to discuss? The *Victoria* docks tomorrow night. When do we move?"

Agent "X" wondered what answers would be given to this. Details, he hoped, would be brought out that would make it possible for him to reconstruct what was passing through their minds. But no one spoke.

Seconds passed. The silence in the room deepened. It grew oppressive, deathly.

"Well?" said a voice at last.

The Agent started then. A slow prickle moved along his spine, reaching to his scalp. He grew tense in his chair, flexing the muscles that the black robe concealed.

For the hooded figures beside him were staring his way—the man who had asked the questions and the other who had just spoken.

He could see a sharp, expectant glitter in the gaze that they fastened on him. And all at once he understood. Professor Morvay had been the master mind of the trio. And, because he had taken the middle seat, they thought he was Morvay. Now they looked to him for guidance and strategy in the crime they planned. He was suddenly placed in a terrible position, with death and defeat as the pitfalls into which he would stumble if the answers he made should be wrong.

CHAPTER XVII

ACROSS DARK WATERS

HE WAITED BREATHLESSLY while the hooded figures at his left and right continued to stare at him with hard, penetrating glances. They, too, were waiting, and Agent "X" cleared his throat.

"I have been thinking—" he said, then paused, his tongue feeling dry against his teeth. It had taken an effort to make his voice sound like Morvay's.

"You said you would investigate—discover where Dunsmark would first be invited," said the man at his right who had first spoken.

"Yes," the Agent spoke slowly, stalling for time. "Many invitations have been sent to him. It will depend upon his own plans. We will not know till he lands."

Aggressiveness crept into the voice of the speaker at his right.

"It has been our method to strike swiftly and depend on surprise and terror. We must not delay too long. We must act while the public and press are still in a furor—while fear of us is rampant. Then Dunsmark's government will pay."

Behind the black hood the eyes of Agent "X" gleamed like bits of steel. He stared from one hooded figure to the other. There was silence in the room again, silence that was pregnant, filled with the greed of men who could not wait. He had learned enough. His voice was low, hoarse when he spoke, but still the voice of Morvay. There was confidence in his tone. They looked to him as the leader, and he would give them leadership undreamed of.

"You are right," he said. "We must strike soon—why not immediately, the moment he lands?"

The man on his right spoke sharply. "We discussed that last night. A police escort will be there and secret service operatives will undoubtedly be guarding him."

Agent "X" made an impatient, deprecatory gesture.

"There is a way. One man can sometimes accomplish what many cannot do. I will capture him myself—bring him here. I have thought of a method."

Exclamations of doubt and amazement followed his words.

"You can't accomplish the impossible. How do you propose to go about it?"

"Trust me," said the Agent quietly.

"We have always gone over our plans together. Three minds are better than one. There may be flaws."

The Agent was stubborn. "I will get Dunsmark alone. Our slaves cannot act in this for us. I will meet him, introduce myself. I will have forged papers from a bank. He will think—"

The man at his left interrupted harshly.

"It is not feasible. It is folly!"

The Agent saw he would have to fight opposition. His voice became aggressive, hard as the rasp of a file on metal.

"I will gamble my share of what we intend to make," he said.

"That is nothing. We are all gambling. We will all lose."

"Have you a better plan to offer, then?"

"Yes." The man at his left spoke now. "The original one. Our slaves will spy on Dunsmark—we will get him to come out alone on some pretext—as we have done with others. We can use the needle and the drug again."

The Agent sneered. "It may be days before that can happen. He may grow suspicious. The police may insist on guarding him night and day. There is agitation against us, my friends. The government is watchful. Have you thought of that?"

The others were silent, and "X" continued, driving home his point.

"Fear of us is spreading. It is good in one way. Fear is powerful and will separate men from their money. It has helped us before. But it may work against us in the case of Dunsmark. There may be no chance unless we act quickly."

There was silence again as cunning brains pondered behind black hoods. The man who had objected spoke at last.

"Very well," he said. "But if you fail, it will end everything. It will be every man for himself." There was a sinister threat behind his words.

"I have as much to lose as any of you," said the Agent quietly.

"You mean then that you will take him as soon as the boat docks."

"Yes," said the Agent, "that is what I mean!"

"And you will bring him here."

"Yes—at once."

"Very well."

The session was over. The Secret Agent had committed himself to a task that seemed impossible; to the task of snatching Sir Anthony Dunsmark away under the very noses of the police and the Secret Service operators who would be watching. It was a task so daring, so unbelievable, that even the members of the hooded trio were skeptical.

One by one they left the council chamber. Agent "X" drove uptown to the old Montgomery mansion, to his secret room, and all through the night he was awake, alert, thinking, planning.

The next day he went to the photograph department of a big metropolitan paper and purchased from their files all available photos of a certain public official—the commissioner of police. He followed it by going to a private photographer who specialized in such things and buying others. He now had fourteen photos of the commissioner in all poses—flash lights of him speaking before a crowd, photos of him in uniform, in private life, and at public functions.

That evening he arranged these photos around the walls of his secret room and studied them carefully. Then with pen and ink, legal-looking paper, and a metal stamp with the seal of the city on it, he proceeded to draw up a document.

THREE hours later, a speed-boat left a secluded dock along the water front and shot out across the harbor. It was a roomy boat, with padded leather seats, and a powerful engine that ran as smoothly as a watch. A muffler reduced the thunderous reverberations of the motor to a subdued musical hum. The boat left a white wake behind it as it threaded its way among the tugs and gliding ferries plying between the down-town docks and the towns and cities across the harbor.

The time was eleven-thirty. At the wheel of the speed-boat was a tall man in a black coat. He had a soft gray hat pulled low, a muffler around his neck. He stared straight ahead across the water, guiding the speed boat with a skilled hand.

Once wind whipped the muffler loose, and the man folded it again over immaculate evening clothes that showed beneath his coat. He was obviously a personage of dignity and importance, a handsome man, ruddy faced, gray at the temples and with a close-clipped mustache lending strength to his firm upper lip. It was the face that was known everywhere—the face of the city's police commissioner.

Any cop would have pointed him out in a crowd. Almost any citizen would have recognized him, for his picture had appeared in the metropolitan papers often. And, in case there might be doubt as to his identity, he carried documents to show who he was and to prove that his tenure of office had the city's sanction.

Yet, miles away in the fashionable mansion of a wealthy political boss, the real commissioner was engaged in an exciting game of poker with several of his cronies. He would have been shocked, furious, terrified if he could have seen the man at the wheel of the boat—the man who would, during the next hour, impersonate himself.

The Secret Agent was gambling again on his mastery of disguise, gambling on a scheme that was incredibly daring.

The speed-boat slowed, began moving in wide easy circles across the face of the dark waters. Once a harbor patrol craft hove into sight and the Agent stilled the motor and extinguished the red-and-green running lights on the speed-boat's sides. The patrol passed by like a gray shadow in the night.

Far down the narrows a blotch of radiance appeared. It came nearer, increased in size. It was the high, many-windowed, super-structure of a great liner—the *Victoria*.

With the majesty of vast bulk and great power under leash, the greyhound of the seas came slowly on. Pigmy tugs nosed along beside it. Soon the great turbines would be stilled, the tugs would warp the huge vessel into the dock where hundreds of excited people waited, friends and relatives of the thousand or more passengers on board. But before that happened, there was official business to be gone through. The *Victoria* would be held at quarantine until doctors had made certain there were no contagious diseases on board. This might take one hour or several. The ship was one of the crack liners. The passenger list held many distinguished names. The routine of quarantine would be as brief as possible.

As the great ship weighed anchor in the narrows, the Secret Agent circled it and watched. He saw the quarantine boat heave to beside the towering sides of the liner, saw the official doctors board her by the stairway that was lowered.

The Agent steered his speed-boat close then, gliding silently alongside the quarantine craft. He made fast a rope and stepped lightly over the quarantine boat's deck.

A sailor stuck his head out of the small hatchway and stared at him in wonder. But Agent "X" offered no explanation.

It wasn't until an officer at the top of the liner's companionway tried to stop him that he drew out the document showing who he was. The officer saluted and stepped back respectfully.

A minute more and he was in the presence of the *Victoria's* grizzled captain. One of the quarantine men and a customs official were with the captain. They recognized the commissioner at once. His papers this time were not necessary. As he drew the captain aside, his handsome face was grave.

"Sir Anthony Dunsmark is on this ship, I believe, captain," he said.

"Yes."

Agent "X" cleared his throat and stared at the *Victoria's* chief officer, frowning. The quarantine man and the customs official looked on in wonder. They could not hear what was being said, but it was evident that something of vast import had brought the police commissioner out across the harbor.

"There is a plot afoot," said the Agent, "a plot to kidnap Sir Anthony Dunsmark and hold him for extortion money. He may be injured, killed. The city can take no chances. It will be better to spirit him away, keep him out of sight until the police have had a chance to investigate. I will take him directly to my home, captain."

The captain nodded instantly. It was not his business to question the wisdom of a move advocated by one of the country's greatest police heads. Agent "X" was led forward through the ship to the expensive suite of cabins that was occupied by Sir Anthony Dunsmark and his secretary. The captain introduced the commissioner.

AGENT "X" saw a tall, ruddy-faced, slightly stout Britisher. Dunsmark had on a baggy gray suit. A pair of eye glasses hung by a cord from his vest. He was vastly flustered at the news the commissioner delivered in a low, tense voice.

His face had paled a trifle. He was a man unaccustomed to violence. Most of his days had been spent in quiet, luxurious offices where people spoke in subdued voices and where there was an air of efficiency and stability.

"I am terribly sorry, Sir Anthony," said the Agent. "But we can take no chances. You had better come with me at once, to avoid danger later when the boat docks."

Puffing with excitement, Dunsmark issued orders to his secretary.

"Your baggage can wait for the customs men," said the Agent. "Your secretary can stay and take care of that. This is all very unusual."

"Very," echoed Dunsmark.

"But it is made necessary by the pressure of circumstances. We must combat crime as best we can."

"Quite!" said Dunsmark.

He was hustled off the boat so quickly and efficiently that he hardly knew what was happening. Sailors from the *Victoria* held the slim speed-boat while he climbed in. If they or the captain thought it strange that the police commissioner should come out alone, they said nothing. This was an extraordinary condition of affairs, met in an extraordinary way.

Speeding back across the harbor Dunsmark recovered some of his composure. He chatted with the man whom he thought was the commissioner.

"You Americans," he said, "are independent fellows. Fancy an English official being able and willing to pilot his own boat like this!"

It was only after they had reached shore by means of an ill-smelling dock and climbed into a parked roadster that Dunsmark began to show signs of nervousness again. Several times he glanced uneasily at the man beside him.

His uneasiness visibly increased as the car rolled into a maze of streets that were dark, rough, and cluttered; streets that seemed to have about them a sinister atmosphere of crime. He spoke at last.

"Look here, commissioner. I don't quite understand this. I thought—"

His words ceased in a startled, choking gasp. His eyes bulged from his head. For the commissioner had drawn a gun. It gleamed wickedly under the glow of the instrument-board light, and it was pointed straight at his side.

"I'm sorry," said the commissioner softly. "You will have to come with me and do what I say, Sir Anthony. Any attempt on your part to cry out or escape will have very serious consequences."

CHAPTER XVIII

THE RAID

A **GENT "X" SENSED** at once that Dunsmark was not a man to cause him trouble. The Britisher was certainly no coward. His many courageous acts and decisions in the world of finance had proved that. But he wasn't used to physical action. And he was still overawed by reports read of crime conditions in America. He sat slumped in his seat, white-faced, silent, ready for the worst.

"X" drove the car on through the night into the shadow of the great warehouse where hideous things had been done and where others would be done again, if he didn't prevent them; where the seeds of murder had been planted and nourished.

He ordered Dunsmark out of the car, and told him to stand quietly in the shadows for a moment.

"There are others about, Sir Anthony," he said. "Do as I tell you. Take no chances. Vital issues are at stake." How vital he did not try to explain. Dunsmark could think what he chose for the time being.

Agent "X" went to the back of the roadster, unlocked the cover of the rumble seat and lifted it. In the spacious compartment in front of the seat was the body of a man doubled up. The man was not dead, only unconscious, for he was breathing regularly. It was the body of Professor Morvay.

The Agent reached in, grasped Morvay, and lifted him out. At sight of his limp figure Sir Anthony Dunsmark gasped with fear. Death, mystery, and horror had met him on his landing in America. He regretted that he had come at all. But the sight of a man who appeared to be dead paralyzed his will. He took pains to obey the Agent's orders.

Carrying Morvay over his shoulder, the Agent motioned Dunsmark to the side of one of the old buildings, and opened the door. He motioned Dunsmark inside, then quietly closed and locked the door, and deposited Morvay on the floor. Then, standing Dunsmark close to the wall, he turned a flash light on his face and studied him for long moments.

"Sorry," he said again. "But you must do as I tell you." His calm voice seemed at odds with his strange actions.

He took the black hood and robe from the closet by the door and adjusted them on his body without even removing the disguise of the police commissioner. He had to work quickly now, make every move count in the desperate game he was playing.

With the hood over his head and his eyes glittering through the slits, he looked far more terrible than he had as the well-dressed police commissioner. Dunsmark's face went a shade paler. He moved forward like a somnambulist as the Agent made motions with his gun.

Carrying the body of Morvay, and thrusting Dunsmark ahead, the Agent went slowly down the corridor. It was fortunate that the deaf-mutes could hear nothing. It was fortunate, too, that Van Houten and Bartholdy entered and left by different ways. He would not encounter them till he arrived at the council chamber.

Twenty feet from the door of the secret room, in a closet under a stairway that he had previously noted, he thrust the still form of Morvay. Then he flicked on his light for a moment and motioned Dunsmark on.

In silence they at last entered the chamber where so much evil had been plotted.

There was a dim light burning in the room; and two spectral black-robed figures sitting on chairs. They gave harsh exclamations at sight of the British financier. Their eyes gleamed with a fierce, avaricious light.

"I kept my word," said Agent "X" quietly.

FOR a moment there was awed silence, then the man at the Agent's left pressed his foot on a bulge in the carpet. The spotlight on the ceiling above flashed on. It bathed Dunsmark's face in brilliant radiance. The paleness of his features, the tenseness of his attitude, the combative look in his eyes, testified to the fact that he had been brought unwillingly. Agent "X" had relied on that. It was why he hadn't dared take Dunsmark into his confidence. The unpleasant interlude had been necessary if his plans were to succeed.

"Does he know the reason for his being here?" came a voice

from behind one of the hoods.

"No," said the Agent. "I have told him nothing. I have kept my word—brought him. Inform him of what we have in mind."

The man at the Agent's right spoke in a harsh measured voice.

"You are an important man, Dunsmark—important to your country and to the world. Neither your country nor the world can afford to lose you. They will, for that reason, take pains to see that you are returned to them uninjured."

The British banker slowly nodded his head. A sudden surge of blood swept across his face. His cleft chin jutted.

"I understand everything, Dunsmark. You understand, of course, that ransom is expected for your safe return. A child could understand that. You can guess that the amount of ransom for such an important person as you will be large, staggeringly large, but not too large—not more than your country will gladly pay. But you don't understand just where you are. You don't realize what will happen if you fail to meet our demands."

Dunsmark's right fist tightened into a ball.

"By Gad, gentlemen—I don't care what your demands are. You've picked the wrong victim. You can't intimidate me!"

A harsh, grating laugh came from behind the black hood.

"Have you followed the news, Dunsmark? Have you heard of that mysterious organization called the 'Torture Trust'? Have you read reports of what happens to men who refuse to meet its demands?"

Dunsmark's face paled again, and its expression showed that news of the terrible series of crimes had reached England.

"I see you've heard of us," continued the voice. "You have heard of dead men, rich men and their sons, being found with their faces gone, eaten by acid. You are a man of imagination. You can picture to yourself no doubt what the slow claws of acid can do. You can understand why you will pay."

"Damn you!" cried the Englishman. "I still say you can't intimidate me. I won't sell my country out to ransom my own carcass."

"No!" the persuasive voice went on. "That is noble of you. That is loyal. You are a man of high ideals, of great principles. You will sacrifice yourself. But have you ever had liquid drops of torture poured on your skin, Dunsmark? Would you want to return to your country marred beyond recognition? Would you want to spend the rest of your life looking so hideous that your friends will turn away from you in horror?"

"Damn you—damn you!" gasped the Englishman. "Let me out of here!"

"That will be easy," said the voice of his tormenter. "We can ask the ransom money without your consent. But everything will be better, more simple, if you will write a note yourself directing your country to pay what we ask. We will make all arrangements for the note's delivery, the delivery of the money, and your safe return. It will be conducted in a businesslike way."

Dunsmark was quivering with fury now.

"All we ask," said the hooded figure, "is a sum proportionate to your high position. A sum which your country, or you yourself perhaps, can well afford to pay. All we ask is five hundred thousand pounds!"

The Secret Agent gasped. They were demanding over two million dollars.

Dunsmark, still trembling violently, remained silent.

"What do you say," came the voice. "Will you cooperate—make things easy for yourself and us? Or must we give you a taste of what hell is like?"

"Go to the devil, all of you," the Englishman cried in a sudden burst of fury. "There are police in America! There is law and order. You'll go to prison and the gallows for this."

The Secret Agent spoke then.

"He will not be convinced, my friends. We will have to take him down below. Call our slaves."

The hooded figure at his right silently pressed the button concealed under the carpet—the button that flashed lights in the deaf-mutes' quarters. A moment later four of them glided in, and the same hooded man flashed orders with his fingers.

The Agent spoke then.

"I am going with him," he said. "Let us all go. Let us see that our slaves make no blunder in this."

Silently they rose and wound through the chill corridors to the cellar below. The door of the torture chamber was unlocked. Struggling and protesting fiercely, Dunsmark was thrust into the metal chair. In a moment the metal cuffs had been clamped over his hands and ankles.

"We have come," said the Agent, "to give you a chance to change your mind—before it is too late."

One of the mutes, precise as an automaton, had gone to a shelf and taken the stopper from a bottle of acid.

"You see it," said the hooded figure standing by the Agent's side. "You see the liquid that no human will can endure."

"God!" cried Dunsmark. "There are decent laws and police in America, I say. You'll go to prison. They won't let this happen."

As though in answer to his words, a sudden sound reverberated through the building. It was a clanging metallic note. Then some-where far above, faint and shrill, a whistle sounded. The noise of a blow came again, repeated, taken up and echoed, till the whole warehouse shook and trembled, as though a hundred axes were crashing through the doors.

"The police," hissed the Agent, fiercely. "A raid. Every man for himself!"

CHAPTER XIX

MYSTERIOUS INSTRUCTIONS

IN HER ROOM at the Hotel Graymont Betty Dale paced restlessly. She lit innumerable cigarettes, took short quick puffs, ground them out. Her eyes were dark with worry. Once she went to the window and stared out across the rooftops. Lights showed on the river far away. In the streets below, after-theater crowds surged and jostled, and the faint blare of taxi horns rose in an uneasy murmur.

There was laughter and gaiety in the ceaseless stream of humanity that flowed on the sidewalks around the hotel like a stream washing the base of a great cliff. There were smiling faces and lightly moving feet. But Betty Dale had a sense of uneasiness, a sense that strange, sinister things portended.

That afternoon she had had a visit from the Agent. He had come to her as H. J. Martin. His card had read: "Credit Manager, Felder & Wright Department Stores"! He was disguised as a sallow-faced, sandy-haired man. She had been fooled as usual until his card had turned black in her hands leaving a glowing white "X" on its surface. Then she had known.

But this time his instructions had surprised her even more than his disguise. He had discarded for the moment his habit of talking in parables and innuendos. He had issued short, crisp statements.

"I want you to do something for me, Betty. If I don't call back before one o'clock to-night, I want you to phone police headquarters. Ask for Inspector Burks and tell him that Sir Anthony Dunsmark has been kidnapped. Tell him Dunsmark has fallen into the clutches of the 'Torture Trust,' and tell him where Sir Anthony and the members of the trust can be found."

He had given her explicit directions then—street numbers that Betty recognized. The place he described was the old warehouse where she had been held and threatened with torture. Her face paled at the recollection.

"And you," she said. "If the police raid the place, where will you be?"

The Agent had remained silent and Betty had noticed that in his eyes was a strange, bright light. When he spoke again his words had not been an answer to her worried query, but further instructions.

"Don't use the hotel telephone, Betty. Go at least four blocks away. Use a store phone booth and leave as soon as you have made your call."

He had gone away then, leaving Betty Dale anxious, uneasy. The hours had dragged by. All evening she had hoped he would call again, hoped that he would countermand his strange orders. How could even the Secret Agent know that Sir Anthony Dunsmark would be kidnapped? The British banker, she knew, had not landed in America. Had Agent "X" wormed his way into the innermost circle of the "Torture Trust," and if so what desperate game was he playing?

Twelve o'clock came with no further word from him. She called the steamship office then. They told her the liner *Victoria*, on which Dunsmark was arriving, was in the harbor, but that it would be held at quarantine for an hour or more.

A quarter of one came and Betty put on her hat and coat. She took an elevator to the lobby, walked through it and passed out into the street. Five blocks away she entered a cigar-store telephone booth and dialed a number. The sleepy voice of a desk sergeant at police headquarters answered her and Betty said:

"I want to speak to Inspector Burks."

"You can't, lady," the sergeant said. "He ain't here. He's gone home."

"I must speak to him anyway. This is very important."

"Who are you?"

"Never mind. Get the inspector. It's a matter of life and death."

The sergeant grumbled and complained, but at the end of a minute he had made switchboard connections. Another voice sounded over the wire.

"This is Inspector Burks. What's it all about? What do you want?"

In quick, breathless sentences Betty Dale relayed the message that the Agent had asked her to deliver—the message announcing Sir Anthony Dunsmark'a abduction—and the inspector's voice rose into a harsh irritable rasp.

"That's impossible! You're lying! The *Victoria,* the boat he's on, hasn't even docked. She's still at quarantine. I know because I've got cops waiting to look out for him. Who the hell are you, lady?"

But Betty Dale didn't answer. She had done her duty, done what the Secret Agent had asked. She hung up quickly and left the store before the police tried to trace the call.

INSPECTOR BURKS at the other end of the wire jangled the receiver futilely. His pale face had turned a shade paler. There was an uneasy look in his eyes. The girl who had called him up and refused to give her name was obviously a nut. What she had told him couldn't be true. Dunsmark couldn't be kidnapped before the *Victoria* landed. But still he was uneasy. And he wasn't a man to let anything pass.

Growling in his throat, still irritable from having been waked up, he lifted the receiver again and demanded the ship-to-shore service.

"Get me the steamer *Victoria*—now in the harbor. Let me speak to her captain."

In a moment the call had leaped through the air across the harbor by wireless telephone. The voice of the captain buzzed in his ear. Inspector Burks asked a blunt question.

"Is Anthony Dunsmark still on board? This is the head of the city homicide squad."

The captain answered quickly.

"Sir Anthony left nearly an hour ago. The police commissioner came and got him."

There was an instant of dead silence, then Burks spoke hoarsely.

"The commissioner—say—he wouldn't do that without letting me know."

"It was the commissioner I tell you—there's no doubt about it"

"What the hell!" exploded Burks. He was beginning to tremble now. He was beginning to sense that something somewhere was terribly wrong. It wasn't like the commissioner to do such a thing without informing the heads of his departments.

With shaking hands, Burks dialed the commissioner's house and got the commissioner's red-haired wife.

"I want to speak to Charlie," said the inspector.

"He hasn't been home all evening. He's out with the boys again—playing cards, I suppose. You'll probably find him at Mac-Dorsey's."

Burks knew who MacDorsey was—one of the city's richest political bosses. He made the telephone dial buzz like an angry bee, and when he got MacDorsey on the wire his voice was a husky croak.

"Better not interrupt the commish," said MacDorsey. "He's drawing for a royal flush."

"I've got to speak to him. It's important."

Burks gulped for air when he heard the commissioner's polished voice, a little chiding now at being disturbed during off hours.

"What is it, inspector? More grief I suppose?"

"Did you go out in a boat tonight, chief, and take that Englishman, Anthony Dunsmark, off the *Victoria?*"

"Did I what? Say, have you gone crazy, Burks? What are you talking about?"

"You didn't get him off about an hour ago?"

"No. Say! I've been here with the boys all evening. What the hell's the matter with you!"

"Dunsmark's been kidnapped, chief. The 'Torture Trust' has got him. The captain of the *Victoria* says someone who looked like you grabbed him off the boat. I've been tipped off to where he is. I'm going to raid the place."

The commissioner's tone was apoplectic.

"For God's sake don't let this get into the papers! We'll all look sweet. I'll sit in at the raid. Where is it?"

In brief sentences Burks told him. Then he made the wires hot. His rasping voice started the various departments in action, got other inspectors on the job. He asked that trucks of the emergency squad be sent out, asked the boiler squad to cooperate, and ordered all available men of the homicide squad rounded up.

Half dressed, with his shoes unlaced and his collar unbuttoned, he sent his own car roaring down town through the night-darkened streets.

THE biggest raid in the history of the city police was under way. Telephone wires were humming. Captains and sergeants were bawling orders.

A green, high-speed truck of the emergency squad, cops clinging to the brass rails on its sides, came hurtling out of a side street
and roared down town with its siren screaming. Two motor-cycle
cops joined it, clearing the way, adding their horns to the din.

Private cars drew aside. Pedestrians scuttled to safety. Inspector
Burks, his face bleak, drove madly, holding his own horn down.

The tip-off, whoever had given it, had been complete. And he
had made his own instructions complete also. No one was to act
until he arrived on the scene to direct the raid.

He found grim-faced men waiting in the dark streets around the
old warehouse. There was the glint of dim light on riot guns and on
the black, wicked snouts of automatics held in steady hands.

Sergeant Mathers, roused from sleep, his eyes bloodshot, came
up for instructions.

"Throw a cordon around the whole building," said Burks. "Circle the block. Don't let any one get out."

Stealthy-footed men approached the building from all sides.
"Those houses in the rear," said Burks. "Watch them, too."

A sleek, official car with a uniformed chauffeur slid to a halt,
then crept through the lines of detectives. The commissioner himself had arrived, his mouth under its mustache a hard, straight line.
Someone had put him in a bad spot. Someone had made him appear ridiculous.

"Let's get going," he snapped.

The raid began then. Men with axes, sledge hammers, and crow-
bars started battering in the doors. Powerful searchlights mounted
on the trucks of the emergency squad flashed on, sweeping the
sides of the big building, making the dark evil streets as bright as
day. Patrolmen and plain-clothes detectives poured in, battering
down doors and racing along corridors.

It was Inspector Burks himself who first saw a spectral black-
robed form ahead of him. The man flashed into sight for a moment
around a passage angle, and Burks saw the evil glitter of eyes behind the slitted hood.

"Halt!" he said. "Stand where you are or I'll shoot."

The hooded man ignored the warning. He tried to spring up a
flight of stairs.

There was the harsh crack of an automatic. Burks had been a
dead shot in his day. The man on the stairway screamed and spun
around. He tottered, clutched at the wall. Then his body slumped

and rolled backwards. He collapsed on the floor of the passage and lay still.

Burks ran forward and snatched the hood loose. Then he gave a swift gasp of surprise.

"God! Albert Bartholdy—one of the D.A.'s snooty assistants. No wonder the cops didn't have a chance."

There was a blue hole in the side of Albert Bartholdy's head. One member of the "Torture Trust" would never plot evil again.

But a patrolman with a riot gun down the corridor cursed in pain. Two sinister gray-clad figures had appeared ahead of him as if by magic. One of them had flung a glittering tube of liquid. It was only by a miracle of good luck that the cop stepped aside in time.

The tube smashed against the wall close to his head. Reeking chemical fumes filled his nostrils. Drops of seering acid struck his cheek.

He cursed again, crouched low, and his finger pressed the trigger of the riot gun. The automatic mechanism jumped and clattered. Flame spurted from the black muzzle.

The two evil, gray forms wilted before it, plunged to the floor, and lay still.

The raiders penetrated to the cellar then. Somewhere ahead a light showed. The inspector ran forward, then stopped. Another black-robed figure lay at his feet. He held his gun steady, but the figure did not move. He stopped, pulled the hood aside, and his face muscles sagged in amazement. For seconds he stared in utter bewilderment.

The man at his feet was not dead but only unconscious. He was breathing harshly, regularly, in the manner of a man under the influence of drugs. But his presence in that place and the black hood he wore showed that he, too, was a member of the "Torture Trust." Burks recognized the features.

"Morvay!" he gasped.

THE inspector turned and ran on toward the lighted room ahead. His gun was in his hand, but he holstered it and breathed a sigh of deep relief. They had not been too late.

A man in an English-cut tweed suit was slumped in a metal chair in the center of the room. His arms and legs were manacled, holding him a prisoner, but he was unhurt. His loud voice showed that.

"Bully for you!" he said. "I told those devils the police would come. There were three of them—murderers, torturers. I told them there was law and order in this bally country."

"Dunsmark," said Inspector Burks.

He recognized the famous banker from the many photos he had seen in rotogravure sections of the papers. There was vast relief in his voice. He and his men had saved the city and the country from disgrace. And the "Torture Trust" had been smashed, trapped—its three hypocritical members caught red-handed and exposed: Morvay, Bartholdy, and Van Houten.

Then Burks saw a small key on a shelf near by. It looked like the key to the manacles on Dunsmark's arms and legs. He tried it, found that it worked, and freed the Englishman.

Sir Dunsmark stood up, stretched his limbs and grinned.

"This isn't such a bad country after all," he said. "I had a scare for a time. Things happened rather suddenly, you know."

"What about that man who came for you on the boat? They say he looked like our police commissioner."

Sir Anthony was apologetic, courteous, but firm.

"I'll tell you all about it later—tomorrow—if you don't mind. I'm a bit fagged by all that's happened. Excitement isn't good for me, you know, and I'm a bit late for a rather important appointment. You gather what I mean?"

"Sure thing! Of course."

Burks knew when to be courteous and when to be hard-boiled. A man like Dunsmark wasn't to be trifled with and told what to do. There might be trouble involved. He personally escorted Dunsmark through the building and turned him over to the commissioner. Cops and plain-clothes men were still smashing doors, and rounding up the last of the gray-clad men.

The commissioner was solicitous.

"You must take my car," he said. "I'll see that you have a police escort."

"Really," said Dunsmark, waving his hand in the air. "No fuss or publicity, if you don't mind. As I told the inspector, my nerves are a bit fagged. I'll just borrow your car and slip out. Thanks awfully."

He got into the car and gave the chauffeur the name of a hotel. The car rolled away on velvety springs. A few blocks from the warehouse and Sir Anthony Dunsmark seemed suddenly to change his mind.

"I'll get out here," he said. "A bit of walk will do me good."

The surprised chauffeur started to object, then closed his mouth.

It wasn't for him to quibble with a distinguished passenger. He stopped the car, hopped out, and opened the door with a flourish.

"Give this to Inspector Burks at once," said Dunsmark.

He slipped a small envelope into the chauffeur's hand.

The chauffeur touched his cap, took the note, and got back into the car. He watched Sir Anthony Dunsmark's tall figure disappear down the street.

"That guy's nuts," he muttered.

Then a faint, melodious whistle reached his ears. It was a whistle that stirred echoes high up in the rooftops and whispered eerily along the faces of the buildings. With a prickle on his scalp that he could not quite explain to himself, the chauffeur turned the car and drove rapidly back to the warehouse. He made his way inside the building, found Inspector Burks talking to the commissioner and gave him the note.

"Sir Anthony Dunsmark handed it to me," he said.

Inspector Burks opened the note wonderingly, then stared in amazement, his eyes narrowing. The sentences of the note were brief and to the point.

Dear Inspector: Look in the closet at the extreme end of the basement corridor. You will find a little surprise. Kindly offer my sincere apologies to Sir Anthony Dunsmark. I regret the inconvenience I caused him; but he is a good sport. I'm sure he will understand when you explain the matter to him.

The note was unsigned. The inspector could make nothing of it. But he ran downstairs again, with the commissioner following him.

There was a door at the end of the lower corridor—a door into a small closet, so flush to the wall that they had overlooked it. They yanked it open now and stood speechless with amazement.

A man clad only in his underclothes sat on the floor of the closet bound with an old piece of rope and gagged with a sleeve of his own shirt. When they pulled him to his foot and drew the gag off, he spoke in a cultured British accent.

"Great Scott! What's the meaning of this?" he said.

"Anthony Dunsmark!" gasped the inspector.

"Yes—and who are you—policemen, or more thugs and murderers?"

"Policemen," said Burks. "This is the commissioner himself!"

"The commissioner," said Dunsmark bitterly. "That's what he told me before. If this is your idea of a bally joke, gentlemen—"

But Burks wasn't listening at the moment. He was staring at the note that the commissioner's chauffeur had handed him. It had been unsigned when he first read it. But now at the bottom of the white page, the outlines of a letter were slowly appearing, turning black as the light fell on it. The letter was an "X"—and it seemed to Burks suddenly that the "X" was like an eye staring up at him and winking in sly, sardonic amusement.

BOOK II

THE SPECTRAL STRANGLER

Silent, horrible as the crushing coils of a serpent were those unseen fingers that blotted out men's lives. A criminal of satanic proportions had risen—the "Black Master," whose victims fell with livid, hideous faces and protruding tongues that seemed a ghastly mockery of the fate they had suffered. Along this terrible murder trail Secret Agent "X" gambled with the Dice of Death.

CHAPTER I

MURDER IN THE NIGHT

WARNING PRICKLES RACED along Federal Detective Bill Scanlon's spine. A hunch told him he was being followed. He was a little man grown gray in the service—gray hair, gray mustache, and thin, grayish features. He looked slight—almost weak. Yet, in the long years he'd worked for Uncle Sam, he'd built up a reputation for courage and ability that few men in the D.C.L. could equal.

He turned his head alertly, stared back, and something seemed to move behind him in the long shadow cast by the trunk of a leafless maple.

For a moment he stood uncertainly, then retraced his steps.

There was no fear on his face, but his eyes were watchful. He slid the flat bulk of an automatic out of his side pocket and held it against his thigh, moving forward cautiously like a man walking on eggshells.

He came close to the big maple, sidestepped around it—but no one was there.

A puff of night wind clattered branches overhead. They were sheathed with ice and made a dry rattle like skeleton fingers clicking together. Bill Scanlon stood waiting.

Then he relaxed. A cat with coal black fur and glowing green eyes spat at him and slunk away. It might have been an evil omen, but Scanlon wasn't superstitious. He thought it was only the cat he had seen.

Pocketing his gun, he set off up the street again. There was someone on it he wanted to see—someone who might be a valuable witness in a mysterious murder and kidnapping in which the government was interested.

A shadow detached itself from the blackness of a house stoop opposite the maple. Slinking spiderlike, the shadow moved after

Scanlon, stalking from tree to tree, hedge to hedge, and stoop to stoop, drawing closer—always closer.

Scanlon turned to stare again, but he saw nothing. The shadow was crouched as still as death. There was something deadly, something horrible, in the purposefulness with which it drew nearer.

Scanlon moved on. The person he wanted to interview lived on this block.

A twig covered with ice snapped behind him. He turned a third time, staring, his breath rising like steam in the cold night air.

Still no one was in sight, but the skin along Scanlon's scalp began to tingle. He grasped the butt of his gun, holding it in his pocket, his finger crooked through the trigger guard.

On his left was a hedge of evergreens shielding the lawn of a darkened house. The evergreens were covered with hoarfrost. There was

While women screamed and men shouted hoarsely, he plunged head first down the slippery hardwood stairs.

a gap between them that seemed as black as the cavernous opening in the front of a skull. Scanlon stared toward it for seconds.

Then the pupils of his eyes widened. He crouched, opened his lips as if to speak—but no words came.

Somewhere in the darkness behind the hedge there was faint, quick movement. It seemed no more than the blurring of a shadow against another shadow. No one appeared. No hand came into sight. But suddenly Scanlon uttered a hoarse, rasping gurgle and reached toward his throat.

His body jerked spasmodically. For a moment he gave the impression of a man dangling horribly at the end of a taut rope. His shadow writhed and leaped on the icy sidewalk beside him. He slipped, skidded, made choking sounds, his finger tightening involuntarily on the trigger of his automatic.

The gun belched flame in his pocket. It made a report that blasted the silence of the winter night. The bullet struck the icy pavement and whined away into the darkness.

Scanlon had both hands at his throat now. He appeared to be clawing invisible, horrible fingers away from his neck; appeared to be fighting a losing battle with some hideous unseen strangler who had held him in an unearthly grip.

But he wasn't a man to give up easily. His struggles became more desperate, more frenzied. He tore at his coat, ripped open his collar with fingers as taut as talons. His shadow mimicked every movement he made, leaping like a dancer pirouetting to some mad, macabre rhythm.

Then at last he slipped and fell to the pavement, his face purpling, his eyes bulging out. He continued to writhe, but he made no sound now except the terrible wheezing of air fighting to escape through an aperture too small for it. The mottled, hideous purple of his skin deepened until his complexion had the hue of an overripe plum. Livid spots appeared on it where veins stood out. They seemed ready to burst sickeningly as blood pumped through them from his wildly laboring heart.

His movements grew slowly feebler. Then from his open mouth his tongue protruded grotesquely, horribly, as though he were mocking the unseen, silent thing that had struck him down.

ECHOES of the shot fired by his dying fingers whispered along the night-darkened street. A light flashed in a house diagonally across from the spot where he lay. A man came out on the porch, peered around, saw Scanlon's body, and ran across the street to it.

For seconds the man stood bareheaded, staring down; then he turned quickly, his eyes dark with fright, and ran back into the house to the telephone.

Silence descended on the street again—a silence that was punctuated only by the skeleton clicking of the ice-coated branches. They seemed to be sounding a monotonous, macabre rhythm—a dirge of death.

The rhythm was interrupted at last by the wail of a police siren up the long street. Headlights flared on the icy pavements. A slim, green roadster shot into view. It was a radio cruiser come in response to the bareheaded man's telephoned message to headquarters.

The cop at the wheel was leaning sidewise, staring out. He jerked the car's nose toward the curb and brought it to a halt beside the body of Scanlon. He and his companion jumped out.

They bent down, opened Scanlon's coat, and pulled papers from his pocket—then stared in surprise. The taller of the two cops spoke grimly.

"A Federal dick. Call headquarters quick. They'll want to know about this."

The other cop obeyed. He started at a run across the street, climbed the steps of the lighted house, and disappeared inside.

In twenty minutes the police cruiser at the curb was joined by a black headquarters' car filled with detectives. It slid to a screeching stop. The men leaped out and crowded close around Scanlon, their breaths mingling in the icy air and their long overcoats making sprawled shadows on the pavement

They stared at Scanlon's credentials and examined his body. Inspector John Burks, head of the homicide squad was among them—a tall man with snapping black eyes and jet-black eyebrows that contrasted sharply with his white hair. He began speaking in abrupt sentences.

"Strangled! Look at his face!"

A police sergeant flashed his light lower, then answered hoarse-ly, a note of fear in his voice.

"There ain't no finger marks, chief. It's like—like that woman who was killed last week, and those other guys—the taxi driver and the feller with him that they found in the vacant lot. Four of 'em murdered now—and all alike!"

Inspector Burks was silent for tense seconds. His thin face was working. His mouth was harsh. Four murders all alike! Four homicides as mysterious as they were horrible! Men strangled apparently by ghost fingers—their lives snuffed out by unseen hands. There had been no mark even on the white neck of the woman, the first victim. Yet her eyes, too, had been, staring and her tongue had protruded in that terrible mockery of death.

This was no ordinary murder case. It was uncanny, baffling, with the police already in a *cul-de-sac* from which there seemed to be no logical way out. A new and hideous crime wave was engulfing the city. Burks struck his clenched fist sharply against his palm.

"There's a man I'd look for in this," he grated. "A man who might do such things—the criminal who calls himself Secret Agent 'X.'"

The sergeant bending over nodded somberly.

"Right, chief. It's the kind of screwy job he might pull. But he's a tough man to lay hold of. He never looks the same twice."

"He'll slip up," said Burks harshly. "He's almost done it a couple of times. And if—if he pulled this job—by God, I'll land him in the hot seat."

Burks's eyes had an eaglelike fierceness as he stared down at the face of the dead Government operative. The distorted features and grotesquely mocking tongue of Scanlon seemed to speak of hideous things.

The medical examiner was still going over the body. He shook his head slowly.

"No doubt about it—it's strangulation. You'd think a slipknot had been tied around his throat, or fingers held there—except that there are no marks."

"Except!" Burks echoed the word bitterly. The ice-coated branches that were like bony fingers above his head scraped together in a sound reminiscent of soft, sardonic laughter.

Then a detective spoke, touching Burks's arm.

"Who's that guy over there?" he asked.

He was looking up the block at a figure that had suddenly appeared. A man swung into sight. He was tall, an overcoat flapped around his heels, and he was coming toward them across the street. Blunt features showed under a slouch hat. He was dressed like a young business man; but his eyes burned with a strange, vivid intentness. He walked up to the group of detectives around Scanlon until one of them stepped forward and barred his way.

"Keep back, guy! There's been a murder. Who are you?"

The newcomer didn't answer. He pulled a wallet from his pocket, fumbled in it and drew out a tattered press card.

"A news hound!" said Burks sourly. "How did you get wind of this so quick?"

The stranger uttered one word then, talking with clipped emphasis as though speech were precious.

"Radio," he said.

"It's tough," snarled Burks, "when every Tom, Dick, and Harry listens in on police calls. Headquarters will have to use code for everything if they want to keep the riffraff away."

THE man with the press card ignored this harsh comment. He pushed closer to the dead man until another detective barked at him to keep back.

When he glimpsed Scanlon's face, he gave an abrupt, horrified start. The hot flame of some deep emotion sprang into his eyes. His hands clenched at his sides. He breathed quickly, deeply. Then, as if afraid he might be betraying himself, he set his face muscles into masklike inscrutability.

He stood silently staring down at the features of Scanlon, but the strange, burning light in his eyes did not abate. Then he asked a few pointed questions which the detectives answered sullenly.

"If you print any phony story about this, I'll have your hide," said Burks harshly. "This is murder—the fourth one like it. Something big is up, see? You'd better be damn careful what you hand out in that lousy sheet of yours."

The man with the press card nodded somberly. He took another long look at Scanlon's face as though that face, even with the distortions that hideous death had wrought, were hauntingly familiar. His gaze wandered over Scanlon's twisted, crumpled body.

Then he lighted a cigarette, puffed on it a moment, and, as if by accident, let it drop from his fingers. But, as he stooped to recover it, his eyes rested for an instant on Scanlon's exposed cuff, where faint markings showed, unobserved as yet by the police. The slain D.C.I. man had written them there with a pencil, jotted down an address. And the stranger, in the flash of a second memorized that address, storing it away in his mind. Then, as quietly and mysteriously as he had come, he moved off into the darkness.

Inspector Burks, occupied with the murder investigation, didn't notice the stranger's absence for a few seconds. When he did, he shot an abrupt, uneasy question.

"Where did that bird go?"

The detective-sergeant at his side looked around in puzzlement.

"I don't know, chief. I thought he was still here."

Burks stood scowling, hands thrust deep in pockets, eyebrows drawn together.

"I wonder—" he said slowly. Then he whirled on the men around him and gave a harsh, quick order. "Don't let him get away. I want to talk to him."

Two cops broke swiftly from the group, spreading out in different directions, searching the street, their flash lights in their hands. They covered the whole block, then came back shrugging apologetically.

"He beat it, chief. We looked. We couldn't find him any place."

There was no one in sight along the dark street; but a sound suddenly rose above the clicking of the ice-coated branches. It was a whistle—faint, melodious, eerie. It had a strangely ventriloquistic quality that seemed to fill the whole air at once.

As Burks stood listening tensely, trying to locate it, it died away. Then, somewhere down the street, an auto engine roared startlingly into life. Gears muttered, whined, grew silent as a fast car swept away into the night.

CHAPTER II

A DARING DISGUISE

THE MAN WHO had displayed the press card didn't go to any newspaper office. He drove swiftly through the winter darkness, staring straight ahead. His eyes were like living coals. His knuckles on the black wheel of the car were white and tense.

Before his gaze, the dead, distorted face of Bill Scanlon seemed to hover. Scanlon whom he had known and worked with in days gone by! Scanlon who had guided him, aided him along the rough road of a perilous profession! Scanlon, loyal to the point of death, who had once even saved his life.

What would Scanlon's wife and young son say when they heard he had been slain? They knew his work was dangerous. They were never sure when he would return. But that wouldn't make their sorrow at his passing any less.

The man at the car's wheel muttered huskily, softly to himself. The words came almost like a chant.

"There's a kid and a woman waiting!" he said.

The glowing light in his eyes seemed to deepen as his lips moved. It grew more steely, more bright, like flame reflected from the polished, gleaming point of a sword. If wise old Bill Scanlon had failed in his mission, fallen a victim to the unseen strangler, then the police must be right. Then this was no ordinary murder menace. The killer back of it all must have the cunning brain of a fiend.

The man of mystery made sure no one was following him. He turned the battleship nose of his roadster into a cross-town street, sped westward toward the river, entering upon a long, smooth drive that followed the curving line of the shore.

Millionaires' homes and huge apartment houses rose on one side of the drive. On the other were paths and a parkway leading down to the water, curtained now in darkness. The man threaded his way through evening traffic, parking at last on a side street.

He leaped out of the car and walked forward, the burning look of intense emotion still in his eyes. He turned a corner, moved faster still, then stopped suddenly to press a hand to his side. A twinge of pain had come for an instant. Under his fingers was the scar of an old wound received on a battlefield in France.

A fleeting, bitter smile played over the tall man's lips. Years ago doctors had predicted that the wound would kill him—that he had only a few months to live. But he had gone on living just the same. There was in his body energy that seemed inexhaustible—energy that even death could not seem to conquer. There was an iron will like a living dynamo that drove him on night and day. He had work to do, strange, secret tasks to perform. He wasn't ready yet to answer the call of the Grim Reaper.

He turned into an avenue running parallel with the drive, walking blocks beyond the spot where he had parked his car before heading back toward the river again. He was on a dark street now—a street deserted, with a high wall on one side of it.

Over the wall, against the night sky, the chimneys and peaked roof of a house were faintly visible. It was a huge pile of masonry, bleak and austere—the old Montgomery mansion left empty by the litigation of heirs who could reach no agreement in the settlement of an estate. It had stood empty for years while the legatees battled like wolves.

The man moved along the wall, creeping deeper into the shadows. Suddenly he stopped. His burning eyes scanned the block in both directions. No one was in sight.

Deftly he inserted a key in a door so nearly the color of the wall itself that it seemed hidden.

The door opened, the man moved inside as silently as a shadow. He was in a place of desolation and ruin now. In the old garden behind the Montgomery mansion.

Statues fallen from their pedestals lay like pale ghosts on the weed-grown grass. A summer house, tumbled down and rotting, showed like the skeletal ribs of a great beast.

He picked his way past a fountain that had long since run dry, entering a rear door of the old house. He moved by feeling alone, moved as one familiar with his strange surroundings.

It wasn't until he was safe inside the house that he flashed on a small light. He was behind the old butler's pantry now. Ahead of him were great silent rooms where moths burrowed in the once rich carpets and where rats scurried across the floors.

He pulled at a tier of shelves against the pantry wall, and suddenly the shelves swung outward. The man stepped behind them into the darkness of a hidden chamber. He swung the shelves after him, touched a switch, and lights in the strange room came on. It was a hideout containing many peculiar and remarkable objects.

SEATING himself before a three-sided mirror with movable rod lights above it, the man's long hands began to do strange, mysterious things to his face. Under their magic touch his whole appearance underwent a transformation.

The blunt, roundish features of the business man melted away, disappeared. The eyebrows changed. The hair of the head revealed itself as an elaborate toupee.

Suddenly the man appeared as he really was—as no one, not even his few closest intimates ever saw him.

The rod lights overhead sprayed radiance on brown hair, on smooth-shaven features that had a boyish cast to them. On gray eyes with a steely glint in their depths.

It was only when he turned to pick something off the shelf that light fell on his face at another angle. Then new lines were brought out—lines that made him seem suddenly older—lines of poise and maturity—with the record of countless experiences and adventures written into them.

He stared at his own reflection for a moment, seeming to salute it grimly.

Secret Agent "X"—the man of a thousand faces—a thousand disguises—a thousand surprises.

The man who was a scourge to the criminals prowling the black alleys of the underworld. The man regarded by the police as criminal himself—even now suspected of murder.

He couldn't set them right, either. He was committed to secrecy and silence; committed to move into terrible dangers and walk into the shadow of the Valley of Death alone.

The police couldn't know what document reposed in the strong box on a shelf above his head. For an outsider to plumb its secrets would have meant death. The lid of the strong box concealed a charge of terrible explosive to protect its contents from meddlers. But every word of the document was emblazoned in the Secret

Agent's mind. He could have quoted it from memory, word for word, paragraph for paragraph.[12]

It was unsigned, but it bore the coat of arms of the United States Government. And he knew that the telegram which had reached him that day by way of the First National Bank had also come straight from Washington, D.C. Before destroying the latter, the Agent read it again, committing it to memory as he had the document.

> Mark Roemer, kidnapped chemist, whose assistant was murdered, employed under cover by Chemical Warfare branch of Army. Was working on important formula. Consequences of his disappearance may be disastrous. Advise you investigate immediately.

This, too, was unsigned; but was couched in a Government code. The Agent alone knew its high source. Between the lines of it he seemed to read a second, more sinister message, written by the trailing claws of crime—claws that were weaving a horrible spider's web of murder—building a menace so great that no man could say what hydra-headed horror might rise from it.

Mark Roemer kidnapped! His woman assistant murdered! A taxi driver and an underworld character slain—their bodies left like carrion in a vacant lot! And now brave-hearted, shrewd old Bill Scanlon murdered, too! A sinister crime pattern ran through it all.

Agent "X" crumpled the telegram viciously, touched a match to it, dropped it into a metal dish to burn. Even before he had received it, he had been watching the Roemer case, scenting the unseen miasma of horror surrounding it.

The telegram did not state what formula Roemer had been at work upon, what strange thing he had discovered. But Agent "X" had an inkling. If he were right, then the four ghastly murders were forerunners of others even more terrible.

He faced the mirror again, looked at himself.

Secret Agent "X." Who was he? No one knew. Whispers there

---

12   AUTHOR'S NOTE: This document of the Secret Agent's is said to have come from some high official of the Government, giving him strange and unlimited powers. These powers are in recognition of services he performed for his country in the Intelligence Division during the World War. It also gives notice that ten public-spirited men of great wealth have subscribed a huge fund for his use, part of the fund being on deposit in the First National Bank, to be drawn by him under the cognomen of Elisha Pond.
The Secret Agent's strange hideout contains a chemical and photographic laboratory, and a small arsenal of bizarre offensive and defense weapons of his own devising. Also the elaborate make-up material used in his uncanny disguises.

were—whispers in a few high places. There were those who said he had the Government's backing, that he was a lone campaigner in the war being waged on organized crime.

His fingers began to move again. From a shelf cluttered with jars and sticks of grease paint, nose and cheek plates, and dozens of ingenious makeup devices, he selected what he wanted.

He dabbed pigments on his face, covered his skin with a strange volatile substance and sculptured it into new lines. Strips of transparent, tissue-thin adhesive tape changed the contours of his face muscles. He covered his own brown hair with a white, cunningly made toupee, blackened and thickened his eyebrows. As he worked, deftly, surely, his keen eyes studied a photograph on the shelf before him.

Tonight, in his efforts to unravel the mystery and horror of the strangler murders, he was prepared to take a daring, desperate step.

When at last he rose from his seat, he had the exact likeness of the man in the photograph—a distinguished public official. There was the same silvery-white hair. The same gaunt, thin-lipped face. The same shaggy, menacing eyebrows. Once again "X's" skilled fingers had achieved a seemingly magical disguise.

He changed his suit and overcoat, dressed carefully, slipped a set of mysterious chromium tools into his pocket, and selected two weapons from his strange arsenal. Then he set out, pausing only long enough to start the mechanism of a hidden seismographic machine which would record the vibrations of footsteps if any one entered his hideout during his absence.

He threaded his way through the desolate garden and out onto the dark street.

Turning his face downtown, he strode swiftly along and hailed a passing cab, being careful to keep his coat collar up and his hat brim pulled down. The light in his eyes showed like a steady, glowing flame. He had started on a vengeance quest for the murderer of Bill Scanlon.

CHAPTER III

MURDER CLUB

THERE WAS GRIM method in the movements of Secret Agent "X" after he left his hideout. Step by step, he began to trace the course of the murder wave that had resulted in his old friend's death.

He went first to a sequestered suburb on the outskirts of the city. Here he dismissed his cab and walked again through the night. He had followed the strangler homicides in the papers as he did all murder cases that threatened to be difficult of solution. He knew what festering spot had first given birth to the cancer of this hideous crime.

He strode swiftly along a street of badly cared for wooden houses, turned a corner, and came to a lot which at first glance appeared to be vacant. But there was a high barbed-wire fence around it. In its center, dimly seen, was a cluster of low, shabby buildings. They were buildings which were huddled together as though drawing away from the scrutiny of prying eyes. They were dark and silent now. Murder had laid its pall of quietude upon them.

Agent "X" had seen pictures of these buildings in the papers. From this place Mark Roemer, the Government chemist, had been kidnapped. Somewhere among those buildings Roemer's woman assistant, Cora Stenstrom, had met death at the hands of the invisible strangler.

There was a barbed-wire gate at one side of the enclosure for coal and supply trucks to enter. There was another smaller gate secured by a heavy lock where Roemer and those who came to see him had been in the habit of going in and out.

The Agent paused beside this. A policeman patrolling his night beat sounded measured footsteps up the block. The Agent waited in the light of a street lamp till the cop came alongside.

*His fist lashed outward and
upward in a flashingly swift arc.*

The policeman stared at the Agent, gave a sudden start, then touched his cap respectfully.

"Good evening, inspector," he said. "Can I be of any help, sir?"

Agent "X's" daring disguise had proven adequate. He shook his head, and, when the cop had gone on, he took the kit of chromium tools from his pocket. There were many of them, seemingly fragile, yet cunningly shaped. He held one in his hand, a glittering piece of goosenecked steel. With quiet efficiency he attacked the lock on the gate. In less than a minute the lock snapped open and Agent "X" passed inside.

He moved like a shadow across the barbed wire enclosure toward the jumbled buildings that loomed ahead. He drew another tool from his pocket kit, approached the door of the largest of the buildings. His hand moved toward the lock, then paused. He was staring at the door's edge.

Someone had been at work here recently. He squinted, nodded understandingly. A burglar alarm had been installed since the murder had taken place. This building was Government property. The work of Mark Roemer had been subsidized by the Government. The Government had taken pains to checkmate any further attempt to pry into the secrets that the building held.

Agent "X" reached into his kit again, drew out a slender band of coiled metal that was like a steel measuring tape. He unwound it from its cylindrical case, probed with the end of it around the door's edge till he found the plates of the burglar alarm.

Forcing the end of the thin steel under the inside plate, he drew the steel to its full length and thrust the other end into the moist ground.

The Agent knew the workings of burglar alarm systems—knew that there were two plates, and that it was the separation of these two plates when the door was opened that caused the alarm to sound. By grounding the inner plate he had prevented the breaking of the electric circuit.[13]

He now opened the door quietly and entered. Once inside, he clicked on a flashlight with a bulb no larger than a kernel of wheat. It threw a tiny spot of radiance through a concentrating lens, a beam that would not be seen from outside but which enabled the Agent to pick his way. His eyes were glowing eagerly.

He located the laboratory in the building. Here were storage tanks for chemicals and jars and bottles of strange, poisonous-looking acids. Here were gleaming, copper-sheathed retorts, crystal refiners, an air-compressing machine, vacuum pumps, and a re-

---

13 AUTHOR'S NOTE: *Secret Agrent "X" has made a study of the various burglar alarm systems just as he has of locks, safes, and vaults. A short time ago a company specializing in the manufacture of protective devices for homes and stores complained that one of their inspectors had been impersonated. There was for a while considerable excitement over it. Then the matter was hushed up. The company stated that it might have been mistakten.*
I asked Agent "X" a few pointed questions on the matter, and I gathered from his evasive answers that he was the man who had done the impersonating. Knowing that he works always for justice, law, and order, I could not blame him for taking whatever means he saw fit to acquire knowledge that would aid him in his pursuit of criminals.

frigeration plant. Here was all the paraphernalia for research into little-known and sinister fields of science. Here was where Mark Roemer and his assistant had worked.

It was from this laboratory that Roemer had been kidnapped. It was in it that the body of his assistant had been found. There seemed to be the dullness of death in this deserted building mingled with the acrid odor of chemicals.

Agent "X" walked to the laboratory's window, the one that newspaper accounts of the crime said had been jimmied. For long seconds he studied it, raising it softly, examining the marks that the intruder's jimmy had made. Then he gave a low exclamation.

Marks in the wood of the window frame showed that the pressure which had caused them had come from *inside* the building. They had been made *after* the window had been opened. Someone had left those marks purposely, made it seem that the window had been jimmied. The police had apparently overlooked this.

Like a flitting wraith, the Secret Agent moved about the big laboratory, studying, sniffing, nodding to himself. A wide field of chemical research had been under way here. It was impossible to say without careful study what angle of it Roemer had been concentrating upon before his disappearance; but the Agent had his own ideas.

FEELING that he had learned all he could, he left; reconnecting the burglar alarm again, leaving the building as he had found it. He made his way down the street toward a brightly lighted avenue, passing the bulky form of the patroling cop placidly walking his beat.

The Agent's next stopping point was a vacant lot a half-mile farther on. It was a dreary spot, filled with rubbish and the rusty bodies of old motor cars. A lean cat whisked from behind a barrel looking back at him with lambent green eyes.

The Agent moved between tin cans and piles of rubbish, pausing at last to stare at a bare spot on the ground.

News photographers a few days before had taken pictures of this spot. The tabloids had published the pictures. A thrill-hungry public had gazed at them. It was a spot of death—the spot where a taxi man and a petty criminal, a lone jackal of the underworld, had been found dead. The bodies were gone now; but Agent "X," reconstructing the crime bit by bit, seemed to see their empurpled faces and outthrust tongues at his feet. They, too, had been killed by the unseen hands of the ghostly strangler.

He looked back at the curb, at the place where the deserted taxi had been found. Then, pondering silently, tensely, he walked on and engaged another cab.

This time he went back toward the city limits.

When he reached the street where the murder of Scanlon had occurred, he ordered the driver to proceed slowly. The Federal detective's body had been removed. The police cruiser and head-quarters car were no longer standing at the curb. But, up the block in front of the address written on Scanlon's cuff, an official car of some sort was parked.

Agent "X" told his cabman to drive on and turn a corner. He paid his fare, got out, and walked cautiously back.

The house that corresponded to the number on Scanlon's cuff was a simple two-story affair. There was a light burning on the ground floor. A hedge ran around the yard.

The Agent walked by the chauffeur who dozed at the wheel of the parked car and slipped quietly into the yard. He moved like a shadow along the building's side. His heart was beating faster now. He was running a great risk. Who was inside?

The shades were closely drawn. He couldn't see. He would have to trust entirely to his disguise. But before revealing himself he wanted, if possible, to learn what was going on.

He slipped quickly to the rear of the house, tried a door. It was locked, but once again he took his tool kit from his pocket and deft-ly picked the lock. Then, so quietly that those inside heard nothing, he entered.

He tiptoed to the closed sitting-room door and listened for a moment. A man and a woman inside were talking. The man had the bullying voice of a routine police officer. The tones of that voice were strangely familiar.

"She must have told you," the man was saying. "We found it on her. She must have known what it meant."

"No—no," the woman replied. "She didn't tell me anything. After Cora went to work for Mr. Roemer I never saw much of her. She was secretive always. I never questioned her."

"It's the only clue," the man's voice continued stubbornly. "If you can tell me what it means, you'll be helping the police. You'll be helping to run down the murderer who killed your sister. Did she ever own a car?"

"No—she didn't drive, I tell you. She never had a car."

"You're sure of that?"

"Yes—yes, I'm sure."

There was silence for a moment, and in this silence Agent "X" quietly opened the door. His eyes were gleaming. His body was tense. The action he planned was high-handed, unusual even for him; but impulse had its place in his working methods. Here was an opportunity! The police had one clue—one he hadn't heard of. What was it? The police might not like it—but, to aid in running down the murderer of Scanlon, he would demand that they share that clue with him.

But, as he opened the door, he paused in sudden, breathless amazement. Fate had played a trick on him. The one man he didn't want to meet was here! Any ordinary dick from the Homicide Squad he could have handled without exciting suspicion. But the man standing in the kitchen facing him was Inspector John Burks, head of the bureau—and his own double!

CHAPTER IV

A CIPHER SOLVED

IN THAT FIRST instant it was evident that the inspector had seen him. Utter stupefaction made Burks's face sag for a moment. His eyes bulged. His thin-lipped mouth opened. So exact was the impersonation that the door might have been a mirror and Agent "X" merely the reflection of himself.

The woman, Cora Stenstrom's sister, was dumfounded, too. Her gaunt homely face assumed an expression of blank amazement.

In the flash of a second, Agent "X's" eyes dropped from the inspector's face to his hand. Burks was holding a slip of paper between tense fingers. On it were letters and figures. Here was the clue that the police had found.

The damage was done now. There was no drawing back. The Agent acted quickly, daringly.

So swiftly that the inspector and the woman could only gape, he crossed the room, gliding up to Burks's side. He uttered an impersonal, coldly clipped sentence.

"Let me see what you have there, Inspector."

It was not a request, but an order. Burks's mouth closed with a snap. His pale, gaunt face flushed to a mottled, furious red.

"Secret Agent 'X,'" he gasped. There was, he knew, only one man in the world who would attempt such a thing or dare such a disguise. His fingers dropped the paper. His hand dived toward his coat pocket The significant bulge there showed that a police automatic was cradled inside the cloth.

But, in that split second, Agent "X" made his decision. Burks would shoot him dead without question, thinking he had killed a notorious criminal. "X" didn't give the inspector a chance to draw his gun.

His fist lashed outward and upward in a flashingly swift arc. A hundred and sixty-five pounds of bone and muscle were behind the fist. The Agent's knuckles struck the point of Burks's chin. It was a boxer's blow, straight to the "button." Without so much as a groan, Burks staggered backward and collapsed. He lay peacefully on the floor, like a man in a deep sleep.

Secret Agent "X" stooped and picked up the paper on the floor. It was only a slip. At first glance the numbers and letters on it seemed simple enough.

"A Green Ford 1920 D EHEC."

While the woman stood frozen, too terrified to speak, Agent "X's" eyes ran over it. He realized instantly that it was some sort of cipher. Burks had questioned the woman about it. She had given him no satisfaction. She evidently knew nothing about her sister's private life. It seemed useless to question her further.

The woman, recovering a little, opened her mouth to scream, but Agent "X" silenced her with an abrupt, commanding gesture.

"Quiet!" he ordered.

With no other word to the amazed woman, he turned on his heel and left the house, striding swiftly through the front door. He walked boldly down the walk and stepped into Burks's car at the curb. Instead of getting in back, he took a seat directly beside the driver.

"Get going!" he said.

The driver, half asleep, snapped into alertness.

"Yes, sir. Where to?"

Agent "X" didn't answer. He was holding the slip of paper under the instrument-board light. His face, the face of Inspector Burks, was a blank, but his pulses were racing with excitement. What was this clue that had baffled the police?

"A Green Ford 1920 D EHEC."

While the chauffeur slid the car into gear and shot away from the curb, Agent "X" studied it.

Those letters at the end of the sentence corresponded to no auto license number he had ever seen. The woman had told Burks that her murdered sister had not even known how to drive a car. Here was mystery. Here was a challenge to the Agent's cunning. Here also was something that might lead him to the door of the murderer of Scanlon.

"A Green Ford 1920 D EHEC."

The clue was now in the hands of no ordinary police official. It was in the hands of a man of brilliant insight, a man trained to look beneath the surface and thread his way through the devious, complex channels of cryptography, code systems, and ciphergrams.[14]

He began in his mind to place letters and figures beneath the sentence. He didn't need any pencil. He had the power of visualization. Seconds passed—and, under the keenness of his analytical brain, the words that had seemed so baffling became understandable.

"Where to, chief?" repeated the driver uneasily. But Agent "X" waved his hand impatiently.

"Anywhere," he said.

As the car rolled on, a perplexed chauffeur at the wheel, the Agent translated the sentence to his own satisfaction.

THERE were five letters at the end of it—EHEC, preceded by a D. The numbers 1920 puzzled him a moment, then made his task easier. There was no letter in the alphabet corresponding to nought. The Agent therefore took 19 and 20, counted along the alphabet and substituted letters for them—the letters "S" and "T." Next he substituted numbers for the letters. This gave him 4, corresponding: to D, and 5853, corresponding to EHEC.

To him it was child's play. The thing was a simple substitution cipher. He now had a telephone number—Stuyvesant 4 5853. He guessed at once why such a simple cipher had been used. The maker of it had counted on the words "A Green Ford 1920" to confuse and throw any investigator off the track. They had so far; but the Agent combined the first words into a name, "A. Greenford."

His eyes were snapping with excitement. Why had Cora Stenstrom, the murdered woman, carried this name and telephone with her? He remembered the laboratory window with its marks of a jimmy meant to deceive. Had Cora Stenstrom herself opened that window? Her dead lips could never tell, but Agent "X" hoped to fathom their secret.

For a moment he fingered the slip of paper tensely, forgetful of where he was. Then he felt Burks's chauffeur's eyes upon him. The man's face was troubled, uneasy.

---

14 AUTHOR'S NOTE: In last month's chronicle of Agent "X's" adventures, "The Torture Trust," I said that he ranked among the world's cleverest cryptoanalytists. There are rumors in Washington that he was at one time associated with Yardley, famous organizer of America's "Black Chamber," during the World War. If so, he must have helped solve the staggering secrets of the German official codes.

"You must 'a found out something, chief. That woman must 'a give you a tip. Where'd you like to go next—if it ain't too much trouble?"

"That's a good question," said Agent "X" grimly. "I'm looking for a murderer."

"Yeah, I know it, chief, bu—"

"A kid and a woman are waiting," muttered "X" again softly, thinking of Bill Scanlon's wife and young son, seeming to see once more the face of a man who would not come back. A sudden harsh look sprang into his eyes.

The chauffeur lifted a hand from the wheel and, in spite of the winter chill, wiped sweat from his forehead. His face was twisted nervously now. He seemed to sense that something was wrong. There was a look of fear and awe in his eyes as he glanced sidewise at his superior.

Secret Agent "X" laughed shortly, bitterly. They were crossing a brightly lighted avenue. Another dark street was ahead.

"Just keep going," he said, "I'll tell you when—"

He stopped speaking. Another sound had cut in upon his words. The short-wave police radio in the front of the car had suddenly come to life. There was a rattle, a buzz. The chauffeur touched the dial.

"Calling all cars!" came the voice of the headquarters' announcer. "Calling all cars. Look out for—"

With a movement so quick that the eyes of the chauffeur could hardly follow it, Secret Agent "X" reached out and turned the dial, cutting off the voice.

"Stop right here," he said quickly.

The car came to a halt with a screech of brakes. Agent "X" jumped put, then paused for an instant, staring back at the wondering eyes of the police chauffeur.

"What is it, chief? What's the matter?" the man asked.

With a strange, sardonic smile on his lips Secret Agent "X" reached into his pocket He drew out the slip of paper with the code upon it, handed it to the chauffeur.

"Give that to Inspector Burks," he said, "with my compliments."

"Inspector Burks! Why—what the hell!"

Words tumbled from the chauffeur's lips; but Secret Agent "X" didn't wait to reply. He slipped around the car, darted across the sidewalk into the shadow of a hedge. The darkness seemed to open up, swallow him.

But behind him, as the excited hand of the chauffeur turned it on again, came the blatant, metallic sound of the police radio.

"Look out for Inspector Burks's official car driven by man impersonating him. Chauffeur believed murdered. Look out for escaping killer. Calling all cars!"

WITH the gleam of sardonic amusement still in his eyes, the Secret Agent ducked between two houses, crossed to another street, and continued on into the night.

He stopped for a moment in the blackness of an alley to change his disguise. As the impersonator of Inspector Burks, he was a marked man now. Police cars would be combing the city. His present make-up would be like a death warrant.

His quick, deft fingers removed it, and pulled other materials from a deep inner lining of his coat. Disguises that took patient minutes to build up could be destroyed quickly. He had other stock make-ups for just such emergencies as this.

Working in the dark by a sense of touch alone, he drew the white toupee from his head, changed it to a gray one, and molded his face into new lines.

He came out of the alley disguised as a man of middle age, with thick lips and sagging face muscles. Then he walked through the night-shrouded streets to the nearest drug store. In a telephone booth, he dialed information. He gave the number he had deciphered and learned that it was the Hotel Sherwood.

Step by step he was creeping ahead. Creeping toward what? Toward the solution of the mystery, toward defeat—death? It was certain that the person who had committed four terrible murders wouldn't stop at committing others. It was certain that menace like a sinister shadow darkened the path that "X" had chosen to follow.

Still disguised as a well-dressed man of middle age, he took a taxi to within two blocks of the Hotel Sherwood. Smoking a cigarette, he walked into the lobby. It was one of the city's smaller, less expensive hostelries. A place where many transient out-of-towners stopped. His presence attracted little attention. And "X" always prepared for small emergencies, acted deftly, swiftly, now.

He fished in his pocket, drew out a complimentary theater ticket that had been handed to him in a restaurant. Dropping this into a yellow envelope, he sealed it and wrote "A. Greenford" on the outside. He moved across the lobby, dropped the envelope on the reception clerk's desk, and, even before the clerk had seen it he went back to a seat beside an ornamental palm. From here he saw the clerk pick up the envelope and place it in a numbered box.

A half hour went by, an hour, while the Agent waited tensely. Many cigarettes passed through his fingers. His nerves were screaming for action. Then, from the corner of his eye, he saw a dark, quick-moving man come out of the hotel's elevator.

The man walked jerkily to the desk and asked a question. The clerk reached into the tier of boxes behind him, drew out the yellow envelope and tossed it on the counter. The Agent's eyes, brightly alert, took in every move.

The dark man opened the envelope, frowned at the ticket and threw it irritably into a cuspidor.

Still frowning, he turned and moved toward a seat in the lobby. He had a brownish, pasty complexion, thin, cruel lips and deep-set eyes.

He stopped suddenly, turning his head toward the door.

Newsboys in the street outside were crying shrilly, shouting: "Extra! Extra!"

One of them came into the hotel's lobby brandishing a paper.

"Extra! Read all about the big murder! Federal man killed! Read all about the big murder!"

The dark-faced Mr. Greenford jumped out of his chair and stepped forward tensely. He fumbled in his pocket, produced coins, and bought a paper. Agent "X" watching intently, noticed the sudden change that came over Greenford's face. Its pastiness seemed to increase. Evil lines showed around his thin mouth. He retired to a corner with the paper in his hand.

Agent "X" quickly signaled the boy and bought one himself.

Here was the terrible story of Bill Scanlon's murder. Here was a picture of him and his wife and small son. Here was the record of his long and faithful service with the Department of Criminal Investigation. Telegraph wires had been humming. The tabloid presses had been busy spewing out a special edition to broadcast this latest strangler horror. The police had been forced to release details to eager reporters. The papers had played it up.

"Unseen Strangler Claims Fourth Victim," the headlines screamed.

But Agent "X" hardly glanced at the story inside. He knew more than these startling lines told. He was watching the man who called himself "A. Greenford."

The dark-faced stranger was devouring the details of the killing, his long, thin hands trembling, one black eyebrow twitching nervously.

MINUTES passed. The man did not move. Then a uniformed telegraph messenger stepped into the hotel lobby. He went to the desk, handed a telegram to the clerk. The clerk signed for it, gave it to a bellhop. The bellhop's voice rose.

"Paging Mr. Greenford. Telegram for Mr. Greenford."

Agent "X" acted swiftly, daringly again. He rose from his seat, held his hand up and signaled to the boy. Before the angry, incredulous eyes of the dark-faced man in the corner, he snatched the telegram and slipped a shiny quarter into the bellhop's hand. Then abruptly, he slit the envelope with his finger and read the message inside.

"Arthur Greenford, Hotel Sherwood," it said. "Come to No. 40 Bradley Square, top floor, rear, midnight. Important. B.M."

The Agent saw that the dark-faced man had leaped out of his chair and was coming toward him. He did not wait. Thrusting the telegram into his pocket, he turned and walked swiftly to the door.

He knew that he was being followed. There was an excited gleam in his eyes. The message of the telegram carried mystery with it. It was almost as mysterious as the sentence found on the body of the murdered Cora Stenstrom—the sentence that Secret Agent "X" had deciphered. Who was B.M.? What motive was behind his midnight invitation? Agent "X" would find out.

Theater crowds were thick on the sidewalk outside. Laughing, jostling people moved along beneath the bright, gay lights. They stared at the gaudy, alluring theater posters, blinked at the flashing neon tubes. They did not sense, as "X" did, the sinister spirit of murder that seemed to stalk through the night.

He mingled in the crowd quickly, but not too quickly. He turned his head once. The dark-faced man behind him was catching up. Agent "X" lighted a cigarette. He strode ahead as though preoccupied with his own thoughts. He did not turn when someone touched his arm. Then a hoarse voice spoke in his ear.

"Wait—you have something of mine!"

Agent "X" looked around then. The man who called himself Arthur Greenford was standing tensely at his side. His face was contorted with emotion. Fear and suspicion glared from the depths of his black eyes.

"That telegram was meant for me," he hissed. "What did you mean by taking it? Who are you?"

Agent "X" faced him squarely. His own eyes were blazing with excitement.

"Perhaps my name is Greenford, too," he said.

"Perhaps—and perhaps not. You will give me that telegram, or—"

There was a sinister threat in the man's incompleted sentence. The Agent smiled bleakly.

"You shall have it if you want it," he said. "A most unfortunate mistake!"

His hand dived into his packet. It came out clutching the yellow telegram. Greenford could not see the small metal tube concealed in the palm of the Agent's hand. The jostling crowd milled around them. Agent "X" held the telegram out. Greenford reached out a hand to take it. The Secret Agent's fingers moved. He held the tube tensely, skillfully. His thumb was pressing one end. From the other, the open end of the tube, a hair-thin needle flashed out. It penetrated the skin of Greenford's wrist, buried itself for an instant in his flesh. The prick of its point was hardly more noticeable than the bite of a mosquito.

Greenford drew his arm away, hardly knowing what had happened. He glanced at the Agent, glanced around. But the telegram was in his fingers. Its message seemed to hold him fascinated. He had not seen ths Agent palm the tube, a miniature hypodermic needle. An instant more and Secret Agent "X" had turned his back and was striding on.

Greenford called after him, started in pursuit again. But he had taken no more than a half-dozen steps when he began to stagger. He fell against a woman at his left, pulled himself up, and swayed to the right. Then suddenly his knees gave way under him. With his face muscles sagging and a look of utter perplexity in his eyes, he fell to the pavement.

Excited shouts went up from the crowd around him. Greenford was sitting on the sidewalk with a dazed look on his face. He was like a man afflicted with a sudden apoplectic stroke. The crowd stopped, drew around him in a ring, staring with dumb, gaping eyes.

"He's drunk," someone said.

"He's sick," said another. No one made a move to do anything about it. A lethargy of curiosity had settled over the people around—the lethargy of the typical city crowd.

Then a man broke through the barrier of gaping people. His face was concerned. He was a dignified-looking man, gray at the temples, heavy featured. He had a professional air about him. The man was Agent "X" come back.

He felt Greenford's pulse—rolled his eyelid down and stared at the iris.

"I'm a physician," he said. "Call a cab—at once. This man seems to be ill."

Someone at the edge of the crowd signaled a taxi. The cab drew up to the curb. Someone else helped Agent "X" lift Greenford to his feet. In a minute he was inside the vehicle. Then, with Agent "X" holding him solicitously, the cab sped away.

CHAPTER V

GREENFORD'S DOUBLE

"TO THE NEAREST** hospital," ordered Agent "X," still maintaining his professional manner. The driver nodded, heading the cab into a long avenue, honking his horn to keep traffic back.

In the interior of the cab, slumped on the seat, Greenford's body joggled like a sack of meal. His head swayed grotesquely on his shoulder. His dazed eyes stared ahead unseeingly.

But as seconds passed, the vagueness of his eyes began to diminish. It was as though a curtain were slowly going up. Agent "X" opened a side window. Cold night air blew on Greenford's face. A little of the laxity left his body. He shook himself, opened his eyes wider. A sound like a sigh came from his lips. Suddenly he moved his head, stared at the man beside him. His gaze met the strangely burning eyes of Agent "X." A snarl came from Greenford's lips, then color rushed back into his cheeks, mottling them darkly.

"Who are you?" he demanded.

Agent "X" did not answer immediately. He reached forward with one hand, slid the glass panel behind the driver's seat shut.

"Silence!" he said harshly.

"See here—" Greenford was crouched back on the seat now like an animal at bay. "Let me out of this cab or I'll—"

There was thickness in his voice, the thickness of some foreign accent carefully hidden. He yanked his arm away from the Agent's grasp, his fingers moved suddenly toward his pocket, then hesitated. The burning, strange light in "X's" eyes seemed to hold his fascinated. "X's" right hand had moved, drawn his gas gun out so quickly that Greenford had been unable to follow the motion. The gun was pointed directly at him now. He could not know that its sinister black muzzle held only sleep, not death. The look in the

149

Agent's eyes was deadly.

The Agent offered no explanation, gave no inkling of his plans. But the look of anger in Greenford's face turned to one of fear. A sickly doughiness came over his features. He began to tremble. There had been murders. Murder was in the air. In the eyes of this strange man beside him he seemed to read a sinister threat.

"Don't shoot," he babbled suddenly. "Don't kill me. I'll do anything you say."

Here was the voice of a coward speaking, a man whose aggression left him when he saw himself cornered. There was contempt in the Agent's eyes. He had met this breed before. He held the gun steadily. Then he slid the panel behind the driver's seat open, again.

"Never mind the hospital," he said. "Drive to the St. James apartments—ninety Jefferson Avenue."

The cabman gave one puzzled glance and obeyed. If he thought at all, he must have concluded that the address given was a doctor's office.

Greenford continued to tremble, staring with terrified eyes at the man beside him. Agent "X" seemed to radiate mystery and power. There was inexorable command in his glowing eyes. Their glance was almost hypnotic. Greenford wilted beneath it.

The cab drew up at the address given. A big but not too expensive apartment rose at the side of the street.[15]

Agent "X" thrust the gas gun in his pocket, but kept the muzzle still pointing at Greenford through the cloth of his overcoat.

"Make any break and—" "X" did not finish his sentence, but he pressed the hard snout of the gun against Greenford's side.

The Agent paid the cabby then, and, with Greenford moving slightly ahead, they entered the apartment building. There was no doorman. A switchboard operator glanced at them casually. Agent "X" pressed the button of an automatic elevator. When the car came into sight, he motioned Greenford into it. He pressed another button, and they ascended to the fifth floor.

Greenford, still trembling with fear, was marshaled down a long corridor and into a simply furnished apartment. The door of the

---

15 AUTHOR'S NOTE: Using his unlimited resources wisely, the Agent, I have learned, has established temporary spots of refuge in several parts of the city; just as he has bought and placed several cars in garages located at different points. He did not tell me, but I surmise that his place on Jefferson Avenue was a furnished apartment taken on a short lease under some pseudonym.

apartment closed after him.

"What do you want?" he asked in a croaking voice. "Who are you? I haven't got—" He did not finish the sentence. He checked himself, stared at the Agent.

The Agent was silent. His burning eyes were still upon Greenford. He seemed to be studying him, seemed to be analyzing every movement that the man made. Greenford spoke again.

"What is it you want. Don't—"

Again he stopped in the middle of a sentence. His lips opened to scream, but the scream ended in a gasp. For, as quickly as the flash of a snake's tongue, Agent "X" had whipped his gas gun out. His finger pressed the trigger. There was a barely audible hiss. A jet of gas sprayed into Greenford's face, filled his mouth. Without a sound, the man staggered back and collapsed on the rug.

THE Agent pocketed his gun; then drew an open-faced watch from his pocket and glanced at it. It was long after ten now. The telegram he had taken from Greenford had given twelve as the hour of the mysterious rendezvous at Bradley Square. Time was a vital element.

He stooped over Greenford, picked him up. Unobtrusive but steel-like muscles in the Agent's shoulders snapped into life. As easily as though he had been a child, he carried Greenford's unconscious body to a big chair and deposited it there, placing pillows behind Greenford's back, propping him.

Then once again he began studying the man's face. He studied it from all angles, noting the planes of it and the lines.

He walked to a closet in the apartment, drew a suitcase out, and turned it upside down. He pressed two brass studs in the suitcase's underside and disclosed a cleverly concealed false bottom that would never have been suspected unless the suitcase's sides and depth were measured. From this secret compartment he took an assemblage of make-up material. Thin vials of pigments and volatile plastic substances.

He locked the apartment door, spread his make-up equipment before a bureau mirror, and set to work. Glancing from time to time at the unconscious man in the chair, his fingers performed the magic that had made the Agent's name one to conjure with. The man of a thousand faces—a thousand disguises—a thousand surprises, was at work again.

For twenty minutes his fingers moved dexterously. When he

turned at last from the mirror, Greenford's double seemed to be in the room. Agent "X" walked across the floor practicing Greenford's characteristic movements. The Agent's disguises went further than make-up. They became a study in muscular coordination as well. He spoke a few sentences, mimicked Greenford's slightly blurred accent.

He searched Greenford then, took a wallet and papers from his pocket and found a money belt strapped around his middle next to his skin. The Agent's fingers were tense as he opened this. It was stuffed with bank notes—bills of high denomination. He looked at their corners. A one and two noughts showed. Century notes!

He counted them. Fifty of them—five thousand dollars! Stacking the bills in a neat sheaf, the Agent pocketed them. They were not for himself. He had no need of money with the account in the First National Bank always ready to draw on. He had never made the test, but he felt sure that his own resources were practically unlimited. But he had a strange outlet for money confiscated from criminals.

There were blank papers in Greenford's wallet. Agent "X" suspected that they held writing in invisible ink. They might give insight into Greenford's strange vocation. But there wasn't time to search for a chemical developer now—and the Agent had already drawn his own conclusions regarding Greenford's character.

He drew the small hypo needle from his pocket again; emptied the colorless liquid from its tubular syringe, and refilled it from a small vial. This he injected into Greenford's arm, close to a vein. The man would stay unconscious for a specific time now, or until "X" chose to administer an antidote.[16]

Next he put Greenford's slumped body into a ventilated closet and locked the door.

It was now after eleven. He descended to the street floor and passed the switchboard operator, who took him for a departing guest. He walked several blocks and hailed a cab. What strange and sinister adventure, he wondered, lay ahead of him at No. 40 Bradley Square?

---

16 AUTHOR'S NOTE: *From hints he has let drop, I know that Agent "X" has done profound research in the field of narcotic and anesthetizing drugs. The opium alkaloids, such as morphine, papaverine, codeine, narcotime, thebaline, and laudanine are known to him; as well as hypnotics of the choral group—veronal, hedonal, trional, barbitonum, and butylchoral hydras. He can figure to a nicety what dosage is necessary to produce a certain period of amnesia or unconsciousness.*

CHAPTER VI

THE HOUSE OF MYSTERY

ONE THING HE saw in his first glimpse of the house, and he gave a start of amazement. The building was closed up. It was a four-story brownstone mansion belonging apparently to the Victorian era. Protective boarding covered the windows on the first floor. The others on the floors above were dark and curtainless. There was a "for sale" sign on the building, showing whitely under the glow of the corner light. Bradley Square had become run down. Its past glories were gone. It was a place of quiet and decay. The once-flourishing park in its center had been turned into a playground for poor children. Deserted swings hung forlornly in the darkness like gibbets.

A drunken man moved tipsily toward the garish doors of a beer saloon at the far end of the square. A few rooming houses on the side where number forty stood showed dim lights through dusty windows.

The Agent walked past the house of mystery several times. What mad thing was this to bring a man to a deserted house? The dark, empty windows seemed to frown down upon him. Were there eyes watching him furtively somewhere in the blackness?

He looked at his watch again. Exactly midnight. A clock blocks away boomed the hour, sending cracked echoes across the square. The icy branches of the trees rattled in the night wind, making him think again of Bill Scanlon's staring eyes and protruding tongue. Death seemed to lurk in the night around him. There was a grimly sardonic gleam in the depths of his eyes. It was into such situations, such places, that his strange commission led him.

He mounted the steps of number forty, pulled the metal end of an ancient bell wire. Somewhere far back in the empty house a thin jingle sounded. He listened. There was no answering sound of footsteps. He pulled the bell wire again. The jangle that awoke faint echoes seemed almost sacrilegious, as though he were disturbing the quiet of a mausoleum—disturbing the dead.

Then the hair on his scalp rose. He held himself tensely. Before him, the weather-worn door of the house opened. There was no one in sight, no sound of a human being, only the faint rusty movement of the hinges. A draft of stale air struck his face. The hallway before him was starkly empty. It was uncanny, awe-inspiring—more so than the sight of any sinister figure. The ghostly movement of the door made him think of the phantom strangler, of the invisible, awful thing that had already snuffed out the lives of four people.

But he moved into the house. It was cold inside with the coldness of a place that has long been empty. Behind him, with an eeriness that made his hair rise, the door swung shut. He was in absolute darkness. Was this a death trap? Had someone planned to lure Greenford to his doom? The Agent smiled bleakly again. He had lived too long in the presence of the Grim Reaper to fear him now. He had cast fear from his heart.

He struck a match, moved forward along the ancient hallway toward a flight of stairs ahead. The paint on the old walls was cracked and blackened with dust. The red plush carpet beneath his feet gave out little puffs of dust as he moved, and ahead, in the doorway leading to the big old-fashioned parlor, tattered, moth-eaten draperies hung, a last relic of decayed and dead gentility.

The parlor was as black as the opening of a tomb. He passed it quickly, ascending the stairs. "Top floor, rear," the telegram had said. He moved past floor after floor, striking matches. In the wavering brief light that they shed, his shadow seemed to pursue him like a stalking fiend. He did not use his flash light. To do so would be out of character. It might throw suspicion on him if unseen eyes were watching.

He came at last to the top floor. Here all street noises were excluded. There was no sound anywhere in the old house. The house seemed to be silent, crouching, like a beast waiting for its prey.

The door of the rear top room was shut. He opened it, passed inside. The curtainless windows admitted a ghostly glow from the light in the next street far below. He saw a few pieces of broken furniture that the last tenants of the house had left behind. A springless iron bed, a chair with one rocker gone, a metal washstand twisted into a shapeless mass of rusty iron. There was no one in the room—no living thing. There was a closet and he opened the

"They must not get us," she cried. "We will shoot—shoot to kill."

door of it, struck a match, looked in. That too was empty, save for a man's old overcoat hanging there like a withered corpse.

BUT as he stepped to the center of the room again, a voice suddenly sounded—a voice so close and so harsh that it was like a dash of icy water thrown on him.

He couldn't locate its direction. It seemed to fill the whole room. It seemed to come from his left; but only blank wall space was there. He listened.

"Greenford," the voice said. "Greenford," it repeated again and again. "You are nearly a minute late, Greenford. It is not wise to come late to this house when an appointment has been made. I expect those with whom I have dealings to be on time!"

The voice ceased as abruptly as it had begun. It was a man's voice, harsh, grating. It was a voice that gave Secret Agent "X" some inkling of the sinister being that he was fighting, a voice that had the assurance and cruel arrogance of supreme power.

Mimicking Greenford's accent, Secret Agent "X" answered.

"The slippery pavements made haste difficult tonight. I am sorry—so sorry."

The voice spoke again.

"Some men learn by their mistakes. Others do not. You will learn to be punctual, or—"

A harsh laugh sounded—a laugh as brutal and evil as the scraping of a poisonous reptile's scales. Then the voice continued:

"I have what you want, Greenford. By murder I gained the thing you sought. Gold would not buy it for you. Death gave it to me. But for gold I will part with it. What amount, Greenford, is your government prepared to pay? Consider well. You have twenty-four hours for cable negotiations. Come tomorrow night at this same time. Take warning! Do not be late! Speak in this room and I will hear. Let me know your answer. I have other customers if your price is not satisfactory. And make no attempt at trickery. You are helpless. You are in the hands of the Black Master."

The voice ceased again, and silence descended on the room, as heavy as the silence of a tomb. Agent "X" pondered a moment.

B.M. had been the initials on the telegram Greenford had received. B.M.—The Black Master. But who was this criminal who held the city in a thrall of fear? Who was this killer who had brutally murdered four people, among them loyal, brave-hearted Bill Scanlon of the D.C.I.?

The silent room and the old house gave no hint.

The fingers of "X's" right hand tautened for a moment, clenched till the knuckles went white. His lips moved slightly, whispered again that phrase that seemed to ring through his head.

"A kid and a woman are waiting!"

He had come close to the murderer of Scanlon—heard him speak. Yet it was as though rocky walls separated them. He dared not strike now, dared not search through that room as he wanted to. He must wait, watch, proceed with the caution and cunning of a fox. A false step—and all would be lost. The horror would go. Scanlon's cruel killing would never be avenged.

He descended the dusty stairs quietly. His eyes held an inscrutable light. He had till tomorrow night to make a decision. But he was still in darkness, darkness as total as that in the black corridor below. The door opened for him again as though the ghost of some ancient, silent servant still lingered in the dim hallway.

He passed out into the street. Night wind struck his face. The ice-coated branches whispered like mocking laughter.

But as he moved along the street, it seemed for an instant that a shadow moved after him. He had trained himself to see such things. He had shadowed men himself and knew the arts of shadowing. He was being shadowed now. Of that he was certain.

For a bare second he paused. His only hope of running the killer to earth lay in seeming for the moment to comply with the voice of the Black Master. He walked on, conscious still of eyes upon him.

He passed beyond the square and came to a thoroughfare. Standing at the curb, he signaled a taxi. His eyes glinted grimly as, looking back, he saw another taxi go to the curb, pick a passenger up and follow.

"The Hotel Sherwood," said Agent "X."

Posing as Greenford, he must play the role of Greenford until—. It seemed now that the cunning of his brain was the only power on earth that could sever the terrible murder chain that unseen hands were forging.

His cab drew up before the bright lights of the Sherwood. The other taxi was no longer in sight. Agent "X" paid his fare and went into the lobby. He picked up Greenford's key at the desk and ascended in the elevator. He was revolving a hundred plans in his mind, wondering what course was best to follow. The man he was battling was a monster—a criminal without scruple, and with infinite cunning. High stakes were at issue. The caution the Black Master had taken proved that. But, even if there were nothing else, the murder of Scanlon was motive enough to drive Agent "X" forward into the very gates of death.

He opened the door of Greenford's room, closed it after him, groping for a light switch. He clicked it on, and the overhead bulbs bathed the chamber in radiance. Then suddenly the Agent held himself taut, holding his breath and with muscles contracted. A woman's voice, sinister as the purring of a sleepy tigress, spoke close to his ear.

"Armand—are you not glad to see me?"

CHAPTER VII

THE TIGRESS!

AGENT "X" TURNED his head slowly, stiffly. For once he had been caught off guard. For once the utterly unexpected had happened.

A woman, blonde and dazzlingly beautiful, stood beside the door. Crimson lips smiled at him. He caught in that first glimpse the feline, arrogant grace that characterized her bearing. She was leaning against the bureau, one hip thrown out, a hand resting on it, the other hand holding an unlighted cigarette. Her close-fitting dark dress revealed the superb outlines of her figure.

Slowly she lighted her cigarette, took a deep puff, blew smoke through her delicate nostrils.

"You are surprised! You did not expect to see me," she said.

Her lips smiled again; but her eyes did not. They regarded Agent "X" with cold, impersonal calculation. The silvery tones of her voice, her sleekness, her beauty, masked something else—something sinister. Here was a woman as dangerous as she was lovely. A tiger woman who lived by her wits and that stinging provocative appeal of her charms. Who was she? The Agent could only guess. He had pulled himself together. He began playing a game—a deadly, silent battle of wits.

"I am surprised—yes," he said. "But a beautiful lady is always a welcome surprise."

She laughed throatily, came nearer. He could smell the faint clinging perfume that seemed to envelop her.

"You used to call me Nina," she said.

"Nina is a lovely name," he replied.

He lighted a cigarette himself, stared at her, waiting and watching, his eyes narrowed. A false move and she might grow suspicious. He must not slip out of his role—the role of Arthur Greenford—the man she called Armand.

"It was clever, changing your name," she said. "But why did you choose the same initials? Arthur Greenford—Armand Grenfort?"

He bowed ironically.

"I did not expect that my initials would undergo analysis by such an astute brain as yours."

She laughed again, but her eyes that were dark and bright as polished agate took on the hardness of agate.

"You are fencing with me, Armand. Do you think I do not know why you are here?"

Her accent and phrasing were foreign. He had catalogued her already. The theft of Mark Roemer's mysterious formula had brought another evil vulture circling about. For in spite of her beauty, the woman before him had in her eyes the look of some predatory bird or beast.

"You are just as subtle as you used to be," he said softly.

She came and laid her hand on his arm, brushing her lithe body against him for a moment. Her lips, smiling up at him, were challengingly close.

"Perhaps," she said, "we can work together—as we did once before."

He tried a shot in the dark then. He made his voice harsh.

"It's too late, my dear Nina. What I seek is gone. It has been stolen. It is in the hands of another."

The woman pushed him away from her roughly. She stepped back toward the bureau again. A transformation came over her. Hate and greed convulsed her face, making her look suddenly older, bringing out wicked lines in her features.

"You lie!" she said, and the two words came from her lips like drops of distilled venom. The beauty of her body was like the sinuous beauty of a cobra swaying, ready to strike.

"You lie!" she repeated.

He stood looking at her, shrugging.

"Listen," she said fiercely. "You will let me work with you—share with you, or—"

Her slim hand suddenly reached behind her. She snatched something from the bureau top which she had concealed under a lacy handkerchief. It was an automatic, flat, polished, small as a child's toy—but capable of dealing death. She pointed the gun at the Agent's heart, held it tensely as though it would give her pleasure to shoot. He did not doubt that she had killed men before.

Again he shrugged.

"What about the kidnapping of Mark Roemer and the murder of his assistant?" he asked.

Her lips slid back from her teeth in an evil smile. They formed a crimson, mocking gash across the front of her white face. She nodded craftily.

"I know," she said. "Mark Roemer was kidnapped. His assistant was murdered—not prettily either. I read all about it. That is why I came to see you. You did it, Armand. You are bolder than you used to be. Men learn by their experience. You murdered that woman— and those others. You have Roemer somewhere and you are guarding his secret. If you are not generous with me, Armand, I will turn you over to the police—right now."

"And if I am—generous?" he asked.

"I will forget what I know about you. What is a murder—between friends?"

THE depth of her wickedness was appalling. It was like finding a deadly, coiled serpent concealed in the soft petals of a flower. She was blackmailing him, ready to wink at murder—if he would satisfy her greed.

He shrugged again, resignedly this time.

"You always had strength of character, Nina. You had a way of getting what you wanted. But I'm tired and there are many things to be gone into. Let us go out and discuss this over a bottle of wine. If we are to work together—we must renew our acquaintance—for old time's sake."

She stood glaring at him, doubt in her eyes.

"Any tricks, Armand—and I will anticipate the law. I will kill you!"

"Are you not a little frightened," he said, "trying to browbeat a murderer?"

For a moment the paleness of her face increased.

"I left a note with certain friends," she replied. "It is to be opened—if I do not return. In it are facts about you—details to aid the police."

"In that case," he said, "we are assured of a quiet evening. I am certain we will get on amicably."

She nodded and put her automatic into a hand bag.

"We understand each other, Armand," she said.

The Agent smiled to himself. He understood her, knew that she was an unprincipled spy in the pay of some government, and that she had once worked with Greenford, or Grenfort. But it was ironic to think how utterly in the dark she was concerning the affairs of the real Grenfort. He had spoken the truth and she had not believed him.

She came then and lifted her lips to his, slipping soft arms around his neck.

"We used to be such good friends, Armand!" Her words were a caress and an invitation.

"Let us not mix business with pleasure," he said coldly.

He saw hatred flash in her eyes again. But she began dabbing powder on her face from a silvered compact. Then she slipped into a clinging fur coat that was thrown over a chair. It made her seem more feline than ever.

They descended in silence to the lobby below and turned their faces toward the street. There was a cab waiting at the curb. Agent "X" ushered her into it and gave the address of a small restaurant.

The woman settled herself beside him.

"Remember," she said, "there is a note waiting to tell the police—everything—if I should disappear."

"Let me repeat that I hold your life as precious as my own," he said mockingly.

She looked at him keenly for a moment.

"You have changed, Armand," she said. "You have more steel in your character than you used to have. That is what murder does for a man."

Suddenly he saw her eyes widen, and a hiss came from her lips that was like the hiss of a startled snake. She was looking back, looking out the cab's rear window. Her fingers tightened over the Agent's arm like clutching talons.

"Armand," she said, "we are being followed. Look—there are men in that car—and they are watching us."

LEADEN THREAT

A **GENT "X" STARED** back tensely. He was not afraid for his own life. He was afraid only that something might impede his progress in tracking down the Black Master—the invisible strangler. In his first glimpse of the men behind, he catalogued them. There were four, grim-faced, clean-cut. One at the wheel of the car, another beside him, two in the back seat.

One was leaning out, signaling for the cab to stop.

Agent "X" bent forward, jerked the glass panel behind the driver's seat open and hissed in the driver's ear.

"Gangsters behind," he said. "Speed up—for your life!"

With a startled twitch of his head, the driver stared back, saw the pursuing car, stepped on the gas. The taxi leaped ahead like a horse under the lash of a whip.

Agent "X" leaned back smiling grimly. The men behind were not gangsters. They were Department of Justice operatives. Of that he was certain. He knew the type well. But it had been necessary to lie to the cabman to save the situation. Nina, the woman beside him, caught the fleeting smile on his face.

"You—you tipped them off!" she hissed. Her hand flashed toward her hang bag again. He caught her wrist.

"Don't be a fool. You accuse me of murder. Would a murderer tip off the law? They must have trailed me."

The woman blanched and began to mutter fiercely. She was no longer beautiful. She was a harsh-faced tigress.

"They must not get us," she cried. "We will shoot—shoot to kill." Again she dived for her weapon. Again he stopped her.

"You will do as I say," he grated. "You came to my hotel. Perhaps it is you they followed!"

"No," she said fiercely. "I came by plane from Mexico. It was night when I landed. They could not have seen me. It is you, Armand, that they are after."

"You are a notorious woman," he answered, again making a stab in the dark. "The American Secret Service has a hundred eyes. Spies are always under suspicion—but they must not catch us."

"No—no," she echoed. "I cannot be found with you. I will be deported—perhaps jailed. They will suspect me of being implicated in the murders you have committed."

"And," he said mockingly, "you will lose the money that I am supposed to divide with you."

He leaned forward, spoke to the driver again.

"Faster—they are catching up."

The man leaning out of the car behind had stopped signaling now. His face under the glow of a street light that flashed past had the grimness of granite. Something gleamed in his hand.

"They are going to shoot!" screamed Nina.

Her sentence was punctuated by the slap of a bullet against the rear of the taxi and a crashing report in the street behind. The cab leaped ahead again as the driver sought frantically for more speed. A second bullet struck the glass in the cab's rear, splintered it, sent it tinkling between the Agent's and the woman's laps. Cold air rushed in. Nina screamed again shrilly. For a moment he thought she was hurt. Then he saw that it was fear. A tiny sliver of glass was sticking in the back of his hand. He pulled it out deftly.

"You don't care," she said. "You don't mind that I may be killed!"

"My dear Nina—" he expostulated. The intense glow in his eyes showed the excitement that steely nerves were keeping under control.

The cab flashed across a street against traffic lights. Brakes squealed madly as another car stopped just in time. A policeman's whistle shrilled. The cab plunged on.

THE driver's neck and cheek—all that Agent "X" could see— were white as a sheet. His hands were wrapped stiffly around the wheel. A third bullet whizzed between the two in back, slapped against the glass partition close to the driver's head. He cried out and the cab lurched and bucked as his arms jerked in fear. It threatened for a moment to go over. Then the driver straightened it out. He pressed the gas button down, put on a final burst of speed. They drew ahead a little. A fourth bullet went wide.

*With a tigerish leap,
she sprang forward.*

"To the park!" barked the Secret Agent. "Turn left—the first gate."

Somewhere behind them now a police siren was wailing. But even the green police cruiser could not catch up. The heavy engine of the taxi was pounding under its metal hood. The rubber tires were whining over the pavement. Traffic was at a standstill. White-faced pedestrians scuttled out of their way, or stood staring fearfully on the sidewalk. The papers had been filled with stories of gang warfare. This looked like an example of it.

The cab's engine began to pound then. It wasn't built for such high speeds. Somewhere a gasket had blown. The cab was slowing down.

Agent "X" looking back saw that the car behind was gradually drawing nearer. Its headlights were goggling like the eyes of a monster. Two men were leaning out now, their faces purposeful, waiting till they were within small-arm range. They were aiming low, getting ready to shoot for the tires. Blown rubber at such speed might be as disastrous as a bullet. The menace of death rode with them in the night.

The woman, Nina, was white-faced now. Her blonde hair was spilling from beneath her hat. She looked suddenly haggish, witch-like, evil as a mad vulture. Her voice had a harpy shrillness.

"They'll get us! We can't escape!"

The Agent made no reply. He saw the park ahead of them. The stone pillars of the gate swept toward them. The taxi hurtled at the gates like a speeding ball headed for two goal posts. It was late. The park was dark and empty. The concrete road ahead was a smooth speedway. But the engine was hissing and pounding at every stroke.

The car behind leaped through the gateway of the park like an avenging nemesis. It roared down upon them out of the night. There was no danger of hitting innocent bystanders now. Three automatics in the black, speeding car spoke in unison. A fusillade of bullets lashed through the night.

One of them ripped across the top of the cab, tearing the fabric into a ribbonlike streak. Another plucked at the cloth of the Agent's coat. In a moment now that centering fire would bring death and destruction. Men in the Secret Service were taught how to shoot.

The Agent's eyes were darting bleakly about. There was a patch of dense leafless shrubbery ahead. The road made a long curve by it. Suddenly the Agent reached forward, gripping the driver's arms. The driver cursed in fear, tried to struggle free. The Agent held on like iron, kept the cab headed for the shrubbery.

The cab lurched off the concrete, taking the low embankment in a careening, rocking bound. Its wheels struck frosted turf, squealed, and bounced. One tire struck a sharp lump of ice and blew with a report like an exploding bomb. The cab slithered around, went sidewise toward the bushes. It would have turned turtle if the tough stems of the shrubbery hadn't cradled it. It ploughed in amongst them while the driver cried out in fear, flinging his hands before his face.

For ten feet it crunched on, breaking branches right and left, ploughing like a tractor through wheat. Then the tough shrubs won out. A cylinder head in the racing engine gave way. The engine came to a clanking, groaning stop, and the cab slid to a standstill.

Blonde Nina was on her knees on the floor, her dress around her silk-stockinged legs. Agent "X" jerked the cab door open, drew her out. The driver was scrambling out also, howling in fear.

A sudden jet of gasoline escaping from a severed feed line bathed the hot cylinders and leaped into a sheet of flame. Agent "X" pulled the woman away just in time. Flame enveloped the cab, crackled and snapped in the bushes, making a blinding intensity of light.

He heard the squeal of madly-applied brakes on the concrete roadway behind. The momentum of the pursuing car had carried it three hundred feet beyond the spot where the cab had lurched off the road.

The Agent clutched at the woman's arm, pulled her through the bushes. They ploughed ahead with the shrubbery tearing at their clothes. Then they came to an open space and ran on till they reached a path. Far behind them the flames of the burning cab made a glow like a torch. Miniature figures, silhouetted against the leaping flames, ran up and stood about. Others beat among the bushes.

The Agent would see later that the cab company was repaid and that the driver was exonerated. He didn't like to drag innocent persons into his dangerous exploits. This time it had been unavoidable.

THEY ran on across the park till they had reached a safe distance. The woman began tucking in strands of loose hair and straightening her disarranged dress. The expression of fear left her face. She was resuming her former tigerish poise.

"Very good, Armand," she said. "I must congratulate you even if you are a murderer and a thief."

Then suddenly, she cried out and looked at her arm. Crimson was dripping from a superficial wound above her wrist.

"I will take you to your home," he said, "or wherever you are staying."

He signaled another cab at the avenue across the park. Nina gave him the address. They were silent now as the cab rolled along, Nina nursing the wound in her arm and darting analytical glances at him.

She had leased a small apartment in the mid-town section and, when the cab stopped, she spoke to Agent "X."

"You may come up," she said. "We will make our arrangements now. There is still the matter of how much you intend to pay me."

He ignored her words, but followed her into the building. They ascended to a suite on the third floor, entered it, and closed the door.

"Let me fix your wound," he said.

He got water, helped her bathe it, tied it up, then rose.

"Where are you going?" she asked.

"Away, my dear Nina. We have had an exciting and pleasant evening. Now it is time to part."

With a tigerish leap she sprang forward, clutched her hand bag, and drew the gun out.

Viciously she jabbed its muzzle toward him. He stood smiling, lighting a cigarette.

"I repeat—it is time for us to part."

"You can't go," she screamed. "I'll kill you and hunt for Roemer myself."

"You are an impulsive woman, Nina—too impulsive for one of your vocation."

He turned toward the door. Behind him the trigger mechanism of the automatic clicked emptily four times. She had tried to pump a stream of bullets into his back—tried to murder him.

He turned and bowed.

"I took the precaution," he said, "of removing the cartridges while we were having our little ride."

She gasped and crouched, glaring at him.

"You will be sensible," he continued, "and wait till I have completed negotiations with a certain party. If you call the police or kill me now, all will be lost. But I see that you are not going to be sensible, dear Nina. You are shockingly intoxicated with the greed for gold. Therefore—"

He reached forward, yanked the cord of the telephone out of the wall, flinging the instrument down. Then, with a mocking bow, he opened the door and walked out, taking the key from the lock. Outside, he locked the door and slipped the key in his pocket. It would be some time before she got out, and meanwhile he had much to do.

CHAPTER IX

THE BLACK MASTER'S THREAT

IT WAS LATE, nearly one-thirty; but the Agent chartered another cab and gave an address on Twenty-third Street. The taxi sped downtown. It drew up in the middle of the block before an apartment house.

The Agent paid the driver, then, before entering the building, stepped among the shadows on the opposite side of the street. Two walls came together here forming a dark recess. From it, unobserved, he could look up at the side of the apartment. Many windows were still lighted. There was a light in a window on the sixth floor.

The Secret Agent moved his lips and gave a strange, low whistle. It was melodious yet eerie with an oddly ventriloquistic note. No one standing even a few feet from "X" could have told where it came from. It seemed to fill the whole air and it echoed in both directions along the quiet street.[17]

The shade of the window with the light in it on the sixth floor moved upward. The window was raised and a girl's head suddenly appeared. From the street her features were visible. She was no more than an enticing silhouette against the light in the room behind her. She looked searchingly up and down the dark block as the Agent repeated the whistle. Then, seeing nothing, she withdrew and closed the window.

The Agent strode quickly into the apartment building, ascended in the automatic lift, and pressed the button of suite No. 6B.

The click of high heels sounded on the parquet flooring inside.

---

17 *AUTHOR'S NOTE: The Secret Agent whistle, as described last month, is a thing peculiar to himself. Once heard, it is never forgotten. On several occassions when he gave it and I knew the Agent was near by, I have tried to trace it down. But I never succeeded. Its source is as hard to locate as the whistling note of certain birds and tree frogs.*

The door opened, and the girl who had looked out the window stood framed in the threshold. She, too, was blonde, like Nina, but she was of an altogether different type.

The small, warm oval of her face held sweetness and poise. Her blue eyes were frank, their keenness softened by long, silky lashes that swept to her cheeks. The gleaming wealth of her hair, alive with the glow of the light behind her, made a sunny halo around her head, blending with the creamy whiteness of her neck. Her *petite* figure was draped in clinging lounging pajamas that revealed its shapeliness. A coolie coat had been flung over the pajamas. She drew this hastily around her and looked questioningly at the man in the doorway.

Her eyes showed no recognition, but her soft warm lips seemed ready to break into a smile. Unable to penetrate his disguise, she was waiting for a signal. He gave it to her, making a motion in the air with his finger—the sign of an X.

Her expression changed instantly. The man before her, whose disguise was so perfect, had revealed his identity by that mysterious gesture. His whistle had told her he was on the way. Now he stood before her—Secret Agent "X."

The girl's blue eyes showed infinite respect. She had never seen the real face hidden behind his thousand disguises. He had fooled her again and again, tested out dozens of make-ups on her. Only on rare occasions, when the old wound in his side gave him a twinge of pain and he pressed his hand to it in a characteristic gesture, had she known who he was without being told by some sign or symbol.

There were reasons for the respect and friendship she felt for this strange man. He had been a friend of her father's—the father who was a police captain slain by underworld bullets. She knew that Agent "X" waged ceaseless warfare on that underworld that she hated and despised.

In her capacity of newspaper woman, a reporter on the *Herald*, she was often able to help him indirectly, give him information about people, or carry out some order that would contribute to the capture of a criminal.

It made her happy to do this, even when by doing so she got into danger herself. And, being human and feminine, she was curious about the real man behind those brilliant disguises. There was in her something that responded to the strange magnetism, courage and daring of Secret Agent "X." She sensed that death was always at his elbow. She knew there was little hope of any romance between them. But by comparison with him, other men seemed tame, uninteresting.

SHE walked ahead of him now into the comfortable living room of the apartment she maintained by her own hard work.

"Sit down," she said. "I'll get you some cigarettes."

The Agent was silent, but his strange burning eyes followed her. She was a girl in a million, as clever and brave as she was beautiful.

"The harvester has been at work," he said abruptly.

Betty Dale turned and looked at him. Agent "X" seldom spoke like ordinary men. There were generally innuendoes, subtleties, and double meanings in everything he said. His speech was as mysterious as his person.

He was holding a sheaf of bills in his hand now. She saw many bank notes of high denomination. He flipped them on the table.

"For victims of the wolf," he said.

She knew at once what he meant. The money that the Agent took from criminals was used to help the victims of criminals. Betty Dale saw to that. Simply, unpretentiously, she distributed what he gave her among people whom crime had in some way left destitute. The wives and small children of men serving prison sentences. Widows and orphans of murder victims.

Was it only to bring her money that the Agent had come?

She saw that tonight he seemed tense and ill at ease. There was an odd light in his eyes, restlessness in the movements of his body.

"Is there any other way I can help yon?" she asked quietly.

He shook his head, blowing quick jets of smoke through his nostrils.

"Ghost fingers are better dealt with alone."

The girl's face blanched at this. Her eyes widened.

"You are fighting the Spectral Strangler then," she said. "There's danger—terrible danger in that. Four people have been killed already. Be careful for my—for every one's sake."

The Agent nodded grimly.

"The trail is getting warm," he said.

She came closer and spoke again.

"I've read about those murders. Every one is talking about them.

They are ghastly, unthinkable. I was going to ask a favor of you—but now, now I won't."

For Betty to ask any sort of favor of him was so unusual that the Agent stared at her keenly. Then he spoke quickly.

"A girl with sunny hair and sunlight in her heart has helped me often," he said. "There are debts that it is a pleasure to pay back. Your favor, whatever it is, is granted."

A flood of color swept into Betty Dale's cheeks. For a moment she turned her face away, hiding the sudden surge of emotion she didn't want "X" to see. Love must never come between them, never interfere with his work. And sometimes in his presence, when he showed the admiration he felt for her, she had to fight love down.

"I was going to ask," she said huskily, "that you go with me to Colonel Gordon Crandal's party tomorrow night. The paper wants me to cover it. There's the society angle—and there's something else."

"Something else?" he echoed, caught by the sudden frown on her face.

"Yes," she said. "Colonel Crandal is rich, aristocratic—and the Crandal jewel collection is famous. He's received threats from some criminal who plans to steal them. The *Herald* was tipped off tonight. There'll be lots of detectives at the party. The police commissioner himself will be among the guests."

"Tell me more about this criminal," he said. "What crook plans such a daring robbery?"

"No one knows. He calls himself the Black Master."

It was Agent "X" who paled this time beneath his disguise. For a moment his long thin fingers tightened over his cigarette, squeezing it until tiny golden shreds of tobacco spilled to the floor.

"The Black Master?" he echoed harshly.

"Yes—do you know of him?"

He did not reply, but the vivid light of deep emotion sprang into his eyes. He was silent for seconds while the girl studied his face. Then he spoke hoarsely.

"Only death could keep me away from Colonel Crandal's party, Betty. You are assured of an escort who will try to match in gallantry the beauty of the girl he accompanies."

CHAPTER X

A BRILLIANT GATHERING

THE CRANDAL NAME was an old and honored one. The Crandal mansion, owned now by Colonel Gordon Crandal, a reserve officer with a distinguished war record, was one of the city's show places. It occupied nearly a whole city block. Great iron gates closed the street entrance except at such times as the owner chose to admit guests.

Tonight was one of those times. The many windows of the Crandal mansion were brightly lighted. An orchestra was playing seductive dance music. The huge ballroom, where presidents and visiting royalty had danced, was open, its furniture dusted, its ancient crystal chandeliers glittering impressively.

The end of prohibition had brought old-time gaiety back. The portraits of long-dead ancestors in tarnished frames seemed to smile down in approval at the handsomely-dressed company. Men were there in tail coats and dinner jackets. Ladies in low-cut evening gowns. Radiant *debutantes* were attired to reveal charms that would lure hesitant bachelors into the bonds of matrimony.

Faithful old servants of the Crandal family moved silently about the polished floors, trays of cocktails in their blue-veined hands. They seemed as much of an inheritance as the house itself.

Betty Dale and her escort came shortly before nine—shortly before the fashionable hour so that Betty, because of her newspaper work, wouldn't miss seeing the arrival of the more impressive guests.

She wore blue slippers and a clinging blue dress, complementing the gold of her hair. A white evening wrap was thrown about her shapely shoulders. Her loveliness rivaled that of any blue blood present.

Girls cast envious glances at her as she entered. Men paused to stare in admiration. Her escort came in for a share of attention, too.

Tall and immaculately dressed in formal evening clothes, his face had the lean, healthy look of an out-of-doors man. It was darkly tanned. His hair swept straight back from a strong forehead. His temples were slightly, becomingly gray.

Betty Dale introduced him to those of the guests she knew.

"I want you to meet Clark Manning, the explorer," she said.

She spoke convincingly. People mumbled that they had often heard of Clark Manning. To admit that they hadn't would have seemed both rude and ignorant. A gushing lady spoke admiringly of Manning's travel books—taking care not to mention any particular titles. Manning seemed like a man worth cultivating. His burning, deep-set eyes were strangely compelling and mysterious.

A friend of Betty's brought Colonel Crandal up to them. The scion of the ancient family was in his late forties, tall, gray-haired, poised. He was still a bachelor and eager, hopeful *debutantes* flocked around him like satellites around a star.

He acknowledged his introduction to Betty Dale and her escort, Secret Agent "X," now posing as Clark Manning, explorer.

The colonel's swift, experienced eyes appraised Betty from her trim little slippered feet to the sunny gold of her hair. Then he spoke debonairly, asked her to dance, and bore her off, leaving a half-dozen disappointed young ladies in his wake.

The girls looked to Secret Agent "X" for consolation. They begged him to tell them about his explorations. But he shook his head modestly. In a few minutes he edged away and strode off to reconnoiter by himself.

HE studied the smiling, gay faces around him. Would they be so smiling, so gay if they knew that the threat of the Black Master hung like an evil shadow over this house? Wouldn't their bright laughter turn to whispers of ghastly fear if they knew that the man who had threatened Crandal was the murderer who killed with invisible, choking fingers?

Among the guests were quiet-faced men in dinner jackets—men who seemed to have no part in the festivities.

These were agency and police detectives detailed to watch and protect Crandal's famous jewels from the menace of a daring criminal. But even they, "X" felt certain, didn't know with whom they were dealing. They didn't know that the Black Master and the dealer in swift, strangling death were one and the same.

Agent "X's" gaze was hawklike. Was it possible that the murderer of Scanlon and those others was somewhere in this brilliant gathering?

His eyes wandered from face to face. He saw the city's tall, suave police commissioner talking to a group of ladies, thrilling them with tales of his police experiences, his successful contests with criminals. Before this night was over the commissioner might have something else to think about—something too ghastly perhaps to relate as drawing room conversation.

Then Agent "X" gave a sudden start.

More guests were arriving. He saw a flash of light on blonde hair. A woman in a flame-colored evening gown came through the ballroom door. She moved tigerishly, sinuously across the floor, a tall, dark man at her side. She was smiling radiantly—smiling with her red lips, but her eyes did not smile. They had the cold, appraising look of an adventuress.

"Nina!" whispered the Agent tensely under his breath.

It was a shock to see her here—a surprise. Yet, staring around at the mixed assemblage, he saw that her presence, was not altogether out of place.

Whispers had it that Colonel Crandal planned to run for the legislature. People of all types and from all walks of life had been invited to this party. A politician and a city commissioner hovered around the punch bowl. A night-club hostess leaned on the arm of one.

Beyond them, fat and baggily dressed, was Nick Baroni, a big shot in the days when gangdom rode to wealth and power on a flood of illegal liquor. He had paid his income taxes, escaped jail. He had reformed, so rumor had it, and was spending his money to gain entree into society. A thin veneer of social polish hid brutal instincts that slumbered behind his oily, massaged face. He was balancing a cocktail glass in fingers that had once tensed around the vibrating trigger of a Tommy gun.

The Secret Agent's lips curled.

Then his eyes swiveled back to the woman in the red dress. He edged close, lighting a cigarette, and heard Nina and her escort introduced.

"Piere DuBrong and the Countess Rocazy," the lady who presented them said.

Nina was carrying it off well. An elaborate *coiffure* had been artfully molded to soften the lines of her face. Her nails were stained a vivid crimson. She held a small fan in her hand, pressing it close against her white bosom. She was capitalizing on her exotic charm, playing on the gullibility of social climbers to whom a European title was a thing before which to bow down and worship. But Agent "X" was not impressed. He believed that her title was bogus.

The man with her, Piere DuBrong, had the alert hungry look of a questing hawk. His glittering eyes indicated a keen, acquisitive brain. The two appeared well matched.

But why were they here?

Secret Agent "X" made discreet queries. Who was the charming countess? Who was the tall man with her? He learned that DuBrong was attached to the embassy and that Countess Rocazy was a friend of his, a lovely woman just over from Europe who could speak excellent English.

On the surface that explained matters. But Agent "X" wasn't satisfied. His sense of impending menace deepened. The gaiety of the gathering impressed him now as gaudy beauty hiding something darkly evil. The bright skin of a poisonous serpent! A blood-hungry beast concealed in a bed of gay flowers! Nina Rocazy was like that—a tigress cloaking her claws behind velvet fur until the moment came to spring.

She and her escort had separated now. Agent "X" was introduced to her and even danced with her. He felt the strange undercurrent of drama as he held the woman in his arms. What would her reactions be if she suddenly learned that her dancing partner was the same man who had accompanied her on that wild taxi ride which had so nearly been fatal? What would she say if he told her he was the same man she had tried to kill and who had locked her in her apartment?

He gasped at her audacity when she asked if he thought it would be possible to see the Crandal jewels.

"I have heard so much of the riches of Americans," she said. "Jewels are riches that even we poor women can understand. They attract us as children are attracted to bright, pretty baubles. There must be other women here who would like to see them, too."

Agent "X" nodded. She did not understand the mocking light in his eyes.

"Such a woman as you would be doubly appreciative," he said.

Beneath her smile, lines of avarice showed. Money, the things that money could buy, were the gods she lived by. But would she have cheek enough to make such a request to Colonel Crandal?

"There has been a threat," he said. "A criminal has announced that he intends to steal the jewels."

He watched her face, but her hard eyes were inscrutable. She shrugged.

"Colonel Crandal is a brave man. He will not fear threats."

THE dance ended and he left her. But he followed her through the milling company and saw her cleverly insinuate herself into the group around the colonel. Smiling radiantly, acting as though the impulse had suddenly come to her, she asked if she might see the famous gem collection.

For a moment Colonel Crandal's face showed surprise. Then he smiled and nodded.

"Certainly, countess, I'll have the jewels brought down. All of you can see them then."

Agent "X" edged close. He heard the police commissioner object.

"What about the threat of that crook?" the commissioner asked. "Isn't it going in the face of Providence to bring them out tonight?"

Crandal made a gesture with his hand.

"That's what your men are here for—to give protection. And a lady has requested that they be shown."

The commissioner flushed and nodded.

"Very well," he said.

Crandal whispered the combination of the safe into the ear of an old and trusted butler who had been with the family forty years.

"Go get them, Wilmot," he said. "But be careful."

The butler protested.

"I wish, sir, that you would come with me. If anything should happen—"

Crandal gave the man a push.

"Do as you're told," he said.

Three detectives followed the butler, after a low-voiced conversation with the commissioner.

In ten minutes the butler returned carrying a square leather box in his hands. His fingers were trembling as he set it down.

"There, sir," he said, and there was a note of vast relief in his voice.

The guests crowded around tensely. Crandal opened the box, exposing the glittering collection of gems that reposed on a cushion of black velvet.

There were rubies that gleamed like drops of freshly fallen blood, emeralds as green as polar seas, sapphires blue as the sky, diamonds that reflected sparkling prismatic lights and gave off rainbow colors. Many of them had come from the crowns of former kings and queens.

Crandal held them lovingly in his hand, then passed them about.

Nina took a diamond necklace and held it in trembling fingers. She placed it against her neck, let the cold stones touch her skin. Her eyes were dark with greed. She seemed reluctant to give it back.

But the other guests were nervous, holding the jewels gingerly, or refusing to take them at all. They appeared to breathe easier when the gems had been exhibited and put safely back in their box. The old butler picked the box up and solemnly bore it away with his escort of detectives. The police commissioner wiped a perspiring face, and Secret Agent "X," watching Nina's every movement, wondered what was going on in her mind.

The butler had taken the jewels up a flight of broad stairs to a second-floor room. Several detectives hung around this stairway for minutes after he had disappeared. The others remained with him on the floor above.

The dancing began again. Liquor flowed freely. The guests and even the police commissioner appeared to relax. But Agent "X" stood tensely staring around. At the moment he could not see Nina, Piere DuBrong, or the pudgy-faced Nick Baroni. He pushed his way through the crowd watching the dancers until the blonde head of the Countess Rocazy came in view. She was in the arms of the politician. He looked about for the others; then suddenly whirled.

A stumbling, horrible figure had appeared at the head of the stairs. It was Agent "X's" hoarse exclamation that stilled the music and attracted the attention of the other guests.

A ripple of tense excitement passed through the assemblage. It increased with the speed of a spreading grass fire. Talk ceased. Laughter died away. All eyes were turned toward the stairway.

The man at the top of them was one of the police detectives. He seemed to be trying to say something. He was waving his arms, staring toward them. Then his hands, clawlike, went to his throat.

He reeled, staggered, clutched at himself. One choking, terrible cry came from his lips. It was silenced as though by the jerk of an unseen noose. The man appeared to be fighting invisible fingers that were wrapped around his neck.

He twisted, swayed, lurched forward. His feet slipped on the top step.

Then, while women screamed and men shouted hoarsely, he plunged headfirst down the slippery hardwood stairs. His body landed with a thud on the rug below. But the man had ceased his struggles now. His face became purple, the terrible livid purple of an overripe plum, the hue which had mottled the dying face of Bill Scanlon. His lips were drawn back in a mirthless, hideous grin. From between them his swollen tongue protruded, mocking, horrible.

While men and women in the room stood frozen with fear, too scared to speak or move, too weighted with horror to do more than breathe, there came a fearful explosion somewhere on the floor above. It rocked the house, rattled the windows.

A *cloisonné* vase dropped off a shelf and rang against the floor. Another of porcelain shattered to fragments as it fell. In the crowd, close to the Secret Agent's side, a woman screamed and fainted. Then pandemonium broke loose.

CHAPTER XI

THE DEAD ARE SILENT

SO TERRIFIC WAS the explosion on the floor above that it seemed as though a bomb must have gone off. Plaster fell from the ceiling. Crystal pendants from the old chandelier followed it in a clattering, tinkling cascade.

Men and women made a wild dash for the doors, jostling each other, crowding, shouting in a mad stampede. Their fear made them forget that they were ladies and gentlemen.

A paunchy man in a dress suit with glittering diamond studs brushed Betty Dale aside with a sweep of his fat arm and charged ahead like a frightened bull.

Agent "X" saw the man's action from the corner of his eye. His lip curled in contempt. The man lurched by him and the Agent thrust a quick foot into his path tripping him, disregarding the fact that the man was the president of one of the city's leading banks. The bank official skidded along the floor carrying a rug with him.

The police commissioner was shouting, too, trying to stem the tide of panic. His voice boomed out. The frenzy began to subside.

Secret Agent "X" leaped up the broad stairway, his eyes burning with excitement. Three detectives, freeing themselves from the milling crowd, followed him.

At the top of the stairs there was a long hallway. Agent "X" looked down it. Another figure lurched into sight. It was the old butler, the man who had carried the jewels down for the guests to see. The butler's fingers were clawing at his throat. He collapsed on the floor as the Agent neared him. His face, too, had the ghastly livid hue of strangulation.

Debris, and the broken panels of a door showed the location of the explosion. Secret Agent "X" needed no one to tell him it was the entrance to the jewel room.

The door was hanging loosely on its hinges. He thrust it open, stepped inside. The force of the explosion had shattered every light bulb. In the gloom he almost fell over another form—another detective.

One of the plain-clothes men behind him flashed on a light. "X" saw then that the man at his feet was dead, too. He had evidently fallen before the explosion had taken place. His body was twisted grotesquely, his features mutilated beyond recognition. Death and horror had struck here.

"The safe's been blown," said the detective behind "X" harshly.

The beam of the man's flash light was focused on the heavy iron box across the room. It was twisted out of line now, its sides bulging, its doors blown off.

"Soup!" said another detective. "A bungling job, too. They used enough nitro to wreck a house."

With drawn guns, both men leaped across the room, running to a window which was open. It gave on a balcony. They turned their lights down on the lawn beneath. Secret Agent "X" heard them cry out. Peering over their shoulders, he saw a fourth huddled form on the icy turf. The detective stationed to patrol the grounds had been killed along with the two others.

Guests, taking courage, now that the police were going to the scene of the explosion, were coming up the stairs, crowding into the hall.

Crandal came into the room, two friends with him. The millionaire's face no longer wore its look of easy assurance. He was tense and pale.

"The jewels are gone," he said hoarsely.

He seemed to forget the dead man lying at his feet, the other men outside. He was staring wide-eyed at the safe.

In front of it was the black leather case that had contained the jewels. It was empty, battered and broken by the terrible force of the explosion. There wasn't a jewel in sight.

Colonel Crandal leaped to the window. He stood speechless, staring out.

The police commissioner appeared in the doorway, a group of guests, including Piere DuBrong and Nick Baroni, with him. The commissioner's collar was torn. His hair was on end. He had been fighting to stop the panic downstairs. He said:

"You'd better go down, Colonel. You'd better go and quiet

your guests. Tell them it's over now. That criminal made good his threat."

There was bitterness, defeat, in the commissioner's voice.

"This has been a terrible night, Colonel," he continued. "Three of my men gone. They tell me MacCarthy outside was killed, too."

THE Secret Agent was listening. His burning eyes were swiveling around the room, staring at the safe and the window. The killer had wiped out clues, wiped out any possibility of identification by leaving a trail of death behind him.

The Agent's gaze came to rest on the faces of DuBrong and Nick Baroni. They both appeared shaken and terrified. But were they? The Agent was baffled. It was as though the Black Master was a being as intangible as the murder weapon he used. Agent "X" stared out the window off across the ice-coated lawn. The commissioner issued a harsh order to those of his men who were left.

"Go out and hunt around. Get some clews that will help Burks."

Hatless and coatless, the Agent dashed out on the lawn. The glow from the lighted windows on the first floor shed ghostly radiance. He supplemented their glow by lighting matches. The detectives came with their flash lights.

But Agent "X" had discovered in his first brief examination of the lawn how hopeless it was to look for clews here. The ground was frozen as solidly as rock. The short turf was matted with ice. Its glass-smooth surface showed no tracks. A hundred men might have walked over it.

He moved up to the dead detective. The man's distorted features showed that the Spectral Strangler had struck him down also. What horror had he seen out there in the semi-darkness? His bloodless lips would never tell now.

Down on his hands and knees. Agent "X" examined the ground around the form of the slain detective. For a moment he bent close, then flattened his palm, rubbed it over the icy coating. Something sharper than ice pricked his skin. He drew his hand up, looked at it. Tiny particles of glass were clinging to it. They were even more fragile than the shell-thin globes of electric light bulbs. A detective came up to his side.

"What's the matter? What the hell are you looking for, mister?"

The Agent held his hand out.

"Glass," he said quietly.

The detective swore harshly, took an empty envelope from his pocket.

"Give it to me," he said.

The Agent passed the glass slivers over. He had forced the police to share a clew with him. It was only fair that he share this one now with them. He believed he understood its significance, but he doubted that it would lead anywhere.

A police siren rose into a moaning wail out in the street. A car turned into the driveway of the Crandal home and drew up before the big entrance-way.

Secret Agent "X" went back into the house. He was there when Inspector Burks of the homicide squad met the police commissioner. The two went into a whispered consultation for a moment; then the commissioner held up his hand, addressing the frightened guests.

"There's a criminal you've all heard of—a criminal I've reason to believe struck tonight, stole Crandal's jewels, and killed these men. I'm referring to the man who masks behind the name of Secret Agent 'X.' It is my belief that he and the Black Master are one."

Betty Dale came close to Agent "X." Her eyes were dark with anxiety.

"We'd better leave," she said. She wasn't thinking of her newspaper work; she was thinking only of the Agent's safety.

His smile reassured her.

"There is work for the lady scribe," he said. "She must stay. But far places call an explorer. He has a rendezvous at midnight."

He looked at the great clock against the wall. It was after ten now.

Some of the guests began to leave. An air of gloom and horror had fallen over the house. The atmosphere of festivity was gone.

Other police cars joined the first one in the drive. Fingerprint experts, Bertillon men, official photographers, the medical examiner and his assistant, and a detail of men from the bomb squad arrived. It seemed that every detective in the city was pouring into the Crandal home.

SECRET AGENT "X," under the guise of Clark Manning, explorer, slipped quietly away. There were deep suspicions in his mind. He intended to investigate Piere DuBrong and the gangster, Nick Baroni. Was it only coincidence that they were there when the robbery took place? But he had a rendezvous at midnight. It could not be postponed. And a question burned in his mind. After such a fiendish and daring crime, would the Black Master still meet him in that silent, empty house that faced Bradley Square? If so, he had a plan worked out. He was ready tonight to take a desperate chance.

He drove quickly to his apartment on Jefferson Avenue, disguised himself as Greenford again. The spy was still unconscious, breathing peacefully in the closet.

The streets were deserted when "X" reached the square. It seemed a place of ghost houses. There was only one light burning. That was across the square in the beer saloon, dimly seen through the jumble of playground equipment. The rusty chain of a swing creaked in the night wind as the Agent passed it. It made a sound like a body swinging on gallows.

With the faces of the three slain detectives and the butler still before his mind's eye, the horror of the empty house seemed to have deepened.

There was not only the chill of mystery as he climbed the steps now. There was a living threat. The brooding, towering menace of death.

He pulled the ancient bell handle, half expecting that this time there would be no result. How could the man who called himself the Black Master be everywhere at once, unless he was the very spirit of evil itself?

Echoes clattered inside the house. A minute passed. Then again the lock of the door clicked and the old door swung open, moved by unseen hands. The Agent entered quickly. As he moved along the black hallways, he struck a match and noticed something that seemed to add to the ghostliness. His own tracks still showed in the dust. They had not been disturbed. There were no others beside them. It was as though he had entered a house peopled only with sinister spirits.

He was slightly ahead of time. He waited in the still top-floor room, waited till a clock somewhere outside boomed twelve strokes. Then suddenly there was a dry rattling in the room. For an instant it was horribly reminiscent of a snake or of some huge reptile uncoiling. Then the voice he had heard before spoke.

"The Black Master salutes you, Greenford. What is your answer? Speak loudly."

Imitating Greenford's foreign accent, the Secret Agent spoke. It seemed as though he were talking to the blank walls of an empty room. It was uncanny, spine-chilling. His own voice reechoed in his ears.

"My government is prepared to pay a large sum for what you have. It is prepared to pay a hundred thousand dollars."

There was an instant of silence, then a harsh laugh broke out. There was bitterness, mockery, contempt in the laugh.

"A hundred thousand dollars! A hundred thousand! You come here and offer me a hundred thousand—for something that will affect the destiny of nations? For something that holds in it the secret of death itself?"

The Agent injected excitement into his answer.

"Give me time then. Perhaps I can make them understand—make them pay more. Perhaps I can raise it to two hundred thousand!"

Again the mocking laughter filled the room.

"Two hundred thousand! The thing that you seek to buy has already snuffed out the lives of eight people. A nation could fall before it as well."

"Eight people!" The Agent gasped the two words, baiting the hidden voice on.

"Yes, eight people. When you read the papers tomorrow, you will understand."

"What is your price then? What shall I tell my government? There must be some reason in this."

"A million dollars," the voice said. "That is my price today. If I am goaded too far, it might rise. Those who do not pay my price will regret it. Tell your government that."

"It is too much—it is impossible," said the Agent. "With governments bankrupt, with revenues lessening, how can you expect so much?"

"Fool!" said the voice. "I ask less than the price of one submarine, the cost of one dirigible. You have seen how I can strike. Beware."

"Give me one more chance," the Agent said. "I'll see what I can do."

"Tomorrow then—at the same time. It is your last chance. I cannot deal with fools and bankrupts. There are other countries that will pay."

The voice ceased speaking. The room was still. The Agent asked another question; but the walls echoed his own voice back. He went into action suddenly, took a short-bladed, gleaming tool from his pocket.

He moved sidewise, ran the sharp tool down the wall, ripping at the paper. It was from there he decided that the voice had come. Was there a secret room beyond, or—

He gave a harsh exclamation. The thick paper had come free. Behind it, sunk in the wall, was the bell-shaped outline of a radio loud-speaker. There was the small circle of a microphone below it. He ripped at the plaster feverishly, saw the compact radio mechanism behind it, and uncovered antenna wires leading to the roof.

The mystery of the voice in the room was solved. But the Black Master was as much a mystery as ever. The trail of the horror killer led on—into a fog bank of terror, eeriness—and doubt.

CHAPTER XII

THE NINTH VICTIM

AS HE LEFT the house he stopped for an instant to examine the door in the lower hallway. The mechanism that operated it was concealed. But he found a wire attached to the old bell cord, leading upward. He pulled this wire and waited. Seconds passed and the door opened. He understood then that the radio impulse sent out from the same station as that of the voice which had addressed him was responsible for its mysterious movements. Battleships and airplanes had been operated by radio control. The Black Master had installed radio controls on a door.

With burning, intent eyes he descended the steps and moved along the street. Again he had the uncanny sense that he was being followed. He paused with a cigarette in his hand, and, before lighting it, stared back through his cupped fingers.

A dark, flitting shadow moved into an areaway behind him.

As though he had seen nothing, the Agent turned and continued his way along the street. But at the next corner he ducked out of sight into a doorway. Skilled himself in all the arts of shadowing, he planned to turn the tricks on his shadower.

Standing in the blackness of the doorway, he looked back. A small man came around the corner, moving with quick, furtive steps. The man stopped suddenly as he saw that the block ahead of him was empty.

For a moment the street light fell upon his face. His features had a vicious, pallid cast. He looked as though drugs had ravaged his body, made him a depraved and inhuman wreck. His eyes were glittering with feverish brightness, his face muscles twitching. Suddenly he retraced his steps, seeming to sense that he had been tricked.

The Secret Agent waited a moment, then came out of his hiding place. Walking close to the side of the buildings he followed the

*They were fighting with the
desperation of cornered animals.*

small man ahead. So deft and sure were his movements that he
seemed no more than a blending shadow.

He caught sight of the small man again as he rounded the corner.
From then on it was the other's turn to try and shake off pursuit.

He seemed to think he had. Six blocks from the square, he came
out into the light, walked across the street, and entered a telephone
booth. The Agent, watching from the other side, could see him
making a call.

Then the utterly unpredictable happened. A movie house next
to the drug store disgorged its audience abruptly. The street became clogged and choked with jostling people. The hophead
slipped out of the booth. His small height made it impossible for
any man to see him.

The Secret Agent elbowed his way quickly through the crowd. But, when he reached the other side of it, the small man was gone.

Agent "X" frowned grimly, bitterly. Twice tonight the law of averages had been against him. Twice he had been disappointed. His search of the room in the house at Bradley Square had yielded nothing but the discovery of the concealed microphone and loudspeaker. Now circumstances beyond his control had made him lose the man he was shadowing. It was a thing that happened to the most skilled man hunters in the world. But the Agent refused to accept defeat.

A swift plan came to his mind. The investigation of Nick Baroni and Piere DuBrong would take time, days even. But perhaps Greenford could tell him something about the latter, give him a quick lead.

SWIFTLY he returned to the St. James apartments on Jefferson Avenue. Greenford was still there. With the spy unconscious in the closet, Secret Agent "X" removed the make-up that impersonated him and again resumed his disguise of a middle-aged man. It was almost time for the effects of the anesthetic he had administered to wear off. But in any event he would have found means of bringing Greenford back to full consciousness.

He injected a liquid containing extracts of adrenaline, strychnine and digitalis into Greenford's arm. A large dose of it would have been fatal. But the Secret Agent was a master of pharmacology.[18]

The hypo injection acted immediately on Greenford's heart It brought him out of the quiet of artificial sleep with the abruptness of an electric shock. He sat up, twitching and glaring about. His eyes fell on the Agent and for a moment he tried unsuccessfully to talk. It was some seconds before he found the power of speech.

"You can't hold me like this," he said harshly. "I've got an appointment tonight."

The Agent smiled. Greenford's appointment was already more than twenty-four hours overdue. The man didn't know he had been sleeping a day and a night.

18 AUTHOR'S NOTE: From casual remarks he has at times made, I am certain that Secret Agent "X" is familiar with the works of Schmiedeberg, Husemann, Stockvis, Brunten, and other experts in pharmacology and Materia Medica. I suppose he was led first into such studies by the need of dealing with toxicology in murder cases.

"What time was it scheduled?" the Agent asked.

"Twelve o'clock."

"It's nearly one now!"

Greenford rose to his feet. Fear had come back into his eyes. He looked at Agent "X" strangely.

"Who are you?" he demanded again.

The Agent shook his head. He was staring at Greenford, and he saw Greeaford's hand go to the pocket where he had placed the telegram of the Black Master. A startled, worried look came over Greenford's face.

"You stole it," he hissed.

The Agent bowed.

"I saved you from an unpleasant interview with a dangerous man," he said.

Greenford made a snarling sound and clenched his fist.

"You're going to tell me who you are and why you are meddling in my affairs."

The lightness left Agent "X's" voice.

He gazed at Greenford in a way that made the other man tremble. There was burning power in Agent "X's" eyes. They seemed to have foresight, uncanny magnetism. They seemed to bore into Greenford's very soul.

"Perhaps you'll tell me why you bribed Cora Stenstrom to betray her employer?"

"I didn't—I didn't," said Greenford in a sudden frenzy of excitement.

"She was in your pay. Do you deny it?"

Greenford's face twitched, his eyes wavered. It was plain that he had been lying. Suddenly he burst forth in a torrent of denials, even before the Agent had accused him.

"I didn't murder her," he shrieked. "She was going to tell me what I wanted. She was going to phone me when all was ready."

"You mean you paid her to leave the window open!"

"Yes—yes, I did, but it wasn't I who killed her."

"No," said Agent "X" sternly. "Another and greater scoundrel preceded you. He took advantage of the path that you had made easy."

"I know it," said Greenford. "My God—who was it?"

"The Black Master," said Agent "X" softly.

He watched Greenford. He could see by the spy's expression that the name meant nothing to him. That telegram calling him to Bradley Square was the first time apparently he had had any dealings with the master murderer.

"Who is he?" asked Greenford trembling.

THE Agent was silent. For seconds his burning gaze rested on the man before him, until Greenford could stand it no longer.

"What are you going to do with me?" he demanded.

"Ask you a question," said the Agent. "Who is Piere DuBrong, friend of the Countess Rocazy—the woman you once called Nina?"

Utter amazement overspread Greenford's face.

"Nina! She is not in this country! She can't be!"

"She is," said the Agent sternly. "Answer my question."

"I know nothing about DuBrong—I swear it! I haven't heard of the man. Nina Rocazy is a dangerous woman—a viper. She is not a countess, but an adventuress—a woman seeking always to prey on men."

The Agent's eyes bored into Greenford's. The spy seemed to be telling the truth. He spoke again.

"I've told you all I know. Now let me go."

"I will," said the Agent, "but on one condition only. It is that you leave the country at once. You made a mistake coming in the first place. Nothing awaits you here—except death."

"You are threatening me!" said Greenford harshly.

"Not threatening—warning you. Will you leave or not?"

The Agent's eyes held inexorable command. Greenford could not meet them.

"You have stolen my money," he said. "My belt is gone."

The Agent took out his wallet, extracted five hundred dollars, and handed it to Greenford.

"It is enough," "X" said. "There's a night plane to Canada. It takes off from the municipal field in half an hour. Your papers are in order—I have seen them. Take the plane and go before death prevents you."

"My luggage!" said Greenford.

"It is too late now to recover it. The American Secret Service is on your trail. Operatives have unquestionably searched your room at the Sherwood. Menace hangs over your head. Your only chance of life is to leave instantly."

Greenford shrugged resignedly.

"I will do as you say," he promised.

But Secret Agent "X" took no chances. If Greenford tried to communicate with the Black Master all would be lost. He wanted to make sure that the spy kept his promise and left. When Greenford went to the street, Agent "X" stealthily followed. Then he frowned in anger and annoyance.

Instead of going to the flying field, Greenford took a taxi to the neighborhood of the Hotel Sherwood. He got out two blocks from it, walked toward it cautiously. Agent "X" followed, keeping on the other side of the street.

He saw Greenford walk furtively along the front of the hotel, passing the entrance three times without getting up enough courage to enter. There was a watchful man reading a newspaper far back in a corner of the lobby—a government operative. The Secret Agent recognized him; but it appeared that Greenford did not.

He lighted a cigarette, pulled his hat brim down, and started toward the main entrance a fourth time.

But he was destined never to enter.

He crossed the open space of sidewalk before the hotel, and it seemed that a noose was suddenly flung around his neck. He staggered on the pavement, clawed at his throat. Agent "X" heard one horrible choking cry and stared aghast at the drama that was taking place.

Greenford's face was becoming purple—the fatal, livid hue that meant death at the hands of the Spectral Strangler.

CHAPTER XIII

GUNS OF DEATH

AGENT "X" SAW a stealthy figure moving across the face of the building. The figure was going away from, not toward Greenford, as would have been the case if it had been a casual passerby. It was the sinister hophead whom "X" had lost sight of in the theater crowd less than an hour before.

By disregarding Agent "X's" warning, by failing to keep the promise he had given, Greenford had walked straight to his death. The emissary of the Black Master had slain him, thinking Greenford was the man who had shadowed him. He had been lurking in the vicinity of the hotel to destroy the life of a man he thought had tried to pry into the Black Master's secrets.

The Agent darted in pursuit of the killer, resolved this time that he would not fail. He would shadow the hophead to his hideout and through him learn the identity of the fiend who employed him; for "X" felt certain that this drug addict was no more than a tool in the hands of the master murderer. As a criminal, he wasn't of sufficient caliber to have plotted and carried out such a campaign of terror.

There was no chance of the hophead being lost in a crowd now. It was late. The streets were deserted. But because of this it was a difficult task to follow him without being suspected. The Agent depended somewhat on his make-up.

Behind him he heard someone come from the hotel entrance attracted by Greenford's dying cry. He couldn't help Greenford now. The man was beyond human aid, destroyed by his own greed and willfulness. He was the ninth victim in the terrible series of murders.

The Agent's eyes were glowing with the light of intense concentration.

The hophead was walking purposefully now like a person who

has accomplished an appointed task. He dived into a subway entrance, rode uptown, and got off in a section cluttered with theaters and cafés. Once again the Agent got a look at the man's face. He saw that he had the features of a rat. There was cruelty in the feverish glitter of his eyes and the twist of his thin mouth.

The chase ended when the man disappeared into the servants' entrance of a notorious night club—the Club Mephistopheles.

This club, the windows of which were curtained night and day, was known to the Agent. It was a place of evil repute, a place where gangsters hung out and where many criminals had made their headquarters. It was a place of vice and debauchery where "slummers" came also, social registerites who wanted to spend money freely and taste the city's wild night life.

There were gambling tables inside. Here the underworld and the world of wealth and fashion rubbed shoulders. It had figured in the papers more than once. Bennie Pomarno, beer runner, had been slain here in the boom days of prohibition. In one of its luxuriously appointed rooms a well-known society matron had committed suicide after losing the last of her fortune at the roulette wheel. It was a club to which the Secret Agent had made it a point to get a card.

But dress clothes were necessary to gain admittance. Crime was hidden beneath the trappings of gentility. The Agent thought quickly, then went to an establishment near a dance hall where tuxedos could be rented. He hired one and entered the door of the Mephistopheles Club.

Though it was long after midnight, the activities inside had not begun to wane. The gambling rooms were crowded. The big dining room still held late diners. A jazz orchestra was playing sensuous music.

The Secret Agent strolled about eyeing the crowd that filled the place. He was waiting for the hophead to appear. Was he employed in this club? And if so in what capacity?

A red-headed, flashily dressed hostess came up to the Agent, but he waved her away. He recognized many faces. Here a society woman. There a crook with a police record. There a small-time politician seeking favor with the big shots of the underworld.

Then he drew back with a sudden, amazed intake of breath. He had glimpsed the fat form of Nick Baroni!

The gangster had evidently come straight here from Crandal's party. Why? To seek solace in a familiar haunt after the terrible and nerve-racking experience at Colonel Crandel's, or for some more sinister reason?

The pastiness of fear still showed on the big gangster's face. The burning eyes of Secret Agent "X" studied him.

Could it be that Baroni was the man he sought—the terrible Black Master? The repeal of prohibition had made it hard for gangs to exist. Rivalry was more bitter. In the days when beer could only be had in speak-easies there had been enough money to support a score of big shots in the luxury that their gross bodies craved. But now this source of revenue had been abolished. The government and legitimate brewers were taking in what the gangsters had formerly regarded as their own. Rackets had narrowed down.

The bitter enmity of the gangs had deepened. They were ready to tear at each other's throats like wolves; and the Mephistopheles Club was in a no man's land between two gang territories.

THE Secret Agent stared and pondered. Baroni had his torpedoes with him now, flat-chested, pale-faced young men who talked without moving their lips and whose eyes were ever watchful; men ready to shoot at the drop of a hat. Rumors that Baroni had reformed were baseless. The fight over the city's slot-machine racket was as fierce as ever. It was centered now between two gangs— Nick Baroni's and Sam Dwyer's river-front mobsters. And now Baroni was on the edge of Dwyer's territory.

Abruptly the Agent's eyes shifted and his body grew tense.

The murderous hophead had made his appearance. He was clad in a black jacket, a wing collar, and bow tie. The man was a waiter in this sinister club, a member of the late night shift. Secret Agent "X" was deeply struck by this.

As an employee here, the man was in a position to get orders from any one of a dozen underworld czars—but he was hovering around Nick Baroni's table. He stepped forward once, struck a match when Baroni skinned the cellophane off a fresh cigar.

Baroni paid no attention to him; but that meant nothing. There were hundreds of prearranged signals by which secret messages and orders could be conveyed.

The Agent watched lynx-eyed. But hours passed and nothing happened. Nick Baroni drank until his face got bloated and mottled. The guests left one by one. Baroni made his exit at last followed by his sinister bodyguards. Secret Agent "X" hung around outside until the hophead emerged again. He shadowed the man to a small furnished room two blocks away.

Then Agent "X" bought all editions of the early morning papers and took them to one of his hideouts. In secrecy and silence he read all available news reports. The story of the murders in Colonel Crandal's home was spread glaringly in headlines across the front pages. The police had made no headway. The famous Crandal jewels were gone. Three detectives and an old family servant had been killed strangely, horribly strangled apparently by unseen hands. There had, the paper said, been another murder outside the Hotel Sherwood. A man named Greenford, suspected of being an international spy, had met death in the same mysterious way.

Through it all a trail of black mystery ran. The police and Government operatives were baffled. There seemed to be no connection between the jewel robbery in Crandal's home, the murder of Greenford, and the four other murders of like nature that had taken place previously.

But the Agent's eyes were grimly alight. He saw a sinister motive, a connection running through it all. But the picture was not clear. Why had the Black Master, who asked a million dollars for the thing he had stolen from the chemist, Mark Roemer, stooped to such a crime as the theft of Crandal's jewels? Was it merely to provide funds for himself until the big sale went through? Wouldn't even the Black Master find it difficult to dispose of such famous gems as Crandal's? And now that Greenford had been murdered, what would be the Black Master's next move? What government would he attempt to negotiate with next?

These were the questions the Agent asked himself as dawn made the sky gray over the city. Milk wagons rattled in the streets outside. Men and women rose to another day of work. The black mouths of the subways became gorged with hurrying people. But the Agent, silent and alone, pondered a murder riddle.

There was one course open to him, one he planned to follow. He would haunt the Mephistopheles Club, watch developments there, shadow Nick Baroni.

WHEN night came, he was among the first arrivals. Disguised as a young man about town, he played heavily at the gambling tables to avert suspicion. He began to win. Here was more money that would go into Betty Dale's fund for crime victims.

But he ceased playing when ten o'clock came and when he saw the gross form of Nick Baroni entering the room.

For a moment the big gangster, puffing on a cigar, swept the gambling tables with cold, alert eyes. Then, while his bodyguards moved quietly into chairs around him, he settled himself before one of the roulette wheels. He began playing with the elaborate, solemn concentration of a man to whom gambling is a serious business.

Tonight, Baroni had more torpedoes with him than usual. There were six of the sleekly dressed, vicious-looking young men. With cigarettes dangling from their bloodless lips, their eyes were ever alert. It seemed that their right hands were never far from their right coat pockets, where flat automatics rested. There was a tenseness about them as though they expected trouble. Had Sam Dwyer, terror of the river front, made some veiled threat, warned Baroni that this was his territory?

The tenseness increased when, toward midnight, Baroni left the gambling room and seated himself at a dinner table. The Secret Agent saw why. He saw Baroni's sloe-black eyes shift across the room. Saw his face muscles stiffen.

There, seated at a table near the wall, was Sam Dwyer, Baroni's hated rival. The river-front gangster was a thinner, younger man. There was a mocking light in his eyes as he looked across the room at Baroni.

Spatted, immaculately dressed, with the corner of a white handkerchief thrusting from his upper coat pocket, Dwyer looked like a fashion plate. But there was a hard, lean wolfishness about him that matched the older man's pudgy viciousness.

Ostentatiously Dwyer rose from his seat and walked across the room. Elaborately he bowed to Baroni and gripped his fat white hand. The two men smiled, stared at each other, and hatred glared from their eyes. Baroni's bodyguards edged nearer, their chalky faces glowing like pale, evil moons against the shadows of the room, their hands tensing like talons. Dwyer's crafty eyes flashed toward them. He smiled again. The Agent couldn't hear what was being said, but he knew that Dwyer was giving vent to some mocking pleasantry. The two men seemed like old friends. It was only the bitter lights in their eyes that revealed the murderous enmity they bore each other. The room grew silent, tense.

But Dwyer walked quietly back to his table. He appeared to have no bodyguards around him. He appeared to have come to the Mephistopheles Club alone; but, while he had been talking to Baroni, the tables around the entranceway had filled. Well-dressed, quiet-moving young men, singly and in groups, had entered.

They paid no attention to Dwyer, or he to them. But when Nick

Baroni saw the newcomers, a pastiness crept over his fat face. The
Agent, watching hawklike, saw the pudgy fingers holding the cigar
begin to tremble.

Smiling slightly, Sam Dwyer was studying his menu. The waiters scurrying about the room looked suddenly like small scared
rabbits. Whispers ran among them and among the guests. There
were covert glances. Frightened gestures. The manager of the Mephistopheles Club walked jerkily across the floor and went up to
Dwyer's table. His face was pale. He remonstrated with the gangster.

Dwyer waved him airily away.

Many guests, still in the middle of their meals, began to rise and
hastily leave. Girls, the color suddenly gone from their faces, asked
their escorts to take them out. The room was slowly emptying, as
the stalking shadows of murder crept out from the walls.

The orchestra on its stand played on, but the music took on a
thin, sickly quality. The eyes of the musicians darted from their
printed notes to the two groups of men facing each other. Their
hands trembled on the keys of their instruments. The rhythm became broken, macabre, like a dance of death.

Baroni was slumped in his seat now. He was trying not to show
the fear that made his features dough colored—trying not to let on
that he was aware of the showdown that faced him. The stubs of two
cigarettes spiraled smoke in the ash tray before him. He lit another
and dribbled smoke through his heavy lips and nostrils. The whites
of his eyes had taken on a yellow tinge as they wandered toward
those tables across the room. He and his bodyguards were outnum-
bered. Dwyer's friends had come in strength of two to one.

The Agent's gaze was upon Dwyer. What would the signal be
that would let hell loose in this room?

The sleek, bland face of Sam Dwyer gave no hint But, as the
Agent watched, Dwyer's well-manicured fingers lifted slowly and
touched the handkerchief in his front coat pocket. He took it out,
wiped his lips delicately. When he replaced it, he thrust it down
out of sight.

It was a slight gesture, almost insignificant; but it was the prearranged gesture that started the fireworks. It was the fuse that
lighted the bomb of human hate and ferocity.

In one and the same moment, the men around him left their
tables and backed against the wall, drawn guns suddenly appeared
in their hands. Dwyer slipped out of his seat as quickly and grace-

fully as a dancer executing a pirouette. With a hoarse bellow of fear, Nick Baroni lurched sidewise in his chair, deliberately flinging himself flat on the floor. He did it to escape the stream of bullets that lashed the spot where his body had been.

CHAPTER XIV

TO THE DEATH

THE AGENT HAD witnessed many gun fights, but never one which began with such deadly sudden ferocity as this. Both sides were shooting to kill, shooting to achieve the greatest slaughter in the shortest space of time.

Baroni had escaped the first blast of bullets. His huge body was half hidden by the table which he had overturned. It was all that saved him. His bodyguards were crouching, their eyes black, evil slits. Like Dwyer's men, guns had appeared miraculously in their hands. They answered the fusillade from across the room with a volley that sent a wave of sound blasting back against the walls.

The musicians left their stand, stumbling off it amid a jumble of hastily dropped instruments. They scurried out of sight. The few remaining guests outside of the members of the two gangs, leaped to safety. Only Agent "X" remained as witness of the crimson carnage that was taking place.

He sat at a table close against the wall. There was a heavy portière near by. He drew it in front of him.

The fighting men paid him no heed; but he knew that he risked a stray bullet any moment.

One of Dwyer's men had fallen to the polished floor of the club. He pressed a hand to his side, screamed, thinly, horribly. A gunman in the employ of Baroni suddenly threw up his hands and took three staggering steps forward. There was a blue hole in the center of his forehead, a surprised look on his evil face. Even before his body hit the floor, there came the vicious *splat* of three more bullets striking him. He crumpled up and lay still, a crimson stain slowly spreading outward.

Dwyer, a gun in his hand, and the look of a demon on his face, was edging forward. He shouted some orders to his men. They spread out, slinking along the walls, creeping closer to the group who faced them. Dwyer himself crouched behind a chair. His gun spat.

Another Baroni man dropped to the floor. Lying with one arm twisted under him, he kept up a murderous fire, until his automatic clicked emptily. Then, painfully, slowly, he began filling the clip from his pocket until a second bullet shattered his wrist. He screamed then and crawled away toward the wall.

Baroni was getting the worst of it. There was no question about that. This was a battle to the death. Dwyer was fighting to wipe out a rival group, to eliminate competition with the quick scalpel of hot lead. And Baroni's small bodyguard was already reduced by two.

Slowly, mercilessly, Dwyer's men moved in fanshaped formation, trying to reach a point where their crossfire would do the most damage. Baroni, his eyes bulging, his face sagging with fright, still lay on the floor. Either the big gangster carried no gun or he was afraid to draw it. He was depending on his men, waiting for death, palsied with terror.

A third Baroni man dropped his gun now. His arm hung limply. He tried to pick the gun up with his left hand, failed. There were only three of them left, crouching, white-faced youths whose lives had been spent under the shadow of fear and quick death. They were fighting with the desperation of cornered animals, knowing that their minutes were numbered.

"Get Baroni," Dwyer hissed. "The yellow-bellied punk is hiding behind that table."

Agent "X" saw the mobsters' fire shift, saw splinters begin to fly from the table behind which Baroni crouched like a sodden, frightened hog.

Then quietly, deftly, the Agent moved his hands. He took a small tool from his pocket—a pair of pliers. They were not ordinary pliers. There was a trough in the middle of them for wires to slip into, a needle point centering in this trough. He snapped the pliers over the cord of the electric table light. His wrist tensed. The needle point was driven through the rubberized insulation, through the strands of copper wire beneath. It formed an instantaneous short circuit. There was a brilliant spark, a puff of smoke. The lights went out as every fuse in the building blew.

The Agent slipped out of his seat. Risking death from the leaden hail of bullets, he crossed the floor, slipped to the side of Baroni. He touched the man's arm, heard him cry out in fear.

"Keep quiet," the Agent hissed. "I put the lights out. I can save you."

He had a reason for this. He felt no friendship, no sympathy for the craven gang lord who had, in his day, ordered the deaths of many men. But there was a chance that Baroni could lead him where he wanted to go—along the trail of the Black Master.

Dwyer's men, taking advantage of the blackness, were circling in like sinister wolves in the night. A bullet plucked at the sleeve of the Agent's coat close to the shoulder.

Then someone, a member of Dwyer's gang, clicked on a flash light, setting it on a chair and leaping back. Its rays illumined one of Baroni's decimated bodyguards. A volley of bullets riddled him, made him collapse like a slumped sack of grain, before he struck. Only two were left now.

THE Agent smiled grimly. Dwyer's men were all around them. Guarding the exits, guarding the windows. Dwyer planned to wipe Baroni and every man of his gang out, leave no witnesses of the terrible battle. He would kill the Agent, too, if he got the chance.

But Agent "X" was busy. From a deep inner pocket, he took a small vial with a screw cap. It seemed a strange thing to bring out at such a time, a strange thing to pit against a dozen flaming automatics. In the vial were a score of tiny pellets, like pills.

He unscrewed the top of the vial with deft, quick fingers, then waited a moment while air seeped in. There had been only a vacuum in the vial before. It had been airtight.

On contact with the air the tiny pellets began to smoke and glow.[19]

Suddenly the Agent made a sweeping motion with his arm. The pellets left the mouth of the vial, scattering around the room, rattling on the floor.

A second later one made a report like a giant firecracker exploding. It seemed fantastic that such force could be contained in such a small body. A second exploded close to one of Dwyer's men. The man screamed with fear, dropped his automatic, and leaped back.

---

19   AUTHOR'S NOTE: The Secret Agent never explained the nature of the pellets to me; but it is certain that they are covered with some compound containing phosphoric acid. Phosphorus ignites on contact with hydrogen in the air. When the coating of the pellets heated up, the thermal stimulus must have discharged whatever sort of explosive they contained. I had known for some time that Agent "X" was a master of certain branches of chemisty.

The firing ceased abruptly. Dwyer cursed and screamed orders.

Then a half-dozen of the Agent's harmless-looking pellets let go, and the room became a crashing, exploding medley of sound. Air waves hurtled this way and that. The windows rattled.

The Agent, calm through it all, spoke sharply in Baroni's ear.

"They are harmless—come with me."

The fat gang leader, shaking with terror, floundered to his feet. He stood dazed, rocking, while the din of the exploding pellets kept up.

Leaving his side a moment, the Agent went to the nearest of his henchmen who was still alive.

"Come," he said.

The man turned with the squeal of a rat, tried to shoot; but the Agent knocked the gun from his hand.

"Fool!" he hissed.

He rounded up the other man, drew them to Baroni's side. The gang leader gave a brief explanation.

"This guy did it," he said. "Let's scram."

They slunk out of the room, passed an exit from which Dwyer's men had fled in terror as one of the Agent's pellets burst close to it. They crept down the stairs unmolested, and out into the street.

An excited crowd was gathering outside. Baroni lumbered through it, scattering people right and left like a hippo ploughing through reeds. His two henchmen and the Agent trailed him.

Down the block two big limousines stood, the fenders of one touching the rear of the other. Baroni piled into the first car. One of his surviving torpedoes took the wheel. Baroni, the other gunman, and the Secret Agent were in the rear. "X" was sticking close to the gangster now, calmly carrying out a preconceived plan.

Gears whined and the car sped away into the darkness. Behind them, police sirens were screaming as a half-dozen radio cruisers, summoned by the frantic appeals from headquarters, converged on the Mephistopheles Club. No doubt the emergency squad cars would be called out, too. It was the biggest gangster battle of the season.

Nick Baroni, slumped and speechless, was mopping his fat face with a silk handkerchief. Rhythmically, monotonously, his plump hands moved round and round. It seemed to afford him relief. His gunman, shivering and crouched like a frightened rat, said nothing as the car tore ahead. But once his eyes shifted strangely, fearfully, to the face of the Secret Agent.

The Agent's features were the bland, even features of a young clubman. His immaculate tuxedo was not even creased. He fingered his tie for a moment, straightened it. Only his burning eyes showed the dynamic fire of hidden emotions.

NICK BARONI spoke then as the speeding limousine carried them to safety, carried them beyond the noise and turmoil of the Mephistopheles Club.

"What's your name, guy—an' what made you chisel in?"

The Agent spoke quickly. This was a question he had been expecting. He was ready for it.

"You seemed to be getting a tough break—and I felt like a little excitement."

The crafty eyes of Nick Baroni, regaining some of their arrogant poise now, focused on him thoughtfully, taking in his patent leather shoes, his sharply creased trousers, his well-fitted coat.

"Just a playboy out for a little fun, eh!" he said.

The Agent stiffened. Irritation leaped into his eyes for a moment.

"Did I act like a playboy?" he asked harshly.

Baroni seemed to wilt. He opened his mouth, spoke quickly. There was a sudden uneasy look in his eyes, as though he sensed for the first time the uncanny power of the stranger beside him.

"Don't get me wrong, mister. You came in at the right time. It's O.K. by me. Those Dwyer rats might have made it a little tough for me. And that popcorn of yours? What the hell was it? How did you think it up?"

"Just a few fireworks," said the Agent quietly. He had slipped back into his role, hiding his dislike for the man beside him, hiding his contempt for the man's arrogance and callousness. For Baroni was pretending now that he would have won the fight with Dwyer anyway. He was ignoring the fact that four of his bodyguard lay dead on the floor of the Mephistopheles Club.

"I'll get that rat, Dwyer," Baroni was breathing. "I'll burn his guts for this." He turned fiercely on the man beside him.

"What do I pay you lice for? Why did you let him get the drop on us?"

"You're talking through your hat, boss," said the gunman sullenly. "Burnie, Monk, Steve, and Fred were wiped out. The rest of us would have got it too, if this mug hadn't edged in."

Baroni lapsed into silence, mopping his fat face again.

"I gotta have a drink," he said presently. "My nerves are shot. Stop at Frenchy's place, Al."

The torpedo driving the car nodded. A block farther on, brakes squealed and the big car slid to a halt before the door of an underworld dive.

"Come in, guy, and I'll set you up a snifter," said Baroni expansively.

The Agent followed the trio to the door of this joint that was still a speak-easy, even though prohibition had been repealed. A slit-eyed man with spiky mustaches opened the door, stared at them through the grating, and admitted them when he recognized Baroni.

"Where's the rest of the boys?" he asked.

"They got into a little trouble, Frenchy. Fix up some Scotch."

Darting an inquisitive look at the Secret Agent, the little Frenchman went off to obey orders. Baroni motioned toward a back room and heaved himself into a chair. He was still perspiring. His hands were trembling. His pasty, soggy face showed evidences of the terror that had almost paralyzed him. He gulped three glasses of whisky before turning to the Agent.

"Now," he said. "What's your name and who the hell are you?"

"James Porter," said the Agent quickly. It was one of his many aliases. He drew a card from his wallet, handed it to Baroni to prove it.

The big gangster stared at the card impressed.

"What do you do for a living?"

"Dabble in the stock market a little."

Baroni's eyes showed cunning.

"You ain't making much money now?"

"No," said the Agent. "You know what happened to the market."

Baroni rested his fat chin on one hand, placed his elbow on the table.

"Listen," he said. "You seem like a good guy. Maybe I could give you a job that would bring in some kale. Then you could hit the high places regular. Four of my torpedoes were wiped out tonight. I gotta get some more. How would you like to be one of them?"

The Agent nodded slowly.

"I'll think it over," he said. This was what he wanted. This would give him a chance to see what, if any, were Baroni's connections with the hideous strangler murders. But he didn't want to appear too anxious.

Baroni took another drink and his self-confidence and suavity increased.

"I got Dwyer's number," he said. "I'm going to get him and take over his rackets. There may not be as much dough as when we was running alky—but there'll be plenty. There's a dope racket that I'm gonna look in on. You could contact the rich guys and high-steppin' dames with that million-dollar manner of yours. We could clean up."

Baroni stared blandly at the Secret Agent, seeming to see in him possibilities for a new type of clean-up—dope peddled to society people who could pay for it. The Agent hid the contempt he felt.

He was about to answer when the three men beside him stiffened. A police siren had suddenly sounded in the street outside. It was followed by the sound of a car sliding to the curb.

Baroni's eyes darted to the windows in the rear of the room. But a thunderous knocking came at the outside door before he could move. Frenchy, trembling, went to the door. They heard him arguing for seconds. Gruff voices sounded outside. Then the Frenchman slid the bolts and stepped back, wringing his hands.

The Agent, looking over the shoulder of Nick Baroni, saw the foremost figure in the group that was entering. It was Inspector John Burks of the city homicide squad.

CHAPTER XV

TAKEN FOR A RIDE

WITH A DEEP scowl on his face, Inspector Burks strode into the speak-easy's back room. He eyed the group sitting at the table distastefully.

"Well, Baroni, I figured I'd find you here," he said.

The big gangster spread his fat hands and shrugged.

"There ain't no law against a guy having a little drink with a few pals."

Slowly, sternly, Inspector Burks eyed the faces of the assembled group. He removed his hat, ran quick, tense fingers through his snow-white hair. His contrasting jet-black eyebrows drew together as he frowned.

"Haven't I got enough trouble with the strangler killings without you gangster rats making more?"

"I don't get you, chief," said Baroni blandly. "Me and these mugs have been here all evening."

"Don't lie to me," cried Burks. "Four of your men were picked up on the floor of the Mephistopheles Club—stiffs all of them. You and Dwyer have been fighting again."

"Maybe we did have a little scrap," said Baroni. "But I ain't admitting it."

"I've got fifty witnesses," said Burks. "You were seen there."

Baroni's voice grew unctuous, smooth as syrup.

"Who started it, chief—did anybody tell you that? If I was there and if I fought, it was only in self-defense. The law says a guy's got a right to—"

Burks silenced him with a wave of his hand.

"Murder is murder, Baroni. Three of Dwyer's rats were killed, too. You were mixed up in murder tonight. It may land you in the pen, or maybe the hot seat. You'd better come clean."

A sickly, pasty hue had come over Baroni's face again. His tone grew whining.

"Listen, chief—maybe I did get mixed up in a little trouble tonight. Maybe there was some guys wiped out. But I didn't start it, I tell you. It was that rat Dwyer. He'll get a bellyful of lead for this. He'll—"

Inspector Burks struck the table with his clenched fist until the whisky glasses leaped and the bottle tipped over, gurgling its amber fluid on the floor.

"I'm going to have a talk with Dwyer, too," he shouted. "I'm going to tell him the same thing. You two mugs are going to make peace, or I'll see that you both go to the hot seat. Prohibition's over. This racket stuff's got to stop. Both of you are going to break up your gangs and go out of business. If you don't, I'll get you on murder charges for what happened tonight."

It was a threat. The Secret Agent knew that. Inspector Burks was taking what seemed the wisest course. There were few convictions for gang killings. It was hard to get witnesses who would testify in court, harder still to pin crimes on the mobsters. They hired the cunningest, most unscrupulous criminal lawyers to be had. Baroni could plead self-defense. He might get off. But by threatening him, Inspector Burks hoped to win his point.

Baroni's face muscles sagged. He had visions of a golden stream from new rackets being diverted from his pockets.

"I'll—I'll think about it," he said.

"You'll do as I say. You'll bury the hatchet with Dwyer—shake hands with him and go out of business. If I find you in any public place again with torpedoes around you—if there is one more killing, I'll railroad you both to the pen on a first-degree murder charge. I'm going to talk to the D.A. about it."

With this ultimatum, Burks turned on his heel and stalked out of the place.

Baroni wiped his face again.

"Let's have another round of drinks, boys," he said.

For minutes he sat brooding, his head sunk into the rolls of fat around his neck. He was lost in thought. Finally he spoke.

"You heard what the inspector said. There's one way of putting it over on that bird. I hate to do it. Maybe I won't. But it's worth considering. If me and Dwyer went in together, stopped fighting, we could clean up on dope. Booze is out; but dope's still good. Now that mugs can get all the liquor they want, they won't want it so much. We'll start 'em on dope and get 'em to like it."

Baroni stopped, took another gulp of liquor. His piglike eyes were gleaming. His shrewdly acquisitive brain was active. He had forgotten the fight in the Mephistopheles Club. Forgotten the dead men on the floor. Forgotten his hatred of Dwyer. Gold took precedence over everything.

"Dwyer and I can open up a swell joint somewhere," he said. "Together we can keep any other guy from chiseling in. If anybody wants snow or coke they'll have to come to us."

The Secret Agent rose.

"Where are you going?" Baroni snapped.

"Out," said the Agent. "I've got some business to attend to."

Baroni eyed him speculatively for a moment. Then he spoke slowly.

"What I said goes," he remarked. "I can use a guy like you in more ways than one. You got class and brains. If I hitch in with Dwyer, there'll be a place for you. Drop around here and Frenchy will tell you where to find me."

"O.K.," said the Agent. There was a mocking light in the depths of his eyes that Baroni didn't get. He was satisfied with the way things were going. If Baroni and Dwyer joined forces, he would have a chance to learn the intimate secrets of both gang chiefs. As a side issue, he'd smash their evil dope racket. But he'd find out first whether either was the Black Master. Now that he thought of it, Dwyer, with his polished manners and suavity, was more the type who might plan such a colossal crime.

BUT, as he stepped into the street outside of Frenchy's place, the Agent's calmness left him. He tensed suddenly, whirled toward the curb. His momentary let-up of vigilance had brought new danger upon him.

A dark sedan with lights out was sliding to the curb beside him. The door was open. A voice addressed him from the interior.

"Come here, guy. Stick your hands up."

The Agent knew the threat of death when he faced it. There was death in that voice. He could see no features; but, just inside the door where the glow of the street light fell on it, he saw the dull, gleaming muzzle of an automatic. He hesitated an instant only, then moved forward.

By the curb he came to a standstill.

"Closer," said the deadly voice inside.

The Agent moved closer still, his scalp prickling.

Then rough hands seized him. He was dragged into the car's interior. Almost instantly gears whined and the car shot away. There were three men in the rear of the car. He caught the silhouette of one and held his breath. He was staring at the sharp, wolfish features of Sam Dwyer, river-front mobster, the man who had butchered four of Baroni's bodyguards.

He did not speak. The car sped on for six blocks. The men beside him were silent; but the hard, cold muzzle of an automatic pressed against his side.

Then the voice of Dwyer sounded again.

"You're the guy," he said, "who cribbed our show tonight. I'd have got that hog Baroni if it hadn't been for those firecrackers of yours. You pulled a fast one—but one of my mugs saw you going out."

Still the Agent was silent.

"What have you got to say about it?" snarled Dwyer. "Who are you, and since when did you start working for Baroni?"

"Just now," said the Agent. "My name's Porter."

"What do you mean—just now? You helped him make a getaway when I had him trapped."

"I horned in just for fun," said the Agent casually.

"Yeah?"

"Yes."

Dwyer was silent for seconds. He turned on a small flash light, studied the Secret Agent's face. There was contempt in his voice when he spoke again.

"Just a dolled-up softy," he said. He swore under his breath and continued. "You shouldn't have done it, fella. Nick Baroni wasn't worth it. He gave you a job, you say?"

"Yeah."

Sam Dwyer laughed thinly, making a sound in his nose that was like a harsh whinny.

"I'm going to save you a lot of trouble, fella. You wouldn't like to work for Baroni. He'd work you hard. He's a bad man. You'd come to a lot of grief. I'm going to save you all that. I'm a good guy."

Dwyer stopped speaking. He laughed again, and one of the others in the car with him laughed, too. Their laughter was harsh, mirthless; it was laughter that held a terrible threat. When Dwyer spoke again, he didn't address the Agent. He spoke gruffly to the driver of the car.

"There's a field at the end of Marigold Avenue," he said. "They're going to build on it when they get around to it. There ain't nothing there now. That will be a good place."

There was coldness, cruelty, in his tone. The driver nodded understandingly and stepped on the gas.

The Secret Agent stiffened. He knew to what use Dwyer planned to put the vacant lot. He knew that they were taking him on a ride of death for the part he had played in Nick Baroni's get-away.

CHAPTER XVI

THE BLACK MASTER'S ORDERS

THE PRESSURE OF the gun against his side increased. The Agent thought quickly. He had often been in the presence of death. It held no terrors for him. But death before his work was done was something he could not face calmly. The gangster killings he had witnessed had been evil, vicious. But they were as nothing compared to the horror of the Spectral Strangler murders. In his mind's eye he saw again the swollen, purple face of Bill Scanlon—the tongue thrust grotesquely between lips silenced forever. He saw, too, the features of those others who had met death in the same terrible fashion.

His own face was calm, but his eyes burned with the deep, glowing light of determination.

Sam Dwyer spoke then, harshly, mockingly.

"Baroni can save the dough he was going to give you. You won't need it; but *he* will—for funeral expenses. A big shot's got to have a decent funeral—an' Baroni comes next—after you."

Dwyer's hard, glittering gaze was fixed upon the Agent. The others were staring at him also. There was sadistic cruelty in these men that made them contemplate murder with fierce pleasure.

"Shall we give it to him now, chief, an' chuck him out afterwards—or wait till we get there?"

The man who had spoken was fingering the cold butt of his automatic. He spoke again, his voice eager.

"It won't make no noise if I put the muzzle close. The rat cheated us tonight. Let's smoke him."

Dwyer answered harshly.

"Pipe down, mug! You're not giving orders—you're taking 'em. There's cops around. We're not taking any chances—tonight."

The car rolled on, nearing Marigold Avenue. The Agent knew

that it was a long, bleak thoroughfare lined with warehouses and factory buildings. There would be no cops there.

Dwyer corroborated this.

"I'll give the word when we turn the corner," he said.

The Agent began to tremble as though in a palsy of fear. They did not know that the man they had captured was a superb actor. The quivering of his arms and body seemed real.

Dwyer's lips curled back from his white teeth in a mirthless grin.

"Can't take it—can you?" he said. "Don't worry, fella—it won't be long now."

The others chuckled evilly. Then the Agent spoke, his voice hoarse, as though terror were constricting his vocal cords.

"How about a smoke?" he asked.

"Wait a minute!" Dwyer's hands felt through the Agent's pockets for a gun. He found none.

"O.K.," he said, "but make it snappy. You ain't got long. The parking ground for rats who don't mind their own business is just ahead."

With hands that shook, the Agent reached toward his vest pocket. He seemed to be fumbling, but his fingers were working purposefully. He drew out a silver cigarette case such as a playboy might carry. He thrust a cigarette between his lips, replacing the case, and drew a small lighter from another pocket.

In the dimness of the car's interior, the gangsters watched his trembling, awkward movements with wolfish satisfaction.

"Soft," said Dwyer. "You never could have taken what Baroni would have handed you. Better thank us for rubbing you out."

Dwyer's gun poked against the Agent's ribs accentuating the remark. Dwyer laughed harshly.

The Agent was silent. With his left hand he snapped open the cap of the lighter. His thumb was on the tiny knurled wheel that made the flint spark. His right hand hung listlessly in his lap.

Then, so quickly that the men beside him could not catch the movements, he whirled the lighter in a swift arc and clamped the fingers of his right hand over Dwyer's gun wrist, pushing the gun away.

No spark came from the lighter. There was a soft, quick hiss. A jet of concentrated tear gas, stored in the base of the lighter under pressure, lashed into the gangsters' eyes.[20]

The man at the Agent's left clawed at his face. Dwyer at his right cursed furiously and pumped the trigger of his automatic. But the gun, deflected, sent bullets into the back of the front seat.

The driver turned a tense, frightened face. A second jet of gas caught him straight in the eyes. He bellowed with fear, took his hands off the wheel, instinctively jamming down on the brakes.

Agent "X" rose, leaped across Dwyer, and thrust open the car's door. It was slowing down, wabbling. The front tire struck the curb. The car rocked and slewed around. Agent "X" leaped out, landing on his hands and knees. In an instant he was up, speeding into the darkness, with Dwyer and his men still cursing and clawing at their eyes.

The Secret Agent's own eyes were glowing. He hoped to get back to the Mephistopheles Club in time to locate the hophead and see what his reaction to the gangster fight had been.

BUT while Agent "X" was still a block away from the club, the hophead was leaving it. He had witnessed the mobsters' battle, but his small animallike face showed no expression. The police had questioned him among other employees. He had answered in adroit monosyllables, telling nothing. And now he was on his way to his sinister employer.

In killing Greenford, he had carried out instructions to the letter—the instructions of a man he had never seen and probably never would see—the Black Master, the man who supplied him with the soul-shattering morphine derivative that his nerves and body craved. His nerves were jumping now, crying out for a fresh shot of the drug.

The hophead had a report to make to his employer also. He feared no pursuit tonight. Greenford was out of the way. No one else, he felt certain, suspected him of being implicated with the Black Master. Nevertheless, he was careful. The Black Master was a man who tolerated no errors, no oversights. Fear of his unseen employer helped, besides his craving for the drug, to make the man

---

20 AUTHOR'S NOTE: One thing I have learned about the Agent's methods. He seldom repeats himself. His ingenious brain is always figuring out new weapons of defense. In his battle with the "Torture Trust," which was chronicled last month, he used tear gas in the stem of a watch in escaping from an embarrassing mix-up with the police. But, being afraid perhaps that the police would ever after be on the alert for a man with a trick watch, he discarded that method of defense for another.

a faithful employee. There was in his heart a dread that amounted almost to superstition for the criminal for whom he worked.

He changed cabs twice, walked along dark, unfrequented streets. On one of them he came at last to a small empty office building. Like the house on Bradley Square, this building was for sale. The neighborhood had run down. It was no longer a business section. The few remaining tenants in the building had been evicted six months before for non-payment of rent. It stood bleak and deserted now, with the chill emptiness peculiar to office buildings that are no longer in use.

The hophead, with a key from his ring, let himself into the front of it. He climbed an old metal stairway to the second floor. Here he entered an office in the center of the building. He touched a switch, turning on overhead lights.

The office was hardly more than a cubbyhole, windowless and airless. The lights he had switched on could not be seen from the street. But, unlike the rest of the building, this office had been renovated. Small as it was, there were indications that someone had recently been at work here.

The place had been dusted, the ceiling and walls had been painted and the light fixtures were new. A huge mirror was set into the rear wall divided in two by a narrow metal panel that ran down its center. The mirror gleamed brightly, reflecting the glow of the lights and sending the dope fiend's own image back to him. There seemed to be two thin-faced, rat-eyed men in the strange little room.

He studied himself for seconds in the mirror, then glanced at the small clock that was clicking on the table. This was a business office; but mysterious and sinister was the business transacted in it.

The clock showed one minute to twelve. The hophead fingered his collar, tried to control his twitching nerves. There were shadows of fear in his eyes. He waited tensely while the hands of the clock moved slowly round to midnight. Once his gaze darted upward to the elaborate, rose-petal design overhead into which the light fixture was set. Then he stiffened.

A voice suddenly spoke to him out of the quiet of the room.

"What have you to report, Taub? Speak and I will hear."

The voice was dry, disguised. It was the voice of the Black Master. It seemed to come from overhead, perhaps from a speaker concealed somewhere around the light fixture. It continued:

"I am watching you, Taub. I see your face plainly. Tell the truth—

about everything. Don't lie to me. Never lie to the Black Master. It is not well. He sees all—knows all."

The dope fiend's face turned a shade paler. His lips moved. He spoke excitedly—in English that had a slight accent.

"Taub never lies, master. Taub always tells the truth. Taub is a loyal servant."

A chuckle filled the room. The dope fiend, Taub, began his report, telling in jerky sentences of how he had caught Greenford trying to shadow him and had killed the spy according to instructions. He mentioned, too, the gangster fight in the Mephistopheles Club.

SILENCE had descended as though the very walls were listening. Taub could feel eyes upon him, but he could not locate the direction from which they came. This, too, filled him with dread. He repeated again and again that he always told the truth. The eyes that he felt upon him were real enough. He was under close, continuous observation by a man watching not ten feet away.

In another small office behind the mirror, which formed a heavy partition, the unseen watcher sat. He was facing the mirror, the back of it. Through its surface, which appeared silvered to the hophead, he could see Taub plainly. The mirror was of Argus glass, the glass used in diamond brokerage offices, the glass that will admit light rays in one direction only. It was eight inches thick—thick enough even to withstand bullets. It formed an invulnerable barrier between the rear office and the mysterious room where Taub stood. But, as an added precaution, the man sitting behind it wore a heavy black mask. His features were hidden. Only his eyes showed, watching the dope fiend. Before him was a tiny microphone connected with the amplifier above Taub's head. He could speak softly into it and his voice would resound in the next room.

When Taub had finished his reports, the Black Master spoke again.

"Greenford was a fool. I do not need him. I have other plans. To make men realize the value of the thing I have to sell, perhaps I shall have to demonstrate it—in a spectacular way."

The Black Master was silent for a moment. Taub waited. Then the Black Master's laughter sounded again. It had the harshness of infinite evil.

"You say these two gangs battled—tried to wipe each other out? What if I aided them in their mutual ambitions? What if I gave the police, the city, and the country a demonstration of wholesale killing that they will remember? Nine murders have taken place already. Would it not be more conclusive to the powers that be if I demonstrated what I can do by wiping out wholesale a nest of rats—two nests of them?"

"Yes, master," said Taub in a trembling whisper.

"I shall destroy Baroni and Dwyer and all those who follow them, Taub. It will be amusing as well as beneficial. As men spray powder on annoying insects and kill them, I shall destroy these criminal parasites. Then—certain men will understand. Then I will get the price I ask for what I have to sell. If not—there will be other murders—till I have made my point clear. You shall aid me, Taub."

"Yes, master. When do these gangsters die?"

The Black Master was silent for a moment. Behind the mask his eyes glittered.

"When conditions are right," he said. "When they least expect it. Go back to the Mephistopheles Club, Taub. Find out Baroni's and Dwyer's plans. Find out what effect the battle tonight will have. Find out where they can be located."

"I will, master."

Taub hesitated after he had spoken. He seemed to be waiting for something—something that he was afraid to mention. The Black Master's laugh rang out.

"I know what you want, Taub! The laborer is worthy of his hire! As long as you are a faithful laborer, you shall be paid. Come close to the panel between the mirrors."

Taub moved forward uneasily. He waited in front of the panel. A section of it disappeared suddenly, disclosing a round dark hole six inches in diameter—large enough for a man's hand to come through. Fingers appeared in this hole, gloved fingers holding a small vial—the fingers of the Black Master.

Taub took the vial. His face was convulsed with the craving that possessed him. Here in this super-potent drug, an opium alkaloid that he could get nowhere else, was peace for his jumping, screaming nerves. It would produce visions that would wipe out the memory of murders he had committed, give him a few hours of rest—and steel him for other murders to come. The Black Master held him in bonds that were stronger than steel chains. He was one of several drug addicts who served the arch criminal. They were safe employees. They would not squeal. To do so would mean an end to their drug supply—with consequent torture to mind and body that would make death welcome.

The Black Master's hand withdrew. The metal plug inside the panel was shoved forward again. The hole was blocked up. The Black Master's voice sounded.

"Go now, Taub. Do as I have ordered. Report here tomorrow night. Baroni and Dwyer and their mobsters shall be destroyed like insects—when the time is ripe. Their deaths shall be a further warning that the power of the Black Master is invincible."

CHAPTER XVII

FLOWERS OF DEATH

TWO DAYS AFTER his escape from Sam Dwyer's death car, Secret Agent "X" received an invitation. It was handed to him by Frenchy, the owner of the speak-easy where Baroni had taken refuge following the battle in the Mephistopheles Club.

The invitation was from Baroni himself. Secret Agent "X," disguised again as James Porter, young man about town, had gone to Frenchy's place seeking news of Baroni. Was there a chance, he wondered, that the two gangsters, Baroni and Dwyer, would forget their animosity and join forces in a new and more sinister racket, as Baroni had proposed?

It seemed possible. The greed for gold was the motive that made gangs organize in the first place. It was stronger than hate—stronger even than the fear of death. And if these two men organized, Secret Agent "X" wanted to watch them. One or the other might conceivably be the terrible Black Master. Or, in contact with them, he might be led to the hideout of this greater criminal.

Baroni's message was short and to the point.

"Porter," it said, "come to my place at eight this evening and come dolled up. Big doings, and I can use guys like you. Frenchy will tell you where to come."

Agent "X" read the note with interest. What was Nick Baroni planning? He spoke to Frenchy, and the rat-eyed, spike-mustached proprietor of the speak-easy gave him Baroni's address. It was in a flashy suburb built up with the gaudy mansions of the newly rich.

Prepared for any emergency, Secret Agent "X" went there at the appointed hour. He had "dolled up" as Baroni had suggested. He was dressed immaculately, dressed in the height of fashion. No one could guess, looking at him, that in the linings of his tuxedo were many small, curious articles that would have no place on the person of the playboy that he seemed to be.

Baroni, as "X" had suspected, lived in one of the most elaborate houses in that pretentious section of the city. It was ornate with bay windows, towers, and colonial columns. A long drive led up to it. Well-clipped shrubbery covered the lawn.

A manservant who had the sneaky look of a gangster admitted him.

The inside of the house was even more ornately elaborate than its exterior. Here the ex-beer-runner indulged his childish impulses and showed his shockingly bad taste. Pictures, art objects, tapestries, and indiscriminate pieces of furniture formed a confusing jumble. Thousands that he had made in illicit enterprises had been spent in decorating this house.

The air was heavy with cigar smoke. There came the clink of glasses from a room opening off the front hall. The squint-eyed servant ushered Agent "X" into this.

Baroni's thick voice boomed out. Surrounded by a group of his underworld followers, gunmen, fences, paid torpedoes, the gang leader was in his glory. Arrayed again in an ill-fitting dress suit, he welcomed Secret Agent "X" boisterously.

"Here's the guy that I was telling you about," he said. "Here's the guy that's gonna throw in with us—him an' his firecrackers."

He was introduced to the circle of men whose bland faces masked depths of evil. The two surviving torpedoes of the night before were there. Four new ones had re-enforced them. In such hard times there were few crooks who were not glad to join in with Nick Baroni. The gangster looked at his watch.

"We're gonna start in ten minutes," he said.

"Start where?" asked the Agent.

Nick Baroni winked at him, broadly, mysteriously.

"I got a little surprise for lots of you guys," he said.

The hired torpedoes hitched the guns in their pockets expectantly, thinking apparently that another battle was in store. Baroni turned on them suddenly. His face was serious now. He waved his cigar in pudgy fingers.

"None o' that," he said. "You mugs are going to leave your rods behind tonight. They won't be needed."

Astounded looks met this announcement. Baroni nodded.

"Yeah, I mean it. Get un-heeled before you leave. If any guy has a gat when he steps out of this house, I'll have him put on the spot."

Glumly the men about him rose and deposited their automatics on a sideboard in the big room, making the sideboard look like a young arsenal.

"How about you, fella?" said Baroni, staring at the Agent. "Ain't you heeled?"

The Agent shook his head.

"I'm not carrying a gun," he said.

Baroni looked sly.

"Don't set off any of them firecrackers, either. You got to act polite where we're going."

Mysteriously he rose then and beckoned for the others to follow.

THEY put on their coats and hats, and, when they reached the porch outside, a collection of limousines awaited them. Some were Baroni's own cars. Others he had hired for the occasion. Their drivers seemed to know where they were going. No directions were given. The Secret Agent had a place of honor in the first car with Baroni. The fat gangster, full of zest tonight, joked and laughed as the cars rolled away.

They headed back toward the city, drove in a procession through the night streets. Then the Secret Agent gave a start of surprise. The cars were drawing up before a familiar entranceway—the door of the Mephistopheles Club. Hadn't Baroni had his fill of bloodshed and violence in this place?

As nonchalantly as though no killings had ever taken place there, as though there had never been bleeding, bullet-riddled corpses on the floor, Baroni entered. His followers came behind him, gaping, wondering.

The club's manager came out to meet them. A few whispered words and he led Baroni across the main floor. They climbed a short flight of stairs, entered the club's biggest private dining room. Then the Secret Agent started again.

A huge table was set in the center of the room. Gleaming plates and silverware showed. Spotless napery spread like a field of snow under the lights. At the table, ranged around it, waiting, was a group of men. But it was the man at the table's head that caught the Agent's eye.

Sam Dwyer!

A sudden tenseness filled the room. Baroni's torpedoes crouched in their tracks, their hands stiffening, forgetting that they had left their rods behind. Baroni waved a sudden affable hand. He spoke suavely.

"This is the surprise I was talking about. Me and Sam here has buried the hatchet. We're gonna behave ourselves now. There ain't gonna be no more killings. All you mugs has gotta make friends and get acquainted. Ain't that right, Sam?"

The thin, dudish gangster at the head of the table rose.

"Business before pleasure," he said. "Maybe Nick Baroni and I would like to sling a little lead at each other, but it don't pay. Times have changed, boys. Nick and I are going into business together. This is a dinner to celebrate our partnership. We both know our stuff. We oughta make good."

Dwyer's eyes focused on Secret Agent "X" for a moment. Sudden malice sprang into them.

"That guy!" he said. "You brought him along, too, Nick?"

"Why not?" said Baroni. "What if he did pull a little stunt here the other night? We gotta forget all that."

"I wasn't talking about that," said Dwyer. "It's something else. I don't like him."

As though in bitter recollection, the thin gang leader rubbed his eyes for a moment. They were still slightly bloodshot from the traces of tear gas that Secret Agent "X" had flung.

"Whadda yer mean?" asked Baroni.

"Nothing," said Dwyer. "But keep him away from me."

"He's gonna sit at my end of the table," said Baroni. "But you fellas has got to be friends, too. Everything's gotta be peaceful from now on. We both gave Inspector Burks our word."

Baroni winked again leeringly. The two gangsters were keeping their word to the head of the homicide squad. They had buried the hatchet, made up with each other. But "X" knew what sinister ambitions filled the breasts of the two men. They hoped to flood the city with narcotics, fatten like vultures on the broken bodies and broken souls of drug addicts.

The men of Baroni's gang eased into their places. Waiters came in. Suddenly Secret Agent "X's" eyes grew intent. Among them he saw the slim, cat-footed form of the dope fiend he had shadowed, the emissary of the Black Master.

The hophead had evidently been detailed by the club manager to wait on the gangster's tables. The rat-eyed man looked around for a second, then disappeared to return a moment later.

In his arms this time he carried a huge floral piece. There was something funereal about it. Roses, carnations, and cornflowers were wired in a big frame. More wire was wrapped around the thick bundle that their stems formed. Maidenhair fern formed a mat around this. But, funereal as it was, it made a gay display.

Baroni and Dwyer turned their heads in surprise.

"For the gentlemen," the hophead waiter said politely.

"Who's it from?" barked Baroni.

The waiter shook his head.

"Bring it here—let's look for a card," Baroni demanded.

The waiter picked the flowers up, brought them close. Baroni looked amid the gay blossoms, shook his head.

"There ain't no card," he said. "It's from the manager of this joint—or maybe the police commissioner himself. Set it down over there, you pasty-faced mug."

The waiter nodded and drew the mass of flowers into a position where all could see them.

"They make me think of a funeral," said Baroni. "But they smell good. Bring on the food and let's eat."

SECRET AGENT "X," watching the face of the waiter, had a sudden, tingling sense of danger that he couldn't quite fathom. But there was a look in the hophead's eyes that was hard to interpret— a look of uneasiness, of expectancy.

It was the hophead who helped serve the soup course, and "X," missing nothing, saw that the man's hands were shaking. Something was wrong with him. Something was in the air. What?

The courses of the dinner progressed. The gangsters ate their food, drank their liquor, and grew noisy. Baroni hurled jokes across the table at his former enemy, Dwyer. The hands of a clock at the end of the room moved toward ten. As the hour approached, Agent "X" noted that the hophead's manner grew more mysterious.

A dusty whiteness had come over the man's already pale face. His small eyes rolled in his head. Twice they stabbed across the room, focusing on the clock. He almost spilled the coffee in serving it.

At five minutes to ten, with the huge meal over, Nick Baroni rose to his feet and proposed a toast.

"To the future of this gang," he said. "To all the dough we're gonna make an' the good times we're gonna have."

They drank gustily, emptying their glasses. Baroni ordered another round and spoke again.

"This has been a swell meal," he said. "I want the guys who cooked it and the guys who served it to come in and drink with us. I want the club manager, too."

The hands of the clock stood at two minutes to ten now. The Agent's eyes were focused not on Baroni but on the rattish, evil features of the hophead waiter. He saw the man's gaze move toward the clock for the dozenth time; then the fellow slipped furtively toward the door. His movements were quick, scared at the last. He seemed to want to get out of the room as though it harbored some terrible evil—something that struck dread to his soul. Baroni saw the man's movements.

"Here," he said: "You gotta drink a toast, too, you dope-eating mug."

The waiter shook his head and jerked open the door.

"Get him—bring him back," roared Baroni. "Just for that I'm gonna pour whisky down his throat till he can't stand up. He ain't no gentleman."

Secret Agent "X" leaped up. More than any one else in this room he was interested in the waiter. What could account for the man's strange actions? He did not want him to get away. He flung out the door after the man, saw him darting down the hall. The hophead was running as though all the devils in hell were after him, running as though to escape death itself.

Agent "X" pursued him as far as the end of the corridor. Then a sound made him turn his head and look back. The door that he had just left, the door of the dining room, had swung open. A man stood in it, a man clawing at his throat.

The man was one of Baroni's henchmen. As the Agent stared in horror, the gangster's eyes bulged, his face grew purple, and, with a hoarse, terrible cry he pitched forward and lay writhing. Another figure followed him, a man who seemed to be fighting invisible terrible fingers encircling his neck.

As he held the door open for a moment, Secret Agent "X" got a look into the room he had just left.

A gasp of sheer horror came from his lips. For the room was a shambles. Men at the tables had risen to their feet. Chairs were being overturned by reeling, staggering figures. Purple faces showed.

Then suddenly the bark of an automatic sounded. It was followed by another and another. Some of the mobsters who had come to the dinner "unheeled" had worn concealed weapons. They were using them now. Each gang held the other responsible for the thing that was happening. Leaden death slugs were being added to the horror of invisible murder.

Two men, clawing fiercely, fighting like demons, lurched through the door. One was a Baroni man; the other a henchman of Dwyer. Tho latter held an automatic. The Baroni man was pinioning his wrist. But the man with the gun jerked free as a sinister purple hue spread over his enemy's face. Before the unseen strangling death could do its work, he sent three bullets crashing into the head of the Baroni mobster.

Then he dropped his gun, clawed at his own throat. In a few seconds he had collapsed to the floor to join the body of the man he had just killed.

Sam Dwyer himself came from the dining room. His immaculate clothes were in disorder now. His sleek hair was streaking down his face. He wrenched at his freshly starched collar as though that were the thing that was cutting his wind off. Then he gave a fearful scream and staggered against the wall. The livid, plum-colored hue of the strangling death spread over his face. His eyes started from their sockets, and he fell forward on the floor.

It was like a glimpse into the mouth of some ghastly inferno. Agent "X" shuddered. The Black Master had struck his most hideously ironic blow.

CHAPTER XVIII

THE MAN HUNT BEGINS

NEWSBOYS WERE SHOUTING in the streets three hours later. They were peddling papers on which were spread headlines telling of the greatest underworld killing in the city's history. Tense-faced men and women were reading the story. The police were staggered by the magnitude of the crime. The Baroni and Dwyer gangs had been wiped out. The two gang leaders and all their followers but one, dining in state at the Mephistopheles Club, celebrating the end of their long feud, had been slain. Two score men had been killed by the horrible strangling death.

Cordons of police still surrounded the Mephistopheles Club. Grim-faced detectives were viewing the scene of this most colossal of crimes.

It was the one surviving member of the gangsters' party that aroused the press and the police to a state of hysterical excitement. Employees of the Mephistopheles Club remembered having seen him coming from the corridor of the private dining room. He had left the building just before the terrible crime had been discovered. The manager of the club had seen him, too. He gave a description to the police.

"Tall, well dressed, even featured—a typical playboy." This was what the manager had said. He remembered having seen this man in the Club Mephistopheles before. He had been there two nights previous when the gangs of Baroni and Dwyer had had their bitter battle. No one knew his name. But dozens of detectives were detailed to comb all the underworld of the city. Descriptions of the man were sent out to every precinct. Every patrolman on the beat was on the watch for him.

Inspector Burks of the homicide squad, called to the scene of wholesale murder, believed that he had seen the man also. He had his own opinion as to the man's identity. He remembered that it was at Frenchy's speak-easy on the night he had warned Baroni not to battle with Dwyer, that he had seen the mysterious stranger.

Detectives were sent to question Frenchy. Trembling and white-faced, Frenchy babbled the truth. The playboy stranger was not a regular member of Baroni's gang. He had helped Baroni in some way. Baroni had invited him to the fatal party. Frenchy had overheard Baroni and the stranger talking. The stranger's name was James Porter.

Armed with this information, the police increased their efforts. They even searched the membership lists of the exclusive clubs. Newspapers gave the man's name to their readers with the request that any reader who heard of him, telephone police headquarters immediately.

But no call came in. No one had heard of James Porter. The name was obviously an alias.

Inspector Burks, hearing this, swore fiercely. The police commissioner of the city was beside him at the moment. The Inspector turned to him, spoke with the bitterness of a man who is baffled and distraught.

"James Porter and Secret Agent 'X' are one and the same," he said. "Secret Agent 'X' is the man behind all these crimes. He's the murderer we want to get. I said so that night at Crandal's home. I say so again now. This city will have no peace until he is behind bars waiting for the electric chair."

The police commissioner nodded gravely, convinced that Burks was right.

And, sitting tensely in a restaurant in an entirely different disguise, Secret Agent "X" was studying the papers. There had been no time to make an investigation of the death room in the Mephistopheles Club. He had his own ideas about how the mass murders had been committed. He remembered that floral piece which had been presented to the gangsters with no name attached. The Black Master's drug-crazed slave had brought it in. The Black Master was behind those terrible deaths. But, in his horror at seeing the shambles in the room, Agent "X" had lost sight of the hophead who had disappeared.

HE knew at whom the hunt was being directed. Toward the man who called himself James Porter—toward himself. There was irony in that. He was fighting the Black Master, risking his life. So far he had come nearer to the truth than any one else; but the police were convinced that he was the murderer. The papers were calling him the Black Master.

From the description that Frenchy of the speak-easy had given, several staff artists on several newspapers had drawn pictures of the disguise Agent "X" had worn.

These were being run on the front pages of the paper as an aid in identifying him. He realized by what miracle he had escaped death in that room. But his own alert faculties were partly responsible; these and the fact that he had been suspicious of the hophead.

A floral offering! "Like a funeral," Nick Baroni had said, and the mass of gay flowers had masked a death more hideous than any one in the room had suspected. Why had the waiter kept looking at the clock? Why had he left like a frightened rat as the hands approached ten? The answer came forcibly to the Secret Agent's astute mind.

At the hour of ten, the Black Master had sent out the waves of radio impulse which had operated some hidden engine of death concealed in that mass of sweet-smelling flowers. The brain of a master criminal had conceived of the terrible plan.

Agent "X" was waiting, reading the papers, wondering when the police would examine the floral offering. But even if they did, he hadn't any hope that it would lead them in the right direction. The Black Master was too clever a man to leave clews that would point the way. The police might guess, as he did, how the murder had been committed, but they wouldn't be any nearer knowing who the murderer was.

As the Agent read the stories of the crime, studying, pondering, a special delivery letter was received at the city headquarters of the U.S. Department of Justice.

It was a letter that brought the chief of the office, working late, out of his chair. A letter that made him strike the desk with a clenched fist. It was a letter from the Black Master.

There at the bottom of the page in typewritten capitals the arch murderer's name was printed. There was nothing phony about it. The contents of the letter showed that it was genuine.

"Gentlemen:" the letter said. "At this moment you are reading newspaper stories and listening to police reports of the murders that have taken place at the Mephistopheles Club. Look at the mailing date on this letter. It was dropped in a post office box at ten o'clock. That was the hour that the murders took place.

"The writer of this letter has a weapon of such terrible strength that the Government cannot afford not to buy it. The Government has seen now what it can do. It has seen men stricken down at a precise hour in a terrible way. I am offering this weapon for sale. It is now on the market. Several countries are interested in it.

"My price is high. But if my price is not paid, other atrocities will follow. I destroyed a nest of rats tonight. The Government, I know, will thank me for this. But, if my price is not paid, a reign of terror will follow in which people who are not rats will die. If that is not sufficient evidence that I mean business, I will move my base of operations to the nation's capital.

"Think well over this. Consult with your superiors. My theft of the Crandal jewels will give me sufficient funds to carry on. I am prepared to wage an indefinite campaign until my demands are met. If some other country buys my weapon first, that will be America's loss."

The Department of Justice official read this letter again and again. He called his colleagues to his side. The city police heads were shown the letter. Messages flashed back and forth between them and Washington. But if the Black Master meant what he said, if he were not a madman, it was a baffling, terrible problem. No civilized country would consider the use of such a terrible weapon even in the chemical warfare branch of its army. The Black Master must be caught, destroyed, before his terrible campaign had reached shocking heights.

A day went by, and no progress was made. That evening, in his office, a public official received a threat. It was from the Black Master telling him that he had been marked for death.

He called up police headquarters. Squads of detectives and Government operatives were sent to guard him. A cordon was thrown around his home to see that no stranger entered. Motorcycle cops rode beside him as he left his office in his own private sedan. The chauffeur was an old and trusted employee. But a detective rode beside him.

When the official reached the safety of his home, he was prepared to stay under cover for days if necessary—for days till the Black Master had been caught. The block was cleared as the official's car rolled up to his house. Detectives watched from all sides.

Then, just before the car stopped, just before the door was opened, the official and the two men with him were seen to rise and clutch at their necks. As detectives rushed forward, they lurched from the car with purpling, hideous faces, clawing at their throats. They staggered, reeled, and fell dead on the sidewalk with their tongues protruding in the mocking, characteristic manner of the strangling death.

A hasty search of the car's interior revealed only one thing. The tiny electric bulb in its roof was broken. Bits of glass lay on the floor. The mystery of the Spectral Strangler was as black as ever.

CHAPTER XIX

THE SPIES' NEST

AGENT "X" READ about this murder in the papers. That night he called on Betty Dale. It was late. She had just returned from the *Herald* office. Her eyes were wide with fright and excitement.

"I was afraid," she said. "Afraid something had happened to you."

The Secret Agent nodded.

"The hounds are chasing a fox while a wolf runs free."

"The Black Master," she said. "Do you know that he made a broadcast to the papers tonight? Do you know he threatened a campaign of terror if the Government does not meet his price?"

The Agent shook his head.

"You wouldn't have heard about it," said Betty Dale. "The broadcast came just before I left the office. It was on a special short wave. They haven't been able to trace it."

"They won't," said the Agent harshly.

She saw by the burning, intense look in his eyes how deeply the news affected him.

"The whole city is hysterical over it," she continued. "Rewards are being offered for the Black Master's capture. My paper has offered ten thousand dollars. Colonel Crandal has offered another ten. The loss of his jewels—those murders at his home—have shaken him. He came to the office tonight. I talked to him. The police commissioner came, too. They all think it's you. If I could only tell them that it isn't!"

"Let the hounds of the law chase the fox," he said bitterly. "The fox will hunt the wolf."

Again fear sprang into her eyes.

"I am terrified," she said. "Terrified for you. He—the Black Master—seems able to strike anywhere. And you were there at the Mephistopheles Club when those awful murders took place, when all those gangsters were killed!"

He nodded and for a moment patted her hand. There was a light in his eyes warmer than the burning glow of the man-hunter. He was human for a moment, glad that somewhere in all the world there was one person who knew he was not a murderer, glad of the friendship and abiding loyalty of this sweet girl.

And the flood of color suffused Betty Dale's cheeks again. The Agent's fingers upon hers made her heart beat strangely. She wanted for an instant to have him put his arms around her, to melt into them and beg him for her sake not to risk his life. But this would be interfering, hindering the strange, important work to which he had dedicated his life. She spoke primly, almost casually, checking the flood of words that sought to pour from her lips.

"Be careful," she said. "Don't take any chances you don't have to."

Secret Agent "X" left her with grim determination in his heart. Three times now he had moved in the wrong direction. Each time, however, he had drawn nearer his goal; yet each time the Black Master had won the point, while Death kept score. The man, whoever he might be, was a monster of cunning as well as cruelty. He was holding the whole detective force of the city at bay, fooling them utterly. And now he had even dared broadcast to the papers, telling them of the campaign of terror he planned.

The Agent knew that the Black Master had a dual purpose in this. It was a free advertisement of the hideous thing he was trying to sell. He was letting the whole world know that the murder weapon he used was on the open market. He hoped by such means to start competitive bidding, to raise its price.

And this made the Secret Agent think of Piere DuBrong and the blonde woman, Nina Rocazy. What were they doing?

He made many discreet inquiries. Countess Rocazy had been staying at the Hotel Imperial for a few days. But she had checked out. It was believed she had gone South. Piere DuBrong had left for Washington. But a long-distance call to the embassy office elicited the fact that he was not expected back for several days.

A grim light showed in Agent "X's" eyes.

He changed his disguise, got one of the cars he kept out of a garage, and silently drove through the night. In the mid-town section, he parked his car and walked along a quiet street. Then he stopped in front of a small apartment building.

This was the place to which he had escorted the blonde after their memorable ride in the speeding taxi.

Was she still here? Was this her hideout when she wasn't playing the role of countess?

HE looked in the mail boxes. The name of Rocazy was not there. Perhaps she had another name, or perhaps she had moved again, gone quietly to some hideout where she could consort with her own kind. He did not believe for an instant that she had left the city.

The Agent remembered the location of her apartment. He stared up the side of the building. A fire escape moved past a window in one of the rooms she had had. The window was dark, curtainless. The apartment seemed empty.

But the Agent moved along the side of the building and drew himself up on the fire escape. Muscles hidden under his well-tailored clothes worked with springlike quickness and precision. Noiselessly he climbed upward till he was on a level with the third-floor suite Nina had had.

His observation from the street below had been correct. Nina's apartment was empty. Not only that. Plasterers had been at work getting the place ready for a new tenant. Small drops of splashed calcimine showed on the inside of the window.

Pressing his face close to the glass, he could see the workmen's stepladders, pails, and brushes standing in the middle of the room. All the furniture had been moved out.

It seemed futile to search for traces of Nina's whereabouts inside. But the Agent hesitated only a moment. His quick mind was working. He never overlooked small bets. He remembered a thing which he had noticed in his one quick survey of the place. The room had an open fireplace. An ordinary detective would have passed this by. But Secret Agent "X" tried to pass nothing by.

He drew his kit of chromium tools from his pocket, thrust the clawlike teeth of one under the window sash. The place was empty. He could risk a little noise now to gain entrance quickly. If there was nothing here, he did not want to waste time.

He pressed down on a rod-like handle which he fitted into the tool. The sudden, tremendous leverage snapped the lock. In a moment he was inside, walking on quick, silent feet. There might be someone in the apartment below. Overhead footsteps would attract attention.

Painters' canvasses, spread over the parquet flooring, helped to deaden the sound. He drew out his tiny flash light, turned its beam on the fireplace. Then he moved forward eagerly. An old broom leaned against the bricks of the fireplace. The painters had carefully swept the floor before starting work.

He had noticed that Nina hadn't been a neat housekeeper. A woman in her dangerous line of work had no time to think of the little domestic niceties. There was a miniature mountain of gray dust and gray ashes on the cold hearth of the fireplace.

The Agent had studied the habits of all types of people—careful people, slipshod people.

Crouching before the fireplace with his small light turned on, he began raking through the ashes and dust with a splinter of wood that the painters had used for mixing plaster.

He worked slowly, painstakingly, missing nothing that the fireplace contained. When he stopped at last, he held three objects in the palm of his hand—the stubs of two cigarettes with lipstick adhering to them, and the crumpled cardboard covering of a package of matches. He discarded the cigarette butts after a close examination of them. They had no name, but a sniff convinced him that they had been Russian.

His eyes glowed when he stared at the match paper. "Café Levant" it said. A border of gold stars and scimitars on a blue background framed the words. The Agent turned back to the ashes and raked again. He unearthed several bits of charred cardboard. These, too, were blue.

He had conclusive proof now that the woman, Nina, made a habit of going to the Café Levant. She bought her matches and cigarettes there. She flung her stubs and empty match papers in the fireplace. All this fitted in with his estimation of her character. She was exotic, slipshod. She might have changed her living quarters, but, if she were in the city, he doubted if she had changed her eating place.

Agent "X" left the apartment quickly and stopped at the nearest telephone. But the Café Levant was not listed. Grimly, purposefully, he called up the service department of the city's lighting company. He was a workman, he said, sent out on a job. Where was the Levant Café located? The girl on duty looked in her books, gave him the address.

The place was far downtown, near the water front. The entrance to it was shadowed by the elevated which snaked overhead like an endless black serpent. There were small cluttered shops of Syrian, Armenian, and Arabian pastries along the street. Agent "X" smiled. If she made a practice of coming all this distance to dine, she would undoubtedly keep it up.

The Agent, looking like a sight-seer who had casually wandered in, entered the grimy doorway of the Café Levant.

It was nothing more than a small, smoky restaurant serving Russian and Oriental foods. The large, greasy proprietor stood behind the cashier's desk near the door. There were a dozen people in the room, sitting at the small, soiled tables, and Agent "X" noticed one thing immediately.

The buzz of conversation ceased as he entered. This was a place where the same diners came night after night. It was a place unadvertized, unknown to the world uptown. The coming of a stranger was noticed at once.

But the Agent sat down casually at a table near the door.

He did not at first return the glances that were directed his way. Conversation began to rise again after a time. It seemed to him that it came in a medley of many different tongues.

His gaze swept the mixed men and women diners, and he saw then that their faces like their voices showed the blood of many countries. The Café Levant was the meeting place of at least a dozen different nationalities—the meeting place perhaps of international spies. And suddenly he bent down, staring at the menu card, hiding the glow of excitement that filled his eyes. For, sitting at a far corner table, talking to a shabbily dressed man, was the woman he sought, the blonde spy, Nina Rocazy.

CHAPTER XX

THE SPY'S BARGAIN

FROWNING AT THE bill of fare as though its exotic dishes were unfamiliar to him, the Agent finally signaled the hovering waiter. He ordered coffee and pastry.

Over the steaming cup of thick Turkish mocha, he furtively scrutinized each face in the room. However shabby their clothing might be, the people around him had a sharpness, an intelligence that seemed out of keeping in this smoky little place. There was a tenseness in their manner, an avid look in their eyes.

He had suddenly the impression that the room was filled with human vultures, quarreling, distrustful, hovering near some prize piece of carrion.

The blonde, Nina, did not glance his way, or, if she did, saw nothing to make her gaze linger. She looked older, more strained. The man with her was as tense and bright-eyed as a hunting hawk. They fitted in with the general atmosphere of this room. It was as though the murders of the past few days had whetted their appetite to possess the Black Master's secret weapon, as the sight of raw meat whets the appetites of a group of tigers. The heads of Nina and the man were close together.

What was she telling him, "X" wondered? Was she attempting to blackmail him also, as she had Greenford? Apparently not, for the man's face had the intentness, the greed, of someone who expects gain.

Agent "X" finished his light meal and left the Café Levant, walking swiftly away. At the end of the block, staring back over his shoulder, he saw the greasy-skinned proprietor come out onto the sidewalk and stare after him.

Agent "X" circled quickly, walked around the block and approached the café from the other direction on the opposite side of the street. There were little shops here, closed up for the night, their windows dark. He backed into the entranceway of one, fumbled a moment with one of his master keys, and opened the door softly.

In the dark interior he crouched, waiting. Looking through the dusty window at a slant he could see the door of the Café Levant. Those coming out of it would never see him, never suspect that they were being spied upon. He could take no chances now. Too many lives hung in the balance.

If the Black Master was not caught soon, the sinister threat of his presence would grow into a horror that would shock the whole nation. "X" had seen the gangsters wiped out like insects. The thought of innocent people being destroyed in the same way made something clutch at his heart as though icy fingers were pressing there.

There was no question in his mind but that those men and women in the Café Levant were spies, here in America to dicker for the Black Master's secret. Just as crooks sought each other's company, so, too, there were places where the undercover operatives of various nations gathered. But these in the Café Levant were, he guessed, for the most part the rabble. Their loyalty could probably be bought by any country willing to pay the price.

Several people entered the Café Levant; several emerged; but it wasn't until nearly an hour had passed that the blonde Nina made her appearance. The hawk-faced man was with her. He was tall, slightly stooped. He was still talking excitedly, leaning over her. They were absorbed, their faces close together in the darkness. This was no mere amorous intrigue. The softness of love in any form was not upon them. They were like two stalking jungle animals, male and female.

When they had nearly reached the end of the block, the Agent emerged. He closed the door of the shop softly after him, moved along in the shadows under the elevated structure. They took a cab down the block, and the Agent followed in his car.

Blocks away, in a Bohemian section of the city, the cab stopped and they got out. Agent "X" parked and got out also. He followed them again until the trail led to one of a row of small, old-time houses on a crooked little street.

Here artists and writers lived, radicals and long-haired poets. Here, too, apparently, international spies found refuge, for the man opened the door of the house with a key and entered with the blonde at his side.

There were no lights in the old house until Nina or the man pressed a switch. Then a glow appeared in a second-floor room. Apparently they had come here to continue the subject under discussion.

The Agent thought quickly. An impulse stronger than a hunch told him that these two were after the death weapon of the Black Master. Nina herself had informed him that that was her purpose in coming to America. She wasn't the type of woman to give up easily a thing she coveted.

SILENTLY as a shadow, the Agent sprang up the steps of the old house and unlocked the door with one of his skeleton keys. Then he checked himself and tensed. He had almost made a fatal error. He could pick any modern lock, open any present-day door, but a protective device on the door of this old house had blocked his way.

There was a heavy brass chain inside, bolted to the wall, its end slipped into a slot on the door. He could not reach it with his fingers. He had almost pushed the door against it. To have done so would have meant a rattle that might have warned the two on the floor above.

Many minutes of patient work would be needed to devise a way of unfastening that chain. The lower front windows were shuttered.

Grim-lipped, the Agent moved swiftly along the block and went around to the rear of the house. The rear door, too, was fastened with a chain. There was no fire escape snaking up the back of the old place, no way of getting to the unshuttered windows on the floor above.

But the Agent wasn't balked. There was still a possible way of learning what those two in the room were discussing. To do so, however, he had to reach the roof of the house they were in.

The houses in the row on the block were all of the same height and period. He walked along till he found another one empty. The old door, with no chain fastened, opened easily under one of the keys he carried. He closed it behind him and swiftly climbed the stairs.

Uncarpeted boarding creaked under his feet. A mouse squeaked and scurried away. There was a smell of dust and mold in the air. It reminded him of his own hideout in the old Montgomery mansion far up the drive.

He reached the attic, found an old iron ladder leading up to a skylight. It was the work of a moment to un-snap the four hooks that held the skylight cover in place. A second more and he was up on the tarred roof, three stories above the street.

Counting the houses as he moved, he crossed swiftly from roof to roof until he was on the building where the two had gone in. Looking cautiously over the coping, he could see the glow of their windows a story below. The shades were closely drawn. From his vantage point he could not look in. The skylight, he knew, was fastened on the inside. The two in the room imagined themselves safe from all listeners. But the Agent drew from his pocket a device which might invade their privacy.

He unfastened a flat, black leather case, took out the delicate mechanism it contained. It was perhaps the smallest telephonic amplifying device in existence—a thing that he had worked patiently on in his spare moments.[21]

A dry battery like that in the smallest flash light gave it power. Wire hardly thicker than thread connected between the single earphone and the amplifying microphone of the instrument. He had fifty feet of the wire strung on a small reel like a spool. This spool was pivoted inside the case itself.

He walked softly to the chimney in the center of the roof, stood on his toes and stared down. It was a two-passage chimney connected with open fireplaces in the front and rear rooms. This he had guessed as soon as he had seen the old house. It had been built in the days when open fireplaces were the only means of heating. There was a faint glow visible far down the sooty throat of the chimney. But it was not the glow of a fire. No smoke or heat was coming up the chimney. It was the glow of the light in the room shining into the fireplace. A gas stove probably supplied heat, and they had not bothered to light a fire.

The Secret Agent held the microphone end of his miniature amplifier in his right hand and slowly lowered it down the chimney. He unreeled the threadlike wire with his left. He dared not drop it all the way. If it appeared in the square opening of the fireplace, it would give warning to those below.

---

21   AUTHOR'S NOTE: *From hints he has let drop during conversations I've had with him, I am certain that Secret Agent "X" has made a profound study of all electrical instruments which might aid in his pursuit of criminals. These include dictaphones, dictagraphs, tel-autography, teletype machines, amplifiers and many types of sound and light reinforcing mechanisms.*

By the length of the wire he had lowered, he estimated the distance. The bell-shaped microphone of his instrument must now be close to the room where the two had gone. It must be hanging just out of sight in the fireplace.

He made a turn of the wire around the chimney to hold it, then stooped and bent over his delicate mechanism. He switched on the small dry battery, the voltage of which had been stepped-up with special chemicals. Two brass screw heads gleamed inside the case. One induced clarity. The other regulated volume.

WITH the receiver of the amplifier clamped to his ear, the Agent crouched in the darkness of the roof and began to listen. At first only a faint blur of sound reached him. He turned the delicate knurled head of the clarifier adjustment. Gradually the blur of sound resolved itself into human voices. But they seemed faint and far away—the voices of pigmies talking in some subterranean cave.

His fingers remained on the clarifier adjustment till the sounds had reached needle sharpness. Then he turned on the volume control.

Like a distant radio station coming into earshot, the voices in the room below grew in size, grew till it seemed that the lips of the people who spoke were close to the Agent's ear. His tiny-microphone, made with exact scientific skill, was doing its work.

He could even hear the extraneous noises that the two in the room made, the faint stirring of their feet, the creaking of a chair, the noise the man made as he cleared his throat.

It was Nina who was speaking at the moment.

"I am nervous, Gustav—always nervous since Grenfort was killed. I am ready almost to give up—and go back."

Agent "X" heard the woman's restless footsteps as she paced. A man's harsh, jeering laughter sounded.

"That is the way of women—brave until danger comes!"

"But Grenfort—"

"Grenfort was a fool, a bungler. You are talking to Gustav Mogellen now. He does not bungle. Grenfort did something to anger this absurd madman who calls himself the Black Master. We don't know what. We cannot say. But I have not angered him. I have treated him with deference like the lunatic he is."

"You are a fool yourself to talk like that, Gustav. The Black Master is not mad. He is a criminal, and he wants money just as you and I do."

"Bah—all Americans are mad."

The man chuckled softly, then spoke to the woman again.

"They will have something to be mad about later when they find that a nation was willing to buy what they scorned and feared."

"You are sure, Gustav? You do not intend to trifle with the Black Master?"

"Trifle! I might, in a gay moment, trifle with you, a charming woman, but I would not trifle with this madman. I tell you Gustav Mogellen is wise. He does not trifle with infants, animals, or madmen. What I have told him is true. My country is willing to meet his absurd price."

"It seems unbelievable," gasped Nina.

"Unbelievable! Unbelievable that a small nation like mine should want to possess a weapon that will give it dominance over others! In the event of war—" There was a slap as the man below struck his fist against the palm. A laugh followed the blow. "In the event of war we should win by the sheer horror we would inspire in our enemies. Armies would refuse to fight. Men would throw down their arms. In my two sessions with the crazy monster in that mad office of his, I have convinced him that I am not fooling. I would not dare fool. Each time I have left it, I have been followed, shadowed. One slip, and I would die like our dear friend Grenfort. Tonight I go to make final arrangements. Tomorrow night, to show my good faith. I will give him an advance payment of fifty thousand dollars—a mere option—but he has agreed to cease his sensational activities and wait quietly till the payments are completed. In a few weeks the weapon that all men fear will be ours."

CHAPTER XXI

THE CHAMBER OF DEATH

FOR NEARLY AN hour, or until the tiny battery in his amplifier began to give out, the Secret Agent listened. The man, Gustav Mogellen, gloating, triumphant, continued to impress the woman with his astuteness.

Agent "X" wondered if her fear were genuine, if she were not playing some deeper game. He wouldn't trust her not to murder the man, say that he had been killed, and take whatever commission his government planned to pay.

But that didn't interest him. It was the immediate future upon which his mind was set. A foreign power was planning to pay the Black Master his price, buy Mark Roemer's stolen formula. This must not happen! The murderer of Bill Scanlon must not escape.

With tense, quick fingers the Secret Agent reeled in the thread-like wire of his amplifier. Carefully, fondly, he put it away in its case. That tiny instrument was all that had stood tonight between America and a plot that might become a menace of world importance.

His eyes were glowing with that strange, burning light as he left the roof by the way he had come. There was much to be done, a hundred chances that he might slip up.

Far down the block he waited, watching the door of that house where Gustav Mogellen had discussed his plans with the blonde. And it was toward midnight that he saw Mogellen emerge. The man, dressed in a dark overcoat walked quickly into the shadows.

Now as never before Secret Agent "X" used his uncanny skill as a shadower. Mogellen looked around once, saw nothing, and strode on. He seemed confident that no one guessed what affairs he was about.

Agent "X" saw him take a taxi at the junction of the street and a nearby avenue. The Agent followed blocks behind in his own car. His sharp, burning eyes, staring ahead, missed nothing.

When the taxi turned a corner, he sped up. When at last it slowed and stopped, he, too, parked, still blocks behind. But he almost ran through the darkness. He was watching as the man, Mogellen, entered a block of empty office buildings. The onward sweep of the city seemed to have left this section deserted. Business offices had been moved farther uptown. No wonder Mogellen in his talk with the blonde had referred to this place as the Black Master's "mad office."

The Agent saw Mogellen look around once, then fit a key into the building's front door. He saw him disappear inside. Two hundred feet ahead, Agent "X" saw another flitting shadow.

He crouched back in the darkness. The man in front was the hophead, the murderous, vicious employee of the Black Master. He saw the man creep forward into the building after Mogellen. He stayed there, no doubt, close at hand, unseen, ready to kill the visitor if anything went wrong.

For twenty minutes the Agent waited amid the darkest shadows on the opposite side of the street. Then he saw Mogellen emerge and move rapidly off. The small, wicked-looking dope fiend slipped out of the building and followed after. The man, probably, had been instructed to shadow Mogellen all the way home, to kill if his actions became in any way suspicious. But Mogellen did not look back. He walked swiftly on, disappearing down the block.

Agent "X" remained in hiding a half-hour longer, then stole forth and quickly crossed the street. He was at the very gates of death now. But he gauged his time. He must search this building while the hophead was away shadowing Mogellen, and finish his search before the man got back.

Noiselessly he fitted a key into the lock and entered by the door through which the spy, Mogellen, had gone. Did the Black Master live here, or was it only his place of conducting business? The cold, damp chilliness of the unheated building made "X" believe that the latter was the case.

Risking sudden death, not knowing what he might find, he began probing with his tiny flash light. In the dust of the floor he was able to trace Mogellen's tracks. He followed them, coming at last to the small, strange office on the second floor. The Agent saw instantly that there was only one door into this office.

He flashed his light, then waited breathlessly—waited for possible death. But nothing stirred. In that one flicker of light he had noticed the mirror covering the rear wall, the mirror with its metal panel down the center.

It had meant nothing to the disordered mind of Taub, the dope fiend. To Agent "X" it instantly conveyed meaning.

He had seen such mirrors in the doors of high-class speak-easies in the days of prohibition. From them the proprietors could look out, but no one could see in. The proprietors could tell just who was ringing the bell, customer or prohibition agent.

Just so the Black Master could look through this mirror at any visitors who came into his office. Was he behind it now? The thought that unseen, sinister eyes might be upon him was spine-chilling. But the Agent gambled all on logic. He felt the surface of the mirror. It was as cold as the rest of the room. It seemed unlikely that the Black Master would linger on in this cold, damp place. He had no doubt left at the conclusion of his interview with Mogellen.

Working on this theory, risking all, the Agent boldly switched his flash light on and began examining the mirror. He soon discovered the round crack in the center of the panel and guessed that there was a secret opening here. It clarified many things in his mind. The hophead had probably never seen the face of his employer. No one, conscious of the fact, had ever looked at the features of the Black Master and lived.

Agent "X" tested the opening in the panel. It was, he saw, fastened tightly on the inside.

He went out into the hallway, investigated, and found that in the remodeling of this office the whole second floor plan had been changed. There was no visible entrance to that room behind the mirror. The way by which it was reached might be from almost any direction. There might be a secret stairway leading up or down, passageways leading even through empty buildings into some other street. To hunt for the hidden entrance would be a lengthy process. Worse still, it would scare the Black Master away.

The Agent knew then that the man must be outwitted if he were to be caught at all. Quickly, quietly, he went away from the mysterious office, leaving it exactly as he had found it. A theory was building up in his mind—a theory that had slowly been dawning. To test that theory he began to construct a startling, fantastic plan.

IT was twenty-four hours later, with darkness again spread over the city that Agent "X" climbed for a second time to the roof of the house occupied by the blonde woman, Nina, and Gustav Mogellen.

Lights burned in the windows of the second floor. The hour was ten. Secret Agent "X" carried a leather suitcase in his hand. He knew that the two were again in the room. He had shadowed them there. He was prepared to risk everything on the plan he had devised.

He took a box from his suitcase, opened it, and again lowered something on a wire down the chimney. But this time it was not a microphonic amplifier. This time it was a small metal cylinder capped at both ends.

One of the caps was held in place by a strip of fusible metal. Electric wires were attached to this in such a way that when current passed through the wires the fusible metal would heat up and melt—releasing the cylinder's cap and the cylinder's contents.

The Agent lowered it swiftly. At the instant that it appeared in the square opening of the fireplace below—the instant a faint shrill scream told him it had been seen, he touched a switch connected with a small but powerful storage battery in his suitcase. Nothing happened apparently. But the scream was not repeated. No sounds came up the chimney from the room below.

The Secret Agent drew his cylinder back up. He rewound the wire and packed it in his suitcase. Then he took out a strong rope. One end of this he fastened to the base of the chimney. The other he lowered over the rear edge of tile roof and climbed down it agilely.

He was not careful to be quiet now. He knew there was no one to hear him. He jimmied a window on the top floor and climbed in, pulling his suitcase after him.

Down through the house he went to the room below. The lights were still on. The Agent held his breath and threw up a window. Then he waited outside a few moments. When he entered again, the night air had cleared the room of the anesthetizing gas it contained—the gas he had released so quietly from his metal cylinder.

The forms of a man and a woman lay on the floor. One was Nina, the other, Gustav Mogellen. Both were breathing quietly, as though in a deep untroubled sleep. They would remain so for hours.

The Agent deposited the woman on a couch, made her comfortable. She was a killer, a murderess at heart, a plotter of evil; but early training made him always more gallant to women than to men.

Gustav Mogellen he propped up in a chair and tied there with a piece of rope.

A small leather brief case was on a table. The Secret Agent went over, opened it, and examined the interior. The brief case contained fifty thousand dollars in United States currency. It was in bills of large denomination, done up in neat packages. The Secret Agent smiled to himself. Here was the "option" money to be paid to the Black Master tonight. He added a package of tens and one of twenties from his own pocket, then put the money back in the brief case, returned to the side of Mogellen. For long minutes he studied the man from every angle. There was no line of the face, no skin blemish, that he did not take note of. Tonight the Agent's very life, the lives of perhaps untold others, depended on his skill.

He set to work then on one of the most masterly disguises of his career. With his make-up materials spread on the small table, with his pigments, face plates and volatile plastic materials before him, his dexterous fingers began to accomplish the seemingly impossible.

With clinging, quick-drying face putty, the Agent duplicated Mogellen's hawklike nose. The planes of his face followed. At the end of half an hour it seemed that two Gustav Mogellens were in that small room. If the blonde Nina could have regained consciousness at that moment, she would have thought the gas that knocked her out had made her see double.

WHEN all was ready, when the Agent had put on the last finishing touches, practiced Mogellen's walk, imitated the sound of his voice as it had come to him over the amplifier, he took the keys from the spy's pocket and picked up the brief case.

He crossed the room, shut the window, slipped into Mogellen's hat and overcoat. Turning out the lights, he descended to the street and locked the door after him. He was going to meet the Black Master tonight for the first time. Even if the Black Master's dope-crazed slave were watching outside, he would not guess that the man he saw was not Gustav Mogellen.

The Agent traveled swiftly through the night in a hired taxi. He left the cab behind him, walked along a block of silent, empty buildings. Whether the hophead was waiting to follow, to spy on him, he did not know or care. At the moment he was not Agent "X." He was Gustav Mogellen, international spy, interested in making a down payment on a secret and horrible weapon that was for sale.

He fitted Mogellen's key into the lock of the deserted building, entered, and closed the door after him. He listened a moment. His sharp ears detected faint movement somewhere in the darkness. The murderous hophead was following close at his heels.

He entered the small strange office on the floor above and turned on the lights. This time as he did so he heard some mechanism in the door click metallically and the lock snapped shut. He was trapped in the room.

He looked at his watch. It showed one minute to midnight. He waited, fingering his tie, registering the uneasiness that a spy might be supposed to feel on such a strange mission.

Then a voice spoke to him out of thin air. A strange, harshly disguised voice that he had heard before. The voice of the Black Master.

"You are on time, Gustav Mogellen. You are anxious to clinch the bargain!"

A second of silence followed, then the Agent answered.

"One does not keep the Black Master waiting," he said, imitating the voice of the man who now lay unconscious in the house a mile away. "I have the money I promised. I am ready to seal the contract. My government has kept its word."

A dry chuckle came from overhead.

"Your government has done well. Yours will be a strong nation. Approach the panel between the mirrors. I am ready to accept the money—and remember! You are locked in this room—a prisoner until our negotiations are completed."

Agent "X," posing as Mogellen, hesitated a second.

"When," he said, "can I hope to receive the secret weapon? I shall have to cable my government for details?"

"When the last payment is delivered," said the Black Master. "The quicker the payments, the sooner the thing that you seek will be given into your hands."

"And you will remain silent and hidden from now until all payments are completed?"

"Yes. There shall be no more killings. The Black Master will appear to be dead. He will appear only in this room to transact his business with you."

The Secret Agent nodded. He came close to the panel between the mirrors. A small, six-inch opening in its center appeared as if by magic. The fingers of a hand reached out. They were black-gloved, almost invisible against the blackness of the opening. The Secret Agent thrust a package of his own ten-dollar bills into the hand. The hand withdrew.

"For your own convenience," the Agent said, "I am making payment in small bank notes. Big bills arouse suspicion and are more easily traced."

"You are thoughtful," came the sneering voice of the murderer.

A package of twenties followed the tens. The fingers of the Black Master's hand seemed to express the inhuman greed that their owner felt. They curled avariciously, reaching for more bills.

Then it was that the Agent's left hand dipped into his pocket and drew something out. So swiftly that it was like a trick of legerdemain he transferred the object he had removed to the palm of his right hand, slipping a package of bills over it. Under cover of the bills, his finger pressed into it. It was a small thimblelike cap with a sharp needle point at its end.

He passed the package of bills to the eager, black-gloved hand of the arch-murderer. Then, quick as the head of a striking snake, he jabbed the needle on the thimble cap into the Black Master's hand.

One faint, harsh cry came through the black hole in the panel

The Secret Agent's hand darted through it—clutched the arm of the man inside, drew it toward him, and turned the beam of a small flash light into the opening that was left.

The light rays fell for a moment on a masked face.

The Agent thrust the mask aside—and gave a harsh exclamation of surprise. For seconds he stared tensely; then he let the inert body of the man inside fall.

As it did so, a signal bell sounded somewhere in the building. To his horror, Agent "X" heard stealthy, quick footsteps answering the bell. He guessed instantly that the hophead he had seen was only one of several vicious degenerates who were slaves of the Black Master.

His scalp prickled as seconds passed. The threat of unseen death stalked through the empty spaces of the dark building. The seconds deepened into minutes—one—two—three. Then suddenly, the lights in the room went out. The Agent was alone in the strange, dark chamber with the knowledge that doom was creeping upon him.

CHAPTER XXII

THE MAN BEHIND
THE MASK

HE WAITED TENSELY till a faint noise sounded over by one wall. There was a scrape of metal, the mouselike squeak of a hinge. A mysterious panel door was opening. He could not see it, but his sharp ears and tensely alert mind told him what was happening.

Agent "X" moved then. He took three silent strides to the wall, flattened himself against it, and inched toward the spot where the noise had come from. His fingers crept ahead of him, feeling, exploring. They discovered a break in the wall surface, and he paused, as still as death.

He could hear faint breathing now. A man was standing only a few feet away, crouched before the opening that the panel had left.

Secret Agent "X" drew back on his toes. Then, using the flat of his hand and his arm like a battering ram, he gave the unseen man a violent shove. At the same instant, he leaped through the break in the wall. With a jarring, sickening thud he bumped into a human body. In one and the same motion he clutched the man, whirled him around, and threw him headlong. Then his swiftly groping fingers found the panel and drew it shut.

As he did so, something crashed against the closed metal—something that had been thrown at him and missed. The tinkle of breaking glass came; then a horrible gurgling scream sounded. It was a scream of terror, of agony, of stark despair. It was followed by the thud of wavering, stumbling footsteps. Clawing fingers slid down the panel, beat against it, but the Agent held it shut. To open it meant death for himself as well as those others now beyond human aid. For faint, acrid fumes seeped around the edges of the oblong of metal. They were burning to the nostrils, constricting to the throat.

The stumbling footsteps inside grew more disordered. Two bodies thudded to the floor. Then silence—the silence of death—filled the strange dark building.

The Agent waited for minutes more, holding the panel shut, until the seeping fumes had thinned and vanished. Then he opened it cautiously. The air inside was still stuffy but breathable. The last of the fumes slipped out of the room into the passageway in which he stood and passed him like an evil spirit escaping.

He turned his flash light into the chamber. Horror met his eye. Two huddled figures lay on the floor, their faces contorted by the strangling death. But the skins of both and the dilated pupils of their staring eyes indicated that they were drug addicts. The tongues of both were thrust from between blue lips as though mocking him. But the Agent had not killed them.

They had died by the force of the evil thing they dealt in—died by the weapon with which they had tried to snuff out the Agent's life. Small splinters of glass lay on the floor by the bottom of the panel. They told a hideous story.

The Secret Agent stooped over the body of one of the dope fiends who would murder no more. He felt in the man's pockets. Wrapped in a nest of cotton was a tiny crystal globe. It might have been a Christmas tree ornament—but it wasn't. The Agent didn't need to be told what it contained.

It was a globe of imprisoned gas—corrosive gas so strange and deadly that it had the power to constrict a man's throat until he choked to death. Gas, however, that would dissipate after a few moments of contact with the hydrogen in the air, losing its power, leaving no trace, its deathly work done. Gas that was Mark Roemer's secret—a horrible weapon which he had discovered during the course of his researches and planned to discard—but which unprincipled governments desired as a weapon of war. It was more efficient than lewisite or mustard gas which left trenches uninhabitable for hours and prevented a conquering army from moving in. It could be used to attack civilian populations, to create a reign of terror worse than long-range guns or air bombs. The Secret Agent shuddered, glad that he had been in time.

HE looked around the room for a moment. The whole story was here. The dead hopheads. The sinister crystal globe. Those glass splinters on the floor—and the unconscious man behind the barrier of mirrors. Who was he? Let the police find out. When they came there would be little to do—except batter through the mirrors and make the most sensational arrest in the city's history—the arrest of the Black Master.

But there was one question burning in the Secret Agent's mind. Where was Mark Roemer—kidnapped chemist? He was a witness needed to complete the amazing denouement. The Agent turned his light into the opening of the wall panel again. The mouth of a passage showed.

He entered this, closed the panel after him, and walked forward till he came to a flight of secret iron stairs leading up. He went cautiously. There might be more of the murderous hopheads. He probed with his flash light, listened every few seconds; but he encountered no one. The stairway led him to an attic of the building. Here were three rough bunks, a table, packs of well-thumbed cards, and a smoky oil lamp. Here were the quarters of the Black Master's slaves. Then he saw a heavy door with a lock upon it at the end of the room. There seemed to be a closet-like room behind it. The lock had been newly placed there. The Agent's eyes gleamed, and he took out his kit of chromium tools. The lock gave him some trouble, but he finally opened it.

As his flash winked on, it illuminated the thin, haggard face of a middle-aged man. The man had evidently been waked from sleep by the Agent's work upon the lock.

He was crouched back on a small, rusty bed in this windowless room—crouched fearfully like a frightened animal. He did not cry out, but his bony hands lifted. There was the fear of death in his eyes. His feet were fastened to the foot of the bed by chains and the bed was bolted to the floor.

"Roemer!" said the Agent tensely.

"Who are you?" The man, who had been kidnapped and held a prisoner for days, spoke in a shaken, terrified voice.

"Never mind! Listen to what I say and all will be well!"

The Agent walked forward, his burning eyes commanding the gaze of the kidnapped chemist. A low-voiced conversation followed. At the end of it Secret Agent "X" left the room, descended by a series of iron stairways to the ground floor, and passed quietly out into the street.

Before changing his disguise Agent "X" did two things. He stopped in an all-night drug store and bought a heavy manila envelope and stamps. Into this he put the packs of bills he had taken from the spy Gustav Mogellen. He placed cardboard around the bills, sealed the envelope up carefully and addressed it in disguised writing:

"To Mrs. William Scanlon, care of U. S. Department of Justice, Washington, D.C."

Once again his lips moved as he whispered that sentence that had rung through his mind like a war cry in his battle with the Black Master.

"A kid and a woman are waiting."

Fifty thousand dollars wouldn't compensate for the death of a beloved husband and father. But it would make life easier for a woman who had a young son to bring up.

"I hope he turns out as swell as his old man," the Agent muttered huskily. Then he turned and moved into a telephone booth.

A HALF-MINUTE later, a mysterious call came into police headquarters. It was a call that brought the sleepy desk sergeant up from his blotter with a jerk. The sergeant tensed as he listened. His hands gripped the telephone like claws.

When the message was ended, the sergeant asked the name of the person who had given it. There was no answer. A low laugh sounded. Then the receiver at the other end clicked up.

The sergeant, red-faced, his eyes bulging with excitement, called Inspector John Burks, head of the homicide squad. He dared even to get Burks out of bed, refusing to listen when Mrs. Burks said her husband had a cold.

"Cold, hell!" said the sergeant. "I got a tip-off. The Black Master's been caught. Mark Roemer's been found!"

When the inspector came to the telephone, the tenseness in the sergeant's voice, and the news that he had, electrified Burks into action.

In ten minutes he was speeding down town in an official car with two police cruisers and a squad of detectives trailing him. He went to the address that the mysterious party who had called the sergeant had given. This was an old and apparently deserted office building on a dark and run-down street.

The next half-hour was one of the most exciting in Burks's whole career.

What the police found in that building Burks told a group of tense press reporters who had gathered like buzzards, following the wailing sirens of the homicide cars.

Burks was still mopping his face from the intense activity of the past few minutes. He knew that the newspaper men were waiting. He knew that he was the man of the hour. With trembling fingers, he lit a cigar and blew smoke from his nostrils before he spoke. They were standing in the Black Master's small office. The double mirrors were broken now, smashed in by police axes. Burks waved his hand toward them.

"That gave us the biggest job, boys," he said. "Those mirrors were eight inches thick."

A tall red-headed reporter edged forward. No one seemed to know him, but he had a press card. There was a faintly malicious gleam in his eye.

"How was it the man behind those mirrors didn't scram while you were breaking them down?" he asked.

"Wait—I'm coming to that," said Burks a little irritably. "First I want you to know that we've got the Black Master and Mark Roemer, the man he kidnapped. Roemer has told us his story. He was being held to make the gas he'd invented when the supply on hand ran out. He didn't want to do it. He would rather have bumped himself off— but Roemer's got a young daughter in finishing school. The Black Master threatened to kill her if Roemer didn't do as he was told."

"And who's the Black Master?' shouted the reporters. "Come on, Inspector—don't hold out on us!"

Burks grinned like a showman about to display a prize exhibit. He waved his hand, gave an order.

"Bring him out, boys!"

TWO perspiring cops came through the jagged opening broken in one of the big mirrors. They carried the limp body of a third man. This man had a black mask over his face. The reporters seethed forward.

"Take it easy," said Burks. "You got a big surprise coming."

With a sweep of his hand, he drew the black mask back.

The reporters tensed. One of them swore harshly.

"God! Colonel Gordon Crandal!"

"That's the boy," said Burks. "He won't do any more murdering now. He's headed for the hot seat or the bug house."

"It can't be! It sounds phoney," said a rosy-cheeked reporter.

"I thought so, too," answered Burks, "until Roemer spilled all the dope."

"But Crandal's own jewels were stolen!"

"I know it. He stole 'em himself to get the insurance. He'd lost all his money in the stock market. He didn't have a cent left—and he was too proud to work. Too proud, too, to sell his house or the jewels. He wanted to keep on being a gentleman. He had to have a lot of money quick—so he figured out a way of doing it. He was in the chemical warfare division during the Big Fuss. He knew what the stuff that Roemer had, the gas, was worth. He must have been shell-shocked, I guess, to turn into the kind of crook he is."

"He's not dead then?"

"No—only knocked out. I wanted to get him alive—make him stand trial."

The troublesome red-headed reporter asked another question.

"You were pretty clever to knock him out before you broke down the glass!" he said.

Burks glared at the speaker.

"The police have a lot of tricks up their sleeves," he said.

"And this joint," went on the reporter, "only a pretty smart bird would have thought of looking here. How did you get wise, chief?"

A slow red spread over Burks's face.

"I've told you guys all I'm going to," he said.

"One more question, chief," persisted the redhead. "Didn't you pass it out a few days back that the bird who committed these murders was a crook named Secret Agent 'X'?"

"I was working on a bum steer," said Burks defensively. "But I delivered the goods in the end, didn't I?"

"All by yourself," muttered the redheaded reporter innocently. His head was bent. He seemed to be writing on his notebook. When he straightened up, Burks was glaring at him. For the space of five seconds the two men's eyes clashed. The reporter carelessly dropped a leaf from his notebook and mumbled:

"I've got to be getting back to the office."

He turned and left while Burks stood staring, frowning and puzzled. His footsteps clattered down the stairway, and suddenly from the night outside an eerie yet melodious whistle sounded.

Burks swore and started for the door. But as he did so, his eye fell on the scrap of paper the red-headed reporter had dropped. On its white surface something had been written, a small penciled letter—the letter "X."

Before any one else could see, biting the end of his cigar nervously, Inspector Burks moved sidewise and planted his foot over it. There he stood, the look of puzzlement in his eyes, while the strange musical whistle in the night outside grew fainter and fainter and finally died away.

BOOK III

THE DEATH-TORCH TERROR

Death hurled a ghastly challenge at Secret Agent "X."
A torch of terror burned above Doom's table where
they played. And charred, unsightly corpses were the
jackstraws dealt him by the grim gamester's boney hand.

CHAPTER I

PLOTTERS OF CRIME

TENSELY, NERVOUSLY, THE four men in the semi-gloom of the padlocked speak-easy waited. Their faces gleamed in the flame of the single candle that flickered and guttered on the dust-laden bar. Their whispers disturbed the stillness of walls that had once echoed to drunken laughter and the clink of liquor glasses.

One of them was pacing restlessly. His quick, jerky steps crossed and recrossed the spot where, months before, the speak-easy's owner had dropped under the flaming snouts of gangster guns—the spot where he had gasped out his life in a hideous welter of blood.

Sinister stains showed on the floor. Ghosts of a harrowing past seemed to lurk in dark, chill corners of the room—ghosts of murder, intrigue, and violent death.

The pacing man was "Monk" Magurren, ex-mobster and beer runner. The three with him were underworld colleagues, banded together tonight in response to a single motive—greed.

Magurren paced on, his shadow moving across the bloodstained floor like a portent of evil to come.

The others were trying to conceal their impatience. "Slats" Becker sat slumped in a chair, a limp cigarette hanging from his lower lip. "Doc" Wiser, sleek and immaculately dressed, examined his nails with studied carelessness. Tony Garino, hair black as night, face as cold and white as marble, was hunched in brooding silence.

They were a sinister crew—human wolves who had followed the lawless caravan of prohibition in the years when King Alcohol ruled the underworld. Each had made and lost a fortune. Now, like wolves denied their accustomed prey, they were hungrily out for whatever fare they could get.

Monk Magurren jerked a jeweled watch from his vest—a relic of former grandeur. His voice rasped with impatience as he glanced at the dial.

"Ten-ten. Why the hell don't he show up? He's got a noive keeping guys like us waiting. He's screwy, I tell you!"

Slats Becker drew a bundle of century notes from his pocket. He spread them on the table in front of him, gestured and shrugged.

"He may be screwy—but these is real leaves he hands out. They look good to a bird who ain't seen a greenback since your Uncle Sam put the skids under old man Volstead."

Magurren stopped before the little gangster, stabbing a bony finger toward his face.

"Did you ever see a big shot like him?" he cracked. "Answer me that, mug!"

The tongue of flame killed the police car's driver.

"So what?" said Becker carelessly. "So what?"

"He's phony, I tell you. That's what. He ain't told us about the job he wants pulled."

"It's O.K. by me so long as there's a little gun play," said Becker. He patted his right-hand pocket fondly where a flat automatic rested. Those snaky, skillful hands of his had written a dozen grim pages in the black book of Death. They were ready to kill again.

"Gun play!" sneered Magurren. "You got that guy sized up wrong. He ain't no big shot, I say. You never heard of him, did you? You never seen him before?"

The others shook their heads. Magurren, arrogant and talkative, was voicing their own secret thoughts. The man who had hired them, arranged for them to meet him here at ten, was a mystery to them. He had them guessing, worried.

Tony Garino spoke, spreading his soft, white hands.

"Maybe he'sa come in from Chi," he said. "Or maybe he'sa just got outa stir."

Monk Magurren snorted.

"I know all the good guys in jail this side of Frisco—an' I don't know this mug. He's just a cheap crook tryin' to get tough. He's got his mitts on a little dough and he thinks he's a big shot. Leave it to me to show him up, I'll—"

The gangster stopped speaking as abruptly as he had begun. Neither he nor his cronies had heard a sound. There had been no creak of window or movement of door. The place had been deserted when they came in. But now a tall, arresting figure walked out of the gloom at the end of the bar and moved into their midst.

"Good evening, *gentlemen!*" The voice that spoke was low, mocking, ironic.

MONK MAGURREN crouched back, snarling in his throat like a startled animal. Slats Becker dropped his cigarette. Doc Wiser slid a tense hand into his right coat pocket, and Tony Garino made a serpent's hiss between white teeth. All of them riveted their eyes on the man who had so suddenly and mysteriously appeared.

"Meester Jones," said Garino, "we didn't 'a' hear you come in!"

The stranger surveyed them silently. His tall figure was clad in a simple, dark suit. His hair was sandy, his face ordinary looking. But there was something in his gaze that made the men in the room shift uneasily. His eyes had a burning, compelling light in them that seemed at odds with the mildness of his features. Force radiated from them. There was a glint of grim humor in their depths as though the stranger called Jones were laughing at the expense of the four gangsters.

It was Magurren who first recovered his swaggering poise.

"Well," he said. "What is it you want us to do? Spill it!"

The stranger ignored this blunt question. He inclined his head toward the rear door of the speak-easy.

"Get going," he snapped.

Magurren bristled.

"I don't go blind on anything, boss. I used to be a big shot myself. I wanta know what's up."

"Yes?"

"Yeah. Don't act like you was the king-pin."

Magurren, sneering openly now, went on when the stranger who called himself Jones didn't answer.

"We know you ain't never had a mob before. We wanta see that you don't get into trouble. Come on—give us the dope!"

The intense, burning light in Jones's eyes silenced him suddenly. Jones motioned toward the door again, and somehow his mild features conveyed a note of inexorable command.

Grumblingly, the four men obeyed, filing toward the rear door of the speak-easy. Jones blew out the candle. In a moment he was ahead of them, guiding them. They crossed a courtyard of broken flags, turned through a door in a fence, and came into a side street. A big limousine was parked at the curb. It was long and low and black, with lines that suggested speed and power. There was something sinister about it, something that made the four men hesitate before getting in.

But Jones held the door open and motioned imperiously. Becker, Garino, and Wiser got into the back. Magurren climbed in front. Jones took the wheel himself.

AN uneasy silence followed as the big car slid smoothly into gear and rolled off. It gathered momentum with incredible swiftness, slipping through the dark streets almost soundlessly. The high-speed motor ran as quietly as a watch. The car was of some foreign make, and Monk Magurren noticed that, whoever Jones was, he could drive like a demon. With an ease that seemed unconscious, he wound his way through traffic, clipped corners, and sped across town.

"Where are we goin', boss?" asked Magurren, his tone a little more respectful now.

Jones didn't answer. He was staring straight ahead, a faint smile on his face, a smoldering light in his eyes. Magurren began to bluster again.

"We want action," he said. "We ain't had no excitement since all the punk grocers in town chiseled into the booze racket."

"Action!" Jones echoed the word softly, and Magurren saw then that the big car was slowing down. They were on a familiar street—too familiar to suit Magurren. He glanced uneasily about as the car stopped. Ahead of them, down the block, was a big, gloomy building, a building with two green lights in front of it.

"Say, what's the idea?" Magurren rasped.

Jones turned in his seat then, faced them. The light in his eyes had an almost uncanny brightness.

"Action!" he repeated. "You don't want a soft job, do you? You want excitement. Well—you're going to get it!"

"Whatta yer mean? Dat's police headquarters down dere!"

"I know it. That's where we're going!"

The sentence was like a thunderbolt. Fury showed on the faces of the men in the car.

"Say, you double-crosser! You—"

Jones held up his hand. "Don't get me wrong! You're not going to have charges pressed against you. You're going there to do a job."

A breathless silence followed. Then Slats Becker croaked a question. "What kind of a job, boss?"

"Kidnap the commissioner!"

Disbelief, bewilderment and utter amazement showed on the faces of the four gangsters. As they saw that Jones was serious, the slow pallor of fear followed. They wanted action, but they hadn't anticipated such an unheard-of, desperate act as this.

"You're nuts!" said Magurren harshly. "You been feedin' on hop if you think—"

The stranger called Jones cut him short. His mild face had suddenly assumed granite hardness. He crouched forward in his seat, seeming to tower over them.

"Four-flushers!" he barked. "Action you want, eh? Tough guys, eh?"

He laughed then, and the sound that came from his lips was like the taunting, insulting smack of fists lashing across their faces. Monk Magurren stiffened. His features became mottled with anger. The suave Doc Wiser trembled and the fingers of his right hand grew rigid as a hawk's claw. Garino bared white teeth in a snarl. His eyes were black pools of fury.

"Listen, boss, you can't talk like that. We'll—"

Jones surveyed them again. His taunting laughter had accomplished its purpose, whipped their pride and conceit, made them ready to face death.

"O.K.," he said shortly. For a moment he fumbled under his seat, and the gangsters started when they saw what was in his hands. Four black automatics. He thrust one toward each man.

"Take these," snapped Jones. "Park the ones you've got in the car!"

He watched eagle-eyed to see that they obeyed. Then he issued swift instructions.

"Becker and Wiser stay outside. Magurren and Garino come with me!"

Wonderingly, tense with excitement, the gangsters followed their mysterious leader.

Two plain-clothes men were lolling outside headquarters. They grew alert as Jones approached with the others trailing him. Police automatics appeared in their hands. Headquarters was under heavy guard, and the four mobsters knew why. It made the job that Jones was trying to pull seem like utter madness.

"What's your business?" said one of the detectives. "Stand back!"

JONES acted so quickly that it left the four gangsters breathless. His hand flashed into his coat, swift as the head of a striking snake. His fingers came out grasping a gun like the one he had given to them.

Before the detective could fire, there was a hiss, a jet of vapor, and without a sound the plain-clothes man collapsed.

Magurren, catching on, fired at the other man. The strange gas gun that Jones had given him worked perfectly. Unharmed, but completely out, both dicks lay on the sidewalk. And Jones passed inside.

He moved with lightning speed now. An alarm would soon be spread. He had to penetrate to the commissioner's sanctum before this happened. The desperate thing he was doing depended for its success on strategy. The desk sergeant bellowed a question. Jones's answer was another jet of vapor from the muzzle of his own gas gun. With a grunt the sergeant collapsed behind his desk.

Jones seemed to know the layout of headquarters. He bounded up the stairs to the second floor, leaving Becker and Magurren on guard below. He made his way along a corridor, burst open a door that was marked: "Commissioner's Office."

A big man with a cigar in his mouth rose abruptly from a chair behind his desk. In one and the same movement, his hand reached toward a signal panel with many buttons on it. But Jones stopped him with a wave of his gun.

"Don't do that, commissioner!"

The commissioner's jaw dropped, his hand hesitated. He had distinguished features, a well-formed face, a carefully trimmed black mustache. His mustache seemed to stand out now in sharp contrast to the whiteness of his skin. Fear of death showed suddenly in his eyes.

"Who are you?" he asked.

Jones, ignoring the question, uttered an abrupt command.

"Come with me, commissioner."

For another second the commissioner hesitated. He looked desperately about. It was late. He had dismissed his stenographer. His own cot, made up at the side of the office, testified to the fact that the police of the city were facing some sort of an emergency, a crisis so real that the commissioner felt his presence at headquarters was imperative every minute. It was this that accounted for the fear in his face. But the compelling look of the man who had burst into his office seemed to move him as much as fear.

His hands dropped limply at his sides. With a shrug he walked across the office to the door.

"Downstairs," said Jones. "There's a car waiting up the block. Walk toward it."

The commissioner started for the elevator, but again Jones's voice gave an order.

"Not that way—use the stairs."

Like a man in a trance the police commissioner did as he was told. When he reached the floor below, he shot one frightened look toward the desk, saw that the sergeant had disappeared, and his face stiffened. A door in the rear opened suddenly. A clerk started to come out, saw what was going on, and paused. Before Jones could fire, the clerk ducked out of sight.

The commissioner swore harshly when he glimpsed the prostrate bodies of the two detectives on the sidewalk. For a moment it seemed that he was going to turn and fling himself on the man called Jones. Cords in his neck stood out. He clenched one fist. But Jones's voice spoke softly.

"Take it easy, commissioner."

THE four gangsters, trembling violently at sight of this highest official of the city's police, closed in. It seemed that they wanted to hide their faces. They were like men clutching a bomb. They feared to keep it—and feared to drop it.

Jones gestured toward the car up the block. The commissioner moved forward mechanically.

When he was still twenty feet from it, there was a sudden sound behind. It was the shrill, ghostly wail of a police siren. A radio cruiser was coming up to headquarters. Jones heard startled cries as the cops in the car saw the two unconscious detectives on the sidewalk.

He flung open the door of the powerful car.

"Get in," he said harshly. The commissioner obeyed, and Jones ran around the side of the car and jerked open the door of the driver's compartment.

As he slipped under the wheel, with Magurren crouched tensely on the other side, hell seemed to break loose behind them. A squad of uniformed cops who had been lounging in the barrack room at headquarters, poured into the street. The frightened clerk had given the alarm. One of the cops had a riot gun. He knelt, aiming for the tires of Jones's car.

But Jones spun the wheel of the big sedan viciously, sent it shooting away from the curb in a dizzy arc. It seemed to spring over the pavement like a live thing. The police cruiser, with headlights glaring and spotlight turned on, came after them. The riot gun in the cop's hand stuttered into life, and a stream of low-flying bullets narrowly missed the big car's tires. One of them struck a hub cap. Metal popped and cracked, and the bullet screamed away into the darkness.

Jones, crouching over the wheel, spun around a corner. The engine under the big hood in front of him rose from a subdued purr into a muffled, throaty whine of gusty power. A hundred foam-flecked horses seemed to be whirling the car ahead through space. Then somewhere in the distance a police siren sounded—a second, third, and fourth gave answer. All the radio cruisers in the city appeared to be converging upon them, rushing to the scene of this most brazen and unparalleled of crimes.

CHAPTER II

THE MAN OF MYSTERY

THE FOUR GANGSTERS and the commissioner in the car with Jones were never to forget that ride. A madman seemed to be at the vehicle's wheel. Yet a madman with such uncanny skill that the big sedan responded as though it had the ability to hear and obey human commands.

It roared past an intersection, and two green police cruisers nosed out of side streets ahead. They came from opposite directions, stopped abruptly with squealing brakes. A score of short-wave radios were picking up the frantic appeals from headquarters. But the cops were in a tight spot. They couldn't fire on the speeding sedan without risking the life of the commissioner.

The patrolmen, therefore, sought to block the street, make the racing car slow down, and perhaps get a shot at the driver. To save the commissioner from what seemed certain death, a desperate gamble of some sort was necessary. They edged in at an angle across the street. The plunging sedan tore on.

At the last moment Monk Magurren, tough killer that he was, swore harshly, fearfully, under his breath. Slats Becker closed his eyes and gripped the tasseled cord that hung from the car's interior. The commissioner sat frozen with a glassy stare, swaying to the movements of the rocketing car like a propped-up corpse. Certain destruction appeared to stare them in the face.

The police cruisers shrieked their sirens in warning. A cop with a gun in his hand leaned out. He waved frantically, ordering the black car to slow down. It came on like a roaring, lurching fury.

The drivers of the cruisers tried to back away. It would have been too late in any event. It was the man at the wheel of the black sedan who saved the situation.

His mild-featured face set in mask-like immobility, he swung the car deliberately toward the curb. His sharp eyes had glimpsed a driveway leading to a garage. The sidewalk was empty. The car's fat tires cut into the driveway at a sharp angle. The car reared up, whizzed forward, and for dizzy, perilous seconds tore along the pavement itself with a wall on one side and the curb on the other. It passed the two glaring-eyed police cruisers.

Then Jones swung the wheel again. The big car leaped back to the level of the street. It left the five men inside bathed in cold sweat. It left the cops in their cruisers paralyzed into inaction. Jones, his face masklike as ever, applied brakes for an instant, whirled into a side street.

Over dark, rutted pavements the car sped forward. It seemed to crouch on each rise, gather speed, and leap ahead. It plunged down into the depressions like a speed-boat taking the swells.

The sirens of the radio cruisers behind resembled the confused baying of hounds that have lost the scent. They faded into the distance as the big car plunged on. Now and again, a new one sounded in front.

At such times, Jones at the wheel, bore away at right angles along some cross street. Once he cut through the uptown theater district, and again the men with him held their breaths and expected death. Grimly Jones held the siren of his own car down to clear the street of innocent pedestrians.

He whirled up a long avenue toward a section of cheap apartments. He bore across town again, till the river showed black and somber under the curtain of night. Then he struck a parkway and followed along it till he was on the edge of the suburbs.

For a moment he slowed the car's speed, quieted the engine, and listened. Somewhere, far behind, the wailing, complaining note of a siren sounded. But it seemed to be going in the wrong direction, taking the wrong route.

Jones smiled, pressing the accelerator again. The big car sped ahead once more. Suddenly he wrenched the wheel, pulled the car's nose around, tore through a sparse hedge that scratched and slapped against the wheels. Abruptly he bumped to a stop, extinguishing the lights.

Darkness lay all around them. They were in a vacant lot at the outskirts of the city. This strange parking space seemed to have figured in Jones's desperate plans.

"Get out," he said.

The gangsters obeyed now, cowed by the ride they had had,

cowed by the crime they had taken part in, and by the strange, amazing actions of their new boss.

Jones himself kept close beside the commissioner. The police chief's face indicated that he expected death. He appeared to think the vacant lot was a prearranged place of execution. But Jones led him on.

He crossed the lot with his little cavalcade following. The streets around it were deserted. A closed-down factory towered on one side, a vast bulk of blackness in the black night. Old, jumbled sheds and warehouses showed ahead. Jones picked his way toward one of these. He stopped, took a key from his pocket, and fumbled familiarly. In a moment he had opened a door and marshaled his men in. He jumped down a boarded passageway, opened another door, and entered a deserted shed.

A small pot-bellied stove was burning at one side of the room. There were bunks along the walls. It was a shed once used by a gang of laborers. Deserted and neglected, it made a snug hideout. Jones lit an oil lamp in a wall bracket. It cast a wan light over the dingy furniture. The windows were boarded up. No glow would show outside.

In brief sentences, giving no explanation of his motives, Jones ordered the commissioner to take off his clothes. When this had been done, he rolled them into a neat bundle and stuffed them under his arm. They contained all the police head's private papers.

Stripped to shorts and an undershirt, the commissioner stood tense and waiting. The four gangsters watched with amazement and wonder. They now seemed to believe that Jones was mad. But his bright, alert eyes held them in a spell of fear.

"I'm going to leave you," he said suddenly. "Hold the commissioner here until I come back."

Abruptly, as though disobedience on their part was out of the question, he went to the door, opened it and disappeared into the night.

The gangsters and the commissioner, listening, thought for a moment that they heard a strange whistle floating through the darkness. It was musical, yet eerie, seeming to fill the whole air at once. Then gradually, like an echo dying in the night, it faded away, leaving only blackness and mystery behind.

THE man called Jones didn't get back into the big car. He left it parked where it was in the vacant lot, concealed by darkness and the sparse, untrimmed hedge.

He walked briskly along the night-shrouded street—walked with the swift, easy stride of a man who has a definite objective. Once a police cruiser flashed by him, its radio crackling, two tense-faced patrolmen at the wheel. They barely noticed the darkly dressed man on the sidewalk with the bundle under his arm.

Once, a little later, Jones paused an instant in his stride to press a hand to his left side as a sudden twinge of pain stabbed close to his heart. But the pain passed and the man moved on. It was the pain of an old wound received in the flaming hell of a battlefield in France—a wound which doctors had predicted years before would kill him, but which his own amazing vitality had overcome.

He turned suddenly, entered the front gate of a house with a "For Rent" sign on it. The house was shuttered and boarded, but he took a passkey from his pocket, opened a side door, and let himself in. He moved across creaking floors, climbed a flight of stairs, and went to an old attic room. Here, under the sweep of low eaves, he was shut away from the whole night-darkened world. It was a temporary hideout that the strange man called Jones had possessed himself of without asking any one's leave.

He fumbled for a moment in a closet, drew out a big suitcase. Snapping it open, he took out an assortment of strange objects. One was an acetylene lamp with an adjustable, parabolic reflector. The current in the house was turned off, but when he lit this lamp, it made the shuttered attic room as bright as day.

He took out a collapsible mirror with three sides, set it up on a shelf, and studied his reflection for a moment. Then his long fingers began to move.

The contours of his face which had characterized him as "Jones" began strangely to disappear. Under the brilliant, violet glow of the acetylene light, a new face came into being. It was a face that not even his few intimate friends had ever seen—a face, the identity of which he kept guarded with a thousand masterly disguises.

The face that stared back at him from the mirror now was not like the gang leader called Jones. The blunt, nondescript features had disappeared. The sandy hair had revealed itself as a clever toupee.

Brown hair showed above a youthful forehead. The even nose, mouth, and chin looked boyish. But, when the man turned suddenly to pick something up, the light fell on his features at a different angle. New lines appeared then, making him look suddenly older, as though, like the disguises that so cleverly concealed him, his own experiences and adventures had numbered among the thousands. It was the face of a mature, poised man of the world—the face of Secret Agent "X."

WHO was Secret Agent "X"? Many people had asked that question. There were those who thought of him as a dangerous, desperate outlaw. The police of a dozen cities suspected him. Yet the underworld itself regarded him with hate and fear—for his life was dedicated to a strange, relentless warfare on criminals.

With unlimited resources at his command, with uncanny skill in the creation of disguises, with an utter disregard of the threat of death, he was a force that the most evil malefactors had to reckon with.[22]

The light in his eyes was burningly intent now. He began taking other objects from his suitcase, working with a definite, sure purpose. There were tubes of plastic, volatile materials. Other tubes of shaded, flesh-tinted pigments. There were tissue-thin nose and cheek plates to change the contours of the features, strips of transparent adhesive tape to draw face muscles into new shape—all the utensils and paraphernalia of the expert craftsmen in the art of disguise.

Along with his materials in the suitcase, Agent "X" removed a half-dozen photographs of a human face. The face was stern, dignified, heavily mustached. It was the face of the commissioner of police whom he had so lately kidnapped. These Agent "X" studied for long moments. They showed the commissioner's features from every angle.

It was a half-hour later that he rose from his seat in front of the three-sided mirror and took off his clothes. As he slipped into those he had taken from the police commissioner, even the commissioner's best friends wouldn't have guessed that the man in that room was other than he appeared to be.

Layer upon layer of the plastic, quick-drying material had molded "X's" face into new lines. It was material so mobile that it fol-

---

22 AUTHOR'S NOTE: An account in the First National Bank, on which he can draw under the name of Elisha Pond, is the source of Secret Agent "X's" vast funds. With a huge amount of money at his command, and with the complete, though unofficial, sanction of high Governmental heads in Washington, Agent "X" often does startling things in his conflict with crime—things so daring and unconventional that no other detective or intelligence operative would attempt them. Yet his actions lead always in the end toward a balancing of the scales of justice.

lowed every movement of the flesh beneath. The man standing there, buttoning up his immaculate coat *was* the commissioner to all intents and purposes. The wallet in his pocket, the various credentials, proved it.

In a moment more, with his hat and overcoat slipped on, he strode out into the street, ready to hurl a gambler's challenge into the very teeth of Fate and Death.

CHAPTER III

THE FLAME OF DEATH

FIFTEEN MINUTES LATER, a cop quietly patrolling his beat saw a staggering, reeling figure coming toward him. The cop gripped his nightstick, held himself tautly alert, then gasped. He leaped forward with a cry of amazement and concern.

The face of the staggering man, seen in the radiance of a street light, was familiar.

"Commissioner Foster!" the cop gasped.

The commissioner seemed too weak and dazed to reply. He collapsed on the sidewalk. His hat fell beside him. The cop saw a red welt on the commissioner's forehead. It was obvious he had been struck down by the men who had kidnapped him. He seemed to be suffering from amnesia.

The cop blew his whistle. An answering blast sounded far down the block. Another cop came running. This second patrolman, when he found what the excitement was, rushed into a house and put in a call to headquarters. The call was answered by two patrol cars and by a special police ambulance.

But by the time they arrived, the commissioner seemed to have regained his faculties. He was standing on his feet, aided by the cop who had first seen him. His hat was back on his head.

He waved the ambulance interns away impatiently.

"Take me back to headquarters," he snapped.

To the nervous, hesitant questions of the cops in the patrol car, he would make no reply. They soon lapsed into awed silence. He spoke once as the cruiser neared headquarters.

"Say nothing about this. If any member of the force lets it out, I'll have his hide."

The cops nodded. Whispers of the police commissioner being kidnapped had gone abroad. A few radio fans with short-wave sets

274

had picked up scraps of the frantic broadcasts that headquarters had sent out. Newspaper men were clamoring to know if there was any foundation in the rumors. But so far the police had stalled. Events of the past week had broken down police morale. For the public to learn that the commissioner had been kidnapped would come close to causing a panic. Now, with the commissioner safely returned, the whole thing could be hushed up. It would be a secret that would never get beyond official circles.

There was a mob of eager newspaper men waiting outside headquarters. Unceremoniously, the commissioner brushed through them. Their jaws dropped when they saw him. They fell back, talking excitedly among themselves. A few bolder spirits hurled questions at him, but he answered none of them.

Back in his office, however, his manner changed. His eyes gleamed with a strange, burning light. He mopped his face with the nervous intensity of a man who has been through a terrible experience.

Inspector John Burks, head of the homicide squad, and six other inspectors were congregated in his office. Their faces had a funereal solemnity. They gazed at him like a man come back from the dead.

"Was it the same gang, chief? Did they try to bump you off—burn you?"

It was Inspector Burks who asked the questions. When he said "burn" he was not using mere underworld phraseology. There was a grimness in his tone, harsh lines in his pale, heavily browed face.

The commissioner nodded slowly. "I think so," he said. "I escaped—I'm not saying how."

Burks leaned forward then. His voice was a hoarse whisper, as though the things he was about to say were too terrible to go beyond the confines of that room.

"There was another robbery early this morning, chief. A cop and a special guard were killed—burned. We thought you'd got it, too."

The others in the room nodded. They looked at each other and shifted uneasily.

The man behind the commissioner's desk knew what was wrong with these men. He knew what accounted for the grim lines in their faces, the haggard, half-furtive expression in their eyes. It was why the commissioner's cot was set up in headquarters. It was why the commissioner had prepared to stay there night and day.

With desperate speed Secret Agent "X" leaped along the hallway and down the stairs.

A CRIME wave more terrible and sinister than any he remembered was facing the city. The whole police force was jumpy, fearful. The department heads were on the point of losing their morale.

"Bring me all the records," he snapped. "I want to go over them again."

An official police secretary went to a huge safe that contained case histories that the public had never seen. There were many volumes in the safe. A miniature rogue's gallery. Letters of confession written by murderers who had long since paid the supreme penalty. Strange records of unusual crimes, and minutes from the latest police blotter.

The burning light in the eyes of the man behind the commissioner's desk intensified as the records were spread before him.

Here was a factual story to make a person's spine crawl. A series of bank and safe robberies unparalleled in the city's history was being committed. Worse still, patrolmen, detectives, and special guards were being killed hideously whenever they got in the thieves' way—killed by being burned alive. Six men had been murdered already. Their charred, hardly recognizable bodies had been found.

"If it hadn't been for their shields," muttered Burks hoarsely, "we'd never have identified Sullivan and O'Reilly tonight. Even their teeth, chief—were gone. How the hell did you escape?"

The commissioner waved the question aside as though it were unimportant. His eyes were fastened on the record books, the careful, unemotional details that had been put on the police blotter. Then he shook his head and looked up. These details told him little. Burks read the look in his eyes.

"There are no clews, chief—no fingerprints—and dead men don't talk."

The man behind the commissioner's desk nodded, staring straight ahead. He seemed to be thinking, pondering. He dismissed the other inspectors and remained closeted for fifteen minutes with Burks of the homicide squad—the man closest to the ever-present specter of death.

In that time Burks went over all that the police knew, verifying each item on the records. He was a little puzzled as to why the commissioner wanted to go over these things again.

Then the door opened as a cop came in. The cop touched his cap, said: "Those news hounds! We can't get rid of 'em. The desk phone rings every minute, and there's a pack of 'em outside. They want to know if you were kidnapped and how you got away."

The commissioner nodded. His face hardened.

"The less we tell them," he said, "the more curious they'll get. We'll have to hand out something. Who's in the mob?"

"A guy from every sheet in town—and that skirt from the *Herald*—Miss Dale. She's the worst of the lot."

"Betty Dale!" The commissioner uttered the name slowly. His face changed. A strange look came into his eyes. "Show her in," he said. "I'll talk to her alone."

IT was known that Betty Dale of the *Herald* had a drag at head-quarters. Her father had been a police captain slain by underworld bullets. As a kid she had roller skated in the very shadow of the precinct houses, sharing her candy and apples with the cops. She had been a favorite and a pet. Now she had grown to young wom-anhood. The commissioner's announcement that he would see her caused no comment. The other reporters made friendly jibes at her "wire-pulling" ability.

The commissioner dismissed Burks, sat back behind his desk, watched the door. High heels clicked in the stone corridor outside. The girl who came into his office had the blue eyes and the golden hair of a stage beauty. But her manner was briskly efficient. There was a worried frown between her arched brows. A pencil was poised in her slim fingers. She spoke with professional abruptness.

"Thanks, commissioner, for seeing me. People are wondering whether there's anything in the rumor that you were kidnapped. My paper would like a story."

For a long moment the man behind the commissioner's desk eyed Betty Dale. His gaze appraised her from her slim feet to the top of her head where her wealth of golden hair had the sheen of imprisoned sunshine. Smartly dressed as always, Betty Dale was a picture of loveliness. Far back in the eyes of the man who looked at her was something deeper and more personal than mere admira-tion. But his first words were startling, making the girl stare at him questioningly.

"The stage is set," he said. "The second act is about to begin."

The sentence seemed strange, meaningless. A slow pallor over-spread Betty Dale's face.

The commissioner smiled, rose, and shut the door tightly.

"Come closer," he said. "There is a fox in the lion's den."

Betty Dale began to tremble now. The man's words seemed to have a strange effect on her. She was staring at him as though she were looking at a ghost. Quietly he tore a corner from a small pad. As quietly he wrote something on it—the single letter "X." He held it up for Betty Dale to see, then dropped it in an ash tray and touched a match to it. As the smoke from it curled up, the girl spoke huskily.

"You!" she said. "It can't be!"

The man behind the commissioner's desk nodded somberly.

"To gamble is to live," he said. "And when death is close, men will gamble at long odds."

"But the real commissioner?" she asked. "Where is he?"

"Safe and sound in the fox's den."

Color began to come back to Betty Dale's face. Slowly she got hold of herself, stopped trembling. They were old friends, these two, Betty Dale and Secret Agent "X."

A hundred times he had fooled her with his disguises, but never in so startling and daring a manner as this. To come and find him sitting behind the desk of the city's police commissioner made Betty Dale feel that she could hardly trust her own senses. She gave one short, shaky laugh, relieving her nervous tenseness.

Agent "X" thought she had never looked so lovely. In that moment, when she was off guard completely, it seemed that there was a light in her eyes answering that subtle something in his.

There was a reason for the emotion that Betty Dale betrayed. This man, whatever his real identity might be, had been a friend of her father's, the police captain slain by murderers' bullets. The rest of the world might consider Agent "X" a desperate criminal, but she knew otherwise. She knew that even behind this daring thing he had done tonight lay some deeply hidden plan for combating crime.

She admired his unshakable nerve, sensed the strange magnetism of the man, and felt drawn to him so strongly that she sometimes had to hide her own emotions. She had vowed that she would never let sentiment interfere with his strange, important work. Now, with a ghastly crisis threatening the city, she disciplined herself more strictly than ever. When he took her hand, she let him hold it only a minute, then drew it away.

"What shall I tell the other reporters?" she asked.

"Tell them you've seen the commissioner," he said. "Tell them he looks all right, and that he speaks lightly of the report that he was kidnapped."

BETTY DALE bent her blonde head, made notes on her pad. Whatever Secret Agent "X" said she would do to the letter. She trusted him, respected him, as she did no other man alive.

"*Au revoir,*" she said; then, raising her voice as someone moved in the corridor outside, she added, "Thank you for releasing a story, commissioner. I'll quash any reports that you were kidnapped."

For a moment her eyes met the strange man's behind the desk. Then she stepped back and her slim, shapely figure vanished through the door. No one could want a more loyal ally than Betty Dale.

But Agent "X's" eyes were harsh. She had helped him many times, but he would not ask her to take part in the sinister struggle now in hand. It was too dangerous, too terrible. A moment later his eyes grew harsher still. For Inspector Burks of the homicide squad reappeared suddenly in the doorway. A gray pallor had overspread Burks's face. His voice shook with emotion.

"A call has just come in," he rasped. "There's been another slaughter, chief, and the worst so far. An attempt was made to rob the Merchants' and Manufacturers' Bank. Four men have been killed! It's the same gang that kidnapped you."

For a moment there was breathless silence. Then Secret Agent "X" stood up, his fist clenched on the desk. It was strangely, terribly ironic that Burks should be telling him this. The blackbrowed inspector who stood before him was one of the Agent's most unrelenting enemies.[23]

Inspector Burks caught his breath, gulped, and spoke hoarsely.

"I'm on my way now, commissioner. I'm going to look things over—and get those damned killers if it costs me my life."

Secret Agent "X" stepped from behind his desk, reaching for the commissioner's coat and hat.

"I'll go with you," he said, and his words were like the crack of a whip.

In silence the two men descended to the street below. The desk sergeant nodded, stared wide-eyed. Two detectives watched their departure grimly.

A closed headquarters car was already at the curb, the inspector's chauffeur at the wheel. Both men stepped into it—the car sped away with a whine of smoothly meshed gears.

Lolling back on the comfortable seat, Secret Agent "X" wondered if their investigation of the crime would bring results. His trip to headquarters, his kidnapping of the commissioner, had been futile. The police, though they had kept all details to themselves,

---

23 AUTHOR'S NOTE: On several occasions, Inspector Burks has accused the Secret Agent of some crime which he did not commit. An honest, stubborn, and hidebound official of the old school, Burks distrusts any but routine methods. Even when Agent "X," working sub rosa, helped him solve two famous murder mysteries, Burks refused to admit that he had been aided. The Secret Agent's brilliant departures from orthodox police technique make clashes between the two men inevitable.

were far from any solution of these terrible murders.

Agent "X" straightened suddenly. His eye had caught sight of something in the chauffeur's windshield mirror. He turned his head, looked out the rear window. Then his elbow nudged Inspector Burks's side.

"We're being followed," he said.

"What!" Burks's head turned, too. For seconds he stared back in amazed silence.

They had turned a corner, left headquarters behind. Back of them, appearing as though by magic, a low-slung dark roadster built like a racing car was following. The sides of the car were high. A black hood swept down to the narrow windshield in front. Side curtains made its interior dark. But Secret Agent "X" caught sight of light glittering on goggles. For an instant he looked into an expressionless, masklike face—a face that was like a crustacean monstrosity, distorted and made inhuman by some sort of weird helmet.

His fingers clenched over Inspector Burks's wrist. He was about to say something, but his words died in his throat.

One of the side curtains of the car behind bellied outward. The helmeted head appeared around the windshield's side. And, in the hands of the man whose features were hidden, Agent "X" saw the gleaming muzzle of some sort of weapon.

Inspector Burks shouted a hoarse warning, but his words were lost in the horror of what followed.

No report came from the weapon in the man's hand. But a blinding, white-hot jet of fire suddenly sprayed from it. It was like a ghastly will-o'-the-wisp, a torch of living, consuming flame suspended apparently in space. With a hiss of scorching enamel and burning fabric, the flame leaped forward and struck the back of Burks's car.

Agent "X" could feel the heat inside. A giant acetylene torch seemed to have been turned on them. He heard the snap of breaking glass, saw a tongue of flame leap over their heads.

The driver of the police car, looking back, glimpsed the bright ball of fire, too. He gave a cry of fear, tried to wrench the car into a side street.

The vehicle turned in its own length and the horrible jet of fire traveled along its side like water from the nozzle of a hose.

The full force of it, sizzling, intensified, touched the window by the driver's seat. The glass melted and ran down in a hissing liquid stream. The tongue of flame licked inward in a blasting wave of heat like breath from the mouth of an inferno.

Before their horrified eyes the driver, with a shriek of fear dying on his lips, wilted in his seat. His head became a mass of ghastly, licking flames. His features disintegrated. His clothing caught fire, and, with a jarring crash, the car, with dead hands on the wheel, plunged across the curb toward a building.

CHAPTER IV

MURDER SCENE

AGENT "X" FELT sickened, paralyzed. The stench and reek of scorching flesh was in his nostrils. Horror pressed upon him like a black, smothering wave. Then something hissed beside him. The flame was probing for the rear of the car again.

Like a coiled spring unsnapped, Agent "X" came to life. He reached forward, grasped the car's wheel, gave it a twist, and slewed the front tires around just as the car struck. It saved them from the full, shattering concussion of a head-on crash.

The big vehicle hit at an angle and scraped ahead to a shuddering stop with its radiator cap almost in a doorway.

Secret Agent "X" was hurled against the front seat, almost on top of the dead chauffeur. Inspector Burks thudded against his back, fell to the car's floor. The inspector was swearing fiercely, trying to pull himself up. The white-hot searing flame of the burning death behind them was seeking them out again.

Agent "X" heard a shrill squeal of brakes as the murder car sought to check its speed. It stopped, began to back, and the snout of the mystery weapon swung around in a murderous arc. The flame hissed brightly, relentlessly, again.

In one and the same movement then, Agent "X" thrust open the car's door that was on the side facing the building and leaped out. Grabbing Burks by the arm he drew the man unceremoniously after him. A space of five feet separated the front of the car from the building's door.

The men in the murder roadster were playing the flame over that space, preventing any escape in that direction. Agent "X" with the inspector beside him crouched behind the big metal body of the car. The death flame licked against the car's opposite side, played a hissing, horrible tune of doom. The wall of the car became red-hot. The fabric began to smoke. Another window gave way and the flames licked through toward them.

The searing torch of destruction was searching them out. The inspector had drawn a police automatic from his pocket. Cursing like a maniac, he began firing back toward the murder car, his bullets going wild. One side of his coat was scorched. His eyes were bloodshot. As the flame ate through the window on their side, Agent "X" drew him down behind the protection of the car's big engine. The tongue of searing death whistled above their heads now. The space between the car and the building's side was getting as hot as a furnace. The horrible threat of being roasted alive faced them.

There came a shriek like a thousand howling banshees. The flame's heat had ignited the car's gas tank. The screw cap had blown and a jet of burning gas was whistling through the vent, mingling with the flame of the death torch in the hands of the murderer.

For a moment the night wind whisked a curtain of dense vapor along the car's side. And in that moment Agent "X" pulled Inspector Burks toward the doorway. He literally hurled the man ahead, flinging himself after, running the awful gauntlet of flaming death.

The murderers in the car couldn't see them. Crouched back in the doorway Agent "X" glimpsed the goggled and helmeted killer leaning far out, playing the death flame on the smoking, crackling police car. Then the car's gasoline tank let go, as the pressure became too great for its metal walls to stand.

The whole rear of the car ripped open. The murder torch licked in and around it until the car became a flaming inferno, a funeral pyre for the dead driver.

The hideous goggled head of the killer withdrew. With a scream of gears the roadster leaped ahead and tore up the street out of sight.

Windows on all sides were opening now. Excited people were screaming. The flames of the burning car were threatening to fire the building against which it lay, as sprayed gasoline ignited.

Burks, with the pallor of a man who has looked into the face of hideous death, drew a shaking hand across his face.

The building in the doorway of which they had taken refuge was a cheap rooming house. Terrified people were opening the inner door: a fat woman in a bathrobe, a man with hair standing on end, two gangling youths. Agent "X" pushed them back.

"A phone! Quick!" he cried.

The fat man made ineffectual gestures. "X" ran on till he saw a coin box phone against the wall. In a moment he was dialing the operator, turning in an alarm. There would be fire engines here presently and cars from headquarters.

He heard the first of the engines from a nearby station roaring up the street. The chassis of the burning police car was glowing red hot. All fabric and upholstery were gone. The driver in the front seat was hardly visible, but there was still the nauseating, horrible odor of burning flesh in the air. Agent "X" had seen many men die, but seldom with such sudden stark brutality as this.

A POLICE cruiser whirled up the block. Hand extinguishers from the red fire truck were beginning to quench the blaze as the crowd gathered. Bedlam reigned in the street. But Agent "X," in the role of the commissioner, spoke quietly.

"We were on our way to look at a murder, inspector," he said. "Let's get going."

Inspector Burks nodded. There was nothing they could do here. The driver of the police car had long since been beyond their help. Other cruisers were arriving and a squad car full of detectives. Agent "X" commandeered it, leaving two cops in charge of the burned and wrecked sedan. Three radio cruisers followed them as escort. Inspector Burks, still trembling, sat back breathing heavily.

"They almost got us," he croaked. "If it hadn't been for you, commissioner—"

He did not finish, but a strange, harsh smile played over the lips of Secret Agent "X." What would Burks say if he knew that the man whose cool-headedness had saved him from that hissing murder flame was the person he had hunted and tried to trap as a criminal?

"We know now how the killers do it," "X" said. "That was some sort of flame-thrower. *Flammenwerfer*. But not the kind the Germans used in the Bois d'Avocourt or those of the British on the Somme in '18. This is something new. It is murder modernized, inspector!"

For a moment a question flashed in the bloodshot, frightened eyes of Inspector Burks. He looked at the commissioner sharply, wondering apparently how the commissioner could give offhand dates like that. Secret Agent "X" had almost made a slip.

"I suspected it from the first," he said, quietly. "I've been doing a little research." The man of a thousand faces was on his guard again. Burks must not know that every weapon of modern warfare was familiar to him.[24]

They plunged on in silence, shaken, sickened, by what they had been through.

THE building in which the Merchants' and Manufacturers' Bank was housed took up half a city block. It was a bulky, old-fashioned flat-roofed skyscraper of twenty stories. The street outside was filled with curious, morbid people now. Ropes had been stretched across the bank's front by the police, holding the crowd back. A dozen or more cars were parked close by.

The police lines opened instantly to let Inspector Burks and the man impersonating Commissioner Foster through.

But Agent "X's" pulses were hammering excitedly. Every faculty was alert. He knew that in coming here he was taking a dangerous chance. His disguise might be perfect, but he didn't know the commissioner's inner thoughts, or all the people with whom he associated. He might make the wrong answers, might arouse suspicion. He planned to get away as soon as possible.

For an instant he glanced at the outside of the bank. It was one of the city's smaller financial institutions, a private bank controlled by five partners. Three of these partners, Burks had said, had been slain. Honer, Osterhout, and Davis were their names. Their bodies were still inside, where, surprised in late conference by the raiders, they had met death under the blast of the terrible *Flammenwerfer*.

But it was the body of the special bank guard in the corridor outside that Agent "X" first saw. He turned his eyes away from the charred, grotesquely sprawled figure. Except for the man's blackened badge, it might have been impossible to identify him. Even the bones of his face and his teeth had been eaten away by the withering heat of the killer's torch.

The bodies of the three bankers, John Honer, Eric Osterhout, and Jerome Davis, in the business room behind the cashiers' cages, were in hardly better shape.

Detectives were checking up, making identification from the blackened, heat-corroded watches, cuff links, and cigarette cases

---

24 AUTHOR'S NOTE: Agent "X" once expounded to me his theory of the course that future wars would take. He mentioned various defensive and offensive weapons used by the Allies and Western Powers in the debacle of 1914-18, showing that he had come in contact with them all in his work with the Intelligence Service.

that lay beside the corpses in the piles of grayish ashes that had once been clothing.

Two of the dead men had been burned on both sides of their bodies, reduced to unrecognizable carcasses. The third, Davis, had received the withering flame on his face and the front of his body only. His features were ghastly but still recognizable.

The Agent studied the position and condition of the corpses for tense moments. Then he looked at the huge vault in the bank's rear. Marks of cutting tools showed around the edges of the locks. It had withstood the onslaught of the raiders' attack, justifying the faith of its builders.

"Has the vault been opened?" he asked. "Is everything all right?"

"We don't know, sir. We're waiting for Marsh and von Blund, the other partners. They're on their way."

Burks, standing at the Secret Agent's side, shot an abrupt question.

"Were there any employees besides the bank guard around?"

Mathers nodded.

"I talked to von Blund on the phone, called him right after I got here. A cashier and one of the bookkeepers were working overtime, too."

Inspector Burks face grew hard.

"Get their names—find them," he barked.

"I'll have to wait, sir, until—"

Mathers didn't finish, for the police lines were opening to let two well-dressed men through.

"That's them now," said Mathers. "They'll give us the dope."

Marsh and von Blund, the surviving partners, gasped with horror as they passed the body of the murdered bank guard. How much had Sergeant Mathers told them? Were they prepared for the added shock that awaited them? Evidently not, for von Blund, the older of the two, a blond, stern-faced man in his early forties, stood speechless at the door of the business room. He swayed, leaned against the wall, his eyes starting from his head. Marsh, shorter, stockier, with the poker face of a typical financier, stood with hands clenched at his sides.

It was von Blund who spoke first.

"Eric!" he gasped. "My God, Eric!"

AGENT "X" saw the man turn his eyes away from that unsightly relic on the floor which had been his friend and partner, Eric Osterhout.

"We went through the war together," muttered von Blund brokenly. "Even that couldn't separate us. But now—" He clenched his fist. "If the law doesn't get those fiends, so help me, I will!"

Agent "X" walked close to the body of Eric Osterhout. Detectives were pulling something from the ashes—a tiny metal pin with the crossed wings of a flyer on it. Agent "X" took it in his palm, stared at it. He spoke quietly to von Blund.

"Your friend must have gone in for aviation," he said.

Von Blund nodded. "In war and peace," he answered, "it was one of his hobbies."

Inspector Burks edged up impatiently and shot another question. "Mathers tells me there were two employees of the bank here with your partners. Where are they?"

For a moment von Blund and Marsh looked at each other, then they stared at the inspector.

"Haven't you seen them?" asked von Blund harshly.

"No."

With quick steps the banker crossed to a desk behind the cashiers' cages. His fingers trembled as he drew out a book giving a list of employees' names and addresses.

"Spencer and Cox," he said. "One was our head cashier—the other was in the bookkeeping department."

"They've disappeared," snapped Burks. "That's evident."

"Call up their homes," said von Blund. "It isn't like them to run away unless—"

"Unless," echoed Burks, "they had something to do with the job that was pulled tonight."

Secret Agent "X" spoke then, pointing to the vault.

"It doesn't seem likely. The cashier must have known how to open the vault. If he—"

But Marsh, the stocky partner, spoke quickly.

"Only the five of us knew how to do that," he said. "But maybe Spencer thought he could. Maybe that was why—"

"It might be a good idea to look inside," said Agent "X." "Perhaps they got in after all—and closed the vault behind them."

Von Blund nodded. But a quick examination of the vault's interior, after he and Marsh had opened the great door, showed that nothing had been touched.

"Thank God for that," said von Blund fervently. "Our depositors won't suffer, anyway!"

But Inspector Burks voiced a sinister thought that was in the Secret Agent's mind also.

"The raiders didn't make the grade this time, but what will stop them from trying again?"

Von Blund clenched his fist.

"We'll land them in hell if they do. I'll hire a squad of special guards. We'll have machine guns posted. Eric, John, and Jerry lost their lives to protect the funds entrusted to them. We'll see that they didn't die for nothing."

There was a quaver in von Blund's voice, but Agent "X" wondered if any stratagem an honest man could devise could checkmate the fiends who put men to death with hissing flame.

SERGEANT MATHERS came back with a frown on his face.

"I've called up the homes of Spencer and Cox," he said. "They haven't returned, but they were here tonight, all right. It looks, Mr. von Blund, as if—"

"I won't believe it," cried von Blund. "They've been with us for years. They were honest, I tell you. Perhaps those fiends kidnapped them."

Inspector Burks, cynical veteran of a thousand homicide cases, spoke grimly.

"Sentiment is a fine thing, von Blund. But don't let it get the best of your reason. Spencer and Cox were probably bribed by the murderers to make things easy. When the raid failed, when they couldn't open the vault, they made a get-away. I'll start a dragnet. I'll have every outgoing train and boat searched and have all roads watched."

The disappearance of Spencer and Cox added further complications to the chain of ghastly murders. Had the cashier and bookkeeper of the Merchants' and Manufacturers' Bank been mixed up in the raids of the flaming torch killers all the time? Or had a bribe or some hidden, sinister threat made the two employees of the bank betray their trust? Agent "X" pondered this.

"The D.A.'s on his way, too," said Burks harshly. "The public's been riding him, and he's got it in for you, commissioner! You know the row you and he had last week!"

Agent "X" nodded, but his eyes grew suddenly bright. What row did the commissioner have with the district attorney? That was something the blotter at headquarters hadn't indicated. It was time he left before he made some slip in the presence of the alert D.A.

"I've got to get back to headquarters," he said abruptly. "There's another angle of this thing I'm working on."

If Inspector Burks felt the commissioner's sudden decision to leave was odd he didn't indicate it. Perhaps he thought the commissioner wanted to avoid unpleasant contact with the D.A. This was the case, but not for the reasons Inspector Burks might have assumed.

The inspector accompanied Agent "X" to the door and mapped out his campaign for trapping the two runaway bank employees.

"If we can catch 'em," he said, "we'll sweat 'em till we find who the guys are that hired 'em. I don't believe they pulled this job alone."

At the door of the bank, Inspector Burks suddenly swore and stabbed a finger toward the street.

"Look! There's that nut, Banton," he said, "trying to get in and pull a snoop act again. He forgets he ain't with us any more and that we don't let four-flushing agency dicks sit in if we can help it."

Agent "X" stiffened. He had never heard of Banton. The inspector spoke as though here were a character well known to the commissioner. "X" turned his head, saw a red-faced, gross-bodied man trying to shove through the police lines, as a cop forcefully restrained him. When "X" opened the door of the bank he heard Banton's angry voice.

"I got offices in this building, I tell you," the man was saying. "You can't keep a guy away from his own place."

As Banton caught sight of Secret Agent "X," a look of sneering familiarity overspread his face.

"Be a sport, commish! Let a guy look around. Just because you kicked me off the force don't mean I'm poison. There's a reward out for these killers. I can use dough as well as the next person— and your gang ain't showin' up so smart!"

There was a bitter slur in that last phrase that Agent "X" caught. The finely tuned mechanism of his memory was working now. Banton! The name stirred recollections. There had been a big police shake-up, a cleaning out of grafters a few years ago. Banton was the name of one of the lieutenants whose resignation had been "gratefully received." "Kicked off the force," Banton had said.

AGENT "X" in the role of the commissioner walked toward Banton. The man's lips curled back from stained teeth and he made another slurring remark.

"A swell bunch of sleuths you got, commish! I been in business myself for nearly two years, and I ain't never been licked on a case yet. That's why I want to look in on this. You can't keep me out either, commish. I got diggin's right in the bank building."

Agent "X," acting as the commissioner, waved his hand.

"Let him look around," he said magnanimously.

"Thanks, thanks," sneered Banton. "Big-hearted of you—commish! You always was a square guy, weren't you?"

The eyes of Banton gleamed with bitterness and hatred, and Agent "X" went on his way wondering. Police were being slain, burned alive. Banton, kicked off the force on a graft charge and now in the detective business for himself, would be worth investigating. Was it possible that bitterness and a deflated ego could account for the brutality and ruthlessness of these strange crimes?

Speeding to headquarters in an official car, Agent "X" tensely pondered these things. He would stay in headquarters just long enough to look up the records of Banton.

Back in the commissioner's office he started to take off his hat and coat, then paused. Following his entrance there came a sudden sound of excitement downstairs. He heard an elevator click open. Then there were louder sounds in the corridor outside—the noise of pounding, running feet.

Suddenly the door of the commissioner's office burst open and an angry, disheveled man stood in the threshold—a man with a shabby overcoat wrapped around his tall, sparse body.

Police Commissioner Foster!

Speechless for a moment, Agent "X" faced the man he had impersonated. He realized in that instant that the weak-kneed gangsters he had hired had got cold feet—let their prisoner go. And, as he stood collecting his thoughts, the commissioner raised a trembling finger and pointed toward him.

"Arrest that man," he said. "He's a criminal and an imposter."

CHAPTER V

A SUSPECT

A **HALF-DOZEN DETECTIVES** crowded in the doorway behind the commissioner. All eyes were focused on Secret Agent "X." The room became charged with a tension that was almost electric.

The Agent met the commissioner's accusing gaze calmly. By no movement or gesture did he betray any indication of nervousness. But he fully sensed what a desperate spot he was in.

Since he worked always beyond the law he could not expect any official support if his identity was discovered. He would be exposed and convicted as an imposter and dangerous plotter, convicted probably as an accomplice of the killers who were terrorizing the police. But his voice was as steady as his manner.

"This is absurd!" he said. "Have you any documentary proof to back up your claims? You must be a madman!"

"Madman!" The commissioner's face became a mottled, almost apoplectic red. He turned, made gestures toward his men. "Arrest him, I say. He's the criminal who kidnapped me."

Agent "X" drew the commissioner's wallet and papers from his pocket, spread them out on the desk in front of him. With a grim smile on his lips he pointed to them.

"Here are papers which give the lie to your wild claim."

The commissioner gritted his teeth in fury.

"You stole them," he cried harshly. "You stole my clothes and my papers. You are an imposter and you know it!"

"Is that so? Can you prove it?"

For a moment a baffled, helpless look crossed the commissioner's face. Then his chin shot forward and his eyes snapped fiercely.

"Yes," he barked, "I can prove it! When I came into office I ordered every patrolman, detectives, and department head fingerprinted. Prints were taken of every member of the city's police including the commissioner. The records are right here in this building. Let them be brought and I'll match prints with you. We'll see then who's the imposter."

A brief, bleak smile came into Agent "X's" eyes. In the person of the commissioner he had a worthy adversary. The man was alert, on the job. Fingerprints didn't lie. Inside five minutes the Secret Agent would be shown up and trapped as an imposter.

But he made a quick gesture, gave an imperious order.

"Get the fingerprints in file F," he said. "Tell Deputy-Inspector Taylor or one of his assistants to come to my office at once."

He spoke with such assurance, seemed so familiar with the routine of headquarters, that the detectives in the door wavered in uncertainty. One of them went to get the fingerprint files. The commissioner, clutching his shabby coat about him, glared fiercely at the man who had usurped his office and duties.

Secret Agent "X" seemed not to have a care or worry in the world. He dipped his fingers into an inside coat pocket, drew out a cigar, and skinned the cellophane wrapper from it. For a moment he ran it under his nose, sniffing the fragrant weed in the manner of a connoisseur. He bit off one end, placed the cigar between his lips, and lit it.

For a second or two he stood puffing, staring back at the furious commissioner with round, quizzical eyes. Then suddenly, as though he had gone through some inner process of counting, he took the cigar from his mouth and tossed it on the floor.

The detectives stared wide-eyed. Police Commissioner Foster, sensing some sort of trick, opened his mouth to give a warning, but he was too late.

The wrapper of the cigar tossed on the floor by Agent "X" burst apart like a firecracker. A blinding cloud of dense white vapor shot into all parts of the room, billowing out into the corridor.

Just before it reached him Agent "X" took a deep breath and marked the position of the door. As the dense vapor cut off vision as effectually as a white curtain, he leaped around the desk and crossed the room in four quick strides.

The detectives had stepped away from the door. Agent "X" brushed through them and out into the corridor. The smoke given off by the cigar was the same as that used by sky writers. A draft had drawn it along the corridor.[25]

WITH desperate speed Secret Agent "X" leaped along the hallway and down the stairs. He had made himself familiar with the layout of headquarters. When he reached the landing below, he turned left and dashed along a lower hallway to a side exit. A cop barred the door, saw the commissioner, and stepped back. The commissioner nodded and passed out into the night.

With quick, cautious steps he skirted the side of the building, and approached the front. A vague hubbub sounded above him. He looked out into the street. The plain-clothes men stationed outside headquarters had been attracted by the uproar inside. They were disappearing into the vestibule.

Agent "X" turned and walked rapidly away down the block. It was late. The street was deserted. He heard a car coming and ducked into an alley between two buildings. Then he moved out and ran on. Two blocks away he crouched for a moment in the semigloom of an unlighted stoop and went over his face with tense, skilled fingers.

The black mustache and most of the characteristics of Commissioner Foster disappeared. Plates plucked from his nostrils changed the contour of his nose. When he reappeared he was a different person. But he still had the commissioner's clothing on. He walked rapidly away, hailed a taxi, and drove to the neighborhood of one of his several hideouts.

Alone, with a portable make-up box before him, he made a careful change of facial disguise, removing the last traces of those things which had made him resemble Commissioner Foster.

He slipped into a new suit, a pepper and salt, loose-fitting tweed. He drew on a slouch hat and a raglan coat. A notebook pencil and Associated Press card completed his disguise. As an inquiring newspaper reporter many channels of investigation would be open to him.

The Agent's work was only beginning. His desperate visit to headquarters in the role of Commissioner Foster had led to an *im-*

---

25   AUTHOR'S NOTE: *To aid his dangerous work of criminal investigation Secret Agent "X" has devised all manner of defensive and offensive weapons. Sometimes it is as necessary for him to slip out of the hands of the police as to escape from the murderous clutches of masters of crime. Since he carries no lethal weapon with him, he must depend on the cleverness and ingenuity of his many strange devices.*

passe. In this sinister business of the *Flammenwerfer* murders the police were working in a black and ghastly fog of mystery.

His eyes were hard and bright as he descended into the street again. One name and one face still remained in his mind. Banton! In a case where clews seemed lacking it was the Agent's method to leave no stone unturned. Banton was worth investigating.

He took a taxi to within two blocks of the bank, then walked forward. Police still held the tense-faced crowd back. The crowd had thinned, but those who hung on were the seasoned and morbid thrill-searchers who would stay all night if necessary.

Agent "X" saw the tall, familiar form of the medical examiner. The official doctor had completed his work, checked up on the charred bodies. A police ambulance was backed up to the door of the bank. Four men with a stretcher between them were moving toward the ambulance. The crowd shuddered, craning collective necks. But the still figure on the stretcher was mercifully covered. The victims of hideous murder were being removed.

Agent "X," displaying his press card, broke through the police lines. But one of Inspector Burks's men barred him at the door of the bank, refusing admittance.

"There's been enough snooping around here tonight," he said harshly. "Orders from the chief! You gotta keep out."

THE sound of angry voices came from inside the bank. Two detectives walked forward roughly propelling a third man between them.

Agent "X" stared intently. The third man had a red face, thick lips, and a fat body. But his eyes were small, shrewd. It was Banton, the ex-police lieutenant. The two detectives shoved him forcefully out. Banton was complaining bitterly.

"The commish himself told me I could look around," he said.

"He didn't say you could poke into all the bank's private papers," snarled one of the dicks. "Give you an inch and you take a mile. Get the hell out and stay out."

There was an ugly gleam in Banton's eyes. He made one of his jeering, sneering remarks.

"Smart boys, eh!" he said. "The whole lousy force will be wiped out before any of you find who the killers are. But it won't hurt the city if a lot of dumb clucks are cleaned up."

"What's that?" said one of the detectives.

"I said you could go to blazes," lied Banton.

He stood mopping his face, glaring toward the receding backs of the two detectives who had ejected him. Secret Agent "X" moved up, displaying his press card.

"They won't let me in at all, buddy," he said. "Give us the low-down on what's happened."

Banton rolled a belligerent eye.

"Go to hell. Find out for yourself."

Agent "X's" voice was wheedling.

"Give a guy a break," he said. "I just got here—couldn't get away from the office sooner. Who do the dicks suspect?"

Banton's lip curled contemptuously. "Ask 'em," he said. "They're hot stuff—always on the inside track, always have the right dope. They'll give you the murderer's address and phone number. Then you can go around and get a signed story."

With a raucous, sarcastic laugh Banton flung off. He passed through the police lines with a jeering word to a cop. Agent "X" watched him a moment, then casually turned and followed. He edged to the outside of the crowd, kept Banton in sight.

The man swung around the block and approached the bank building from the other side. There was a side entrance there, leading up to the scores of office floors above.

Banton, lumbering like a huge, ill-tempered bear, went into the building. His office could evidently be reached from this side, too. Since the police had barricaded the front, he had come around this way.

When Banton had disappeared Secret Agent "X" increased the speed of his steps. He moved out of the shadows, crossed the street. An instant more, and he had slipped into the bank building, following the belligerent ex-police lieutenant.

CHAPTER VI

THE BLUE LIGHT

THERE WAS ONE all-night elevator still running, operated by the janitor in the basement. This could be summoned by a bell. The door of it was just clicking shut. Banton was ascending.

Agent "X" walked back along the corridor and looked at the directory board. Searching under "B" he found the name "Banton. Detective Agency." The suite was No. 428.

With quick decision he turned and made for the stairway. Silently and swiftly he moved upward.

When he reached the fourth floor, the broad, lumbering form of Agency Detective George Banton was just disappearing down a corridor that swung at right angles. He did not look back. He didn't know that he was being followed. Agent "X," master of shadowing, seemed almost a part of the dark wall as he proceeded after the ex-police lieutenant.

When he came to the angle of the corridor he peered around it. Banton was thrusting a key in a lock, opening his office. He disappeared inside, snapped on a switch, and shut the door. Through the frosted plate glass Secret Agent "X" saw the man's shadow for a moment and saw the large gilt lettering that proclaimed the man's profession to the world.

He wondered if Banton was what he appeared to be. As a police lieutenant Banton's record had been unenviable. He had indulged openly in graft and had been asked to resign from the force. Some private detectives made a precarious living on the ragged edge of the law. They had been known to frame innocent people, obtain false testimony, and perjure themselves on the witness stand. Banton looked like the type who would know every trick by which a private dick might turn a dishonest penny.

Agent "X" was about to enter the Banton Agency to see why its owner was up so late. But suddenly he stopped. Far down the end of the corridor something diverted his attention.

There was an open transom above a closed office door. Through this transom an odd light showed.

The light had a strange quality to it. It was blue and wavering like the glow from a spark gap. It sent weird reflections along the sides of the corridor, cast flickering shadows around the edge of the transom.

Agent "X" moved toward it wonderingly. As he came close he could hear a faint crackling sound. His body tensed. Then another sound came above the lightning-like crackling. It was the whir of some sort of machinery. This stirred his curiosity even more.

The room at the end of the corridor couldn't be one of the building's power stations. The name card on the door said: "A. J. Darlington." It was obviously a private office.

On a night when the bank below had been attacked, when four men had met horrible deaths, anyone working as late as this in the building was worth investigating. Secret Agent "X" pressed the button beside A. J. Darlington's door.

The whir of the machinery inside began to diminish. The crackling blue light in the transom above the Agent's head got dimmer and faded away. Only the glow of an electric bulb showed. Footsteps sounded inside.

The door was opened and a head thrust out. Agent "X" was prepared for the unusual, but he tensed as he stared at the figure which stood just inside the threshold.

The man would have been arresting anywhere. He was tall, white-haired, and gaunt, with a leathery face and deep-set eyes. Clad in a stained smock, with his sleeves rolled up over skinny, hairy arms, he stared at Agent "X" questioningly.

"What do you want?" he demanded.

His tone was gruff, irritable, the tone of a man who wishes privacy and resents interference. The word "crank" was written all over him—in the unpleasant harshness of his voice, in the peevish, discontented lines of his face. And especially in the antagonistic light in his eyes.

Agent "X" cleared his throat, smiled. He took his press card from his pocket, thrust it under Darlington's nose.

"I'd like to ask you a few questions, Mr. Darlington."

As he spoke Agent "X" edged forward, his sharp eyes stabbing into the room. Then he tensed inwardly. Beyond Darlington, through an open door, he glimpsed a completely equipped laboratory, filled with expensive scientific paraphernalia. There were glass retorts for distilling chemicals, strange-shaped jars, metal cylinders, static electrical machines, and a large, complex optical instrument on a tripod. Each object registered in his lightning-fast brain, and roughly he estimated that they must be worth thousands of dollars.[26]

BUT the gaunt man before him drew the door closer and shook his head violently, suspicion in his eyes.

"I've nothing to say to you newspaper men. When I'm ready to talk, I'll talk. You can't pry into my affairs and misrepresent me. You're all too dumb to understand what my studies into the nature and action of light may mean. Good-night, sir, and don't bother me again."

Darlington tried to close the door, but Agent "X" deftly thrust a foot into it. He pressed forward, shoving the tall man back. Darlington's eyes blazed angrily. But Agent "X" stood his ground.

"Just a few questions," he insisted. "I believe you're going to be disturbed more than once tonight."

"What do you mean, young man?"

Agent "X" eyed Darlington steadily. "Perhaps it will interest you to know that an attempt was made to rob the Merchants' and Manufacturers' Bank downstairs. Four men were murdered."

Darlington skinned his lips back from long, rodent-like teeth and made annoyed gestures with his hands.

"A bank robbed! What is that to me? It is the gold of the sunlight I'm interested in—gold that travels at the incredible speed of one hundred and eighty-six thousand miles a second. The laws of infinite space—the mystery of electrons billions of miles away—are what I am concerned with."

"Murder can't be dismissed," said Agent "X." "Four men were killed, I tell you—burned alive in a room less than a hundred feet below you."

---

26 AUTHOR'S NOTE: The battle between criminals and the law is becoming a battle of scientific analysis as well as action. Secret Agent "X" in his contact with Bertillon experts, fingerprint men, and skilled medical examiners, has done research in many branches of science. All types of scientific equipment are familiar to him and it was easy for him to recognize the scope and value of Darlington's.

Darlington raised his eyebrows. "Shocking!" he snapped. "But no concern of mine. If men would forget their mundane troubles and contemplate infinity there would be less crime. The life of man is brief—and according to Mr. Einstein's law of relativity—"

Agent "X" cut him short. "At what time did you come into this building tonight? Answer me that, Mr. Darlington."

Their eyes clashed for a moment, then Darlington spoke sulkily.

"I always come at eight—after the clammering crowd has gone. I come then so that I can have peace and quiet in which to work."

"Doesn't murder mean anything to you?"

"A sordid sociological phenomenon," said Darlington pompously. "Something for the criminologists to deal with. My labors lie in the field of abstract science."

"You saw nothing unusual then when you entered this building tonight?"

"There was a light in the bank. I saw that. These are hard times for the fools who slave their silly lives away in the marts of gold. When I saw the lights in the bank's windows I recalled that magnificent proverb of Marcus Aurelius: 'He who gazes on the farthest star learns more than—' "

Agent "X" interrupted the strange man's discourse again. "I can quote you as saying then that you saw the lights in the bank at eight o'clock?"

"You can quote me as saying nothing, young man. And now, if you'll please leave, we'll terminate this fruitless and unpleasant interview."

Agent "X" made no move to go, and Darlington suddenly bent his angular body and leaped forward. Seizing Agent "X" by the shoulders he shoved him through the door in an effective "bum's rush." The tall crank was amazingly spry and powerful for all his white hair.

Agent "X" tried suddenly to check himself. For, as the door opened and Darlington thrust him out, he saw two men close at the end of the corridor. One was Sergeant Mathers of the homicide squad. The other was a detective from the same department. Before he could stop he slammed into them, nearly knocking the breath from their bodies.

CHAPTER VII

FIND THE WOMAN

IF AGENT "X" hadn't clutched Mathers, the mastiff-faced detective would have fallen. He gasped, swore, and banged against the wall.

"What the hell!" he growled.

Agent "X" heard the door of Darlington's office close with a bang. A harsh, mocking laugh floated through the transom overhead.

"What's going on here?" barked Mathers pulling himself together, recovering his dignity.

Secret Agent "X" drew out his press card again.

"I was looking around, chief. I saw a funny light in that office and knocked. There's a crank in there named Darlington. I asked him some questions and he got sore. You know the rest."

"What did he say?"

"He says he isn't interested in murder—and doesn't know anything about it."

"Isn't interested, eh!"

Sergeant Mathers stepped forward and pounded on the door. "Every tenant in this building is in for a questioning by the police."

Agent "X" jerked his thumb toward the door of the Banton Detective Agency. "What about him, then?"

Mathers shook his head.

"We know all we need to know about Banton."

Agent "X" relapsed into silence.

There was no sound in Darlington's office at Sergeant Mathers' knock. Not until the detective took out his automatic and began to hammer on the panels with the butt, did the door open again. Then Darlington's face was contorted with fury.

"Can't you leave a man alone?" he snarled. "Do you want me to call the police?"

"You're talking to the police now," said Mathers grimly. "You're going to answer a few questions that will go down on the official records."

"I'll answer no more of anybody's questions," snapped Darlington.

"No?"

"No!"

Sergeant Mathers nodded and thrust out his jaw. "Just for that, Mr. Darlington, you'll take a little trip down to headquarters and talk to the inspector himself. I've orders to round up all suspicious characters."

Grasping his opportunity Agent "X" crowded back into Darlington's office, his eyes veiledly alert. He identified the big instrument on the tripod supports as a spectroscope. That upheld Darlington's claim that he was investigating light. But what about his complex, costly chemical equipment? It seemed to indicate that sunlight wasn't his only line of research. Deftly, unobtrusively, Agent "X" began a cursory examination of the laboratory's contents.

Here was a vacuum pump with a chamber for experiments in rarified air. There was an oxygen storage tank. There a high-pressure Bunsen burner. He lingered a moment over this, his eyes deeply speculative.

Darlington interrupted his meditation, stabbing an accusing finger in his direction.

"Take that young man along, too," he said bitterly. "He's an impertinent trespasser."

Mathers snorted scornfully. "We got troubles enough without getting fussed over every snooping news hound in town. Get out of here, you! Scram!"

He shoved Agent "X" out of the laboratory, hustled Darlington into his hat and coat, and, with his colleague, drew the gaunt, protesting crank into the corridor. Then he locked up.

But as they pushed along the hallway Banton's door opened. The fat detective stood in the threshold, his small, cunning eyes narrowed.

"What's all the racket?" he asked,

"None of your business, Shamus," snapped Mathers.

Darlington held back, jerking a thumb toward Banton, and raising his voice.

"He's a neighbor of mine—a friend. He'll tell you this is outrageous. He'll vouch for my good character."

"Somebody will have to vouch for his first," said Mathers sneeringly. "Come on, Santa Claus—the inspector's waiting." He gave Darlington's arm a vicious jerk.

Secret Agent "X" pretended to follow them, but stopped when he reached the head of the stairs. Banton had gone back into his office, and "X" retraced his steps quickly. Would this be a good time to talk to the detective again, or would it be better to wait and watch?

WITH a shrug the Agent turned and opened Banton's door. Then he paused in brief surprise. The detective's offices were more luxurious than he had anticipated. The green rug on the floor was soft as a grassy lawn. Crystal clear mirrors lined the walls. The woodwork was highly glossed. The furniture of the latest modern design. It might have been the sanctum of a millionaire broker. What was the basis of Banton's evident prosperity, strangely at odds with his whining, seedy look? And was it pure coincidence that Banton was friendly with Darlington, who did secret research in a laboratory filled with chemicals?

Then he caught a glimpse of Banton through the open doorway of an inner office. The man was sitting back in a handsome swivel chair, hat tipped over his eyes, a cigar stuck between thick lips.

The agency detective seemed to be in deep and troubled thought, but he took his feet down, swung around, and glared as Secret Agent "X" entered.

"What the hell do you want? I thought I told you to run along."

"X" assumed the tone of a disgruntled reporter.

"You didn't give me a break. Now I got some more questions to ask you."

"The cops wouldn't tell you anything, eh—so you come back to me?"

"That's right. I thought you looked like a good guy."

"Well you can high-tail it back where you came from! Let the cops hand out their own dirt. I ain't spillin' anything tonight. I'm busy."

Banton didn't look busy, but there was malignant hostility in his shrewd, piglike eyes.

"That guy Darlington that the dicks just took down to headquarters says you're a friend of his," said the Agent. "I thought you could give me a little dope on him."

Banton burst into raucous and jeering laughter. Then his face clouded.

"Friend, my eye! He's just an old coot with some money and a lot of crazy ideas."

"What sort of ideas?" asked "X" softly.

For a moment a look of fury blazed in Banton's eyes. His face muscles twitched. He gripped the arms of his chair as though holding himself down.

"Find out for yourself, mug," he rasped. "What the hell do you think I am—an information bureau? If you want to hire a detective, let's see you come across with the fee—half down and half when the case is finished is my way. Now shut up and get out."

Agent "X" drew a cigarette from his pocket. He lighted it, sat down on Banton's desk, and flourished his notebook.

"It won't hurt you to give me a little dope," he said stubbornly.

Cords in Banton's neck stood out. He rose suddenly, made a threatening movement toward Secret Agent "X." Then he paused. His eyes turned toward the door, and Agent "X" turned, too.

The door of the outer office had opened and closed quickly. A girl stood just outside. She was a strikingly pretty girl with hair as black as jet, eyes like agate, and a smooth, olive complexion.

She moved forward on exaggeratedly high heels, swinging her lithe hips with the smooth, easy grace of a dancer. She was a girl who would have attracted attention anywhere. The paleness of her face seemed accentuated now by some deep, hidden emotion. There was emotion in her black eyes, too, making them snap and sparkle like fire seen through dark glass. Her hands were white and tense on the smart beaded bag she carried.

She looked from the agency detective to Secret Agent "X" and back again.

"I would like to see Mr. Banton," she said, "alone."

Agent "X" hesitated for only a moment. In that moment he was filled with wonder as to why the girl was here at all. And his gaze lingered an instant on her exotic, brooding face. Then Banton's voice sounded harshly.

"Can't you see I got a client? Didn't you hear what she said? Scram!"

Agent "X" shrugged and rose. He jammed his notebook in his

pocket, pulled his slouch hat down with a vicious tug, manifested all the mannerisms of a disgruntled reporter. With his cigarette dangling from his lips he went out the door and slammed it after him; then took pains to make a noise in the corridor as he walked away toward the stairs. But, as he looked back, he saw Banton's shadow on the frosted glass and heard the click of metal. The agency detective had taken no chances. He had locked the door.

IT was then that Agent "X" paused and retraced his steps a second time. Banton and Banton's client interested him strangely. How had the mysterious-looking dark-faced girl known that Banton was in his office so late at night? Who was she? Had she, too, been waiting outside and seen Banton enter? If so, what was her business with the ex-police lieutenant turned sleuth? Had it any connection with the hideous bank murders?

No one was in the corridor. Coming close on tiptoe to the door of Banton's office, Agent "X" pressed his ear against the frosted glass. But he heard nothing, not even the low buzz of voices. The two inside had retired to the inner room.

Agent "X" might have picked the lock. But he didn't want to be discovered prowling by Banton. If there was any reason to suspect Banton it would not do to arouse the detective's own suspicions. There were other ways in which the Agent could work.[27]

He took from his coat an article which looked at first glance like a small pocket Kodak. Opened up, the illusion was still maintained. But there were nearly twelve feet of what appeared to be the camera's black cable release. On the end of this was a circular disc.

Agent "X" unwound the cable, opened the instrument's back, and placed it to his ear. Then, standing on tiptoe, he thrust the end of the black cord up over the door through the ventilating transom. The instrument he held in his hand was not a camera, but an electric amplifying device, sensitive and delicate as a watch. He turned a rheostat control which corresponded to the film wind of a camera.

The voices of the man and woman now came to his ears as a confused buzz. They were talking evidently in the closed inner of-

27   AUTHOR'S NOTE: Ingenious portable mechanisms of various types are a part of the Agent's equipment. With the magic of science supplementing his courage and resourcefulness, he is able often to bridge gaps which carry him far ahead of the law's representatives.

fice. Through the thickness of a doorway and through many feet of air the vibrations of their voices came to him. But not even the ingenious amplifier in the Secret Agent's hand could reduce their conversation to perfect clarity.

He listened tensely, ready to snatch the amplifier away if steps should sound along the corridor. His fingers moved the tiny control lever, reaching the most delicate adjustment possible, making the girl's voice more distinct.

"—to help me," she said. "I know what I'm talking about."

The girl was silent. Banton's voice came, confused, rumbling, making the diaphragm of the amplifier tremble so that words were blurred. Banton seemed to be arguing.

As Agent "X" worked with his control, the girl spoke again. The first part of her sentence was lost, but the last four words were arresting, making the Agent's eyes brighten, glad that he had taken pains to come.

"—Davis was my friend."

Davis—that was the name of one of the bankers who had been killed. Other words, caught here and there, verified this—words such as "murder," "dead," "robbery."

The girl's visit to Banton then had some direct connection with the raid tonight on the Merchants' and Manufacturers' Bank. Her agitation was an outgrowth of that terrible crime. Here was a steer that any detective would have followed. To Agent "X" it was a path that might lead to almost any unexpected thing. The girl hadn't gone to the police. She had gone to Banton. This meant that she had something to hide. Agent "X" pondered tensely.

Darlington with his strange laboratory. Banton, combative, shrewd and suspiciously prosperous. This girl who had known Davis.

They formed a trio worth watching—and one of them might well lead him closer to that trail of hideous murder.

CHAPTER VIII

WINGS OF MYSTERY

THE GIRL AND man inside sank their voices to even lower pitches. Twice more "X" caught the name Davis. But the sentences were disconnected and confusing.

When talk ceased, when he heard the stir and scrape of chairs inside, he drew his microphone from the transom, coiled it up, and stepped back.

Quickly he moved to the angle of the corridor and waited there, crouching in a dark doorway, till the girl came out of Banton's office and hurried to the stairs. He got one glimpse of her face. There were crimson spots of excitement in her olive cheeks. Her dark eyes were snapping like fire. He heard the click of her high heels as she moved down the stairs, and, like a shadow, he followed.

Banton he could locate any time. But who was the dark-eyed girl, and what was her interest in the dead banker, Davis? It was this that Agent "X" wished to find out.

When he reached the street floor, moving silently down the stairs, he saw the girl standing in the shadow of the building's vestibule. He saw her look along the street in both directions before moving out, saw her slink into the shadows and walk like a person who does not want to be observed. He followed, taking care that she should not see him. Four blocks away, he saw her summon a cruising taxi.

The crowd around the bank, still tense, talking excitedly, was beginning to disperse. Cabs were hovering about, anxious to pick up a few late fares. Even death had its profits. Agent "X" signaled one of the circling taxis.

"Follow the cab ahead," he said. "Keep it in sight."

The driver cast a frightened look at his fare, then nodded. There was nothing sinister about "X" in his present role. His appearance was that of an intent young newspaperman.

The cab lurched away along the dark street. It was after twelve. Much had happened in the past two hours. The period had been a veritable cyclone of danger, death, and mystery. And the excitement was not over. The pieces of the ghastly murder puzzle lay scattered on the face of the darkness. Agent "X" was trying to gather them up.

The cab bearing the strange black-eyed girl turned into an uptown avenue. It sped quickly, as though its passenger were impatient. In ten minutes it turned east, followed a cross-town street, and entered upon the plaza of a big interborough bridge.

Its red tail-light winked up the long slope of the bridge, reached the summit and went down the other side. It left the bridge and entered a wide thoroughfare. They were in a different borough now. The chase had led away from the scene of murder. But Agent "X" had learned that the ramifications of murder lead far.

For a half-hour more the chase continued. Agent "X" was getting uneasy. What if the girl in the cab ahead got on to the fact that she was being followed? He wished he were driving one of his own cars. There would have been less chance of his being seen.

They came to the suburbs, at last, followed a long concourse. The Agent breathed easier. There were many cars here despite the lateness of the hour. Romantic couples out for a night drive. Theatergoers returning from shows in town.

He ordered the cab to creep closer.

Then the taxi ahead swung off the boulevard, plunged down a smoothly paved side street between wooden suburban houses. "X" knew where he was now. A sudden premonition came. He sat forward tensely in his seat.

Against the night sky, the great beam of a searchlight swept back and forth with rhythmic monotony. It was like a huge waving arm. It was an airbeacon. Ahead of them lay the newly equipped municipal flying field, the field where night mail planes landed and took off, where there was always alertness and a bustle of activity. The great hangars housed many small planes. Agent "X" had visited the field often, flown from it himself.[28]

Was the girl going there now?

There could be no doubt about it. Her taxi turned into the wire enclosure, headed into the parking space, with the black bulk of the hangars beyond. Landing lights were on. The deep-throated roar of an airplane motor sounded.

Rutted mud made the Agent's taxi jounce like a ship in a stormy sea. "X" ordered the driver to stop. He glanced at the meter, leaped out. It had run into several dollars, but he paid the driver twice the amount. Then in the semigloom surrounding the big, lighted field, he strode after the other cab with the girl in it. It had stopped, too. The girl was getting out.

The swinging, persistent arm of the air beacon lighted Agent "X's" face. The bright, excited glow in his eyes wasn't entirely the reflection of the searchlight's radiance. The cab which had brought the girl moved off, swung around, bumped by in the darkness. It was headed back toward the city. The girl strode on.

"X" got a silhouetted glimpse of her figure. It seemed to express determination, hurry. He saw her go into the field's operations office and speak to the man at the desk. Night planes were coming in and leaving on regular schedule. But the field's sightseeing, joy-riding ships were shut in their hangars, housed for the night.

THE man in the operations office shook his head as Agent "X" watched through the window. Then "X" saw the girl display a roll of bills. He saw her toss them down on the desk. The man in the operations office smiled and finally nodded. He motioned the girl to a seat, picked up a telephone. The girl sat smoking, holding a cigarette between her long, carmine-tipped fingers. Her slimly shod foot tapped impatiently. There was worry in the dark, heavily lashed eyes.

A half-hour went by and a pilot came into the office. He looked sleepy, sullen. There was a helmet with goggles on it hanging carelessly over his arm. His sleepy eyes brightened as he saw the waiting

---

28   *AUTHOR'S NOTE: My first intimation that Agent "X" was a skilled pilot came under peculiar circumstances. I saw him face a desperate emergency which I shall never forget. We were speeding to Washington, D.C., on a night plane, a huge, bimotored low-winged cabin job, when the left engine blew a cylinder head, A piece of metal smashed the front vision window, injuring the senior pilot. The junior pilot lost his head. The plane, with bad air conditions, got out of control, began to lose altitude and threatened to wreck us all. It was Secret Agent "X" who took one of the big dual wheel controls, nursed the plane alone on one motor, and made an expert landing at the nearest emergency field.*

girl. The droop left his shoulders. He had been waked from sound sleep, apparently, to take a passenger up. Now he showed interest.

Agent "X" stiffened. There was no doubt as to what the girl was going to do. She had hired a plane and was going up. Why?

Only the dark night, sky or the girl herself could answer that question. But he didn't wait to ask it.

He turned, looked out across the wide field. A mail plane was on a dolly, being wheeled out and loaded. Mechanics were swarming around its engine. His eyes went beyond it.

A private hangar was open. Lights showed inside. Two planes were out on the dead line, one was warming up. It was a small, two-seated ship, a sport plane belonging to some rich playboy. No doubt he was going to take his girl for a night ride.

Agent "X" struck out at a run toward it. Employees of the flying company were wheeling another plane from a hangar, one of the regular company ships. Orders had gone out from the operations office. A mechanic turned the handle of the inertia starter. The motor coughed, sputtered, broke into a roar.

It was almost warm by the time Agent "X" reached the vicinity of the smaller plane. The pilot was helping the girl in. She had on a helmet and goggles provided by the company.

Agent "X" looked toward the open door of the hangar before which the smaller plane squatted. He saw figures inside; the playboy who owned the plane was adjusting his helmet.

The motor of the small plane was humming sweetly now. And behind "X," down the field, the company ship leaped away to taxi into the wind.

Like a swift, silent wraith, Agent "X" darted from the shadows. He reached the small sport plane, drew the chocks from under its fat air wheels. In a moment he had vaulted into its cockpit.

He looked behind. The owner of the ship hadn't even left the hangar.

As the company ship pivoted far down the field, nosed into the wind, and rushed forward with a song of power, Agent "X" pushed the throttle of the sport plane home.

He raised the tail off the ground, raced forward with a steady hand on the stick. The amazed shouts of the plane's owner in the hangar behind were drowned in the engine's blasting crescendo. The lights of the hangar rocketed away. The lights of the other ship were passing overhead.

Agent "X" taxied forward, kicked left rudder, turned.

The sting of the night wind lashed his unhelmeted head. He crouched behind the low wind cowling, fed gas to the motor. A moment more and he had drawn the stick back, drawn the plane off the ground, and was roaring up into the black night sky.

THE SKY KILLER

THE EYES OF Agent "X," sharp as a hunting hawk's, spotted the exhaust glow of the other ship. He began to climb. The small sport plane, built for speed and aerobatics, had the swift grace of an arrow. A connoisseur of fine planes as he was of cars, Agent "X" knew that Fate had been good to him tonight. The high-speed radial motor in front was pulling the ship up like a rocket. Already he was on a level with the sky craft ahead.

He climbed higher still, getting above it, keeping that tiny, flickering exhaust plume in sight. Where was the other ship going? What strange objective did the mystery girl have that she needed to take this midnight flight?

The two-place ship ahead didn't even circle the field. It climbed steadily into the wind, then turned at right angles in a steep bank and bore away toward the city. This surprised Agent "X." He didn't know what he had expected, but it had seemed likely that the girl would fly away from town. Instead she was flying toward the heart of it.

The miles that had taken nearly an hour to traverse by land were flown in a few minutes on the wings of the wind. The altimeter of the Agent's ship showed two thousand feet. He was mounting still. Far below, he saw the smooth ribbon of the boulevard with lights strung along it like bright pearls. The speeding cars were crawling beetles.

Wispish, low-flying clouds swept across the sky. The Agent took advantage of them, nosing up out of sight from time to time, dropping again to keep the other ship in view. It flew steadily toward the city, until the thin silver band of the river was beneath them. He saw the bridge they had crossed, with the crawling lights of motors and trolleys on it.

Then he caught his breath. The other plane, climbing now, was headed straight toward that section of town where the Merchants' and Manufacturers' Bank was located. Against the sky line for a moment, against the farther river which made an island of the city, he saw the flat-topped, eighteen-story skyscraper that housed the bank.

Then he drew back on his stick to keep above the other plane. Once again he rocketed up into the low-flying clouds. He swept through them, climbed on into the clear, cold starlight.

He let another thousand feet register on the altimeter, waited, and saw the hired plane burst through the layer of clouds like a monster breaking the surface of some white sea. For a moment he nosed down, shutting off his motor. He heard the engine of the plane beneath pop once, and saw the ship nose down, its motor silent, too. It swept back toward the clouds in a long, descending bank.

Agent "X" pushed the stick forward and dived. With his propeller still ticking over, but the engine silent, he shot down toward the clouds with the wind whistling a chant through the struts and flying wires. The clouds rushed up to meet him. He saw the other plane disappear.

Alert, tense-faced, he followed it. The whip of the mist around his head was like a cold plunge. Then he broke through. The other plane was below and ahead. It had flattened out now. In a long, silent glide it was headed toward the bank building.

Like a winged wraith Agent "X" followed. There was small chance that they would see him against the clouds. Little starlight came through. The lighted streets against which he could glimpse the plane below formed a better background.

But what did this strange maneuver signify? In his anxiety to find out, he steepened his glide, picked up speed, and swept closer to the ship ahead. Did the girl plan to drop something on the bank?

But no. As the plane below swept over the bank he was not more than five hundred feet behind. For a moment, against a street beyond, he could see the helmeted head of the girl scanning the top of the bank. But she dropped nothing, made no movement. The plane continued, banked away, nosed down till it had picked up speed again. Suddenly the roar of its motor sounded. It shot up toward the clouds.

Agent "X" waited, then switched his own motor on. In the dull drone of the ship above, the sound of his own engine would be lost. He passed over the bank, looked down. All was black on the flat-topped roof. The big building seemed peaceful. There was no hint of the appalling thing that had happened in it tonight. He wondered if Banton were still in his office—and if he knew that his client was sailing the night skies far above him.

The two-place ship disappeared into the clouds. The Agent's sport plane was answering its propeller, rocketing up in a magnificent burst of speed.

Back in the clouds again, he kicked right rudder, bore away. When he burst through them he was flying at a different angle from the other plane. He swung around in a wide circle and followed, climbing above it once more. Afraid that he would be seen, he continued to climb till his altimeter registered eight thousand feet, until the air was still and cold and so thin that his ears began to ring, until the plane below was a mere speck on the white surface of the clouds. Then again he shut off power and nosed down over it.

IT was headed away from the city, but not back toward the flying field. The mysterious girl passenger had not finished her night flight yet.

Through holes in the clouds Agent "X" could see the glint of water now, and the lights of ships. They had nosed out over the harbor. The clouds became more ragged. The other ship was harder to see. He nosed lower.

The ship with the girl in it was following the shore line of the harbor now. It began to circle, and, diving low with motor shut off, Agent "X" saw the girl leaning over the side, peering down. The plane went down through the clouds. Agent "X" followed.

He hung just under the clouds while the other ship continued dropping. He could follow its exhaust flare once more. Then he saw lights strung along the shore in a curve—the lights of a harbor. He strained his eyes to see through the darkness. The water below cast wavering reflections. The night seemed filled with mystery. What was the other plane doing?

It continued to circle, going three times around the harbor as though the girl were looking for something, or familiarizing herself with the location of this place.

Agent "X" made out gray shapes on the water now. Boats. But the ship ahead was not a seaplane. It couldn't land. Again he watched for some signal, saw none. The clouds drifted more thickly. He could see only the feathering exhaust of the plane below.

The plane left the harbor at last, started back along the shore again toward the city. Then Agent "X" caught his breath. He was gliding with motor at idling speed. It seemed to him suddenly that he detected another sound. The air seemed to be filled with a throbbing note. He looked up, started.

For an instant he saw a firefly spark against the black under surface of the clouds.

The spark winked, disappeared, came on again. He closed his own motor entirely, glided down toward the water a thousand feet below. Then the hair on his neck began to rise.

Far above him he heard the thin, high wailing of wind shrieking through speeding wires. A ship was coming down from the clouds in a fast dive.

HE looked ahead toward the two-place company plane. The feather of its exhaust was still visible. Then, as though the curtain of the night had opened up, the long, lavender beam of a search-light stabbed down from the clouds. It leaped across space like a lightning bolt, focused on the plane with the girl in it.

In that first glance Agent "X" could see the white goggled faces of the girl and the pilot staring up. The beam of the searchlight narrowed. The other plane was sweeping close. What did it mean?

In an instant the answer came.

A series of stuttering, rhythmic reports sounded in the sky above. Agent "X" saw a winking, vicious pin point of light close to the spot where the searchlight came from.

The mysterious plane that had dived out of the clouds was shooting, firing mercilessly at the girl and the pilot ahead.

He saw the pilot bank to the left, sideslip away. An instant the searchlight lost it, then picked it up again. Like a terrible, all-seeing eye the lavender beam held its mark. The pilot ahead had apparently had no wartime training. He knew nothing of defensive air tactics. It made sweat crawl along Agent "X's" spine. This was butchery, slaughter, murder he was witnessing.

He fed gas to his own ship, raced forward. But there was nearly a thousand feet of intervening space. The horrible *rat-tat* of the machine gun on the plane above sounded again. The finger of the searchlight was focused on its mark.

Then, as Agent "X" came nearer, he saw, under the searchlight's glare, like a horrible tableau, that the pilot had been hit. The man was jerking in the cockpit. The plane gave a crazy lunge forward, sheered off on one wing. The merciless death beats of the machine gun continued.

The pilot ahead flung out one arm, turned up an agonized face. Then he gripped the stick, pushed it forward, dived toward the water.

Agent "X" knew it was the worst thing he could have done. Wartime pilots were trained never to fly away in a straight line. "X" remembered brilliant wing-overs, rolls and Immelmann's he had seen—the strategic air maneuvers of skilled aces who could throw an enemy off. Even for him it would have been a simple matter to avoid that groping searchlight's beam.[29]

But the pilot ahead was helpless, wounded, and ignorant of combat tactics.

At last the plane sideslipped, did a falling leaf maneuver, then nosed into the surface of the water with a burst of billowing spray.

---

29   *AUTHOR'S NOTE: At a flying club dinner which Agent "X" attended in the disguise of a reporter I once heard him engage in conversation with a group of ex-service pilots. He showed an intimate knowledge of all wartime planes and equipment, and related inside stories of famous aces which none of us had heard before. When questioned afterwards, he shrugged and said he'd picked up a bit of information along the Western Front in his intelligence work. But later still, in a book I borrowed from him, I accidentally discovered the impressive silk ribbon of the French Croix de Guerre being used carelessly as a marker.*

CHAPTER X

GROPING BULLETS

FOR ONE HORRIFIED instant Agent "X" watched. The searchlight still played over the crashed ship. The air spaces in the wings were holding it up—holding it till bullet holes filled and the plane sank from sight. The figure of the girl was visible. As the spray subsided he saw her struggling desperately in the rear cockpit.

The searchlight shifted. The murder plane nosed up from its dive, and Agent "X," eyes bright and bleak as steel, thrust his control stick forward.

There was no hesitancy in his movements now. There was only one thing he could do. In a matter of minutes, seconds perhaps, the heavy engine of the crashed plane would pull it beneath the surface, dragging the girl with it.

Wind howling through struts and wires, Agent "X" roared down. He had no searchlight to guide him. But horror had marked the spot where the other plane rested. Faintly against the gray surface of the water he could see the distorted floating mass. He put on a burst of power, plummeted in a dive that made the wings shudder. At the last he flattened out, pulled the nose of the ship up and pancaked into the cold swells. On the chance of saving a human life he was deliberately wrecking a four-thousand-dollar plane.

The fat air wheels struck first, ploughed through the water. The landing carriage groaned as though in resentment of this harsh treatment. The engine's hot cylinders took water with a boiling, bubbling hiss. And Agent "X," cleared of his safety belt, leaped the instant the plane began to settle. He had unlaced his shoes, kicked them off. He struck out toward the spot where the other plane had landed. The water was cold, freezingly chill against his body. And his movement in it was a strange transition from the swift sky progress he had been making.

He took a half-dozen quick strokes and listened. Something slapped against the top of a wave. The wing of the fallen plane. He heard a faint, shrill cry that sent the blood racing through his veins.

He didn't try to explain to himself the reasons behind the thing he had seen. There would be time for that later. His one thought now was to save a human life. There had been enough of murder already.

Something rose out of the water ahead of him. It was a wing of the plane, canted. That meant that the other one was broken—or else the ship was already beginning to sink. The cry came again. There was a note of horror, fear, in it that wrenched his heart.

He gripped the wing, pulled himself along it hand over hand, racing his body through the water. He passed a strut top, two, neared the fuselage of the plane. Then dimly he saw the girl ahead. She had gotten out of her safety belt. She was clinging to the coaming of the cockpit. He couldn't see her face, but he called to her.

A smothered intake of breath answered him. There was a moment of silence. Then her voice sounded, scornful, fierce as a trapped animal's cry. "Murderer! Butcher!" There was in her speech, too, the faint trace of some foreign accent.

Her words were like a blow. Agent "X," treading water, gathered his thoughts. Who did she think he was? What did the girl mean?

"I heard your plane crash," she said bitterly. "I hoped you'd been killed. Now I suppose you intend to finish your work!"

The Agent spoke softly. "I'm not the person you think. You've made a mistake."

"Who are you then? You've killed my pilot. He's dead—dead, I tell you—and you are going to kill me!"

"It wasn't I who shot at you," he said. "I saw you crash and came to help."

A harsh, scornful laugh came out of the darkness. "You expect me to believe that—butcher!"

There was another moment of tense silence, then Agent "X" spoke again.

"Listen!" he said.

He could almost feel the girl in the darkness straining. Then she cried out.

"It's someone coming to rescue me. You can't kill me now!"

She gave a sudden, piercing scream, a cry for help, waving her

The horrible "rat-tat" of the machine gun on the plane above sounded again.

arm and beating against the canvas cockpit of the plane. Agent "X" reached forward and caught hold of her. She screamed again and tried to wrench loose.

"Be quiet!" he hissed. "They aren't coming to help us. They are coming—"

He didn't finish the sentence. The roar of a plane's motor was louder now. Once again the bright, questing beam of a searchlight flicked on. It swept across the water, centered on the wrecked plane.

AT almost the same instant the Agent's ears caught the horrible, rhythmic tattoo of a machine gun again. Bullets slapped into the water in a burst not fifty feet away.

In the glaring glow of the searchlight's beam he saw the girl's white, terrified face. He looked beyond her, got one ghastly glimpse of the dead pilot slumped over his controls, his body riddled with bullets.

For one tense instant the girl turned toward him.

"I was wrong," she said. "I'm sorry—they are going to kill us."

"Not if we can help it," he grated. "Quick! The plane's sinking!"

She gave a moan of stark terror then. "I can't swim," she said.

It was as though all the hideous fiends of hell were chuckling, conspiring to create a nightmare there in the darkness. They were almost a mile from shore! The girl couldn't swim! And now armed killers above their heads, relentless, purposeful were trying to slay them as the pilot had been slain. Agent "X" spoke quickly, harshly.

"Put your arms over my shoulders—so. Hang on—but don't throttle me."

Trembling, the girl obeyed. For a moment he felt the softness of her body against him, then they were free of the plane. But before he had taken two strokes, the searchlight had swept close.

It seemed like some terrible, monstrous eye, leering at them. The thunder of the plane's motor was a deafening cascade of sound in their ears. It even drowned out the measured beat of the machine gun.

But bullets snapped and crackled into the wreckage just behind them. Bullets beat around them in the water. The girl screamed again, shrilly, close to his ear, and he thought for a moment she had been struck.

Another salvo of shots fanned the water just ahead. He felt his lips moving, felt himself cursing at the murderous fiends overhead. The plane swept on, so close that he could feel the wind of its propeller. He turned his head, saw to his horror as the plane was outlined for a moment against the glow of its own searchlight in front, that it had pontoons. It was a small, swift seaplane.

The searchlight clicked off, the plane was banking now, getting ready to land and make sure that its terrible work was done.

With all the strength in his body Secret Agent "X" forged ahead through the water, carrying the girl on his back. The steady clutch of her fingers showed that she was unharmed. But he knew that their danger wasn't over. There was the threat of death by drowning ahead, the threat still that the murderer in the seaplane would find them and riddle them with bullets.

For that reason he almost burst his lungs to put as much distance between them and the wreckage as he could.

He heard the other plane come to rest on the water, heard the pontoons squash, and the motor cut to idling speed. The plane was taxiing over the surface now. The searchlight stabbed on again, swung around toward the wreckage, focused on it. Then the plane came forward.

Hardly daring to breath, Agent "X" swam on. He didn't go straight toward shore. Instead, he moved off at an angle. In a second he was glad he had done so. The searchlight on the plane began to swing around. It swept across the water, straight toward the shore. For a moment he pulled the girl beside him and held her there with only her face out.

A reflected glow from the searchlight was playing over them. He feared the terrible lash of bullets, feared death not for his own sake, but because he had a life to save and work to do. He could feel the wild pounding of the girl's heart close to him.

THE searchlight shifted, turning back on the wreckage again. For seconds the unseen killer in the plane examined his handiwork. He still seemed unsatisfied. A red flare came from the plane's exhaust stack. It streaked across the water, taxiing again.

It circled in a wide arc, came back. This time its searchlight bobbed over the water so closely that Agent "X" gave up hope and waited. But the slow-rising swells served as a precarious, protecting barrier.

The plane taxied by, with the two of them just outside its searchlight's path.

Agent "X" swam on. The plane circled again. It had become a wild, desperate game of hide and seek out on the blackness of the water. The pilot, hideous criminal that he was, wanted apparently to make sure that no one survived. Some tremendous issue appeared to be at stake.

Seconds passed and "X" saw another light far off on the horizon. Another plane seemed to be coming, perhaps from some coast guard station or army field, or perhaps the owner of the ship he had borrowed.

That ship would have to be replaced now. Betty Dale with her newspaper connections would find out the owner's name for him, and he would see that an amount large enough to cover the loss of the ship was sent to the man anonymously. To save a human life, to come closer perhaps to the solution of this ghastly murder mystery, beside this the loss of a plane was nothing.

He saw the murder ship leave at last, frightened perhaps by the approaching light. But the light on the horizon passed far overhead. "X" concluded it was a coastwise mail plane on one of the big transport lines.

The long swim to shore began. Agent "X" didn't try to hurry. He was too experienced a swimmer for that. Minute after minute he made his long, clean strokes tell. The girl seemed to be beyond speech. She was clinging to him as if frozen. When at last he heard the sound of waves breaking on the beach, he thought perhaps she was chilled to the point of death.

His feet touched sand. He reeled through low surf to the shore, staggered up a beach. Then for a moment he laid the girl down. She sagged limply. He felt her face, rubbed her hands.

"Your name?" he said. "What's your name? Where do you live?"

She groaned, stirred. He repeated his query, again and again, shouting it in her ear. As though it had reached her from a long way off she answered at last, mechanically, feebly.

"Rosa Carpita," she said. "Rawleigh Apartments."

She muttered something else, something that "X" couldn't understand. She sank back limply into the unconsciousness from which his shouted questions had half aroused her.

HE looked tensely about. There was a bluff at the top of the beach. He saw it silhouetted against a glow in the sky. The glow seemed like lights. He picked the girl up bodily, cradled her in his arms, and strained forward up the sand. He labored up the bluff.

There *were* lights beyond—a cross roads with a spray of three electric bulbs strung on a pole. Far down one of the roads two spots of radiance were approaching. He ran with the girl in his arms across a rough field. Holding the girl beside him, he waited and signaled the car whose lights he had seen.

It was a farmer's truck, coming into the city with crates for early morning shipment. The man on the driver's seat stared at "X" skeptically, then saw the girl.

"We capsized in the water," said Agent "X." "This girl has fainted. I've got to get her back to the city."

The farmer nodded. "Get in," he said.

For many minutes they bumped and jounced over the dark night road, coming at last to the outskirts of the city. Agent "X" saw a taxi. He thanked the farmer and transferred his burden to the swifter vehicle.

The driver didn't know the address, but a directory in a drug store telephone booth gave it.

In twenty minutes the cab drew up before a large apartment house. It was a luxurious place, with a canopy over the sidewalk and a gilded foyer. The doorman had long since gone off duty, but the night switchboard operator let Agent "X" and his limp burden in. Rosa Carpita was breathing regularly. She was in a state of exhaustion from the fright she had had and her long submergence in the water.

The switchboard girl summoned a janitor who showed the Agent to Miss Carpita's apartment. "X" turned to the man, spoke quickly.

"Get a doctor," he said. "This young woman almost drowned. She needs care at once."

The janitor hurried off. Agent "X" deposited the black-eyed girl on a couch and made her as comfortable as he could. She was unwounded, unhurt. He had saved her life. But she might be unconscious for hours, and, if she came to, she would be in no condition to talk. He doubted if she would anyway. Whatever her mission into the night skies had been, it was veiled in mystery. He would send Betty Dale to question her in the capacity of a *Herald* reporter, and later he would come to see her again himself.

He looked around her apartment a moment. There were many pictures of stage celebrities on the walls, some of them autographed. There were some of the girl herself in costume. He found a sheaf of press notices stacked under a paper weight. He scanned them quickly.

The girl was Rosa Carpita, Spanish dancer, who had appeared in many revues and night club skits. The luxury of her apartment attested to the fact that she was successful.

Then Agent "X" gave a start and stepped forward. On a table at the end of a room a large photograph was set between two upright lights. It was the photograph of a man, a face familiar to Agent "X" who never forgot any face that he had once seen actually or in the press.

It was the face of Jerome Davis, one of the three murdered bankers, and on it was an intimate line: "To my dear Rosa from Jerry."

CHAPTER XI

PLUNGING DEATH

WITHOUT WAITING TO see more, Agent "X" left the Rawleigh apartment. A doctor would soon be there to take care of the girl. There would be inquiries, perhaps a police investigation. The Agent was wet, uncomfortable. He took a taxi to the nearest of his hideouts.

There he changed his clothes and lay down on a couch for a few hours sleep—an unusual thing for him.[30]

But the close call with death under the merciless flame of the *Flammenwerfer,* the wild ride in the night skies, and the long swim through icy water had left him utterly exhausted.

When morning dawned, newsboys in the street began crying scare-head editions. Black headlines were spread across the front pages telling of the ghastly bank murders, and the disappearance of two bank employees. There had been another robbery and murder, too, another charred corpse left behind. A jewelry store in an outlying part of the city had been robbed and a cop who had gone to the scene too soon had been killed. The city was in the grip of an appalling crime wave.

Agent "X" visited the scene of this robbery also, saw the safe which had been blasted open by some cracksman who knew his job.

Why, he wondered, hadn't the same men, raiding the Merchants'

---

30   AUTHOR'S NOTE: *The rules of life which other men follow do not appear to apply to Agent "X." Possessed of almost inexhaustible energy, and of peculiar nervous sensibility, he can, when the need arises, do with amazingly little sleep. The same applies to food. I have known him to use nothing but capsules of synthetic, concentrated foodstuffs for periods as long as forty-eight hours, without suffering any loss of energy. He has worked out a series of setting-up exercises, based on the principle of dynamic tension, which he claims keeps him always in good form.*

and Manufacturers' Bank, used a nitro charge, too? If they made a second raid they probably would. He hoped the special guard would be adequate.

There were many other things in the paper to interest Agent "X." There was the story of a passenger plane leaving the municipal field and not returning, and of another plane being stolen.

Both were insoluble mysteries.

A young woman, Martha Rollins, dark-eyed and exotic, the paper said, had hired the plane the night before under strange circumstances. Pilot Steve Howden of the field's flying service had flown her. It was feared that they had cracked up somewhere.

The girl then, Rosa Carpita, had used an assumed name on the company's books. Agent "X" read the other story, the tale of the stolen ship. The paper could ascribe no motive for the theft of that unless some bandit was making a get-away. The plane had belonged to a millionaire's son named Kirkland.

Interesting also to Secret Agent "X" were the details of the three bankers who had been slain, especially the short life history of Jerome Davis. Davis was married, the paper said. His wife was abroad. From what "X" gathered, their marriage was a social affair with little love between them. He thought again, then, of the dark-eyed girl, Rosa Carpita.

Calling Betty Dale on the phone he asked her if, in her capacity as *Herald* reporter, she would go to the Rawleigh Apartments and make a few inquiries. Betty did so, but her report was disappointing. Rosa Carpita had left her home early that morning. The doctor had been in attendance upon her. It was believed she had perhaps gone away to the country as she had taken a grip with her.

He called next on the families of Spencer and Cox, the vanished bank employees. The police had been unable to locate these men. For hours their families had been besieged by detectives and newspaper reporters. Spencer had a wife and six children. His absence was a tragic mystery. But Agent "X" had heard of other bank employees, married and apparently honest, who had embezzled funds and left.

Cox had only a brother living. He was the operator of a garage. From him "X" gathered that the other bank employee had been a rather fast-living fellow, a bachelor who liked his good times. The papers, he noticed, played this up. It was even whispered that Cox was fond of the races.

In connection with this, and in the guise of an enquiring reporter, Agent "X" called on the two surviving bankers, von Blund

The Agent stepped back, and as he did so, something slapped the pavement where he stood.

and Marsh. Grave-faced and strained-looking, they were in their offices in the bank.

"You will understand," said von Blund, "that after such an experience as we have been through we cannot give you much time. You are the twentieth reporter who has already—"

Agent "X" nodded and waved the protest down. He stared into

the clean-cut, smooth-shaven face of von Blund. The piercing blue eyes, aristocratic features, and blond hair showed the banker's Germanic stock.

"Tell me," said Agent "X." "It is a highly personal question. You may not care to answer it. But it is being hinted in newspaper circles that there were things in one or more of your deceased partners' lives that their families would wish to cover up."

For a moment von Blund started. "What do you mean?"

"Women, for instance. Unconventionalities."

"You're talking rot. My partners have unblemished records in every way."

"There are reports that Mr. Davis was seen—"

Von Blund struck the desk sharply. "It is true that Mrs. Davis is in Europe. It is true that they spend a great deal of time apart. But that is neither here nor there. To my knowledge Jerome Davis was a man of impeccable morals and highest honor."

Agent "X" nodded. He thanked the banker and left. Von Blund's manner indicated that he knew nothing of any intimacy between Davis and the dancer, Rosa Carpita. But, since Davis had been married, and since his profession was such that he couldn't risk any breath of scandal, it was quite natural that the affair should be kept under cover.

There were other lines of inquiry Agent "X" wanted to follow. He visited the family of the slain bank guard and questioned many people employed in the vicinity of the bank.

Then Secret Agent "X" did a strange thing. Retiring to one of his hideouts he disguised himself as a prosperous, middle-aged business man—a ruddy-faced individual with gray hair, eye-glasses, and lumpy features. He dressed himself in a suit of clothes to match the type and got from a near-by garage one of several cars he kept.[31]

In a smart, expensive coupé, he drove directly to the building which housed the Merchants' and Manufacturers' Bank.

Business was going on as usual The bank's doors were open. An armored truck stood close to the curb. A load of cash was being

---

31 AUTHOR'S NOTE: Each car of the Agent's is registered under a different name. The fund in the First National Bank is for the purchase of combating, crime, and Agent "X" isn't niggardly in the way he spends it. The pursuit of the Death-Torch Killers had already cost thousands. There was the money he had given to Monk Magurren and his gangsters to aid him in kidnapping the police commissioner. There was the amount he had already set aside to pay for the airplane he had destroyed. And he stood prepared to spend thousands more if it would help in running down this band of brutal murderers.

taken in, while grim-faced guards watched alertly from a distance. Depositors and business men were displaying their faith in this bank which had withstood the bandits' raid.

Agent "X" went to the renting manager of the building. He presented himself as Andrew Balfour of the Midland-Central Utilities Company and, under this guise, rented an office on the fourth floor—one he had previously noticed was vacant.

IN the next hour, posing as Andrew Balfour, he acted the part of a slave driver. Like a man accustomed to getting things done at high pressure, he ordered immediate deliveries of typewriters, desk equipment, and office stationery.

He had a letterer put the name "Midland-Central Utilities Company" on the frosted glass of the door. He had his own office marked: "Andrew Balfour, Private."

Then he visited an employment agency and hired several girl office workers.

As a business man of apparently substantial resources, Secret Agent "X" wandered again into Banton's office, just across the corridor.

The private detective's manner showed that he had already checked up on the building's new tenant. He was suave and deferential with the oiliness of a man who hopes to get a new client.

Puffing a cigar, hands in vest pockets, Secret Agent "X" leaned back in the padded chair that Banton courteously provided him.

"There is a chance," he said, "that I may need some investigating of an intimate nature done for me. I would like an idea of your fees and facilities."

Banton was more than willing to oblige. While Agent "X" watched, listening and sizing the man up, Banton talked.

"My regular policy," he said, "is one half down and one half when the case is finished. But for a man of your standing I'll be willing to undertake any investigation with no thought of remuneration until the affair is finished. I have many competent assistants."

Agent "X" got a glimpse of these—shifty-eyed men of the stool-pigeon type, men who could be trusted to climb in porch windows and steal evidence if it could not be obtained in any other way.

He thanked Banton and left, with the detective's card in his pocket.

Darlington didn't show up that day. Inquiries revealed that he had been released from headquarters. But Agent "X," in the role of Balfour, stayed on in his office after his girls had left. To spy on Banton and Darlington without arousing suspicion had been his purpose in renting the place. Through Banton he expected to check up on Rosa Carpita, also. His engaging of an office force had been an elaborate blind.

In his shirt sleeves, surrounded with papers and files, he appeared to be furiously busy. Banton wandered in once to exchange pleasantries with the new tenant who gave promise of becoming a client. At intervals Agent "X" went to the mail chute in the corridor and kept his eye on both men's offices.

It was toward nine that he saw again the flickering blue light in Darlington's transom. The crank had returned.

Agent "X" ran up and knocked at Darlington's door. When the elderly crank thrust his head out Secret Agent "X" bent forward excitedly.

"I beg your pardon," he said. "I saw an odd light. I thought perhaps there was a short circuit—danger of fire, you know."

"Who are you?" rasped Darlington.

"A new tenant—a neighbor of yours on this floor. I moved in today. Sorry if I disturbed you."

Darlington was clad again in his stained smock. He seemed as busily absorbed as he had the night previous.

"You'll learn to mind your business," he snapped. "Good night, sir."

With that he slammed the door in the Agent's face.

For nearly an hour the wavering light in Darlington's office continued while the crank pursued his nocturnal labors. Then, as Agent "X" made a trip to the mail chute, he saw that Darlington's transom was black. The crank had apparently left.

All the offices on the floor except Banton's were empty. The corridor was still.

Agent "X" walked quickly to Darlington's door and knocked. There was no answer. He paused a moment, listened, then took a cleverly shaped pass-key from his pocket. With a twist of his wrist he opened the door and entered.

A window was raised, but the office was deserted.

Swiftly Agent "X" searched the place with his flash light. The probing beam covered every part of the room. It fell on the rows of books, the scientific instruments, the retorts and jars of chemicals.

Over these the Agent lingered longest, a questing glint in his eyes. The terrible *Flammenwerfer* gun was a chemical weapon. Was there sinister significance in the hidden researches of Darlington?

In a worn notebook Agent "X" discovered figures that Darlington had jotted down. They seemed to pertain to the velocity of light. Apparently the man was what he claimed to be. And apparently he had completed his investigations for the night.

Then Agent "X" saw an open leather case belonging to some sort of instrument—a camera it seemed, but one equipped for special purposes. There were holders for lenses and ray filters, metal frames for film packs. Where was the camera itself? Had Darlington taken it with him?

"X" left the office, went back to his own. When he came out again, Banton's office, too, was dark. Agent "X" took a chance and slipped into it, but the papers in the detective agency gave no clew as to the man's connection with Rosa Carpita.

Agent "X," still in the role of Balfour, left and descended to the street. There were a half-dozen lines of investigation open to him— one to learn the whereabouts of Miss Carpita. He didn't doubt his ability to do so. He anticipated a night of feverish activity.

Then suddenly he held his breath, pressed back against the side of the bank building. The blood in his veins seemed to run cold. From the darkness above him came a bloodcurdling human cry. It was a cry of fury and stark fear. The Secret Agent looked up.

He could see nothing, but echoes of that hideous cry whispered along the face of the building.

Then something that seemed like a giant bat with outspread wings hurtled down out of the darkness. It was ghastly, uncanny. The Agent stepped back, and as he did so something slapped the pavement at almost the precise spot where he had stood. It was the body of a man—the body of A. J. Darlington.

MYSTERY CLUE

W**ITH A SENSE** of crawling horror Agent "X" stared. The awful *smack* of Darlington against the pavement told a story of its own. Every bone in the man's body was broken. He lay face downward, a sprawled and hideous blob, arms and legs spread out. After that terrible cry, after the sight of him falling, the sudden silence that ensued was like a ghastly vacuum of death.

Then the vacuum was punctuated by the sound of thudding footsteps. One of the special guards stationed in front of the bank came running around the corner.

Secret Agent "X," in the role of Balfour, pointed. He heard the guard's horrified exclamation. The man's face was a sickly white. Gingerly he bent over the prostrate form of the crank experimenter. Agent "X" was marshaling his thoughts. This was a development that in his wildest dreams he hadn't anticipated. But even in that moment of surprise and horror he didn't forget that he was playing a role.

"It's Darlington," he said. "The old gentleman who has an office on the same floor as mine."

The special guard nodded.

"You'd hardly know him. He must have fallen or committed suicide. His office is right above here."

It was true. Agent "X" looked up. The windows of Darlington's room where he worked so late were directly above the spot on the sidewalk where the man had met such a ghastly end.

The guard stood erect, mopping cold sweat from his face.

"I heard him cry—I won't forget it. This place gives me the creeps. Four guys murdered the other day—and now this bird tumbles out of his window."

Agent "X" stood frowning, his eyes fierce and bright. He had been in Darlington's office five minutes ago. He couldn't tell the guard that. But Darlington hadn't been there then. Yet here he was, dead, a blob of shattered flesh beneath his own window. It was mystery added to mystery.

The guard drew a whistle from his pocket, blew it. A police detective stationed outside the bank came to the spot also. Agent "X" had seen him before. Curry was his name.

"It's enough to drive a man nuts," said the special bank guard. "The old bird on the fourth floor has bumped himself off."

Curry stood staring down, then began questioning the man he thought was Balfour.

Agent "X" answered mechanically. He was staring at Darlington's body. The crank's desperate cry and the sickening sound of flesh striking stone still echoed in his ears. It troubled Agent "X." Even more than the actual horror of it was a question that repeated itself again and again. Where had Darlington been when Agent "X" was in his office? How had he gotten back so soon?

"Stay here," said Curry to the bank guard. "I'll go up and take a look at his place. Maybe he left a suicide note. He was a nut anyway. They had him down at headquarters last night. I guess the sweating they gave him was too much for his nerves."

The detective strode off. Agent "X's" first impulse was to follow. Then something detained him. He stared at Darlington's body again, stared up at the face of the building. His eye traveled along floor after floor, lingered on the fourth, continued on up. Suddenly he tensed. The answer to his own secret question had come! The law of increasing velocity was at work here. The shapeless hulk that had once been a man formed a terrible and startling clew.

Agent "X" turned, went back into the building. The guard thought he was following Detective Curry.

But Agent "X" didn't go to the elevator. He didn't want even its operator to see him. What he had to do must be done alone. Swiftly for a man who appeared as old as Balfour, he began ascending the building's stairs, going cautiously when he reached the fourth landing.

A light shone in Darlington's office. Curry was there, searching for a possible suicide note. Eyes glowing brightly, Secret Agent "X" crossed the corridor and continued up. He was convinced that Curry would find nothing. He believed he knew the answer to the state of Darlington's body. He had seen other men fall—seen them afterwards.

FLOOR after floor he ascended, winding his way up through the building's interior. Once he tiptoed softly to pass the open door of an office where a scrub woman labored. Once he heard the voices of a group of late workers standing by the elevator. He continued to the building's top floor. This was dark and deserted. There were two vacancies in it, and two offices that were occupied, but they were closed for the day.

Moving stealthily as a shadow, Agent "X" found a stairway that led to the roof above. It was a metal door and it was unlocked. Agent "X" tensed.

A flight of iron stairs led to a skylight. He climbed them quietly, examined the skylight. This, too, was unfastened and he pushed it slowly up.

A blast of cold night air struck his face. Overhead he saw the clear, brilliant twinkle of the stars.

He closed the skylight, stepped out on the tarred roof. It was broad and flat with a strip of coping around it that made a border of shadow black as jet. The roof seemed as big as a field. Two or three ventilators thrust up starkly, standing like still, watching figures.

Agent "X" stared alertly about him, but could see no movement. All seemed quiet.

Like a man unsure of his ground, he stole forward. His feet made no noise on the black tarred surface. He came to the edge of the coping, looking over.

Far below he could see the spot on the sidewalk that was a man's body. Darlington! The guard was still there, too, and other figures were moving up.

Rising through the walled canyon of the street in a weird and mournful moan came the siren of an ambulance.

Agent "X" turned away. His eyes were like steel points. There were uneasy prickles along his spine, a warning of danger.

He had his flash out. With its pencil-thin beam he began searching the roof. Then he stooped and picked something up.

It was a small brass screw head, knurled at the edges. It was polished, uncorroded—showing that it had been freshly dropped. Even one night of dew would have given it a thin coating of verdigris.

A little thing, but to Agent "X" it was concrete evidence that he had been right. The thing in his hand was the screw of a camera's focusing adjustment.

Darlington hadn't fallen from his window. He had been up here. His researches had led him to the building's roof. And from this height his body had rocketed down.

Agent "X" recalled that empty case he had seen in Darlington's office—the case he had felt certain belonged to some sort of camera. The camera wasn't on the sidewalk. It was nowhere on the roof. It had disappeared completely—and this, coupled with the small brass screw in his hand was significant to the Agent's alert mind. It was evidence that Darlington hadn't fallen or committed suicide—evidence that the man had been pushed off the roof—murdered!

Breathless over his discovery, every nerve alert, Agent "X" probed farther with the beam of his flash light.

Foot by foot Agent "X" continued to search. Then he paused abruptly again. His toe had struck against something. He flashed on his light.

Screwed into the surface of the roof was some sort of socket. It was dark-colored, inconspicuous, almost flush with the tarred covering.

HE searched and found others. They seemed to form a mysterious pattern. They were strung along at intervals of ten feet or more.

Under the inner edge of the coping he made another discovery. A wire ran the length of it. At intervals along this wire electric lamp sockets were fastened to the boarding. Every six feet he found one of them. All were empty.

Down in the street the siren of the ambulance rose again as it bore Darlington's body away. Echoes reverberated like ghoulish laughter, mocking those whom mystery baffled.

Were these sockets more of the slain crank's handiwork? Was he in the habit of setting his strange equipment up here and gazing at the stars by night?

Somewhere in that string of sockets showing under "X's" flash like challenging, unwinking eyes was the answer—the solution perhaps of the terrible *Flammenwerfer* murders. For the death of A. J. Darlington seemed to link up with those other horrible killings at the bank.

But Agent "X's" investigations were suddenly, rudely interrupted. He was following the coping, heading toward the spot where it angled away along the west side of the building. The two sides formed a dark corner.

So quickly that "X" was caught off guard, a shadow detached itself from this pool of blackness, bounded toward him. He tried to swing his flash as he heard the scrape of feet on the tarred roof, but a balled fist knocked it from his hand. A man tried to dash by him, and Agent "X" leaped in and grappled. He realized then that someone with a coat drawn up to hide the whiteness of his face had been squatting in that corner all the time.

The man was big, powerful. He fought with savage ferocity to break away. The Agent couldn't see his features—the roof was too dark—but Agent "X" had an uncanny sense that he knew who it was.

Locked like boxers in a clinch they fought desperately, exchanging short, swift body blows, swaying and panting. The movement of their feet made a dry scuffing on the roof. They lurched to the right, edged nearer the coping.

The big man whose face was hidden gave a harsh cry of fear. Agent "X" tensed and pressed his body back. For, in a fleeting instant of horror, he saw the lighted streets below him. They were battling close to the coping, their torsos hanging over.

Repeating his cry "X's" assailant jerked away. Terror gave him frenzied strength. Agent "X" was unbalanced, pulled forward away from the coping. He toppled through the air, crashed to the dark roof, and the black upright finger of a steam-escape pipe struck against the side of his head. For a moment his body went limp and it seemed that the sky was settling upon him, dropping with a rush and a roar that threatened oblivion.

A DETECTIVE THIEF

FOR PAINFUL SECONDS he seemingly battled to hold the sky at bay, to keep the stars from burning him. He struck at them, felt them burst and fly off like sparks from an emery wheel. Then he came to his senses.

He was lying on his back on the cold roof. Something slammed somewhere. It was the skylight cover. He tried to rise, fell back, then got groggily to his feet. For the first time he became conscious that he was gripping something. It was small and round and hard.

He saw his flash light case gleaming ten feet away, staggered over and recovered it. He clicked it on and looked at the thing in his hand.

The muscles along his hunched shoulders grew rigid. His eyes became bright. For the thing he held was a pencil with a metal clip. It was painted blue and red. There were no initials on it—nothing extraordinary about it—but the Agent knew he had seen it before. He had an uncanny memory for details, seldom forgot anything that had once registered.

The pencil belonged to Agency Detective George Banton.

Leaving the roof he descended the building's many stairs rapidly. He saw nothing of Banton, and the fourth-floor offices of the detective agency were dark. Agent "X" hurried to the street.

For an instant his gaze swivelled along the sidewalk. There was still a dark, ghastly stain where Darlington's body had fallen. He shuddered and the lights in his eyes became bright as polished steel.

At a pace rapid for a man of the apparent age and dignity of Andrew Balfour, he set off up the street. Three blocks away his roadster was parked. He got in, drove to the nearest of his hideouts, and made a rapid change of disguise. When he reappeared this time he was dressed as a young and dapper man—derby hat, trim dark suit, topcoat—a man who would be presentable anywhere without attracting particular attention to himself.

He sped to Detective Banton's home address listed in the telephone book. It was a luxurious apartment in an expensive section of the city. There, confident of his disguise, Agent "X" asked bluntly to see the detective, ready with a pretext for his visit that would allay Banton's suspicions. But an attendant in the foyer informed him that Banton hadn't been back all evening.

Agent "X" turned away abruptly. Banton was the hottest lead along that trail of death and terror. But there were other channels of investigation open. To burrow in from all angles until the crimson edges of the crime picture were complete was the Agent's method. And time was precious. He would return to Banton later.

His next point of investigation was the home of Jerome Davis, murdered banker. With Davis dead and Mrs. Davis still in Europe, there should be no one there but the servants.

A daring plan came into Agent "X's" mind. It was imperative that he learn more if possible of the banker's connection with Rosa Carpita. Then he might discover why Rosa had engaged Banton.

Agent "X" parked his car a full block away from the Davis home, approaching the house from the opposite side of the street. Caution had become instinctive with him.

He crossed the pavement, slipped through a hedge, and circled the house. A dog growled somewhere. Agent "X" paused. Then he sounded his strange, melodious whistle. It was faint now, too faint to reach those inside. It was meant for the dog's ears alone. The dog's growling, which had been about to burst into a bark, ceased. Agent "X" saw the twin phosphorescences of the animal's eyes. The dog was coming toward him stiff-legged, inquiring.

Agent "X" made a clucking sound in his throat. He stood waiting for the dog, then gave his low, strange whistle again. The animal approached, sniffed, wagged its tail. In a moment he was patting the dog's head and the two of them were on the best of terms.[32]

There was a dim light in the vestibule of the house, another in the kitchen. Coming close to a window, Agent "X" saw a middle-

---

32   AUTHOR'S NOTE: *The Agent has an uncanny faculty for making friends with animals. They seem to sense the strange magnetism of his personality. And his whistle, a peculiar, ventriloquistic, birdlike note, first arouses the interest, then gains the confidence, of dogs particularly.*

aged couple sitting forlornly at a table. These appeared to be the only servants.

THE upper floor of the house was dark. A porch roof on one side of a rose trellis leading up to it offered a way of access. But, with the couple preoccupied in the kitchen, Agent "X" took an easier course. He quietly and swiftly ascended the front steps, produced one of his delicate pass-keys, and in a moment was inside the house,

The dog, whining softly, tried to follow him. Agent "X" smiling shook his head and motioned the animal back. He left the beast squatting on its haunches puzzled as to why it couldn't enter the house with its new-found friend.

On rubber-soled shoes Agent "X" crossed the front hall of the house and climbed the stairs.

Investigation of the five bedrooms on the second floor soon revealed the one Davis had occupied. There was a set of golf clubs in a man's clothes closet. Just off the bedroom was a den. The probing beam of the Agent's flash light went eagerly into this, disclosed an easy chair and a heavy mahogany desk.

He began examining the desk drawers. Would Davis keep letters from another woman in the house where his wife might find them? Possibly, considering that Mrs. Davis was away now. Then "X" stooped eagerly. Built directly into the heavy desk was a small safe.

He got down on one knee, put his ear to the safe, and moved the dial gently. His ability to discover the combination of a safe by hearing and touch alone was uncanny. In less than five minutes the small door of the safe swung open.

There were letters inside and confidential reports. He went through them quickly, selected two letters with feminine handwriting on them. They were brief notes from Rosa Carpita, accepting luncheon dates. A third, written several weeks later, showed that her friendship with Davis had progressed. He had invited her to take a ride in a plane with him.

Agent "X" put the letters in his pocket. Then suddenly he started. His ears had detected a sound outside. It was the abrupt, low growling of a dog. He closed the safe quickly, strode to the window. The growling stopped as he listened, ending in a strange little yelp of pain. Then all was quiet.

But the Agent, staring out of the dark room, saw a flitting shape cross the lawn below. He saw the figure pause, stare up at the house. It was a man.

Agent "X" waited. The man suddenly and surprisingly began to climb the rose trellis under Davis's window. A bleak look came into the Agent's eyes. His pulse beat faster. He tip-toed out of the den, went behind a screen in the farthest corner of the bedroom, and waited there, gas gun in hand.

Seconds of tenseness passed. Something moved by the window. There was a faint scrape, a squeak of wood, then a snap. The window was raised, and a bulky form stepped into the room.

Agent "X" could hear the man breathing heavily after his exertions. All was silent in the house. The man turned on a flash, swivelled it around the room. Then he walked cautiously toward the door of the den.

As the light from the man's flash fell on the wall ahead of him, Agent "X" got a glimpse of his silhouette. He tensed and held his breath. The man was no ordinary burglar. He was a gross, thick-necked figure. He was Private Detective Banton!

THE Secret Agent watched to see what Banton would do next.

In a moment he found out. The detective, too, made the discovery of the safe in Davis's desk. He twirled the dial for a moment, then drew something from inside his overcoat. It was a leather kit of safe-breaking tools. Banton put a pair of gloves on, selected a diamond-pointed drill, and bored a series of holes around the lock. He probed and pushed with a metal pick through these holes.

At the end of half an hour, with prodigious sweating and labor, he succeeded by main strength in doing what the Agent had done by skill and knowledge.

With the safe finally open, Banton seemed shaken and nervous. He stopped to listen, fearful apparently that he would be caught in his act of safe-breaking. He didn't wait to go through the papers in the safe. He began stuffing its entire contents in the deep pocket of his overcoat.

Agent "X" catted silently from behind his screen, crossed to the corridor door, and slipped out. Swiftly he descended the stairs, crossed the front hall, and left the house as he had come.

He moved around it toward the rose trellis, stopped. His foot had touched something. For a brief moment he bent down and flicked on his flash. Then he scowled and muttered harshly.

The dog that he had made friends with a short time before lay stunned at his feet. Banton had silenced the animal by a cruel blow on the head with a blackjack. Gently Agent "X" stroked the dog's silky ears and soft muzzle. He wished he had time to stay and revive the animal, but there was already a faint sound above his head. Banton was coming out the window.

Agent "X" crept into the shadows of a hedge. There he waited tensely. The bulky form of Banton appeared as a dark blotch on the roof, came down the rose trellis, crossed the lawn. Agent "X" followed.

When Banton had gotten a block away from the Davis home he moved with the confidence of a man who is satisfied with the job he has done. He walked two blocks, got into a little closed flivver, and drove off. The Agent sprinted for his own car, climbed in, and drove along a street paralleling the course Banton had taken. Then he swung toward it, saw Banton's flivver pass, and followed it.

Banton went first to his own apartment. Agent "X" waited outside tensely. The fact that the detective had left his flivver parked at the curb directly in front of the building indicated he was not through with his nocturnal prowlings. The car, shabby like his clothes and out of keeping with his evident prosperity, was a means of remaining inconspicuous.

In twenty minutes Banton reappeared and drove off. This time Agent "X" stepped out of his hiding-place and signaled a taxi cruising past. Banton might become suspicious if he saw the same roadster behind him again.

The chase led across town and Agent "X" ordered the taxi to slow up when he saw Banton's flivver stopping. Banton got out, looked around once, then moved off, walking on the balls of his feet with the pussyfooting gait of a professional sleuth.

He turned into a dark side street, moved more slowly. Agent "X" stayed as far behind as he dared and kept to the shadows. Banton looked uneasy. He slowed down still more. Suddenly Agent "X" tensed.

A figure stepped out of a doorway and joined Banton. It was the figure of a girl. She took Banton's arm and they moved off together. Agent "X" crossed the street and followed them.

They continued for two blocks and entered a small Italian restaurant. Agent "X" strolled by and looked in. Then he nodded to himself and his eyes gleamed. The girl who had met Banton was Rosa Carpita.

She hadn't left town after all. She was in hiding, and, far from her regular haunts, she had met Detective Banton by prearrangement.

Agent "X" meditated a moment. He wanted to hear what they were saying, just why the girl had engaged the professional services of Banton, but it was important, too, that he find out where she lived. In the restaurant it would be impossible to use his microphone. They might become suspicious if he took a table too near them.

He engaged a taxi and had it wait around the corner, heading into the street the restaurant was on. Then he took up a position where he could watch the front entrance. His nerves and brain cried out for action, but this was a situation that called for patience and care.

It was a long wait, nearly an hour, before the two reappeared. They parted at the door of the restaurant, Banton going one way, the girl going the other. This meant that they had concluded their business, whatever it was.

THE girl set off on foot. Agent "X" paid off his disgruntled taxi driver for the time spent in waiting. He himself followed the girl on foot, shadowing her to a shabby, low-class hotel, five blocks from the restaurant. It was very different from her own swanky apartment, proving that the girl was taking no chances of being seen by anyone she knew.

He waited till she had passed through the lobby and had taken the old-fashioned elevator upstairs. She must have checked in here that very day.

Leaning over the desk, Agent "X" made inquiries as to rates in the hotel. As he did so he stared at the register. The only entry of a single party made that day was "Marie Rosa, Washington, D.C." The Agent nodded with a faint, grim smile on his lips.

He thanked the clerk for his information, then turned and left. A plan had come to his mind. Now that he knew Rosa Carpita's whereabouts and had seen her in close confab with Banton, he might go to her disguised as the private detective. But first he would have to learn from Banton himself some inkling of what their business was.

He took a taxi to the block where he had parked his own roadster, and headed back toward Banton's apartment, devising alternate plans according to whether Banton was in or out.

Almost mechanically he sent the powerful car racing across town, his mind battling with the hideous murder mystery that was costing men's lives.

Suddenly the Agent turned his head. The high-pitched wail of a police siren sounded. He drew toward the side of the street. A green radio patrol car shot past, going like the wind.

There was a frenzied note in the blast of its siren, recklessness in its speed. Wrenching the wheel, the Agent turned and followed. He heard another car join the first, racing in the same direction. A crawling sense of horror filled him. A hunch told him it could mean only one thing. The torch-killing band of robbers had struck again!

CHAPTER XIV

MELTING MURDER

CROUCHING OVER THE wheel, he pressed the gas button down until his own long, low roadster was eating up the distance that separated it from the nearest radio cruiser. The red taillight of the police car increased rapidly in size.

It was headed toward the mid-section of the city. Then brakes squealed in sudden protest. Rubber snarled on the pavement. The cruiser was slowing down.

Agent "X" saw why. Down the block another car was coming—a long, low roadster with a narrow windshield and flattened hood.

In his first horrified glimpse of it, Agent "X" recognized the car. It was the same one that had followed him when, disguised as Commissioner of Police Foster, he had nearly lost his life with Inspector Burks. Its terrific rate of travel indicated that it was speeding away from the scene of some other crime.

Agent "X," a cold chill clutching at his heart, wished he could cry out a warning to those cops in the car ahead. He tried to do so, but they didn't hear him. Then he jammed on his own brakes, watched like a man in the midst of a nightmare over which he has no control,

One of the cops in the cruiser thrust a submachine gun out of the vehicle's side, pressed a trigger, sending a stream of bullets toward the oncoming roadster. But it was a speeding target no man could hit.

It careened toward one curb, leaped back toward the other, came roaring on. Suddenly the Agent's knuckles went white on his own steering wheel. A wicked black snout poked out of the roadster's side-curtain. There was a hiss, a streak of light through the air, and a blinding, crackling jet of flame played over the police cruiser that had tried so staunchly to bar the murder car's way.

The cruiser, still moving, swerved and crashed into the curb. The cop with the machine gun tumbled out as the door burst open. He fell on his knees on the sidewalk, and the roadster roared by, its hideous weapon playing over the cruiser, killing the cop at the wheel, making a funeral pyre out of the trim headquarters car. It was gone up the block at express train speed before the fallen cop could arise.

Agent "X," trembling, slid into the curb behind the burning cruiser. The man inside was dead, beyond aid. The cop with the gun was just getting up. Agent "X" called out harshly and made a quick motion.

The cop hesitated only an instant, his face as white as parchment. Then he understood. He leaped onto Agent "X's" running board, and even as he did so, "X" sent his own car forward with a screech of quickly meshed gears.

The cop was silent as "X" hurtled ahead. The engine under its polished, streamlined hood rose to a vibrant roar of power. The clack and hiss of the tires made talk impossible. The Agent's eyes were focused far in front. He passed a police cruiser, outdistanced it. His knuckles were white, his eyes gleaming points of steel. For the moment he was acting on impulse. In a cold, unreasoning fury, now, he was doing the one thing that seemed possible, chasing the killers, hoping to give the cop with the gun another chance to use it.

Driving as he had never driven before, driving like a madman, he sent his roadster hurtling through the night-darkened streets. Then far ahead he saw the murder car. There was, he knew, some special motor under its low hood. His own cars were custom built, bought for the highest speed, the most exceptional usage. Pressing the gas button to the floor boards, risking death every instant, he crept up on the car before him.

The street no longer seemed like a street. It was a whizzing, hissing band of black asphalt, ripping back under the tires, threatening, it seemed, to tear them from the rims.

The cop beside him leaned out the side of the car. He was shaking, his face was deathly white. But his hands were holding the submachine gun steadily. The department heads might be getting nervous, losing their morale, but these men in blue were fighting like true soldiers. Agent "X" warmed to the man beside him. For the moment he was proud to be battling shoulder to shoulder with the law which had so often hunted him.

HE was gaining on the murder car now. The suburban streets were flashing by. Houses seemed to leap at them out of the darkness. In a moment he heard the stuttering report of the machine gun in the cop's hand. An acrid whiff of smokeless, powder filled his nostrils, lashed back by the wind. The ejector of the gun was spitting empty shell cases.

Then with breath-taking suddenness the murder car seemed to be coming toward them. Agent "X" knew what it meant.

He applied the brakes, shouted a warning to the man beside him. He wasn't thinking of his own life. But nothing would be accomplished if the killers in the car, now slowing down, were allowed to slaughter again.

Then, in the air directly ahead, shutting out view of the murder car, blinding like a blazing sun of death, appeared a fiery eye of flame. The cop swore fiercely. The jet of flame came nearer. Its heat was scorching. In another instant it would be upon them. The cop flung down his gun and jumped.

Agent "X" crouched, jammed on the brakes. The sickening smell of scorching rubber filled his nostrils. The front tires of the car blew with reports like miniature bombs. The roadster bumped and sagged on tire rims. He opened the door, flung sideways, just in time.

The jet of flame descended on the car, melting the windshield as though it were a sheet of ice, firing the padded leather cushions inside. With the cop beside him, "X" raced for the protective shadows beside the street.

The murderer's car drove on, leaving Agent "X's" roadster a burned and ravaged wreck.

Crouched in the chill darkness, waiting for the other radio cruisers to come up, the cop told Agent "X" what had happened.

"I don't know you, buddy, but you got guts," the cop said. "We didn't get 'em—but we tried. They blew the safe of the Graybar Jewelry Company and got away with a half million in ice. They burned the guard, just burned the guy, too. Schroder and me got it over—the guy that was driving me, a good guy, too. Schroder and me got it over the air from headquarters and tried to head 'em off. But a swell chance a fella's got against that heat gun they use."

Agent "X" nodded somberly. A direct attack against the torch killers was suicidal. His face was bleak in the wavering glare of his burning roadster. He heard other motors down the block—radio cruisers coming. The murder car had sped on—no one knew where.

Cold fury at the killers possessed him. He didn't wait for the cruisers to come up. There would be questions, delay. He wanted to get back to the city, back to his own line of investigation at once. Without any explanation to the surprised cop he flung off into the shadows and disappeared.

He crossed a lot, put two blocks between himself and the light of his burning roadster, then he located a taxi. The police would have another mystery to probe as to the owner of the burning car. The name it was registered under would tell them nothing. There was no such person.

Agent "X" sat still and tense as the cab sped back along the route over which he had pursued the murder car. The night had been a chain of apparently unprofitable episodes. But he had gained something—learned the whereabouts of Rosa Carpita, and caught Banton in strange actions. Banton!

"X" leaned forward, spoke to the driver. The cab stopped in front of the private detective's apartment. It was late, getting close to midnight. Banton's flivver wasn't outside the building. "X" hoped the man was in. He would have some sort of show-down. There must be an end to these death-torch horrors, and, if Banton knew anything, "X" would find a way to make him talk.

He located Banton's suite number in the mail slot and went directly up, letting himself into the building with a pass-key. The switchboard operator merely glanced at him as he passed by, thinking he was a tenant or the friend of a tenant.

AGENT "X" pressed Banton's buzzer and waited. But there was no answer. Banton was out. Unceremoniously, then, Agent "X" entered.

The apartment was small, unattractive, cluttered. He searched with the thoroughness of a trained investigator, worked with the frenzied speed of a man driven on by a single motive. But the results of his search were disappointing.

He located a safe, opened it, and came upon the papers Banton had stolen from Davis's house. There were also records of Banton's more shady transactions for various clients. But there was nothing which threw light on his dealings with Rosa Carpita. That must be gotten from the man himself. There were two courses open to Agent "X." To wait here for Banton's return, or to go in search of him.

Agent "X's" nerves cried out for action. It was possible Banton had gone back to his office. He could make the trip there, then return if he failed to locate Banton.

"X" went to the nearest of his hide-outs and changed back to the disguise of Andrew Balfour. As he drove in a cab to the bank building he mapped out a course of action.

"X" left his cab and walked swiftly to the side door of the bank building.

He entered with his tenant's key, ascended quickly to Banton's office. But it was dark and empty. "X" let himself into his own suite, then switched on the lights and paced the floor, thinking.

He hated to involve Betty Dale in any way. Yet in the present situation she could help him. It would be easier for her than for him to check up again on the movements of Rosa Carpita. He knew that Betty, as always, would be willing to aid him, and, late as it was, he didn't hesitate to call her.

But, as his hand reached out for the telephone, he paused. Faintly through the thick walls of the room a strange scraping sounded. Another man might not have heard it. But the Agent's hearing was uncannily keen. The scraping noise was followed by a thud that was hollow, ghostly. The Agent leaped to his feet.

He strode to the door, opened it, thrust his head out and listened. Banton's office was dark, but once again he heard the eerie scraping. It filled the corridor with a thin whisper of sound, faint as the rustling of a serpent's scales sliding over stone. It set his teeth on edge. Then the noise ceased.

The Agent stood puzzled a moment, went to the door of Banton's office and let himself in with a skeleton key. Tensely he searched the place, but no human thing was there.

He went back to his own office, got out his sensitive sound amplifier and pressed the disc microphone to the wall. Then he trembled with excitement. A turn of the rheostat control and the scraping sound reached his ears again. It seemed to be on the floor above now, or even higher. With a sudden hiss of breath the Agent put his amplifier down. He leaped into the corridor and started at a run for the stairs that led upward.

CHAPTER XV

DANGER FLIGHT

THERE WERE MANY of them. The building towered sixteen stories above the floor his own office was on. But he dared not use the elevator, dared take no one into his confidence. There were secret and sinister things in the wind.

He climbed the stairs three at a time, floor after floor. Near the top he paused an instant to rest and listen. He no longer heard the scraping noise. The great building was still. But gradually as he waited a new sound intruded upon his consciousness. It was the muffled, far-off beat of an airplane motor, and it seemed to be approaching. Once again the Agent was electrified into action.

He took the last flight of skylight stairs in a reckless leap, crouched tensely. Then, as he cautiously raised the glass cover, he heard again the faint deep-throated mutter of a plane somewhere in the dark sky overhead.

The cloud ceiling was low. Swirling, trailing vapor threatened wind and rain. The glow of the streets was reflected in this mist. The ship above seemed to be nosing down through it, feeling its way. Perhaps it was only a mail plane, perhaps—

But Agent "X" strained forward. His gaze left the clouds, went to the roof. His eyes grew wide with intent interest.

There were times when his swift actions were based on so-called "hunches"—really the quick interplay of deductive faculties working below the conscious level of his mind. It was such a hunch, such a subconscious deduction, that had made him suspicious of the sound in the wall and brought him up to the roof. And it had not led him wrong.

For the roof had undergone an amazing transformation. From the under edge of the coping on each side a bright glow of light was now flaring out—light from bulbs, the sockets of which he had discovered on his previous visit.

And, from the roof's center, set in the strange socket clamps, was a collapsible framework of slender tubular steel.

There was a pulley, a sliding truck, a spring releasing device—with something set in a metal holder that caught and held the Agent's eye.

The thing was a big canvas sack like a mail pouch.

In one rushing, clear-visioned flash of understanding the Agent grasped the significance of what he saw. It linked up with the strange death of Darlington, and brought him one step nearer to the death-torch killers.

The device in the center of the roof was similar to that used in airmail pickup. The airplane circling overhead, feeling its way down through the low clouds, was coming to get that sack. What the sack contained, Agent "X" could guess. The crank, Darlington, had been murdered because, in his lonely studies of light, he had come up to this roof to look at the stars, photograph them, perhaps, and had accidentally interfered with the plans of a fiendishly clever band of thieves and killers.

The Secret Agent leaped forward to the waiting canvas sack. A knotted cord fastened the neck of it. A stout braided wire cable was bolted to a series of metal rings sewed directly to the heavy canvas, sufficiently strong to stand the jerk when the sack was swung into the air after a catapult device had thrown it forward.

The Agent unknotted the cord at the sack's mouth. He moved with lightninglike speed, knowing that any instant the plane above might swing into sight. The poor visibility, the lowness of the clouds, was all that made possible the desperate thing he planned to do.

Many packages of bank notes were there, and smaller canvas sacks of gold and silver coins. Here was a haul of stolen loot waiting to be relayed to some safe hiding-place—loot that had been taken at the cost of men's lives.

There were a dozen big ventilators jutting from the roof. With an armful of packages containing bank notes the Agent ran to the nearest of these. Unceremoniously he dumped the cash in. He wasn't sure where it would fall, but it could be located and recovered afterward. Frenziedly, working against time, he made four more trips, dumping the bags of coins into the ventilator, too, emptying the big canvas sack hooked to the catapult.

He heard the airplane in the clouds above shut off its motor. He knew the significance of that. The ship was getting ready to dive below the clouds, glide in to make its pickup. His experienced ears told him that its motor was muffled, that the pilot was taking no chances of having someone in the street hear him.

With eyes bright as pin points of polished steel the Agent moved close to the sack. The thing he was about to do seemed almost suicidal. It required sheer nerve, fearlessness of death—characteristics that the Agent possessed to an extraordinary degree.

The instant before the plane above broke through the under edge of the clouds, Agent "X" stepped into the sack, replacing with his own body the bulk of the bills and coins he had taken out. The weight was not greatly different. Perhaps he was twenty or thirty pounds heavier. But the sack was big, the catapult device should be strong enough. He hoped so, waiting silently, with the cord he had removed once again looped around the mouth of the sack, its ends drawn inside. He tied them just as he heard the first thin whistle of rushing air sweeping through flat wires.

IT seemed an eternity while the whistle mounted into a wavering screech. Then the pilot of the approaching plane flattened his glide. The screech lessened, became a thin wail. The wail grew steadily louder.

Blood pounded through the Agent's temples. He could hear the beating of his heart as though it were sledgehammer blows. He had been in many strange and desperate situations, but never one quite like this, when seconds seemed to stand still, when he waited for the grappling cable of the oncoming plane to sweep him into the very jaws of death.

He could hear the clank and swish of the still revolving propeller, like the beat of great ghastly wings. Then there came a click, a snap. The Agent held himself tautly, gripping the cord of the sack mouth in fingers that were white and steely.

Abruptly he toppled sidewise, pressed against the side of the sack. The sack was rushing forward. His neck was snapped back, his head was pressed against the canvas, too, as though a thousand pounds were holding it there. Breath hissed from his lungs.

There was another snap, a nerve-shattering, forward lurch, a dizzy sense of being whirled in an arc as though he were on a giant pendulum. Then a rush of upward movement at express-train speed.

Now he was pressed to the bottom of the sack, glued there apparently, his only conscious hold still on the end of the cord, and the cord was straining into his fingers, cutting them. That upward movement was familiar. He had felt it before, though never like this. He knew he was free of the roof now, sweeping upward into the sky on the end of a slender cable—sweeping with the threat of death imminent.

There was a sudden low mutter of sound, a jarring tremble that the cable transmitted down to him. The plane's engine had been switched on again. He was yanked skyward at a steady, breath-taking pace. The sides of the sack grew clammy as it was drawn through the clouds.

Then the plane leveled out. There was a metallic grinding sound—the sack being reeled in.

Agent "X" waited. The suspense now was as great as when the plane was gliding in to pick him up. Would the pilot discover the amazing substitution that had been made—a living man instead of a sackful of stolen loot?

The grinding continued. The sack swung from side to side in dizzy, breath-taking sweeps that told of the plane overhead rocking and dipping in a windy night sky. The side of the sack struck something with a cracking blow that almost knocked Agent "X" unconscious.

He gasped, recoiled, felt the top of the sack flattened against a hard surface that pressed down on his neck and shoulders. His face was pushed forcibly into the canvas, but the grinding noise had ceased. There was only the steady vibrating roar of the plane's motor. The sack no longer swung. It had been snugged fast under the belly of the ship.

For almost a minute Agent "X" didn't attempt to move. He rested in his cramped, contorted position, breathing in great lungfuls of musty air. The last few seconds had been the most desperate of his entire career. He was still in the shadow of destruction suspended in a canvas sack under the fuselage of a madly racing bandit plane, flying toward an unknown objective.

But he was closer to the killers than he had been since their terrible raids started—closer perhaps to learning the secrets of their fiendish organization.

He began slowly limbering his cramped muscles while the plane hurtled on. The sweeping rocking movement of the tightly clamped sack told him that the air was rough, stirred by stormy winds. Only the lure of gold would have influenced any pilot to make such a daring pickup on a night like this.

THE Agent freed his left hand from the place where it was pinned under his own body. He worked it up toward the top of the sack.

With both hands he tugged at the cord fastening. But it was impossible to undo it, useless even to try, with the top of the sack wedged against the underside of the plane.

The Agent freed his right hand from its hold on the cord. He worked the fingers down to his pocket; fumbled for seconds in the numbing cold that was beginning to seep into the sack in the hundred-mile-an-hour slipstream.

His fingers came out at last holding a jackknife. With infinite effort he succeeded in opening it. Cautiously he drew the blade up until it was on a level with his eyes. He turned it, edged it sidewise, cut deftly through the canvas, making a small peephole. But he could see nothing.

A blast of wind struck his face with the force of some solid substance. He made the hole wider, edged the knife blade down. To stay in the sack in his present position until the plane landed would be suicidal. The killers who had snuffed out the lives of a dozen men would unhesitatingly butcher him.

But he had no definite plan of action. His one thought had been to find where the plane was going, who was piloting it, and to what secret hideout the stolen money was being taken.

He worked the slit in the sack until it was large enough for him to thrust an arm out. Feeling in the icy darkness and cutting blast of the slipstream, he verified what he had already guessed.

The ship was a seaplane, equipped with twin pontoons. It was the same plane from which the bullets had been fired that had shot Rosa Carpita from the skies, killed her pilot. The sack was snugged between its pontoons. He reached up, felt the cable on top. It disappeared through an eyelet in the fuselage of the plane, connecting with a reel somewhere in the pilot's cockpit.

For seconds he deliberated. The wind blast was getting terrific. The air was growing more and more bumpy. Wisps of chill fog whipping past, beaded his face with icy moisture. What should he do?

HE felt around the mouth of the sack with tense, groping fingers—felt for the rings that were sewed to the canvas. There were many of them; but if the stitching should become loosened, if the sack was gone when the plane landed, its loss would be attributed to the jerking, whipping lash of the wind. And the loss would cover his tracks. First, however, he must get out of the sack himself.

With the blade of the knife he slit the sack from top to bottom, and, regardless of the tearing blast of the wind, slowly crawled out, wrapped his legs around pontoon struts. Minutes passed before he was entirely independent of the sack for support.

Bracing himself in the full blast of the slipstream, with the hungry fingers of Death seeming to reach for him, he began systematically cutting the stitches around the metal rings.

Not until they were free, with no trailing thread whose cut end would tell that a knife had been used, did he stop to rest.

Not until he heard the empty sack whip back between the pontoons and go sailing off into the darkness behind the plane.

Then, braced and panting, he rested after his terrible exertions. Yet it was hardly a rest that a man would choose. For the force of the wind seemed bruising, and the numbing beat of the cold was making him ache all over. There were moments when the lulling voice of Death seemed bidding him to let go—find relief in a swift fall into the dizzy spaces below.

Suddenly he felt the ship's nose tilt downward. A sensation came like that of going earthward in a fast elevator. A cloud of mist beat up against his face. Holding tightly to the struts, he waited.

Minutes seemed to pass as the plane lost altitude. Suddenly lights showed through the swirling masses of vapor beneath. They were lights stretching in a semicircular ring, lights that the Agent had seen before. This was the harbor over which Rosa Carpita had circled in her hired plane.

The Agent's pulses quickened. The plane was coming down for a landing. There was purposefulness in the way it was descending.

It swung around in a great bank. The riding lights of ships, the lights strung along the shore, whirled in a strange kaleidoscope of luminescence. The hidden pilot above switched off the engine. For a moment he flicked on a searchlight—the same searchlight whose ruthless eye had picked out Rosa Carpita's plane in those terrible seconds when her pilot had been killed.

Looking down, Agent "X" saw storm-tossed water. Great swells were coming in from the open sea. The harbor seemed too rough for a landing. The pilot of the engine seemed to think so too. He hesitated, switched on his engine, came nearer shore. But, driven on by the lust for gold, men will do desperate things. The Agent knew this. It was evident that the pilot intended to land.

The Agent held his breath. This killer above him possessed infinite skill. No doubt of that. He handled the little plane like a master. His flying spoke of long experience in the air.

The plane circled again, descended till its long pontoons were almost touching the tops of the swells. The roar of breaking waves mingled with the beat of the throttled motor.

The Agent wrapped arms and legs around struts. Then the plane came down, touched.

To the Agent it seemed to crash with the force of a battering ram. The water seemed to have a rocklike hardness. An icy crest drenched him, battered him. But the plane was only on its first step. It settled still more, nosed into a breaking swell, driven by the gale. A half ton of water smacked against Agent "X." No man living could withstand it. It tore at his arms and legs. He felt himself slipping. Frantically he clutched, but a second wave followed the first. With a smothered, choking cry the Agent was swept from his precarious hold, swept into the black water as the plane settled to its landing.

CHAPTER XVI

THE AGENT INVESTIGATES

HIS HEAD FLICKED a strut as he was swept by. For an instant he fought the blazing, whirling lights that flashed in his brain. Then he struggled with the mountainous seas that seemed to crash in on top of him in glittering cascades. He sank beneath the surface, bobbed up in the wake of a hissing swell.

With numbed muscles and dazed brain he began the battle of his life. The sense that he was drowning spurred him on to fight with the water as though it were a living thing. He'd come too far to go under now, even though it would be easy to slip beneath the waves. Who would be the wiser? No one—but Agent "X" had work to do.

On the crest of a wave he gazed shoreward. The seaplane had disappeared in the blackness, its motor sound sinking to a low rumbling mutter, then ceasing entirely. It was somewhere resting on the water, but he couldn't see it.

He could see lights along the beach, however, and here and there the riding lanterns of vessels. Sensing the direction of the wind he allowed himself to go as the waves went, in toward the shore, husbanding his strength.

The huge steel side of a yacht loomed out of the darkness, shutting off his view of the shore. It seemed endless as he slid along its length. A single red riding light winked down at him. He might have called for help, but he didn't.

The plane had landed in this small harbor. Here somewhere was the solution of the terrible mystery of the torch murderers. In this vicinity they had stored their loot. He would not risk his chances of finding them by calling anyone's help now.

But the last half-mile to shore was a nightmare. Part of the time Agent "X" was half unconscious. He was battered, bruised, swirled by the waves. He felt as though he were swimming along some limitless watery treadmill, climbing numberless swells, descending into the hollows, rising to the top again. The sting of salt spray in his eyes almost blinded him.

When at last his feet touched bottom and he reached the shore, he could only crawl up it on hands and knees. He fell forward on his face, lay still, then heaved himself up again. This wouldn't do! He mustn't be discovered here. He struggled to his feet, stumbled up the beach. Then his knees bumped something. He groped blindly until, through smarting lids, he saw the dim bulk of a big shed against a background of light beyond.

He moved along it until his fingers found a door. It seemed loose, and, tugging against it, he found that it slid back on rollers. The air inside was warmer. It was heavy and musty with the scent of twine and tar. He sank again to his hands and knees, groped, and his fingers encountered a pile of old sails. On the rough canvas, with the wind shut out, he sank into exhausted slumber.

THE cold, gray light of dawn was filtering into cracks in the sail shed when Agent "X" awoke. He had the remarkable faculty of sleeping as soundly as a child when he slept at all, and of restoring weary nerves and muscles. In spite of his wet clothing and the exhaustion of a few hours before he stretched, rose, and felt fit again.

With quick, cautious steps he strode to the wall of the old sail shed and looked through a crack. A stretch of cold, gray harbor with boats floating on it met his eye. But the seaplane was nowhere in sight. For a moment he stood debating.

He knew that, wearing the disguise of Andrew Balfour, he must be an incongruous sight. The salt water had ruined the shape of his suit. Wet and wrinkled it was draped around his body. But, so perfect was the material used in his facial make-up that even the submersion hadn't washed it off.

He was still Andrew Balfour, still the middle-aged business man—but a man in appearance very much the worse for wear. If he were seen around here it might arouse the suspicion of the very people he didn't want it to. He couldn't say who they were. But he was certain now that the hiding place of the stolen jewels and currency that the torch robbers were taking in their wholesale banditry was somewhere around here—perhaps on one of the yachts.

That was the most logical place for it, and it instantly gave him an idea, a plan of action. But first he must get away and change his disguise.

He walked to another wall of the shed, looked along the shore. There were many bungalows and cottages, closed because of the earliness of the season. Smoke rose from the chimneys of a few built for all-year-round use. But no one was in sight. He judged it was still very early in the morning. His watch had stopped.

He opened the door of the shed, slipped around its side, and, keeping it between himself and the harbor, walked inland as fast as he could. Not until he got five hundred feet away from the water did he spy anyone. Then he saw a sleepy-looking milkman making his rounds. He ducked out of sight till the man and his horse and wagon passed by. There was a trolley track, but no trolley seemed to be running. The Agent wanted to get away from here as quickly as possible. But how?

There was no way out except to borrow someone's car. It could be returned later. He saw several parked before houses along side streets. One was in front of a hedge, hidden from the windows of the house. It was a touring car with the side curtains down. The ignition was locked, but Agent "X" quickly raised the engine hood, found the ignition wires, broke them off, joined their ends together, and established a circuit.

While the people in the house still slept he got into the car and drove off rapidly. He could leave it anywhere, and the police, through the Motor Vehicle Registry, would see that it was returned to its owner. To catch the band who had taken the lives of over a dozen men, Agent "X" felt he was justified in commandeering this car.

Back in the city, in one of his own hideouts, he changed his disguise to that of Elisha Pond, the mythical character in whose name a vast sum of money was on deposit in the First National Bank.

When the bank's doors opened at nine Agent "X" presented himself at the paying teller's window and drew out ten thousand dollars, asking mainly for bills of large denomination. The bank was accustomed to the eccentricities of "Mr. Pond." His account was of such size that all employees had been instructed to be especially respectful.

With the money in his possession, Agent "X" made another quick change. He put on a suit of expensive, sports tweeds, molded the lines of his face into the appearance of a well-groomed, well-fed, prosperous-looking bachelor in his late thirties. He placed a handkerchief in his upper coat pocket, the corner showing jauntily, put a huge solitaire diamond ring on his finger, and selected a Malacca walking stick. Attired thus, he set out again.

IT was nearly ten. He called Betty Dale and asked her as a favor to him to keep an eye on a certain Marie Rosa, registered in a down town hotel, the address of which he gave.

He next called up the offices of "Andrew Balfour" and told his office managers that he expected to be out of town for part of the day. He considered dropping in on Banton, but gave up the idea as profitless. First of all he wanted to establish a base at the yacht harbor from which he could operate without arousing anyone's suspicion. To do that he was prepared to splurge on a grandiose scale.

Under the name of K. K. Parker, one of many aliases he was accustomed to using, he hired a large limousine and chauffeur for a week, to be at his beck and call whenever he might want them.

In this handsome vehicle, reclining on the soft cushions, Agent "X" drove back along the suburban roads to the yacht harbor where he had so nearly met death a few nights before. His eyes were hard and bright as he stared through the speeding limousine's crystal-clear windows. A glow of excitement filled him as the harbor came into view.

Sunlight was breaking through the clouds now. The water was blue and sparkling. The storm winds were subsiding, but, to Agent "X," that bright expanse of water held sinister significance. There somewhere, killers lurked. There loot that had been paid for in men's blood was hidden.

As K. K. Parker he had his limousine draw up before the office of the town's boat works. A sign in the window read: "Reconditioned Yachts For Sale."

Smoking a cork-tipped cigarette, Secret Agent "X" strolled into the office and presented his card. "I'd like to look over some of your boats," he said.

His name obviously meant nothing to the manager of the shipyard, but the limousine standing outside, the cut of Mr. Parker's clothes, his appearance and commanding air were impressive.

The manager nodded, spoke deferentially. "Come this way, sir, I'll show you what we have."

On this lengthy tour of inspection the Agent asked endless questions. What was the seaworthiness of this boat, the speed of that, the fuel oil consumption of such and such an engine.

At last he located a craft that seemed to please him. This was a large cabin cruiser that had formerly belonged to a millionaire shoe manufacturer. The Agent paid a five-hundred-dollar option on the vessel, announcing that he intended to arrange for certain alterations and redecorations. The manager didn't know that the man who called himself Parker was interested in the cruiser solely because of its position.

From its portholes Agent "X" could command a view of the harbor in both directions. With a pair of compact, high-power prism binoculars he read the name on every yacht within sight. There were nearly a dozen drawn up beside piers, covered over as this one had been. These drew his particular attention.

Having established a base to which he could come unmolested and without rousing anyone's suspicions, Agent "X" started back for the city early in the afternoon. First he put in a long-distance call to Betty Dale.

Her answer wasn't too satisfactory. The girl, "Marie Rosa," or Rosa Carpita, was still registered at the hotel where Agent "X" had seen her, but she had slipped out before Betty had got there and had not been back as yet. Her luggage, Betty had ascertained, was still in her room.

Frowning, Agent "X" went back to his parked limousine. The patient chauffeur backed the car around, headed for the road that led to the city. But he had gone only a mile when Agent "X" barked abruptly into the speaking tube. His eyes, looking out of the car, were suddenly steely with alertness.

"Stop," he said. "Turn around and go back."

The chauffeur nodded glumly. The whims of rich men were never very understandable.

But it wasn't a whim that had prompted Agent "X's" sudden change of plan. A small flivver was parked in a side street. Agent "X," who missed nothing down to the smallest detail, had got a glimpse of the car's license plate. It was the flivver belonging to Private Detective George Banton.

DEATH CLUE!

AGENT "X" SPOKE to his chauffeur as the car approached the harbor town's central parking space.

"Stop here," he said.

At a swift stride he struck off along the street. But, once out of sight of his chauffeur, he went back toward the spot where he had seen Banton's car. The car was empty. The side curtains were down. Agent "X" touched the motor hood. It was cold. This meant that the flivver had been parked there for some time.

The side street in which it stood led up toward the summit of a small hill overlooking the harbor. Summer bungalows on wooden foundations lined each side of the street. They appeared to be empty.

Flicking his cane, smoking a cigarette, and strolling like a stranger looking over the town, Agent "X" walked up this hill. When he reached its top he ducked out of sight between two deserted cottages. Peering through a screen of leafless bushes he stared in both directions. The harbor lay peaceful at his feet, dotted with yachts at anchor. A path led along the shore to another cottage colony on a neighboring hill.

Agent "X" waited, watched, then raised his small, powerful glasses to his eyes. He might have been a rich sightseer looking over the yachts in the harbor. But he turned his glasses away from the harbor toward the many bungalows. For minutes he searched, then suddenly tensed.

On the side porch of a bungalow a quarter of a mile distant were two figures—a man and a woman. He caught sight of the woman's head first. It was heavily veiled. No features were visible, but the set of the head, the carriage, were familiar to Agent "X" who noticed such things.

Before Agent "X" could duck, the blackjack struck him a blow on the side of the head.

The man's face came sharply into focus. It was Detective Banton. And the girl with him, "X" was certain, was Rosa Carpita. He became more certain as the girl touched her companion's arm and said something. The lithe swing of her body, the studied poise of her which had become unconscious and instinctive, gave her away in spite of the heavy veil.

They, too, were looking out over the harbor. But "X" saw that the porch on which they stood was screened by a low bluff with bushes on the top. Only their heads would be visible from the water. They didn't want to be seen.

Excitement tingled through Agent "X's" blood. Step by step he was creeping closer to his goal. Two of his chief suspects were here before him. Somewhere out on the blue harbor was one of the bases of operations of the torch-murdering band. His face set grimly. He must move cautiously now. Everything depended on stealth and strategy until he was sure of his ground.

When he saw the two on the bungalow porch leave at last and start back toward the hill on which he stood, he preceded them down the narrow street. He went back to his own car, got in, and told the chauffeur to drive slowly ahead and stop. Not until he saw Banton's flivver back out of the side street and head toward the city, did he give further instructions.

"Keep that car in sight," he said, "but don't get too close."

The shadows of afternoon were lengthening into evening. Banton's little flivver was making good time, lurching and bobbing over the road. Agent "X" felt secure in the belief that his own presence in the limousine with the chauffeur would not arouse suspicion.

WHEN they reached the city, Agent "X" considered whether to follow Rosa Carpita or Banton. He was certain they would separate, and he decided on the latter. Betty Dale would keep watch of Rosa Carpita's movements for him. Banton seemed the more sinister.

He was right about their separating. Rosa Carpita got out in a dark block and hurried off. Banton continued on to his office in the bank building. Agent "X" drove by in his limousine, then dismissed it, telling the chauffeur he would not be needed until the next morning. At a brisk stride Agent "X" went to the nearest of his hideouts.

He changed quickly to the disguise of Andrew Balfour and hurried to his office. In his pockets this time he secreted many strange objects—not knowing what emergencies he might have to meet in the next few hours.[33]

The girls were just leaving his office, their day's work done. He nodded to them curtly and went to his own sanctum with the air of a man preoccupied with weighty business matters. But when the last of his help had gone, he tiptoed quickly to the door and peered out into the corridor. As he stood watching he saw two of Banton's

---

33 AUTHOR'S NOTE: *Various defensive and offensive weapons, materials for quick changes of disguise, sound-recording devices are some of the things Agent "X" carries in the linings of his clothing. For this reason he always avoids being caught and searched by the police. To be found with such things on him might prove fatal to his career as a hunter of criminals.*

assistants go into the private detective's office. In ten minutes, two more arrived. There seemed to be a gathering of the clan.

Banton had evidently summoned them. What for?

Agent "X" was glad he hadn't been able to locate Banton the night previous, directly after seeing the flaming torch murderers kill another cop. At that time he had been all for bluntly approaching Banton and making him talk. Now, calmed down after his strange experience of the night, he was ready to use caution and strategy again—ready to look first and leap afterward.

When another of Banton's sinister-looking aides had come, Agent "X" saw the detective's shadow on the frosted glass of the door, heard the click of the lock. Banton had assembled his men for a secret conference.

Agent "X" worked quickly. People were passing by in the corridor every few minutes, leaving their offices. They would be doing so for the next half-hour. To stay outside Banton's door listening with the portable amplifier that he had used effectively before, would be courting detection and disaster now. But there was another way.

Agent "X" took a spool of insulated wire from his pocket, wire as black and thin as thread. There were small copper terminals at each end. It was a slender electric cord which he carried for just such emergencies as this—to extend the range of his amplifier.

With the small disc-shaped microphone in his hand he stepped quickly across the corridor to Banton's door. No one was in sight. He reached up, dropped the microphone through the transom, took a turn of the threadlike wire around one of the transom rods, and then backed toward his own office.

He threw the other end of the almost invisible wire over his own transom and pulled it taut. It now stretched across the corridor, but far above the height of people's heads. In the semigloom it wouldn't be seen.

With tense fingers he connected the terminal at his end to the portable amplifier in its cameralike case.

A TURN on the rheostat control and he was listening in on the secret conference in Banton's office.

It was disappointing in some respects, importantly significant in others. Banton was issuing orders, not giving away secrets. His voice was rumbling, aggressive.

"Don't ask me why," he was saying, arguing down an over-cautious aide. "Do as I tell you. That's your job. That's what I pay you for—an' you can't afford to be choosy. There ain't one of you I ain't got something on. I could send you all back to the gutters where you came from—or worse."

Banton's sneering laugh sounded.

"You know where the toughest guys hang out. Round 'em up— get a gang together. I need a dozen anyway, and when I say tough, I mean tough. See that every man jack of 'em is heeled—an' see that he knows how to shoot."

"You ain't never done this sort of thing before, boss," said the voice of an assistant complainingly. "You'll get mixed up with the law."

Banton's answer was a fierce snarl. "Maybe I ain't never had good reason to. The law won't know anything about it."

Instructions followed, instructions to which Agent "X" listened closely. Banton was ordering his own men to round up a dozen of the fiercest gunmen and killers they could find. He was stepping out of his role of licensed private detective. He was ready to hurl defiance into the law's face.

But Banton wasn't telling his men what his secret purpose was. He was leaving them in the dark. He spoke again arrogantly.

"There's a guy named Becker and another named Garino who'd be good. The cops want them for kidnapping the commissioner a coupla days ago. They're hiding out and I know where. The other guys with them that pulled that crazy stunt skipped town. Get Becker and Garino."

There was the whisper of money changing hands. Agent "X's" eyes were bright, eager. "Slats" Becker and Tony Garino! Two of the very men he himself had hired. He, too, knew where they were hiding out. He had underworld contacts, systems of grapevine telegraphs. Now Banton was hiring them for some sinister purpose of his own. It opened another line of investigation for the Agent. Things were coming nearer and nearer a climax. The voice of Banton came through the amplifier again.

"Give 'em a hundred bucks apiece. Tell 'em there's twenty times as much if they stick with me and use their rods right. And tell 'em to wait close. When things are ready I'll give 'em the high sign."

"When will that be, boss?"

"Tonight, maybe. Two of you guys come along with me. We're going on a little trip. There's more things I want to tell you."

Agent "X" opened his door, stepped across the corridor, and re-trieved his microphone. Tensely he coiled it up, then left the build-ing.

He strode swiftly up the block, turned. He had left one of his cars parked beside the curb in front of an empty house.

Before entering it he retreated into the shadows, and his skill-ful fingers made quick changes in his face. He drew out the cheek plates that had given his features the sagging contours of middle age. He changed the hue of his complexion. He was no longer An-drew Balfour. He was younger, more dapper again. Banton would never recognize him as his fellow tenant in the bank building, and it was Banton Agent "X" was thinking of.

He got into his car, turned around, and waited close to the end of the block with the engine running, until he saw Banton and two of his aides emerge. They got into Banton's flivver. The little car lurched off.

Agent "X" followed, and at the end of fifteen minutes he felt certain that he knew where Banton was going—so certain that he dared drop far behind. Banton was turning into a boulevard that led toward the suburbs, heading toward the distant yacht harbor that was a three-quarter-hour run from the city.

IN fifteen minutes more there was no doubt about it. Agent "X" loafed along behind. Single-handed, he was by degrees getting closer to the strange, sinister action that impended.

When they reached the town where the yacht harbor was lo-cated, Banton parked his flivver in the same side street. He led his two colleagues up on the hill.

Agent "X" instantly stopped his own car, climbed out, and cut through the darkness. The process of shadowing was easy for him now. He was crouched near the street that ascended the hill as Banton and his assistants passed. He followed them up the hill, and was near enough to see them standing on the bluff and hear Banton give low-voiced instructions. But what these instructions were Agent "X" missed. He saw Banton stride away, leaving his two men there. The agency detective walked into the little town, turned down an alley, and prowled along the shore.

Agent "X," like a grim nemesis, followed. But Banton seemed to be on an aimless scouting expedition. On a clear patch of beach, where any moving figure was visible, Agent "X" had to let him get ahead.

Then suddenly Agent "X" stopped. Something black was heaving in the small turf that the harbor swells kicked up. It showed like a blotch, against the sand. It might be a box or a hat, but it stirred his interest.

He walked down the slope of the beach quickly, stopped. The thing was a box, but a leather-covered box—a camera.

It was no ordinary camera, either. The Agent saw that. He was a man experienced himself in all types of photographic equipment.

His fingers tightened over the water-logged, leather-covered box that had apparently been flung carelessly into the harbor. He snapped open the front, saw the fine, elaborate shutter mechanism, the special, many-glassed lens.

He felt along the surface of the camera with hands that trembled slightly—felt until he came to a screw pivot, the head of which seemed to be missing. From an inner rear pocket he took out a tiny screw that he had picked up two nights before on the roof of the bank building. He tried it on the pivot post of the camera, found that it fitted. His eyes were pools of light.

This was Darlington's sky camera, the one that had been hidden the night he had been thrown from the roof, murdered.

And, in a flash of deductive reasoning, Agent "X" understood why it was here. Darlington's murderer had hidden it in the quickest and most convenient spot—the canvas pickup sack that he had that night been getting ready. It had been brought to this harbor, tossed into the water by the killers. It confirmed the Agent's belief that they were close at hand.

He had forgotten Banton for the moment. The camera occupied his thoughts. But his reverie was interrupted by the soft crunch of sand. The Agent whirled, but not quickly enough.

With the suddenness of swooping shadows, two figures leaped at him out of the semidarkness. One was brandishing a blackjack.

Before he could duck, the blackjack struck him a blow on the side of the head, and it seemed that a thousand multi-colored stars and comets showered down upon him from the black depths of the sky.

CHAPTER XVIII

THE LAST RAID

IN THAT FIRST instant of agony he fought against the sense of dizziness and pain that possessed him. He let himself collapse, deliberately, then twisted sidewise with a swift, rolling motion. The second blow of the blackjack missed him.

His hand flashed out with the speed of a striking snake, gripped the man's wrist. The man let out a smothered, harsh cry. His companion fell on top of Agent "X." Together they pressed him to the cold, wet sand, while the man with the blackjack tried to free his wrist and swing a death-dealing blow.

Agent "X," interpreter of men's motives, read murder in the silent, tigerish attack of these two. They had come upon him looking at the camera, caught him prowling, snooping. He was to be destroyed as a menace to some criminal plot.

Sensing his closeness to death, Agent "X" summoned his keenest faculties, mental and physical. The man's blackjack might not be the only weapon.

With his free hand, Agent "X" struck a crashing blow at the nearest man's face. He couldn't see any features. There was only a black head outlined against the faint grayness of the sky.

The man grunted, relaxed his clutch. Agent "X" twisted again with a motion like a steel spring released. His fingers still gripped the wrist of the blackjack holder. The man cursed, relaxed his clutch on the weapon. Agent "X" broke free, leaped to his feet and kicked the blackjack toward the water.

Both men rushed him, tried to force him toward the surf. The clenched fist of one caught him in the jaw, snapping his head back. He struck out again, and knocked one of the men in the sand; then he leaped away and ran in a zigzag course up the beach. As he did so there was the thudding report of a silenced gun and a bullet screamed close to his head. The next moment he was in the black shadows under the broken piles of an old pier.

The two men ran up the beach and stood in the shadows of a shed. He couldn't see their faces. Their voices were two low for him to hear. It was only his phenomenally keen eyesight that made it possible for him to see their outlines at all.

At a fast stride they struck off along the beach, keeping close to the wharves and sheds, keeping away from the lighter sand. But the Agent followed as persistently as he had trailed Detective Banton. Perhaps, for all he could tell, one of them was Banton.

He held his breath a moment later. The two men leaped up on a wharf that ran out into the harbor. He heard the creak of boards faintly under their feet. He followed, creeping along the wharf, stopping often to get the men's silhouettes against the faint grayness of the horizon.

A covered yacht, apparently out of commission and laid up for the season, was snugged fast to the side of this wharf. In an instant the two murderous figures blended with the darker shadow of this and disappeared.

Agent "X's" pulses hammered. He believed he was close to the secret of the murderer's hideout. But, when he approached the yacht in the darkness, he could see nothing except boarded doors and carefully closed canvas coverings. To flash a light would be suicide. He had a feeling that eyes were straining there in the darkness.

He thought of Banton. Was one of these men the agency detective, and if not, had Banton gone back to the city?

He left the wharf and went back into the town. It was now pitch dark. But he located Detective Banton's flivver, just backing out of the side street. Banton at the wheel.

Agent "X's" face furrowed. If the yacht he had seen was the hiding-place of stolen loot there must be other accomplices in the city, and he didn't want to strike till he could bring about the round-up of the whole murderous gang. If one or more escaped, the death-torch terrors might continue. The inner hunch which had so often directed him along the right track urged him to stick to Banton's trail.

He got into his own car and followed the detective back to town. But he was not even careful now to keep the red tail-light of Banton's car in sight. A daring plan had suggested itself. Two men whose addresses he knew would be offered jobs as gunmen in the mysterious gang that Banton was about to assemble—"Slats" Becker and Tony Garino. Becker was almost a head shorter than the Agent, but Garino was approximately his size.

Back in town he drove swiftly to the neighborhood where Garino was lurking, hiding from the police after the kidnapping of the commissioner. Knowing the greediness of the man, Agent "X" felt certain that he would not turn down Banton's offer.

The place where Garino stayed like a wolf in hiding was a shabby rooming house in a tough neighborhood, a rooming house kept by a woman who specialized in the harboring of criminals.[34]

The location of every room was familiar to Agent "X." It was here that he had come to get in touch with Tony Garino, Monk Magurren, and the others in the first place.

He parked his car and moved forward confidently now. Diving through an alley, he crossed several cluttered back yards by the simple expedient of vaulting over their fences. He counted the fences, came at last to a yard where he stayed.

There was a light in the basement of the house. A witchlike old woman was puttering around in a dirty kitchen. But it was a room in the third floor that held the eye of Agent "X." A light burned in this. There was a crack beneath the shade. It was the room where Tony Garino dwelt.

With the silence and agility of an ape, Agent "X" crept forward and drew himself up to the first platform of the rusty fire escape that snaked down the rear of the house. He ascended cautiously, testing each rung of the iron ladder to be sure that no squeaking bar betrayed him.

Just under the window of the third floor he paused. Raising his head he looked inside. He had come in good time.

Tony Garino, the white-faced black-haired gangster, was in earnest confab with one of Detective Banton's men. They were just finishing their deal apparently. A hundred-dollar bill changed hands. Banton's man handed the gangster a slip of paper. Garino talked with much gesticulating of his hands.

Ten minutes passed during which the Agent got hints through a lot of vivid pantomime. Then Banton's man left. The actions of

---

34   AUTHOR'S NOTE: *To find out about this place Agent "X" had once disguised himself as a thief and taken a room there. To disarm the landlady he had even shown her a suitcase full of allegedly stolen silverware and had, at her artful insinuations of blackmail, divided some of it with her.*

Garino showed that he was getting ready to leave at once, too.

He went to a shabby bureau, took a big automatic from a drawer, examined the clip, and shoved the gun into his coat. He knelt before the rusty gas stove that heated the room, turned it out, and, after it had cooled a moment, ran his fingers over the blackened burner. With the soot he had collected he made smudges on his face.

This clumsy attempt of Garino's at disguise brought a sardonic gleam to the Agent's eyes. The gangster was trying to guard against recognition by the police. But, to the Man of a Thousand Faces, it seemed rather ridiculous.

THE Secret Agent descended the fire escape as silently as he had come up it, crossed fences, and turned into the street. Garino was just coming out the door of the rooming house as he did so. He set off at a brisk pace up the street keeping well into the shadows.

Agent "X" followed, ducked through a side street, skirted ahead of Garino, and waited beside a porch stoop, as silent as the night itself. In the Agent's hand now was the small, gleaming cylinder of a hypodermic needle. The reservoir of the instrument contained a highly concentrated, liquid anesthetizing narcotic of his own mixing.

Tony Garino never knew what had happened to him. The arm that flashed out of the shadows, the point of the needle that pierced his skin, were synchronized like an act in some well-rehearsed play.

Garino was drawn into the shadows and deposited with his back against the stoop just as the drug in his veins began to thrust him down into the depths of unconsciousness.

Leaving him there, Agent "X," as though nothing had happened, came out of the street and walked swiftly to the spot where he had parked his car. He drove ahead to a point opposite the place where he had left Garino and stopped close to the curb.

A moment he scanned the street in both directions. A single pedestrian was hurrying along.

Agent "X" got out, raised the hood of his motor, and pretended to be absorbed in engine trouble until the pedestrian passed.

Then he closed the engine hood and raised the cover of the car's rumble seat. He turned, darted into the shadows. When he came out he was carrying a limp burden—the inert body of the gangster.

The Agent now drove to one of his most accessible hideouts. Each was chosen with great care to give as much privacy as possible in regard to entrances and exits. This was a deserted house, like the one he had used when he had disguised himself as Police Commissioner Foster. He had possessed himself of it without asking anyone's leave.

He carried Tony Garino into it, deposited the gangster in a ventilated closet, locked the door, and changed to the disguise of Andrew Balfour.

By kidnapping Garino he had gained for himself a method of entering Banton's mysterious gang. In Garino's pocket he had found the slip of paper that Banton's man had given the gangster, telling where the gang was to be assembled. It was a water-front address. Time was precious. Garino was due there any time. But first Agent "X" wanted to find out what Banton was doing. Was he still in his office?

Completing the disguise of Andrew Balfour, he went out into the street again. He drove to the vicinity of the bank, parked his roadster, and strode forward, headed for the side entrance that he and Banton usually used. Then he paused, prickles of horror traversing his spine. A man staggered past the corner of the building into range of the Secret Agent's vision. He wore the light-blue uniform of a special bank guard.

A light was playing in the air behind him, a wavering spectral light, like a pursuing will-o'-the-wisp. It became a jet of hissing flame that descended on the guard's back and sent him writhing to the pavement where he lay, a charred and inert heap.

With a hoarse cry on his lips Secret Agent "X" leaped forward. He dashed around the corner of the bank building, risking the flaming death himself, and a scene of terror and disaster met his eyes.

The flaming torch bandits had returned. The Merchants' and Manufacturers' Bank had been raided, and the goggled, helmeted figures were escaping in their long, low roadster after a grisly carnival of robbery and death.

CHAPTER XIX

MURDERERS AMIDSHIPS

IT WAS A second before Secret Agent "X" understood the full horror of what had happened.

The front doors of the bank were open. Every window was smashed. Special detectives, driven back by the raiders, began running forward again as the murderers' roadster shot away. But the terrible work had been done thoroughly.

A bank guard, shouting like a madman, was dashing toward the doors.

"They're in there," he screamed. "Marsh and von Blund! They must have got it, too! Those devils burned them like they did the others."

The man's face was twitching. His eyes were red-rimmed, staring. Other guards and detectives came slinking out of the shadows across the street, trembling, sheepish.

Agent "X" saw another blackened corpse lying up the block. A big guard, his face dripping with sweat, spoke hoarsely, close to the Agent's ear, as though answering an unspoken accusation.

"We couldn't help it—we had to scram. They drove us off with that flame gun of theirs. That poor fella tried to stick—and look what they did to him!"

Discipline had broken down. The demoralizing force of fear lay upon the survivors of the raid. Inside the bank, the icy hand of terror had fallen like a blight. Agent "X" entered with the first group of detectives. He heard the cursing cry of one of them.

"Look—they got them!"

The man was pointing through the open door of the bank's business office. A sprawled, unsightly figure lay just inside the threshold. Beyond, close to a big desk, was another.

A detective bent down, fumbled with trembling fingers, and

lifted the heat-corroded wreck of what had once been a handsome gold watch. Its crystal had melted under the blast of the death-torch, making the figures on its face as unrecognizable as the grisly horror from which the detective had taken it. But the monogram on its back was still visible: "F.M."

"It's him—Francis Marsh," said the detective in an awed voice. "The killers got them both. That other's von Blund."

So thoroughly had the terrible death-torch done its work, that the blackened pieces of jewelry were the only means of identification. But they established the grim fact that the partners who had survived the first unsuccessful raid had met death in this second one.

"The safe was blown wide open," said another detective. "They used enough nitro to sink a battleship. You could hear it ten blocks away."

Agent "X" saw that the great vault of the bank had been cleaned out. Its door had fallen outward, the quadruple hinges ripped, the lock bolts cracked as though they had been brittle clay. Every bit of the cash was gone.

"Marsh asked for a special guard tonight, too," said one of the surviving guards brokenly. "A big lot of cash had come in. They were getting their books straightened."

Inside the office, with the remains of the two bankers, was a third corpse, identified as the body of an elderly bookkeeper.

Police sirens sounded outside. Agent "X," in the guise of Andrew Balfour, was there when Burks of the homicide squad arrived with a battery of detectives. The face of the homicide squad head was bleak. His voice was bitter.

"I warned them the killers would be back," he said. "I warned them to keep away from here at night."

THE Agent's eyes held steely brightness. He stood, his body rigid, staring down at the ghastly remains of this biggest of raids. Then he turned and slipped quietly out. If he stayed, there would be questions. It was only because of the confusion, the demoralization of the police, that his presence hadn't been noticed. As a tenant of the building, he might be held as a material witness. And he had other reasons for going.

The lightning of the death torch had struck twice in the same spot. The significance of this filled Agent "X" with grim purpose, spurred him on to action. It was as though Banton had had secret warning of what was to happen tonight. Where was Banton?

Swiftly and silently Agent "X" slipped away from the police, away from the excited, tense crowds that were coming, attracted by the explosion. He found his parked car, drove furiously back to the hideout where he had left Tony Garino.

The gangster was still unconscious, and, removing him from the closet where he was breathing in peaceful unawareness, Agent "X" studied the man's features.

He studied them with the close, detailed intentness of an artist and craftsman, even opening the mobster's thick lips and staring at his teeth.

Two gleaming gold bicuspids characterized Garino's smile. The Agent had not forgotten these.

As he began his deft, ingenious impersonation of the unconscious gangster, working under the brilliant glow of his portable acetylene lamp in front of his triple mirrors, he imitated Garino's mouth first of all.

This was a simple matter. He opened a box filled with shells of thin, resilient gold alloy, shells that corresponded to each of his teeth. He snapped two of these over his own bicuspids and flashed a gold-toothed smile at himself. Then he began the quick impersonation of Garino's features. His own face changed like magic under the deft touch of his fingers. When the face was finished, when Tony Garino seemed to be sitting there before the mirror in that hidden room, he slipped a toupee over his own brown hair, and smoothed it down to shiny sleekness with Vaseline.

Then he undressed Garino and assembled the man's clothing. Before putting it on he got out another suit of special, thin material and attached it with spring clamps to the lining of Garino's coat. When he had put on the mobster's flash suit, the other beneath it did not show. Its bulk seemed only the stockiness of the gangster. He pushed Garino back in the closet, locked the door, and filled his pockets with an assortment of the mysterious objects that he was in the habit of carrying.

Then he turned his collar up, pulled his hat down, and hurried to the street. The address on the slip of paper that Banton's man had given Garino was within walking distance. It was in a westerly direction toward the river.

As Agent "X" approached it, moving at a fast walk, the neighborhood grew steadily worse. He was in a street of junk shops and dark, dilapidated warehouses, busy places in the daytime but dark and sombre now.

He came to the street that fronted the water, crossed it, and saw the oily gleam of the river ahead. He passed between two pier sheds, walked down a boarded alley, and came to the flat expanse of another smaller pier that was used as a base for tugs out of service.

A group of dark-clothed men stood whispering in the gloom at the end of this dock. He saw them before they did him, watched them a moment intently, then retraced his steps and ran quickly to the nearest cigar store where there was a telephone. Closeted in the booth he made a mysterious telephone call to Betty Dale, asking her to relay a message from him to police headquarters.

WHEN he returned to the dock the men were still there, and their low whispers hushed as he approached. He could see the stiffening, suspicious attitudes of their bodies,

He walked as he had often seen Garino walk—for his disguises went further than merely assuming the features of the man he impersonated. He made each disguise a study in muscular co-ordination as well. A voice that he had heard before spoke hoarsely out of the darkness.

"It's that mug, Tony!"

The Agent, peering intently, saw the pale face and slumped body of "Slats" Becker. The little gangster grinned wryly.

"We thought yer'd got cold feet, Tony!"

Another voice cut in, thick with anger, the voice of Banton's man who had made the arrangements with Garino.

"Where the hell you been? What's the idea? Didn't I tell you to come right away? We expect the boss any minute!"

Agent "X" shrugged in Garino's characteristic gesture.

"Excusa me! Maybe I no come back. I hadda say gooda-by to the skirt."

Harsh laughter echoed his remark. Banton's man hissed for silence. Looking around at the men who stood on the dock, Agent "X" saw the toughest bunch of gorillas he had ever found collected in one spot. Banton's assistants were bad enough, but they were the sneaky stool-pigeon type. The men they had assembled were cutthroats, gunmen, the city's most dangerous riffraff—rats who could be lured out of hiding only by the smell of blood or the glint of gold—beasts who prowled in the night. The pockets of each bulged. They were armed to the teeth.

Suddenly, off across the black water, a light winked. Three times—a space of darkness—another flash.

"That's the boss now," said Banton's right-hand man. "Come on, you mugs—get ready to go aboard."

Out of the blackness that lay over the face of the water, something long and gray appeared. It nosed toward the dock, cutting the swells silently, showing no lights except that one signal which had been doused.

It came nearer, showed like some monster of the deep. It was a huge, gray-painted motor cruiser. Its rakish lines, the sharp swell of its bows, proclaimed it a former rumrunner; one of the fastest, most sinister-looking boats that Agent "X" had ever seen. How Banton had acquired it, what black history lay behind it, he didn't know. But, on the forward deck, cradled under a canvas tarpaulin, he saw the ominous shape of a mounted machine gun. The boat slid into the dock noiselessly, and the Agent's expert ear knew by the faint, rumbling purr of the motors amidships that this craft was superpowered.

It had been built to outdistance the fastest patrol boats of the coast guard fleet. It had the lines of a destroyer; it was a destroyer in the full sense of the term.

Awed by the impressive craft, the cutthroat crew that Banton's men had assembled swarmed silently down to the deck. The harsh, lumpy face of Banton himself looked out of the pilot house window. He and a single engineer had brought the boat from its former berth.

"Keep your traps closed!" Banton warned. "Any mug who talks will get a crack over the head. This isn't a picnic!"

As silently as she had come, the long narrow boat nosed away from the dock, nosed out into the river, and slipped like a gray wraith across the water. The engines, Agent "X" knew, were only at idling speed. Banton was careful not to leave a wake. Once a man from the deck of a passing tug hailed them, staring in surprise at this craft that showed no lights.

But Banton paid no attention. Two of his men on port and starboard sides were watching intently, alert, it seemed, for danger. But the boat slipped on unmolested, and the lights of the city fell away behind.

IT was only then that Banton opened the motors to their mid-speed, and the gray craft seemed to lift out of the water and shoot ahead on throbbing wings. A white, hissing wake trailed behind it.

Banton came down from the pilot house, turning the wheel over to his most trusted assistant. He went forward, peeled the canvas off the machine gun, fingered the synchronized mechanism. The black snout of the gun seemed to thrust ahead like a finger, warning of evil to come.

It was then that a shrill cry sounded somewhere amidships. Agent "X," in the group around the gun, turned. Banton turned, too, a fierce oath escaping him. A slim figure came running along the throbbing deck of the boat. Two other figures followed.

Banton stood, legs wide apart, amazement written on his heavy features. Agent "X" saw a white, tense face; the curves of a lithe body. Rosa Carpita!

The dancer came up to the group around the gun, up to Banton.

"Call your gorillas off," she said scornfully. "They're chasing me."

"You!" Banton hissed, amazement and anger in his voice. "How did you get here?"

"You wouldn't tell me your plans so I followed you. I don't trust you, Banton. I'm sorry I let you in on—"

"We found this skirt stowed on board," said one of the men who had chased her, "She was hiding in a closet."

The girl, Rosa Carpita, drew herself to her full height. Her black eyes were snapping fiercely. Her face, lovely before, was contorted into harsh lines.

"Don't forget, Banton, that I am your client—and that I employed you!"

Banton's little eyes were gleaming. He took a step forward.

"You've no business here," he said. "You'll hafta go ashore."

"I won't," the girl said. "I demand to know what your plans are."

Agent "X," witnessing this strange drama, began to understand. Banton made a harsh gesture. He scowled at the men around him.

"Keep still," he warned. "Don't talk in front of these rats. Come to the cabin!"

He turned, lumbered off, and the girl followed. There was a mutter of low-voiced speculation behind him.

Agent "X" followed softly, but Banton and the dancer went down to the cabin amidships. The door was locked. There were curtains over the ports. He could see or hear nothing of the strange conference that the two were having. His eyes gleamed, however. His alert brain was at work. When Banton came back alone ten minutes later, he wasn't surprised.

"What did you do with the skirt, boss?" asked one of Banton's men.

Agent "X" heard the harsh answer.

"Locked her up like the cat she is."

It was plain to the Agent that Banton was in some way double-crossing his client, Rosa Carpita. The girl had followed him, come on board to find out what was going on. All this was consistent with Banton's character as the Agent had sized it up.

Banton went back to the pilot house. For nearly an hour the speed boat rocked in the swells, its engines muttering idly, while Banton swung it in slow circles.

Banton's voice came down from the open window of the pilot house at last. He gave an order that his assailants understood. They walked among the men on deck, marshaling them like soldiers.

Agent "X" saw the gleam of hidden weapons being brought out. Four submachine guns were taken from a locker. One of Banton's men manned the tripod gun up forward.

"All you mugs get ready," Banton said.

Off on the night-darkened horizon, in the mouth of the harbor, Agent "X" saw a shape moving, a boat slipping out, showing no lights. His nerves tingled with excitement. It came toward them like a sea ghost.

For an instant, as it was silhouetted against a short light, he saw that canvas still mantled its deck, that it was the same covered yacht he had seen tied up. It passed them a half-mile away, slipped out to sea. And then he heard the engines of the speed boat beneath him throb into life. Its bow swung, it seemed to leap ahead across the dark waters. The chase of death had begun.

CHAPTER XX

KILLER'S PACK

LIKE A SNARLING gray wolf of the sea Banton's speed boat lunged ahead. Its prow was the snout of a wolf worrying a bone in bared fangs. The wake it kicked up was the lashing plumed tail of a marauding sea beast.

And Banton, wide-legged in the pilot house, was the man-demon who urged the beast on to the kill.

A tenseness had crept over that murderous crew. Agent "X" saw clawlike hands fondling gun butts; he saw the blood lust in the rolling whites of eyes. He heard short, barking sentences hurled from beneath bared teeth. A huge wolf with a pack of lesser wolves! There was blood on the moon tonight.

He was glad that the girl was below decks, glad that she was to escape the horror that lay ahead. For the whole fantastic outline of the deathly enigma he had been fighting was beginning to take shape. His own pulses were racing. His eyes were points of shimmering light.

The sea itself was silent, seemingly deserted. It was the silence before a storm—the dreadful silence that bore in it the threat of doom.

The covered yacht ahead was speedy. But Banton's gray speedboat was faster still.

The distance lessened minute by minute. The white ghostly canvas covering the yacht's deck showed. Those on board, whoever they might be, were keeping up the farce that the vessel was empty. What would Banton's method of attack be?

The answer came soon.

"Stand ready to give 'em hell!"

It was Banton's voice calling down from the pilot house. Agent "X" caught a glimpse of the man's red face. Banton's eyes were gleaming slits of wolfish cruelty.

"Rake her from stem to stern," he bawled. "Now!"

One of Banton's men crouched behind the tripod-mounted machine gun, pressed the firing lever. The gun leaped on its fastenings. Bronze-jacketed bullets sped across the night-shrouded waters. The cartridge belt writhed like a gleaming snake uncoiling, spitting its venom. The man behind the butt had once handled a Tommy gun for a mob of rumrunners. His fingers were practiced. His aim was true.

The bullets were riddling the canvas covering in a death-dealing stream. If men were there they would meet their doom. But the covered yacht sped on. There was no sign of life on board, only that grim white wake.

Cursing, as though steeled to something expected which did not come, Banton ordered two of the submachine gunners to open fire. The deathly, bone-rattling tattoo of the Thompson guns joined the clatter of the heavy-caliber weapon up front. Their snouts sprayed lead on the craft ahead.

THEY were close astern of it now. Banton twisted the wheel. Like a huge gray wolf circling its prey, the speed boat heeled over and went around the larger yacht. It tore past the yacht's side while Banton's henchmen kept up their withering fire.

Behind the bows of the yacht, the pilot house showed. The leaden spray from the muzzles of the Tommy guns concentrated there. Glass smashed. Sheet metal crumpled. Boarding was ripped as with a thousand fangs. The yacht suddenly heeled over. Its white spray lessened. It lay wallowing in the trough of the seas like a still gray ghost.

There was something ominous about its stillness. No moving thing showed. Banton began to swear like a madman. He bellowed another abrupt order. A man dived into a locker of the ex-rumrunner. He reared up clutching two corrugated missiles—hand grenades, "pineapples." These were Banton's aces in the hole.

"Give 'em hell," he said again, and the man with the grenades hurled one across the space that separated the two craft. With unerring aim it dropped on the yacht's deck.

A blast of orange flame came. A roar sounded. Pieces of wood and strips of canvas rose into the air. The bomb left a gaping black hole in the yacht's deck, but Agent "X" doubted that it had penetrated below decks.

The yacht seemed to wallow like a great, still beast, watching, crouching.

Banton circled her again, making the engines of the speedboat roar as though by this display of sheer speed and power he could cow those on board the yacht.

"Get the grappling hooks out," he shouted.

From another locker, two-pronged hooks were brought with ropes attached—relics, too, of rumrunning days—relics that had been used by hijackers.

With a burst of speed Banton cut into the yacht's stern again. This time he didn't sheer off. He held the speedboat's bow straight for the other craft, turned slightly and ran alongside, so close that the metal sides of the two vessels scraped. Then he reversed the engines, backed water in a smother of foaming spray.

"Fling 'em," he snarled.

The grappling hooks dropped on the yacht's decks, caught in scuppers, hatchways, and capstans. The ropes were made fast. Then a gangster shrieked a hoarse warning. Like rats, the men, ready to board the yacht, fell back.

For a point of brilliant flame stabbed out from the yacht's super-structure. It was a hissing, scorching will-o'-the-wisp of fire, that dropped like a lightning bolt on the speed boat's deck.

Where it fell, sizzling flame burst up. The deck boards smol-dered, crackled, flamed. The gray enamel turned black. The fright-ened yells of men mingled with the hissing of the flames.

Banton alone seemed calm. He had snatched up a submachine gun himself. He sprayed lead at the spot where the flame came from. The jet of flame flickered, forked out. It touched the cruiser's pilot house.

With a howl of fear Banton left his perch, clattered down the iron stairs into the boat's interior. The wicked tongue of flame licked the pilot house. It heated the metal sheathing, turned var-nished boards and framework into crackling embers. It reduced the pilot house into a smoking ruin.

Banton's men had taken refuge in the offside of the cruiser. Here, protected by twenty feet of the boat's cabin, they were safe. Banton appeared among them, sweat streaming from his face, his lips curled back from his teeth, his eyes the eyes of a devil. He still held the machine gun in stubby fingers.

"We'll get 'em," he said. "Stand ready to board her, you rats."

He walked stiff-legged through the cabin, smashed a port, and thrust the muzzle of his machine gun through. As a police lieuten-ant he had had practice with Thompson guns. He was a dead shot.

His fingers tightened on the trigger of the Tommy gun again. Its muzzle bobbed and clattered.

There came a sudden scream from the spot on the yacht where the flamethrower had sprayed fiery death. The jet of flame lowered, went wild, hissed into the sea, sending up clouds of white steam.

In the light of it the men on the cruiser seemed like crouching demons. Banton, with his clattering submachine gun, was the high priest of hell.

Agent "X," climbing up an iron ladder to the sleek cruiser's top deck, saw a man pitch headlong from the bridge of the yacht. He saw the strange, horrible weapon in the man's hand clatter down.

"I got him!" howled Banton exultantly. "Now, you rats, come on—we'll board her."

Like a pack of howling, bloodthirsty wolves the gunmen and murderers of Banton's assembled gang followed their leader. Up over the sides of the yacht they swarmed, a living wave of death.

CHAPTER XXI

STRANGE SIGNAL

IN THE MAD tumult of the raid no one noticed the actions of Secret Agent "X," the man they supposed was Tony Garino. He was on his hands and knees on the top of the cruiser's cabin now. He was fastening two black cylinders to the gray-painted woodwork, thrusting them, into the hard pine boarding with needle-sharp spikes.

They pointed aloft like miniature gun muzzles, pointed toward the black night sky. He pulled a wire on the top of each, struck a hidden sparker, and, in the interior of the black cylinders, foot-length fuses sputtered and glowed.

Then he dropped back off the cabin roof, leaving the cylinders where they were, black, silent fingers lifting to the clouds.

He started for the deck of the yacht, then stopped. Banton and his gangsters had boarded her, but they had not won the battle.

Like a waiting, wounded beast, the yacht came to life again. One of the men on board had been killed, but others remained. A round porthole along the top deck snapped open. Another black snout projected.

Agent "X" saw the streak of light that hissed from it. He saw the light burst into flame, heard the gangsters howl with rage and fear. Like rats taking cover they fled to the yacht's stern deck and crouched there behind metal life boats and capstans—behind any refuge they could find.

One, a burly gunman with the face of an ape, knelt behind a coil of rope, trying to level his Tommy gun. The man in the open port-hole saw him. It was the gunman's undoing and death.

The gushing flame from the hideous *Flammenwerfer* leaped across space to the coil of rope. The rope became a mass of seething flame. The man behind it, jumping to his feet, shrieking with fear, became a human torch. He stumbled across the deck, then dropped, an inert, horrible mass of smoking cloth and flesh. The flame played over him until he no longer resembled a man.

A gangster, losing his nerve, screaming with terror at what he had seen, jumped from his place of hiding and dived over the yacht's rail. Banton cursed like a madman.

He was crouched behind a heavy capstan. The flaming torch killer sought him out. The *Flammenwerfer* splashed liquid flame on the rounded metal surface of the capstan. Flame hissed on both sides of Banton, hissed over his head. He crouched, cursing, palsied with fear, until one of his men turned a Tommy gun on the open port where the liquid death came from.

Then the head of the flame-thrower disappeared. The flaming jet dribbled off, ceased. The gangsters stole out of cover again. A man with a pineapple bomb hurled it, and the side of the superstructure where the flame-thrower had been became a twisted mass of iron.

Banton, jumping from behind his capstan, white and trembling snatched two of the hand bombs from his henchman's fingers. He dropped his machine gun held the pineapples at his sides, and crept forward like an enraged gorilla.

But the jet of liquid flame appeared in another spot, farther astern, sending the gangsters running like scared rabbits. They fled along metal alleyways, fled beneath the canvas, while the flame sought to follow them, burning the canvas covering above their heads. Another went down, wrapped in flaming shrouds. But the rest reached the forward deck of the yacht.

Banton hurled his pineapples. They missed their mark, struck a lifeboat, bursting it apart like the pod of a pea. The other fell into the water, sending up a geyser of white spray. Then Banton cursed and leaped forward with a gloating light in his eyes.

A strange, squat weapon lay at his feet—a weapon with a blunt muzzle, a pressure tank behind it, another tank where concentrated, inflammable liquid was stored.

Agent "X," on board the yacht now, saw Banton lift the thing up. Banton held one of the flame-throwers in his hands. He gave the curved lever that served as a trigger a tentative press. The thing spouted a clot of flame that hissed and splashed on the deck. The pressure tank roared like escaping steam.

"Come on," bellowed Banton, "we got 'em now!"

As though in answer, a jet of liquid fire sprayed down from an open window. Banton leaped aside just in time. Where he had stood the deck boards seethed with flame.

Banton, crouching behind a steel stanchion, turned the muzzle of his own weapon upward. The jet of flame wavered, went true. The other flame-thrower ceased firing. The port where he had stood became a circle of hissing fire.

The fear-stricken gangsters took fresh courage. The staccato beat of the submachine guns sounded again. A gang of men, under the direction of Banton, who held his flame-thrower ready, began tearing at a battened-down hatchway. Others struck with axes on the steel doors of the nearest entrance.

A WINDOW smashed in. A gangster hurled a pineapple bomb into the gorgeously furnished interior of the yacht. The explosion lit up the inside of the boat so that its ports looked like the red eyes of a monster.

Then a man pointed.

"What the hell's that!"

From close by in the darkness a sputtering crackle sounded. A gangster screamed in fear as something rushed upward as though an imprisoned ghost of the sea were escaping.

They could hear the thing screaming higher and higher up, into the dark sky. Then, far above their heads, almost in the clouds it seemed, the darkness was ripped apart. Balls of fire, brighter than the flame-throwers, made a dazzling glow over the whole face of the sea.

"A rocket!" gasped Banton. "It's that girl—she's sending 'em. She's signaling."

He started for the side of the cruiser, stopped. Another rocket went up. But it rose from the top of the cruiser's cabin. It left a visible trail behind it. The girl was not there. No one was there. The coming of the rocket seemed uncanny. It howled upward like a banshee, burst at last into red balls of fire that the sea wind whipped into myriad sparks. The sparks fell seaward in a shower, dimmed, faded, went out.

"It's some double-crosser," hissed Banton. "We'll get him later! Now—"

He turned his flame-thrower on again as a shadow moved behind another port. He squirted liquid death along the superstructure of the yacht, until an answering jet of flame sent him howling back.

Like a battle of demons in the mouth of hell the two *Flammenwerfers* competed with one another, while the gangsters cowered back. The hideous flaring glow of the gushing jets of flame lit up the whole deck of the yacht. Banton's face was the face of a devil, a man driven on by hate and greed.

Agent "X" caught sight of a hideous goggled head. The men on the yacht were fighting to keep their ghastly secret intact—fighting to retain the mysterious cargo below decks. Agent "X" knew what that cargo was. He could guess the identity of these men who fought with liquid flame, these men who spread terror and death behind them, leaving a trail of charred and blackened corpses.

But Banton was hardly better. He drove the other away at last, silencing the hissing snout of the *Flammenwerfer* above him.

Agent "X" was watching the fight, seeming to take part in it. The automatic in his hands gave barking reports from time to time. His bullets clanged off the steel sides of the yacht's superstructure. He hadn't forgotten that he was Tony Garino, gangster. He gave the appearance of being one of the battlers. But he was watching, waiting, his eyes sweeping the dark waters.

BANTON'S men were swarming into the luxurious cabin now. One of the steel doors had given in, loosed on its hinges by a pineapple bomb. At the head of the stairs, leading down to the saloon below, a helmeted figure appeared. Then the worst carnage of the battle took place.

Three gangsters, murderous rats from the city's water fronts, were caught off their guard. Agent "X," looking through a window, saw what happened. The jet from the *Flammenwerfer* reached them as they made a rush for the stairs.

It struck the foremost of them in the chest, and the man's body seemed to disintegrate before the seething gush of flame. He stumbled backwards, his features disappearing. The others went down, too, became huddled hulks of men. The cabin's interior was filled with the sickening odor of scorched flesh.

Then a submachine gun chattered from one of the cabin's rear windows. Its quick death leaped across space before the man with the flame-thrower could change the direction of his jet. He dropped his weapon, stood at the head of the stairs for a moment like some goggling, hideous apparition. Then with a cry he threw up his arms and fell backwards, riddled with bullets—dead.

Banton was almost master of the ship now. His big face was bloated, red, his eyes bloodshot. The fear and carnage around him seemed only to whet his appetite for the thing he sought. He ran across the cabin, callously leaping over the grotesquely slumped forms of what had been three of his men. He started to plunge down the stairway, a flame-thrower in his hand. Then he paused. A shout had come from outside. It was a cry of fright and warning.

Above the crackle of automatics, above the sharp tattoo of a Tommy gun still playing, came another sound. It was a sound that sent prickles of fear racing up Banton's spine. It was the eerie, wailing note of a siren—a note that he had heard often before in his life. Words came to his lips.

"The cops!" he gasped.

The siren's note was joined by another—a third and a fourth, Banton stood trembling, white as a sheet. The sirens outside seemed to be clamoring like dogs, like hounds on the hunt—the hounds of the law.

He staggered to a window, looked out. From all sides it seemed, across the face of the dark waters, searchlights were stabbing, converging on the two boats that rolled and wallowed side by side.

He heard the throb of powerful motors, heard sharp bows cutting the swells. A gray shape like a leaping hound cut through a searchlight's beam. It was a slim, fast coast guard patrol boat, and its decks were black with armed men.

With a hoarse cry of fury and fear Banton fell back.

"We're trapped," he said, and the words came from his lips as though wrenched by the quivering hands of Greed.

CHAPTER XXII

KILLERS UNMASKED

THE GANGSTERS WERE like stricken men in that first moment of confusion while sirens wailed and searchlights stabbed upon them. They stood stunned, dazed—jaws slack, eyes wide. Then they took refuge in the yacht's cabin with Banton.

He began cursing at them, ordering them to fight, telling them they would be killed if they didn't. He lashed them with his tongue, put fear into their hearts. They commenced snarling like cornered beasts, then they crouched and fired at the patrol boats. A screaming, clattering volley of machine-gun bullets answered their shots.

Banton was almost like a maniac now. He saw himself cheated of the thing he sought. He lifted the captured *Flammenwerfer* gun, thrust its snout through a window of the cabin and squirted liquid fire across the water. He was making a desperate attempt to keep the patrol boats at bay.

The jet of flame missed its mark. Its line of trajectory became an arc. It hissed into the water, sending up billows of steam. Just beyond it, circling like slim greyhounds, the patrol boats edged nearer. Banton raised the gun higher. His face was a living fury. He had double motives now. He had never forgotten that the law had humiliated him, forced him to resign. And, wolfishly, he was ready to murder in order to guard the thing he had fought to possess.

The jet of flame almost struck the gray prow of a coast guard patrol.

Then the man disguised as Tony Garino made a slight movement with his left hand. He was in the cabin of the cruiser, crouched behind its steel walls with the others. No one noticed the darting motion of his fingers. No one noticed either the small glass vial that flashed through the air and shattered with a barely audible tinkle against a metal table leg. The colorless liquid in it seeped out.

But invisible fumes filled the air. A gangster nearest the table felt them first. He began rubbing his eyes. Then he dropped his gun, put both hands to his face and staggered across the floor, seeking air. The fumes were growing sharper, more astringent. They were the smarting fumes of concentrated ammonia that got into the eyes and made them burn and water.

A cloud of fumes drifted around Banton's head, sucked through the draft of the window. The flamethrower waved his stubby hands. He howled with rage, screamed an oath. The gray boats in the sea before him became confused shadows as tears blinded his eyes. He lost all sense of aim, sprayed flame on the deck of the yacht. Then with a cry he flung the terrible weapon from him and put his hands to his eyes.

The gangsters' fire had fallen off. The cabin was becoming untenable as the fumes filled it and thickened. One by one the gangsters stumbled through the exits to the deck. Some still clutched their guns, firing fiercely, aimlessly. A volley of machine-gun bullets smashed into one and he collapsed into a thrashing heap, then lay still. Others dropped their guns and raised their hands above their heads in token of surrender. The gray patrol boats began to edge closer.

AMONG the larger coast guard craft was one harbor police patrol. It was far from its accustomed beat tonight, but strange things were in the wind. Two of the most important officials of the city police department were on this boat, the commissioner himself, and Inspector Burks of the homicide squad. The trails of murder know no boundaries, and, though this sea battle was far outside the police boat's territory, both men were following a murder path. Tense, rigid, standing beside the rail, Inspector Burks spoke.

"I thought it was phony when that tip-off came. The skirt wouldn't give her name. She hung up on me—but after the killing at the bank tonight I was ready to try anything."

The tall commissioner was silent a moment, then he touched Burks's arm.

"They've had enough! They're quitting. They know when they're licked."

He was pointing to the yacht, from the cabin of which the gangsters were stumbling, lifting their arms. The police boat came nearer and Burks let out a harsh curse.

"That fat guy—it's George Banton, chief. What the hell's he doing out here? Maybe he sent up those rockets!"

Both men were puzzled. All that had happened tonight was puzzling to the law. The tip-off had come into headquarters in a girl's voice, informing the police that the death-torch murderers were planning a sea getaway. It had sounded fantastic, but a half-dozen coast guard boats had responded. The mysterious message had told them to wait until rockets went up. Those rockets were mysterious, too. Who was responsible for them?

Burks, standing at the rail of the police boat with the commissioner at his side, was trying to dope it out—and wasn't getting far.

As the gangsters stood in a huddled group, still blinded by the ammonia fumes, the coast guard boats and the police patrol closed in. Searchlights played on the two vessels that were locked with grappling hooks. The dead men on the decks, the havoc caused by the flame-thrower, showed how fierce the battle had been.

Agile coast guardsmen were the first to leap to the deck of the yacht.

INSPECTOR BURKS swore harshly again and stared in amazement, for Banton was fighting like an enraged beast. Blinking through watery eyes he tried to yank an automatic from his pocket and fire at the coast guardsmen.

A balled fist knocked him flat. If he had tipped off the police and sent up rockets for help what was the matter with him? Inspector Burks couldn't figure it out.

He climbed to the deck of the yacht with Commissioner Foster at his side. The coast guard boats had pushed in, surrounding the two locked vessels. Their crews were swarming up from all sides. Six cops from the harbor patrol joined them.

Banton was yanked to his feet by the man who had knocked him down. The private detective stood blinking, sullen. Burks hurled a harsh question at him.

"What the hell's going on here, you rat?"

"Find out for yourself!" yelled Banton.

"You sent up those rockets, didn't you?"

"Rockets! Do you think I'd call any of you lily-livered cops in to help me! The girl did it—the little—"

"What girl?"

Banton shook his head and sneered into Burks's face. But at that moment two coast guardsmen brought a kicking, struggling figure between them up from the cabin of Banton's ex-rumrunner. It was Rosa Carpita, the Spanish dancer. She wasn't speaking English now. She had lapsed, screaming, into her native tongue.

"We found her locked in a closet," said one of the men. Sweat dripped from his face. He was panting. "She don't like being rescued," he said.

Burks, growing more perplexed, bawled a question.

"How in damnation could she send up rockets locked in a closet?"

But he didn't question the girl at the moment. A more important matter claimed his attention. The tip-off had been that the band of death-torch murderers were escaping in a yacht with their fortune in loot. It was to see the murderers rounded up that Burks and Commissioner Foster had come out here.

There were pungent fumes of ammonia inside the cabin, keeping the coast guardsmen back. Here was another mystery. Who had thrown them? The murderers on board the yacht, Burks decided.

The fumes began to clear. The cops and coast guardsmen entered. They held machine guns, automatics and sawed-off shotguns ready. There must be life still on the yacht, more of the flame-throwers. They were taking no chances.

Three hideous hulks that had once been men were sprawled on the floor of the cabin. They went on to the head of the stairs, then shouted. At the bottom of the stairs lay another figure, helmeted and goggled. One of the torch murderers—dead. The mystery of their identity was at last to be disclosed to the police.

Inspector Burks was trembling with excitement. The police had had little part in catching this band of sinister raiders, but he was in at the finish. If there were any left alive they would have to stand trial for the murders they had committed in the city.

It was Burks himself, gun in hand, who saw a face ahead of him along a passageway of the yacht. His features grew white. He thought he was looking at a ghost. Then the face disappeared, a door slammed. From behind the door Inspector Burks heard a single pistol shot and the thud of a falling body.

He leaped forward, yanked open the door, and stood, gun in hand, staring down.

A tall man lay at his feet, a man with stern, aristocratic features, blue eyes and light hair. The blue eyes were blazing now. The features were setting into the immobility of death. There was a cruel sneer on the aristocratic mouth.

"Von Blund!" gasped Burks.

He leaned against the wall, rigid, dumfounded. The man who lay at his feet was supposed to be dead already, slain in the last raid on the Merchants' and Manufacturers' Bank, a charred and hideous corpse identified by his cuff links and jewelry. Understanding of this ghastly mystery began to filter into Inspector Burks's mind. With a harsh oath he stumbled back along the passageway, stooped over the goggled and helmeted figure at the foot of the stairs.

While Commissioner Foster watched, he ripped off the helmet and goggles exposing the dead face beneath. It was the commissioner's turn this time to gasp in surprise.

"It's Francis Marsh, inspector! In God's name, what does this mean? He was killed tonight—burned!"

"We thought he was!" barked Burks. "Von Blund's in there, too. He shot himself when he saw he was trapped, when he saw the game was up!"

"You mean—"

"I mean that the cleverest bunch of thieves and murderers in the history of the city pulled the wool over our eyes, chief."

"What about Osterhout, Davis and Honor—the partners killed in the first raid?"

THE answer to that question came before Burks could speak. Two coast guardsmen came into the cabin carrying a sprawled figure on a piece of canvas. He, too, was goggled, helmeted. But the helmet, ripped off, exposed the face of Eric Osterhout—von Blund's wartime partner, the man whose supposedly charred corpse found in the Merchants' and Manufacturers' bank had shown the wings of a flyer. He, also, was dead, riddled by bullets from the guns of Banton's raiding gangsters. And a group of cops herded a shaking, thin-faced man into the cabin following the corpse.

It was Honer—the fourth bank partner. He had little stomach for action, and they had found him hiding in a closet.

But he wouldn't speak. His bloodless lips were locked tight.

It was the black-eyed girl, Rosa Carpita, taken from the closet on Banton's cruiser, who answered vehemently when Burks asked a question.

"What about Davis?" the inspector said. "He must be around here, too."

The girl, standing in the door of the cabin, stamped her foot.

"Fools!" she said. "Bunglers! He is not here. He was killed—murdered!"

"That's what we thought about the others," answered Burks.

"But he was murdered, I tell you. I know. He was the only honest one. He told me terrible things were going to happen. He suspected, but he was afraid to go to the police. They, the murderers, hated him after he had been approached and had refused to aid them. Their bank was going to pieces. They were desperate men. So they killed him—because he knew too much."

"And you were sweet on him, weren't you, girlie?"

Color flooded Rosa Carpita's dark face.

"You are impertinent," she said coldly. "I shall not answer that question."

"Why didn't you come to the police if you knew so much? Why did you wait to tip us off tonight?"

"Tip you off?" Rosa Carpita pouted in puzzlement. "I did not tip anyone off. You are talking crazy. I employed that big pig, Banton, to catch these men. I wanted to be revenged."

Banton spoke then, sneering through clenched teeth.

"She wanted to get her paws on the reward money that was up for the killers' capture. But she got cold feet and called on you cops at the last minute."

"You liar! You double-crosser! I didn't get cold feet! I didn't call the cops! But I would have if I could—after you locked me up and threatened to kill me."

She turned to Inspector Burks, flinging a volley of words at him.

"This man is a crook, not a detective. I hired him to help me catch those murderers. I showed him the place where they were hiding what they stole. Jerry—Mr. Davis—had whispered many things to me. He was a good man—I wanted to see him revenged— and there was big reward out for his murderers. This pig, Banton, is right. We were going to split it. But he found out that they had so much money on board their boat. He was like the greedy hog. He was going to steal it—what you call hijack it—and then put me out of the way—whoof—so I would never tell nothing."

"Now I get you," said Burks. "Up to your old tricks, eh, Banton? You're hooked on a murder charge now. You and you're little pals here have been killing guys tonight. They were murderers, but the law don't even allow that."

He turned to Rosa Carpita.

"You better come clean—all the way, sweetheart! You did tip us off tonight, didn't you? You figured your big boy friend, Banton, was going to cross you?"

Rosa Carpita started to speak, then held her tongue for a moment. A crafty look came into her dark eyes.

"It is right," she said haltingly. "I did what you call tip you off. I knew that the big brave cops would be more generous than this fat pig, Banton. I knew that the reward would be mine for catching these murderers."

Banton exploded into a scornful abuse. His voice was a sneer.

"She's lying," he said. "She's got a tongue like a corkscrew. I thought she'd done it, too, first off. But she was in the closet, you say. That's where I put her, an' she didn't have a chance to send up any rockets. One of my own mugs must have done it because he loved me."

Inspector Burks scratched his head. The whole thing was mystifying. It would take hours to unsnarl. Rosa Carpita had changed her story suddenly—changed it when she saw a chance of getting the reward money. Burks's puzzled speculations were abruptly interrupted.

From somewhere below decks a thumping noise sounded. It increased in violence, became steady, monotonous.

Thump, thump, thump!

It sounded like spirit knocking; like some of the ghosts of the dead come back to haunt the ship. The cops and coast guardsmen stared at each other in startled wonder. Then Burks voiced a harsh question.

"What the hell's that?"

CHAPTER XXIII

MAN OF MYSTERY

THE THUMPING CONTINUED, and Burks gathered his men and went with them to discover its cause. They followed a passageway that led from the stairs at the foot of the yacht's saloon, and the thumping grew louder.

"It's somebody pounding," said Burks. "Some guy's trying to signal us."

They walked quietly, tracing the thumping at last to the metal door of a closet. The door was locked, apparently on the outside. The thumping was repeated as monotonously as before. Then a man's hoarse voice spoke behind the door, faint, muffled.

"Help—let me out! Help!"

Two stout-muscled cops seized the knob of the door and succeeded in forcing the lock. The door opened. Behind it was one of the yacht's storage closets, and there, standing against the wall, hands and feet bound, was a man. He was a tall man, white-haired, well dressed, distinguished-looking. His face was honest. He was obviously a prisoner.

"Thank heaven," he groaned. "I thought they would murder me, too."

Burks was aggressive at first. "Who are you?" he said.

Then his manner became more respectful. When the tall man's hands were untied, he fumbled in his pocket, brought out a wallet, and drew forth a card. This he presented to Inspector Burks.

On it was the name: "Carleton Madder, State Bank Examiner."

Madder drew credentials from his pocket, adding these to the card.

"They kidnapped me," he said. "They wanted help in disposing of stolen bonds. Then they planned to murder me afterward. They locked me in the closet when the attack began."

Madder's manner and appearance carried conviction. His credentials were above reproach. Burks nodded and handed them back.

When Madder was brought to the cabin above, Honer, the only surviving banker, stared at him blankly, but, whatever his thoughts, he kept them to himself.

The police and coast guardsmen continued their search of the yacht. They found hundreds of thousands in stolen cash, securities, and jewels—the loot of the murder band. It was transferred to the police boat, kept under heavy guard, to be rushed back to city vaults for safe-keeping before being returned to its owners. Coast guard boats attached hawsers to the two battle-ravaged vessels and made ready to tow them back to port. The death-torch killers would never rob or kill again.

Inspector Burks, Commissioner Foster, and the tall, dignified bank examiner named Madder, smoked in the cabin of the patrol boat as it sped away, its quest ended.

Inspector Burks voiced a question which seemed to be preying on his mind, and Madder, the bank examiner, hazarded an answer.

"I'm wondering about Spencer and Cox," the inspector said. "Those were the two bank employees who were supposed to have made a get-away after the first raid. If they weren't guilty what happened to them? Do you suppose—"

Madder, staring at the inspector, nodded.

"I suppose just what you do, inspector. They were the corpses found by the police alongside Davis's body. The murderers had transferred their own watches and jewelry to their victim's pockets to make it seem that they themselves were the ones who had died instead of the two employees whom they brutally murdered."

"And the last two corpses—the ones we thought were von Blund and Marsh? Who could they be?"

THE tall bank examiner shrugged. "Underworld characters probably. The murderers must have had one or more criminal aides in such a well organized plot. We know now that they brought their loot directly to the bank in an ordinary armored car. Who were its drivers? I became suspicious myself when I saw the car come with a load which wasn't accounted for on the books of the bank. I wasn't satisfied with the explanation. They probably killed these criminal aides when they were of no further use and would only be in the way. Those were the corpses you found in place of von Blund and Marsh."

Burks shook his head vigorously, offering an objection.

"What good would it have done, man, to take the cash to the bank vault? Answer me that?"

The tall bank examiner was leisurely in his reply. He lit a cigarette, blew smoke through his nose.

"It's only a theory, of course," he said. "But I overheard a few things. Osterhout and von Blund were former Prussian officers. One was a flyer. Both were men of action and daring. It is my belief that they transferred their loot to the roof of the bank building through a special shaftway leading from the vault. On the roof it was picked up by a plane and taken to the yacht."

"Impossible! Fantastic!" said Burks.

"Perhaps—but I think subsequent investigation of the vault and the roof may prove that my theory is correct."

Burks was still pondering this amazing explanation when the boat docked. The bank examiner was fidgeting to be off.

"I've a report to draw up and turn in," he said. "You can call me later if you want me to testify."

Unmolested, he leaped to the pier and strode away into the darkness, while the cops began to unload the loot to waiting armored cars summoned by radio.

For a moment Inspector Burks was preoccupied, then suddenly he stiffened and listened.

A faint whistle, eerie yet melodious, floated back across the dock. It seemed to fill the whole air, seemed to have a strange, ventriloquistic note like the call of some wild bird.

Inspector Burks's eyes gleamed in quick understanding. He had heard that whistle before. He recognized it. It was the whistle of the "Man of a Thousand Faces," the man whose identity was an eternal mystery.

A small boy came dashing through the police lines that cut off the end of the dock. A cop tried to stop him, but he ran on, clutching something in his hand. He sped up and thrust the thing in his hand under Inspector Burks's nose.

"Here, mister," he said. "A guy ast me to give it to you."

It was a note, and in the boy's pocket was a bright half dollar. His eyes were shining with the excitement of so much sudden wealth. Inspector Burks's eyes shone, too.

The note was brief, explicit in some spots, mystifying in others.

"Darlington was murdered," it said. "He did not commit suicide.

Ask Rosa Carpita about the plane she hired under the name of Rollins, two nights ago. Ask her why she took the flight and what happened on it. And search the ventilators on top of the bank." The inspector bent closer, staring intently. A faint "X" was visible at the bottom of the note—its only signature.

But the "X" and the writing above it, like the strange whistle sounding through the night streets, grew steadily fainter as Burks watched, and finally faded away, leaving only the blank paper in his trembling hand.

BOOK IV

AMBASSADOR OF DOOM

A monster of evil came to the nation's capital. A green-masked ambassador from Hell's own legation, followed by a horrible horde versed in the poison torments of the Far East! Even the police who sought to trap him did not guess the ghastliness of his real motive. That remained for Secret Agent "X" to discover as he prowled through a dark and sinister labyrinth of Washington espionage.

CHAPTER I

TERROR'S WEAPON

DARKNESS LAY OVER Washington. Darkness that was a smothering black blanket ripped apart by sinister knife blades of lightning. A jagged streak empurpled the sky. It bathed the dome of the Capitol at the end of Pennsylvania Avenue. It etched the classic columns of the White House in lurid silhouette.

Thunder rolled in like a savage war drum. When it died away, echoes raced across the Mall toward the distant ghostly spire of the Monument. Trees moaned in the night wind. Rain lashed the empty streets in chill torrents.

The city seemed deserted. Its residents had taken refuge in their snug homes. They were ignorant of the strange, secret conference in session at the State, War and Navy Building. They were unaware of the nerve-racking tension that filled a locked and windowless room where seven men sat.

Five of these men were United States senators. One was a cabinet member close to the President. The seventh was an army officer attached to General Staff.

The army officer was concluding an amazing speech. He stared from face to face of the tense circle around him.

"Let me repeat," he said, "that the discovery of Doctor Browning's just before his death was quite accidental. His life was given to the study of radioactive substances. He was an authority on radium, thorium, and uranium. It was a radium-induced cancer that sent him to an early grave. But the destructive possibilities of radioactivity didn't concern him. He was interested only in its therapeutic effects."

The young officer paused, cleared his throat, and fingered the papers on the table before him.

"When Doctor Browning sensed the sinister powers of the ray

Agent "X" gripped the knife-man and hurled him forward at the one who held the deadly captive.

amplification mechanism he had built, he was profoundly shocked. To make sure that his fears had a basis in fact he tested the mechanism on animals. He found that it caused complete and permanent paralysis of all nerve centers. He found that it turned living things into horrible hulks with a bare spark of life still remaining. He found, moreover, that it was effective at a great distance. He was about to destroy it when he was stricken by death himself. Fortunately, the United States government saw fit to confiscate the

mechanism and the blueprint plans."

The army officer sat down abruptly. In spite of the chill of the room, beads of sweat glistened on his forehead. He wiped them away and his hands shook nervously. A peal of thunder boomed far off on the horizon like deep-toned mocking laughter.

The gray-haired cabinet member at the table's head rose. For a moment he, too, stared at the five senators. Then he spoke in a voice that seemed unnaturally dry:

"You've heard Captain Nelson's testimony, gentlemen. You've heard reports and seen statistics showing what the mechanism of Browning's can do. There's no question, gentlemen, but that the United States has in its possession one of the most terrible offensive weapons on the face of the earth. A weapon, let me remind you, so ghastly, so inhuman, that it appears to be outside the pale of civilized warfare. The purpose of this meeting is to decide whether or not this weapon should be preserved or destroyed. What are your feelings in this matter, gentlemen?"

FOR a moment there was silence punctuated only by the faint footfalls of the armed guard outside and the muffled rumble of the thunder. The senators were grappling mentally with the appalling horror of what they had heard. They were visioning armies going down under the force of an invisible ray. Visioning strong men being turned into paralyzed, corpselike wrecks; men speechless, motionless, yet still alive—legions of the living dead.

White-haired, ruddy-faced Senator Blackwell, chairman of the committee, rose to his feet, fists clenched. He struck the table a terrific blow. His finely molded face was quivering with emotion.

"It must be destroyed!" he cried. "Get rid of it for all time. Burn the plans, sink the machine into the deepest depths of the sea. I don't care how you do it—but destroy it!"

He sat down, breathing heavily. Three other senators—Dashman, Foulette, and Cobb, nodded instant agreement. But the fifth, Senator Haden Rathborne, a pale, saturnine man, shook his head. There was a fire in his eyes as he faced the others.

"Gentlemen," he said harshly, "I understand your feelings. But war is war—and the instruments of war must be effective. We have machine guns, explosives, poison gas. Why not a paralyzing ray?"

Again Senator Blackwell became the spokesman for the others.

"Why not?" he shouted. "Because, as we've just heard, it's inhuman, ghastly. Because we know that paralysis is one of the most horrible things that can afflict a man. Because it is a fate we wouldn't wish even upon our enemies."

Senator Rathborne jumped to his feet. The light in his eyes had become a living flame. He thrust his short-necked head forward, hunched his shoulders, and drew up his hands in a gesture of angry impatience. His voice rose in sudden, fierce emphasis:

"With war threatening in a dozen countries it is madness to destroy such a weapon. The interests of humanity? Very pretty, gentlemen—very pretty! But we have the interests of our own country to consider. If war should come we can't afford to be white-livered and squeamish."

Senator Cobb entered the discussion now. A round-faced little man, immaculately dressed, he stabbed a shaking finger at Senator Rathborne.

"Remember, sir," he said hoarsely, "that civilian populations will suffer, too. You can't prevent it. Do you care to contemplate women and aged non-combatants becoming paralytics? Do you care to picture thousands of innocent children made hopeless cripples for life?"

Rathborne instantly gave answer, his whole lean body trembling with fanatical zest.

"I've never sought popularity, Cobb," he snarled. "I'm not a vote-snatching, favor-currying politician like some gentlemen I could name. I'm a man who speaks his mind. I advocate retaining and developing the Browning ray machine into an efficient weapon of war. In the next world conflict, the nation which inspires the greatest terror will win—the nation that breaks its opponent's morale."

Cobb stood speechless, confused. It was Blackwell who addressed the meeting for the third time. His face looked apoplectic. He struck the table, threw his shoulders back, and spoke in a voice that made the walls ring.

"Rubbish, Rathborne—utter rubbish!" he shouted. "It was Germany's terroristic tactics—her submarines, her Zeppelins, her poison gas—that made the nations of the earth rise up to crush her in the World War! Countries will always combine to defeat a common enemy. Even if this were not so, the proud history of these United States wouldn't allow us to stoop to the use of such a weapon. I move, gentlemen, that the Browning ray mechanism be destroyed for all time."

Senators Dashman, Foulette, and Cobb leaped to their feet, cheering Blackwell. The cabinet man joined them. Captain Nelson, looking relieved, nodded his approval.

Only Senator Rathborne remained silent. His face wore the obstinate, sullen expression of a man who cannot accept defeat gracefully. But the motion was carried over his head. It was agreed by the senatorial committee that Doctor Browning's hideous ray mechanism be destroyed.

RATHBORNE was the first to leave the conference room. He placed his broad-brimmed hat on his head with a vicious slap. He stalked angrily from the building. The others made their exits in pairs.

Rain lashed their faces. Wind pressed their garments to their bodies. But they didn't mind the fierceness of the weather. They felt they had done a good night's work. They thought they had settled an unpleasant problem. None of them guessed how soon the unseen spirit of horror was to stalk through the dark, deserted streets of Washington. None of them sensed that the lightning was like a demon's winking eye and the thunder that followed it a peal of devilish, sardonic mirth.

But a few minutes after they had left the committee room a human cry stark with agony sounded in the night. It rose piercingly above the mutter of the thunder, died away into a weird echo that whispered along the now deserted street.

A patrolling cop two blocks away heard it. He turned alertly, staring into the murky gloom from beneath the dripping visor of his rubber-covered cap. The glistening black rubber of his cape swished wetly as he ran toward the spot from which the sound had issued.

There was no one on the sidewalk. His flash beam probed areaways; and suddenly he stooped down.

A sprawled, inert figure lay at his feet—a man. Under the glare of the electric torch, livid rivulets of crimson showed. They streaked the man's cheeks, mingling with the rain, coming from a hideous wound in the left temple. The cop's fingers groped hastily for the man's pulse. There was no heartbeat. The man was dead.

One shrill blast on the cop's whistle summoned the patrolman on the next beat. Then he ran to the phone box on the corner.

His call was relayed over many wires. It caused consternation in high circles. Hardly had the five senators reached their homes when a strange message was flashed to each.

"The Secretary of War requests your presence immediately!"

Wondering, filled now with a deep sense of foreboding, the senators responded. One by one their fast cars sped back along their tracks, and at the State, War and Navy Building they entered the same windowless room they had so recently left.

The secretary greeted them silently, his face grave and strained. There were odd, haunting shadows of uneasiness in his eyes. Not until they were all assembled did he speak. Then he stared fixedly into the faces of the five senators seated before him. He licked his lips, fumbled a moment with his watch chain, cleared his throat noisily.

"Gentlemen," he snapped. "I have terrible news for you. You heard tonight the report that Captain Nelson gave us on the Browning ray mechanism. You heard what a devastating weapon it could become. You were shown the unpleasant statistics of experiments made on animals. Gentlemen, Captain Nelson has been murdered—the plans of the ray machine have been stolen!"

SHADOWS IN THE NIGHT

AT THE MOMENT this terrible news was being spoken, a fast sport roadster came to a screeching stop before the Army Air Corps base at Mitchell Field, Long Island.

A tall man muffled in a heavy overcoat leaped from the car. There was a suitcase in his hand. He walked with quick strides through the field gate toward a two-place army plane warming on the deadline.

Sparks from the throttled motor issued like a swarm of fireflies from the end of the hot exhaust stack. The pilot turned his head, nodding, as the tall man came up. He watched as the tall man climbed into the gunner's cockpit. He listened for the snap of the safety belt, then bent over his controls.

The plane tore down the field, leaped into the night sky in a roaring zoom of power. It banked, straightened out, and began to climb. Its destination was Bolling Field, Anacostia, D.C.

The pilot had no idea as to the identity of the man riding behind. He was only obeying orders which had instructed him to wait for and pick up a passenger. If he thought at all, he supposed that the man was an embassy attaché or an important witness in some fresh financial scandal the Government was investigating. The pilot's one concern was to see that the trip was made safely. It was a wicked night for flying.

Only one or two people in the world knew the identity of the plane's mysterious passenger. These few were pledged to secrecy and silence.

In the passenger's pocket was a telegram couched in secret government code. It was addressed to Elisha Pond, care of a bank in New York. It summoned him to Washington. Arrangements for the army plane had been made at the order of a high Government official.

He lashed out with his fists, tried to fight free, then something was thrown over his head.

Tonight the mysterious passenger in the gunner's seat was a man of destiny. His movements in the next few hours might influence the lives of thousands of people. They might conceivably influence the future of a nation.

In appearance there was nothing extraordinary about the man. He was youngish, well built. He sat erectly in his seat, staring ahead into the dark night. The only odd thing about him was the intent, burning light in his eyes. This light seemed to indicate depths of intelligence, magnetism, and power.

Yet, inconspicuous as the man's features appeared, they held infinite mystery. For the face that showed was not his real one. The man was disguised, so cunningly that not even the sharpest eye could have detected a flaw. The man was, in fact, a master of disguise—a master of a thousand faces. The man was Secret Agent "X."

Who was Secret Agent "X"? For months past people had been asking that question. Criminals along the black byways of the underworld had asked it. They had learned to fear his name. Rumors had even spread behind prison walls, spread to the darkest and most evil dives. Gangsters had heard of Secret Agent "X." Murderers had trembled at mention of him.

The police forces of a dozen cities had asked to know who he was. Detectives had suspected him. He had been hunted as a criminal. Crimes that he had never committed had been pinned on him until subsequent facts proved him guiltless. Yet no one could give an accurate description of him, for he never appeared twice alike. He was a man of a thousand faces—a thousand disguises—a thousand surprises. A man who was feared, hated, suspected, hunted. A man who guarded his identity as a precious secret.

There was the snapping of excitement in Agent "X's" eyes tonight. Under the cognomen of Elisha Pond, in care of the First National Bank, he had received many telegrams from Washington. They came from a high Government official whose identity was also a secret.[35]

Sometimes they asked that strange facts be unearthed. Sometimes they asked him to investigate mysterious crimes. But never before, since his perilous career as Agent "X" had begun, had he been summoned to the capital. Something unusual was in the wind. Some case of greater import than any he had ever tackled impended.

Blood raced through the Agent's pulses as the swift plane tore

---

35   AUTHOR'S NOTE: The exact source of Secret Agent "X's" unlimited powers as an investigator of crime has never been revealed. He holds a document of commendation from someone high in the Nation's trust. A fund was subscribed for him by ten public-spirited men of great wealth, and placed on deposit in the First National Bank, to be drawn by him under the name of Elisha Pond. From a study of case records and from things the Agent has let drop, I know that his career has been strange and varied. He made a distinguished record in the Intelligence Service during the World War. He has a vast knowledge of police methods. He is past master in the art of disguise. All these facts are upheld by his amazing exploits as a hunter of criminals.

through the sky. Its whirling propeller sliced the sheets of rain. Lurid flashes of lightning began to show on the horizon. They shed a ghostly light on the wings; made the pilot ahead look like some crouching, helmeted monster.

And the Agent watched the ship's course with the eye of an expert. If anything should happen to the army flyer up front, Agent "X" was capable of flying the ship himself.

They were following the shining ribbon of a straight double-tracked railroad. A fast passenger train showed beneath them. It was forging ahead at seventy miles an hour. But it seemed like a crawling, phosphorescent caterpillar as the army plane overtook it, and left it far behind.

In less than two hours a searchlight beacon showed on the horizon. It swung rhythmically across the heavens in conflict with the lightning. Peering over the plane's cowling, minutes later, Agent "X" saw the flood lights of a Government field below. He saw the Washington Monument on his left, saw the gleaming surface of the Potomac River.

The plane began to descend. It banked, nosed into the wind, slid downward out of the night like a huge bird. Landing lights on its wings winked on and off. Other lights answered below.

The velvet-smooth surface of the field swept up. It was glistening with rain. The plane's air wheels touched the ground. They lifted, touched again, settled. The plane taxied up to the hangars, fishtailed to a stop.

AGENT "X" leaped out. For a moment he looked around. A curious mechanic was moving forward. An officer, protected from the chill drizzle of the rain, stared at him from an open doorway. Then he saw a man in a glistening slicker running toward him.

"X," who never forgot a face, stared intently. When light from the hangar's open doorway fell on the man, "X" nodded to himself. The approaching figure was someone he knew—a trusted Department of Justice operative named Saunders; a man who had often been active in the dangerous field of counterespionage. On at least a half dozen occasions in the past, Agent "X" had talked to him.

But Saunders' face was a blank when he came up. He didn't recognize Agent "X." The Agent's masterly disguise fooled him. Saunders, thick-set, powerfully built and sandy-haired, peered under his wet hat brim.

"Are you Mr. Pond?" he asked.

The Agent nodded.

"I was told to meet you when you landed. I've got a car out in the street. But first, if you don't mind—"

Again the Agent nodded. He knew what Saunders wanted. Caution was ingrained in the men who worked for the Federal bureaus. "X's" hand dived into his pocket, came out grasping a wallet. From it he drew a card bearing the name of Elisha Pond. Saunders didn't know that this was one of a dozen aliases. He didn't know that the man called Pond carried other cards which he could have produced just as readily. He didn't know that the man before him was Secret Agent "X." He was merely obeying orders from a superior, as the pilot of the army plane had done.

"O.K.," he said. "Step this way if you please, sir. It's a nasty night, isn't it?"

"Yes," said the Agent grimly. He had an idea it was nastier than Saunders realized. He sensed strange, dark things in the air. He followed the stocky form of Saunders to the waiting car, a small, weather-beaten coupé.

"My own bus," said Saunders proudly. "She doesn't look so nice, but she's a sweetheart on the road."

Both men climbed in. Neither of them saw the shadow that moved along the hangar wall. Neither of them saw the dark, intent face that gleamed for a moment under the splashing drops of the rain.

There was a public telephone booth in a small cigar store opposite the field gate. As Saunders' car splashed away, the shadow by the hangar wall ran over to the booth. In a moment he was speaking softly into the mouthpiece of a phone, using a foreign tongue. Another man, a half-mile away, was answering him, also in the same tongue. The second man hung up, slipped out into the dreary darkness.

Saunders tried to make conversation as he and Agent "X" sped along. "X" answered only in monosyllables. He was oppressed by a sense of impending trouble, wondering about the mysterious reason for his summons to Washington. He liked Saunders, but the man was only a small cog in some vast thing that was under way. The sandy-haired Federal operative lighted a cigarette. He sent the little car whizzing along, driving with careless ease.

It was Secret Agent "X" whose eyes roved the street ahead with the closest attention. It was "X" who first saw the dark car pointed at a crazy angle toward the curb. For a moment his fingers closed over Saunders' arm.

"Someone's skidded," said Saunders. "And nearly smashed up."

A man in a chauffeur's uniform was bent over one wheel of the car ahead. He straightened, raised a hand in signal.

"They're in trouble," said Saunders. "Let's see what's the matter."

He braked his little car, began to slow down. The Agent's eyes had become burningly bright. But the chauffeur looked all right. He was dark-skinned. He seemed to be a mulatto. Saunders brought his car to a stop, cranked down a window.

"What's the trouble, fellah?" he said.

The brown-skinned chauffeur came forward, holding something in his hand.

"Look," he said. "Broken!"

He thrust his hand through the side window of Saunders' coupé, opened the fingers. Then it was that Agent "X" hissed a sharp warning; but he was too late.

Something crackled in the brown-skinned man's hand. It was like a dried puffball. A jet of brownish powder squirted from its collapsed sides. The powder filled the interior of the car. It went into the two men's faces, blinded them as though hot needles had been thrust against their eyes. Saunders swore fiercely and lashed out with his fist.

"You double-crosser. I stopped to help you and—"

WORDS choked in his throat as the brownish powder passed between his lips. Agent "X" did not try to speak. He jerked at the car's door, tried to get out, hoping that the night air and rain would clear his vision. He rubbed at his eyes with one hand, but it only seemed to drive the hot needles deeper into his nerves.

Dimly then he heard the sound of running feet around him.

He heard crisp orders shouted in a foreign tongue that made him start. A master linguist he had a basic knowledge of many languages. This was one he had heard before, but it seemed out of place, fantastic in his present surroundings. The brown-skinned chauffeur had been joined by others.[36]

---

36 AUTHOR'S NOTE: The science of linguistics is invaluable to an intelligence operative. It was his aptitude for languages, combined with his brilliant insight into codes and ciphers, that made the part "X" played in the World War so remarkable. There are rumors that, after America entered hostilities on the side of the Allies, Agent "X" was sent to many fronts. I believe he saw service in the Dardanelles when Allenby, in conjunction with sea forces, made an ill-fated drive. There is a rumor, also, that he performed a successful mission for Lawrence in Arabia.

Hands caught hold of Secret Agent "X." He lashed out with his fists, tried to fight free; then something was thrown over his head. A noose was jerked around his neck. He had a sense of enveloping cloth. A pungent, smothering smell was in his nostrils. It was like a strange, Oriental incense; but the sweetish odor of it was cloyingly oppressive.

He raised his hands, tried to pull away the hood that had been flung over his head. The dizzyingly sweet odor in his nostrils was filling his lungs now, choking off breath, making him reel on his feet.

Saunders beside him gave a hoarse, gurgling cry. He, too, had been attacked in the same way.

Blinded, smothering, Agent "X" was at a hopeless disadvantage. The onslaught had come before he had been on his guard, before he had conceived of the possibility of any enemy being present.

Cold fury filled him. He battled desperately to keep his faculties, to free himself from the smothering hood before darkness came. But the fumes in his lungs were mastering him. He slipped on the wet pavement, sank to his knees. His legs seemed to crumple under him. As blinding lights danced before his pain-racked eyes he fell into the black depths of unconsciousness.

CHAPTER III

DEATH BY TORTURE

HORROR BEAT UPON him when he woke up. He had a sense of appalling catastrophe. He had lost all track of time. He seemed to be in a dark, still room. Then he became conscious of a sound. A man's voice, low-pitched and precise.

The Agent's eyes still burned, but when he raised inflamed lids he found that he could see. He started, and breath hissed between his teeth. He was in a room. It was a man's voice he heard. And he saw in that first instant of returning consciousness that both he and Saunders were prisoners. There were steel handcuffs on his ankles and wrists. These were attached to rings in the wall behind; Saunders looked like a man stretched out on a crucifix. His head still hung down.

Then "X's" eyes swivelled again to the man who was speaking. His attitude was as calm as the quiet tones of his voice, but his appearance made the Agent's body grow rigid. For the man wore a green mask over his face. It was a livid, poisonous green, like the scales of some reptile, and, through slits in the mask, his eyes glittered as coldly and evilly as the beady eyes of a snake.

"You have waked," the man was saying. "Your friend is waking also. You will now be able to answer questions I shall ask."

Agent "X" turned his head. Saunders' eyes, red and inflamed, were opening.

"What the hell—" he muttered. "Say, what's this. You—"

The man in the green mask held up his hand. His eyes glittered behind the green of the cloth that covered his face. There was a measured inhuman dryness in his speech.

"Wait," he said. "It is not for you to ask questions. That is for me. You need only answer."

"I'll answer nothing," said Saunders. "I'll see you in hell for this."

"That may be," said the green-masked man quietly. He chuckled, and there was something about the sound of that chuckle that tightened the skin along Agent "X's" spine. He had been in the presence of some of the world's most desperate criminals—men without heart or soul. He sensed now that he was in the presence of a murderer. He muttered a warning to Saunders.

The green-masked man turned on him.

"You need not be afraid to talk—Elisha Pond," he said. "Your secrets are known already. You were summoned to Washington tonight for a special reason. You are the man about whom strange rumors have circulated, I think. You are called—"

The green-masked man stopped speaking for a moment and walked forward. He probed with tense, inquisitive fingers, picked at the lifelike plastic material on the Agent's face.

"That is a disguise you are wearing—a most remarkable one. It is my belief that you are the man called Secret Agent 'X,' the man, they say, who can make himself up in a thousand different ways." Green Mask's chuckle came again. "Whether you talk or not now, Elisha Pond—it is unimportant. You will talk later, when I am ready—and if I give you another chance. Look!"

The man lifted his hand. In it was the telegram that had brought Agent "X" to Washington.

"Code!" the green-masked man said. "Government code. Very ingenious, isn't it? Very difficult to read—but listen."

In a clear voice the man who had captured Agent "X" and Saunders began to decipher the message on the telegram—the message instructing "X" what to do in a certain room of a certain house upon his arrival there. It was from a high and mysterious Government official. The green-masked man read it as easily as though it had been addressed to him. Then his voice grew harsh.

"This paper has saved you some unpleasantness. If I hadn't seen it, and if you still refused to talk, I would take means to make you. For you are an important man, Elisha Pond. Otherwise you would not have been summoned to Washington. You are expected to perform a great service for your country. But it is evident to me that I know more at the moment than you. The rest I shall learn from the sender of this telegram—and from your friend here."

Again Saunders spoke, fury mottling his face. "Not from me, you won't—you double-crossing mug."

"I don't like your speech," said the green-masked man quietly. "You were instructed to take this gentleman, Elisha Pond, to a certain address. You will now give me that address."

"You heard me," said Saunders. "Come over here and I'll give you a poke in the eye."

"Fool!" rasped the Green Mask. He clapped his hands suddenly. The door of the room opened. Four figures glided in. The eyes of Secret Agent "X" stared at them burningly. Saunders gaped in amazement. If this had been a weird, drug-distorted nightmare, the four who had entered could not have been more grotesquely horrible. They, too, wore green masks, but not a simple cloth mask like the man in the chair. Hideously carved devil faces of some thin wood covered their features. They looked savage, barbaric. Leering mouths, huge noses, distended nostrils—with the sinister glitter of their own eyes flashing through holes in the wood. One of them spoke—and Agent "X" recognized again the foreign tongue he had heard before.

The man in the chair gave answer, using the same strange dialect.

"Chinks!" breathed Saunders—but "X" knew he was wrong.

The man in the chair turned again, faced Saunders.

"I give you one more chance," he said. "Will you talk or shall the *Kep-shak* be used—the pollen of the blossom that loosens men's tongues?"

A cold sweat stood out on the Agent's forehead. Some inkling of what was to ensue filled him. He turned his head toward Saunders.

"Talk," he said. "Tell him what you know!"

This wouldn't be much—only an address. Its concealment was not worth a man's agony. But Saunders shook his head. He was a powerful man, arrogantly confident of his own physical endurance.

THE green-masked man in the chair clapped his hands again. The four others stepped forward. One of them drew a knife, slit the sleeves of Saunders' coat from shoulder to wrist, laying bare his arms. Another drew something from behind his back that was like a tiny devil's claw. With an abrupt, expert stroke he drew it across Saunders' skin, leaving a line of red scratches. A third man came forward with a metal box in his hand. He lifted the cover, drew out a pinch of grayish powder.

"Talk!" said the Agent again. "Talk, Saunders."

The thick-set Federal man gritted his teeth. His lips remained locked.

The man with the pinch of powder made a swift motion. He tossed the powder on the scratches along Saunders' arm, rubbed it in with his thumb, stepped back. A slow change came over Saunders' face. The muscles in his cheek began to tense. His body began to move. He writhed in the steel bracelets that held him, bucking his shoulders up, trying to tear his wrists loose. But the cuffs were locked tightly. The strong steel held.

His lips opened then. Breath whistled between his teeth.

"God!" he muttered. "God!"

The ruddy glow of his face was paling slowly now. Beads of sweat stood out on his skin. Agent "X" tried desperately to work loose, to aid him. But the steel of the handcuffs bit into his own skin. They held tight.

"I'll talk," said Saunders with a sudden groan. "You win, Green Mug. I'll talk."

The words were wrenched from his lips by pain. He was a brave man, but the agony of a strange, exotic drug seeping into his veins through the scratches in his arms was too much. He babbled the address to which he had been directed to take Agent "X." The green-masked man in the chair nodded. Agent "X" listened. Then the green-masked man spoke.

"You are a fool, Saunders. I don't like fools. And you would be a nuisance if you lived. Also your death will be a lesson—to Elisha Pond!"

Horror crawled along the spine of Agent "X." He had feared something like this. A cry sprang to his lips.

"If you do, Green Mask—I'll see that you die yourself."

Green Mask bowed ironically. "Another fool," he said. "Look—and profit by what you see!"

He gave a low signal. The man with the powder stepped forward. Another pinch of the hideous gray stuff landed on Saunders' tortured flesh. A groan came from his bloodless lips. He writhed horribly, tried to speak, but only a discordant babble came from his quivering mouth.

Agent "X" strained until veins stood out on his forehead, until the handcuffs bit cruelly. He called harshly for this terrible thing to stop. Green Mask did not answer. The four others were silent, their glittering eyes turned upon their victim.

At the last, Agent "X" did not look. Horror, nausea, weighed him down. The hissing gasps that came from Saunders' throat seemed to lash the still air of the room. The walls seemed to throw the sound back in whispers of hellish laughter. Then silence followed, and when Agent "X" looked again, Saunders' powerful body hung slack in the steel cuffs that held him. Saunders was dead.

Weak himself from the ghastliness of what had taken place, Agent "X" sagged in his fetters. He had faced death and torture in his life, but he could not calmly see others suffer.

The green-masked man spoke a low order. The four who had performed his bidding disappeared as they had come. Green Mask arose calmly. He slipped into a hat and coat he had thrown over the back of the chair. His glittering, evil eyes became fixed on Agent "X." Agent "X" answered the look with fierce, silent hatred. The green-masked man buttoned his coat leisurely, turned his hat brim down.

"Let this be a lesson," he said. "I go now to receive the instructions meant for you. I go to learn exactly why you have been summoned by plane to Washington. And if the reason is what I think, I will have use for you later."

With a mocking salute, the man turned and strode across the still room. An instant later a door opened, closed, and was locked. It was followed by the sound of receding footsteps.

CHAPTER IV

THE LIVING DEAD

AGENT "X" STARED at his surroundings. The room he was in was bare, except for the one chair and a small table. There were no sounds, no street noises. Apparently the green-masked man had taken the others with him, left no guards, trusting to the strength of those forged steel handcuffs.

The Agent tested them. They were locked so closely to the flesh that they made painful pressure against his skin. The metal rings behind him were bolted into beams in the wall. He was apparently a hopeless captive. He rolled his eyes toward the still form of Saunders, cursed silently under his breath. He had seen many men die, but few as horribly as this.

Then Agent "X" began to move. He arched his body backwards. He thrust his hands down and brought his heels up. He could touch his shoe with his finger tips now. The steel cuffs cut cruelly into his wrists. He ignored the pain, stretched down farther still.

The fingers of his right hand groped along his left shoe sole. They paused, pried the leather of the sole apart at a point just in front of the heel. Working laboredly in his cramped position, he slipped something out. It was a four-inch piece of metal—a file. One side of it was highly tempered steel. The other side had a crystalline black substance set into it, held by grooved edges and mineral cement. It was a sliver of black diamond, thin as isinglass, but with a finely toothed cutting edge that was fashioned to rend the hardest of metal.[37]

---

37 AUTHOR'S NOTE: *The Agent is alert always to defeat, the possibility of capture and imprisonment. In his warfare on criminals the law is a constant threat, for the law misunderstands his motives. The diamond-set file, with no duplicate perhaps in all the world, is one of many protective devices he carries to free himself from handcuffs and to escape, if necessary, from a barred cell.*

Turning this file in his hand, holding it in tense fingers, Agent "X" pressed the diamond-set edge against the connecting links of his handcuffs. With a steady, rhythmical movement he drew it back and forth and felt the tiny crystalline teeth bite into the metal. Minute flakes of steel fell away. The groove that his diamond file made grew deeper and deeper.

At the end of ten minutes of patient effort, the links of the handcuffs parted. He breathed deeply, flexing his cramped arms. The metal bracelets were still on his wrists. There wasn't time to sever them now. He bent and attacked the steel links that connected the fetters on his ankles.

He had more room to work now, more leverage. Muscles in his arms and shoulders stood out as he drew the diamond-studded file across the metal in short, powerful strokes. He freed himself of the ankle cuffs in half the time it had taken to do the others. He stood erect—free—and the burning light in his eyes became like a hot flame. He moved close to Saunders, felt the man's pulse to see that he was surely dead. The glassy, staring eyes of the Government operative were proof enough. Standing erect, face muscles rigid, Agent "X" seemed to be making a silent pledge.

Then, with the steel bracelets unconnected, but still on his wrists and ankles, he strode across the room. The door was locked on the outside, but locks were no impediment to the Agent. He drew a set of slender chromium tools from the lining of his pocket. With the head of one, bent like a blunt fishhook, he picked the lock and opened the door.

There was a hallway outside. It was dark and still. The Agent picked up his suitcase which stood in a corner. The disordered state of its contents showed that the green-masked man had gone through it.

Agent "X" turned it upside down, pressed metal studs on the bottom, then breathed quickly.

The mysterious criminal had missed the narrow, cleverly hidden false bottom where many of Agent "X's" elaborate make-up materials were hidden. Only careful measurement of the sides of the suitcase would have revealed that.

With his luggage in his hand, Agent "X" catted into the dark hallway. He passed along it cautiously, ears and eyes alert. He encountered no one. He was in an old, deserted house. The masked torturers had gone.

AT the end of the hall he came to a street door. Lightning showed a vivid purple streak across the bottom of the door. He heard the dull and distant rumble of thunder.

He opened the door cautiously, stared out. The house faced on a dark old street in a part of Washington he was not familiar with. But there was no one in sight. The Agent slipped down the steps, crossed the street, and moved quickly ahead. He hated to leave Saunders behind, but the man was beyond aid now—and there was strange and vital work to be done.

He walked five blocks, then plunged into a corner drug store. He found a telephone booth and made a quick call, dialing a number not listed in the public directory.

A masculine voice answered him. It was a deep voice, with a note of quiet power in it, a voice known to Agent "X" only as "K9."

In clipped sentences Agent "X" told of their capture, Saunders' brutal murder, and his own escape.

The deep voice of "K9" gasped out a hoarse curse. "Saunders killed!" A silence followed. "X" could hear the harsh breathing of the man at the other end. Then the voice resumed: "Your impersonator failed to pass the tests. I grew suspicious, gave him no information, but—"

"He escaped!"

"Yes!"

"And your orders for me?"

"Come immediately to the appointed place. There is no time to lose now—after what has happened. We don't know who this man is—or what he'll do next."

Agent "X" left the telephone booth quickly. He found a taxi. In it he was whirled through the night-shrouded streets of Washington to the address that was on the telegram.

He stopped the cab a block away, got out, and walked ahead cautiously. His quick brain was active. The green-masked devil would hardly be waiting here to intercept him—for he would suppose that the man he knew as Elisha Pond was still a prisoner.

Tense and alert, the Agent ascended the steps of a big old-fashioned house. At his ring an elderly servant opened the door. With a brief nod to the man, Agent "X" entered and walked directly to a room on the third floor. The room was furnished, but there was no one in it. Agent "X" closed and locked the door.

HE strode to an old-fashioned desk against one wall, seated himself in a chair before it. He knocked on the desk four times, a space, then four times more, as the telegram had instructed him. Then he waited.

As though ghostly fingers were moving it, a small drawer in the desk was pushed out toward him. From a hollow space behind the drawer a voice issued. It was the same deep voice that had spoken to "X" on the telephone.

"The countersign?"

"The thirteen original States," answered "X."

The drawer moved back, its front coming flush with the edge of the desk. There was a second of silence, a slight rustling sound, then the drawer moved into sight again.

It contained a piece of paper this time. On the paper a strange, disordered arrangement of numbers and figures were written. They belonged to no known Government code or cipher. They had been devised to fill a unique and special need.

"Read," said the voice behind the desk.

Agent "X" took the paper from the drawer, studied it an instant, and spoke in a clear voice: "He is trampling out the vintage—"

With a pencil he wrote beneath this sentence, using the same strange symbols, "where the grapes of wrath are stored." This line from the "Battle Hymn of the Republic" was the oral and written test the deep-voiced man had mentioned.

Agent "X" pushed the paper back into the drawer and the drawer disappeared. There was another moment of silence and the voice behind the desk spoke again: "Correct!"

"I am listening," said Agent "X." He had given proper identification. He was in communication with a trusted Government official, one of the few persons in the world who knew the real nature of his desperate and dangerous work.

The deep voice began to utter short, swift sentences.

"Two men have been killed tonight. Saunders was not the only one. The first was a Captain Nelson of General Staff, a man bearing important papers—the loss of which form a terrible threat to the safety of this country."

At mention of the officer's name, Agent "X" tensed, and asked a sudden question.

"Was it John Bernard Nelson?"

"The same—you knew him?"

"Yes."

A shadow came into Agent "X's" eyes. He had known Nelson back in the days when the world was bathed in the red carnage of war. He had known him as a high-spirited officer, brave, honest and loyal. And "X," who never forgot a face, saw the features of Captain Nelson in his mind's eye now. It added a personal touch to the mystery and horror of what had occurred tonight. Was this man another victim of Green Mask?

"How was he killed?" asked "X" harshly.

"By a blow on the head."

The voice of "K9" began to give details then, details of the Browning ray mechanism, and the theft of the plans. When he had finished, "X" asked an abrupt question.

"Who are the suspects?"

A pause followed this query. The man who spoke through the drawer seemed to be thinking, pondering.

"It is a delicate matter," he said at last. "That is why you were summoned, Agent 'X.' It is a matter that cannot be handled in the regular way. Five senators were in that room. Until this thing is settled, until the stolen plans are recovered, suspicion rests upon them all."

"Their names?" asked Agent "X" quickly.

"Blackwell, Dashman, Foulette, Cobb, and Rathborne."

"What line of investigation do you recommend?"

Again the voice was silent for a second. The answer it gave was tentative, reluctant.

"Senator Dashman was a friend of Captain Nelson's. It was he who was influential in getting Nelson appointed to General Staff. He of the five would have been most likely to know in advance any movements the captain might make."

"Anything else?" asked the Agent.

"One more thing! Captain Nelson has been seen in the company of a woman named Lili Damora. Investigate her, also."

"I will," said "X" quietly.

HE was beginning now to understand the importance of his summons to Washington. He was beginning to realize the extreme difficulty of this task that had been wished on him. The deep voice of the man behind the desk came again, quivering with suppressed emotion.

"You now have the facts, Agent 'X.' The rest is up to you. Terrible as the death of Saunders was, your task is greater than the mere pursuit of a murderer—a thousand times greater. It may be too late. Doctor Browning's secret may already have left the country. In any event, menace hangs over America. If these plans fall into the hands of an enemy country—if war should come with that country—then untold horror will befall your fellow citizens. Do all you can to recover them. Leave no stone unturned. Stand ready to give your life, if necessary. That is all, Agent 'X.'"

The voice ceased speaking. The drawer closed slowly. Trembling slightly, Agent "X" arose. It was not fear of death that made him tremble. Death he had faced often—on the flaming battlefields of France, in strange, dark alleys of the underworld, high in the air, deep in the sea. Years ago doctors had predicted that death would come from the wound in his side where he now bore a livid scar. The only fear that influenced him was the fear of possible failure—the fear that he was too late.

He descended the stairs of the house, left it as he had come. He strode off resolutely into the night. Down the block he signaled a cab. He gave the junction of two streets as his destination. There he changed to another cab. He did this twice more, keeping a cautious watch behind, taking precautions against the possibility of pursuit. The man in the green mask was constantly in his mind.

AT an address in a street of furnished apartments Agent "X" stopped at last. He took a key from his ring, entered the door boldly, went to an apartment on the second floor. Here was proof of the far-sighted policy he pursued in his strange warfare on crime.[38]

The apartment was small but completely and comfortably equipped. Dust on the floor and furniture showed that it hadn't been occupied for months. The Agent went to a closet, drew forth a wardrobe trunk. In it, packed closely and carefully, were dozens of suits and uniforms. It might have been the wardrobe of some master character actor.

He drew from it a trim army uniform. It had a captain's insignia on the shoulders. The silver star and gold coat of arms of the

---

38   AUTHOR'S NOTE: With the unlimited funds at his disposal, Agent "X" has established hideouts in many different cities where the trails of crime may lead him. In fashionable apartments, in underworld localities, in medium-priced dwellings he has bases from which to work. The hideout in Washington was one of the first he hired at the outset of his career, anticipating that some day he might be called to the nation's capital.

General Staff were on the collar. In the pocket of the uniform were papers denoting the fact that its wearer was Captain Stewart Black. They were in good order and would pass inspection anywhere. As an army officer of General Staff, "X's" movements were less liable to be questioned.

Before putting the uniform on, he opened the false bottom of his suitcase again. From it he took a small, collapsible, three-sided mirror, then an array of pigments, transparent tissues, and volatile plastic substances. Here was all the paraphernalia of a man who was a master of disguise.

He made sure the door was locked, set his mirror up. Then his long, powerful fingers went to work. He removed the disguise he had worn upon his arrival in Washington. For a moment, under an overhead light, his real face was revealed—the face that not even his few intimates ever saw. It was a singularly youthful face except when the light fell on it at an oblique angle. Then new planes were brought out. They showed marks of maturity and strength, with lines that were faint but recognizable records of countless strange experiences and adventures.

On these features that were really his own, he began building up a new face. The pigments came first, changing the color of his skin. Then strips of tissue-thin adhesive, creating new muscular contours. Then the mysterious volatile substance that dried almost instantly. The substance so flexible that it responded to every facial move-ment. He had the rugged, blunt features of a hard-bitten army officer now. Once again Agent "X" had wrought a masterly disguise.

In his natty uniform he seemed to have stepped straight from the General Staff offices, or from some drill ground. But even the uniform was not as simple as it looked. It contained secret, hidden pockets. Into these Agent "X" transferred certain small things that he carried in his other suit. There was even material for a quick change of disguise, if that became necessary.

Leaving his apartment quickly, he summoned another cab and gave the address of Senator Dashman's home.

Rain still spattered on the pavement. Lightning flashed on the horizon. The storm that refused to leave the vicinity of the city seemed an expression of the menace that hung over the nation's capital.

The cab sped along wet, glistening streets, came at last to a big house in a fashionable suburb—a house that expressed the dignity of a man who was one of the country's lawmakers.

Agent "X" strode up the steps and pressed the bell. He had begun his campaign of action. He had a pretext for his visit to Senator Dashman carefully thought out. His inquiries about Captain Nelson would seem natural and in order. But it was seconds before his signal at the bell was answered.

Then a scared-faced, trembling servant came to the door. He was a colored man with features that showed the dusty grayness of fear. He stood on the threshold, making ineffectual motions for "X" to enter.

"X's" muscles grew rigid. He sensed in that first instant that something was wrong.

In quick strides he brushed past the servant, entering the carpeted front hall. A group of white-faced people were crowding close to a doorway across the hall. They turned as Agent "X" came toward them. He grasped the arm of a young man.

"What is it?" he barked. "What's the matter?"

The young man's voice rose hoarsely. He raised a trembling hand and pointed through the doorway.

"There has been a robbery—and—look!"

Agent "X" followed the direction of the man's shaking finger. An older man was seated at a desk in the room beyond, a man whose face "X" had seen in the papers many times. A man whose photograph he had in his possession, as he had the photos of all important Government officials. Senator Robert Dashman.

In that first swift glance Agent "X" saw why these men and women in the hallway were crowding close with a look of fear in their eyes. For Senator Dashman was toppled sidewise in his big armchair. His eyes were wide-open, glassy. His skin had the leaden hue of putty, and from his distended nostrils and open mouth came the hoarse sound of stertorous breathing. Senator Dashman was paralyzed—a horrible living corpse.

CHAPTER V

WHISPERING DOOM

AGENT "X" STOOD stunned for a moment. There was a ghastly suggestion in Dashman's stricken state. Was this the work of the terrible Browning ray? Doubt came instantly. How could it be, since only the plans of the ray mechanism had been stolen?

Agent "X" pressed forward into the room where the senator sat. A white-faced, trembling girl whose features showed a family resemblance hovered by his chair. "X" looked at the girl and said quickly, "A doctor should be called at once."

The girl nodded. "One is on the way. He will be here any moment. And you—"

"Captain Stewart Black," said the Agent. "I came here to question your father about—"

He paused and turned to stare at the group in the doorway. In the first moment of excitement he had made no close inspection of those in the house. Now he stood rigidly transfixed, his face muscles stiffening.

A blond, powerfully built man was in the group. There were three others—two young women, one of whom he knew by sight, and the dark-haired young man whom "X" had first questioned. But the blond man was the focal point of interest.

The man's face, too, was familiar to "X." There had been a change, a drastic one. Plastic surgery had evidently been used. The chin and nose were different. But to "X," who had made a life study of facial lines and planes, even the magic of the surgeon's scalpel was not sufficient to conceal true identity. He had seen this man before.

Names, faces, dates flashed through his brain. The years unrolled like the faded page of a parchment strip. He found the name he sought.

Karl Hummel—Prussian spy! The brain of Agent "X" raced with excitement. He was gazing at a man who had played his part in the World War with ruthless cunning, the cunning of a person who believes the end justifies the means.

The Agent's manner grew studied, calm. He turned back to the young woman again, the girl he guessed was Senator Dashman's daughter. He started to ask a question, stopped. The front door was opening. Three men were entering the house.

"Doctor Stoll!" cried the girl. "Hurry! Something terrible has happened to dad! The house was robbed a little while ago—and now—"

A sob choked off the girl's speech. She pointed to her father.

The foremost of the three men strode forward, a physician's case in his hand, deep concern on his face. The Agent's glance wandered past him, rested on the second man.

This man was thin, sharp featured, with eyes that showed penetrating intelligence. A small, carefully clipped mustache darkened his upper lip. His features were familiar to one who knew the city and its environs as Agent "X" did. Inspector Clyde of the Washington municipal police!

While Doctor Stoll began his examination of the senator, Inspector Clyde spoke to the senator's daughter in the abrupt manner of a man accustomed to authority.

"Your servant reports there has been a robbery, Miss Dashman. The city, as you may know, is experiencing a wave of robberies. I came myself when I heard your father had been injured. If you will please give me the details."

But the girl shook her head and turned from him. The doctor's coming had relieved her of the need of keeping her emotions in check. She gave way to sobs and another young woman in the group stepped forward. This was the girl whose face was familiar to "X"—a girl who was a college chum of the Agent's closest and dearest friend. She touched Inspector Clyde's arm as the Agent looked on.

"Valerie's in no condition to answer questions, inspector. The rest of us will tell you what you want to know. We were here, too."

"And who are you?"

The girl's answer was haughty. She stared at the inspector with chin held high.

"Suzanne Blackwell," she said.

"Go ahead," said Clyde gruffly. "I'm listening."

"Sam, Lili, Otto, and I dropped in a little while ago to see Valerie. Her father was in his study here. The door was closed. Valerie sent Thomas, the butler, to tell the senator that guests had arrived. He didn't answer Thomas's knock. Valerie became uneasy because her father has been under a strain from overwork lately. She opened the door and found him as you see him now. The safe was open, papers scattered about. It seemed like a robbery—the window was open, too. That's all we know."

Inspector Clyde had a notebook in his hand. He spoke crisply: "These three friends of yours, Miss Blackwell. I haven't had the pleasure of an introduction. Let's get them straight. One at a time, please."

AGENT "X" was paying close attention. The inspector's brisk questioning was saving him trouble. Suzanne Blackwell's next words startled him. She pointed toward the girl who stood between the two men by the door—a stunning, lithe-bodied brunette.

"Miss Lili Damora," she said, "of New York, Budapest, and Washington."

This was the girl Agent "X" had been asked to investigate, the black-haired beauty who had been seen in the company of Captain Nelson. She teetered self-consciously on high heels and patted her sleek *coiffure* with an affected gesture. She had luscious, pouty lips and the languorous air of a society belle.

Suzanne Blackwell indicated the two men next, giving the name of the dark one first, then the blond ex-spy.

"Mr. Sam Barkley, American sportsman, and Herr Otto von Helvig of the German Legation."

Inspector Clyde wrote down these names and turned to the Agent.

"And you?"

"Captain Stewart Black—just arrived, inspector, to do a little questioning on my own account."

In clipped sentences Inspector Clyde issued an order to the sergeant of detectives who had followed him in.

"Look around outside, Quane. See whether there's anything on the lawn."

The inspector himself walked across the study to the small safe that stood open, its papers strewn about. He hurled a question over his shoulder.

His skin had the leaden hue of putty. He was paralyzed—a horrible living corpse.

"What seems to be the matter, doctor?"

Doctor Stoll answered quickly. "A slight stroke, I should say. Some of you help me get him upstairs. Send for a trained nurse at once. Call this number."

As Agent "X" stepped forward to assist, the front doorbell sounded again. There was a furious, impatient note in it this time. The Negro servant hurried to open it and two men burst into the hall.

One was short-legged, immaculately dressed, his round fat face pink with excitement. The other was taller, thinner, a gauntly saturnine look about him, a fanatical light in his eyes. Senators Josephus Cobb and Haden Eathborne.

Valerie Dashman, getting a grip on herself, went forward to meet them. Cobb spoke abruptly, words trembling from his lips.

"Rathborne and I have been arguing. We've come to have a talk with your father. We must see him at once, we—"

The senator's voice ended in a fat wheeze. His eyes grew round with horror. The color slowly drained from his face and was replaced by the pallor of deep-rooted fear. For the Agent, Doctor Stoll, and Otto von Helvig were carrying the limp form of Senator Dashman out of his study.

Cobb's eyes rested on his senatorial colleague's sickly hued features. Then he gasped a sentence that seemed wrung from his lips.

"Good God—the ray!"

Inspector Clyde, following the procession, turned sudden, sharp eyes on Cobb.

"What was that you said, senator?"

Added fear leaped into Cobb's eyes. He shook his head with abrupt emphasis.

"Nothing—nothing—I was only talking to myself. What on earth has happened here?"

"Robbery," said Inspector Clyde. "And Senator Dashman has suffered a stroke."

COBB stood speechless, swaying on his short legs as they carried Dashman upstairs. A faint sardonic smile showed on the face of Haden Rathborne. Suzanne Blackwell's face had gone white.

The eyes of Agent "X" were tensely alive. Cross-currents of human drama had made the atmosphere of Dashman's home electric. "X" hadn't missed Cobb's explosive mention of the ray.

As they laid the senator on his own bed, the Agent's eyes rested on Dashman's neck. A tiny red mark showed there. The skin around it was slightly swollen. The Agent pointed toward it.

"Look, doctor—what's that?"

Doctor Stoll glanced down quickly, shook his head. "I don't know," he said. "I saw it. I'm wondering. It looks as though the senator had pricked himself. His pen perhaps."

"Perhaps," said the Agent, but his voice sounded skeptical. Then his eyes narrowed. A sudden horrible thought flashed into his mind.

That mark was part and parcel of the ghastly mystery, the folds of which seemed to be growing deeper and denser as he went along. He had noticed something else, and he hurried downstairs after they had laid Senator Dashman on his bed. The senator was in the doctor's care now. All that could be done for him would be done.

"X" was thinking of the strange look of terror that had come over Suzanne Blackwell's face when Senator Cobb had mentioned the ray.

Evidently she, too, had some knowledge of Browning's creation.

She was putting on her hat and coat when Agent "X" reached the hallway below. He saw that her fingers were trembling. She was no longer the poised, self-confident girl she had been when he first entered. Cobb's blurted utterance had shaken her for some reason.

Sam Barkley and Otto von Helvig hovered anxiously near her. Valerie Dashman was at her elbow.

"I must go home at once," Suzanne was saying. "You'll excuse me, won't you, Valerie? I know your father will be all right. You won't think I'm running away?"

"No—but why—"

"I can't tell you now—but I feel—that I ought to go home."

Sam Barkley laid his hand on her arm. "I'll take you," he said. "My car's outside."

Von Helvig intruded himself quickly. His tones were smooth but firm. There was a challenge in his eyes as he met those of Barkley.

"I was leaving anyway. I must get back to the legation. There is much work tonight. I will take Miss Blackwell with me, if she will be so kind."

Barkley shrugged and stepped back. Von Helvig captured the girl's arm. With a quick good night to the others, Suzanne Blackwell left. The Agent's eyes followed the tall figure of Karl Hummel, alias "Otto von Helvig." The man he had known as one of Europe's most cunning spies. Here was a lead he could not neglect in his quest of the stolen plans. He must follow it, but not immediately. There was still Lili Damora.

He turned, looked about him. The woman from Budapest was in close confab with Senator Rathborne. It seemed to the Agent that she was using her charms upon him, attempting to dazzle the senator with her exotic beauty. Her lashes rose and fell coquettishly, sweeping her delicately tinted cheeks. Every gesture she made was for effect. The lithe balancing of her body on one graceful hip. The movements of her slim, carmine-tipped hands. Admiration gleamed in Rathborne's narrow eyes. He seemed to lean over her predatorially.

Now was no time to question the woman—not with Senator Rathborne listening. Not with so many strange cross-currents in the air. He would see her alone, later. His eyes roved again.

SAM BARKLEY and Senator Cobb were standing together by the study doorway. The senator was mopping his fat face nervously. The pinkish flush of excitement had given way to a pallor that lingered. His glance swept the stairway up which they had so lately carried Dashman. He was waiting tremblingly for the doctor's full report—waiting with a fear that "X" could well understand.

"X" walked up and introduced himself.

"I'm told," he said, "that Captain John Bernard Nelson was murdered tonight. He was a friend of Senator Dashman's. But perhaps you can tell me something, senator. What was the meeting in the State, War and Navy Building from which Nelson was returning when he was killed?"

Fear leaped into Cobb's eyes. "I am not at liberty to speak," he said quickly. "I know nothing about Captain Nelson. I never saw him before tonight."

"Then you were at the meeting?"

"I did not say that!" Cobb gasped. "Really, captain! If there is a Government investigation into this matter and if I am called as a witness, I will answer questions at the proper time. Now—"

"I beg your pardon," said Agent "X" suavely. "Since Senator Dashman has been unfortunate enough to have a stroke, it seems that my visit here tonight was timed badly."

He excused himself, murmured a wish to Valerie Dashman that her father would soon recover, and left the house.

Once outside he moved quickly. The rain had stopped, but the sky was still overcast and fitful lightning flickered on the horizon. The Agent summoned a cruising cab and gave the address of Senator Blackwell's house. Why had Suzanne Blackwell been so alarmed when Cobb had mentioned the ray? Did she fear an attack of like nature on her father? And what part was the former spy, Karl Hummel, playing in his new rule of embassy attaché?

These were the questions Agent "X" asked himself as the cab sped along. At the moment, there was no one in all Washington to help him. He had undertaken a tremendous task single-handed. And he seemed to be working in a confused and black night of impenetrable mystery.

He dismissed his cab a block from Blackwell's home. It was farther along in the suburbs than Dashman's residence had been. A wide lawn stretched around it. Wet shrubbery glistened on the lawn.

Agent "X" moved toward the house like a wraith. He had played his hand openly so far. Now he was going to play it secretively— look and listen before he made any further move. He climbed an iron fence, dropped onto the lawn. He moved across it through the wet grass toward the house where a flicker of light showed.

Fifty feet from the house Agent "X" paused with an abrupt tingling along his spine. Something had moved in the darkness, something that was fleeting, sinister. A sudden premonition of danger telegraphed itself to his ever-alert brain. With a motion that was instinctive he jerked his body to one side.

As he did so, something like a swift-winged insect whispered past his head. It struck the trunk of a tree with a soft *spat,* and stopped, ten feet away.

Agent "X" whirled, then fell to the ground. Out of the darkness of a mat of shrubbery, four figures leaped toward him. The sense of imminent, hideous danger warned him that he could only escape death by some quick ruse.

CHAPTER VI

MEN OF MYSTERY

HE LAY STILL as the figures moved up. Their feet were uncannily silent on the grass. They walked like savages, bent forward, shoulders hunched. He caught a glimpse of the face of one in a shaft of light filtering from the street. That face was brown-skinned. Not negroid. The bones were too high, the lips too thin, the eyes too small and bright.

These, he felt sure, were the same men who had worn the green masks in the chamber where Saunders had been poisoned. These were the killers who had carried out a master murderer's will.

The truth of this was verified a moment later. One of them spoke in the strange tongue that "X" had heard before and recognized. They closed in around him like wolves.

His stillness, his appearance of death, was all that saved him. Knives gleamed in the hands of two of the men. Another carried something else, a tiny, slender pipe, mysterious, sinister.

They muttered in their monosyllabic language. Two of them reached down, the ones with the knives. There was horrible purpose in the way their hands groped.

"X" hurled himself sidewise then with an abrupt movement that was timed to within a fraction of a second. A master of disguise and strategy, he could use physical force, too, when necessity dictated. His feet swept in a circle, knocking two of the killers to the ground—those with the knives. His powerful hand caught the ankles of the other two, hurling them off their feet.

There was something ghastly about their stoical silence. He had taken them by surprise, tricked them, by playing possum, but they made no noise as white men would have done. They showed the training, the discipline that an exacting master had instilled into them.

They sprang back toward "X." For a moment one of their knives swept downward in a whistling arc.

The Agent struck then, lightning fast, with the tips of his fingers only. It was a strange blow, a thrust of his wrist forward. His hard finger tips jabbed the knifeman just under the armpit. The brown-skinned killer gave a grunt of pain. His knife slipped from his hand.[39]

For a moment after the Agent had struck him he lay writhing in pain, his lips locked together. The second knifeman tripped over him. But the man with the strange pipe in his hands was stepping back. His hands were taut as talons. His eyes glittered with an evil, murderous light.

The Agent saw him raising the pipe to his lips. Here was death. The threat of the knives was as nothing compared to this new device. For "X" knew what that insectlike whisper past his head had been. He knew what it was that had struck the tree trunk.

With a movement like a wrestler, Agent "X" clutched the fallen knifeman, raised him above his head, and hurled him forward toward the other who held the pipe. There were steely muscles beneath "X's" well-fitting uniform. He knew the secrets of leverage and suddenly applied strength. The man he had flung struck the feet of the other. Both rolled to the ground with a serpentlike hiss of breath.

A guttural order came from the lips of one who seemed to be their leader then. In an instant all four of the strange brown-skinned men were slinking away into the darkness. It was as though the night had swallowed them. One moment they were there. The next they had gone, and "X" could not hear even the sound of their feet. But, holding his head close to the ground, looking along it, he saw four shadows flitting across the iron fence that bordered the estate. A moment later he heard the sound of a motor starting up, heard it purr away into the night. Single-handed he had defeated them, but he did not fool himself. Sooner or later he was destined to meet them and their devilish master again.

THE Agent rose to his feet. The elbows and knees of his uniform were wet and muddy. Mud smeared his sides and back. But

---

39 AUTHOR'S NOTE: *Among the other means of self-defense, the Agent has mastered the technique of jiu-jitsu, which depends largely on using an opponent's own strength and weighth to disable him. But the blow struck with the finger tips was not jiu-jitsu. It was based on his knowledge of the position of important nerve centers. The underarm area is a region where sensitive neurons come close to the skin.*

he hardly noticed it. He moved forward for a moment, turned on the beam of a miniature flashlight with a bulb hardly bigger than a grain of wheat. He pointed it toward the ground, stopped and picked something up.

In his hand was a featherweight pipette—a hollow reed, open at both ends—seemingly harmless. It had dropped from the brown-skinned man's fingers when he had fallen. One end of it had been stepped on and crushed. It was useless now, but the Agent knew it had been more deadly than the fanged jaws of a snake. It was a blowpipe, a savage assassin's weapon, simple as it was terrible.

He walked back to the spot where he had been when the strange whisper sounded so close to his head. Again his light flashed on. Sticking in the trunk of a tree was a tiny dart, a, brilliant green feather at one end, a bone point at the other with a black, gummy substance adhering to its surface.

He drew it out, broke a section of the blowpipe as a guard against the deadly point, and put it in his pocket. His mind flashed back to that small mark on Senator Dashman's neck. Here was the answer. It had not been the paralyzing ray, but something almost as sinister. Two horrors hung over Washington: the threat of one still unleashed; and the real, ever-present menace of a band of hideous poisoners whose motives were veiled in mystery.

Eyes harsh as steel points, Agent "X" moved on across the lawn toward the house. This was what he had come for. The four brown-skinned killers had delayed him, but had not turned him from his course.

There was a light in the room that seemed to be the library. The rest of the house, save for the servant's quarters, was dark.

Agent "X" again took his chromium tools from his pocket. He had not forgotten the words of the man who had spoken to him through the desk—the man who had summoned him to Washington. "Your task is greater than the mere pursuit of a murderer—a thousand times greater."

The threat of murder was a side issue. He was here to battle an unseen threat to a nation.

With swift, tense movements he came close to the house. A light showed over the vestibule of the front door. He went to a side entrance where no light showed in or out.

Silently, deftly, utilizing all the skill he possessed, he used his steel implement to pick the lock and enter the house. He found himself in a narrow hall that seemed for the use of servants alone.

He moved along it, remembering where the lighted library was. He heard servant's voices in a room at his left. He passed through a door at his right, the dining room. He crossed a hall, saw the library ahead. The door of that was ajar. Voices came from behind it. Agent "X" crept close.

The voices came plainly now. Risking the possibility of being seen he moved closer still. The door of a writing room showed near by. He would duck into that if a servant should come.

There were three persons in the library—Suzanne Blackwell, a young man, and the senator, her father. Von Helvig was not there. He had apparently taken Suzanne only as far as the door.

There was tense drama in this expensively appointed room. The Agent's eyes snapped. The girl, Suzanne, was speaking, her face still white, her slim hands clenched. She was talking fiercely to her father.

"It was the ray, I tell you," she was saying. "The ray you told us about. Senator Cobb said so. I heard him. If you had been there to see Senator Dashman you would believe me. It was horrible. I remembered what you had said and I was afraid—for you."

THE ruddy face of Senator Blackwell was contorted. A cigar was clamped in his mouth. He was pacing the room. There was a strange, haunted look in his eyes. His daughter's words seemed to be affecting him strangely, but he spoke with explosive emphasis.

"What you say is impossible! Do you hear? I should never have told you about the ray. It put silly ideas into your head. The plans of it only were stolen—just a few hours ago."

"They *were* stolen, then?"

"Yes—but you mustn't breathe a word of it to anyone. No hint of it must reach the papers."

The young man in the room spoke suddenly. Agent "X" had been watching him. He looked like Suzanne in feature, but he hadn't her spirit or haughtiness. There was weakness in his mouth, lines of dissipation around his eyes. His complexion was bad. The muscles of his face were twitching. His hands shook, and the tones of his voice had an hysterical quaver.

"They'll get us all," he said shrilly.

The senator turned on him fiercely. "You're a fool, Ferris. As a son you disgrace me. If you can't talk sense, shut up. Don't frighten your sister more than she is. I want both of you to forget this thing.

You're going away, Ferris—back to the sanatorium for another treatment."

It was painful to see the twitching of the young man's face now. To the eyes of Agent "X" the evidence was plain, Ferris Blackwell was a drug addict of some sort. Here was tragedy in a high place.

"I can't go yet," said Ferris. "Not until I've seen someone!"

The senator answered sternly. "Doctor Claude says that one more treatment is necessary. I spoke to him today. He's coming for you—and you are going with him tonight."

The eyes of the two men clashed strangely. Ferris Blackwell's lips began quivering violently. Then he cried out and hunched back as though trying to escape his father's penetrating stare. Suzanne Blackwell suddenly straightened her shoulders.

"I'm sorry, Dad. I'll buck up. It's bad enough to have one weakling in the family. I was scared tonight—that's all. I left right away after Senator Cobb mentioned the ray. Otto von Helvig brought me home."

"You didn't tell him your fears?"

"No."

"Well don't. I don't like him, Suzanne. He asks too many questions. He's the last person in the world who should hear about any of this."

"Why?"

"Because he works for a foreign government, and because I don't trust him as an individual. Stick to Barkley—if you must have a man hanging around. He may be a loafer—but he's harmless."

"And you don't think Otto is?"

"No—I tell you I don't trust him."

Senator Blackwell jerked his watch from his pocket.

"It's ten-thirty now," he said. "Doctor Claude will be here any minute. Get your things packed, Ferris. You've got to go with him. Try to behave like a man."

Agent "X" withdrew quietly. He had heard enough. He was determined now to trace Otto von Helvig and see whether this man was still engaged in espionage activities. If so, the stolen blueprints of Browning's hideous mechanism might have passed through his hands.

CHAPTER VII

A DANGEROUS MOVE

THE EYES OF the Secret Agent were gleamingly bright. A desperate plan had occurred to him. Not to confront von Helvig at the legation. That would be futile. Disguised, he could interview the man. But there was an infinitely better way.

He would get at the very heart of Washington's espionage activities, find the center of that spider web of spy work which is spun about every capital in the world, even Washington. Along its threads would travel whatever whispers there were concerning von Helvig and Lili Damora.

The Agent deliberated a moment, frowning. There was no one in Washington to help him; no one upon whom he could depend for information concerning the movements of the five who had sat on the senatorial committee.

Beneath the peaceful surface life of Washington lay a dark underworld of espionage, a dank, unwholesome labyrinth. While he investigated this, he needed someone to contact the stratum above. The future safety of America hinged on the return of the Browning plans.

Yet in all the world there was only one person who *could* help him. Only one whom he could completely trust. That one was Betty Dale. Blonde and lovely, daughter of a police captain who had fallen victim to underworld bullets, Betty hated criminals as much as "X" did.

She was a lady of the press now, a society reporter, forging ahead by her own hard efforts. She would come to Washington if he asked her to. The paper would give her leave.

It would be a simple matter, too, for her to move in the very circles "X" wanted watched. For Betty had invested her father's life insurance money in a college education—and at college Suzanne

Looking over his shoulder, Agent "X" saw the bloodhounds' gleaming eyes.

Blackwell had been her roommate. When in Washington Betty always stayed with Suzanne. There was nothing more natural than that she should come to Washington now, to cover for her paper the ball that Senator Marvin Foulette was giving tomorrow night. A wire from "X" would bring her.

But Agent "X" had qualms. What right had he to ask her? The theft of the plans had brought horrible forces into play. Was he justified in risking Betty's safety in the slightest degree?

It was minutes before he could decide this question. He knew that if she ever found he had needed her and not called her, she would be hurt. She'd asked him to promise once that he would always tell her when she could be of use to him. Often in the past she had helped him. At the times when he took money from crooks he distributed it for him among the helpless victims of crime; among the innocent children of men sent to prison; among widows left by assassin's bullets.

And, with America itself menaced, she would be eager to take any risk. He finally made his decision. On the way to his hideout Agent "X" sent a carefully worded telegram to Betty. It would bring her by plane the next day. He instructed her to proceed directly to Suzanne's house, not letting Suzanne know that her visit had any purpose except to cover Senator Foulette's ball.

At his hideout "X" swiftly examined the tiny dart which had so nearly imbedded its point in his flesh. He scraped the black, gummy substance from the tip and sniffed at it. Then he took a small box from the false bottom of his suitcase. It held a compact chemical outfit—miniature vials of acids for chemical tests, a tiny collapsible retort for making distillations.

He put the substance from the dart in a test tube a quarter inch in diameter and used the flame of his cigar lighter in lieu of a Bunsen burner.

TEN MINUTES of analysis confirmed his suspicions. The gum on the dart was poisonous black resin from the deadly Rengas tree, known also as Singapore mahogany. Agent "X's" eyes reflected hot pin points of light as his mind flashed back to that tiny mark on Senator Dashman's neck, his strangely paralyzed condition, his stertorous breathing.[40]

The brown-skinned men spoke a Malayan dialect. The Rengas tree was found commonly in the Malay peninsula. This upheld his belief that the murderous Green Mask headed a band of Malay poisoners. The blinding powder loosed in Saunders' car was probably Malay. So also was the *Kep-shak* torture which had ended Saunders' life.

---

40 AUTHOR'S NOTE: Agent "X," a student of toxicology, knew that the action of Rengas was often similar to that of "Aconitium Napellas" in its last stages—namely, dysphea or respiratory paralysis, with the skin cold, livid, and covered with sweat.

Agent "X" replaced his miniature laboratory, and shed the army captain's uniform. He stripped the makeup from his face; with swift precision began to create a new disguise. Beneath his skillful fingers an inconspicuous-looking young man emerged—a man with a smooth-shaven face and sandy hair; a man who carried the cards of H. Martin, Associated Press reporter. He had credentials, travelers' checks.

He left his hideout and went to a "drive-yourself" garage, hired a smart roadster with a roomy compartment in the rumble seat. He sped along the night-shrouded streets of Washington, eyes bleakly alert.

It was nearly midnight now. A chill drizzle still fell. Lowering clouds hung low over the city. Danger seemed to lurk in the darkness.

He followed Massachusetts Avenue to Stanton Square. He cut into Maryland Avenue, circled the Capitol grounds, then headed down Delaware Avenue toward that point of land bordered by Washington Channel on one side and Anacostia River on the other.

Ahead of him was the Army War College, but he stopped before he reached it, turning into a dark, nondescript side street. Here, within a half-mile of the War College, was a place known to "X" as a hotbed of espionage. Perhaps spies chose this spot because it was close to some of America's military secrets, past and present. Perhaps it was to keep an eye on the men at Uncle Sam's fighting college.

Agent "X" did not know. But he knew that at a certain address in this dark, badly lighted street was a clearing house for spy information. Here a sinister personage conducted a sinister traffic. Here secrets for which men risked their lives and women risked their honor were bought and sold. Here dwelt a man who was a veteran operative of espionage.

Agent "X" had long known of his existence. So had men of the D.C.I., but they did not know his address and "X" did. He had long hoped that this knowledge might prove useful. Now the time had come to test it.

He parked his roadster a block away, proceeding along the dark street as silently as a shadow. The house he sought was a wooden, three-story affair. He saw it looming darkly, no lights in its windows, something unprepossessing about its misshapen lines.

Its infamous occupant had apparently gone to bed. But one

could never be sure—not with the man who used the business name of Michael Renfew. He was as cunning as a fox, as spineless as a rabbit, except—

Agent "X" knew Renfew's character. The man was an espionage merchant. His own active days were over. He was a coward at heart, but a sly, sneaking jackal of a man; and a man still to be feared.

The Agent didn't go to the front door. He went to the rear of the house, creeping along its side, moving like a wraith. At the rear door he took out his tool kit again. Never had he been so careful as now. A man like Renfew would have ears that would detect any sound. His dangerous work would make him fear for his life. He would take means to safeguard it.

The Agent, before he opened the rear door, took a small metal disc from his pocket. He drew from its side a ribbon of gleaming copper that was like a measuring tape. But it had no numbers on it. It served another purpose.

He thrust one end of it in the moist, rain-wet earth. With a thin tool like a knife blade he probed cautiously around the door's edge till he heard the faint scrape of metal. There he wedged the knife blade. He attached his metal disc to it, and opened the door.

By doing this he had disconnected an ingenious burglar alarm, which operated on a broken circuit when the door was open. Agent "X" had seen to it that the circuit remained unbroken.

He entered the house and closed the door after him. He took off his shoes, laid them on the floor, and moved forward on his stocking feet.

Was it possible that Michael Renfew was not at home? Agent "X" planned to see—and wait for him if he wasn't.

A second door he came to was closed. With the caution of a man whose dangerous life had taught him eternal vigilance, Agent "X" explored this also.

HE found two tiny electric wires, hardly larger than threads, running along the frame. The door had an alarm system, too. He scraped the insulation from the wires, connected them with a small piece from his own pocket, and opened this door. He was convinced now that the spy was at home.

A flight of stairs that had a tendency to creak gave him trouble. Once he paused, thinking he heard movement above. Then he continued upward, stepping on the sides of the stair boards to prevent movement.

He came at last to the door of a bedroom, closed like the others. It was many minutes before he found means to open it, found the location of the last electric alarm. There wasn't a burglar alive who could have entered that house without waking the tenant. But Secret Agent "X" was no burglar.

An old-fashioned four-poster bed was in the room. A man was sleeping in it. So silently had the Agent approached, so trustful was the man of his alarm system that the Agent crept to the bed and bent over the sleeper and still the man slept on. The Agent clicked on his tiny flashlight, then leaned forward to wake the sleeper.

As he did so Renfew stirred. He was a gaunt, wizened man with a bald head and a face as wrinkled and leathery as a turkey buzzard's. He opened his little eyes, gave a sudden scream of fear.

Quick as a striking snake his hand reached out toward a cord beside his bed. He yanked it, and in the same instant Agent "X" leaped forward, sprawling across the bed. As he did so the floor beside the bed where he had been standing a second before dropped away. A trapdoor fell downward, a yawning black hole leading all the way to the cellar opened up. How many people visiting Renfew had taken this terrible plunge?

"X" grasped the wrinkled spy's body, held him fast by the arms, while his eyes glared into Renfew's.

The spy screamed again, and the Agent shook him as a terrier would shake a rat.

"Silence," he ordered, and his strangely compelling voice seemed to affect Renfew like a blow. The spy lay back gasping.

"Who are you," he croaked, at last. "Don't kill me. I have nothing!"

The Agent had drawn a gun from his pocket. It was a gun that fired only a small charge of anesthetizing gas, but Renfew didn't know that. The muzzle of the gun was pressed against his chest.

"Get up," said the Agent, "and get dressed."

"Who are you? What do you want?" the man repeated.

"Never mind! Get up!"

"X" moved across the bed to the other side, avoiding the black pit left by the trapdoor. He kept his eyes fixed on Renfew, alert for tricks. He kept his gun against the spy's body. He pulled the cord of a small electric bulb, flooding the room with light.

Renfew stared at him with glittering eyes. His face showed no recognition. The Agent's disguise was a perfect blind. He took his press card from his pocket, held it before Renfew's face.

"A newspaper reporter," the spy gasped. Then his eyes became crafty. "Perhaps we can make a deal. There is no need for violence."

Remembering the trapdoor, "X's" eyes grew steel hard. "A broken neck is rather violent," he said harshly.

"I thought you were a burglar," said Renfew.

"Dress and come with me," was the Agent's order.

"You are a fraud," screamed Renfew suddenly. "You are not a press reporter. You are going to kill me."

"Not if you obey my orders," said the Agent. "Otherwise—" He gave the spy a jab with the muzzle of his gun.

WITH trembling arms Renfew began to dress. There was something inhuman about the dryness of his face. He had the complexion of a mummy, but the eyes were wickedly alive. "X" wished he could turn the man over to the police. But that could not be done now. He must use Renfew's establishment and Renfew's reputation.

When the spy had dressed, "X" motioned toward the door.

"I am leaving," he said. "And you are coming with me. Make any move to escape and—" Again he gave the man a vicious jab with his gun.

Keeping his light switched on, he pushed Renfew ahead of him down the dark stairs. The man's voice shook with terror as he asked a question.

"The alarms—how did you get through them?" His eyes rolled back toward Agent "X." He looked with awe into the steady, steely gaze of the Agent. "X" did not reply and Renfew seemed to wilt, sensing that he was in the power of a man who possessed supernatural powers.

"X" pushed Renfew out into the night, keeping a grip on his arm. He held the muzzle of his gun close as they moved along the street. When he came to the spot where his car was parked he made Renfew get into it. In silence he drove off.

The spy's face had gone a sickly white now. The paleness of his complexion, overlaid with its network of wrinkles, was hideous. He kept glancing sidewise at "X."

Agent "X" drove quickly, plunging along the dark quiet streets. The city seemed to have gone to bed. Once the whistle of a patrolling cop shrilled at "X" to slow down, but he sped on.

Not until he came to his hideout did he stop. Then he took a firm grip on Renfew's arm. He pressed his gas gun close to the left side of Renfew's body.

"Quiet!" he warned.

Renfew moved forward shivering.

"X" had a key. He entered and went into his small furnished apartment without anyone seeing them. Renfew stood trembling, his eyes darting about, as though not knowing what strange thing to suspect.

"Sit down," said "X" suddenly, and pushed Renfew into a chair. He turned then and locked the door. The spy sat shaking, looking up at him like a cornered rat.

"I know all about your work," said "X." "I know that you sell Government secrets as other men sell merchandise. I know that you are loyal to no country in the world, but give what you have to the highest bidder."

The Agent stopped speaking, took a wallet from his pocket. From it he drew a huge sheaf of bills. There were notes written in four numerals on the top, many others in three. Renfew's eyes bulged. Greed took the place of fear. He licked his lips, then smiled.

"Perhaps we can make a deal yet," he said.

"Perhaps," said the Agent. "What great secret was stolen from America within the past twenty-four hours?"

Renfew was silent a moment, his eyes stabbing the Agent's. He began to fence.

"Many rumors have come to me."

"One thing—more important than any," said "X."

"Perhaps the building of the new D10 submarines," said Renfew. "I have been offered—"

"No," said "X" harshly. He held a thousand-dollar bill forward, watching Renfew's face fixedly.

"I'll give you this as a down payment if you tell me what I want to know."

Renfew's eyes stared avidly at the bill. His lips moved again.

"Perhaps the secret commercial treaty with—"

"X" stuffed the bill in his pocket "You do not know," he said. He was convinced of it. News of the stolen Browning plans hadn't reached Renfew's ears as yet.

HE did not question Renfew further. The man's secret records would give him the leads he sought. He looked at Renfew fixedly for a moment. The spy's face began to pale again, losing the color that had come back at the sight of money. He sensed something speculative and coldly impersonal in "X's" attitude.

"What you going to do?" he cried.

"This!" said "X"—and before Renfew could move he raised his gun and pulled the trigger. The spy opened his mouth to give a piercing scream, but a cloud of gas from the gun's muzzle filled his throat, choked him.

One gurgling whisper came from his lips, then slowly he slumped forward and fell to the floor. He was not dead, merely knocked out, and he would remain so for many minutes.

The Agent looked at his watch. It was nearly twelve-thirty.

He wanted to make sure that Renfew stayed unconscious for a good while to come. He could take no chances with the spy now. A method of getting him out of the country had occurred to the Agent. But there was no time to effect it. He went to his suitcase, opened the false bottom and took out a minute hypo needle. Expertly he jabbed this into Renfew's arm. For twenty-four hours, unless the Agent chose to wake him sooner, Renfew would remain unknowing.[41]

Next the Agent propped Renfew back up in the chair and studied him. For long moments he looked at the man from every angle. Then he got his make-up materials and began to work on his own features. This was his object in capturing the spy. By stepping into Renfew's shoes he hoped to gain information that could be gotten in no other way. The disguise he now undertook was in many ways the most difficult he had assumed for many months. Small strips of the transparent adhesive were necessary to simulate Renfew's wrinkles. The Agent plastered his own brown hair down with a special liquid that evaporated on contact with the air.

Before it had a chance to disappear, and while his hair was still close to his scalp, he slipped a rubber cap over his head, giving an impression of baldness. He added plastic material around the edges, smoothed it out—and when he had finished, Renfew's double seemed to be standing in the room.

---

41   AUTHOR'S NOTE: The Agent has many times proven his knowledge of hypnotic and anesthetizing drugs, particularly the opium alkaloids. By varying the quantity and using different types, he can figure to within a few minutes just how long a man will remain under a drug's influence.

"X" went through the spy's pockets carefully, took out all papers and keys that might be helpful, and carried Renfew's inert body to a big clothes closet. He had had an eye to this in selecting the apartment. There was a wide crack under the door. Renfew would not suffocate. "X" put him in and locked the door.

Then he went quickly out into the street again and climbed into his roadster. He made the trip back to the dark section of town where Renfew lived in fifteen minutes.

He parked his car, walked forward, and quietly entered the spy's three-story house.

His first act was to return to Renfew's bedroom and close the trapdoor. A breath of dank, moldy air rose upward from the cellar as he pulled the door shut. He fastened it and carefully arranged the cord by the bed again.

Then he searched around the room till he found an old safe concealed inside a big desk. At the end of ten minutes the Agent had opened this. With eyes intent he began going through the spy's private papers.

Most of them were in code, but he remembered the tattered, well-worn book he had taken from Renfew's pocket. He would have been able to decipher the code without it, but time was an important element.

He opened the book, found the code key, and began reading the papers.

Here were brief reports of espionage deals that would have shocked the State Department. Records of military secrets being bartered, records of the bribery of public officials. Entries that hinted at dark, unspeakable things done to gain information which could be sold.

Then Agent "X" suddenly raised his head. He listened a moment, thrust the papers back into the safe and closed it.

The faint jingle of a bell had sounded eerily in the still house. Someone was at the front door.

CHAPTER VIII

DEATH CRY!

THE BELL'S NOTE was repeated as he tiptoed down the dark stairs. He might be facing a bad situation. This might be one of Renfew's friends. Would his disguise work?

Strange echoes were still sounding through the old house as he reached the front door. Small leaded windows were set in its side frame—more of Renfew's precautionary measures.

Agent "X" used one of them now. At first he could see nothing. Then his eyes got used to the gloom of the street outside. It was at least brighter than the room he was in. Light from a distant pole lamp filtered along the pavement.

A man was standing outside. He was hunched over. His collar was turned up. His hat pulled down. Agent "X" caught a glimpse of his profile. He had never to his knowledge seen the man before. The man was just about to turn away when "X" opened the door. He started violently, peered forward.

"I was afraid you weren't in, guv'nor!" the man said.

His accent seemed to indicate cockney extraction.

"A fine time to wake a man up," said Agent "X," imitating Renfew's cracked voice. "What do you want?"

"I'd like a few words with you, Mr. Renfew."

The man stared behind him along the street. There was a look of uneasiness in his squinted eyes. When "X" told him to come in, he entered the house with the quick, slinking gait of a furtive animal.

"Now what is it?" said "X." He turned on his little light. It was pointed straight into the man's face. In his other hand was his gas gun.

"It's all right," said the stranger hoarsely. "You ain't never seen me before, guv'nor—but I've heard of you. Don't get excited."

"What's your name?"

"It ain't important, guv'nor—if you don't mind—I'll—I'll tell you later—after we've had a talk."

"What is it you want of me?"

The man came closer. There was an odd, hungry look in his eyes. "We might as well play square with each other," he said. "You buy—things. I know that. I ain't no fool, and I've got something to sell—information you might call it."

"Information?"

"Yes."

"Follow me," said Agent "X."

He led the stranger up the stairway and to a room on the second floor which had served as Renfew's office. He pulled down the shade, turned on a light, and seated the stranger before a cracked desk. He took a seat behind the desk himself.

"Now what is it?" The Agent's burning eyes were watching the stranger's face. The man was at least not dangerous. But he was furtive, tricky-looking—a type common no doubt in this house of espionage.

"Well, guv'nor," the man said, "there was something stolen tonight right here in Washington—something important enough so that the bloke that stole it killed the bloke that had it. And maybe if I wanted to I could tell the Government where to find it. I ain't saying I could, but maybe I could."

The man stared at Agent "X," licking greedy lips now. The hungry light in his eyes was itching avarice.

"I'm a poor man," the stranger continued. "I work hard and don't get nowhere. If it just happens that I get information that somebody else might buy, there ain't no harm in my selling it, is there?"

"No," said the Agent. He tried to keep back the excitement that he felt. Here was a development apparently more quick and fortunate than he had dared hope.

"It ought to be worth a lot of dough to someone," the man said. "Thousands."

His thin fingers moved as though he were already enjoying the feel of many bank notes. "I could leave this bloomin' country and go back where I came from," he added.

"Just what is this thing that was stolen?" said the Agent. "If you'll tell me what it is perhaps I can give you a better idea of its worth."

THE man leaned forward. His voice was a hoarse, dramatic croak.

"A thing that could turn a whole army into stiffs in a second," he said. "A thing so 'orrible that 'alf the countries in the world would like to get it—'cause they love each other so much!" A shrill cackle of laughter came to his lips. He spread his fingers, struck his hands together. "They'd go down like that—the sojers—if you turned this thing on 'em. An' the country that gets it can wipe out the rest."

"You are English," said "X." "I should think you'd want to let your country have this thing." He was baiting the man now, seeing what else he could learn. The man shook his head.

"England ain't never treated me no better than America. I'm like you. I'll sell to any bloke who has the price. An' I didn't say I could get this thing—I said I knew maybe where it could be got."

"Did a man named Browning invent it?" asked the Agent suddenly.

The man recoiled, fear veiling his eyes. Then he cackled again. "You old fox, Mister Renfew! You're smarter than I thought—pretending like you didn't know. Yes, it was a bloke named Browning. You know about it then. You know how much it's worth. You—"

The man stopped speaking suddenly, turned his head toward the window.

"Did you hear anything?" he said.

"No," said the Agent.

"I thought I did. Pull that shade down—all the way. There's a crack! I thought some bloke followed me here."

The Agent rose, walked to the window, drew the shade farther down. He saw that the stranger's face was white with fear.

"Tell me your name," the Agent said calmly, "and perhaps we can do business. I deal in the sort of thing you have to sell. I have wealthy customers."

"No," said the man, "I can't tell you my name—not now. I'm hired by a bloke who's a big gun in this city, an' the country, too. I work fer him, you understand. I happened to hear him make a threat against the bloke who was killed tonight—the bloke that had what was stolen. When the bloke was killed it wasn't 'ard to figure who killed him. It wasn't 'ard either to figure who 'ad the thing that was stolen."

"What's your employer's name?"

A crafty look came into the stranger's eyes. "Say, listen—not too fast!"

The Agent extracted two thousand-dollar bills from his wallet.

He flung them down on the desk.

"Maybe this will make it easier to talk."

The man swallowed twice. He stared at the money. His hands twitched as though he could hardly contain himself. His voice was a husk when he spoke.

"I can't tell you nothin' now," he said. "It's all got to be arranged businesslike. I just wanted to find out—whether you was in the market. You are—I can see that. I got to have papers drawn up—a lawyer an' everything—to see I don't get into trouble."

"Right!" said the Agent. He saw that the man wasn't going to talk. He shoved one of the thousand-dollar bills forward. "Take that," he said, "just as a mark of good will—and as a sort of option. Don't tell anybody else what you've told me, will you?"

The man grabbed the bill, fingered it lovingly.

"No, sir," he said. "It'll stay between you an' me. But I gotta have a lot more of these, an' everything's got to be businesslike, the way I said."

"When will I see you again?"

"Tomorrow night," the man said.

The Agent nodded. He rose and showed the man downstairs.

"Tomorrow night," he said softly, then opened the door and the strange, furtive-faced man slipped into the darkness.

Agent "X" knew he would be back—unless something intervened. It was this possibility that made the Agent move quickly after his visitor had gone. Too many sinister forces were in the wind to take any chance. Too many unscrupulous people wanted the information the stranger had to sell. The Agent dared not wait.

Snatching a hat and coat, he ran to the back of the house, slipped out the rear door. Ten seconds after the man had left the front, Agent "X" was on his trail. The man did not know it. He did not know that one of the most masterly shadowers in the world was following him. He used several common ruses to throw off pursuit. He dodged around corners, kept to the dark side of the streets. But Agent "X" did not lose him.

The man got into a small car, drove off. The red tail-light of his auto bobbed up the street. In less than a minute the Agent was following in the fast roadster that he had hired.

It was a long chase, through the night-darkened streets, then out into the still darker suburbs.

ON the highway, almost deserted now, Agent "X" turned off his headlights. For nearly a mile he followed the car ahead, keeping on the road by the dim light reflected from the rain-wet macadam. Trees and fields began to flash beside the road at last. A golf course, silent and deserted, stretched away under the night sky. The road began to cut through dense woods. Rich men's estates formed little oases of green turf in this forest.

Then "X" saw the car ahead draw to the side of the road, turn and jounce into the bushes. Its red tail-light disappeared, winking off suddenly.

"X" stopped his own car. He left it parked far off the road, sprang out and walked ahead. A distant boom of thunder sounded hollowly across the still, wet woods. He stopped when he came near the spot where the stranger had parked. He listened and could hear the faint sound of footsteps, the rustle of small bushes as someone moved away. The man had struck off through the woods.

"X" entered them cautiously. Shadowing would be difficult now. The woods were black. He could not see the man. He was on unfamiliar territory.

Stooping, he felt the ground with cautious, exploring fingers. The bushes were denser in spots. Less so in others. He continued to feel; made a discovery. A narrow path began here.

This helped. He walked along, feeling his way. Again he stopped. The man's footsteps were softer now. They grew fainter still and died, as the Agent listened. The man evidently knew his way along this path. The Agent risked flashing his tiny light. The denseness of the woods would hide its glow. He made sure of the path he was on.

For the space of fifteen minutes he lost all sight and sound of the man ahead. But he made sure he was following the path. He was confident where the man was going. A chill dampness came out of the wet woods around him. Once a frightened bird gave a shrill cry. Once a small animal, a squirrel perhaps, skittered away among wet leaves. The Agent continued his way.

Then at last he saw a light ahead. He moved on along the path, and the light became two—the windows of a small house. Beyond them he could see another faint light which seemed to be a larger house. He was approaching one of the rich men's estates from the rear.

But, as he neared the lights he had first seen, the Agent suddenly paused. A scream cut through the stillness of the damp, night woods. It was a fearful scream that sent prickles along "X's" back. It held fright, horror. And, as he moved ahead again, running now, every muscle tense, the screaming mounted into a cry of sheer agony that beat upon the eardrums intolerably.

The Agent raced toward the spot. Fearful and shrill as the scream was, he sensed that it was muffled by walls. It had come from inside the cottage where the lights showed. As he neared this the screaming died to a ghastly gurgle, then faded away entirely.

The Agent burst through a patch of shrubbery that marked the path's end. For a moment he paused, almost tripped.

In the light that flared from the windows of the cottage he had caught sight of a face against a background of wet tree trunks. It was turned toward him, eyes glittering. It was the horrible, green-masked face of the man who had murdered Saunders.

CHAPTER IX

DEATH TO THE AGENT

THE FACE VANISHED before "X" could move. There was no sound in the darkness. The face and its owner seemed to melt into the woods and be swallowed up by tree trunks. Any attempt at pursuit in that Stygian blackness would be futile—and fatal. "X" sped ahead and jerked open the door of the cottage. Perhaps he would be in time.

But he saw in his first horrified glance that he wasn't. A ghastly sight met his eyes.

A man was stretched out on the floor. His coat, shirt and undershirt had been ripped open. Livid scratches made a network of crimson lines across the bare skin of his chest. Grayish powder showed around the edges of the lines. The man's face was contorted into a hideous mask of agony. But, distorted as it was, the Agent recognized it.

This was the same man who had come to Renfew's place with a secret to sell—and the man was dead.

The brutal *Kep-shak* torture had been used. A large amount of the death-flowers' pollen had been rubbed into his wounds. So much that the man had died after a few moments of excruciating agony. But not before, "X" guessed, he had babbled his secret to Green Mask. Once again Green Mask had gotten ahead of "X," wrung a secret from a dying man's lips.

Cursing harshly, fists clenched, Agent "X" stood for a moment staring down. The menace of Browning's stolen plans was bad enough without having the added horror of this green-masked killer ever present. The murderer's move tonight convinced "X" of one thing. Green Mask did not have the stolen plans in his possession. He, too, was after them. It was a race between himself and Agent "X." A race that had become a titanic struggle.

The Agent looked quickly around the room. There was nothing here of interest. Even the man's name was not important now. He would never satisfy his greed to sell the information he had obtained. He was a mercenary, disloyal rogue, but he did not deserve such a death as this. No human being did. Again the Agent's curse was like a pledge.

He turned toward the door of the cottage, opened it cautiously. The night outside seemed dark. But when he stepped across the threshold, a harsh voice spoke close to his ear.

"Hands up! Don't move, fellah—or I'll blow your damned head off!"

Slowly, stiffly, the Agent raised his hands. A man with a double-barreled shotgun was moving around the edge of the cottage. The gun was pointed straight at "X's" head. He knew what a load of buckshot would do at such close range. He waited, hands held stiffly aloft, and another man followed the first. This second man was clad in a chauffeur's uniform. The first one wore overalls and looked like a gardener.

"We seen you slip into the cottage," the man with the gun said. "We heard Peters hollerin'. What's goin' on here?"

"Look and see," said "X" quietly.

The man in the chauffeur's uniform did so, while the other held the gun unwaveringly on "X." A hoarse, horrified curse came from the open door of the cottage.

"Good God!—Peters has been murdered!"

"Murdered!" the gardener's eyes glinted. "We got the killer here, Jake. Hold the gun on him while I take a look."

The chauffeur came out, trembling violently. The whites of his eyes were showing. His lips were blue. When he took the gun, his hands shook so that "X" thought he might pull the trigger accidentally.

The gardener went in. He, too, swore and came out like a man who has seen a ghost.

"Tortured," he said. "This devil scratched him up first and killed him afterwards."

He jerked the gun from the chauffeur's hands, jabbed its heavy muzzle against "X's" body.

"Who are you? What did you do that to Peters for?"

Agent "X" spoke quietly again.

"I didn't. It was another man—a man in a green mask!"

The gardener's voice was a disbelieving snarl. "A likely story. Get going, you buzzard. We'll wake the senator up—an' tell him about this. We'll turn you over to the cops."

The Agent's eyes burned like fire. He said nothing more—and he did not try to break away. He wanted to learn whose estate this was—which senator it belonged to. The dead man, Peters, had said that he worked for a "big gun." In a moment "X" would meet the man—the person whom Peters thought had stolen the plans.

The gardener and the chauffeur conducted "X" along a path to the big house which loomed in the trees ahead. A light was burning in one of the top-floor windows.

"The senator's still up, Jake," said the gardener. "Run and get him down. Then open the back door. I'll take this killer in."

He held the shotgun close as the chauffeur sped off.

"I'd like to pull the trigger," he snarled. "I'd like to blow you in two after what you did to Peters."

TWO minutes passed. Lights flashed in the lower floor of the house. The kitchen door swung open.

"Bring him in. The senator's down," the chauffeur called out.

The gardener, still prodding "X" with the gun, marched him into the house and through the kitchen.

In a front room, a gaunt, saturnine-looking man in a dressing gown and slippers was waiting. Agent "X" recognized him at once. Senator Haden Rathborne.

The man's deep-sunken eyes were burning. His thin lips were twisted. He fixed his piercing gaze on "X."

"Who are you? What's the meaning of this? They tell me you murdered Peters."

Agent "X" was silent, and Senator Rathborne strode across the floor and came close.

"Keep the gun on him, Benstead. Shoot if he makes a move."

Chin thrust forward, eyes glaring, Rathborne seemed to be trying to bore into "X's" very soul. Agent "X" returned his stare calmly. He in turn was sizing up the senator. It was a dark rumor he had heard about Rathborne. Peters had said that the senator had threatened Captain Nelson's life. But was it possible that Peters had made some mistake?

"Speak up," said Rathborne. "Who are you?"

Still "X" was silent, and Rathborne gave an abrupt, harsh order.

"Search him, Jake."

The chauffeur went through "X's" pockets, brought out a wallet. But there was no name in it. He shook his head and passed it to the senator. Rathborne cursed angrily.

"I never saw him before. Did you, Jake?"

"No, sir."

Senator Rathborne strode to a table, opened a drawer, and took out a gleaming revolver. There was a hard light in his eyes as he came back. He fingered the gun, came close and jabbed it against "X's" chest.

"Speak now," he said, "or I'll kill you. What did you murder my superintendent, Peters, for?"

The expression on "X's" face did not change. His disguise was still that of Renfew, the spy. So perfect was his make-up that even at close range it was not detectable as such. His eyes burned with a steady flame as he returned Senator Rathborne's gaze. The man was strong-willed, almost a fanatic. "X" knew his political reputation as he did those of all United States senators. He made it a point to follow such things. He had well-catalogued files, innumerable notes.

He was facing one of the hardest-headed lawmakers in the country. Rathborne was a man of great independence, a senator of the old school. But would he dare kill a man in cold blood, even a man he thought was a murderer? Agent "X" spoke then, his voice a soft drawl.

"I wouldn't shoot if I were you, senator," he said. "Circumstantial evidence isn't always reliable. You'd have a lot of explaining to do if you killed me—and perhaps your own life may not bear investigating."

It was a shot in the dark, bait thrown out, and Senator Rathborne rose to it. A trembling seized his body. His head came forward on his short neck like the head of a predatory bird.

"What do you mean?" he shouted. "What is there in my life that I can't tell the whole world about?"

"You know better than I do, senator. But if you should kill two men—"

The Agent's eyes were probing the senator's, trying to read his thoughts. A mottled hue of fury came over Rathborne's face. It did not seem to be the fury of a killer. It was the fury of outraged pride.

"The man is crazy," he shouted.

He lowered his gun, stepped away, then strode swiftly across the room to a table. With trembling hands he picked up a phone, clattered the receiver on its hook. He put his white lips close to the mouthpiece, barked into it.

"Get me the police!" he said.

CHAPTER X

HOUNDS OF THE LAW

A **THIN-LIPPED SMILE** twitched the corners of Agent "X's" mouth. Either Rathborne was the finest bluffer in the world— or else Peters had been wrong. "X" was inclined to believe the latter. There was no time to verify it now. He must get away before the police arrived. They might recognize him as Michael Renfew. If they did, it would put an end to his espionage work.

But the shotgun in the gardener's hand was still pointed at his heart. A slight twitch of the man's finger would literally blow him in two.

Rathborne, his face still mottled with fury, lighted a cigar. He had laid his gun on the edge of the telephone table. He advanced toward "X" again, blowing a cloud of smoke from his nostrils.

"We'll see about your circumstantial evidence," he said harshly. "They'll send you to the chair or to an asylum where you can't commit any more such atrocities."

Agent "X," face expressionless, slowly let his body sag. The movement was calculated, almost imperceptible. His arms were still raised above his head, but his knees were bent.

"Stand still," said the man with the shotgun.

The Agent's eyes had swivelled side-wise. He saw that a window in the room was half open. Suddenly he tautened his lax muscles, leaping to the left, toward the spot where Rathborne stood.

The gun in the gardener's hand roared. The noise, in that confined space, was terrific. It seemed that a bomb had gone off. The charge of buckshot whistled past the place where "X" had been. It crashed into a glass-doored bookcase, shattered the glass, and riddled the books. Before the gardener could swing his gun, "X" had grabbed the senator.

Rathborne was a vigorous man, but Agent "X" was stronger. He

464

literally whirled the senator off his feet, drew his body around as a shield.

When the gardener had once more got his gun into position, Agent "X" was behind the senator, holding the senator's arms pinioned at his sides. If the gardener fired again, he would kill his employer.

The gardener's face turned a sickly white. The gun in his hands wavered. Rathborne struggled fiercely and tried to kick back with his heels. The gardener shouted hoarsely.

"I can't shoot—go and knock him out, Jake."

The chauffeur sprang across the floor; but "X" pulled Rathborne back toward the window, dragging the senator's heels over the floor as if he were a dummy. For a moment he held Rathborne with one arm only, reached behind with the other and raised the half-open window.

He suddenly released his clutch on Rathborne, shoved him straight forward toward the gardener with the gun, and stepped backwards out of the window.

He dropped on his hands and knees, moved close to the house, and darted along its sides. The head of the gardener appeared in the window just as "X" made the corner of the house. The shotgun roared again, but the bullets whistled harmlessly by "X's" head. He was already around the building.

He had the whole night to hide in now. He sprinted for the dark woods that composed half of Rathborne's estate. In an instant he was in their protective cover.

Stopping and looking back, he saw the gardener and the chauffeur come out with lanterns in their hands. They ran confusedly around the house, flashed their lights into the woods. They seemed to realize the hopelessness of trying to find the man who had escaped.

Tense and silent "X" waited. He had the idea of going back into the house and searching Rathborne's safe after the police had come and gone.

A speeding automobile came up the long drive. Its headlights goggled weirdly through the wet shrubbery. It came to a stop before the front of Rathborne's house. Four men leaped out. There was a hurried conversation on the front steps that "X" couldn't hear. He could see the angry form of Rathborne still in his dressing gown and slippers.

THE police began scouting around the house. When they came dangerously near, Agent "X" stole back into the woods. He wasn't afraid of being caught. He could see them in the lights from the house. They couldn't see him.

They went back along the path that led to Peters' cottage, and "X" followed. He wanted if possible to hear what the police said when they saw the torture victim. But the gardener with his shotgun was still alert. His face was white. He was more to be feared than the police. "X" couldn't get close enough to hear.

Suddenly he stiffened and listened. Ten minutes had passed. Another car was coming into the drive, a second load of cops apparently.

"X" circled through the woods and peered from between the trees. Then suddenly his lips tightened grimly.

It was another police car, but the police were not alone. Three huge dogs leaped from the car ahead of the men. They had monstrous heads, powerful jaws, flapping ears. Bloodhounds.

This was something he hadn't anticipated. Evidently Rathborne had put in another telephone call. The hounds were on chains. A beefy-faced man led them forward under the window from which "X" had leaped.

The great dogs sniffed the grass. Suddenly one of them lifted his head and gave tongue. The sound echoed through the still night woods. It was like a devil's cry. The other two answered, strained at the leashes that held them. The beefy-faced man snapped them loose, and, with a bound of powerful legs, the three monstrous animals leaped forward toward the woods where "X" was watching.

With a sudden hissing intake of breath Agent "X" turned and fled toward the path along which he had come from the spot on the highway where he had left his car. The police and the gardener with his lantern and gun would follow the dogs. "X" was trapped if he didn't outdistance them. He suspected that he would be shot on sight this time.

The dogs had gone to the spot where he had first crouched in the woods, watching. They bayed excitedly, then struck off, following his footsteps with the grimness of fate itself. He could hear them crashing and leaping in the wet woods behind him, hear the excited shouts of the men urging them on.

"X" flashed his tiny light, found the path. He sped along it, but the dogs, able to see in the dark, were plunging forward at twice his speed. Every second they drew nearer. They were outdistancing the men, leaving them far behind. They were overtaking Agent "X."

The blood pounded in his veins. The old wound in his side ached. The baying tongues of the great hounds seemed to echo directly in his ears now. Their crashing grew louder and louder. He looked over his shoulder and saw the gleaming phosphorescence of their eyes. They had found the path, too. They were speeding along it, noses to the ground, great jaws slavering. "X" knew he would never make the car before the dogs reached him.

He stopped suddenly in the very center of the path. His lips moved in the darkness. From them issued a strange whistle, a note that was both melodious and eerie, a sound that seemed to fill the whole air at once. It was the whistle of Secret Agent "X"—unique in all the world.

It penetrated the deep woods, reverberated weirdly. It seemed to have a strange effect on the dogs. They stopped baying. They dashed up to Agent "X," paused in a ring around him, their greenish phosphorescent eyes staring curiously. He spoke softly then.

"Nice fellows," he said. "Quiet there! It's all right."

The leader of the great man-hunting beasts, trained to follow human scent, shuffled forward on padded feet. He thrust a wet muzzle against the Agent's hand, licked his skin.

A bleak smile touched the Agent's face. He had demonstrated again the strange power he had of inspiring friendliness in animals.[42]

Another low-spoken word and the Agent turned and continued along the path. The men had found the path, too. They were shouting and running behind. But the dogs remained silent. As though the Agent had been their master they padded quietly at his heels, a strange and awe-inspiring escort.

He reached the highway with the police still three hundred feet behind. Moving swiftly he found his car still parked in the bushes. The hounds seemed loath to leave him. He patted their heads, snapped his fingers, and pointed back into the woods. Then he leaped into the car and backed out.

When the police broke through the highway the red tail-light of his roadster was nearly a half-mile distant.

---

42 AUTHOR'S NOTE: This is the second recorded instance of the Agent's extraordinary power over animals, especially dogs. At sound of his odd whistle they seem to recognize him as a friend rather than a foe.

Agent "X" lurched backwards, as though the force of the lead had pushed him off his feet.

But, though he had escaped the police, mystery and horror still hung heavy in the night. The sinister man in the green mask had beaten him to the secret that Peters held.

Hours later, that night, "X" went back to Rathborne's house, entered, and searched the safe. But he found nothing to indicate that the stolen plans were there.

THE next morning newsboys were shouting in the street. The Secret Agent, still in the disguise of Renfew, bought a paper. Then his hands grew tense and his eyes blazed.

The story of Peters' torture and death was spread across the front page. But that was not all. Senator Rathborne's house had been robbed during the night. The safe and desk drawers in the senator's library had been ransacked. A butler who had heard a noise and come in had been stricken with some strange form of paralysis. The paper said it was shock.

Both the murder of Peters and the robbery were attributed to the man who had escaped daringly through Rathborne's window, using the senator as a shield. They were combing the city for a person referred to as the "Fiend Killer." No mention was made of a man in a green mask. The police were looking for Secret Agent "X."

"X" went back to Renfew's office and paced the floor. Senator Rathborne had given an accurate description of him. There was danger if he appeared abroad in the disguise of Renfew, danger that he might be held and questioned. There was no doubt that Rathborne would identify him. It complicated matters. But he felt fairly secure in Renfew's house.

He again took up his study of the code papers which Peters' visit had put a stop to the night before. And again he was interrupted. This time by the jangle of a telephone somewhere in the house. Agent "X" had not known of its existence. He located it concealed inside a cupboard in an otherwise empty room on the second floor. He took the instrument out. It was evidently a private wire. His hands were tense as he put it to his ear.

A husky voice came out of the receiver: "This is Shank reporting. Anything for me to do today, boss?"

Agent "X" thought quickly. He understood now. A man in Renfew's position would have some sort of secret organization, someone to help him collect the things he bought and sold.

"Yes," "X" said. "I think so. Come over."

"O.K.," said the voice at the other end. "How about Zeb?"

"Where is he?"

"Right here."

"Bring him along, too."

The Agent hung up, eyes gleaming. In disguising himself as Renfew and coming to this establishment, he was acquiring a ready-made following. Shank and Zeb. There might be others, too. He wanted to see them. It was possible they would be of aid in finding out what he wanted to know. But it was ironic that he should be using Renfew's men.

They came within twenty minutes, two shifty-eyed, dapper individuals. He watched closely to see whether his disguise would arouse their suspicion. But it didn't.

Shank was hatchet-faced, flat-chested, with a stooping, furtive sort of gait. Zeb was smaller, stouter, an inoffensive-looking little man, except for the cold gleam in his eyes.

"X" wondered what dirty work they had helped Renfew in. Their clothes indicated he had been able to pay them respectable salaries.

Zeb grinned, took out a file, and commenced manicuring his nails. He turned them this way and that, inordinately proud, it seemed, of their glistening polish. Shank chewed gum steadily.

"Stick around, boys," said "X." "I've got irons in the fire."

They went to a rear room of the house, drew a pack of dirty cards from a table drawer and began a listless game of pinochle. The Agent went back to his reports.

But the bell of the hidden telephone jangled again. This time when he answered it was a woman's voice. There was a note of excitement in it.

"Hello, boss. There's a gent wants to see you," the woman said.

"Is that so?" The Agent spoke cautiously. He would have to watch his step. A slip, and one of these mongrel hangers-on of Renfew might grow suspicious.

"Yeah!" the woman said.

"Whereabouts is he?"

"Here in the restaurant. He was asking for you. I said I'd call you up."

"What's his name?"

"He won't give it. He says you'll know him."

Agent "X" pondered tensely. He didn't know where the restaurant was. If he asked the girl it would give his ignorance away, excite her suspicions. And "X" wanted to make sure who this man was who had called for him. It might be a police detective or a Government operative looking for Renfew. It might even be a trap.

"Tell him to go to Garfleld Park," "X" said suddenly. "Tell him to take a bench in the west end. I'll meet him there in twenty minutes. I'd like to look him over first, you understand?"

"Yes, boss."

Risking police detection, Agent "X" slipped out of the house. The roadster he had hired was still parked down the block. He got in and drove to the east end of Garfield Park, where he stopped again.

His movements became as cautious as a stalking cat. He lighted a cigarette, turned his collar up and his hat brim down and shuffled slowly along imitating a weary down-and-outer. His eyes were piercingly alert.

Then, as he approached the west end of the park, his pulses quickened like suddenly released triphammers. There was a figure on one of the benches—a well-dressed man, wearing spats and carrying a stick. He was big, blond, and he had coldly penetrating blue eyes. Agent "X" recognized him at once.

The man was Otto von Helvig, embassy attaché and ex-Prussian spy.

CHAPTER XI

AMBUSHED!

FOR THE MOMENT Agent "X" continued his role of down-and-outer. Half of his face was hidden by the collar of his coat. He moved toward von Helvig at the same slow shuffle. When he came opposite the attaché he spoke in a husky croak.

"A few pennies for a cup of coffee, mister?"

Agent "X" thrust out one hand, shaking it as though he were afflicted with palsy.

Von Helvig cursed under his breath and waved him away. But "X" stood his ground, staring at the attaché fixedly. The Prussian lifted his head angrily, glaring at the man he took for a panhandler. Then his expression changed. He leaned forward, smiled suddenly, showing gleaming white teeth.

"You old fox, Renfew! You fooled me—even though I was expecting you."

"Herr von Helvig," said the Agent respectfully. "This is a great pleasure!"

The attaché eyed "X" sharply.

"You've changed very little since I saw you two years ago, Renfew! And you're still up to your old tricks."

Agent "X" bowed. "A man must make a living, Herr von Helvig."

Von Helvlg touched "X's" arm. "I am due at the legation now," he said. "My time is brief. But there's something I want to ask you, Renfew. You are a man who keeps his ear to the ground. You are a fox who listens at the rabbit holes. You don't miss much. Have you heard recently of any great theft from the United States Government?"

It was a surprising question coming from von Helvig. "X" knew that the man's clean-featured blondness and the babylike candor in his blue eyes hid a cunning, crooked brain. He hedged.

"Perhaps," he said. "Why do you ask?"

"Just a matter of curiosity," said von Helvig evasively. He opened his wallet, took out two century notes, folded them, and held out his hand.

"Here is the price of your cup of coffee, Renfew. Now come on— loosen up and tell a fellow what you know."

"X," playing the role of Renfew, waved the money away.

"I have changed, my dear von Helvig, since we last met. My business, if I may say so, has grown. I no longer accept—ah—small gratuities."

Anger reddened von Helvig's blond face. He hastily pocketed the money.

"My mistake," he said. "I'll be frank with you. A lovely woman has come to me with a certain proposition. She claims to know where something of singular importance, stolen from the Government, may be recovered. She has asked my cooperation in securing it. Do you know to what she is alluding, Renfew?"

There was an odd, avaricious glitter in von Helvig's eyes. "X" was puzzled. Was von Helvig really seeking information; or was he trying to lay a trap? "X" must watch his step, impress von Helvig with his knowledge. He bowed very low and spoke softly.

"If the lady in question is very lovely, she has done well to ask the cooperation of the gallant—Karl Hummel."

It was as though "X" had struck von Helvig a blow. Every muscle in the man's body tensed. His eyes narrowed to points of steel. His hand moved across his face where a miracle of plastic surgery had been performed. Only the tiny scars in his cheek were reminders of it.

"You are crazy, Renfew," he said harshly. "What do you mean by calling me that name—Hummel?"

"Nothing," said the Agent blandly. "Just a whimsy of mine. Perhaps it was a mistake."

For a moment von Helvig sat in tense silence, his eyes probing those of the Agent's. Then he took out his wallet again, adding three more century notes to the two he had offered the Agent before, and held them out.

"I must insist that you take this small token of my good faith," he said. "I am going to take you completely into my confidence, Renfew. I want you to meet the lady in question tonight. I want you to hear her story—and be my adviser. You are a man of even more remarkable talents than I had estimated, but—" Von Helvig suddenly leaned forward and laid steely fingers on the Agent's arm. His blond face became a mask of cruelty. His eyes were pin points of murderous light. "If you value your life, Herr Renfew, you will keep faith with me. I am no man to trifle with."

"Nor I," said the Agent. "I think we understand each other."

"This evening then," said von Helvig. "We shall have dinner together—you and I and the lady I spoke of. Be in this same spot at six-thirty. I will drive by and pick you up."

"Very good, Herr von Helvig."

Conscious that the man's eyes were still boring into him, Agent "X" turned and shuffled off. His pulses were racing. The lead that the murdered Peters had brought him had apparently been false. This one promised results. Unless von Helvig was setting a trap for him, he might learn, within the next twelve hours, the location of the stolen plans.

BACK in Renfew's house, Agent "X" gave instructions to Shank and Zeb.

"I've got a job for you," he said. "Go to the German embassy. Wait outside and watch for the attaché, Otto von Helvig. He is tall, blond, blue-eyed. There is a slight scar on each cheek. If he leaves the building at any time during the day, follow him. Check up on every movement he makes—and report back here at six this evening."

The two men rose from their listless card game.

"We got you, boss," they said.

When they had gone "X" paced the floor a moment. His nerves tingled for action. He seemed to be getting closer to what he sought. His disguise as Renfew had been a wise move. It had brought him in contact with von Helvig. Was it possible that the lovely lady he mentioned was—

"X" smiled grimly to himself. Then he looked at his watch. Ten o'clock. At twelve the plane he had asked Betty to come in would land at Washington Airport. He'd had no answer to his telegram. He'd expected none. But he wanted to make sure of her arrival. He could not meet her openly; could not, at this time, run the risk of being seen with her, but he could see whether she was on the plane.

At a little before twelve, his disguise changed to that of a sallow-faced young man, Agent "X" crossed the Potomac on the Highway

Bridge and turned into Military Road. Arlington was beyond. The Hoover Airport was at his left. The Washington at his right. The deep-throated hum of airplane motors filled the sky. Out-of-town tourists were going up from Hoover Airport on short sight-seeing hops over Washington.

The sky had cleared. The sun was shining. But to "X," who knew the strange events of the past twenty-four hours, a sinister menace hung over the city. It wasn't dispelled by the bright sky nor the sunshine.

He found where the tri-motored E.A.T. plane bearing Betty Dale was to land. He waited at the edge of the field, saw the huge ship appear, a great dark bird on the horizon. He saw it come down to a stately landing, taxi up to the field office.

An attendant unrolled a carpet. Steps were set in front of the big plane's metal door. A laughing group waited for the arrival of friends and loved ones.

In this group Agent "X" saw Suzanne Blackwell. It meant that Betty had sent her a wire. It meant that Suzanne was here to meet the Agent's blonde ally.

His pulses quickened as the plane's door opened and the passengers piled out. The loveliest of them all was the trim-figured little blonde who stepped to the turf of the field and ran toward the spot where Suzanne Blackwell was waiting. Hair the color of imprisoned sunlight peeped from under her blue *cloche* hat. Her fresh young lips were softly red. Her blue eyes were dancing. This flying trip to Washington was a lark to Betty Dale.

Fondly the Agent watched as Betty and Suzanne embraced. For a fleeting second he saw Betty's eyes rove over the crowd, lingering on each face. He knew she was looking for him, knew also that his disguise had fooled her. He would not make himself known till the time prearranged for their meeting. The time when furtive, crafty eyes which might be watching would be least suspecting.

With her arm linked in Suzanne Blackwell's, Betty walked toward Suzanne's waiting roadster. "X" wouldn't see Betty again until night fell. But he knew now that she was in Washington. He knew that she was ready to help him.

He frowned a moment, a shadow in his eyes. Her fresh, blonde beauty seemed a contrast to the dark forces now in motion. A strange sense of uneasiness filled him, a foreboding, as though some secret voice were warning him. He regretted at that instant that he had asked Betty to come.

Then he remembered that he was Secret Agent "X," pledged to aid his country. He must put all fear aside, even fear for others, as he had fear for himself. He turned and strode back to his own waiting car.

At six that evening, disguised again as Renfew, he received the report of Shank and Zeb.

"We spotted von Helvig, boss," Shank said. "We didn't lose him all day. He had lunch with two guys, one from the Mexican embassy, another who was a newspaper gent. He left the embassy on Massachusetts Avenue, and stopped for a half-hour in a joint on Thirteenth Street. There he talked to a guy in a back room. It was screwy, boss! This guy looked like von Helvig's twin. He left by the back way and von Helvig went to the Wilmott Hotel. He's there now!"

"Good work," said Agent "X" softly. "Thanks."

AT shortly after six that evening a closed car slid to a stop at the curb near Garfield Park. A tall man was driving. He was dressed in the height of style, a soft gray hat on his head, spats on his ankles, yellow pigskins on his hands.

He was a man who bore a marked resemblance to Otto von Helvig of the German embassy. But there was a hardness about him, a wolfishness, that the more polished von Helvig managed most of the time to conceal. This man was definitely a member of the underworld.

There were three others with him, harsh-faced, flat-chested young men, overly dressed. As the car stopped, the driver asked a question.

"Everything ready, boys?"

The three men with him were busy for a moment. They took wicked-looking automatics from their pockets. Over the ugly snouts of these they slipped awkward cylinders that made the guns seem grotesquely long—silencers.

"All O.K., Al," one of them said.

"You can handle 'em all right that way?"

"Say—you oughta know us." There was a note of evil pride in the voice of the man who spoke. "We've knocked off bigger mugs than this."

"O.K. But any slip—and there won't be a pay-off. The big shot behind this is a hard bird to please. Wait till I give the signal—then do your stuff!"

The blond and dapper man who looked like von Helvig showed his teeth for a moment in a wicked smile. He motioned with his hand for the others to get out.

They left the car and vanished into the shadows along the square like slinking gray wolves.

The man in the car glanced at the clock on the dashboard. It was now a quarter past six. He took a cigarette from his pocket, lighted it. Inhaling luxuriously, he, too, got out of the car and sauntered toward the west end of the park.

Now more than ever he looked like the Prussian attaché. Anyone seeing him from a distance would be fooled. When he arrived at the park's west end, his sharp eyes swiveled. He seemed to be counting the benches.

He turned, walked up to one and sat down—the very bench that von Helvig had occupied that morning. He crossed his legs, blew smoke from his nostrils, leaned back comfortably. The three men he had brought with him crept noiselessly closer, the silenced automatics in their hands. They were awaiting his signal. The stage was set for murder.

A bell across the park struck a single booming note. Six-thirty.

Even as the stroke died away on the night air, a man's shuffling figure appeared. He came from the direction of the park's east end. Hat brim turned down, collar turned up, the man had the wrinkled features of Michael Renfew, dealer in espionage. The man was Secret Agent "X."

FIVE hundred feet away, he saw the figure on the bench. Piercingly bright eyes stabbed out from under the Agent's hat brim. The figure ahead looked like von Helvig. The German attaché had apparently kept the appointment. Tonight, it seemed, "X" was going to meet the "lovely lady" who knew where the Browning plans could be discovered.

Simulating a down-and-outer, "X" continued to shuffle forward. The man ahead, smoking on the bench, did not turn his head. He seemed to be deep in meditation.

The Agent was within a hundred feet of him now. Fifty feet—twenty-five. The Agent moved toward the bench—and not until then was the suspicion he had had confirmed. The man on the bench wasn't Otto von Helvig. The man was a perfect stranger to "X."

"A penny for a cup of coffee, mister?"

The Agent's voice was the cracked, querulous voice of an old panhandler. His skinny fingers trembled. The stranger on the bench lifted cold eyes and shook his head.

"Not tonight," he said. "Beat it."

The panhandler dropped his skinny hand, turned and shuffled on. The man on the bench followed him with eyes that were suddenly bright. His lips skinned back in a mirthless grin.

Abruptly he took a white handkerchief from his coat pocket, opened it and blew his nose loudly. As he tucked the handkerchief back into his coat, three figures moved out of the shadows that made blotches on the park's grass plot.

Their dark clothes blended with the shadows; their feet were noiseless. Swiftly, murderously, they crept upon the man disguised as Michael Renfew.

It was at the juncture of another asphalt path that they came close enough to fire. Simultaneously then they raised their guns.

At the last minute, as though some secret sense had warned him, the shuffling figure turned. But he appeared to be too late. The three hired killers fired.

There were no smashing explosions in the night. Only faint flickers of flame and three muffled reports. Then the sharp *spat* of lead striking where the guns were aimed.

Agent "X" lurched backwards as though the force of the lead had pushed him off his feet. One gurgling cry came from his lips. His knees bent under him. He sank to the asphalt, twitched a moment, and lay still. The gunmen pocketed their weapons and slunk away. The man on the bench, humming softly to himself, rose and sauntered in the opposite direction.

CHAPTER XII

SINISTER SMOKE

FOR NEARLY FIVE minutes, or until the slow measured steps of a patrolling cop sounded, Agent "X" lay just as he had fallen. Then, magically it seemed, he rose to his feet, moving quickly into the shadows. His eyes were gleaming like living coals. His lips were harsh. There was the trembling pulse of excitement in his body.

In the semigloom beside the path he reached up with tense fingers, feeling the front of his coat. There were three holes in the cloth. He probed in one; probed down to the hard resilient material of the bullet-proof vest he wore.

Half expecting trickery, Agent "X" had come prepared. The vest, cleverly molded to his torso, covered the whole of it. It had witnessed the shock of bullets many times before. He had established one thing tonight. Otto von Helvig didn't stop at murder.

But the Agent wasn't sure he had played his own hand wisely. In this desperate game, with so many crosscurrents, no man could proceed in a straight course. The Agent was a gambler. A high adventurer in an underworld of terror. A man who took chances with death itself in an effort to balance the scales of justice.

He sped across the park silently, swiftly. In the darkest shadows, amid a clump of shrubbery, his fingers roved over his face. His movements in the next hour called for a new disguise. Michael Renfew, supposedly dead, must stay dead.

It was a relief to get the rubber cap, imitating baldness, off his head. It was a relief, too, to peel the transparent tissues, creating a network of wrinkles, away from his skin. He took a few other materials from the lining of his coat. He used them with the skill of a man who was master of a thousand faces.

When he emerged from the shadows, he was young again, utterly unlike the man who had gone down under a volley of murderers' bullets.

He got in his car and drove swiftly through the night to the Wilmott Hotel, the hostelry where von Helvig was stopping. He was not an instant too soon.

Otto von Helvig, tall, immaculately dressed, suave as only a diplomat can be, was just leaving his key at the desk. No one looking at his bland blond face would have guessed that here was a man who, less than an hour before, had engaged assassins to kill a fellow human being. But "X," posing as Renfew, had dared to bring up a ghost from von Helvig's past—dared to call him Karl Hummel. That in itself, "X" guessed, had been reason enough for the attempted murder. Perhaps there was a still more sinister motive.

He watched von Helvig go to the street, saw the doorman signal a taxi. The taxi sped along Pennsylvania Avenue. The Agent followed in his own hired car. Again his pulses throbbed with excitement. He believed he knew where von Helvig was going—to keep a tryst with a beautiful lady. Was it possible he knew the lady's name?

Von Helvig's taxi drew up before a building of fashionable apartments. He paid the driver, walked nonchalantly into the elaborate foyer.

Agent "X" drove on, parking a full block away. He walked briskly back. Von Helvig had disappeared. In the bronze directory Agent "X" looked for a name—and found it. Lili Damora! This, he believed, was the lovely lady von Helvig had come to see.

The eyes of Agent "X" were snapping. Lili Damora's apartment was 4E. He must learn what was said at this meeting between von Helvig and the sinuous-bodied woman from Budapest. To do so he was prepared to gamble with fate again.

He walked boldly past the uniformed doorman. The girl at the telephone desk stopped him.

"Miss Damora is expecting me," "X" said. Experience had taught him that a confident manner allays suspicions. He went directly to the elevator, ascending to the fourth floor.

Here he became more cautious. The corridor was empty. Faint sounds of radios and conversation came from behind the closed doors.

Agent "X" walked forward to 4E. His eyes darted alertly about This was evidently a large apartment. There were two doors. One marked with the letter and number. The other blank. That would be a bedroom. The first probably opened on an entrance hall with the living room off it. To go in there would be inviting disaster.

He stopped by the first door, listened. The faint sound of voices reached his ears. He moved on to the second, and could hear nothing.

The Agent worked quickly then. Keeping a sharp eye out along the corridor, he used his compact tool set with its implements that would open any lock. In a few seconds, with hardly a sound, the door moved inward, and he found himself as he had expected, in a bedroom. Von Helvig's coat, hat, and stick were on the bed. Voices came from a room beyond—the living room.

THE Agent's nerves were tingling. He crept forward across the dark floor. Perfume bottles and powder jars stood on the dresser. There was the vague odor of scent in the air. This was the exotic Lili's chamber. A strange place for Agent "X" to be.

He put his ear to the door, listened intently. He hoped he would hear enough in the next few minutes to size up the situation. The throaty voice of the brunette reached him. His eyes shone.

"Don't be impatient, Otto. I am hungry. Let us have dinner first. We can discuss this afterwards."

Von Helvig's answer was harsh.

"It is safer here—where there are none to listen. You know as well as I that every restaurant in Washington is a hotbed of espionage. Tell me what you have to say. Then we can enjoy ourselves at dinner—and at the ball afterwards."

"Yes—the ball," said Lili, speaking in a husky drawl.

"Come—come, Lili, don't fence, or I shall think you are stringing me along, as the Americans say."

"Perhaps I am," said Lili softly. "Perhaps I pretend to know things I do not know just to enjoy your company, Otto."

Von Helvig gave an angry exclamation.

"Don't," said Lili. "You look so fierce that I am afraid. I shall be frank with you. I must have two or three days more."

"You don't know where they are then?"

"Not precisely—I told you that. But I think I know how to go about finding them. Two or three days more, Otto, with your help, and we shall have them."

"They are here in Washington then? They haven't been taken away?"

"If it were otherwise how could I expect to get them," said Lili evasively.

"I hope you realize, Lili, that I'm not a man to be trifled with?"

The Agent's mind leaped back. That was what von Helvig had said earlier in the day to him—and the man had proved it. If Lili was fencing, she had better watch out.

What "X" had heard was not encouraging. Lili herself did not seem sure. Perhaps she was only playing a game with von Helvig. Or perhaps she really knew. In that case it would mean hours, perhaps days of patient shadowing. Could either Shank or Zeb be trusted? Wouldn't Betty Dale be more of a help? Lili Damora moved in the diplomatic set. He would ask Betty to discover if possible exactly who her friends were and how she spent her days. He listened a moment more.

"I am disappointed," von Helvig was saying. "Very disappointed."

"Don't be sulky, Otto. Trust me—and remember—keep your eyes open tonight. Every one of importance in Washington will be present at the ball, including Senator Cobb!"

The Agent started. Was Lili merely trying to confuse von Helvig. It almost seemed so.

"X" moved back across the bedroom to the door. Von Helvig would be coming for his coat presently—and "X" had heard enough to convince him that a fog of mystery still hung over the stolen Browning plans. It was still a race between himself and the green-masked murderer who had killed Saunders and Peters.

AMONG the brilliant guests at the home of Senator Marvin Foulette that night was a young man introduced as Raphael Sancho, descendant of a wealthy South American family and the nephew of a president.

He was here in Washington, it was said, to study the American form of government at close range. He was an ambassador of good will. It was at the request of a high government official that the Foulettes had invited him at the last moment.

They welcomed him at the door. Mrs. Foulette, a dignified, white-haired lady, murmured a conventional phrase of greeting. The senator shook his hand perfunctorily. He passed on into the ballroom of the senator's big home, now ablaze with lights, and filled with people. A few *débutantes* cast admiring glances at him, but otherwise he was unnoticed. There was no representative present from the particular country from which he came.

The young man, however, appeared perfectly at ease. He strolled about the big room and, using excellent Spanish, engaged the Brazilian ambassador in a conversation concerning South American tariffs.

As his tongue rattled off dry statistics, his alert eyes scanned the main door. The even flow of his words ceased for a moment as Senator Blackwell and his party arrived. Suzanne Blackwell was with her father, escorted by Sam Barkley. Suzanne's college chum, Betty Dale, held the arm of the senator.

It was upon her that the eyes of Raphael Sancho dwelt. And in their veiled depths was a look of fondness and admiration.

The girl whose hair held the golden glint of imprisoned sunlight was radiantly beautiful tonight. A simple green dress set off her dainty figure. Her eyes held a sparkle of excitement, making them seem as bright as the single jewel at her throat.

Others arrived, Lili Damora, dark, almost serpentine in her lithe grace, with full, pouting lips and a dazzling smile; Otto von Helvig, wearing the ribbon of a military order across his chest, courtly as a prince of the blood.

Upon these, too, the eyes of Raphael Sancho rested for a moment, while a thin smile twitched the corners of his mouth. Senator and Mrs. Foulette left their position by the entranceway and circulated among the guests. They took pains to introduce Raphael Sancho to a number of eager young women. It wasn't long before he was gliding around the ballroom to the strains of a languorous dance from the Argentine.

But his eyes still followed the form of the girl in the green dress, the girl with golden hair and a single jewel at her throat.

Betty Dale seemed at times preoccupied, too. Once her eyes met Sancho's and looked beyond him. Again he smiled thinly. Not until a series of formal introductions led him to the side of Suzanne Blackwell did he mention what was on his mind.

They had danced to one number. He was leading Suzanne back toward her father. He spoke softly.

"The girl in the green dress, with the golden hair. Is she not a friend of yours, Miss Blackwell? Did she not enter with your party?"

Suzanne Blackwell laughed. "Yes," she said, "and I am jealous, *Señor* Sancho. I believe you danced with me just to get an introduction to her. My friend Betty Dale is always pulling the choicest plums out of the pie."

"Plums?" said Sancho vaguely. "Pie?"

"That's right," said Suzanne. "A nice kind of fruit, you know, and an American form of pastry. But come—here's Betty now. I'm sure you'll find her a more accomplished dancer than I."

The young *Señor* Raphael Sancho bowed low over Betty Dale's slim hand.

"Miss Dale," he said. "I am so happy to meet. Is it that you will dance with me?"

Betty's voice was perfunctory as she accepted. Her expression was slightly worried. Someone she had hoped to see was not here. Raphael Sancho whirled her into the rhythm of a sinuous bolero. His tones were ingratiating as he talked with his charming Spanish accent. But she hardly listened. To her he was just another of the indolent young men to be found in the gay society of America's capital. Betty Dale, for all her youthful appearance, had the keenness of maturity and experience.

It wasn't until Raphael Sancho uttered a sudden mysterious phrase in perfect English that Betty became electrified.

"There are shadows beneath the sunlight," Sancho said.

The blue eyes of Betty Dale grew bright. She tensed in the arms of Raphael Sancho. Her gaze met his.

"Careful," he added. "Wolves lurk in the shadows." Then, as the music stopped, he drew her to a seat in the corner. "Let me show you a picture of my country, Miss Dale."

HE drew from his pocket a small photograph of a South American capital. Betty Dale stared with wonder. Suddenly the man called Raphael Sancho flipped the photograph over, holding it in his palm so that only Betty could see. In that moment she held her breath in excitement. A single letter showed on the back of the picture, written in some strange ink. It was the letter "X," and under the glare of the lights it slowly began to fade.

"You!" she said. "I did not guess!" Then, in spite of her effort at self-control, the color in her cheeks deepened. Her eyes became ever more bright. The man whom she most respected and admired in all the world was at her side. The man whose real face she had never seen, but whose strange, dynamic personality had cast a spell over her emotions so that all other men by comparison seemed lame. The man, whom, deep in her heart, she loved.

But Betty Dale knew that "X" had only his work to think of. She knew that the time might never come when they could be more to each other than they were now—loyal, trusting friends and allies.

She knew that she had no right ever to interfere with his strange, caring career.

The Agent pocketed his photograph. He looked quickly around.

"There is a small alcove at the end of the room," he said. "Perhaps we can continue our discussion of South America there."

They circled the dance floor, a youthful, graceful couple. Eyes followed Betty Dale enviously because she had apparently captured the interest of the dashing Raphael Sancho. Other eyes looked with envy upon Sancho because he was holding the attention of the room's loveliest girl.

They sat on a bench in the alcove and Betty Dale spoke quickly.

"I have found out nothing except that both the senator and Suzanne seem upset. Ferris has gone to the sanatorium again. But I don't thick that's what's worrying them. It is something else."

"Yes," said the Agent. "Be careful, Betty. Be on your guard even when you are talking to Suzanne. She has friends. It is these friends I want you to watch. Find out all you can about Lili Damora, and the German attaché, Otto von Helvig. Find out also about Senators Foulette, Cobb, and Rathborne: Remember anything you hear."

"I will," said Betty. "Is it something very important?"

"Very," said the Agent.

"And dangerous?"

A shadow came into the Secret Agent's eyes for a moment. He was thinking of Green Mask.

"I have said be careful, Betty. Be on your guard every instant."

Betty touched his arm suddenly. "Nothing will happen to me. It is you I am thinking of. I read about the terrible murder of Senator Rathborne's man. Had that anything to do with what is worrying you?"

The Agent nodded. "Yes, Betty, it had. But my reason for being in Washington is more vital even than the hunt for a murderer. It is something which concerns the safety of America. It was that which made me ask you to come."

Betty started to answer, then suddenly stopped. She stared across the ballroom, eyes wide with amazement. Something strange was happening. It was a warmish spring night. Windows on both sides of the ballroom were open. Now a smoky haze was coming through these windows. People were moving back.

A man's voice was raised in sudden excitement.

"Fire!" he said.

The soft throb of the orchestra came to a stop. Low conversation was hushed. Agent "X" rose to his feet, stepped forward. He moved quickly toward one of the open windows which gave on a wide lawn outside. Then he paused and sniffed, nostrils dilating.

A strange odor was in the air. The haze of smoke was curling in ghostly streamers through the whole big room. This was not fire—it was something else. A girl near "X" gave a cry and swayed against her escort.

"I'm fainting," she gasped. "Air—please."

But she did not reach the door. She had taken only two steps when her knees gave way and she collapsed on the polished floor. Others were staggering, too. The smoke in the air made a dim veil, blurring faces. Or was it the effect of the strange scent? Agent "X" did not know. This time he leaped toward the window.

But his leap ended in a drunken sort of stagger. For a fresh breath of the strange smoke had entered his nostrils. It made his senses swim. He heard other cries around him; saw, as through an awful fog, that men and women in all parts of the room were sinking to their knees, collapsing on the floor.

He turned back toward Betty Dale, tried to reach her. She, too, was collapsing, slumping sidewise in the seat, her head falling forward on a wilting neck.

Chill horror grasped Secret Agent "X." In a frenzy of effort he tried to go to her, get her out of this room. But his muscles would not respond. Like a man caught in the grip of a horrible nightmare that paralyzes while a danger he cannot avoid creeps upon him, Agent "X" fell to the floor. There he lay, immobile, unable to move—slipping closer and closer to the borderland of unconsciousness.

CHAPTER XIII

THE THREAT

AGENT "X" STRUGGLED fiercely, his iron will urging him on. He would not give up as other men did. Physically helpless, he fought to retain that spark of consciousness which still made him able to see and hear. Turning his head he breathed through his cupped hands, holding them across his face, drawing the air through tense fingers to purify it.

Numb in every muscle, his eyes could still focus. And he was amazed at what he saw.

Hideously evil faces appeared in the windows as the strange haze began to clear. Sinister brown-skinned figures glided into the room. There were at least a half-dozen of them, and they began robbing the inert guests with calculated thoroughness.

They stripped rings from fingers, links from men's cuffs, necklaces from the white throats of women, tiaras from their hair. Jewels were all they seemed to seek. Everything that glittered they fell upon and pocketed as a flock of hungry vultures might pluck flesh from bones.

"X" could not stop them. He could not even cry out. The single small jewel that Betty Dale was fond of, an heirloom from her dead mother, was taken from her throat as he looked. Then fresh horror came.

Two of the men were lifting Betty Dale up. He saw as in an unbelievable nightmare her body rise from the floor, saw her blonde head hang limply, saw her borne toward the door.

Icy hands clutched at the Agent's heart then. Frantic blood surged in his veins. He tried to move, but still the drug held him. An invisible net seemed spread over his whole body.

His lips moved to form words: "Betty Dale! Betty Dale!" But they made no sound. He alone of all the guests was witness to her abduction. And he was unable to prevent it. It was plain to him who these brown-skinned men were. This was the poisonous Malay horde whose master was the green-masked killer. These were the men who had tried to murder him with the dart on the lawn of Blackwell's house, the same who had tortured poor Saunders to death with the hideous *Kep-shak*. And now they were taking Betty Dale away.

More terrible than torture of the body was the mental torture that gripped Agent "X." Except for him, Betty Dale would be safe in her own home city hundreds of miles away. If he had not called her, this would not have happened.

As he lay, fighting for the power to move, bathed in cold sweat, a shadow fell on the floor beside him. He could not turn, but his eyes rolled feebly. The shadow belonged to one of the brown-skinned men.

The man stooped, pinned a note to Agent "X's" coat. Then he moved after the others, and the Agent caught a last glimpse of Betty Dale's golden head. A last glimpse of her pale, lovely face.

There came times when the Agent's dauntless spirit seemed to master his flesh. This was one of them. Overcome like the others by the strange smoke that had filled the room, Agent "X" refused to let it conquer the fighting heart within him.

The fingers of his right hand began to move. A quivering set their tips in motion. They curled up slowly until his fist was clenched. Then his arm moved also, beginning at the elbow, drawing toward his chest. The fingers plucked the note that the brown man had left. His eyes scanned the words that the note held. And the words seemed to burn into his senses like fire, eating away the coma that held him.

"You cannot win, Agent 'X,'" the note said. "You saw Saunders die, and were horrified. You were horrified, too, when I killed Rathborne's man, Peters. But you have not seen all. It is terrible to die, but a living death is worse. There are poisons that act quickly. There are others that gnaw at the nerves themselves—destroying what can never be repaired. And my slaves are masters of their art. I have your friend Betty Dale, who came to Washington to aid you. Through her I issue a command. Make no further investigation into this case. Leave the city at once—or my slaves will practise their art on her. She will be stricken, paralyzed for life, her mind and body shattered forever. Take warning and obey. The Green Mask."

A groan came from the Agent's lips. Horror pressed upon him. But the note was the last thing needed to drive him to a frenzy. He had seen the green-masked man's tactics. He knew that even if he did drop the case and leave, Betty Dale would not be safe.

His other hand was moving now. His legs were beginning to obey. He was fighting the battle of his life. Even before he could stand, he crawled toward the door through which Betty had been taken. It opened on a tiled porch with the lawn beyond.

HE reached the door, thrust his head into the darkness. The chill of the night air helped him. He felt new life coming into his veins. Clutching the side of the door, he drew himself to his feet, stumbled out onto the lawn. Once he fell on his face, striking his head on the ground, but he was up in an instant.

Through shrubbery he saw a glint of water and then he understood. Beyond the lawn was the river, and it was toward this that the dark-skinned men had gone. It was from the river that they had come.

He crept forward toward the spot where the senator had a boat wharf, and he saw skulking figures ahead. There was a dark shadow at the right of the wharf. The figures merged suddenly with this. Then came the sound of a muffled engine. The dark shadow moved out.

It was a boat, long and low to the water. It backed away from the wharf, turning in a half-circle. White foam, appeared under its bow. A white wake showed behind it. And the sight of it moving away spurred Agent "X" to fresh action.

At the left of the wharf was another shadow. Senator Foulette himself was a yachtsman. "X" leaped along the wharf, eyes stabbing the darkness. Water lapped against a polished hull. A runabout was moored to the wharf, securely fastened with ropes.

The Agent drew a knife from his pocket. No time to untie lines now. He slashed, freed the moored craft, and jumped down into it.

Familiar with all types of engines, he slid into the padded seat up front. Then a harsh exclamation came from his lips. A locked ignition switch met his groping fingers and each second of time was precious. Face set, eyes burning, he fumbled under the seat, drawing out an engine wrench. He leaned forward over the rounded wind glass and smashed at the plywood deck. He struck at it like a man in a frenzy till the thin boards gave way. Then he tore at the wood with his bare hands and reached inside.

Under the decking, in front of the instrument board, he found what he sought—the wiring of the ignition. He pulled two flexible cables out, joined their ends together and completed the circuit. As he did so his eyes strained off across the water. He could still hear the engine of the boat ahead.

Then he pressed the starter, heard its muffled whine. He moved the spark forward, drew the throttle back, and his own engine broke into life. Afraid that its starting roar might be heard, he let it idle for a moment, backing slowly from the wharf.

He eased the runabout's nose around toward the white wake that the other boat had left. His eyes burned with a hot, tense light. His fingers pushed the throttle forward, and the boat he was in moved ahead.

He followed the white wake that showed on the water. His eyes sought each bit of foam, each breaking bubble. He could no longer see the other boat. It had no lights. But he was following it, following Betty Dale. He swept on to where the river widened and the shores became less populated. On by salt marshes and tiny islands.

IT was toward one of these, grass-grown and covered with dense shrubbery, that the wake of the boat ahead led. "X" cut his speed and crept along. A minute after he had done so he heard the engine roar of the other boat diminish in volume.

He kept out of its wake now, afraid that his own craft would be seen as a black shadow in the foam. With his engine barely turning over, he nosed in near enough to see the other boat thrust between shrubbery that grew close to the water's edge.

Five hundred feet distant he circled the island. Caution was all that would save Betty now. Beyond the island the mainland showed. A channel separated the two. The Agent crossed this and brought his boat among the trees. To one of them he tied it, and slipped out of his coat and shoes.

If there were eyes watching, he dared not take the boat to the island. It would be too great a risk—for Betty Dale. Instead he dropped over-side, silently as an otter. In long swift strokes he swam ahead, slowing when at last the thick vegetation of the island loomed up.

Then his feet touched; he moved up to a narrow sandy shore. Bushes higher than his head grew here. He skirted them, moving along the beach until they thinned.

His eyes were growing used to the faint light of the stars. He could see more plainly now, and as he pushed forward toward the island's center the dark bulk of a building rose. It seemed a huge old barn.

Then Agent "X" stopped dead in his tracks. A shadow rose before him. Green Mask was behind all this and Green Mask did not do things by halves.

A Malay word was grunted at him. He answered in the same language; but what he said did not seem to be the right thing, for the shadow moved toward him inquiringly and "X" backed away.

His muscles were tense as coiled springs. He knew that death was close at hand. But for Betty Dale's sake he must not die. Deliberately he drew the man away from the building. If there were other guards "X" did not want them to hear.

The Malay spoke again. "X" was almost at the water. He crouched behind a bush, waited, and the brown-skinned man came up slowly. Then abruptly, as though his eyes could penetrate the dark, the Malay turned and leaped. As he did so, he pulled something from his belt. A curved knife glittered wickedly in his hand.

CHAPTER XIV

ISLAND OF TERROR

THE MAN'S ATTACK was like the death lunge of a hooded cobra. He struck for the Agent's heart, seeking to bury the knife blade to its hilt; struck with the quick ferocity of some jungle creature to whom killing is a natural act.

The Agent's sidewise lurch was all that saved him. He saw the knife flash by, clutched the wrist that held it, and with his free hand gripped the Malay's face, pressing his palm across the brown-skinned killer's mouth. There must be no outcry. Any disturbance would cause a murderous horde to descend upon him.

But the Malay was a cyclone of destructive fury. He twisted like a snake, tried to bury his teeth in the Agent's hand, tried to wrench his own fingers loose and slide the knife along "X's" straining neck.

The Secret Agent's fingers clamped like steel over the man's jaw. They dug into his cheek, bent his head forward. But bushes cracked and rustled beneath their moving bodies. This sound, too, would bring disaster.

"X" drew the Malay toward the water then, down the small, sloping beach into the chill river. The man tried once to cry out. But only a hissing grunt came. The Agent let his body sink, pulling the man in after him. He kicked his legs in powerful scissors strokes, pushing violently away from shore.

The current caught them. They began to drift downstream. But the Malay was like a squirming, thrashing fish. He reared up, bringing his full weight down on "X," forcing his head under. They sank below the surface together, fighting furiously.

With a sudden vicious thrust, the Malay caught "X" in the stomach with a knee. Racking pain shot through the Agent's body. For an instant his grip weakened, and in that instant the Malay broke away.

In the black water "X" felt a slithering foot slide past. The brown-skinned man was rising to the surface to call for help. "X" clutched again, warding off the knife blow that swung down at him. A grim foreboding told him that this was to be a battle to the death.[43]

He clutched the man's arm again, struck with his fist under water, felt his knuckles hit yielding flesh. But the water deadened the force of his blow. The Malay suddenly wrapped muscular legs about him. It was like being caught in the tentacles of an octopus. Breath bubbled from the Agent's compressed lungs. Nothing seemed able to break the brown man's viselike grip.

"X" drew the Malay's knife arm downward and held it, twisting slowly, turning the knife blade inwards.

The Malay's body stiffened suddenly. For seconds "X" could not understand it, could not understand the strange shrinking movement the man had made. For the knife blade had barely touched his flesh. Then he felt the brown-skinned killer's muscles growing lax. Strangely the man's struggles were beginning to cease.

They rose to the surface slowly. Then the Agent understood and horror gripped him. The knife blade had been poisoned. The Malay had been struck with his own venomous steel.

The man was floating on his back now. A hoarse breath came through clenched teeth. He squirmed like a wounded fish, lay still. The man was dead.

For a moment only, the Agent hesitated, then his face grew grim. A swift plan came to his mind. Under the dim starlight, close to the water, he stared at the dead Malay's features. Here perhaps was his one hope of saving Betty Dale. But it was a plan so desperate that it seemed like a challenge hurled into the very face of death.[44]

Turning suddenly he began towing the corpse of the Malay toward the mainland's shore. It was slow work against the river's current. The bobbing head of the dead man behind him touched grue-

---

43　AUTHOR'S NOTE: *Hardly ever in his strange and adventurous career has the Agent slain an adversary. The ingenious defensive weapons he uses are not lethal. He prefers, with few exceptions, to work by wit and courage and his masterly disguises.*

44　AUTHOR'S NOTE: *Two of the Agent's greatest problems in the masterly disguises he creates are the difficulties of changing eye color and height. The former he has met in various ways. By expanding his pupils with drops of Belladonna when his eyes must appear dark. By using other drugs he lightens the irises. To some extent it is possible to give the appearance of lower height by lax posture; bending of the knees, drooping of the shoulders, etc. Special shoes with thick inner soles are an ingenious method of adding height. The Agent uses both these methods as well as others.*

somely against his back. But fear for Betty Dale overbalanced all else. These were not ordinary criminals. They seemed the spawn of some wild nightmare—a horror horde under the control of a ruthless fiend. They could not be combated in any ordinary way. The police could not help him. To tell them where the island hideout was, would, he felt sure, bring hideous disaster on Betty Dale. The green-masked devil would vent his fury upon her.

HE reached the shore five hundred feet below the spot where he had moored his boat. Lifting the lifeless Malay to his shoulder, he carried the man through the sparse woods, laying him at last in the bottom of the boat. Then "X" cut loose and let the current drift the craft downstream.

Not until the island was a half mile behind did he start the motor. Then he headed for the opposite shore, giving the island hideout a wide berth. His eyes were gleaming now. The plan he had conceived was built on desperation. Showing no lights, he sped back along the course he had come. His eyes strained across the dark water until he saw a small river town ahead.

He passed it, tied his boat under the black shadow of a sandy bank, and walked away from the river. He was fighting not only for Betty Dale's life, he was fighting for the safety of his country. If he did not conquer now, this green-masked killer would beat him in the final show-down.

Without compunction then, the Agent acted swiftly. He must get the Malay to his own hideout. Wet and hatless, still in evening clothes, he knew that if a policeman saw him he would be held as a suspicious character. There would be questions, explanations, and time was vital. He prowled till he saw an auto stop before a house, waited till the owner got out, leaving the engine still running. In a second Agent "X" was behind the wheel, gliding off up the dark street.

He stopped by the river, transferred the body of the Malay to the car, leaving Foulette's speed boat still tied among the trees. He was helping himself to other people's property tonight. But there was justification for everything he did.

He sped along a road that edged the river, came at last to the suburbs of Washington, then to the city itself. The Malay's body was slumped on the floor of the car. It would not be seen unless a policeman stopped him. That was a chance, too, he must take.

But he reached his hideout safely where Michael Renfew was

still his prisoner. He doubled the Malay's body up, wrapped it in a lap robe, and took the outside way to the hideout he had hired—the dark fire escape where none would see.

Once inside he set feverishly to work. There was no time to lose—not with Betty in the hands of the green-masked killer's horde.

All the artistry of the Man of a Thousand Faces would be needed in the thing he planned to do. For long moments he studied the dead Malay's face, studied its contours and its color, noticed the man's clothes. The man was wearing a cheap cloth suit. Then "X" began one of the most difficult disguises of his life.

The high cheek bones were not hard to simulate. Strips of transparent adhesive pulling his own flesh did that. But the strange pigmentation gave him trouble.

Stripped to the waist he rubbed brown liquid into his skin, covering his whole torso. He had been in the water once. He might have to swim again. The coloring fluid he used was waterproof. But he carried a vial of liquid that would take it off.

IT was nearly an hour before his task was done; nearly an hour before Secret Agent "X" had turned himself into a brown-skinned savage. He found a suit in his own wardrobe like that the Malay wore. When he left at last, using the fire escape again, one of the green-masked murderer's own men seemed to be emerging from that house.

Swiftly the Agent got into the car that he had taken in the river town, and went back along the route he had come. Not all the way, however. His eyes grew alert. He wore dry clothes now. They must remain so. If he arrived on the island wet it would mean suspicion, exposure, and the end of his desperate plan. But he could not go in the motor boat. He must have some silent craft.

He stopped at a place along the road where low-roofed buildings rose close to the river. They were dark, deserted, but the Agent walked quickly to them. Once again that night he helped himself—this time to a light canoe.

He broke into a boat shed, took the frail craft out, launched it. He was no more than a mile from the island now. The river current was with him. It would be better this way than going in the stolen car. Motorcycle police were probably looking for its license plates even now.

His pulses raced as the island loomed ahead. He sent the canoe forward under the swift thrust of his paddle. At the last he let it drift with the current.

Silently as a shadow it bore him forward. The dark vegetation of the island loomed before his bow. He brought the canoe in, waited breathlessly, ready to leap at the slightest sound. But none came, except for the faint stir of branches in the night wind and the lapping of the water.

The Agent was trembling as he set foot on land; trembling not for himself, but from the fear that filled him for Betty Dale. He drew the canoe up, turned his face toward the center of the island.

Each foot he moved he half expected to feel the prick of a death dart, or see a man with a knife leap toward him. Would his desperate disguise work?

The starlight shone through the branches on his brown-skinned face, revealing its Malaysian contours. His eyes probed the darkness ahead. Then he made a discovery. The building in the island's center was no barn. It was an old storage warehouse, built at the time of the war, taken over now by a man who was a vicious enemy of society.

A dark figure moved suddenly at "X's" left. He waited, pulses hammering, felt eyes upon him. One of the Malay killers came slowly up. Then he saw others, coming in from different angles. And suddenly his body grew rigid. For out of the darkness ahead came the faint, mysterious note of a deep-toned gong. It seemed to be a signal, summoning the dread clan together, and Agent "X" moved forward—into the very citadel of terror.

CHAPTER XV

GREEN GOD OF DEATH

HIS PULSES RACED as he crept close to that great gloomy building. His daring disguise had worked so far. He had not been questioned. He had been accepted as one of this poisonous Malay horde. But what of the gong? What did it signify? And where was Betty Dale?

There was one small door in the building ahead. Agent "X" entered this along with other of the brown-skinned men. A dim oil lamp burned at the end of a long passage. Boarding clattered underfoot, rousing ghostly echoes in this shadowed corridor. The odor of some strange incense deepened in the air as he neared the light ahead. Then the gong's note sounded once more, closer this time, and the faces of the Malays around him seemed to change. They contracted into masklike immobility, eyes glittering strangely, heads stiffly held.

There was a doorway to the right of the dim lamp. One of the brown men opened this. A heavy curtain showed, with the glint of more light beyond.

Before entering this curtained chamber the Malay lifted a mask of carved wood from a peg and placed it over his features. These were the masks the torturers had worn when Saunders had been slain. They hung like grinning skulls upon the wall. Agent "X" took his.

Then the man ahead thrust the curtain aside. Agent "X" followed him, and felt a sudden pulse-beat of excitement.

In those few steps along that dark corridor and through this curtained doorway, he seemed to have been transported to a world fantastic as a nightmare. It seemed impossible that he was within a few miles of Washington, D.C., America's capital.

For the scene before him was barbaric, amazing. The room, one of the ground-floor chambers of the old warehouse, was hung with the skins of animals and bright, Oriental tapestries.

Oil lights flamed and flickered around the walls. At the end of the big room, on some sort of wooden base, a hideous idol rose grotesquely. From its flaring nostrils streams of incense vapor rolled in slow spirals to the ceiling, as though the idol were breathing fire. It had huge, batlike ears, a long nose, wide-open, staring eyes.

Before it was an altar made of a slab of stone, and upon this a live sheep was tied. The note of the gong sounded again, muffled, mysterious, seeming to come from the idol's very mouth.

The Malays, moving forward in the manner of sleepwalkers now, arranged themselves before the idol in a worshipful semi-circle. There was a pungent odor mixed with the incense. Agent "X" recognized it as *Bhang*, or hashish. The leader of the Malay group passed cigarettes filled with the same drug. The men began to smoke, their eyes glazing as they puffed.

The frightened sheep at the altar let out one quavering baaa. In that high-ceilinged room echoes came back like a fiend's insane laughter.

Then suddenly the Malays commenced to chant. A strange, barbaric, age-old song of the jungle—a devil song that the high priests or *bomors* of *Kelantan* had handed down from father to son through the centuries. Brown arms and bodies swayed; the pulse-beat of savage rhythm rippled muscles like serpents' coils.

Agent "X," drawing sparingly on the hashish cigarette that had been handed him, watched the ceremony tensely behind his mask. The Malays seemed to be working themselves up to a pitch of ecstasy. Their chant rose in volume. Suddenly, at its height, the gong sounded still again, and the chanting ended in a long-drawn sigh. Then they prostrated themselves, arms stretched out, heads on the floor, and "X" from the corner of his eye saw why.

A trapdoor opened beside the idol. A tall figure appeared. A man with a weird headdress, ornamented with green plumes, and a robe of the same hue. A man with a mask more hideously wrought than any of the others.

He mounted a flight of steps slowly, seeming to rise out of the very earth, and not until he had reached the altar before the idol, did the Malays lift their heads. They gazed raptly then. The masked *bomor* addressed the evil spirits, turning first to the hideous idol, then to the men before him, then to the tethered sheep. Again the animal bleated, pulling back with braced hoofs against the rope that held it.

The *bomor* spoke in words that Agent "X" could understand.

"You have done well, O men of Kelantan," he intoned. "The great god, Tuan, is pleased. You have taken jewels from the white devils. You have laid them at the feet of Tuan. You have killed white devils, and this also pleases Tuan. Soon we shall take a boat across the water. Soon we shall return Tuan to his native land and he will reward you for the precious things you have so graciously laid at his feet."

The green-robed priest then walked slowly toward the idol, lifting a cloth pouch from his belt. He thrust his hand into this, drew forth a glittering collection of jewels, and solemnly dropped them at the idol's feet. A few sparkling necklaces he slipped over the idol's upraised arms.

THE Malays around "X" chanted again, strange words that formed a jewel song. The eyes of Agent "X" gleamed behind his mask. Here, apparently, were the jewels stolen in Washington over a period of weeks.

His eyes riveted once more on the high priest. The man's mask hid his face, but Agent "X" was certain that this was the one who had ordered Saunders' death, the man who had killed Peters—and captured Betty Dale.

When the green-masked priest had finished decorating the idol, he turned and walked toward the tethered sheep. The creature was to be a living sacrifice. A strange chill of horror filled Agent "X" as the *bomor* stood above the animal, knife gleaming in his hand.

The song of the Malays to their devil god rose again, pulsed in the incense-heavy air with the slow, insistent beat of jungle tom-toms. At intervals the *bomor's* hollow voice gave answer to the chorus.

The frightened sheep repeated its trembling cry, but was silenced by a thrust of the high priest's knife. Briefly it struggled, then lay still. Crimson from its slashed throat stained the altar stone.

The ghastly ceremony was completed. Leaving the idol still glittering with jewels, the green-masked *bomor* backed slowly away. As he did so he committed the slain sheep into the hands of the Malays. The earth seemed to open up and swallow him. He disappeared as he had come—through the hidden trapdoor. The hideous idol had taken the sheep's soul. Its worshipers had been given the animal's flesh.

But the brown men were still under the influence of hashish. For nearly an hour they chanted. "X" had to remain. His thoughts were with Betty Dale—but to break that strange half-circle would have meant rousing suspicion.

AT last the chanting ended. The Malays rose, "X" among them. Each went first to the idol, bowed down, fingered the jewels. Agent "X" followed the example of the others, but when his turn came to bow he stared keenly at the glittering heap before him. Then he caught his breath, bent forward sharply.

These jewels were not real! They were cleverly made paste imitations. The green-masked high priest was tricking his followers, keeping the real gems himself.

The Malays seized the dead sheep then. They carried it out of the chamber into another smaller room. Here they removed their masks. Their faces no longer showed the rapture of devil-worshiping fanatics. They looked with brutish appetite on the sheep, and drawing knives from the wall they began cutting it up.

On a huge charcoal brazier they roasted the pieces and ate with savage gusto. Here were men who had been taught by their master to wear European clothes, but they were still savages at heart. There was something horrible about their ravenous, smacking greed as they fell upon the sheep. Again, as when they had snatched the jewels that evening, they reminded "X" of hungry vultures. But now the flesh they ate was real.

One by one they began to nod drowsily after eating. The hashish was still heavy in their blood. Their heads nodded. Sleep overcame them, stretched them out on the floor.

It was then that "X" rose and slipped from the room, ready to risk death to find Betty Dale. He knew that he hadn't long. These men, closely resembling animals, would sleep like animals. In a short time they would waken. Any unusual sound would rouse them now.

Agent "X" stole into the room where the idol was. He examined the jewels for a moment, verifying what he had glimpsed. They were every one paste. He found the trapdoor through which the *bomor* had disappeared, tried to lift it. It was fastened on the under side. It must lead to some secret passage. The followers of the green devil god had probably never seen their *bomor's* face.

Agent "X" hunted for another door. But there was none in this room. He went back into the smoky corridor where they had first entered. Here, a door led into another passageway.

Silent, tense, he began systematically searching every room of the old warehouse. He came upon one filled with rusty machinery, relics of the World War. Then at last he saw a faint light ahead.

He moved forward more stealthily still, pushed open a door, and caught his breath.

The light came from a smoky lamp. In its gleam a girl sat upright in a rickety old desk chair, bound hand and foot. It was Betty Dale, and at the same moment he saw her, her eyes riveted upon him and dilated with fright. Before he could stop her, or indicate who he was, her lips opened and she gave a piercing scream that echoed startlingly through the whole great building.

CHAPTER XVI

THE IDOL'S VICTIM

AGENT "X" LEAPED forward tensely, and as he did so he made motions in the air, indicating the letter X. He put a finger on his lips for silence.

Betty Dale's face turned white as death. A great trembling seized her. She stared at the man before her with amazement. Agent "X" had come to her in many disguises, but never one seemingly as impossible as this. Her lips framed words, words that were almost a moan.

"My God—it can't be! It can't be!"

"It is, Betty!" The Agent's voice was low, vibrant. He knew what catastrophe that one scream of hers might cause. She, too, realized. Her eyes held infinite remorse.

"I didn't mean to—I was frightened. I thought—"

"I understand, Betty!"

The Agent drew a knife from his pocket, stepped forward, then paused. He was about to sever the ropes that held her. But quavers of her scream still echoed. A confused hubbub followed it. His worst fears had been realized.

"They are coming," Betty said hoarsely. "Go quickly—before they find you here."

The Agent meditated. He wasn't afraid for himself. Long ago he had cast out fear. But Betty's life depended on his own actions. If the green mask fiend discovered his real identity, Betty would pay for it in a way too ghastly to contemplate. If he freed her now there would be questions.

His mind worked swiftly. The hubbub in the building had grown silent now. The silence was ominous. He knew that sinister forms were running through dark chambers and corridors toward them. He came close, spoke hoarsely.

"They must not learn who I am, Betty. Everything depends on that. Scream! Scream again!"

"I don't understand," she whispered brokenly.

"You will. It is too late to try to escape now. Scream, Betty—now! It is the only way."

The Agent's orders were as law to Betty Dale. She trusted him. He had never failed her yet. She didn't know what desperate plan he contemplated. But she screamed again loudly. The Agent raised his hands above her as though to clamp strangling fingers around her white neck.

"Again!" he commanded. "Scream!"

A second piercing cry tore from her lips. The brown men heard it. They plunged through the door, knives gleaming in their hands. They paused, animal faces intent on Betty Dale, who crouched as though in fear of the man before her. The Agent lowered his claw-like hands, cringed back, and stared at them.

The man who was their leader, next to the green-masked *bomor*, advanced.

"What is this?" he demanded in Malay.

The Agent did not answer. He made his body tremble. He did not meet the headman's eye. Betty's life depended on his acting now. He seemed a cringing Malay, caught where he should not have been found. When at last he spoke it was hoarsely, and Betty Dale started as the strange Malay words came from his lips—words unintelligible to her.

"This girl is one of the white devils," said Agent "X." "I was going to kill her."

The headman looked at him sternly, doubtingly.

"Did not the great *bomor* say she was to be left alone?"

Agent "X" hung his head. The other continued.

"It was because of her beauty that you came here. Do not lie. You have gone against the vows of Tuan. You have sought the company of a white devil woman. You have sought company of one who is taboo."

A fanatical light glittered in the headman's eyes. He lifted bony hands toward the ceiling.

"Tuan, here is one who has broken his word to thee. Here is a foolish one who must be punished."

BETTY DALE'S eyes sought those of the Agent. Words trembled on her lips. He silenced her with a movement of his hand behind his back. The Malay headman came forward, seizing Agent "X" by the arm.

"Come," he said. "Leave the chamber of this white devil woman. It is for our *bomor* to make the decision of what shall be done with her. When the time comes to dispose of her, he will so order it. She will suffer—but the hour is not come. It is you who must suffer now. It is you who must die first."

Die! The Agent was glad Betty could not understand. Her fear for him might have made her forget. She might have cried out. He walked quickly to the headman's side. He bowed his face.

"I come," he said. "I yield to Tuan's will."

He dared not give even a backward glance at Betty. His heart was pounding fast. He would rather die than have them learn he was not what he seemed. If that should happen, their fanatical, idol-worshiping fury would include the girl.

They led him back along the way he had come. The Malays around him set up a slow and terrible chant.

"The wrath of Tuan is mighty! O great is the strength of Tuan! Swift is the punishment of Tuan!"

The light of fanaticism spread to their faces, also. Barbarians under the skin, emotion swayed them. This man had broken his vow to the hideous green idol. This man must die. Agent "X" sensed the cruelty of innate sadism in their voices and expressions.

They drew the curtains aside, put on their masks again, and entered the chamber of Tuan. The great squat idol stared down, nostrils seeming to flare in derision. Its eyes glared as mercilessly as its human followers.

The voice of the headman came again harshly.

"Our *bomor* has gone back into the earth from whence he comes. We cannot summon him now. We cannot wait. It is the law that those who break their vows to Tuan shall meet swift punishment. The *bomor* would want it so if he were here. A faithful servant of Tuan shall see that the law is carried out."

There was human ardor in the headman's voice now. Here was a chance to act with the *bomor* away. Here was a chance to assert his own authority over the followers of Tuan, and to placate the idol as well. He made a sudden, imperious gesture. Agent "X" was seized. Before he could resist he was thrown on his face by four of the green-masked men. He heard the headman's voice again.

"Bring cord, O followers of Tuan!"

Tentatively, the Agent struggled. But he saw the hopelessness of that. Knives were pressed against his back. The headman's voice addressed him harshly.

"Act wisely and your death shall be slow. There will be time to make your peace with Tuan. Your cries will please him. But be a fool and you shall die by the knife swiftly, like a sheep that is slaughtered. You shall be cast among the lowest devils."

Agent "X" lay still. But he made his muscles expand rigidly as they bound him; and he held them so, even though the Malays tightened the cords until they bruised and broke the skin. He held them rigid until his body was cold with sweat which his captors took for the sweat of fear.

Four of them lifted him to the altar stone before the grinning idol—the smeared slab on which the sheep had died. It was cold and wet with the animal's blood. The Agent's flesh recoiled from the contact. The headman's next command came harsher still.

"The claw," he said. "Bring that and the dust of *Kep-shak*. It shall be spread thinly that the man may suffer long."

A Malay left the group. The others crowded closer. Brown hands ripped the clothes from Agent "X's" chest and arms. His heart stood still. Would his dyed skin betray him? Would it stand the test? That for the moment worried him more than the threat of the terrible *Kep-shak*.

He did not wince when the claw-like implement was drawn across his skin, leaving its long crimson scratches. The Malays began to chant again. Weirdly their voices rose into the high-ceiled room. The headman led the macabre chorus, lifting arms toward the idol that stared down with glassy eyes.

"O Tuan, Great One. One who has broken faith with thee is now to die. Let his screams fall upon your ears. Let his groans make penance for the wrong he has done. Do not blame his sin upon those who have kept the faith."

The headman himself took the metal box that contained the *Kep-shak*. He reached with clawlike fingers into it, withdrew a pinch of the grayish powder. There was a gloating light in his eyes, the lust of one to whom cruelty is natural. The other Malays stood tensely watching. Then the headman reached forward, raised his hands.

"Behold, O Mighty Tuan—the pollen of the flower of pain now falls upon the guilty."

He opened wide his fingers, let the gray powder drift down onto Agent "X's" skin and rubbed it into the scratches with a sudden vicious sweep of his hand.

CHAPTER XVII

THE IDOL'S WRATH

THE TINY ABRASIONS became like raw and throbbing wounds. A burning brand seemed to have been laid on them. Pain leaped along the Agent's nerves. Pain reached into his body with twisting fingers of red torment.

As through a haze he saw the hideous idol and the faces of the Malays gathered round. The men set up a low chant. Their voices rose and fell, seeming to blend with the pulsing waves of agony that made a cold sweat bathe the Agent's face.

He clenched his teeth, determined to stay silent. Then suddenly he changed his mind. They wanted him to suffer. They wanted him to suffer visibly. If he did not it would only bring more of the dread powder, diminishing his chances of escape.

He let a groan roll from his lips. The headman's eyes glowed evilly. The Malay's chant rose higher.

"Tuan, O Mighty One! Just punishment has come to him who wronged thee. Behold how he cries out in pain!"

The Agent groaned again, writhing in his bonds, gambling with hideous death, suffering agony that they might not learn who he was.

For seconds, while the grayish powder burned into his flesh, he turned and twisted, acting as he thought a Malay would. These brown men didn't know with whom they dealt. They didn't realize the Spartan courage of their victim.

At last "X" lay still; breath whistled between clenched teeth. The brown men nodded, as though pleased. The headman again addressed the idol.

"He is weak, O Tuan. It will not be long before the *Kep-shak* has done its work. It will not be long before thou art avenged."

Agent "X" remained as if nearly dead, as if the astringent poison had already conquered his will. He let his mouth hang open, rolled his eyes.

Then his pulses leaped. The brown-faced men were moving toward the door. They thought him far gone now. They were going to leave him to suffer his last agonies alone, let the *Kep-shak* finish its deadly work. It was on this he had gambled. On it he had built a desperate hope. It was why he had chosen torture rather than death by the knife.

He watched the brown-skinned men withdraw. Pain racked his body. The sweat on his forehead was real enough. Blood beat in his temples like cruel hammer blows. The *Kep-shak* was seeping slowly into his bloodstream. A few minutes more and it would be too late. The powder had been sprinkled thinly, his torture slow, but human flesh and human will could not endure it long. He thought of Saunders, fettered and dying; of Peters, stretched dead on the floor of his cottage. Soon his own face would be like theirs.

But the Malays were going back to their sleep, back to their savage hashish dreams. "X" waited until their low-voiced chanting faded away.

Then he moved again. Not in pain-constricted jerkings such as he had allowed himself for the benefit of his torturers, but purposefully. Slowly he drew his right hand from the rope that seemed to press tightly into his flesh. The Agent had used a well-known trick.[45]

By stiffening his muscles, holding them rigid when they bound him, he had increased the diameter of arms and legs. Now, as he relaxed them, they slipped back to normal size. But escaping from his bonds was not the most desperate part of his battle. That was the battle between the poison and his own iron will. A battle once more of flesh against spirit. For his limbs were growing numb. Pain wrenched his muscles.

When, after seconds of agony, his right hand was free, he loosened the ropes more quickly. Weak and shaking, he lay still a moment on the altar slab. Then he forced himself to his feet. His eyes were burning with a light that was almost feverish. He stumbled toward the curtained door; paused to listen.

---

45 *AUTHOR'S NOTE: By a system of carefully thought out exercises Agent "X" keeps himself marvelously fit. His physique is not the muscle-bound disproportionately developed one of a wrestler or professional strong man; but rather the physique of a boxer. Each muscle is coordinated and smoothly functioning, and his reflexes are lightninglike.*

There was no sound in the building now. But he could not go to Betty immediately. The poison powder was still on his arms and chest, being absorbed through the tiny cuts. "X" tried to brush it off, then stopped. At the first contact of his hand new stabs of pain thrust into him. But he must get rid of the stuff quickly, or die.

He followed the passage he had first entered, reached the small outside door, and slipped out into the darkness. His eyes would hardly focus. Breathing was getting difficult. Cold fingers seemed to be pressing around his heart

Through the night he staggered, stumbling, falling, getting up. He knew where he was going, but the way seemed endless. His knees were almost giving under him. His body was a quivering mass of pain.

Then he saw the glint of water. With a desperate plunge, he reached it, immersed himself in the river. Its chill was like a merciful poultice. He lay breathing hoarsely, till the poison began to thin as the powder dissolved. He moved his hands across the scratches now, washing the hideous stuff away; washing till each tiny abrasion was clean.

It was minutes before the pain began to abate. It was like the slow withdrawal of burning wires that had been driven into his flesh.

A HALF-HOUR passed. Then again he crept toward the building where he had suffered such torment. The poison of the *Kep-shak* had left his muscles weak. He didn't let that stop him. Silent and tense he slipped into the building, crept along the dim corridor to the chamber where Betty was imprisoned. On the threshold he paused, looking in. Fear chilled him for a moment.

Betty's Dale's eyes were closed. Her face was pale as death. But she wasn't dead. Her eyelids lifted at Agent "X's" cautious hiss. Again he made the mysterious sign—the "X" traced in the air. In spite of this she almost cried out at the sight of his torn clothing and scratched skin.

"X" put his finger to his lips for silence, then drew a knife from his pocket. Quick slashes severed the ropes that bound her, and the Agent motioned Betty to follow him.

But the girl was unable to walk. She took an uncertain step across the floor, then sank down with a little moan.

"In a moment," she whispered, "I'll be all right."

There was no time to wait. One of the Malays might take it into his head to prowl.

Swiftly Agent "X" stooped and gathered Betty in his arms. He was glad she couldn't see his face, or the sweat that started on his forehead. The effort of picking her up brought gruelling pain back into his muscles. Half of his strength seemed to be gone.

With Betty in his arms, he moved stealthily along the shadowy passage. Once he thought he heard a sound and paused, tensely alert. Then he continued. Outside at last, he stood Betty gently on her feet. He rested a moment, breathing heavily, gathering his spent strength.

"I can walk now," Betty whispered.

"Wait," he said. "Later," and picked her up again.

He moved straight toward the river, planning to skirt its bank. But a whisper of sound came from the building behind them. A human call! One of the Malays was awake!

The sound was repeated, taken up by other voices. The Agent's blood seemed to freeze in his veins. His escape from the idol's chamber had been discovered.

He turned and cut into the woods. Seconds were precious. He must locate his canoe. He dared not even think of the consequences if they were captured now.

In spite of Betty's insistence that she could walk, the Agent continued to carry her. The ground was rough, with bushes and vines clogging the path. Everything depended on silence now. His own sure-footed tread, making their progress as quiet as was humanly possible in the underbrush, now and then rustled a leaf, snapped a dry twig.

There came a savage cry from the darkness behind. It was not loud, but held infinite evil. Betty Dale tensed in the Agent's arms.

HE did not try to reassure her. Every breath, every ounce of strength he possessed must be saved for what he had to do. The canoe lay somewhere ahead where he had left it hidden under the river bank. His sense of direction had never failed him. He knew that even though his brain was still dazed by poison he was heading toward it.

But a tangle of vines impeded his way. They scratched his ankles, clutched at his feet and legs. He had to slow down. Once he tripped and, lacking the freedom of his arms for balance, almost fell.

There were definite sounds of pursuit now. Guttural grunts, low-voiced orders. Bushes rustled perilously close behind. It was like a ghastly nightmare, with the vines clutching at his legs like the fingers of an enemy intent on impeding his progress.

He broke through the mat at last, saw the gleam of water beyond. But the rustlings behind were coming closer. He put Betty down, found that she could walk, and took her hand. Then suddenly he thrust her ahead of him.

"Straight toward the water, Betty."

He did not tell her why he made her walk ahead. But an instant later he ducked and thrust Betty Dale frantically to one side as something whispered by in the darkness with the thin hum of an insect's wings. Their brown-skinned pursuers were shooting at them with poisoned darts.

Agent "X" saw the canoe, then, a slim dark shadow among the bushes. He drew Betty down, and they crawled on hands and knees toward the water. "X" shoved the canoe free of the slimy mud edging the shore, then whispered to Betty Dale to get in.

"Lie down," he said, "flat."

Betty obeyed. "X" seized a paddle, balanced precariously in the frail craft's stern, and thrust strongly away from shore. The canoe shot out, sharp prow cutting the water with a knifelike sweep.

But as it did so, winged insects seemed to be following them. Horror crawled along the Agent's spine as something plucked at his coat sleeve. There was a soft *spat* as a dart hit one side of the canoe. It quivered there, its sinister green-feathered end showing in the faint starlight.

Agent "X" glanced back toward the island, saw shadows moving along the shore. He dug his paddle into the water, and a powerful back-thrust sent the canoe shooting ahead. Then he, too, bent down, holding himself on braced hands that gripped the canoe's gunwale.

Two more darts spatted into the canoe's sides. Others hummed above his head. Then the current caught them, whirled the light craft around. He rose and sent it swiftly downstream.

But a cry rose from the shore. Another low-voiced order. A second later the Agent turned his head and tensed. Something was moving out from the island's edge—something that lay black on the surface of the river.

Machinery whined. An engine barked into life. The dark shadow turned and glided toward them. The Malays had taken to their motor boat. Death was hurtling out of the darkness behind them.

CHAPTER XVIII

RED DEATH

IT SEEMED THAT all the hideous forces of the night were conspiring against them. It seemed almost that the idol, Tuan, had the evil power attributed to him by his followers—and was reaching out fingers to snatch them back.

The Agent's mouth was set. Pallor spread beneath the disguise he wore. His eyes were points of burning light. The motor boat behind them had turned now. It was plunging down the river's channel in pursuit.

Muscles in the Agent's back stood out like knots. He leaned forward at each stroke, dug in, sent the canoe shooting ahead under his paddle thrust.

"If there were only another paddle," Betty whispered. "I could help you, then. You came to the island to save me."

"I would have come anyway, Betty. It might as well have been tonight as later."

There was a note of buoyancy in "X's" voice. He would not let the girl know the fear he felt. She was being brave—as always— putting his safety ahead of her own. Under the faint starlight he caught the golden glint of her hair, saw her eyes, bright as stars themselves, turned upon him.

"They are coming," she whispered tensely. "They must know now you are not one of them. They will kill you."

"The fox knows many tricks," Agent "X" answered, lapsing once more into the mysterious, indirect form of speech he was fond of. His eyes strained through the darkness. The shore was two hundred feet away. But if he turned, going side-wise to the current, he and Betty would be overtaken before they reached it.

Agent "X" thought quickly. The roar of the motor boat behind was like the pulsebeat of some drum of doom. Caught by the Malays again, he could not hope to escape. Neither could Betty. She would be taken back, and the green-masked criminal would make good his threat. She would be tortured horribly, and left paralyzed for life.

Breath hissed between the Agent's teeth. He leaned over then, spoke hoarsely.

"There is one way," he said. "You must slip out and swim to shore, Betty—while I lead them after me."

He knew that Betty was an expert in the water. The river would hold no terrors for her. She could make the shore easily. But she made a protest that sounded almost like a sob.

"I can't," she said. "They will catch you—and kill you. Let me stay with you—and be caught—too."

For a moment her words betrayed a secret of her heart; the secret that she felt more than friendship for this strange man; the secret that he had become part of her own life. Her eyes were misty. Her voice trembled as she leaned out and touched his arm.

"Let us fight—together," she said.

The Agent caught the significance behind that word "fight." Die was the word she should have used, the word she really meant. He kept the tremor from his voice as he answered.

"It is our only chance, Betty. And more than our lives is at stake. There is the work that brought me to Washington."

"Then *you* swim!" said Betty eagerly. "Let me lead them off. They won't hurt me if I am caught. They'll just hold me prisoner till the police come."

"X" didn't frighten her by repeating the green-masked killer's threat, but his voice was firm.

"No, Betty—we must both escape. And perhaps we can."

He looked behind him, touched Betty's arm quickly. "Now! In a moment it will be too late."

A sound like a sob came from Betty Dale's lips. She reached forward, drew her high-heeled slippers from her slim feet—the same slippers that had moved so gaily over the dance floor at Senator Foulette's house a few hours before. She was still clad in evening dress, white arms and shoulders bare.

The Agent's fingers touched hers for a moment, gripped them reassuringly.

"It will be all right," he said. "But you must promise, Betty, to leave Washington at once."

"Then how will I know—if you are all right?" she asked.

"Call the *Herald* as soon as you can. I'll do the same. You'll hear from Raphael Sancho. Now, Betty—good-by."

The Agent leaned far over, bracing the canoe against his paddle. Betty Dale, slim and lithe as a nymph, slipped overside into the dark water. He saw her dive beneath the surface, saw her blonde head reappear twenty feet distant. For an instant that frightened him. What if the Malays saw her, too?

He swung the nose of the canoe around, paddled back, screening Betty's movements. Then he swung again in the other direction.

A DARK shadow bulked on the river's rim behind. He could see the speed-boat now. That meant they could also see him. His heart leaped with relief, for the other craft's nose was turning. Betty Dale was safe.

He bent over his paddle. With Betty no longer in the canoe it seemed to leap over the water like a skimming bird. He dug the spruce blade in, gripping it in powerful fingers. He thrust savagely, turning toward the opposite shore.

The thunder of the speed boat crept closer. Death rode the wind behind, death in its most hideous form. But Agent "X" was fighting to escape; fighting the battle of his life. Now, with Betty Dale safe, he was free to pursue his strange work in Washington; free to continue his quest for the stolen plans.

But could he make the shore? The motor boat was plainly visible now. He could see the white froth at its prow, froth that was like foam flecking the mouth of a snapping, snarling beast. He was nearer shore than he had realized. The smooth surface of the river was broken by a mat of reeds—a marsh. Last year's dry growth still raised thick stems. He could plunge among them and be hidden from the poison darts behind. But they were still a hundred feet away.

He swung his paddle to the other side, strained fiercely, cutting across the current. He calculated the best angle to make it, but still the speed boat was gaining on him. A guttural shout rose behind him. A strange chant followed. The Malays in the boat were singing their song of death.

They were sure of victory now; sure they would recapture him. But an instant later their chant turned to shouts of anger. They, too, had seen the dark barrier of reeds. The motor's roar reached a higher note. It swept down out of the night like a savage demon's growl.

Something struck the water close to "X's" canoe. For an instant he saw a tiny feathered stick before it sank out of sight. A dart! The high wind had made the Malay's aim poor. He must gamble now—on the wind, to send the darts wide of their mark; on the reeds ahead, to shelter him.

His lips were white as he swept forward over the last fifty feet of dark water. The thunder of the speed boat-beat in his ears. A dart sang past his head, buried its deadly point in the canoe's gunwale. There was a *spat* against his paddle, and, looking down, he saw another quivering in the soft spruce.

A *swish* and the canoe's bow slipped in among the reeds. Thick stems closed in behind it. For a moment he was safe from the flying darts, protected by a mat of vegetation.

But he leaped from the canoe, floundering ahead toward boggy land. And as he moved, the speed-boat lunged in amid the reeds also. Agent "X" lurched sidewise, heard the boat's sharp prow crunch against the canoe's frail side.

Swiftly, determinedly, he plunged ahead, deeper and deeper into the reeds. Dry stems cracked and broke. He was making noise, but the speed-boat's throbbing motor drowned it out. Let them follow if they wanted! He had a start now. His own legs would be as fast as theirs. A great purpose spurred him on.

The speed-boat's engine slowed. He heard the suck and slap of its propeller as it backed out. Then he stiffened. Raising his head, he sniffed the air, then turned startled eyes behind. In that instant new horror clutched his heart.

Between the thick reed stems he saw a faint glow. It brightened. A slim flame shot skyward. Above the speed boat's throttled motor rose a vicious crackling sound.

Fire! The Malays had put a light to the dry marsh reeds! And the wind was sweeping off the river toward him!

Like an evil ghost a gray cloud of smoke drifted overhead. It seemed to spread huge arms above him. It was torn, thinned by the wind, but more followed it. Then the first glow became a crimson, blazing light. The speed-boat's motor ceased. Across the still river, above the crackling hiss of flames, the death chant rose again.

"O Tuan, Great One, the gods of fire have aided thee in thy wrath! He who is guilty shall be punished. He shall be consumed in hot flames."

As the strange chant rose, the fire seemed to spread its hungry arms. It leaped along the river's edge and swept forward toward the spot where Agent "X" was floundering. And each instant the threat of its red fangs increased.

CHAPTER XIX

FLAMING PERIL

HORROR CONSTRICTED AGENT "X's" throat. The crackling flames seemed to sound a death knell to the victory that had been so near. This was a peril he had not foreseen. Had the devil god, Tuan, won after all? The deepening smoke clouds seemed to form a curtain lowering upon the defeat of Agent "X."

He turned fiercely and floundered on through the marsh. But he could not outdistance the wind. It drove the flames coiling through the dry reed stems like red, hungry serpents. The fire gathered fury with every foot it covered.

The Agent came to a hummock of hard ground. On his toes, he stared forward across the marsh. He groaned. As far as he could see, the waving tops of the dry cat-tails continued—an undulating plain, lurid now with the red glow of the fire.

A billowing breath of smoke swirled about him. He choked, stumbled on toward a slight break in the reeds ahead. Here he sank waist deep in the water. A channel cut through the marsh at this point.

He started to climb out, turned back. The roaring of the fire had shut out the Malay's chanting now. The Agent was alone in a world of smoke and flame. Only a thin barrier of reeds stood between him and a blazing inferno. The flames were fast devouring that. On each side, where the reeds were thinner, arms of the conflagration shot out. He was being encircled in a fiery embrace—an embrace of death.

The water in which he stood was his only hope—and the Agent's mind flashed back. Years ago, as a boy, he had been caught in a forest fire. He remembered how he and an old woodsman had saved themselves.

With quick tense fingers the Agent drew his knife. He bent forward, slashed at the reed stems, drew one out. With his knife blade

516

he trimmed the ends. The reed was hollow. He put it to his mouth, drew air through. A grim smile made his eyes grow bright. A human life hung upon that slender reed—and a nation's destiny, perhaps.

The fire was close now—thirty feet. Clouds of hot air swept forward. The Agent wet his reed in the channel's water, then lay down on his back. Raising himself on one elbow, he kept his face above the surface of the water.

The fire swept onward in a roaring, red glare. Reeds on the channel's edge began to smoke and curl. The top of one burst into flame, dropped as the stem bent and broke.

Heat quivered above the water. Blazing stems and gray ashes hissed as they fell. Then like a red, destructive wave, the full force of the fire advanced.

The Agent wet his reed again, put it between his lips. He lay flat, submerging his face now, sucking breath through the hollow stem. He opened his eyes. Water made his gaze blurry. But overhead all was brightening. The red glow intensified to orange. Wavering arms of fire swept across the channel.

Smoke beat down. The Agent drew in a lungful through the reed and choked. Terrible seconds followed in which it seemed nothing could survive that flaming holocaust. Acrid smoke cut his lungs like knives; the water above his face grew warm.

But the reed stems were consumed quickly. When it seemed that he could no longer live without a breath of clean, cool air, the fire glow began to fade. The air he sucked down through the reed became purer. At last "X" raised his head.

The channel now was rimmed with coals. Reed roots still smoldered. Powdery white ashes sifted down. He could hear the fire behind him, still roaring downwind. But he was alive. He had beaten Tuan again.

Far off across the river, he heard the chanting of the Malays. He could not make out the words, but he knew they must be reciting a victory song for the devil god. They believed "X" was dead.

He waited till even the ashes of the fire began to die. Then he rose from the channel that had saved him. Slowly he followed in the charred wake of the fire. There was danger that he might be silhouetted against its glow. Bnt he took that chance. The Malays were probably too far away to see him.

He must get back to Washington now. He must learn all that happened at the raid. The green-masked devil priest had told his followers that they would soon take a ship across the water. Did that mean he had the plans?

Fire was still burning far back along the marsh. There might be other channels and deep bogs to cross. The Agent walked parallel with the river, then turned downstream. A half mile below the spot where his canoe had landed, he again approached the shore.

After the hot fire a long swim held no terrors. He slipped into the cold water and struck out. Long swift strokes brought him at last to the farther side of the river. Somewhere here Betty Dale had also landed.

He followed the river shore upstream for a mile, passing the sinister island which lay peacefully beneath the starlight now. The Agent continued to the spot where he had moored Senator Foulette's speed boat. Here was a ready means of getting back to the city. The thundering roar of its motor woke echoes along the dark river. The blast of cold night wind cleared the Agent's faculties. His eyes were alert as those of a hunting hawk as he sped up the dark river toward the nation's capital.

THREE quarters of an hour later a swift roadster turned into the driveway of Senator Foulette's estate. A nattily-dressed army officer was at the wheel, an officer with the insignia of General Staff upon his collar. Papers in his pocket bore the name of Captain Stewart Black. The Agent had gone to his hideout and made a quick change in his disguise.

It was one-thirty, yet lights still showed in the senator's big mansion. Sleep was impossible in that household where crime's black shadow had so lately fallen. Washington's greatest jewel robbery had taken place—and more. Inspector Clyde had men still stationed on the spot. The Foulettes' servants had been grilled for hours.

The Secret Agent quickly parked his car beside the others in the drive. His eyes were penetratingly bright. There were things he must learn quickly. What conclusion had the police reached? What had been the aftermath of the brown-skinned Malays' raid?

A group of reporters were congregated on the porch. No longer allowed admittance, they waited, hoping for fresh developments. Their cigarettes made red pin points in the darkness. Agent "X" walked swiftly toward them. Here was as good a way as any of learning the facts.

He spoke abruptly, playing the role of brusque and hard-boiled army officer.

"What's going on here?"

Silence followed his inquiry. Then a chuckle sounded.

"Where have you been, general?"

"I know there's been a robbery," said "X" impatiently. "But tell me about it. I've just arrived in the city."

"Robbery's right," a reporter said. "Enough sparklers were lifted tonight to cover a circus queen's wedding dress. But that ain't all! A guy and two janes has disappeared. There's a mystery a mile wide and twice as high. The police are playing left-handed poker with stacked cards. This will be hot copy for a week."

The reporter's colorful description brought more chuckles from his comrades. But Agent "X" tensed with interest.

"Three people disappeared? Who were they?"

"A senator's daughter, her girl friend, and a spik named Sancho. It looks like some guys were going into the wholesale kidnapping racket."

"What senator's daughter?"

"Old man Blackwell's. The crooks knocked everybody out with giggle gas. They took the janes and the spik along with the rocks they lifted. But we ain't got nothing out of Blackwell. He's been hit hard and won't open up. His dopey son was bumped off tonight, too."

"What—Ferris?"

"Yeah, you know him? Sorry if I made a break, general. But he was parked at a sanatorium where they hand out cures to snow-birds. A nurse heard him screeching and thought he had the D.T.'s. She got a doctor. His door was locked and when they got in he was all scratched up and dead."

The light of interest in the Agent's eyes became like a snapping flame. "Scratched up?"

"Yeah! And a guy in a green mask was seen making a get-away. The same guy, I guess, that bumped off Senator Rathborne's hired man last night. The bird they call the 'fiend killer.' Tie that if you can! Washington's getting as good as Chicago used to be. How do you figure it, general?"

The Agent didn't answer. His mouth was grim. Suzanne Blackwell kidnapped and Ferris murdered! Both the work of the green-masked killer. There was strange significance in this. He asked another question:

"How do they know Miss Blackwell was kidnapped?"

"She was gone when the police got here. She ain't been seen since."

"And everybody else was here?"

"Yes—except them other two."

"X" turned suddenly and strode back toward his roadster. The reporter's voice drifted after him.

"Say, general, give a guy a break. I handed you a lot of dope. How about spilling something yourself?"

BUT "X" had reached his car. Gears whined. He spun around the drive and headed toward the street, without having entered Foulette's house. He had all the information he needed at the moment.

"That bird's got something on his mind," the reporter growled.

How much, he didn't know. The eyes of "X" were steely bright. Out of this night of horror and mystery had suddenly come a startling revelation. Behind the green-masked murderer's actions, Agent "X" read a hidden motive.

He sent the swift car roaring through the streets, racing as though with death itself. Suzanne Blackwell kidnapped. She had not been taken to the island with Betty. That he knew. Where, then? And why had she been abducted? This, coupled with the death of Ferris, brought an abrupt, amazing theory to the Agent's mind. It was like the answer to an algebraic problem suddenly revealed.

He slowed his speeding car at Senator Blackwell's drive, whirled in. This time he didn't steal across the lawn. He went straight to the big front door. Another car was there, one from headquarters. A trembling servant answered his ring.

"Who are you, sir?" the man asked.

"Captain Black. I'd like a word with the senator, alone."

The servant shook his head.

"Inspector Clyde is with him now, sir. He's given orders not to admit anyone else tonight."

"This is important. I'm from General Staff."

The servant looked doubtful but impressed. "Step in then," he said and stood aside uncertainly. "I'll ask him. Perhaps he'll see you."

The Agent waited in the big outer hall. Low voices came through a closed door beyond. The servant knocked, disappeared, then returned.

"He says he'll see you, sir—in a moment."

It was several minutes later that Inspector Clyde appeared, his face drawn and worried. The butler motioned toward the library door and "X" walked in.

Senator Blackwell was pacing the floor, his ruddy color gone. He seemed years older than when the Agent had last seen him. There were deep lines in his face. His eyes held shadows of haunting fear. His voice shook as he addressed the Agent.

"You're from General Staff, Wilbur says. What is it, Captain Black? Be as brief as you can. I'm a worried man tonight. And Inspector Clyde is waiting. I really shouldn't see anyone. You've probably heard—"

"Yes," said Agent "X" quietly. "And I'm very sorry, senator."

The older man motioned to a chair.

"Sit down, captain. What can I do for you?"

"First tell me about yourself. Your daughter has been kidnapped, they say; and your son—"

"Murdered," said Blackwell harshly. "I'd rather not talk of that, captain, if you don't mind. I've told Inspector Clyde all there is to tell."

"All?" The Agent spoke the word abruptly. It seemed to have a strange effect on Senator Blackwell. He stiffened, stared at the Agent with sudden furtiveness. His eyes were alert, guarded.

"Yes—what do you mean?"

For seconds the Agent didn't answer. His eyes, burning with an uncannily intent light met those of the senator.

"Just what I say, senator," he replied at last. "There are things that the ordinary forces of the law can't handle. Things so important to the country's welfare that they must be accomplished in absolute secrecy."

THE pallor of Blackwell's face deepened. He tried to light a cigar, but the trembling of his hands prevented it. The Agent snapped his own lighter and held it out. Blackwell puffed, sat down heavily.

"I don't understand what you're talking about," he said.

"Those plans of Doctor Browning's ray mechanism that were stolen when Captain Nelson was murdered," said "X." There was a pause, then he added softly, "Also the kidnapping of your daughter and the strange death of your son. A connection is apparent there."

Blackwell ran a trembling hand across his face. "The police are hunting for her now," he said. "Every way out of the city is being watched. Every air line, every railroad, every boat pier. They'll bring her back to me."

"And your son's death?"

"Horrible! But why are you harping on it? Do you want to torture me?"

"No," said "X," "not torture you. But I believe you realize, senator, that something greater than even the lives of your son and daughter is at stake. That something is the present welfare and future safety of our country!"

The senator clenched his hands, spoke huskily. "The theft of the plans was terrible, captain. I voted that they be destroyed. I was the leader of the opposition. Now I dare not think what their theft may mean—but what have they to do with my own personal trouble?"

Agent "X" leaned closer to the older man, eyes steady.

"A great deal, senator. Aren't you perhaps putting your personal troubles above the welfare of your country?"

A sound like a sob came suddenly from Blackwell's lips. "I love Suzanne, captain. They've taken Ferris. I can't let Suzanne go, too. I must get her back! Nothing shall stand in my way!"

"What if I told you, senator, that the man who has her is utterly without scruple. What if I tell you he will play you false—even if you accede to his demands—as I believe you have already done."

FOR a moment it seemed that Senator Blackwell might have an apoplectic stroke. His eyes shone like those of a cornered animal. His face was a ghastly hue.

"My God, captain! Who told you that—" His voice trailed off. He stared at "X" horrified.

"Correct me if I'm wrong," said "X." "Your son, Ferris, killed Captain Nelson and took the Browning plans. He wanted money to buy more of the drug that enslaved him. He was the thief and the murderer! Am I not right?"

It was seconds before the senator could find his voice. Then he nodded brokenly. "I don't know how you learned this, captain! I never thought—" he broke off, struggling for control. "Ferris was a poor, mad fool. But it was the drug, believe me! It was the drug! He never would have done it otherwise. It was my fault for telling him about the thing beforehand. I shouldn't have taken even my children into my confidence."

The senator had admitted Agent "X's" amazing accusation! He continued hoarsely: "Ferris didn't mean to kill poor Nelson. That I know. He only meant to stun him—he told me so. When he found what he had done, he brought the plans to me and—"

The senator paused again, shaking like a man stricken with palsy.

"Where are they now?" demanded Agent "X." "Quick, senator, tell me that."

Blackwell's voice was hardly audible. "If you had a daughter, captain, and she were kidnapped— If you never expected to see her again, unless— If I can only get her back! I'll make any sacrifice! I'll stand trial before the whole country. Let them impeach me if they want to. I was afraid of shame before—when Ferris told me what he'd done. I was aghast. I hid the plans, waiting for a way to return them. Then Suzanne—"

"You mean the Green Mask has them?"

Senator Blackwell wilted suddenly, seemed on the point of collapse. "Yes," he said dully. "He came tonight and demanded them. I don't know who he is, but he'd got the truth from Ferris—tortured the boy. Don't look at me so, captain. I gave them to him! It was the only way!"

"And when did he promise to bring back Suzanne?"

"Tonight sometime. He wasn't clear."

A harsh, mirthless laugh came from the Agent's lips. But he stepped forward, laid a hand on Blackwell's shoulder.

"I understand, senator. Keep quiet about this. Say nothing to anybody. Nothing at all, do you understand?"

Agent "X" picked up his army cap. He turned toward the door— looked back as the senator's voice rose.

"What are you going to do, captain? How can I save Suzanne? How can I be sure?"

"There is no surety," said "X." "There's only hope. I'm going to talk to the inspector. I want to see him alone."

The senator spoke in sudden panic. "You're not going to tell him—about Ferris—and the plans? Wait—the police don't know!"

"It's something else entirely, senator," said "X" harshly. "You may trust me—to keep silent."

He strode through the door, crossed the hall quickly, and entered the drawing room. Inspector Clyde turned at sound of his step. His sharp face was palely set. The Agent nodded, spoke abruptly:

"We've met before, inspector. At Senator Dashman's home, you may remember. I'd like a word with you?"

Inspector Clyde nodded surlily. His pride was ruffled apparently because the Agent's visit had interrupted his own interview with Blackwell.

"What is it you want?" he snapped. "I'm a busy man tonight."

AGENT "X" asked a blunt question. "When you reached Senator Foulette's after the robbery this evening, just what did you find, inspector?"

"Jewels had been stolen and three persons were missing. Miss Blackwell, Raphael Sancho, and a girl named Betty Dale. We believe they were kidnapped."

"Who called the police—the servants?"

"No—they were knocked out, too. A man named von Helvig called us—an attaché of the German embassy."

"He revived first, you mean?"

"Yes, he was among the first."

"And when did he leave?"

"After we'd finished questioning him."

"Did you make a list of all those present, inspector?"

"Certainly, as a matter of routine. They'd been robbed and filed normal complaints."

"Did you happen to talk to a Miss Lili Damora?"

"Yes, she'd lost a diamond ring valued at five hundred dollars. She was with von Helvig. Was she a friend of yours?"

"Yes, inspector, exactly. And I sympathize with her loss."

Inspector Clyde shrugged coldly. "What's a bit of a jewel compared to human lives. Three people were kidnapped, I tell you. We have every reason to believe they are in danger,"

The irony of the situation held grim humor. Clyde was talking to one of the supposedly kidnapped people now. But the Agent's face was masklike.

"Thank you, inspector," he said. "I appreciate your information."

A sly gleam of curiosity came into the inspector's eyes now. "You're not trying to cast suspicion on von Helvig, are you? It doesn't seem likely that a man attached to a government legation would be a jewel thief, does it?"

"It doesn't, inspector. You are right. Thanks again, and goodnight."

Secret Agent "X" turned and strode quickly from the room. The light of excitement was in his eyes now. There might be nothing in what the inspector had told him; but again, there might. Von Helvig was a murderous criminal. He had been a ruthless spy, and he had been the one to summon the police. Suzanne Blackwell hadn't been taken to the island. Where was she—and was von Helvig responsible for her abduction?

"X" went straight to the Hotel Wilmot and was told that von Helvig hadn't been in all evening.

The Agent pondered a moment, then left the hotel and drove swiftly through the night streets again. This time he went to the fashionable apartment where Lili Damora had her suite. The doorman had long since gone off duty. Agent "X" didn't announce himself to the sleepy-eyed girl at the switchboard. He walked past, ascended in the all-night elevator, pressed the bell of Lili's apartment. But there was no answer to his ring. Seconds passed. He pressed the button again. Still no answer.

The Agent took his tool kit from the lining of his coat then and entered the apartment by deftly and silently picking the lock.

The place was dark and quiet. An inexplicable sense of eeriness hung over it. He turned on his tiny light, moved cautiously. The bed hadn't been slept in. It was not even turned back. He went into the drawing room next, stood still a second looking about, them bent sharply forward.

The place was in good order, but something on the rug caught his eye. A dark, sinister spot that was crimson, and still damp.

He examined the rug carefully, eyes brightly alert. Another spot of crimson showed near the hall entrance. He passed across it, opened the door of a guest room, entered.

The bed there hadn't been used, either. The room was spotlessly neat. But he noticed a slight roughed-up place on the carpet. Beyond this was the door of a clothes closet. The Agent moved forward, touching the knob. It was locked.

With suddenly tense fingers, Agent "X" removed his compact tool kit again. He selected a steel implement to suit, forced the lock, and pulled the door open. Then he gave a sudden hissing exclamation.

A huddled figure lay on the floor of the closet. A white face with glassy eyes stared up at him above a crimson-stained shirt front. The face was that of Karl Hummel, alias Otto von Helvig, ex-Prussian spy and embassy attaché. One glance at his still, marble-pale features showed Agent "X" that he was dead.

CHAPTER XX

A LIVE CORPSE

HERE WAS A turn of events as unexpected as a sudden blow in the dark. The Agent was staggered.

For tense seconds he stared down at Karl Hummel. One of Europe's most cunning spies lay at "X's" feet—dead. A man who had served his country during four years of bloody strife, outwitting many opponents, winning many triumphs. A man who had played the desperate game of espionage with all the strength of mind and body. And now, in time of supposed peace, he had succumbed to a criminal too terrible for him to cope with.

For a moment Agent "X" forgot Karl Hummel's ruthless past— and saw him only as a victim of their common enemy. He felt a touch of sentiment for this brilliant old-time adversary of his, who had rolled the dice—and lost. Then he stooped and lifted Hummel up.

Stretching the dead man on the floor, he went through his pockets with swift thoroughness. Careful examination of a wallet in Hummel's pocket disclosed a sheaf of bills, a few calling cards. "X" tossed these impatiently aside, then felt through the dead man's vest. He paused to scrutinize another card. This bore the name of an undertaking firm—David Daniels & Son. Unimportant, it seemed—or was it? The Agent stared at it for tense seconds.

There was gruesome irony in finding a mortician's card in a dead man's pocket. But there was no amusement in the Agent's keen eyes. The murder of Ferris Blackwell, the kidnapping of Suzanne, had sent his mind leaping to conclusions which had been right. Now a macabre hunch was building itself about this bit of pasteboard in his fingers.

He left Hummel stretched out on the floor and went back into the hallway where a telephone stood on a small table. He dialed quickly, reading the undertaker's number from the card. It was after two in the morning—but undertakers keep all-night phones. They expect calls at any hour. Death does not wait upon human convenience.

A voice answered at once. Agent "X" spoke cautiously.

"Von Helvig speaking. You delivered a casket this evening, I believe."

Silence for a moment, then: "Yes—the delivery was made about nine o'clock—a hurry call. But Von Helvig wasn't the name. There must be some mistake."

"What was the name?"

There was another silence before the voice spoke again: "Hummel."

The Agent's body stiffened. His fingers gripped the receiver tightly. This must mean that Lili knew the spy by his real name.

"Karl Hummel?"

"Right."

"My mistake. The same party wants some flowers. There's been a mix-up. Will you please give me the address?"

"It's out in the suburbs," answered the voice. "But they've gone. They wanted to ship a body tonight. That's why we had to rush the order through."

"You did the embalming, too, I suppose?"

"No, another undertaker did that. We delivered the casket and called later to make shipment. They left by the Congressional Express."

"Thanks! I've got to catch them if I can."

The Agent's voice was quiet. But his fingers trembled as they replaced the receiver of the phone.

Karl Hummel, alias von Helvig—the man who lay dead in the next room! A casket quickly bought and shipped by train. The Congressional Express. These were new and sinister angles in a mystery already bafflingly black.

Agent "X" looked at his watch. Already that train was miles away, speeding northward over night-shrouded rails. There wasn't time to catch it by car!

"X" picked up the telephone again. The number he called this time was listed in no book, but at last a deep voice answered—the voice of the man known to the Agent as "K9."

Briefly Agent "X" made a strange request. Then he plunged to the street and sent his roadster leaping from the curb.

Minutes later he braked savagely before the gates of Bolling Field. An air beacon still shone, but the field's hangars were dark—all except one. Here sleepy-eyed mechanics were rolling out a ship. A two-place attack plane, high-powered, swift, dual-controlled. As mechanics whirled the prop a man slipped a flying helmet over his head—one of the army's crack pilots.

He peered curiously as the man called Captain Stewart Black approached. Respect showed in his eyes when he recognised the insignia of General Staff. He saluted.

AGENT "X" scrutinized intently the man who was to fly his plane. "K9" had promised him a special pilot. This man who stood before him was Lieutenant Draper, an instructor in aerial acrobatics, a racer and dare-devil flyer. Here was a pilot as expert as the Agent himself.

"X" touched his arm.

"I've got to catch a train, lieutenant. The Congressional Express, on the Pennsylvania line. I want you to overtake her and land me."

"Where?"

"On her."

Draper's face expressed amazement.

"You want me to land you—where?"

"On the train, I said. When you spot her, nose down and straighten out. I'll manage the rest"

"You mean you're going to transfer?"

"Exactly!"

Shaking his head doubtfully, but apparently realizing that it was no use opposing the will of his superior, the pilot climbed into the rear cockpit. He let the ship warm five minutes more. The life of a captain on General Staff might be on his hands tonight.

The swift ship zoomed up off the field and climbed like a rocket. Agent "X" slipped goggles over his eyes. His pulses seemed to beat to the radial engine's roar. He knew the pilot thought him insane. But Draper could be trusted to do his stuff.

They wheeled over the city, headed northward, and picked up the line of the railroad within ten minutes. At twice the train's speed the fast ship forged ahead. Mile after mile through the black night sky.

It was Agent "X" who spotted the Congressional Express first. There was a cut through the hills. He caught the glint of lighted windows, like a string of brilliants snaking along the earth. He turned his head and signaled the pilot behind him, motioning downward with one hand.

Draper's face was white. But he obeyed instructions, diminishing altitude sharply and leveling.

The Agent rose in the cockpit, the windblast striking his body with the slapping violence of a huge palm. He stood poised until he grew accustomed to its thrust, then threw one leg over the side and stepped out on a wing. A tense calmness directed his movements—the calmness of a man who knows the safety of his country depends upon the success of his desperate plan.

He grasped the sharp struts firmly, slipped backwards and groped downward with his feet. His toes found the plane's landing carriage. He climbed down, twisting his body around the strong steel rods. Six feet ahead the propeller cut like a gigantic scythe, death in its whirling blades.

The wind blast tore at him as the plane nosed down again. The ground billowed up. Lieutenant Draper, wild though he considered the attempt, was doing his stuff. He would have something to tell his buddies about, though they would undoubtedly think he was lying. His face was white as he bent over the controls, brought the plane down slowly, throttled the engine.

Plainly visible now, the train was almost directly below them. A rushing serpent in the darkness, with a brown top and a hundred fiery eyes glowing in its sides. It was toward that brown top that Lieutenant Draper flew, dropping the plane's nose gradually, expertly.

Agent "X" clung to the landing gear, waiting tensely. Not till the train had rounded the curve and was on a long straightaway did Draper try to get close. Then he dropped altitude swiftly, leveled out a hundred feet above the train. It was a roaring monster now, flashing through the darkness at eighty miles an hour. Draper cut his own speed to match it, held steady.

Then, foot by foot, the plane seemed to drift down toward that gliding brown-backed serpent. Lieutenant Draper was peering over the side, goggled head thrust out, hands steady on the sensitively responsive controls. The train's top crawled slowly back. A strong wind at their tail was making it difficult to synchronize speed.

A GRIM smile twisted the Agent's lips. One slip—and it would mean death and the end. He must not fail now. He must wait till

that backward motion of the train ceased. Fields, trees, dark houses fled beneath them. Draper came lower still until the ship's air
wheels seemed almost to touch a car's top. And now the train appeared to be standing still. Its speed and the plane's were matched.
The moment had arrived.

Eyes steely bright, the Agent opened his fingers and dropped.
For a second he seemed to hang in space between the roar above
and below him. Then, on hands and knees he struck the roof of a
car. He slid. The rushing wind pushed at him with hostile strength.
For an instant he was helpless in its grip, nearly swept from the
surface of the speeding train. Then his fingers caught in a ventilator opening, curled in a viselike grip. He was safe.

He crouched, looked up at the climbing plane. Lieutenant Draper's goggled head peered over the side. His hand lifted in salute.
Then the ship soared upward like a bird and vanished into the
aerial blackness.

Secure, steady now, Agent "X" crawled forward along the top of
the swaying car. He covered two Pullmans, a string of day coaches,
came at last to the baggage car which was coupled to the tender.
Steam and smoke from the big locomotive belched in his face, raining gritty cinders.

Thankful for the night darkness that hid him from the engineer
up front, Agent "X" prepared for the dangerous maneuver that
faced him. He must get from the roof of the baggage car to its forward end. Here was his only means of entering the car. Its rear was
coupled with a closed-in hood to the express car behind.

He steadied himself for an instant on the swaying roof, near the
front then sprang to the tender, grasping the ladder attached to its
end. His pulses were hammering fast. This mad evening's work was
drawing to a climax. The jar and rattle of the plunging train made
opening the locked door of the baggage car difficult. But finally he
accomplished it, and a moment later was inside.

In the comparative quiet within the baggage car, a dim light
burned. Trunks and suitcases were stacked along its sides. The
Agent's keen eyes probed. Then he started. A chill prickled along
his spine. He had found the thing he sought—a coffin. But there
was more than one. There were four!

"X" walked to them. Long, low, the four pine boxes held their
cargo of the dead. Four bodies being shipped back to their homes.
The Agent did a strange thing. Stepping back, he reached into his
pocket. Certain things were always on his person—implements

that aided him in his arduous work as hunter of criminals. Now he drew forth what seemed to be a small pocket camera.

HIS mind was working swiftly now. A wild theory had evolved in his brain. The coffin ordered by von Helvig, under the name of Karl Hummel, lay at his feet. One of the four pine boxes held that coffin. But which one?

Everything depended upon his find-out. If his theories were right, the coffin held a key to the whole mystery. He fingered the thing in his hands, drew a black cord from it with a circular disc at the end. This contrivance was not a camera, but one of the smallest, most sensitive sound amplifiers in the world. The disc at the end of the cord was a tiny microphone.[46]

The instrument had aided him many times, but never had he put it to such a strange use.

Kneeling on the car's floor. Agent "X" placed the amplifier's disc on the nearest coffin top. The box containing the small dry batteries and the receiver was against his ear. He crouched like a ghoul, listening—listening for the heartbeats of the dead.

The roar of the train was a Niagara of sound. "X" turned the delicate rheostat dials, adjusting for selectivity. He heard the rumble of the wheels, the couplings scrape, but no other sound. The occupant of that coffin would be forever still.

Sweat beaded the Agent's forehead. This was gruesome work, and fear gnawed at his heart—fear that he was perhaps too late—or that he had been wrong in his deductions. He passed to the next coffin. But his listening brought the same result.

His hands trembled slightly as he approached the third. He lowered the disc of his microphone, moved the dials. His amplifier was like a stethoscope now, and a sudden intense light brightened the Agent's eyes.

Out of this wrapping of the dead came a living sound—the slow, regular beat of a human heart! A live person was in that gruesome box.

Swiftly the Agent straightened, thrust his instrument away. He walked to the front of the car. No one in sight. But the coffin was

---

46 *AUTHOR'S NOTE: There have been many times in his exciting career when this sensitive amplifier has been of use. With the cord extension it has enabled him to listen in on secret conversations. It was utilized in the case of the "Death-Torch Terror," chronicled last month. In tracing down clews which led to the capture of the hideous "Flammenwerfer" murderers.*

marked for unloading at Baltimore. And Baltimore was only a few minutes away! He must work quickly!

His tool kit disgorged a hacksaw of thinnest razor steel. With this he cut the nailheads in the outer box. He lifted the board free. Screws in the coffin's top came next. Then he raised the lid and in the dim light stared down tensely.

A girl lay inside the coffin. She was inert, colorless. But her features did not show the marble rigidity of death. Her breath came with slow regularity. It was the unconscious form of Suzanne Blackwell.

QUICKLY Agent "X" lifted her from the coffin. He shook her gently, but she did not rouse. She was like a person under the influence of an anesthetic. Obviously she had been drugged. "X" rubbed her wrists and hands; he took a tiny hypo needle from his pocket and plunged it into her white arm. It contained a powerful stimulant—one of the Agent's many secrets.

A minute passed—two. Then faint color began to show in Suzanne Blackwell's cheeks. Agent "X's" probing finger detected a quickening of her pulse. It was as though he had worked a miracle in the dimly lighted baggage car; brought a corpse back to life.

At last Suzanne opened her eyes, as "X" held her in his arms. He spoke gently, reassuringly, but the girl opened her mouth to scream. Awakened from her deep drugged slumber, she was like one roused from a nightmare.

"Don't," he said. "Be quiet, Miss Blackwell. You are safe."

His hand covered her soft lips momentarily. Then he saw intelligence dawn in her dilated eyes. She stared up at him.

"Don't be afraid," he said. "It's all right now."

"Who are you?"

"A friend—a friend of Betty Dale's. You've had a terrible experience, but you're all right now."

"Where am I? What has happened?"

"You're on a train. You were—in this."

Suzanne followed his gesture, gasped shudderingly.

"A coffin! Oh—"

"Listen!" "X" said tensely. "Criminals did this. They must be caught and punished. You can help me. Will you?"

She eyed him doubtfully, terror still in her eyes.

"Yes—if you are a friend of Betty's—"

She could stand now, and her mind was fully awake. But she recoiled as her eyes discovered the other coffins.

"This is horrible," she whispered. "It will haunt me—always."

"It is horrible," "X" said quietly. "But you will forget."

He got into the empty coffin himself, under the girl's amazed eyes. The train would soon be coming into Baltimore. There the coffin would be unloaded—and Agent "X" wanted to go with it. He must find out its destination. The fact that Suzanne had not been killed proved that she was being held as hostage in case of police pursuit.

He gave her quick instructions.

"Close the coffin. Then stay out of sight. Wait here in the baggage car or hide outside the end door if necessary. Get off when the train stops and run forward beyond the engine. Don't let anyone see you. You might be taken prisoner again. Is it clear?"

"Yes," the frightened girl whispered. "It is clear."

The coffin's lid came slowly down over Agent "X." It was a big casket, meant for a larger person than Suzanne. "X" had plenty of room. And he would not have long to wait. Baltimore was only fifteen minutes away.

In the close darkness, vibrating with the rumble of the train, the Agent lay, his brain racing. If Suzanne did her part, all would be well. If not—but that possibility he refused even to consider. This last move had been a desperate one. But he could get out of the coffin whenever he wanted to. He had made sure of that. Only a few of the coffin's screws had been replaced. They were sawed nearly through. The boarding of the pine box would be easy to lift.

But the air inside was strangely close. A faint odor came from the lining pressed against his face. He turned his head sidewise, breathing lightly in order to conserve the oxygen.

Minutes dragged by. The air grew more and more oppressive. It made him giddy. He fought against it, but he seemed to be back on Lieutenant Draper's plane. He seemed to feel its lurch and sway.

Five minutes passed. Ten. The train was slowing down. Agent "X" felt drowsy now. He shook himself sharply, then tensed as air brakes hissed and a shudder jarred the train. He listened, identifying each sound.

THE express rolled to a stop. The door of the baggage car squeaked as it slid back. From inside the coffin, "X" heard the sound of men's voices. There was the scrape of feet on boarding, the sudden sense of being lifted.

The coffin moved. A bump as it dropped, his oblique position, and the crunch of wheels on gravel told the Agent that he was now on a baggage truck, moving forward. Then the truck stopped and a moment of silence followed, until he heard the train get under way again, wheels screeching, engines puffing. Men's voices came indistinctly. The Agent used his microphone once more. He'd planned this. It worked as well inside as out. But the speakers were only baggagemen.

An auto rumbled up. The coffin was moved again, carried to the auto, shoved inside. "X" realized he was now in a van. A long, jouncing ride followed.

It lulled the Agent dangerously close to sleep. He fought to keep awake. But his lids felt strangely heavy, and it was only the van's squealing stop that roused him. A man spoke close to the coffin.

"Catch hold—easy now."

The truckman's voice, but it was answered by another that made the Agent tense suddenly, as it directed, "This way, boys—careful!"

He'd heard that voice before!

The coffin was carried forward, bumped down. "X" heard the soft wash of water, retreating feet. The coffin was stationary once more, but there was a rocking motion. Voices came from a distance, a woman's among them. He could not distinguish words.

More minutes passed. Then came a pulsing roar of sound that almost split his eardrums. He quickly tuned the amplifier down. Listening tensely he identified the roar. Those were airplane motors. He was in a plane again! But that hissing slap of water against a hulk—it must be a flying boat or seaplane. The hissing stopped. He felt a long sweep upward, the dizzy rocking of the air.

More than ever now he was conscious of the stuffiness inside the casket. Lethargy seemed to have him in its grip. The microphone slid from his fingers.

Something warned him suddenly. Desperately he tried to rouse himself. But he slipped back. His throat felt dry. His tongue seemed huge in his mouth. The roar of the strange plane's motors was like a roaring in his own head.

A tingling sense of horror spurred him to new effort—but no effort could rouse him from the lethargy now. He was slipping down—down—and he couldn't move. Then at last the awful real-

ization came into his numbed brain. There was a lingering drug inside the coffin—remnant of the drug that had held Suzanne Blackwell in its grip. But now it was too late. Agent "X" fell helplessly
into a black pit of unconsciousness.

CHAPTER XXI

TRAPPED

A GENT "X" AWOKE as from a terrible nightmare. He awoke with horror clutching at his throat. His mind was filled with a sense of appalling catastrophe. He had not anticipated the drug in the coffin. Luck had been against him. He had been outplayed at every turn. Now the last hand had been called—and he had lost. There was coldness on his face. The airplane's engines no longer sounded in his ears. In their stead a voice was speaking. It was a taunting voice, harsh, inhuman as the scrape of metal. It was the voice of the man in the green mask.

Agent "X" opened his eyelids slowly. He was still lying in the coffin and fingers were poking at his face, exploring his disguise. Over him a man's head hovered. He saw the startling hue of poisonous green. He saw lips moving; heard harsh words clearly now.

"This is a pleasure," the green-masked man was saying, "and a surprise. I hope you have slept well—Elisha Pond. I hope your bed was comfortable. I hope you liked the trip." A chuckle followed the words.

The Agent lay silent, too stunned to speak. This was no nightmare. It was reality more terrible than any dream.

"The coffin's perfume—was it not pleasant?" the harsh voice taunted. "Very clever, Agent 'X'! You gallantly rescued a fair lady in distress. But in doing so you got into distress yourself. Shall we call it that?"

The cold gray light of dawn shone in "X's" eyes. He was staring up at the sky. He was on a ship's deck. Still he did not sit up. He was seeking to clear from his brain the fumes that had knocked him out. The green mask's voice continued.

"It has been an exciting game, Agent 'X.' I appreciate the clever moves you've made. You freed your blonde friend from the island. You gave my Malay colleagues a pleasant chase. Even when they thought they'd burned you, you had the laugh on them. And then—just how did you trace the coffin? That would be interesting to know. Perhaps you'd like to tell me."

The man laughed again. "You can afford to talk now. The game is ended. You have lost. We can chat like old friends, until—"

The laugh that came now was as sinister as death. Looking into those eyes behind the green mask Agent "X" read his doom. But before he could speak another voice sounded—a woman's voice close by. The Agent swiveled his eyes and saw the sinuous dark form of Lili Damora.

"Don't trouble him, Ito," the woman from Budapest said. "I can tell you how he traced the coffin. He found Karl Hummel in my apartment. It was my fault. I forgot about the fool's having that undertaker's card."

The green-masked man bowed. "Very pretty, Agent 'X.' Your deductive faculties are good. You played me closely all the way. How unfortunate that in the end you were one move behind!"

"Don't gloat, Ito," Lili Damora admonished. "It is such frightfully bad taste."

"But it pleases me to vanquish a worthy adversary," the green-masked man replied.

Secret Agent "X" stared keenly now. "Ito," Lili had called Green Mask. That was Japanese! "X" spoke for the first time.

"You were in doubt, too, about the plans until you tortured Ferris Blackwell."

"But I hit upon the truth at last. And you are still in doubt." The green-masked man laughed with grim amusement. "Is it not a pretty game, Lili? Let us show him how very close to the plans he is."

Green Mask clapped his hands. Like sinister wraiths, four brown-skinned Malays moved out of a hatchway and glided up.

"Get up," Ito said to Agent "X." "You see where you are—on board my ship. And I have my friends with me. You know their tricks by now, I think."

Agent "X" rose slowly. He saw the Malays facing him, knives in their hands.

"Perhaps," said Ito, "I can't convince them that this is the man who cheated their god, Tuan. Your disguise was too good for that. But they will be glad to kill at a word from me. Let me show you now where the plans are."

ITO crossed to the coffin that "X" had vacated. He reached between the lining and the frame, drew out a long envelope. He held it up an instant. Then he shoved it in his pocket.

"I was careful to the last, you see. I paid a compliment to your secret service. If I should be caught I didn't want the plans found on me."

The Agent adopted the same suave manner as Ito now.

"And what do you intend to do with me?" he asked.

"Compliment you still further," said Ito. "Flatter you with death. If you were not so clever I might let you live. But I shall be courteous. You may choose one of several ways. You had a taste of *Kep-shak*. Would you like to complete the experience?"

Lili Damora shivered slightly and spoke with a note of contempt.

"Can't you be civilized, Ito? Why not shoot him as I shot Otto? It is so much easier and quicker."

The green mask turned on her quickly.

"Did I ask for your advice, dear lady? You know how I hate Americans. And I have a right to speak since my father was one. Don't try to cheat me of my fun. If you don't like my ways go below!"

Lili Damora flounced off and Ito laughed. The cruel bantering note was still in his voice.

"Choose," he said. "How do you wish to die?"

The eyes of Agent "X" roved desperately—roved over the cold morning sea, over the faces of the men around him, along the deck of the vessel he was on. He was searching for a way out. And his mind told him there was none; his mind told him he was beaten.

How did he wish to die? This fiend was calmly asking him that. Death held little terror for Agent "X." He had been schooled against it. But defeat in this, the greatest thing he had ever undertaken, was a bitter, ghastly pill to swallow. Worse even than the sting of the *Kep-shak* torture. His country, his chief in Washington relied on him—and he had failed. This masked criminal was sneering at him—this man who had the Browning plans. Revolt flared in the mind of Agent "X." His eyes turned upward, and suddenly he tensed.

Thin, ghostly wires stretched across the sky between the vessel's masts—wires that were his last link with the world he knew. Radio! This was a tramp steamer he was on. He'd seen the type before and knew them well. His eyes dropped. He was silent for a moment. Suddenly he raised his hand.

"Look! Over there!"

It was an old trick. He was pointing out across the sea. But he was counting on its very simplicity to fool the man who used elaborate tortures on his victims. He would not suspect "X" of using a ruse so crude. Moreover, Ito was swollen with the feel of victory—arrogantly sure of himself. Agent "X" had calculated well. At his sudden gesture, the tenseness in his voice, Ito and the Malays turned their heads.

IN that moment, Agent "X" leaped. He heard the shrill cry of anger that lifted behind him. A knife whistled through the air. He sprang aside. The knife hissed close beside him, landed with a thud against the deckhouse.

He sped forward along the vessel's deck. A desperate plan had formed in his mind. He climbed an iron ladder, ran ahead. The bridge rose before him. He found the door he wanted, burst in. A man who was not a Malay crouched over his instruments in the ship's radio room. A man who was a weak-eyed river rat. A white man, but a man enslaved by drugs. One of Ito's craven slaves.

The Agent closed the door behind him. He barred it with a chair. His fist flashed out, crashed into the face of the wireless man. The man slumped to the floor, head lolling.

For a bare second the Secret Agent paused. He studied the dials along the wall, the complicated instrument board. He threw a switch, leaped to the small table where the man had sat. His fingers touched the radio key.

Quickly, expertly, he gave the signal of the Hampton Roads naval station. Seconds that seemed eternities went by. Then there came an answer to his call.

Shouts sounded outside now. Running feet. The Agent paid no attention to them. Bent over his key, eyes burning, he sent a message that might influence a nation's destiny. For three minutes he used a secret naval code, then stopped. Men were beating on the door.

He switched the light off as evil faces were framed in the wireless room's small window. The glass broke behind him with a crash.

The Agent leaped across the floor. There was another door beyond, an officer's room. He ran through this, out to the deck again, doubling back along his tracks. A Malay saw him and gave a howl. "X" plunged into a doorway, down into the interior of the ship.

Death stalked on all sides of him now. But he must fight for time—time. Where was Ito now? "X" didn't know. He ran forward to the cabin where Lili Damora had gone. A Malay appeared in his path, knife gleaming. The Malay hurled the knife. "X" dodged and fired his gas pistol into the man's face.

Then he saw a door ahead of him and flung it open. A woman's piercing scream sounded. Lili Damora stood before him.

"You!" she hissed. A gun appeared in her hand. The Agent sprang aside as it lanced flame. He leaped forward tigerishly, wrenched the weapon from her fingers. She cowered back.

The Agent's lips curled. Here was the creature who had been playing with the green-masked criminal all the time. She had even used Karl Hummel, outwitted him, and slain him when he was of no further use. The Agent read the whole ghastly story now. Karl Hummel in her hands had been a mere tool.

"Go to the door and lock it quickly," he ordered.

She obeyed, sliding a heavy bolt home. "X" knew the door had iron cleats across it. It and the room's partitions formed a stout barrier.

As Lili stepped back a voice came through the wood—the voice of green-masked Ito.

"Clever again, Elisha Pond! You sent a wireless message. But even that is too late. This boat is fast. They will not catch us now. And if they should overtake us, we have a plane on board. Long before help can arrive we shall have broken in—and you will be dead."

"Leave him alone," cried Lili. "He will kill me if you don't."

The green-masked man laughed.

"You are a dear lady, Lili. But let me make it clear that a threat to your life cannot save Pond. High as I hold you in esteem my enemy comes first."

As though to emphasize this, Green Mask fired through the door, and the bullet whistled between Lili and Agent "X." Then there came a series of thuds as Malays battered axes on the door.

Lili hissed like a venomous snake, furious that Ito was willing to risk her life to get at "X." She turned to the Agent and a torrent of angry words came from her lips.

"I'll tell you who he is," she cried. "You'll understand the sort of animal you're dealing with. He's a half-caste—a mongrel—half Jap and half American. Because his father deserted his mother she taught him to hate America."

A shower of ax blows drowned out her voice for a moment. The door shook and creaked. Lili screamed above the noise so that her words would reach Ito's ears, too.

"I hate him as much as he hates Americans. I'd like to destroy him as he would destroy them. I tolerated him only because he promised me wealth when the stolen plans were sold."

Lili Damora looked like a sinister harpy now. Fury distorted her face, drove her beauty from her, seemed to add years to her age. She screamed a curse.

"Ito with his high-society airs! Ito who calls himself—"

TWO more pistol shots rang out as Ito fired furiously through the door. Ax blows half deadened their reports. But Lili stopped speaking and gave a piercing shriek. She clutched her left side, crimson staining her fingers.

"You've hit me—you devil! You've—"

The words choked in her throat. She took a staggering step forward, then collapsed and lay still on the floor—a murderess slain by her own partner in crime.

Whether it was intentional or not "X" didn't know. He stood aghast, tense and silent as the Malays hacked the door to pieces.

Five minutes—ten—went by. Death would come soon now—death—

Then a new sound came, filling the air, rising above the ax blows. It was a sound that pulsed through the Agent's blood, thrilled him. The roar of airplane motors—the planes the Agent had summoned by radio. They circled the ship, signaling for it to stop—but the vessel forged ahead. Then suddenly the Agent started.

There was a noise out on deck. The staccato rattle of a machine gun. This sinister craft was armed. He stared from an open port.

One of the planes, sweeping low over the gray sea, suddenly tilted, thrusting its broad wing toward the sky. A column of black smoke trailed behind it. Its engine coughed, sputtered. There was a blinding, rending flash of flame. The gray plane was torn apart before his horrified eyes, its gas tank hit and exploding.

The other navy planes rose higher. One of them swept down over the ship. Something black dropped through the air. It struck the sea close by. There was an explosion, a geyser of water. The Malays howled in fear. "X" heard the machine gun chattering again. Now was the time he had waited for.

He crept back to the cabin door, unlocked it. The arrival of the planes had taken the Malays out on deck. Ito was with them, urging them to fight.

The Agent charged across the deck, a bounding, leaping streak. Before Ito knew what was happening, Agent "X" had caught him in his arms. His swift charge carried them both over the rail. Thay went tumbling head over heels down into the sea. Malays lined the deck above, blowpipes in their hands, sinister darts ready. But they dared not shoot for fear of hitting their master.

The two below were locked together, but Ito fought like a trapped animal. In a frenzy at being defeated he scratched, kicked, and bit. His eyes behind the mask glared with inhuman hate. His fingers were like clutching talons as he sought for "X's" throat. But Agent "X," spurred on by the great cause for which he fought and with victory close at hand, battled with every nerve and muscle in him, battled—and finally won.

As in a daze he saw the swooping gray planes overhead. A bomb struck the vessel's stern. Flame leaped out.

Then one of the big planes landed on the water and taxied over to the spot where "X" held the furious Ito, now subdued. "X" pulled the green mask from Ito's face—and was not wholly surprised at what he saw. The face before him was that of Sam Barkley—supposed American sportsman—the man who had pretended to be an ardent suitor of Suzanne Blackwell's. It was from her no doubt in some indirect way that he had finally guessed the truth about Ferris.

The Agent's hand reached into Barkley's coat, drew out the Browning plans and transferred them to his own pocket. They were wet; but the water-proof ink wouldn't run. The plane came up and stopped. It was a big naval amphibian.

"Ahoy there!" cried a voice.

THE plane carried a crew of four. Strong hands reached down for Agent "X" and Barkley; but, as they did so, one of Barkley's arms moved suddenly. A gleaming vial was in his fingers. Before "X" could stop him he put it to his lips, pulling out the cork with his white teeth. With a movement swift as lightning he swallowed the vial's contents, made a choking sound, then gave a strange, harsh laugh.

"X" smelted the fumes of bitter almonds—prussic acid.

The scared men in the plane swore fiercely and yanked Ito up. But they were too late. Barkley's face was changing color. He coughed, writhed a moment, and lay still.

"What in hell does this mean?" one of the navy men asked.

"It means a master spy and murderer has committed suicide," said "X."

"And who are you?"

"That can wait until later."

"We were told to go out and halt this ship, the *Kelantan*. She wouldn't stop. She fired on us—brought down one of our planes. What were you doing then? How do we know you're not a spy, too?"

"You don't," said the Agent quietly. He knew that, in spite of his army uniform, nothing he could say would convince them. There would be questions asked when he arrived on shore. They'd want to see his papers, find out how it happened that an army officer knew the secret naval code that had brought the planes out. He couldn't afford to reveal his identity even though he now had the Browning plans. His career wasn't ended yet. He was still Secret Agent "X."

He watched breathlessly as the gray planes stopped the *Kelantan* with another well-placed bomb. The Malays ran for cover, their machine gun abandoned, but the ship was sinking by the stern, its bow reared up. It listed, water pouring through a gapping hole in its plates that the bomb had made—and suddenly it slid bottomward, air bursting through bulkheads and whistling up through the waves above. The *Kelantan* and its murderous crew were gone forever.

The plane "X" was on rose from the water, heading back toward land. There was a cabin in it. Two pilots sat up front. The flight commander began questioning "X" in the cabin. A member of the crew stood by. Sam Barkley's body rolled grotesquely as the big plane lurched and dipped.

The gray shore line came out of the landward mist, then the plane sailed over Chesapeake Bay. But, to the navy man's questioning, Agent "X" answered only in monosyllables. Then, as the plane began to glide downward, he did a strange and sudden thing. He whipped his harmless gas gun out, sent a puif of vapor into the faces of the two men in the cabin.

As they collapsed, Agent "X" reached above him and pulled a 'chute pack from a rack. He slipped quickly into the harness, thrust the side door open against the wind blast.

An instant he poised, then leaped, his tumbling body forming a black receding dot. It was a delayed jump. He didn't want the other planes to see him, or, if they did, he wanted to be too far down for them to catch. He didn't pull the rip cord till he had fallen nearly two thousand feet and the water was a thousand feet below him. Then his 'chute blossomed out. He had figured carefully, and the high wind off the sea bore him toward land.

Later that same morning a mysterious message reached the high Government official known in the secret files as "K9." The message was in code. It was brief and to the point, and it came from a town near Baltimore.

"Browning plans recovered," the message said. "All is well. On way."

There was another sentence telling Department of Justice agents to go to a certain address in Washington. Fast cars filled with armed operatives hurried to the spot. There they found a notorious spy named Michael Renfew, a man the D.C.I. had long been wanting to catch because of his subversive espionage activities. They also found a dead Malay whose presence Renfew could not or would not explain.

At almost the same moment Senator Blackwell received a telegram which helped to lift the gray pallor of fear from his face.

"Don't worry," it said. "All is safe—and secret." It was signed "Black."

The senator had his daughter back now. She had arrived by auto; brought from Baltimore by friends of the family.

Silently, devoutly, Senator Blackwell blessed the name of Captain Stewart Black, the dapper officer from General Staff who seemed to be a clairvoyant and the very soul of discretion, all in one. He did not know that the man behind it all, the man he had to thank, was Secret Agent "X"—master of mystery, and man of destiny.

Made in the USA
Las Vegas, NV
25 March 2025

20085816R00312